WINGS OF FIRE

THE BRIGHTEST NIGHT
THE GRAPHIC NOVEL

For Wyatt — talented artist, expert
Minecrafter, and hilarious friend
—T.T.S.

For Tui, Barry, Rachel, and Maarta — I'm
incredibly honored to be a part of this team!
—M.H.

Story and text copyright © 2021 by Tui T. Sutherland
Adaptation by Barry Deutsch and Rachel Swirsky
Map and border design © 2012 by Mike Schley
Art by Mike Holmes © 2021 by Scholastic Inc.

Library of Congress Control Number Available

ISBN 978-1-338-73086-9 (hardcover)
ISBN 978-1-338-73085-2 (paperback)

10 9 8 7 6 5 4 3 2 1   21 22 23 24 25

Printed in China   62
First edition, December 2021
Edited by Amanda Maciel
Coloring by Maarta Laiho
Lettering by E.K. Weaver
Creative Director: Phil Falco
Publisher: David Saylor

WINGS OF FIRE

THE BRIGHTEST NIGHT
THE GRAPHIC NOVEL

BY TUI T. SUTHERLAND

ADAPTED BY BARRY DEUTSCH
AND RACHEL SWIRSKY

ART BY MIKE HOLMES
COLOR BY MAARTA LAIHO

AN IMPRINT OF
■SCHOLASTIC

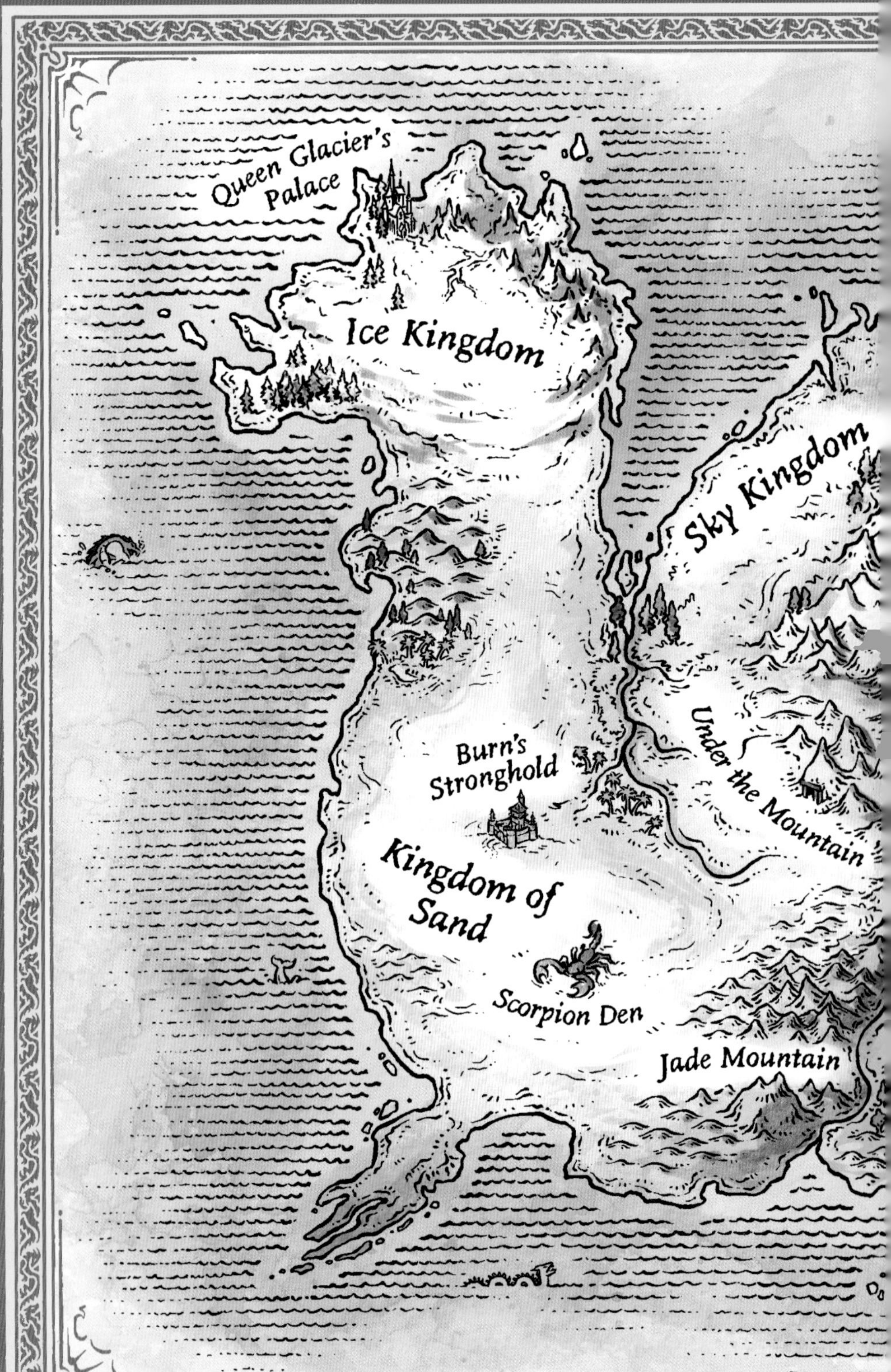
Queen Glacier's Palace
Ice Kingdom
Sky Kingdom
Under the Mountain
Burn's Stronghold
Kingdom of Sand
Scorpion Den
Jade Mountain

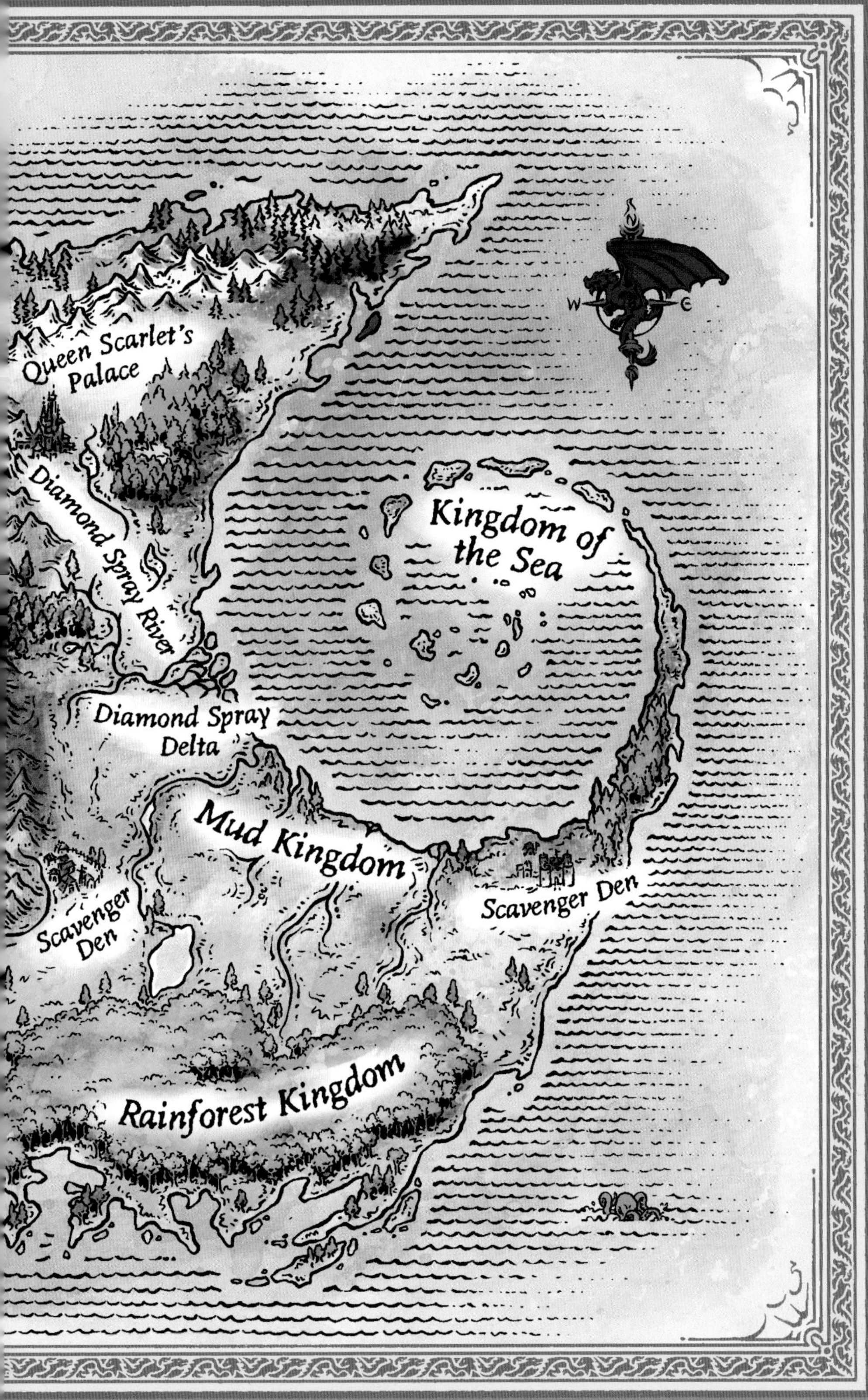
Queen Scarlet's Palace
Diamond Spray River
Kingdom of the Sea
Diamond Spray Delta
Mud Kingdom
Scavenger Den
Scavenger Den
Rainforest Kingdom

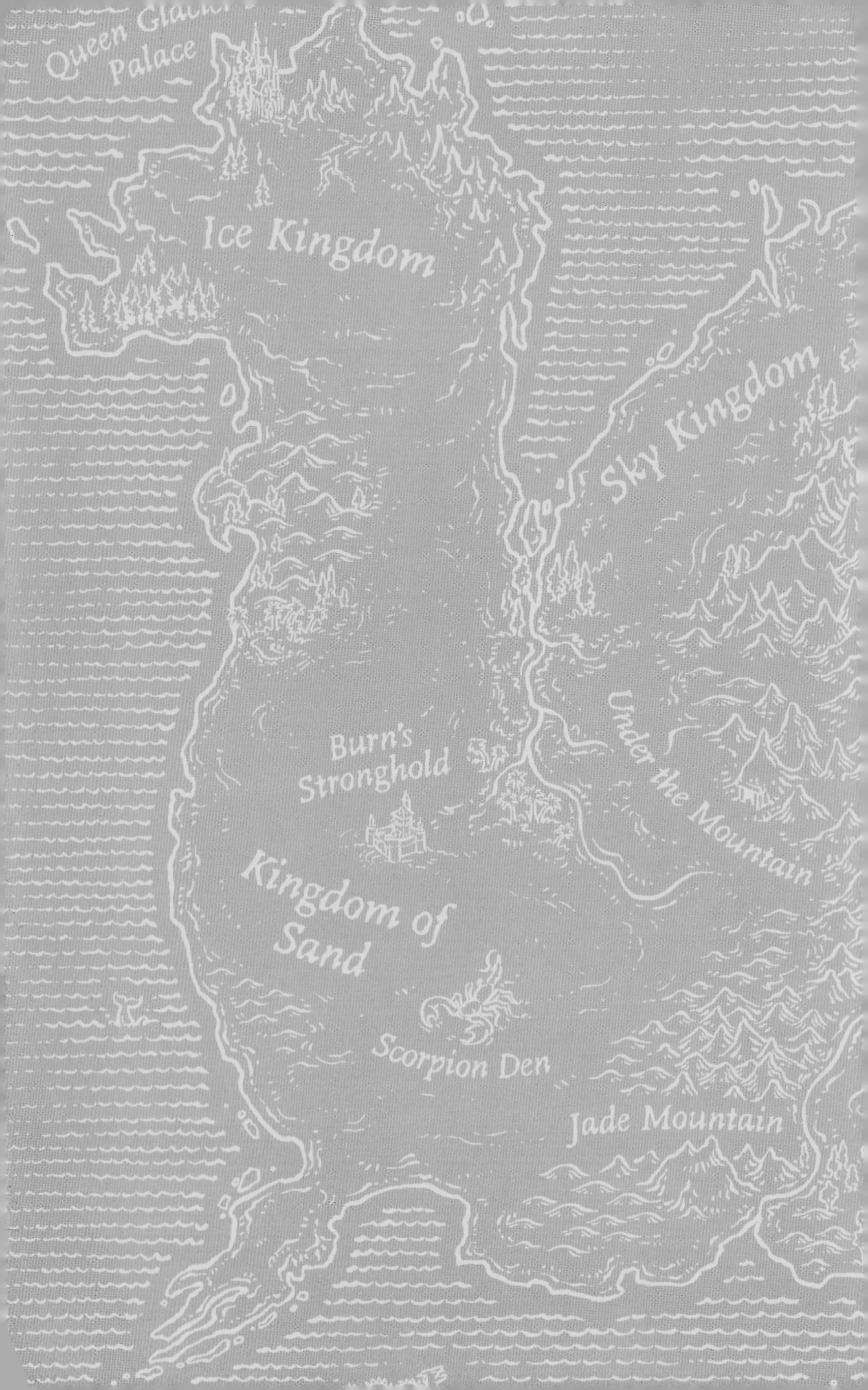
Queen Glacier's Palace
Ice Kingdom
Sky Kingdom
Burn's Stronghold
Under the Mountain
Kingdom of Sand
Scorpion Den
Jade Mountain

THE BRIGHTEST NIGHT

THE DRAGONET PROPHECY

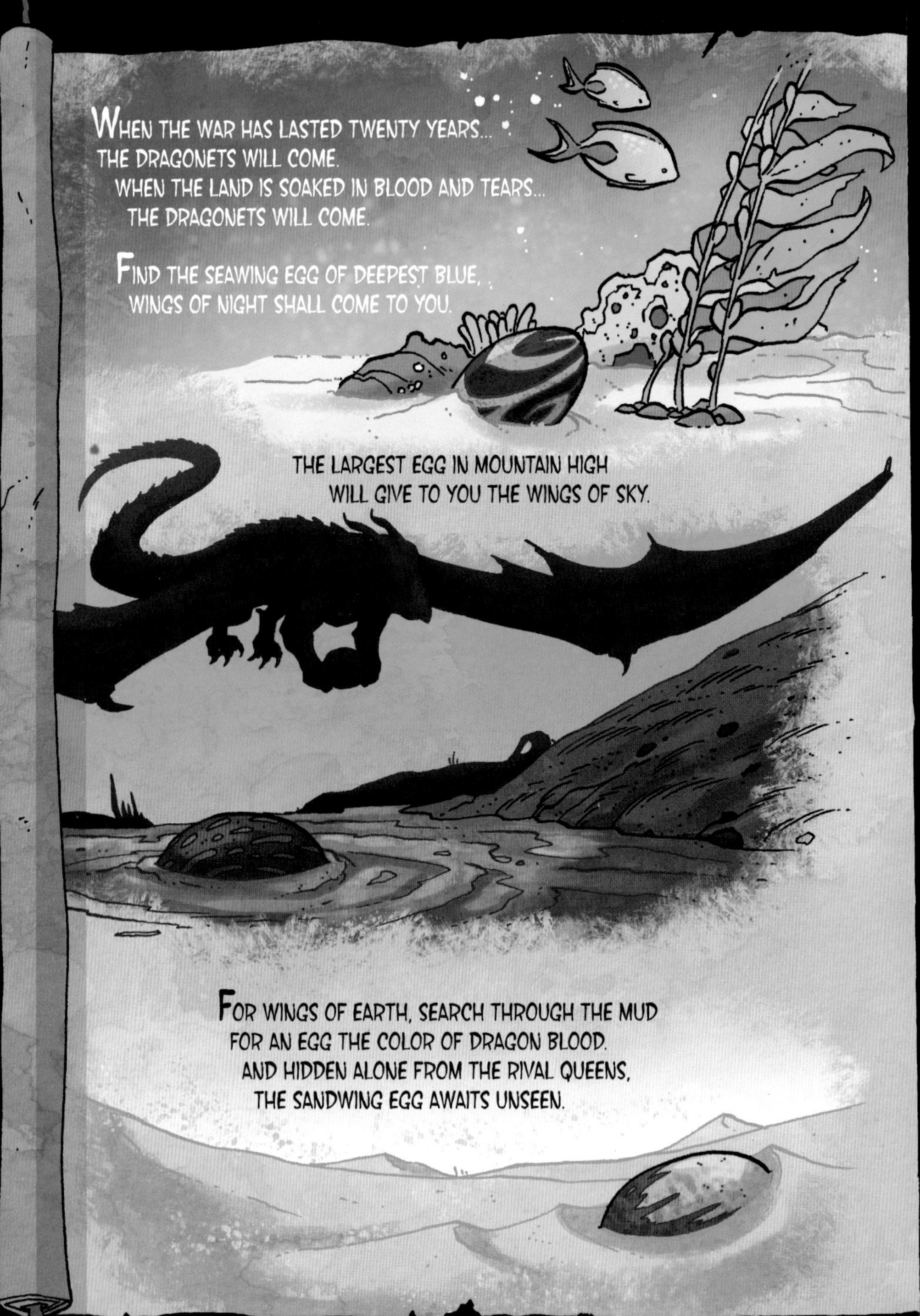
WHEN THE WAR HAS LASTED TWENTY YEARS...
THE DRAGONETS WILL COME.
WHEN THE LAND IS SOAKED IN BLOOD AND TEARS...
THE DRAGONETS WILL COME.
FIND THE SEAWING EGG OF DEEPEST BLUE,
WINGS OF NIGHT SHALL COME TO YOU.
THE LARGEST EGG IN MOUNTAIN HIGH
WILL GIVE TO YOU THE WINGS OF SKY.
FOR WINGS OF EARTH, SEARCH THROUGH THE MUD
FOR AN EGG THE COLOR OF DRAGON BLOOD.
AND HIDDEN ALONE FROM THE RIVAL QUEENS,
THE SANDWING EGG AWAITS UNSEEN.

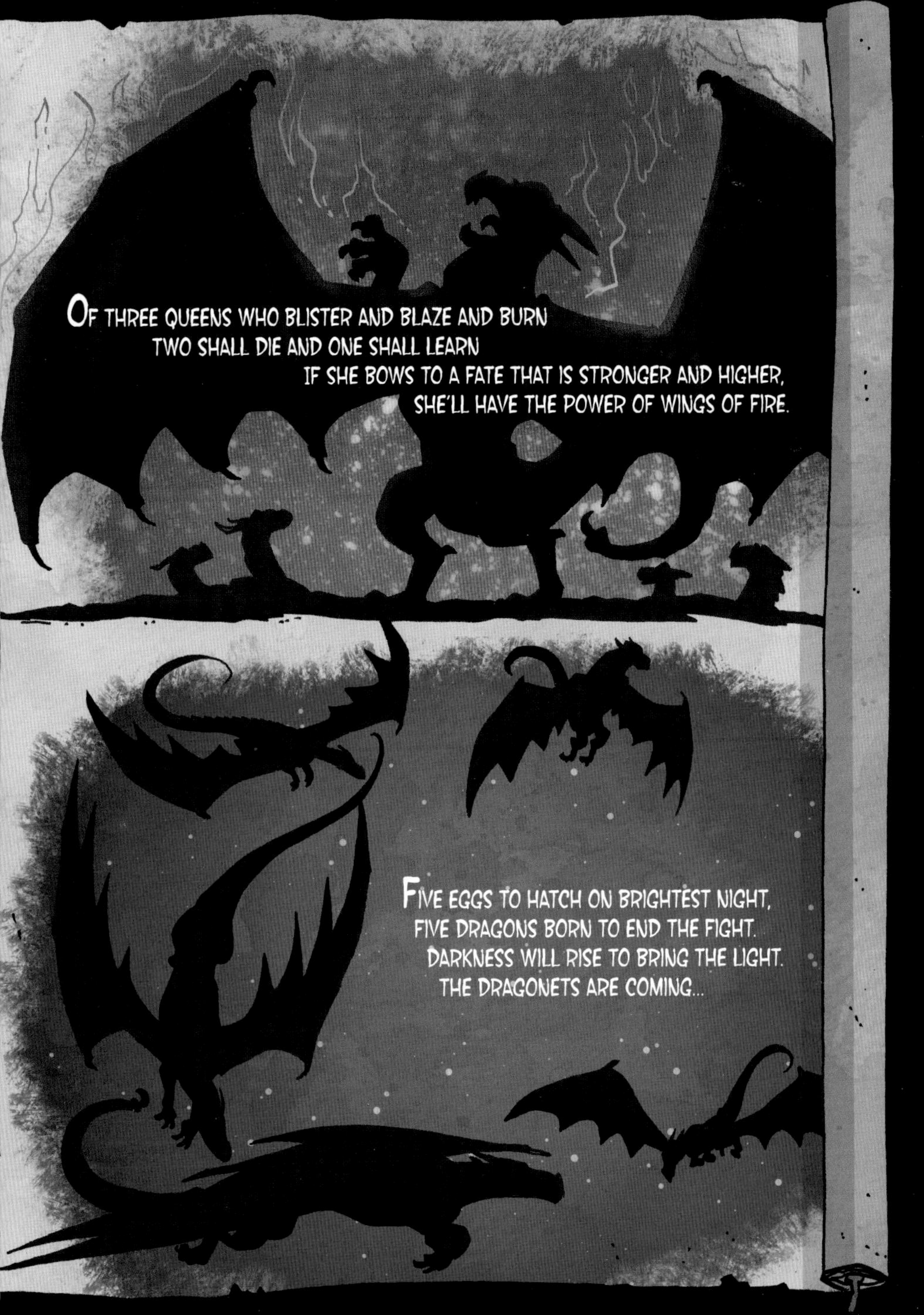
OF THREE QUEENS WHO BLISTER AND BLAZE AND BURN
TWO SHALL DIE AND ONE SHALL LEARN
IF SHE BOWS TO A FATE THAT IS STRONGER AND HIGHER,
SHE'LL HAVE THE POWER OF WINGS OF FIRE.
FIVE EGGS TO HATCH ON BRIGHTEST NIGHT,
FIVE DRAGONS BORN TO END THE FIGHT.
DARKNESS WILL RISE TO BRING THE LIGHT.
THE DRAGONETS ARE COMING...

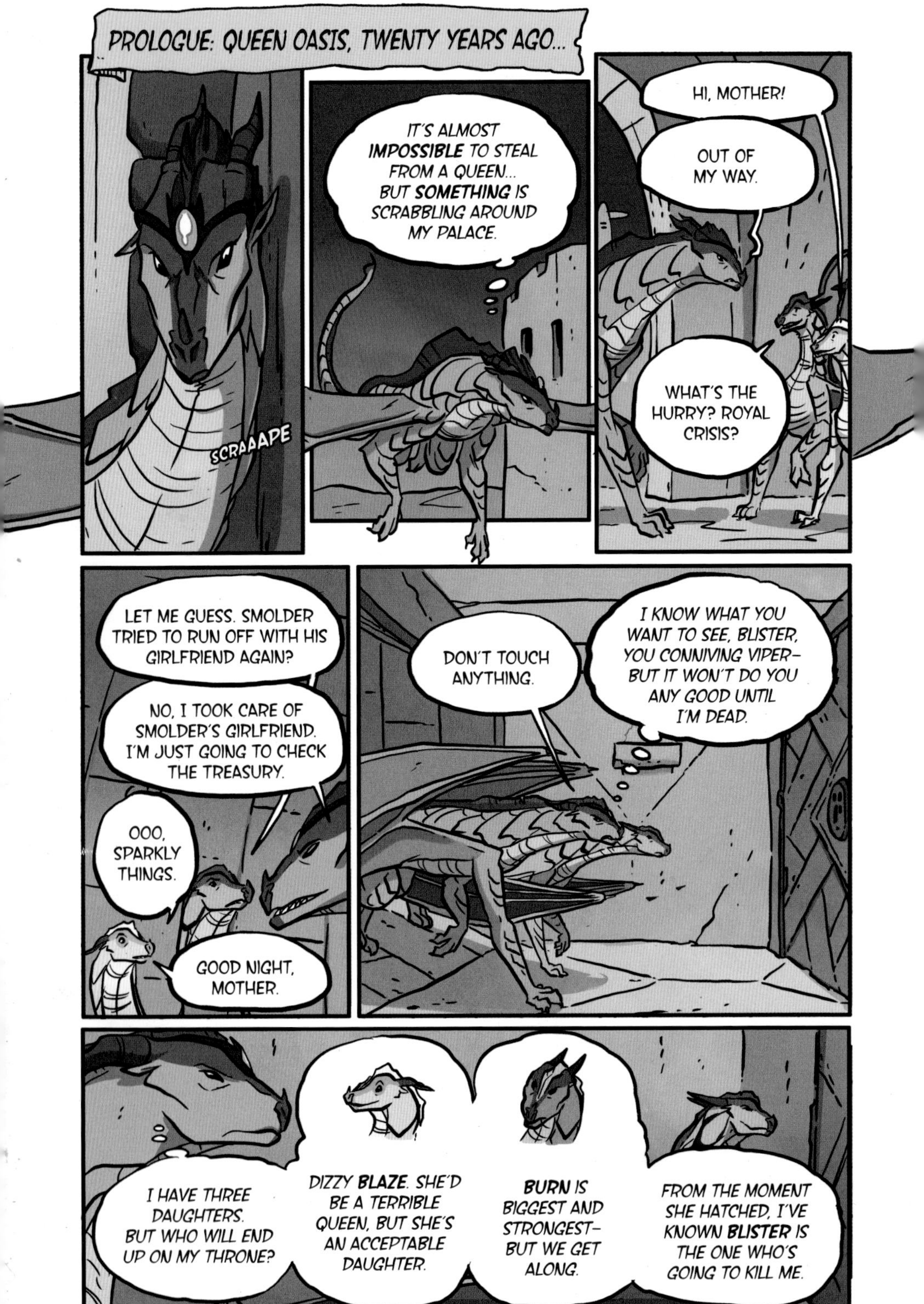
PROLOGUE: QUEEN OASIS, TWENTY YEARS AGO...
SCRAAAPE
IT'S ALMOST IMPOSSIBLE TO STEAL FROM A QUEEN... BUT SOMETHING IS SCRABBLING AROUND MY PALACE.
HI, MOTHER!
OUT OF MY WAY.
WHAT'S THE HURRY? ROYAL CRISIS?
LET ME GUESS. SMOLDER TRIED TO RUN OFF WITH HIS GIRLFRIEND AGAIN?
NO, I TOOK CARE OF SMOLDER'S GIRLFRIEND. I'M JUST GOING TO CHECK THE TREASURY.
OOO, SPARKLY THINGS.
GOOD NIGHT, MOTHER.
DON'T TOUCH ANYTHING.
I KNOW WHAT YOU WANT TO SEE, BLISTER, YOU CONNIVING VIPER— BUT IT WON'T DO YOU ANY GOOD UNTIL I'M DEAD.
I HAVE THREE DAUGHTERS. BUT WHO WILL END UP ON MY THRONE?
DIZZY BLAZE. SHE'D BE A TERRIBLE QUEEN, BUT SHE'S AN ACCEPTABLE DAUGHTER.
BURN IS BIGGEST AND STRONGEST— BUT WE GET ALONG.
FROM THE MOMENT SHE HATCHED, I'VE KNOWN BLISTER IS THE ONE WHO'S GOING TO KILL ME.

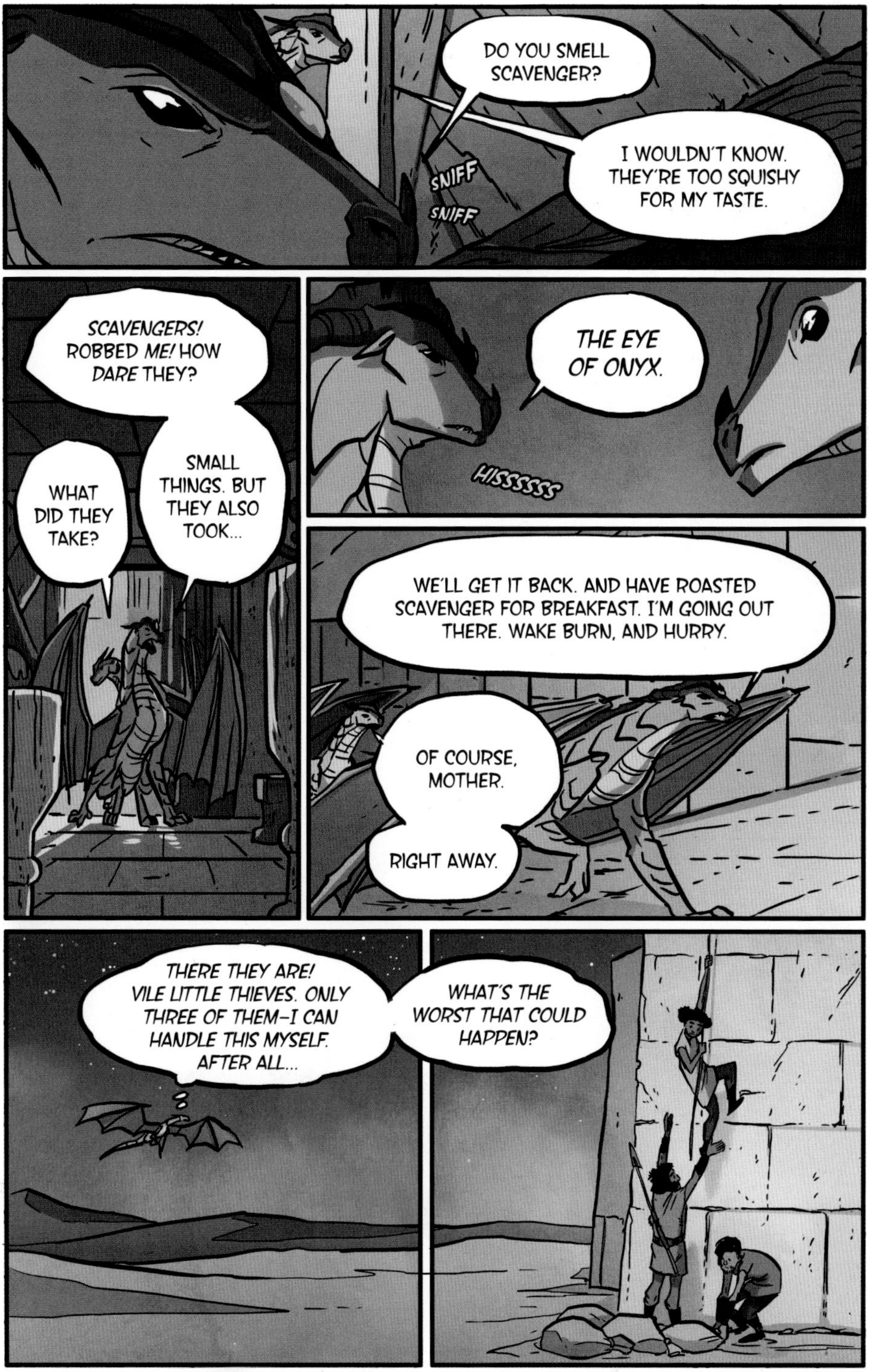
DO YOU SMELL SCAVENGER?
SNIFF
SNIFF
I WOULDN'T KNOW. THEY'RE TOO SQUISHY FOR MY TASTE.
SCAVENGERS! ROBBED ME! HOW DARE THEY?
WHAT DID THEY TAKE?
SMALL THINGS. BUT THEY ALSO TOOK...
THE EYE OF ONYX.
HISSSSSS
WE'LL GET IT BACK. AND HAVE ROASTED SCAVENGER FOR BREAKFAST. I'M GOING OUT THERE. WAKE BURN, AND HURRY.
OF COURSE, MOTHER.
RIGHT AWAY.
THERE THEY ARE! VILE LITTLE THIEVES. ONLY THREE OF THEM—I CAN HANDLE THIS MYSELF. AFTER ALL...
WHAT'S THE WORST THAT COULD HAPPEN?

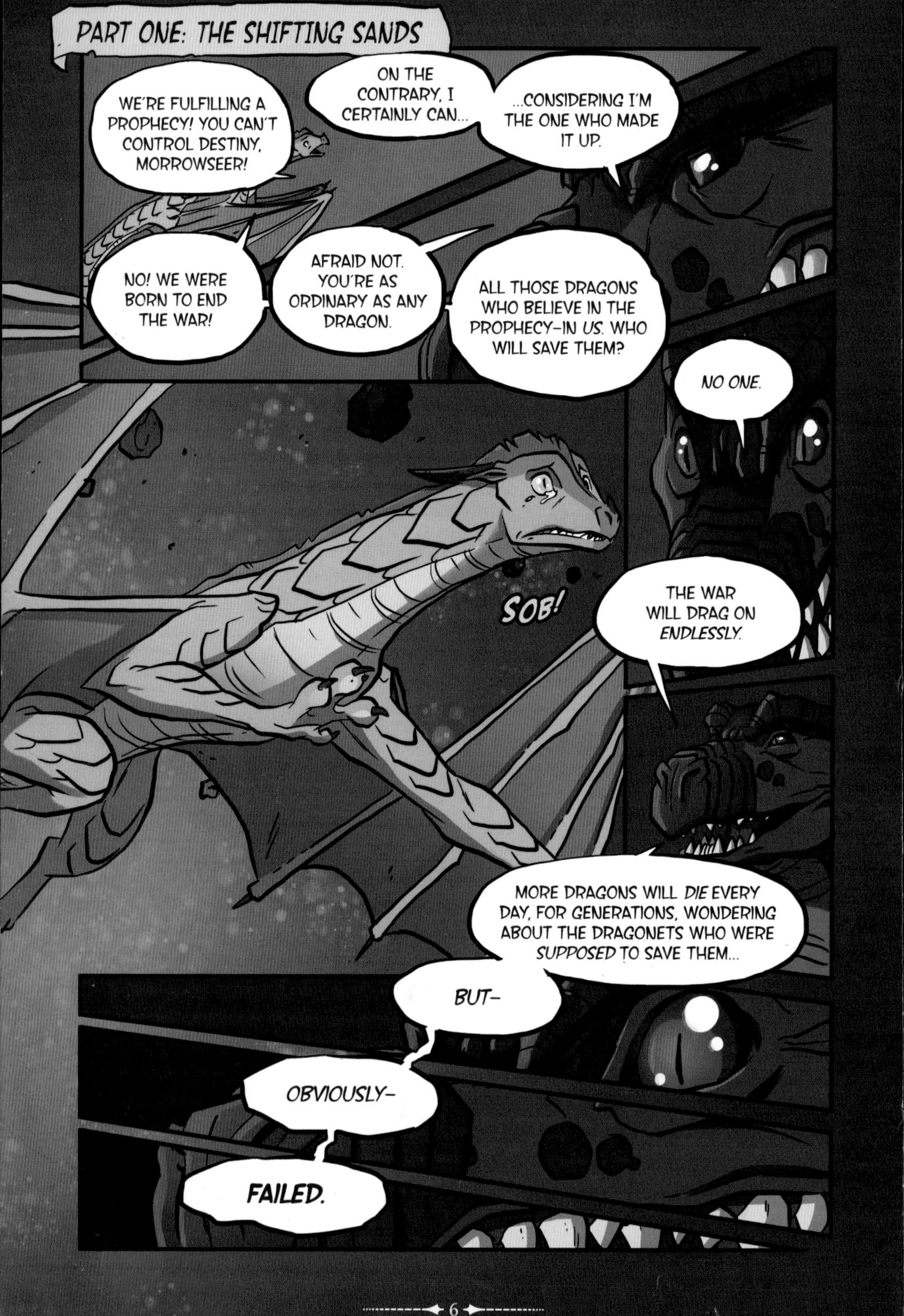
PART ONE: THE SHIFTING SANDS
WE'RE FULFILLING A PROPHECY! YOU CAN'T CONTROL DESTINY, MORROWSEER!
ON THE CONTRARY, I CERTAINLY CAN...
...CONSIDERING I'M THE ONE WHO MADE IT UP.
NO! WE WERE BORN TO END THE WAR!
AFRAID NOT. YOU'RE AS ORDINARY AS ANY DRAGON.
ALL THOSE DRAGONS WHO BELIEVE IN THE PROPHECY—IN *US*. WHO WILL SAVE THEM?
NO ONE.
SOB!
THE WAR WILL DRAG ON *ENDLESSLY*.
MORE DRAGONS WILL *DIE* EVERY DAY, FOR GENERATIONS, WONDERING ABOUT THE DRAGONETS WHO WERE *SUPPOSED* TO SAVE THEM...
BUT–
OBVIOUSLY–
FAILED.

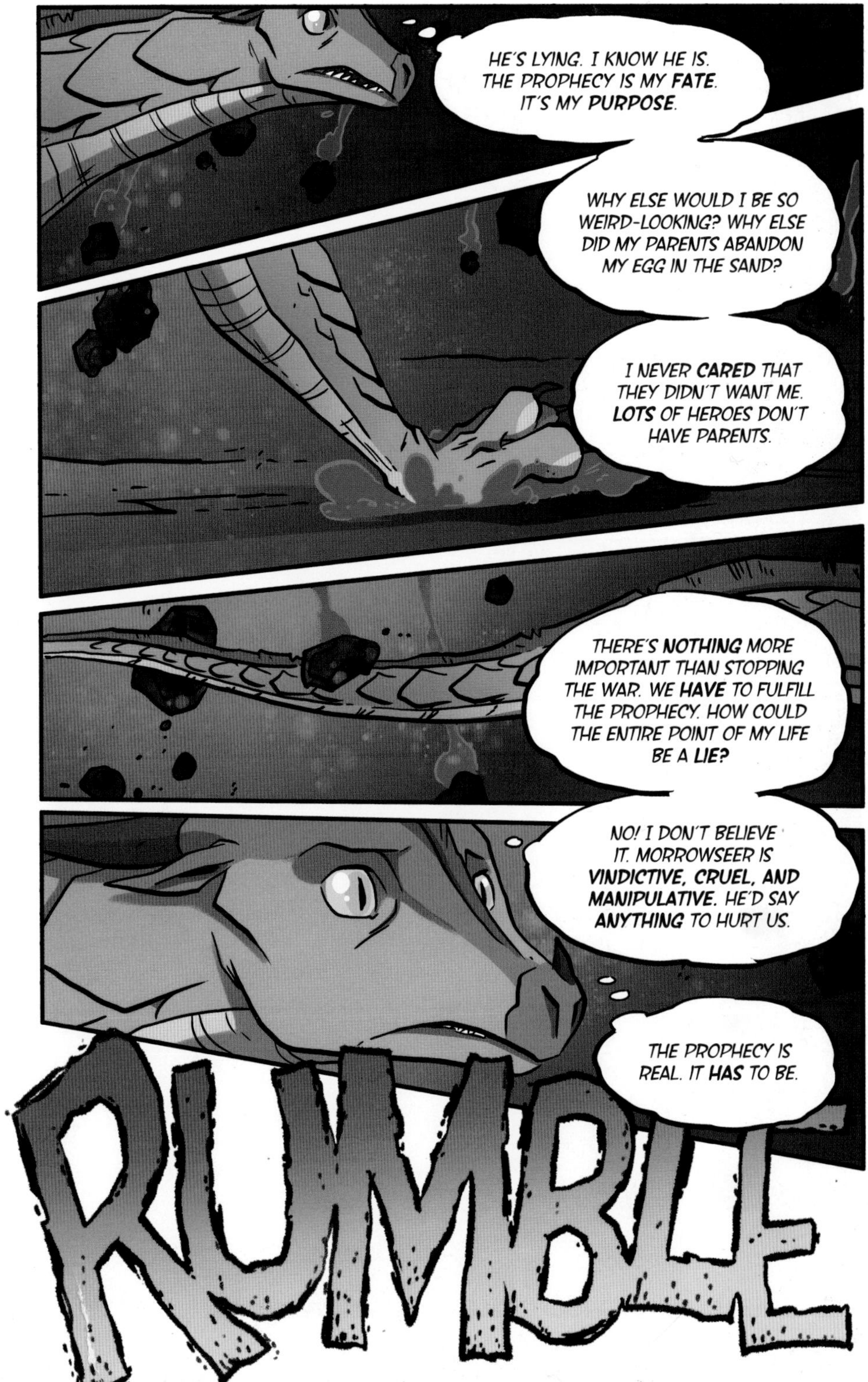
TTW
HE'S LYING. I KNOW HE IS. THE PROPHECY IS MY **FATE**. IT'S MY **PURPOSE**.
WHY ELSE WOULD I BE SO WEIRD-LOOKING? WHY ELSE DID MY PARENTS ABANDON MY EGG IN THE SAND?
I NEVER **CARED** THAT THEY DIDN'T WANT ME. **LOTS** OF HEROES DON'T HAVE PARENTS.
THERE'S **NOTHING** MORE IMPORTANT THAN STOPPING THE WAR. WE **HAVE** TO FULFILL THE PROPHECY. HOW COULD THE ENTIRE POINT OF MY LIFE BE A **LIE?**
NO! I DON'T BELIEVE IT. MORROWSEER IS **VINDICTIVE, CRUEL, AND MANIPULATIVE.** HE'D SAY **ANYTHING** TO HURT US.
THE PROPHECY IS REAL. IT **HAS** TO BE.
RUMBLE

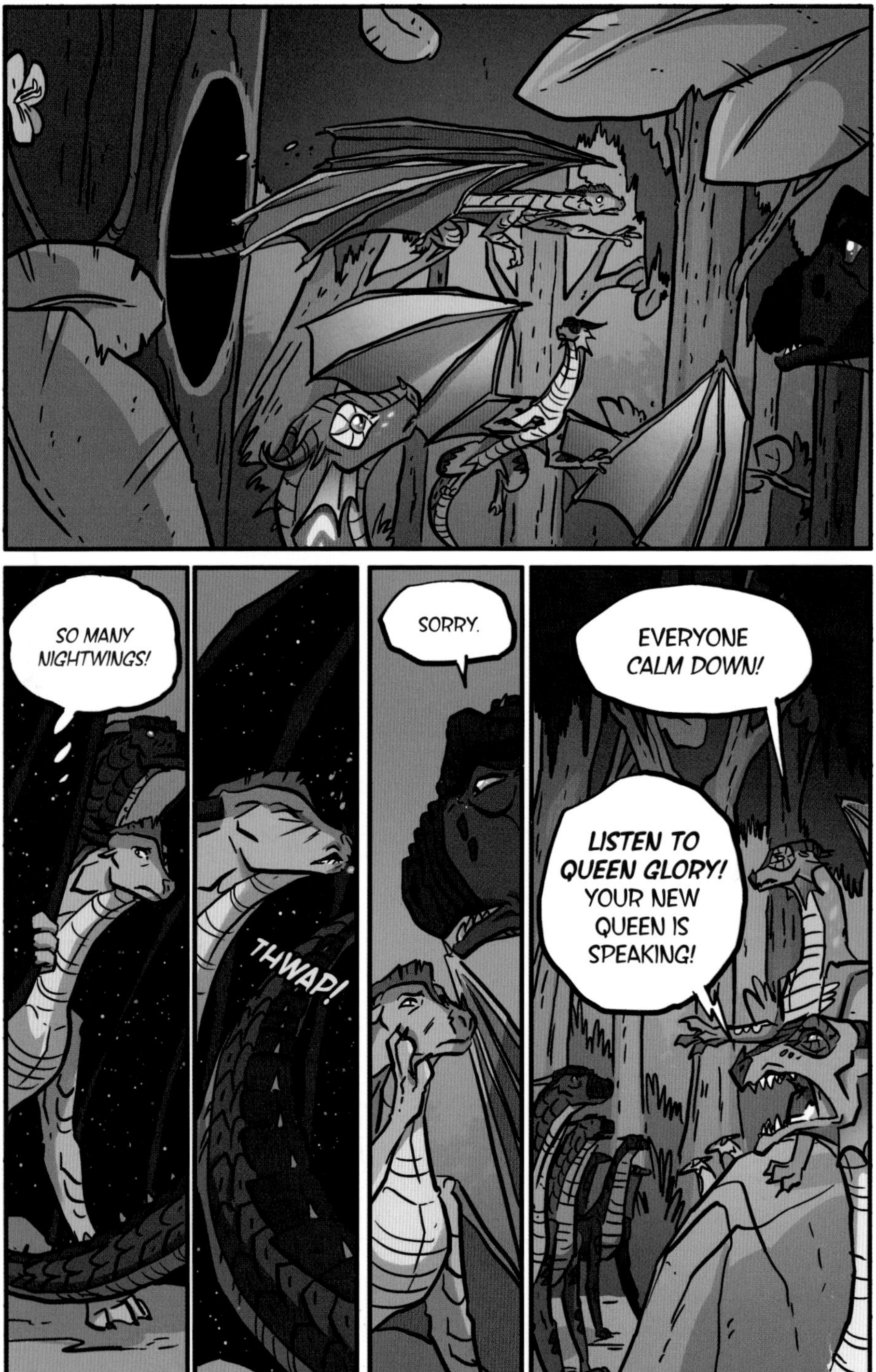
SO MANY NIGHTWINGS!
THWAP!
SORRY.
EVERYONE CALM DOWN!
LISTEN TO QUEEN GLORY! YOUR NEW QUEEN IS SPEAKING!

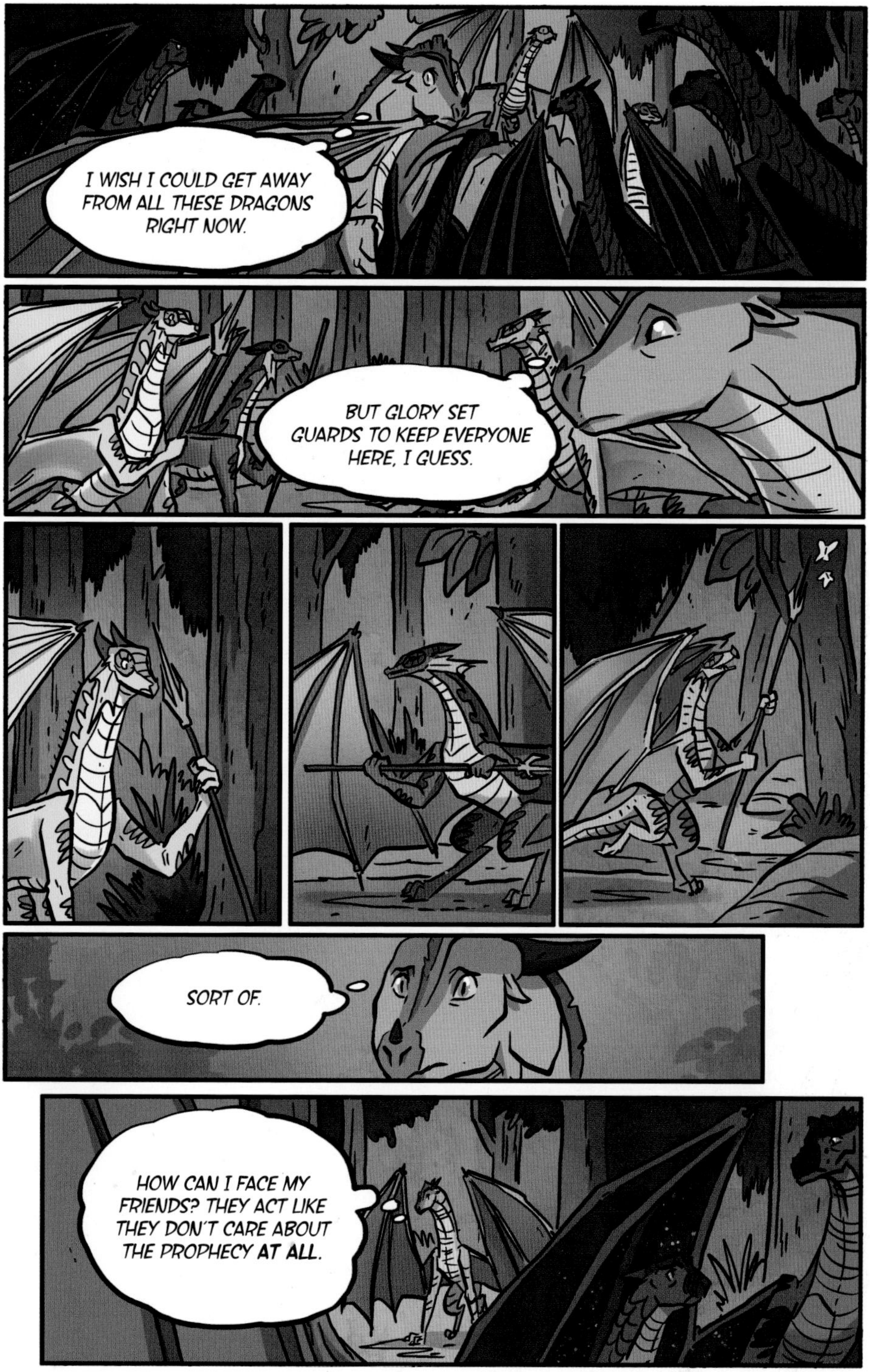
I WISH I COULD GET AWAY FROM ALL THESE DRAGONS RIGHT NOW.
BUT GLORY SET GUARDS TO KEEP EVERYONE HERE, I GUESS.
SORT OF.
HOW CAN I FACE MY FRIENDS? THEY ACT LIKE THEY DON'T CARE ABOUT THE PROPHECY AT ALL.

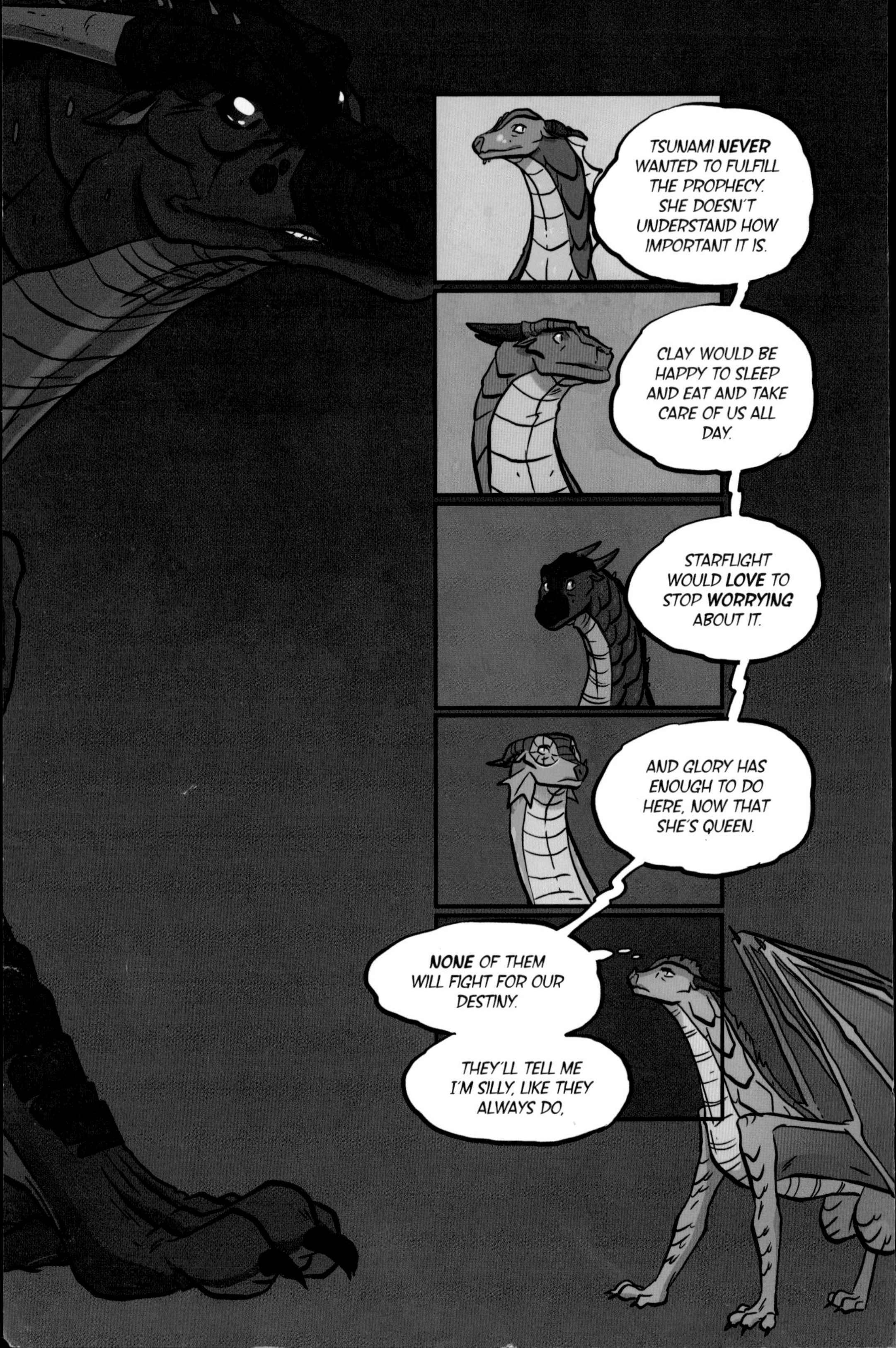
TSUNAMI NEVER WANTED TO FULFILL THE PROPHECY. SHE DOESN'T UNDERSTAND HOW IMPORTANT IT IS.
CLAY WOULD BE HAPPY TO SLEEP AND EAT AND TAKE CARE OF US ALL DAY.
STARFLIGHT WOULD LOVE TO STOP WORRYING ABOUT IT.
AND GLORY HAS ENOUGH TO DO HERE, NOW THAT SHE'S QUEEN.
NONE OF THEM WILL FIGHT FOR OUR DESTINY.
THEY'LL TELL ME I'M SILLY, LIKE THEY ALWAYS DO,

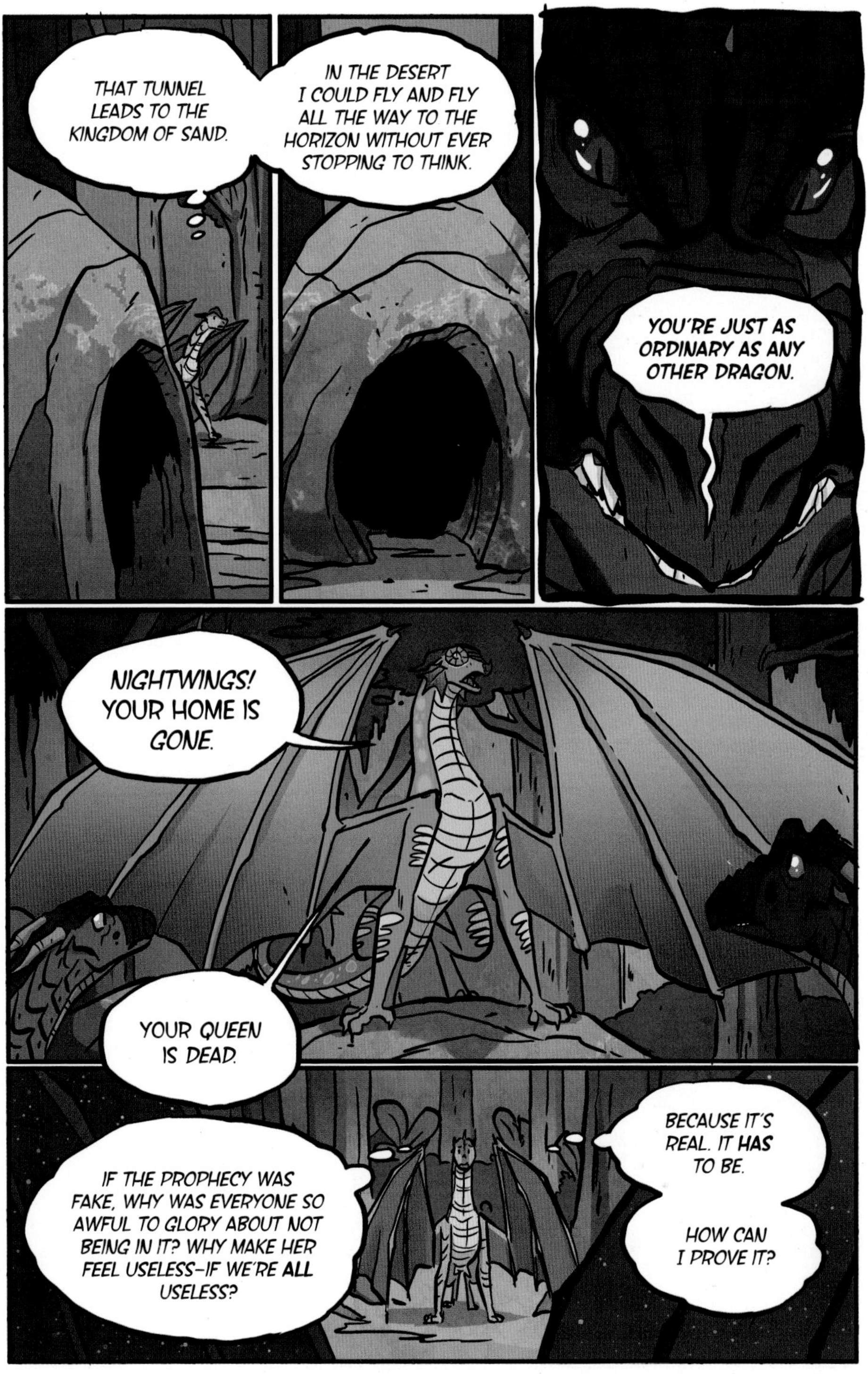
THAT TUNNEL LEADS TO THE KINGDOM OF SAND.
IN THE DESERT I COULD FLY AND FLY ALL THE WAY TO THE HORIZON WITHOUT EVER STOPPING TO THINK.
YOU'RE JUST AS ORDINARY AS ANY OTHER DRAGON.
NIGHTWINGS! YOUR HOME IS *GONE*.
YOUR QUEEN IS DEAD.
IF THE PROPHECY WAS FAKE, WHY WAS EVERYONE SO AWFUL TO GLORY ABOUT NOT BEING IN IT? WHY MAKE HER FEEL USELESS—IF WE'RE **ALL** USELESS?
BECAUSE IT'S REAL. IT **HAS** TO BE.
HOW CAN I PROVE IT?

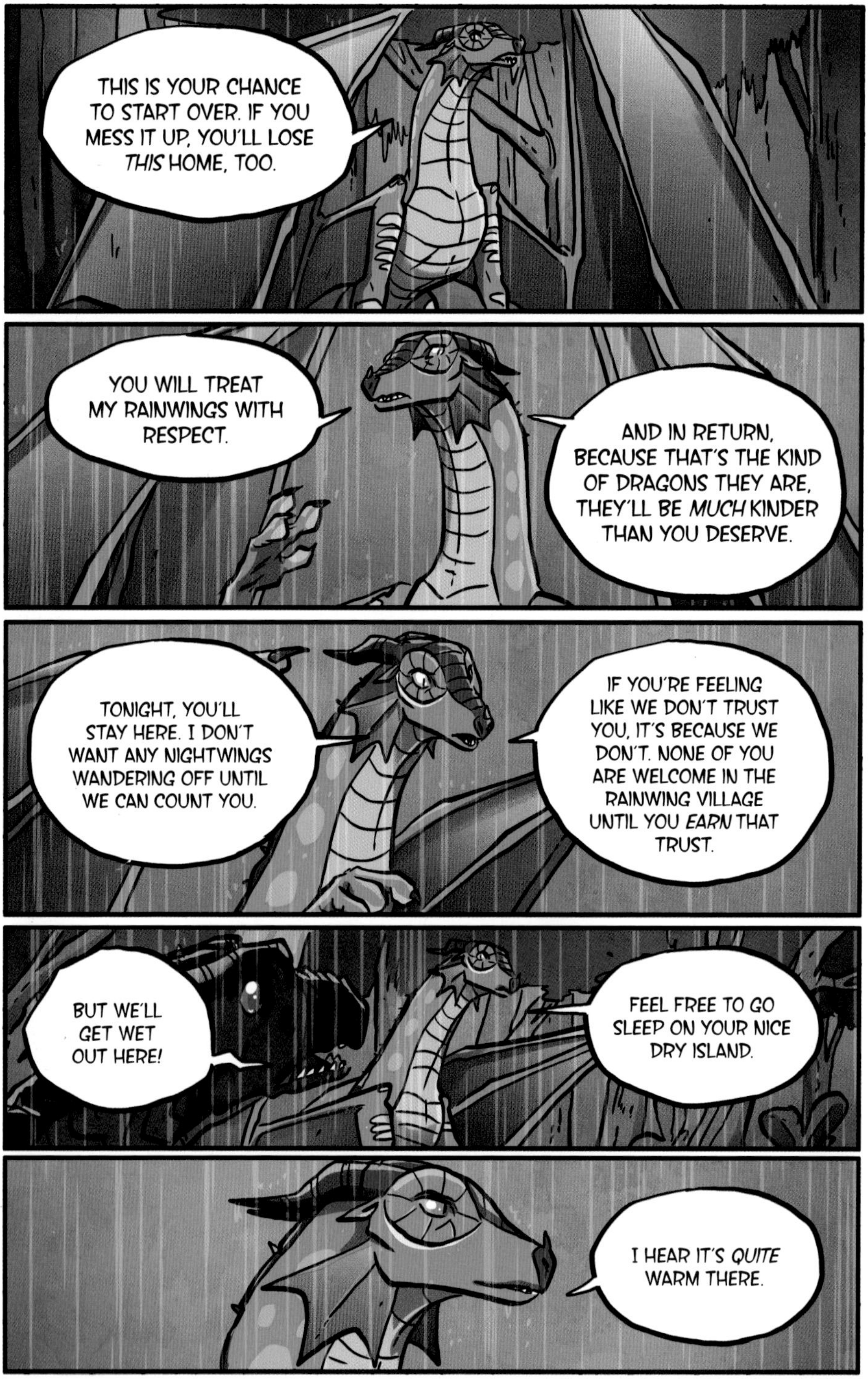
THIS IS YOUR CHANCE TO START OVER. IF YOU MESS IT UP, YOU'LL LOSE *THIS* HOME, TOO.
YOU WILL TREAT MY RAINWINGS WITH RESPECT.
AND IN RETURN, BECAUSE THAT'S THE KIND OF DRAGONS THEY ARE, THEY'LL BE *MUCH* KINDER THAN YOU DESERVE.
TONIGHT, YOU'LL STAY HERE. I DON'T WANT ANY NIGHTWINGS WANDERING OFF UNTIL WE CAN COUNT YOU.
IF YOU'RE FEELING LIKE WE DON'T TRUST YOU, IT'S BECAUSE WE DON'T. NONE OF YOU ARE WELCOME IN THE RAINWING VILLAGE UNTIL YOU *EARN* THAT TRUST.
BUT WE'LL GET WET OUT HERE!
FEEL FREE TO GO SLEEP ON YOUR NICE DRY ISLAND.
I HEAR IT'S *QUITE* WARM THERE.

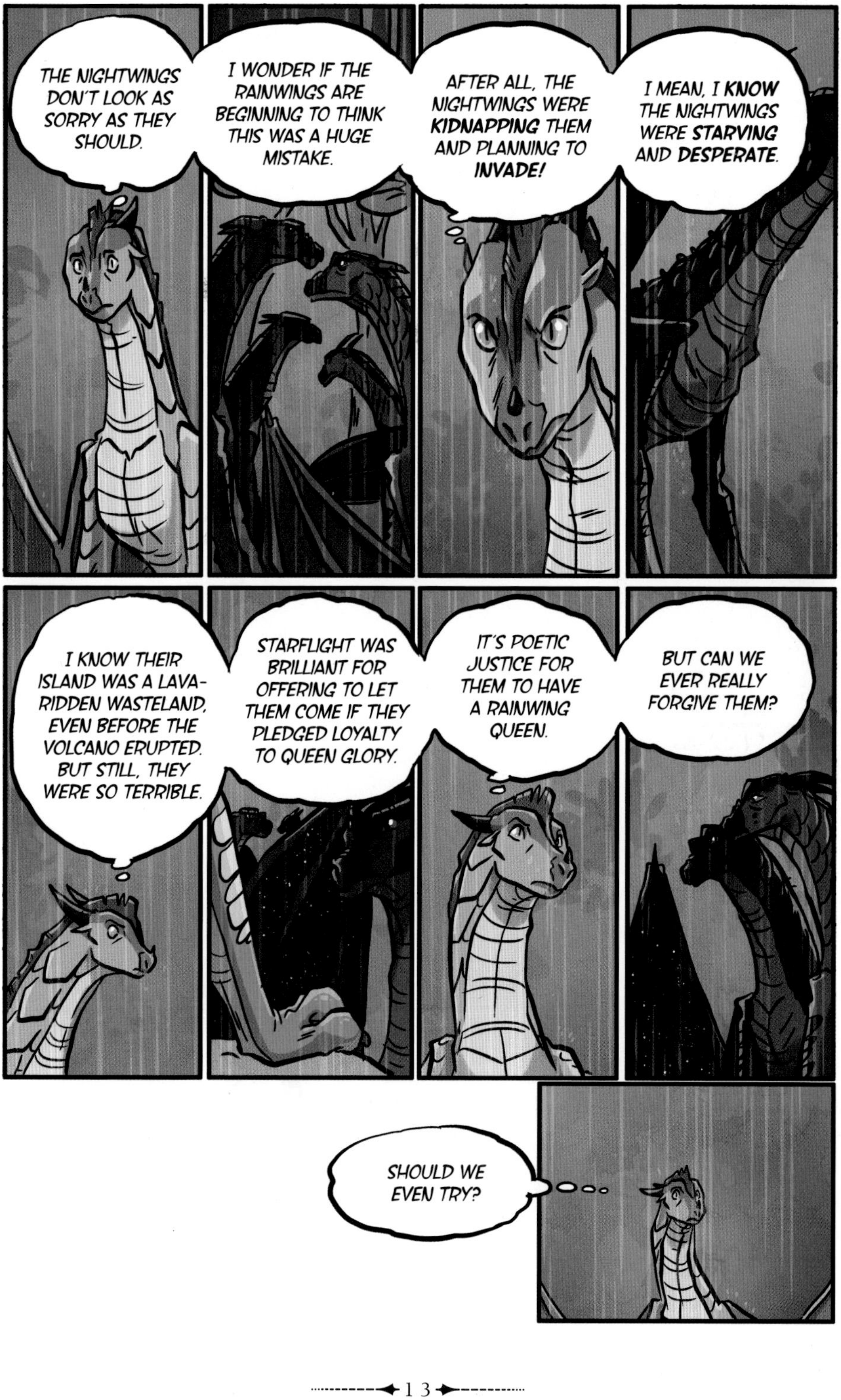
THE NIGHTWINGS DON'T LOOK AS SORRY AS THEY SHOULD.
I WONDER IF THE RAINWINGS ARE BEGINNING TO THINK THIS WAS A HUGE MISTAKE.
AFTER ALL, THE NIGHTWINGS WERE **KIDNAPPING** THEM AND PLANNING TO **INVADE!**
I MEAN, I **KNOW** THE NIGHTWINGS WERE **STARVING** AND **DESPERATE**.
I KNOW THEIR ISLAND WAS A LAVA-RIDDEN WASTELAND, EVEN BEFORE THE VOLCANO ERUPTED. BUT STILL, THEY WERE SO TERRIBLE.
STARFLIGHT WAS BRILLIANT FOR OFFERING TO LET THEM COME IF THEY PLEDGED LOYALTY TO QUEEN GLORY.
IT'S POETIC JUSTICE FOR THEM TO HAVE A RAINWING QUEEN.
BUT CAN WE EVER REALLY FORGIVE THEM?
SHOULD WE EVEN TRY?

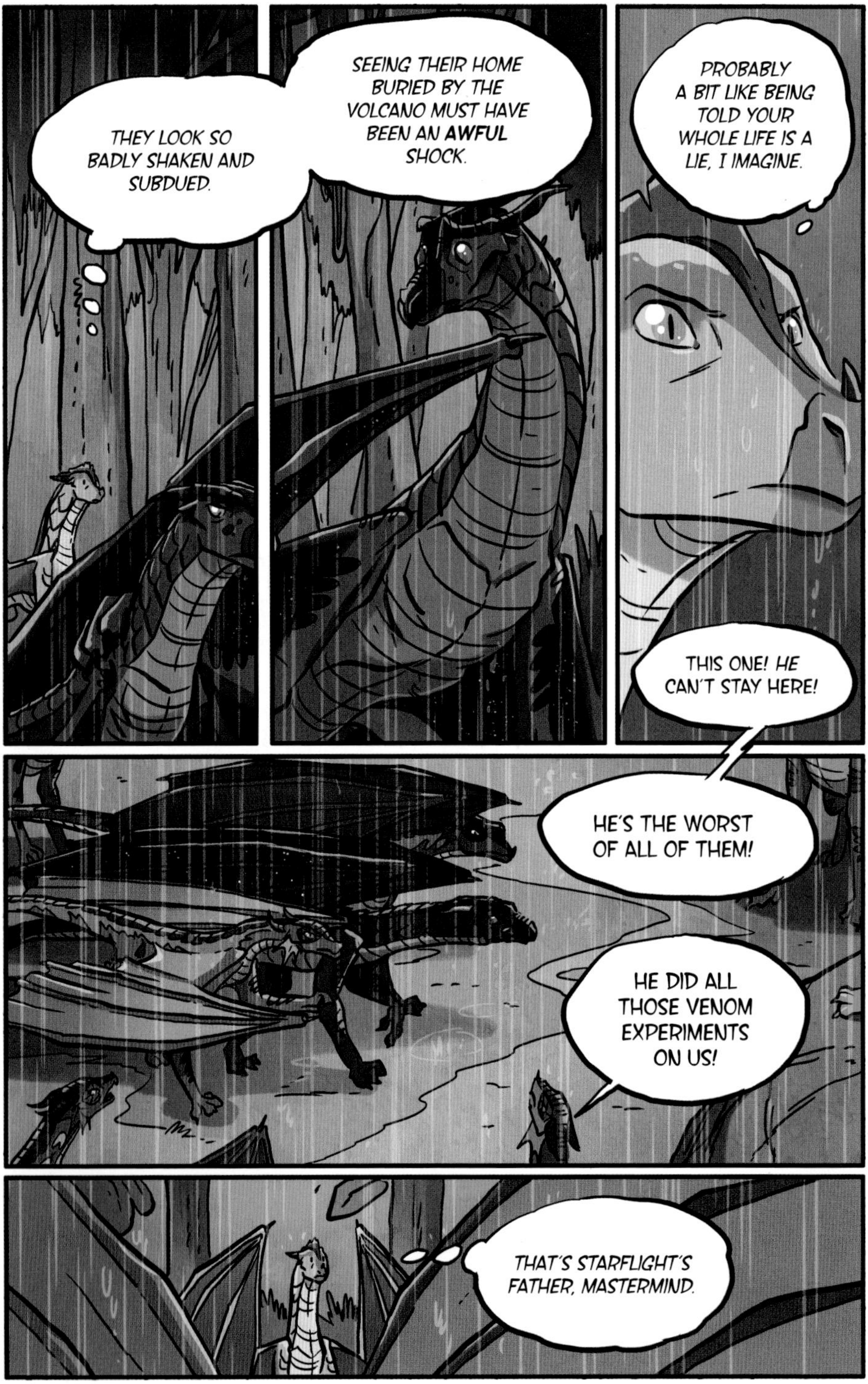
THEY LOOK SO BADLY SHAKEN AND SUBDUED.
SEEING THEIR HOME BURIED BY THE VOLCANO MUST HAVE BEEN AN **AWFUL** SHOCK.
PROBABLY A BIT LIKE BEING TOLD YOUR WHOLE LIFE IS A LIE, I IMAGINE.
THIS ONE! HE CAN'T STAY HERE!
HE'S THE WORST OF ALL OF THEM!
HE DID ALL THOSE VENOM EXPERIMENTS ON US!
THAT'S STARFLIGHT'S FATHER, MASTERMIND.

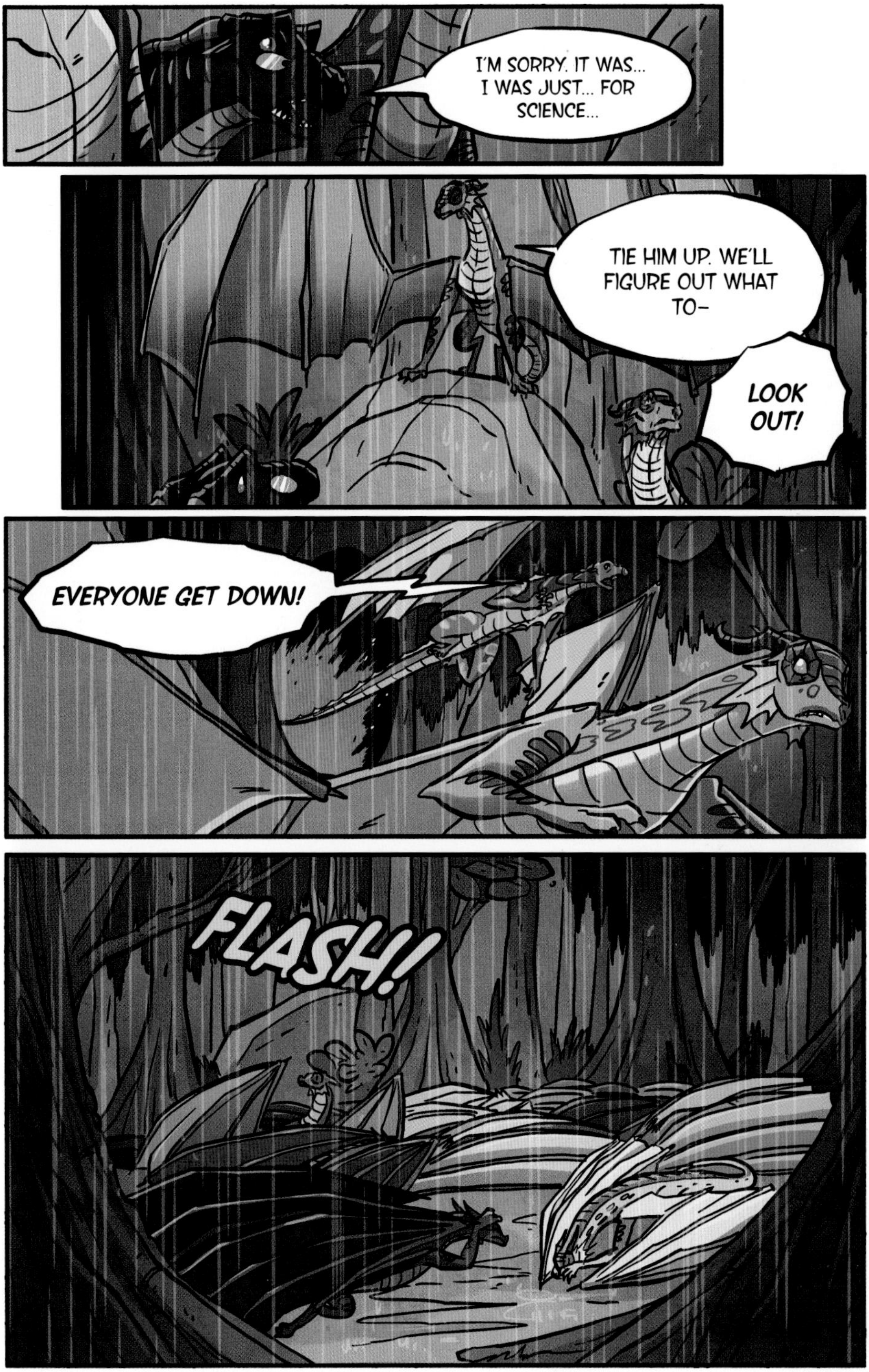
I'M SORRY. IT WAS... I WAS JUST... FOR SCIENCE...
TIE HIM UP. WE'LL FIGURE OUT WHAT TO–
LOOK OUT!
EVERYONE GET DOWN!
FLASH!

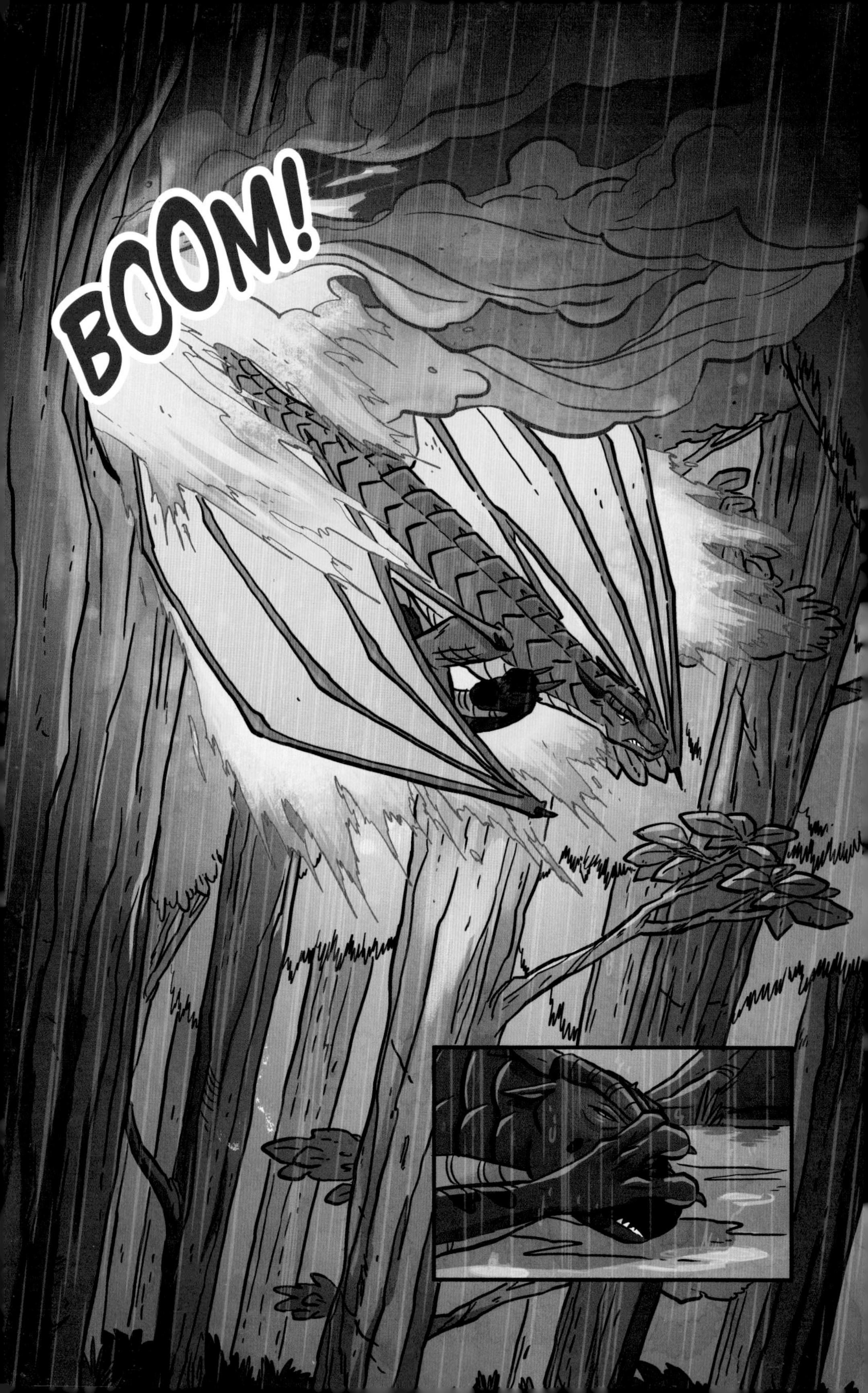
BOOM!

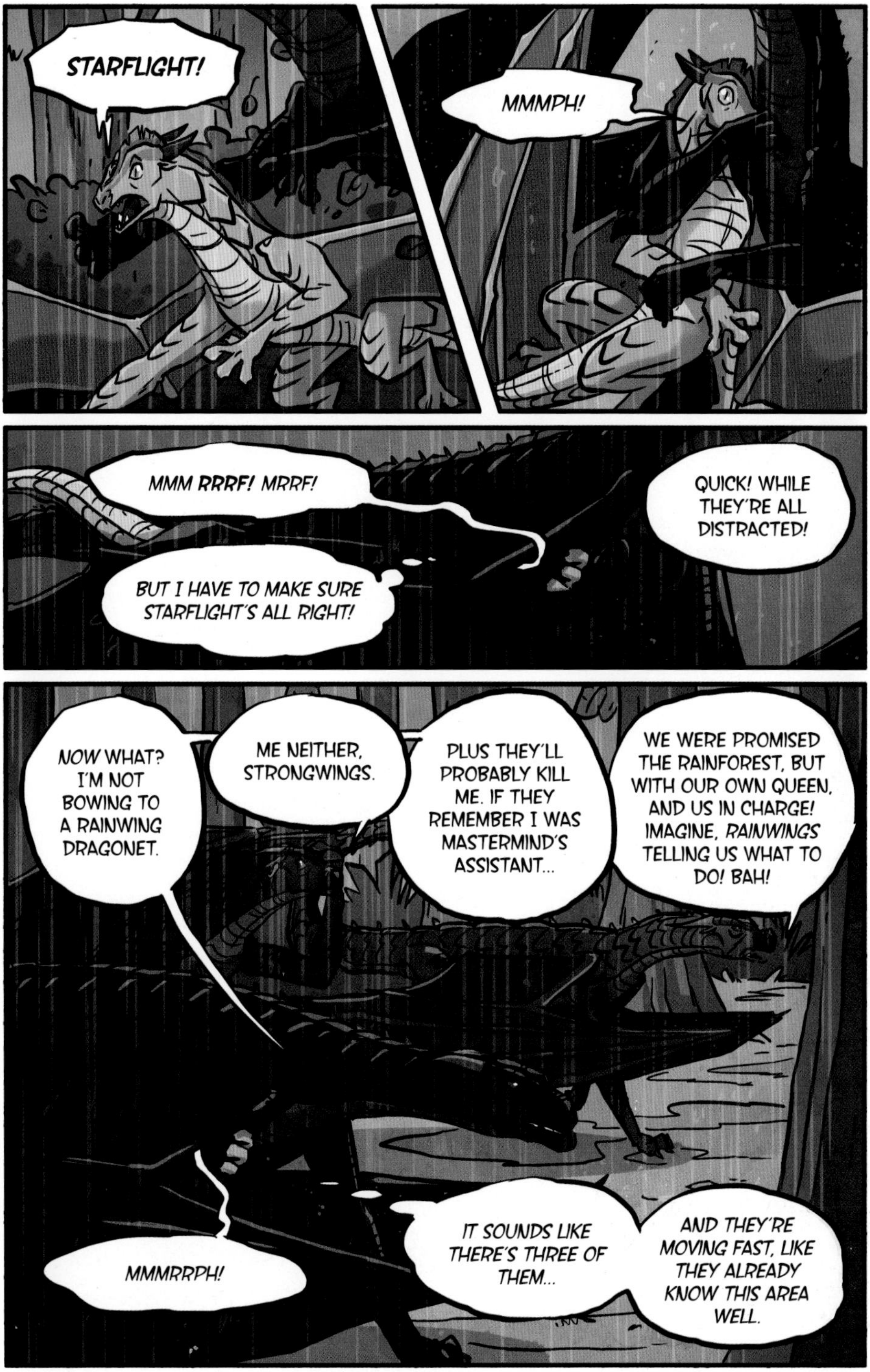
STARFLIGHT!
MMMPH!
MMM RRRF! MRRF!
BUT I HAVE TO MAKE SURE STARFLIGHT'S ALL RIGHT!
QUICK! WHILE THEY'RE ALL DISTRACTED!
NOW WHAT? I'M NOT BOWING TO A RAINWING DRAGONET.
ME NEITHER, STRONGWINGS.
PLUS THEY'LL PROBABLY KILL ME. IF THEY REMEMBER I WAS MASTERMIND'S ASSISTANT...
WE WERE PROMISED THE RAINFOREST, BUT WITH OUR OWN QUEEN, AND US IN CHARGE! IMAGINE, RAINWINGS TELLING US WHAT TO DO! BAH!
MMMRRPH!
IT SOUNDS LIKE THERE'S THREE OF THEM...
AND THEY'RE MOVING FAST, LIKE THEY ALREADY KNOW THIS AREA WELL.

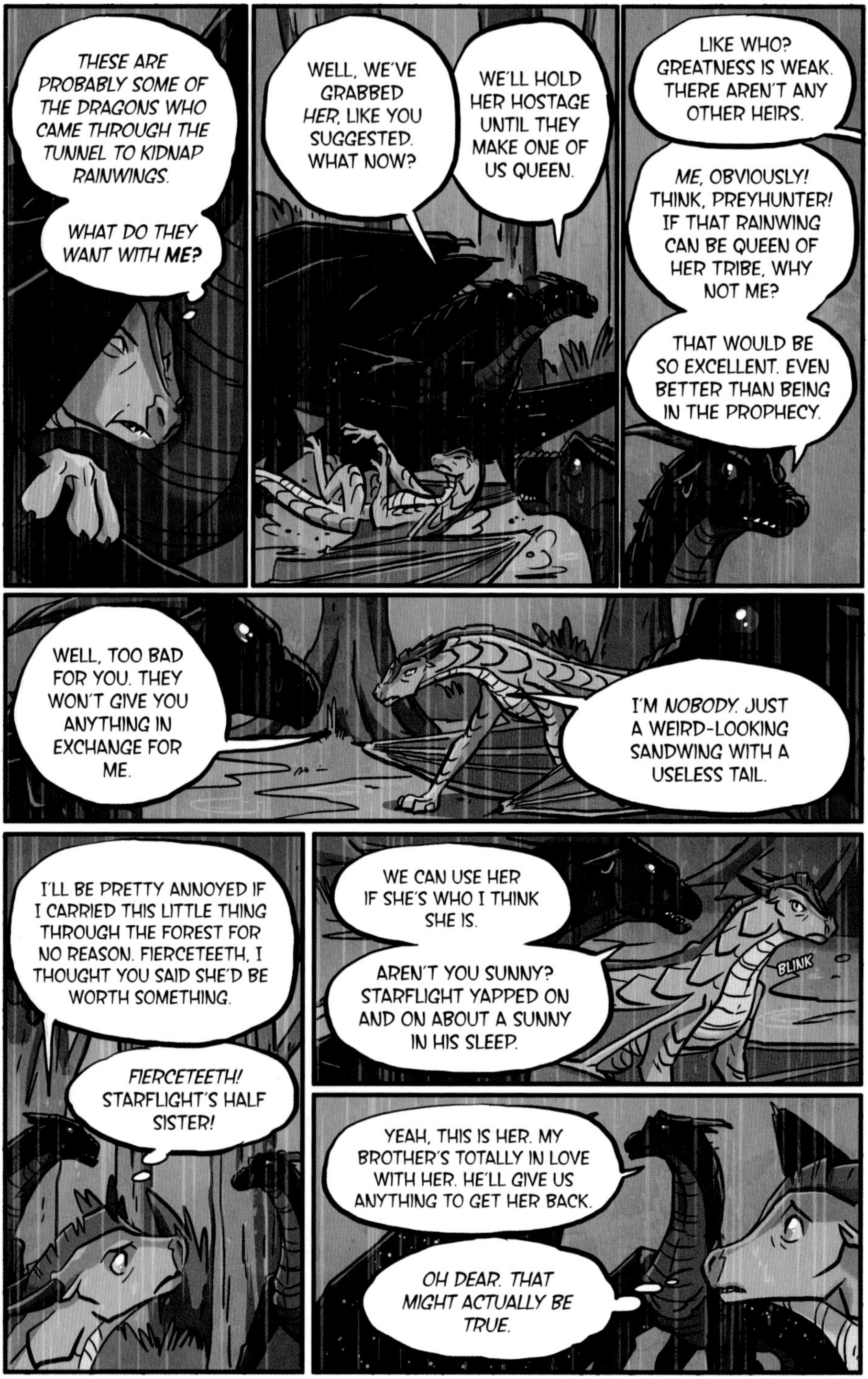

THESE ARE PROBABLY SOME OF THE DRAGONS WHO CAME THROUGH THE TUNNEL TO KIDNAP RAINWINGS.
WHAT DO THEY WANT WITH ME?
WELL, WE'VE GRABBED HER, LIKE YOU SUGGESTED. WHAT NOW?
WE'LL HOLD HER HOSTAGE UNTIL THEY MAKE ONE OF US QUEEN.
LIKE WHO? GREATNESS IS WEAK. THERE AREN'T ANY OTHER HEIRS.
ME, OBVIOUSLY! THINK, PREYHUNTER! IF THAT RAINWING CAN BE QUEEN OF HER TRIBE, WHY NOT ME?
THAT WOULD BE SO EXCELLENT. EVEN BETTER THAN BEING IN THE PROPHECY.
WELL, TOO BAD FOR YOU. THEY WON'T GIVE YOU ANYTHING IN EXCHANGE FOR ME.
I'M NOBODY. JUST A WEIRD-LOOKING SANDWING WITH A USELESS TAIL.
I'LL BE PRETTY ANNOYED IF I CARRIED THIS LITTLE THING THROUGH THE FOREST FOR NO REASON. FIERCETEETH, I THOUGHT YOU SAID SHE'D BE WORTH SOMETHING.
FIERCETEETH! STARFLIGHT'S HALF SISTER!
WE CAN USE HER IF SHE'S WHO I THINK SHE IS.
AREN'T YOU SUNNY? STARFLIGHT YAPPED ON AND ON ABOUT A SUNNY IN HIS SLEEP.
BLINK
YEAH, THIS IS HER. MY BROTHER'S TOTALLY IN LOVE WITH HER. HE'LL GIVE US ANYTHING TO GET HER BACK.
OH DEAR. THAT MIGHT ACTUALLY BE TRUE.

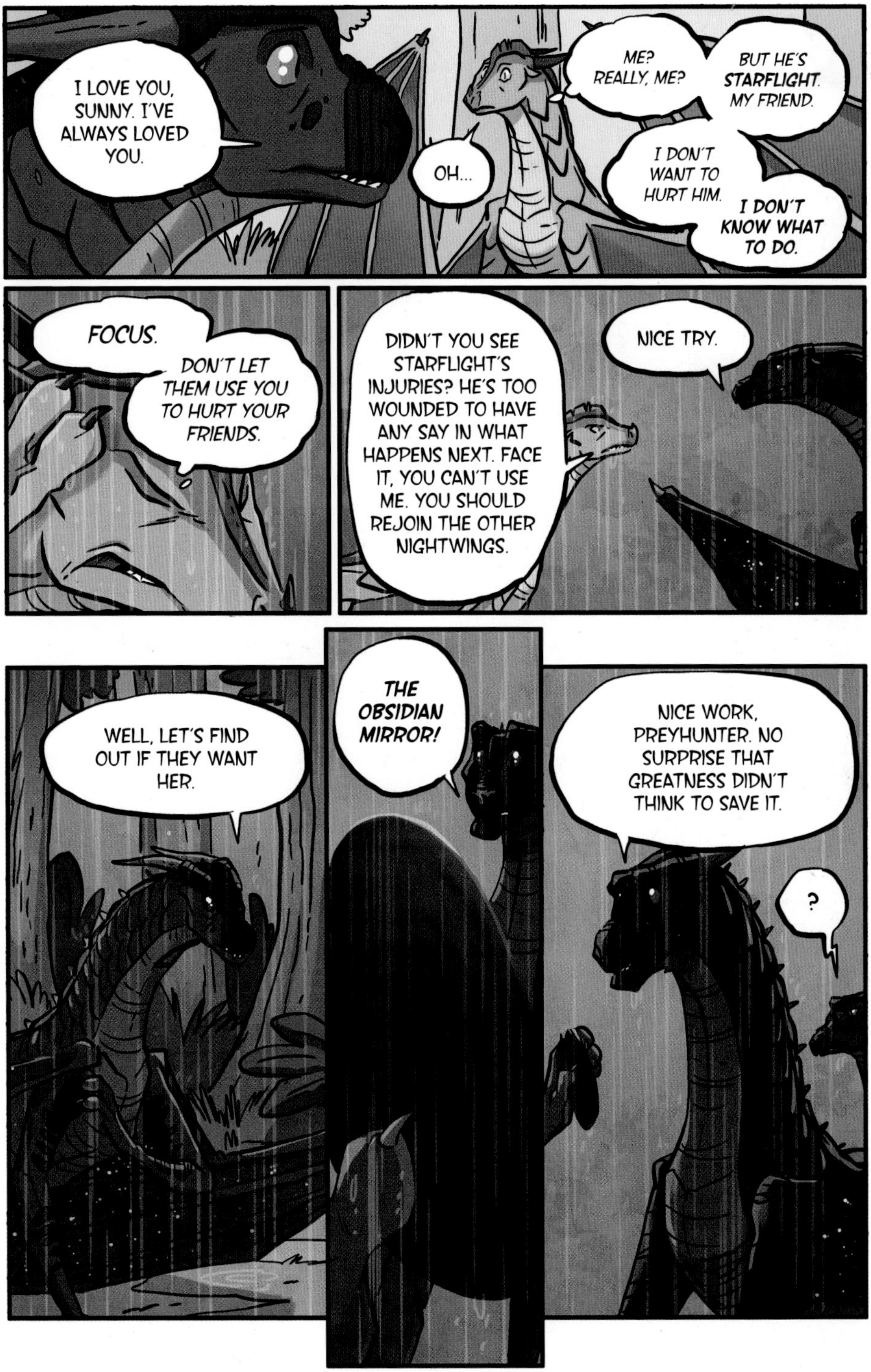
I LOVE YOU, SUNNY. I'VE ALWAYS LOVED YOU.
OH...
ME? REALLY, ME?
BUT HE'S **STARFLIGHT**. MY FRIEND.
I DON'T WANT TO HURT HIM.
I DON'T KNOW WHAT TO DO.
FOCUS.
DON'T LET THEM USE YOU TO HURT YOUR FRIENDS.
DIDN'T YOU SEE STARFLIGHT'S INJURIES? HE'S TOO WOUNDED TO HAVE ANY SAY IN WHAT HAPPENS NEXT. FACE IT, YOU CAN'T USE ME. YOU SHOULD REJOIN THE OTHER NIGHTWINGS.
NICE TRY.
WELL, LET'S FIND OUT IF THEY WANT HER.
THE OBSIDIAN MIRROR!
NICE WORK, PREYHUNTER. NO SURPRISE THAT GREATNESS DIDN'T THINK TO SAVE IT.
?

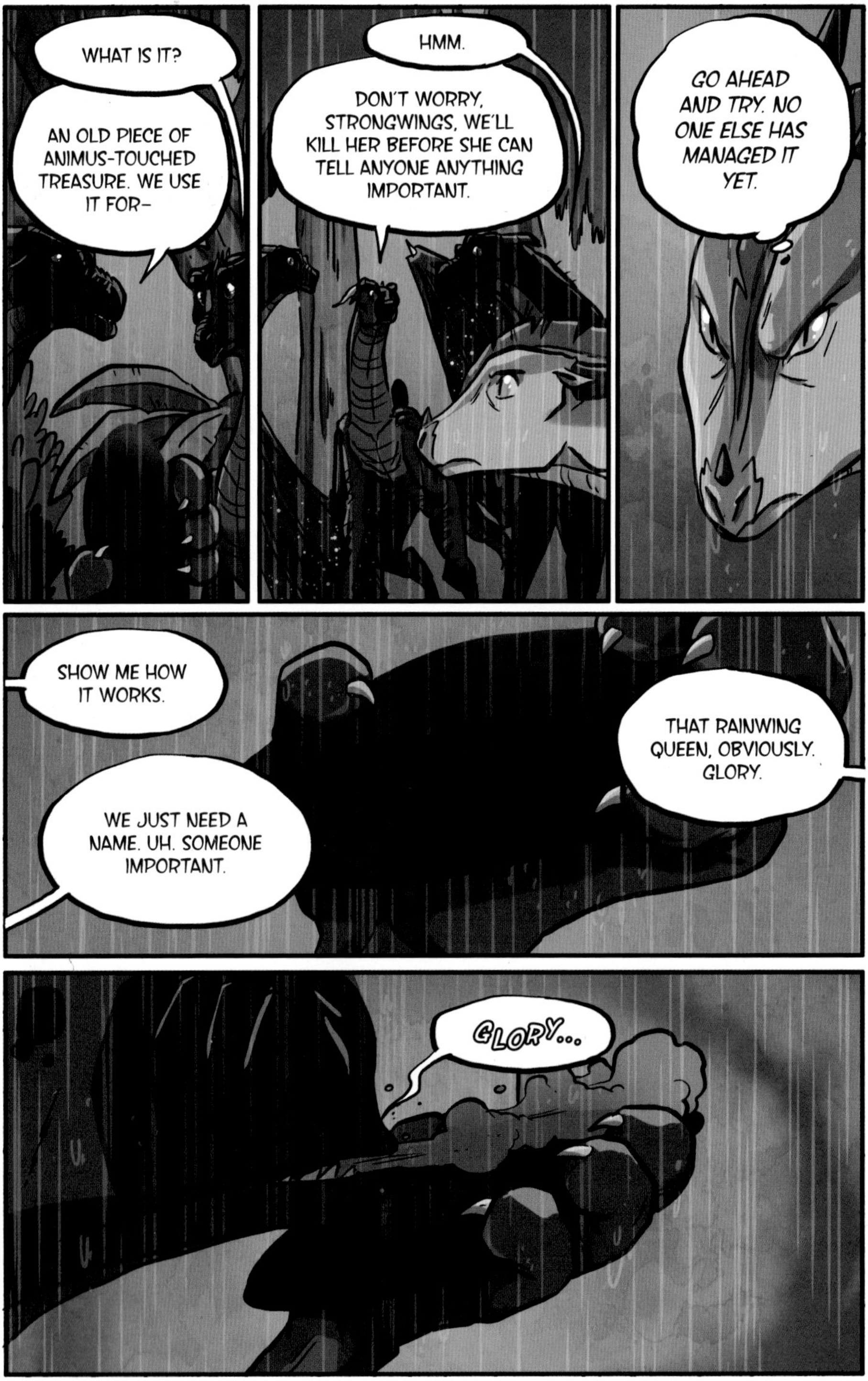
WHAT IS IT?
AN OLD PIECE OF ANIMUS-TOUCHED TREASURE. WE USE IT FOR–
HMM.
DON'T WORRY, STRONGWINGS, WE'LL KILL HER BEFORE SHE CAN TELL ANYONE ANYTHING IMPORTANT.
GO AHEAD AND TRY. NO ONE ELSE HAS MANAGED IT YET.
SHOW ME HOW IT WORKS.
WE JUST NEED A NAME. UH. SOMEONE IMPORTANT.
THAT RAINWING QUEEN, OBVIOUSLY. GLORY.
GLORY...

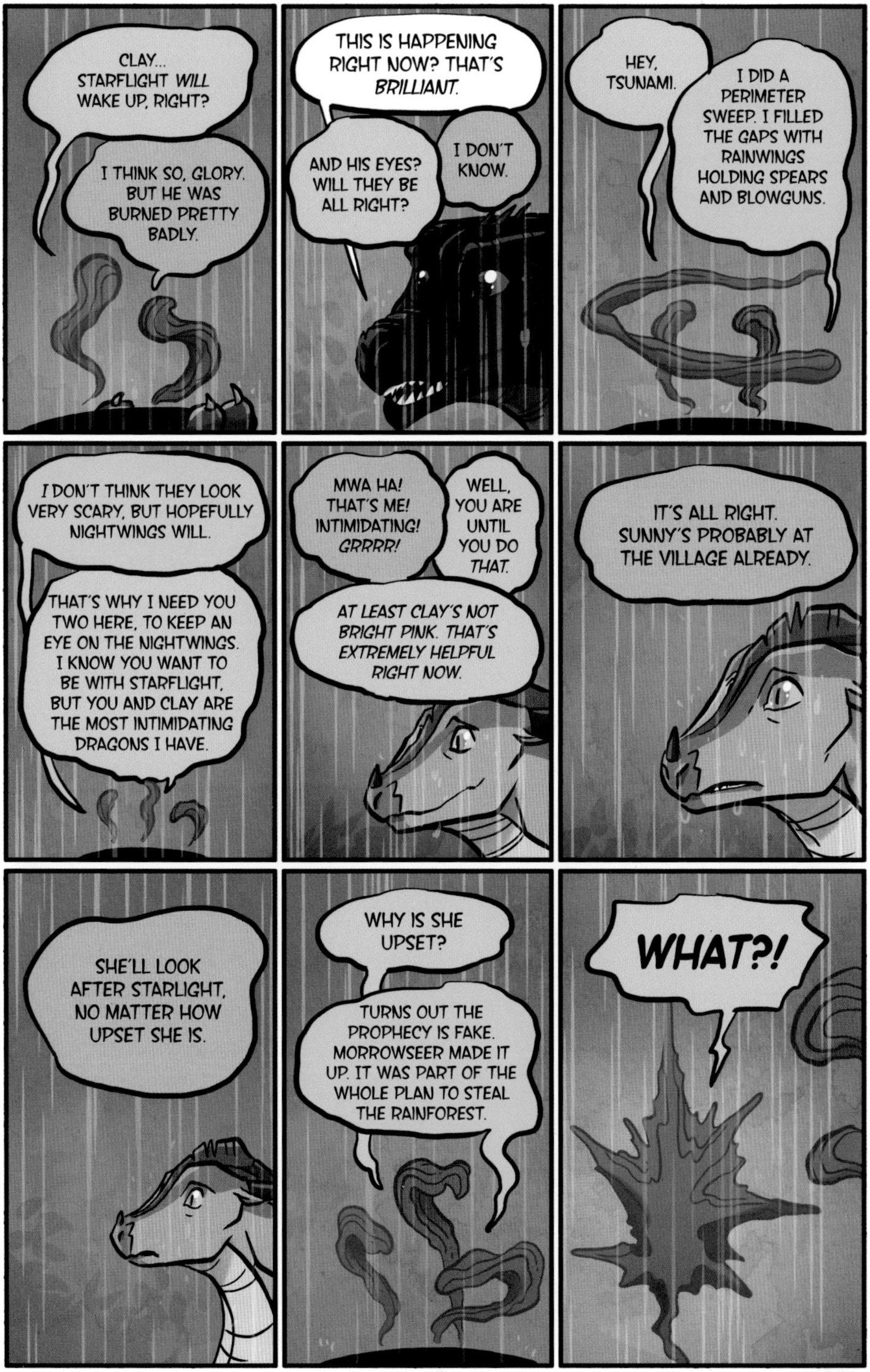
CLAY... STARFLIGHT *WILL* WAKE UP, RIGHT?
I THINK SO, GLORY. BUT HE WAS BURNED PRETTY BADLY.
THIS IS HAPPENING RIGHT NOW? THAT'S *BRILLIANT.*
AND HIS EYES? WILL THEY BE ALL RIGHT?
I DON'T KNOW.
HEY, TSUNAMI.
I DID A PERIMETER SWEEP. I FILLED THE GAPS WITH RAINWINGS HOLDING SPEARS AND BLOWGUNS.
I DON'T THINK THEY LOOK VERY SCARY, BUT HOPEFULLY NIGHTWINGS WILL.
THAT'S WHY I NEED YOU TWO HERE, TO KEEP AN EYE ON THE NIGHTWINGS. I KNOW YOU WANT TO BE WITH STARFLIGHT, BUT YOU AND CLAY ARE THE MOST INTIMIDATING DRAGONS I HAVE.
MWA HA! THAT'S ME! INTIMIDATING! *GRRRR!*
WELL, YOU ARE UNTIL YOU DO *THAT.*
AT LEAST CLAY'S NOT BRIGHT PINK. THAT'S EXTREMELY HELPFUL RIGHT NOW.
IT'S ALL RIGHT. SUNNY'S PROBABLY AT THE VILLAGE ALREADY.
SHE'LL LOOK AFTER STARLIGHT, NO MATTER HOW UPSET SHE IS.
WHY IS SHE UPSET?
TURNS OUT THE PROPHECY IS FAKE. MORROWSEER MADE IT UP. IT WAS PART OF THE WHOLE PLAN TO STEAL THE RAINFOREST.
WHAT?!

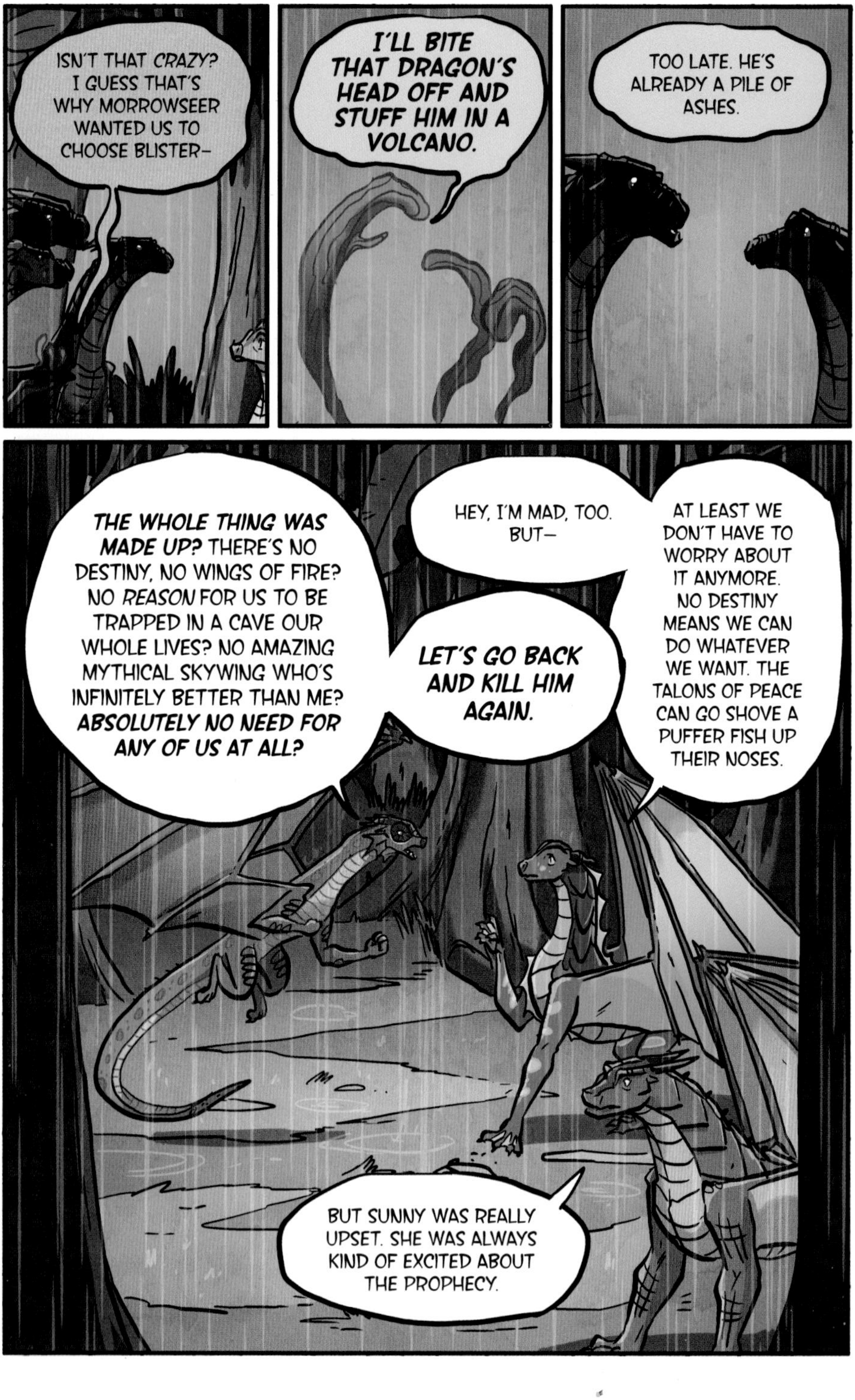
ISN'T THAT CRAZY? I GUESS THAT'S WHY MORROWSEER WANTED US TO CHOOSE BLISTER—
I'LL BITE THAT DRAGON'S HEAD OFF AND STUFF HIM IN A VOLCANO.
TOO LATE. HE'S ALREADY A PILE OF ASHES.
THE WHOLE THING WAS MADE UP? THERE'S NO DESTINY, NO WINGS OF FIRE? NO REASON FOR US TO BE TRAPPED IN A CAVE OUR WHOLE LIVES? NO AMAZING MYTHICAL SKYWING WHO'S INFINITELY BETTER THAN ME? ABSOLUTELY NO NEED FOR ANY OF US AT ALL?
LET'S GO BACK AND KILL HIM AGAIN.
HEY, I'M MAD, TOO. BUT—
AT LEAST WE DON'T HAVE TO WORRY ABOUT IT ANYMORE. NO DESTINY MEANS WE CAN DO WHATEVER WE WANT. THE TALONS OF PEACE CAN GO SHOVE A PUFFER FISH UP THEIR NOSES.
BUT SUNNY WAS REALLY UPSET. SHE WAS ALWAYS KIND OF EXCITED ABOUT THE PROPHECY.

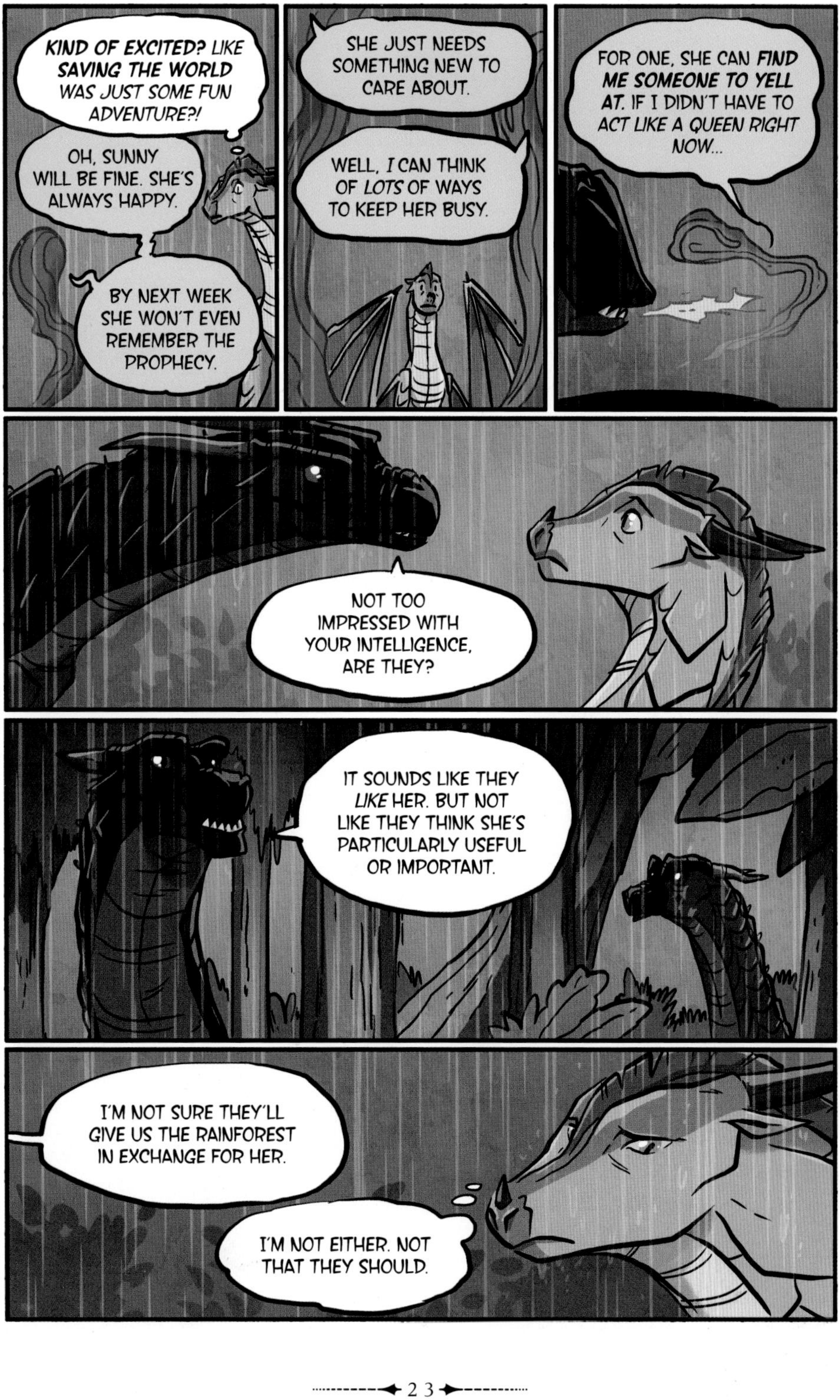
KIND OF EXCITED? LIKE SAVING THE WORLD WAS JUST SOME FUN ADVENTURE?!
OH, SUNNY WILL BE FINE. SHE'S ALWAYS HAPPY.
BY NEXT WEEK SHE WON'T EVEN REMEMBER THE PROPHECY.
SHE JUST NEEDS SOMETHING NEW TO CARE ABOUT.
WELL, I CAN THINK OF LOTS OF WAYS TO KEEP HER BUSY.
FOR ONE, SHE CAN FIND ME SOMEONE TO YELL AT. IF I DIDN'T HAVE TO ACT LIKE A QUEEN RIGHT NOW...
NOT TOO IMPRESSED WITH YOUR INTELLIGENCE, ARE THEY?
IT SOUNDS LIKE THEY LIKE HER. BUT NOT LIKE THEY THINK SHE'S PARTICULARLY USEFUL OR IMPORTANT.
I'M NOT SURE THEY'LL GIVE US THE RAINFOREST IN EXCHANGE FOR HER.
I'M NOT EITHER. NOT THAT THEY SHOULD.

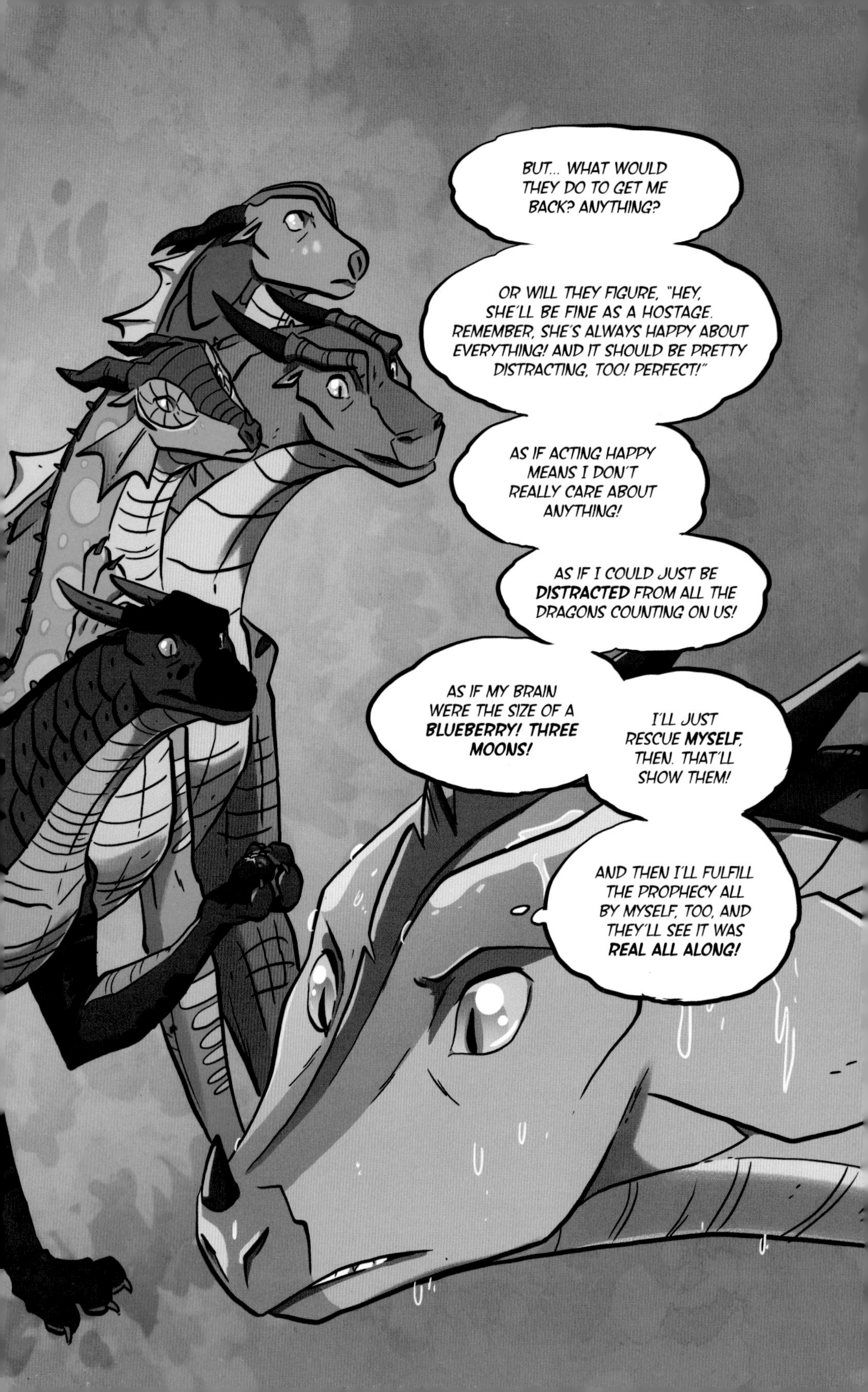
BUT... WHAT WOULD THEY DO TO GET ME BACK? ANYTHING?
OR WILL THEY FIGURE, "HEY, SHE'LL BE FINE AS A HOSTAGE. REMEMBER, SHE'S ALWAYS HAPPY ABOUT EVERYTHING! AND IT SHOULD BE PRETTY DISTRACTING, TOO! PERFECT!"
AS IF ACTING HAPPY MEANS I DON'T REALLY CARE ABOUT ANYTHING!
AS IF I COULD JUST BE **DISTRACTED** FROM ALL THE DRAGONS COUNTING ON US!
AS IF MY BRAIN WERE THE SIZE OF A **BLUEBERRY! THREE MOONS!**
I'LL JUST RESCUE **MYSELF**, THEN. THAT'LL SHOW THEM!
AND THEN I'LL FULFILL THE PROPHECY ALL BY MYSELF, TOO, AND THEY'LL SEE IT WAS **REAL ALL ALONG!**

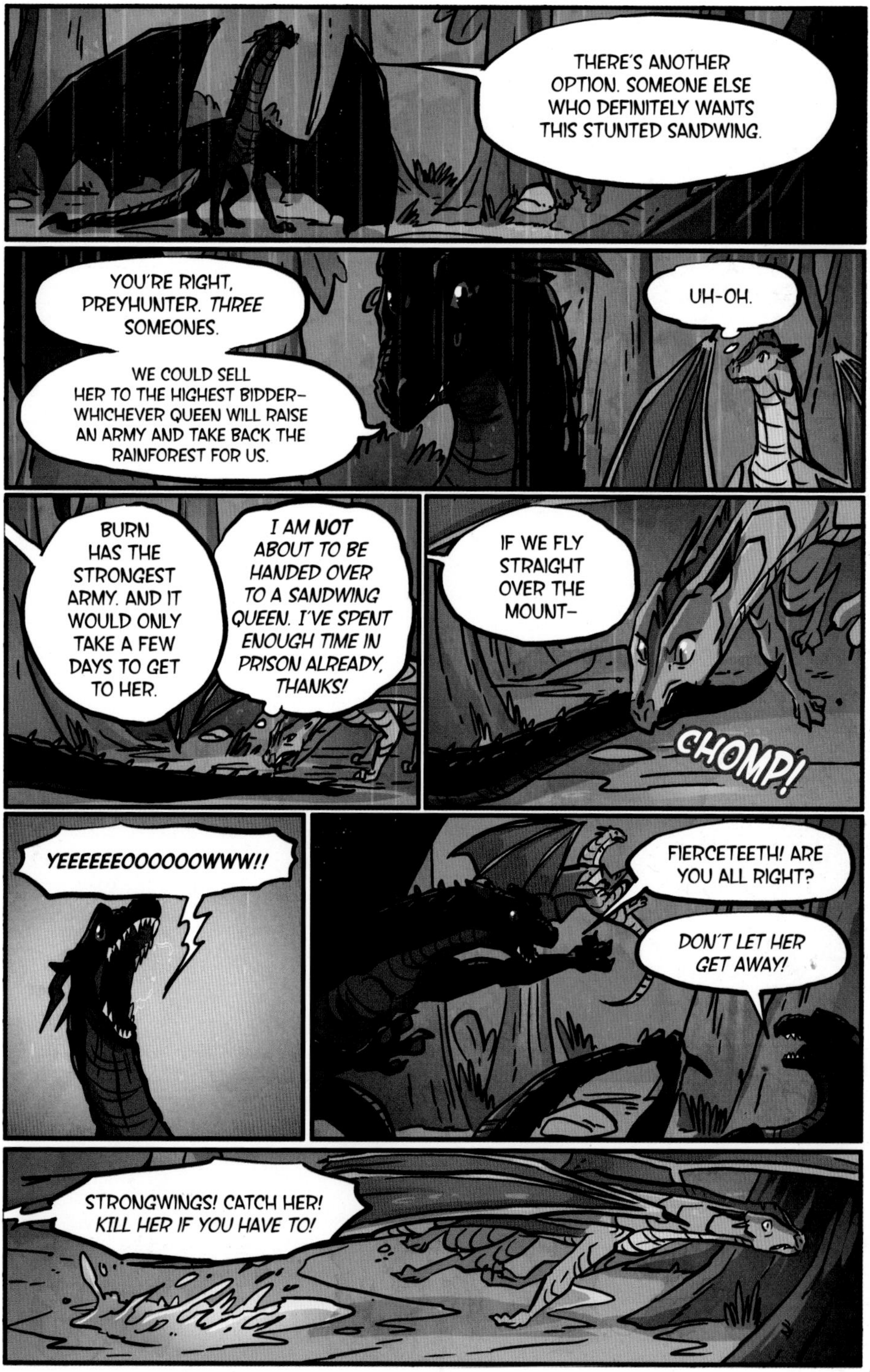
THERE'S ANOTHER OPTION. SOMEONE ELSE WHO DEFINITELY WANTS THIS STUNTED SANDWING.
YOU'RE RIGHT, PREYHUNTER. *THREE* SOMEONES.
WE COULD SELL HER TO THE HIGHEST BIDDER– WHICHEVER QUEEN WILL RAISE AN ARMY AND TAKE BACK THE RAINFOREST FOR US.
UH-OH.
BURN HAS THE STRONGEST ARMY. AND IT WOULD ONLY TAKE A FEW DAYS TO GET TO HER.
I AM **NOT** *ABOUT TO BE HANDED OVER TO A SANDWING QUEEN. I'VE SPENT ENOUGH TIME IN PRISON ALREADY, THANKS!*
IF WE FLY STRAIGHT OVER THE MOUNT–
CHOMP!
YEEEEEEOOOOOOWWW!!
FIERCETEETH! ARE YOU ALL RIGHT?
DON'T LET HER GET AWAY!
STRONGWINGS! CATCH HER! *KILL HER IF YOU HAVE TO!*

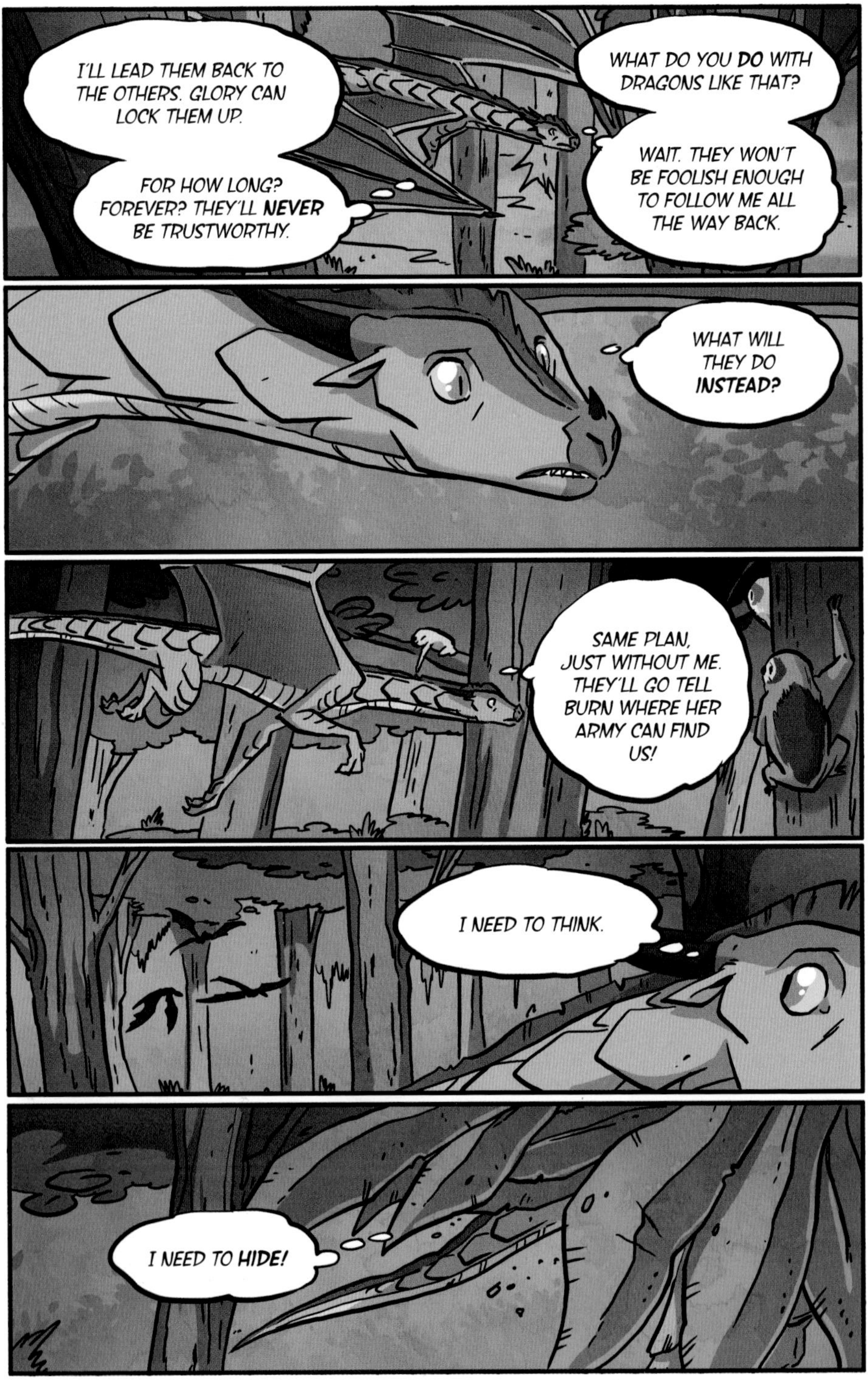
I'LL LEAD THEM BACK TO THE OTHERS. GLORY CAN LOCK THEM UP.
FOR HOW LONG? FOREVER? THEY'LL **NEVER** BE TRUSTWORTHY.
WHAT DO YOU **DO** WITH DRAGONS LIKE THAT?
WAIT. THEY WON'T BE FOOLISH ENOUGH TO FOLLOW ME ALL THE WAY BACK.
WHAT WILL THEY DO **INSTEAD?**
SAME PLAN, JUST WITHOUT ME. THEY'LL GO TELL BURN WHERE HER ARMY CAN FIND US!
I NEED TO THINK.
I NEED TO **HIDE!**

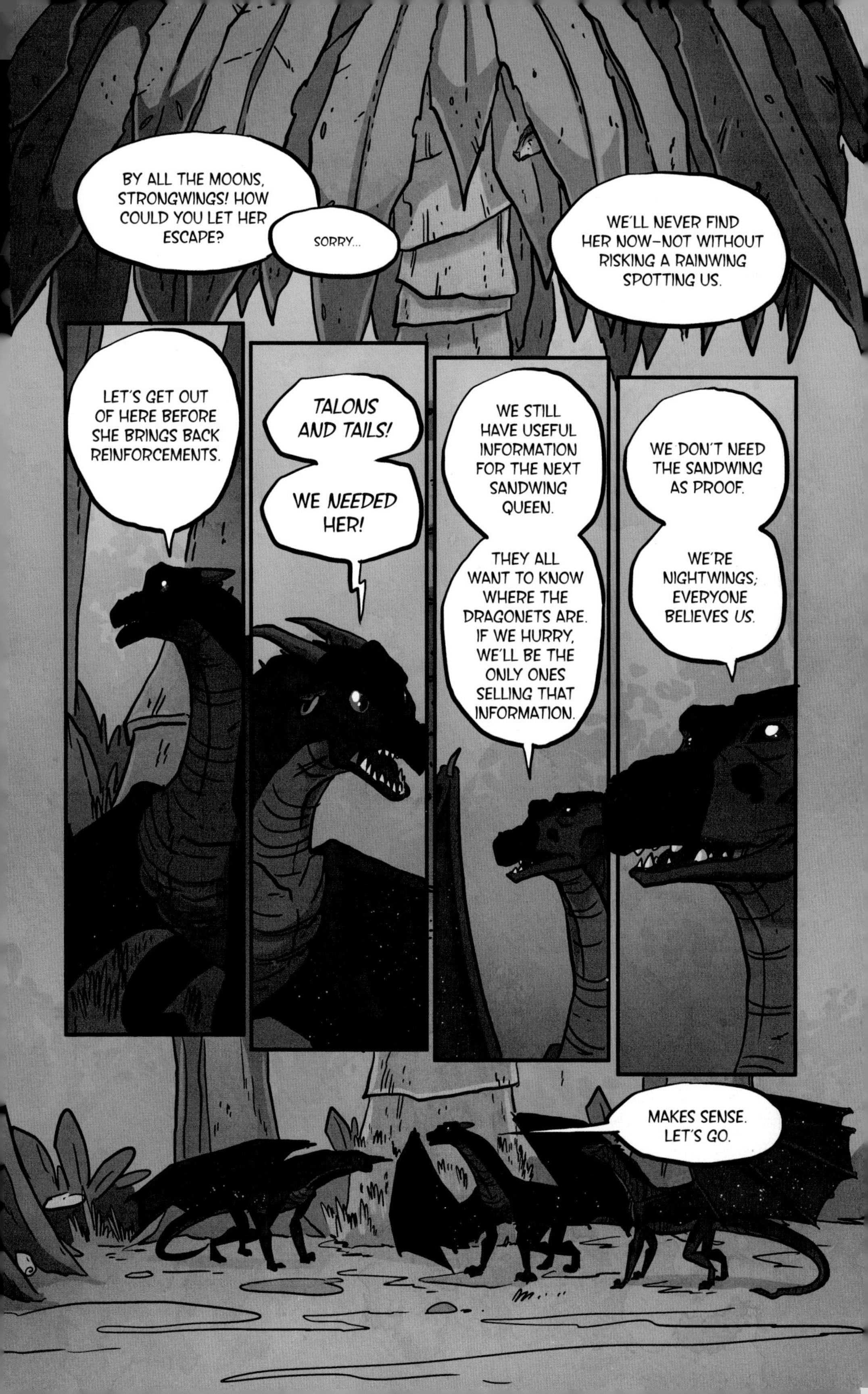
BY ALL THE MOONS, STRONGWINGS! HOW COULD YOU LET HER ESCAPE?
SORRY...
WE'LL NEVER FIND HER NOW—NOT WITHOUT RISKING A RAINWING SPOTTING US.
LET'S GET OUT OF HERE BEFORE SHE BRINGS BACK REINFORCEMENTS.
TALONS AND TAILS!
WE *NEEDED* HER!
WE STILL HAVE USEFUL INFORMATION FOR THE NEXT SANDWING QUEEN.
THEY ALL WANT TO KNOW WHERE THE DRAGONETS ARE. IF WE HURRY, WE'LL BE THE ONLY ONES SELLING THAT INFORMATION.
WE DON'T NEED THE SANDWING AS PROOF.
WE'RE NIGHTWINGS; EVERYONE BELIEVES *US*.
MAKES SENSE. LET'S GO.

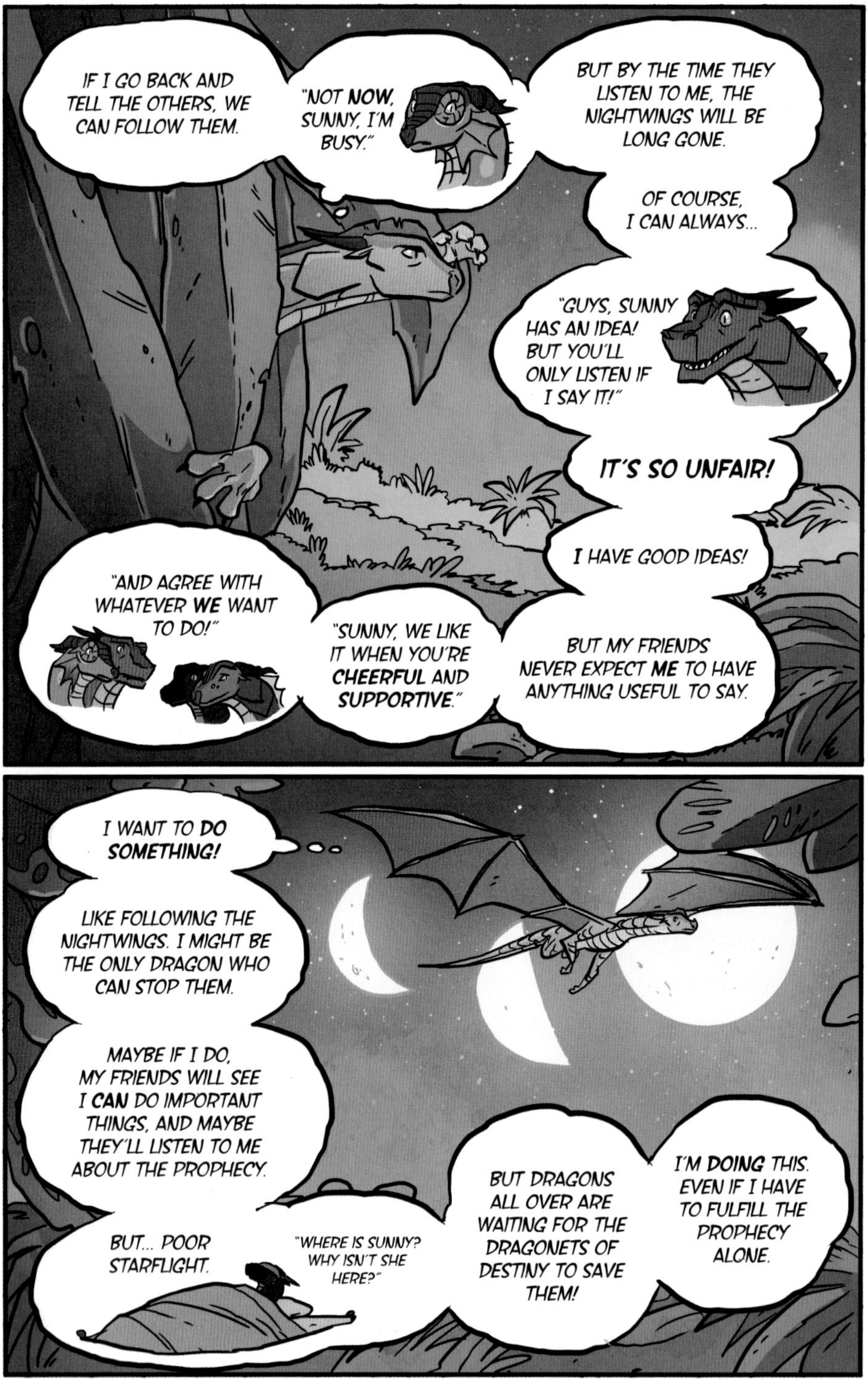
IF I GO BACK AND TELL THE OTHERS, WE CAN FOLLOW THEM.
"NOT NOW, SUNNY, I'M BUSY."
BUT BY THE TIME THEY LISTEN TO ME, THE NIGHTWINGS WILL BE LONG GONE.
OF COURSE, I CAN ALWAYS...
"GUYS, SUNNY HAS AN IDEA! BUT YOU'LL ONLY LISTEN IF I SAY IT!"
IT'S SO UNFAIR!
I HAVE GOOD IDEAS!
"AND AGREE WITH WHATEVER WE WANT TO DO!"
"SUNNY, WE LIKE IT WHEN YOU'RE CHEERFUL AND SUPPORTIVE."
BUT MY FRIENDS NEVER EXPECT ME TO HAVE ANYTHING USEFUL TO SAY.
I WANT TO DO SOMETHING!
LIKE FOLLOWING THE NIGHTWINGS. I MIGHT BE THE ONLY DRAGON WHO CAN STOP THEM.
MAYBE IF I DO, MY FRIENDS WILL SEE I CAN DO IMPORTANT THINGS, AND MAYBE THEY'LL LISTEN TO ME ABOUT THE PROPHECY.
BUT... POOR STARFLIGHT.
"WHERE IS SUNNY? WHY ISN'T SHE HERE?"
BUT DRAGONS ALL OVER ARE WAITING FOR THE DRAGONETS OF DESTINY TO SAVE THEM!
I'M DOING THIS. EVEN IF I HAVE TO FULFILL THE PROPHECY ALONE.

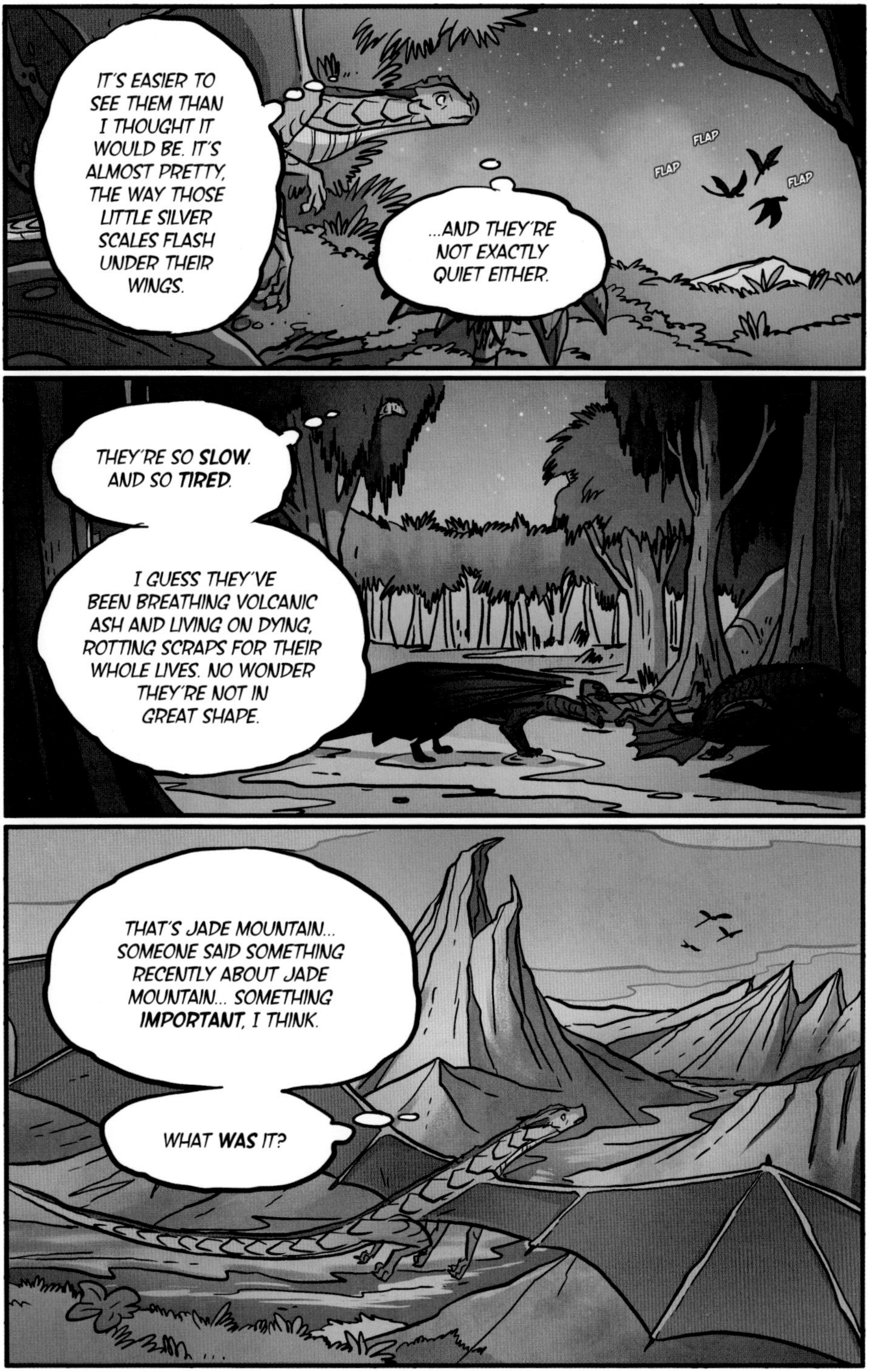
IT'S EASIER TO SEE THEM THAN I THOUGHT IT WOULD BE. IT'S ALMOST PRETTY, THE WAY THOSE LITTLE SILVER SCALES FLASH UNDER THEIR WINGS.
FLAP
FLAP
FLAP
...AND THEY'RE NOT EXACTLY QUIET EITHER.
THEY'RE SO **SLOW**. AND SO **TIRED**.
I GUESS THEY'VE BEEN BREATHING VOLCANIC ASH AND LIVING ON DYING, ROTTING SCRAPS FOR THEIR WHOLE LIVES. NO WONDER THEY'RE NOT IN GREAT SHAPE.
THAT'S JADE MOUNTAIN... SOMEONE SAID SOMETHING RECENTLY ABOUT JADE MOUNTAIN... SOMETHING **IMPORTANT**, I THINK.
WHAT **WAS** IT?

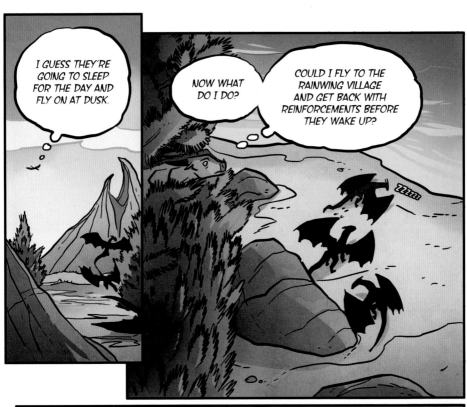

I GUESS THEY'RE GOING TO SLEEP FOR THE DAY AND FLY ON AT DUSK.

NOW WHAT DO I DO?

COULD I FLY TO THE RAINWING VILLAGE AND GET BACK WITH REINFORCEMENTS BEFORE THEY WAKE UP?

NO. IT'D TAKE ME ALL DAY JUST TO GET SOMEONE TO PAY ATTENTION TO ME.

I CAN DO THIS MYSELF. I **HAVE** TO.

YESTERDAY I WOULDN'T HAVE WORRIED. I'D HAVE KNOWN FOR SURE THAT WHATEVER I DID WOULD TURN OUT ALL RIGHT.

MORROWSEER IS THE **WORST**. MAKING ME DOUBT EVERYTHING. STUPID NIGHTWINGS WITH THEIR **DECEITFUL, ALL-KNOWING, HIGH-AND-MIGHTY—**

ALL-KNOWING.

THERE IS SOMETHING I CAN DO TO SLOW THEM DOWN.

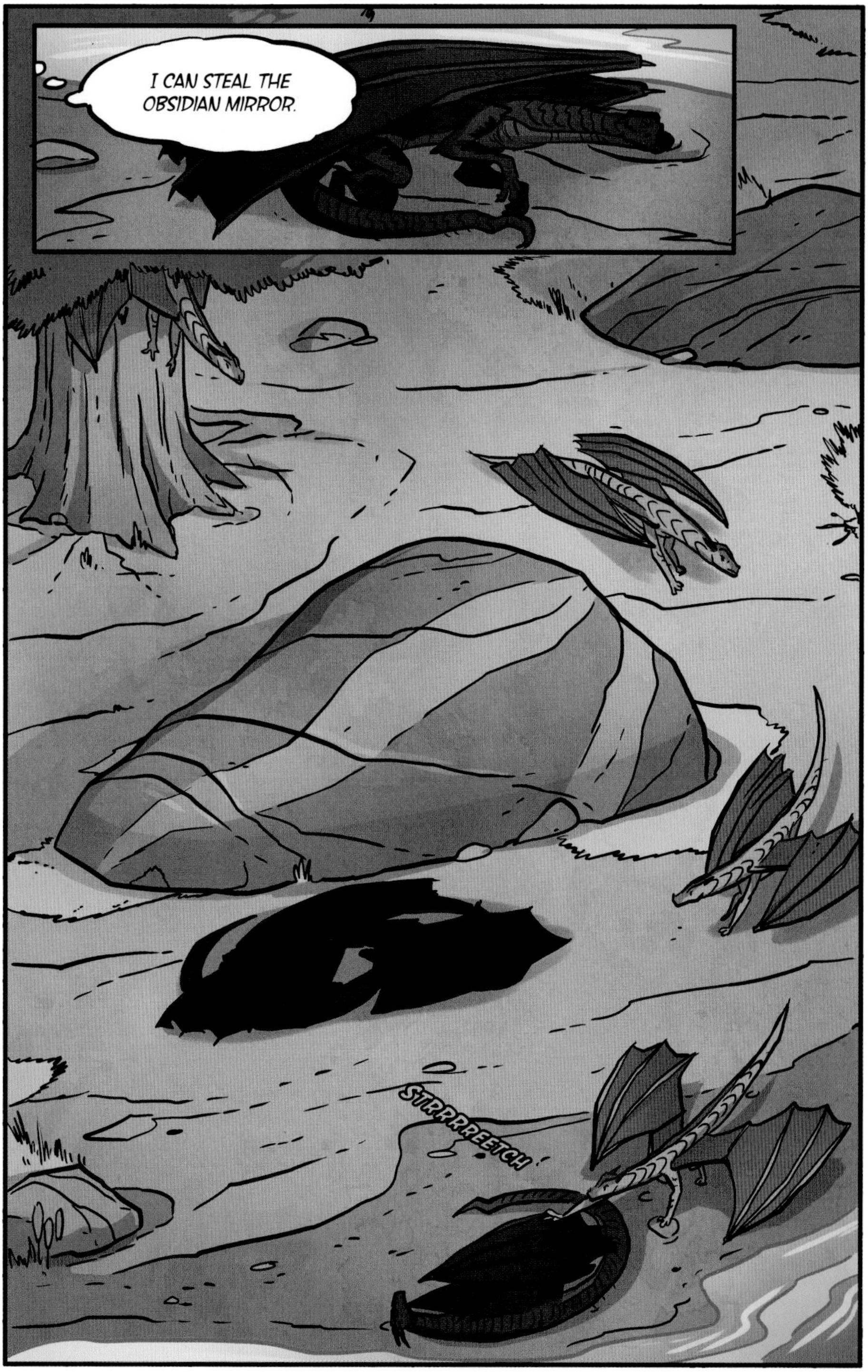
I CAN STEAL THE OBSIDIAN MIRROR.
STRRRRREETCH

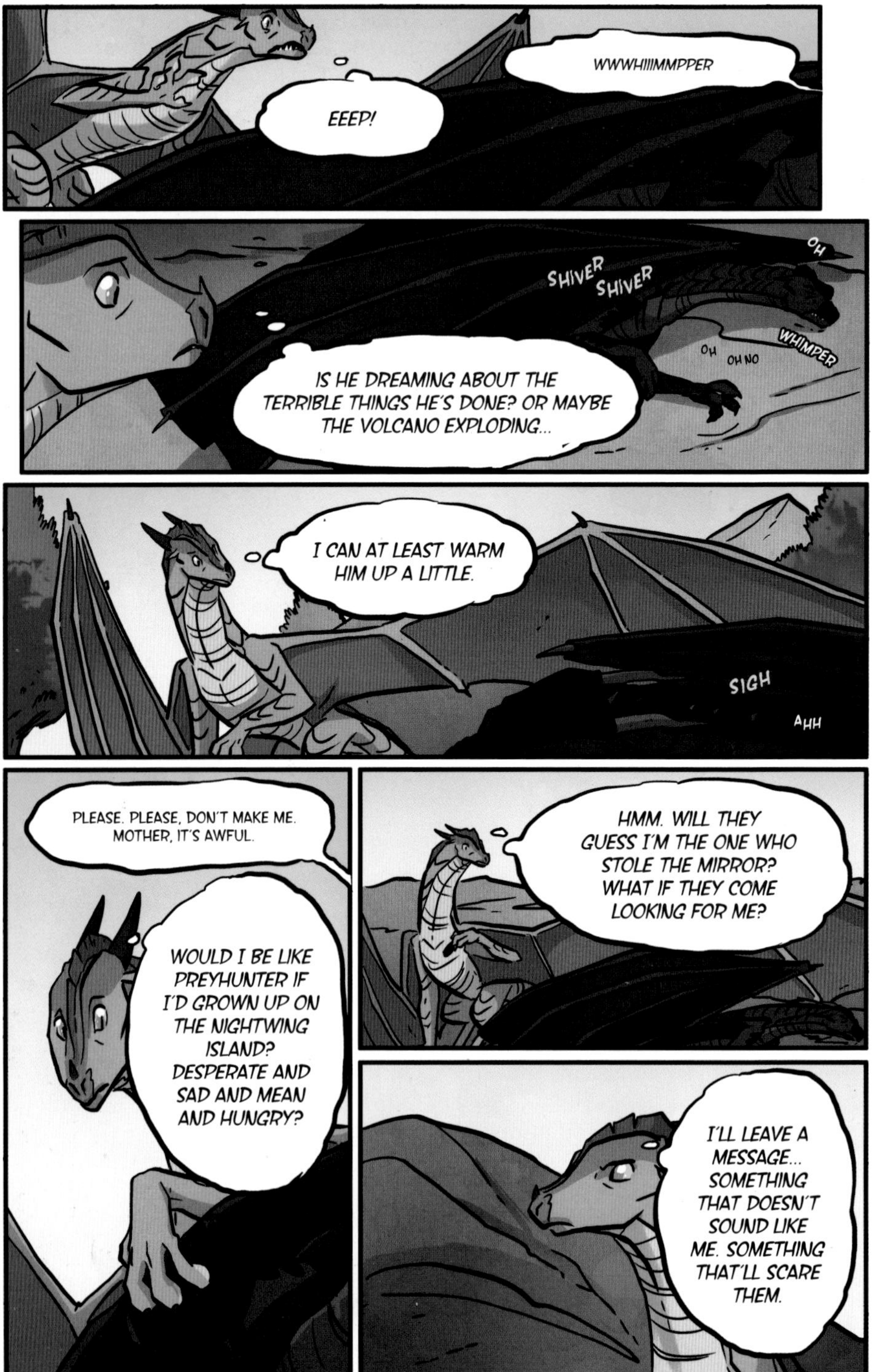
WWWHIIIMMPPER
EEEP!
SHIVER SHIVER
OH
WHIMPER
OH OH NO
IS HE DREAMING ABOUT THE TERRIBLE THINGS HE'S DONE? OR MAYBE THE VOLCANO EXPLODING...
I CAN AT LEAST WARM HIM UP A LITTLE.
SIGH
AHH
PLEASE. PLEASE, DON'T MAKE ME. MOTHER, IT'S AWFUL.
WOULD I BE LIKE PREYHUNTER IF I'D GROWN UP ON THE NIGHTWING ISLAND? DESPERATE AND SAD AND MEAN AND HUNGRY?
HMM. WILL THEY GUESS I'M THE ONE WHO STOLE THE MIRROR? WHAT IF THEY COME LOOKING FOR ME?
I'LL LEAVE A MESSAGE... SOMETHING THAT DOESN'T SOUND LIKE ME. SOMETHING THAT'LL SCARE THEM.

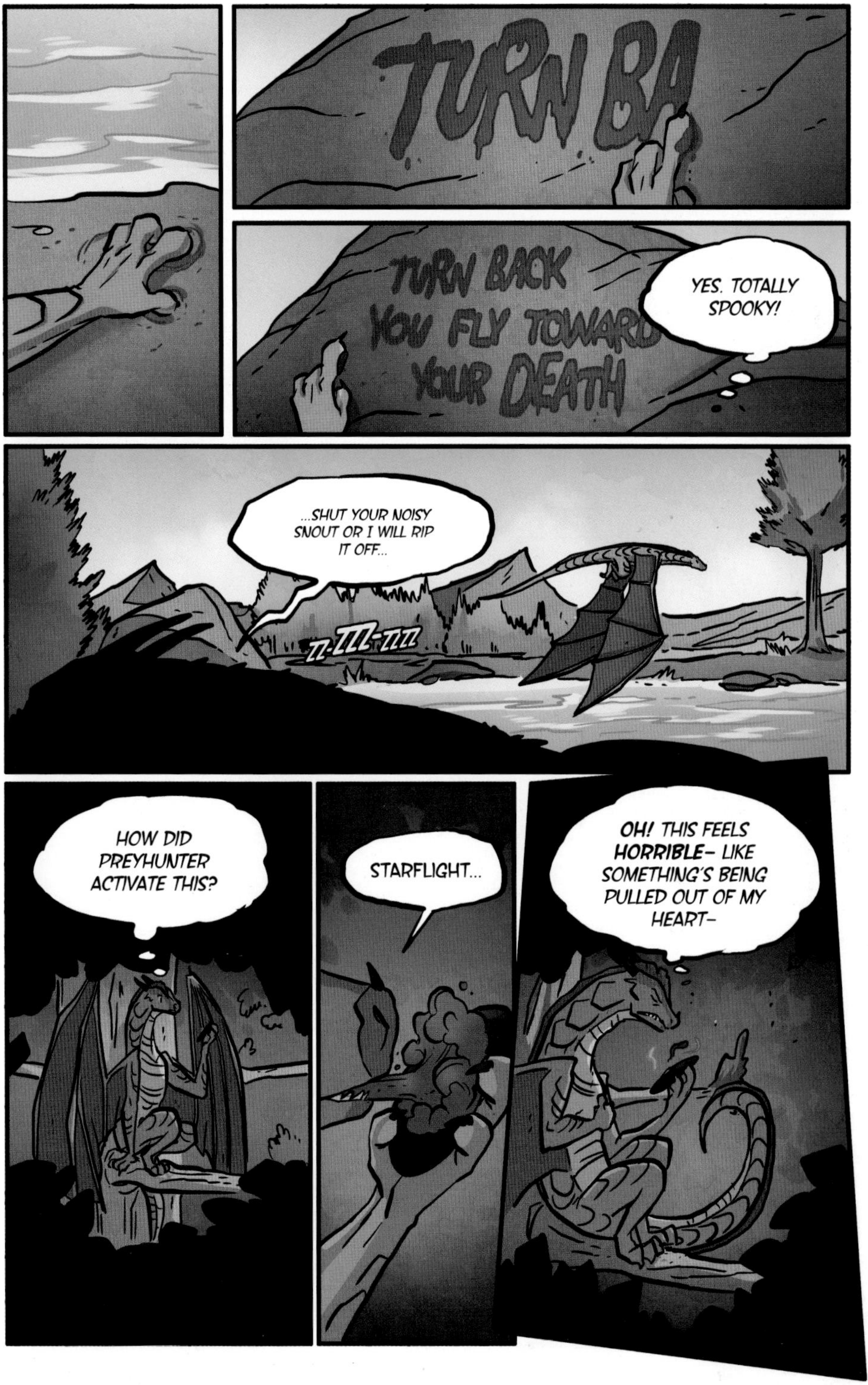
TURN BA
TURN BACK
YOU FLY TOWARD
YOUR DEATH
YES. TOTALLY SPOOKY!
...SHUT YOUR NOISY SNOUT OR I WILL RIP IT OFF...
ZZ-ZZZ-ZZZ
HOW DID PREYHUNTER ACTIVATE THIS?
STARFLIGHT...
OH! THIS FEELS HORRIBLE– LIKE SOMETHING'S BEING PULLED OUT OF MY HEART–

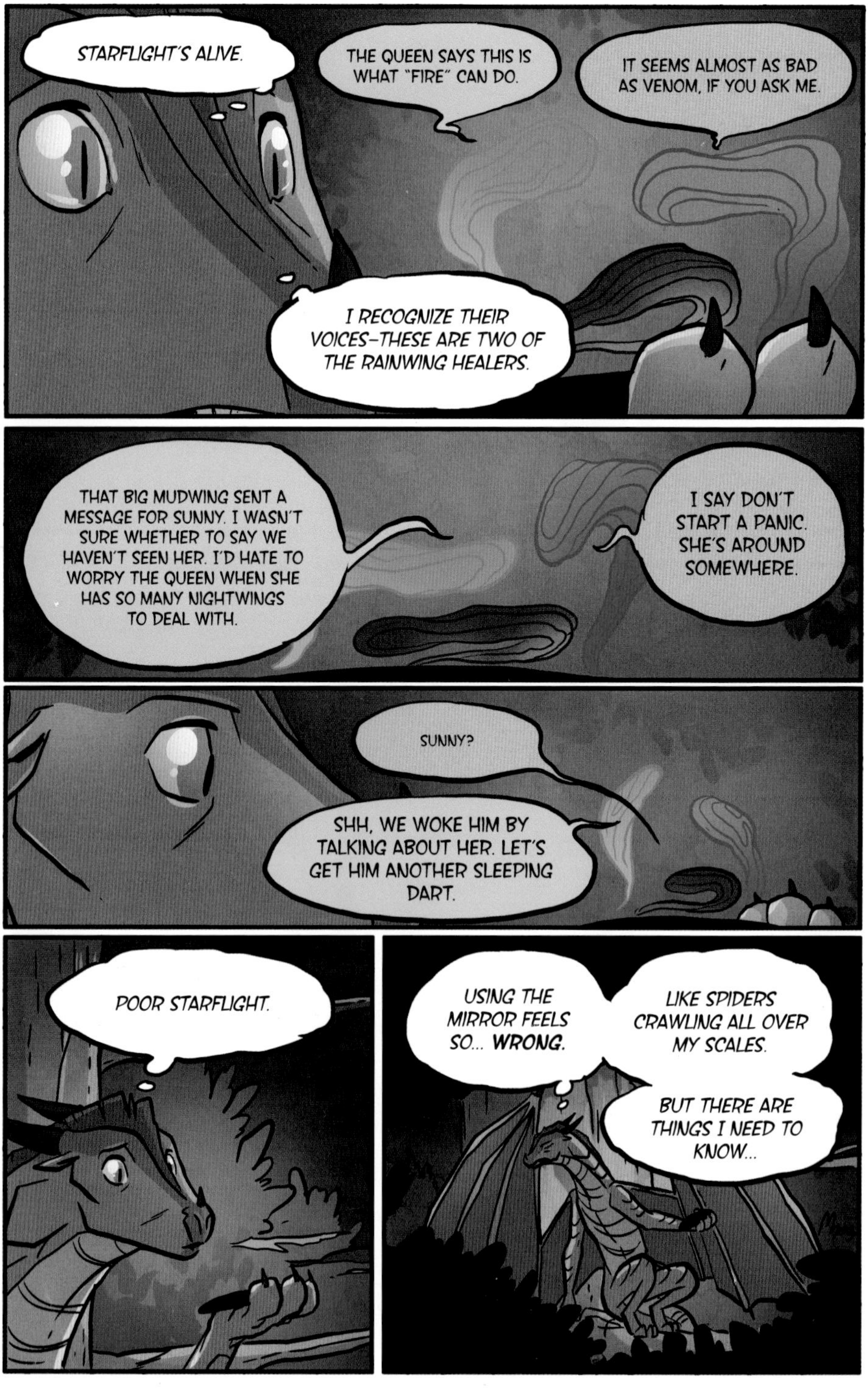
STARFLIGHT'S ALIVE.
THE QUEEN SAYS THIS IS WHAT "FIRE" CAN DO.
IT SEEMS ALMOST AS BAD AS VENOM, IF YOU ASK ME.
I RECOGNIZE THEIR VOICES–THESE ARE TWO OF THE RAINWING HEALERS.
THAT BIG MUDWING SENT A MESSAGE FOR SUNNY. I WASN'T SURE WHETHER TO SAY WE HAVEN'T SEEN HER. I'D HATE TO WORRY THE QUEEN WHEN SHE HAS SO MANY NIGHTWINGS TO DEAL WITH.
I SAY DON'T START A PANIC. SHE'S AROUND SOMEWHERE.
SUNNY?
SHH, WE WOKE HIM BY TALKING ABOUT HER. LET'S GET HIM ANOTHER SLEEPING DART.
POOR STARFLIGHT.
USING THE MIRROR FEELS SO... **WRONG.**
LIKE SPIDERS CRAWLING ALL OVER MY SCALES.
BUT THERE ARE THINGS I NEED TO KNOW...

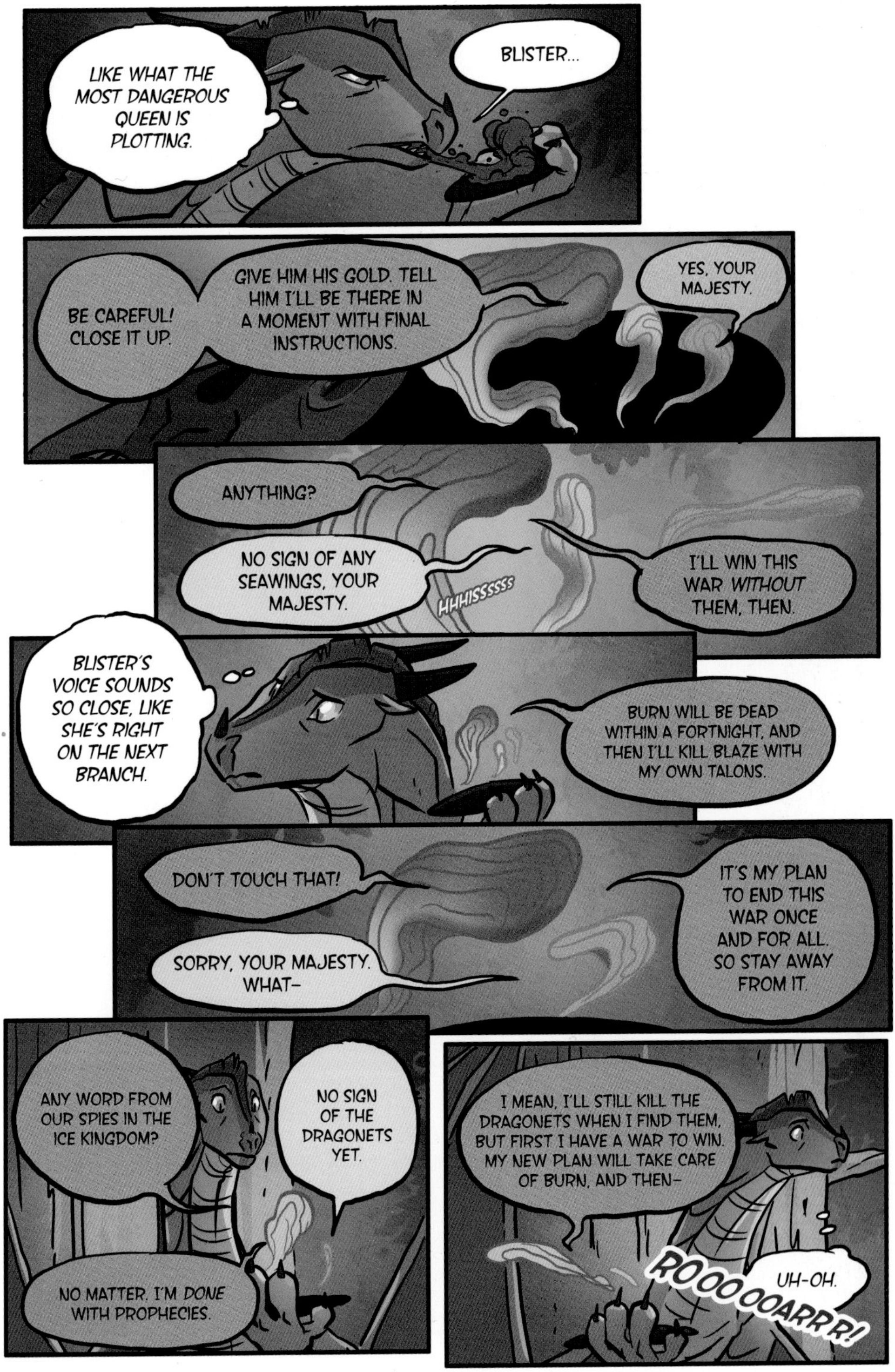
LIKE WHAT THE MOST DANGEROUS QUEEN IS PLOTTING.
BLISTER...
BE CAREFUL! CLOSE IT UP.
GIVE HIM HIS GOLD. TELL HIM I'LL BE THERE IN A MOMENT WITH FINAL INSTRUCTIONS.
YES, YOUR MAJESTY.
ANYTHING?
NO SIGN OF ANY SEAWINGS, YOUR MAJESTY.
HHHISSSSSS
I'LL WIN THIS WAR WITHOUT THEM, THEN.
BLISTER'S VOICE SOUNDS SO CLOSE, LIKE SHE'S RIGHT ON THE NEXT BRANCH.
BURN WILL BE DEAD WITHIN A FORTNIGHT, AND THEN I'LL KILL BLAZE WITH MY OWN TALONS.
DON'T TOUCH THAT!
SORRY, YOUR MAJESTY. WHAT–
IT'S MY PLAN TO END THIS WAR ONCE AND FOR ALL. SO STAY AWAY FROM IT.
ANY WORD FROM OUR SPIES IN THE ICE KINGDOM?
NO SIGN OF THE DRAGONETS YET.
NO MATTER. I'M DONE WITH PROPHECIES.
I MEAN, I'LL STILL KILL THE DRAGONETS WHEN I FIND THEM, BUT FIRST I HAVE A WAR TO WIN. MY NEW PLAN WILL TAKE CARE OF BURN, AND THEN–
ROOOOOOARRRR!
UH-OH.

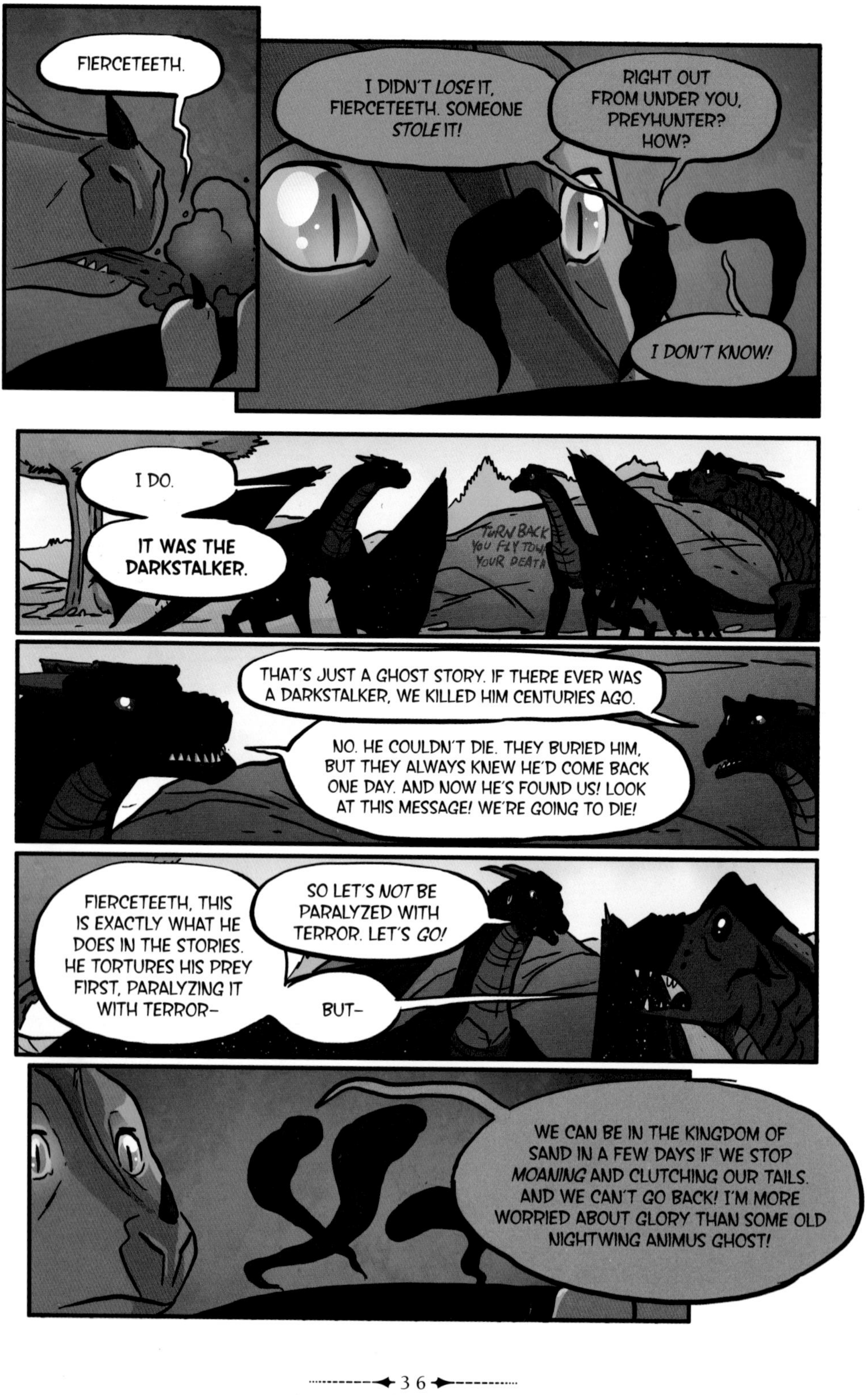
FIERCETEETH.
I DIDN'T *LOSE* IT, FIERCETEETH. SOMEONE *STOLE* IT!
RIGHT OUT FROM UNDER YOU, PREYHUNTER? HOW?
I DON'T KNOW!
I DO.
IT WAS THE DARKSTALKER.
TURN BACK
YOUR DEATH
THAT'S JUST A GHOST STORY. IF THERE EVER WAS A DARKSTALKER, WE KILLED HIM CENTURIES AGO.
NO. HE COULDN'T DIE. THEY BURIED HIM, BUT THEY ALWAYS KNEW HE'D COME BACK ONE DAY. AND NOW HE'S FOUND US! LOOK AT THIS MESSAGE! WE'RE GOING TO DIE!
FIERCETEETH, THIS IS EXACTLY WHAT HE DOES IN THE STORIES. HE TORTURES HIS PREY FIRST, PARALYZING IT WITH TERROR–
SO LET'S *NOT* BE PARALYZED WITH TERROR. LET'S *GO!*
BUT–
WE CAN BE IN THE KINGDOM OF SAND IN A FEW DAYS IF WE STOP *MOANING* AND CLUTCHING OUR TAILS. AND WE CAN'T GO BACK! I'M MORE WORRIED ABOUT GLORY THAN SOME OLD NIGHTWING ANIMUS GHOST!

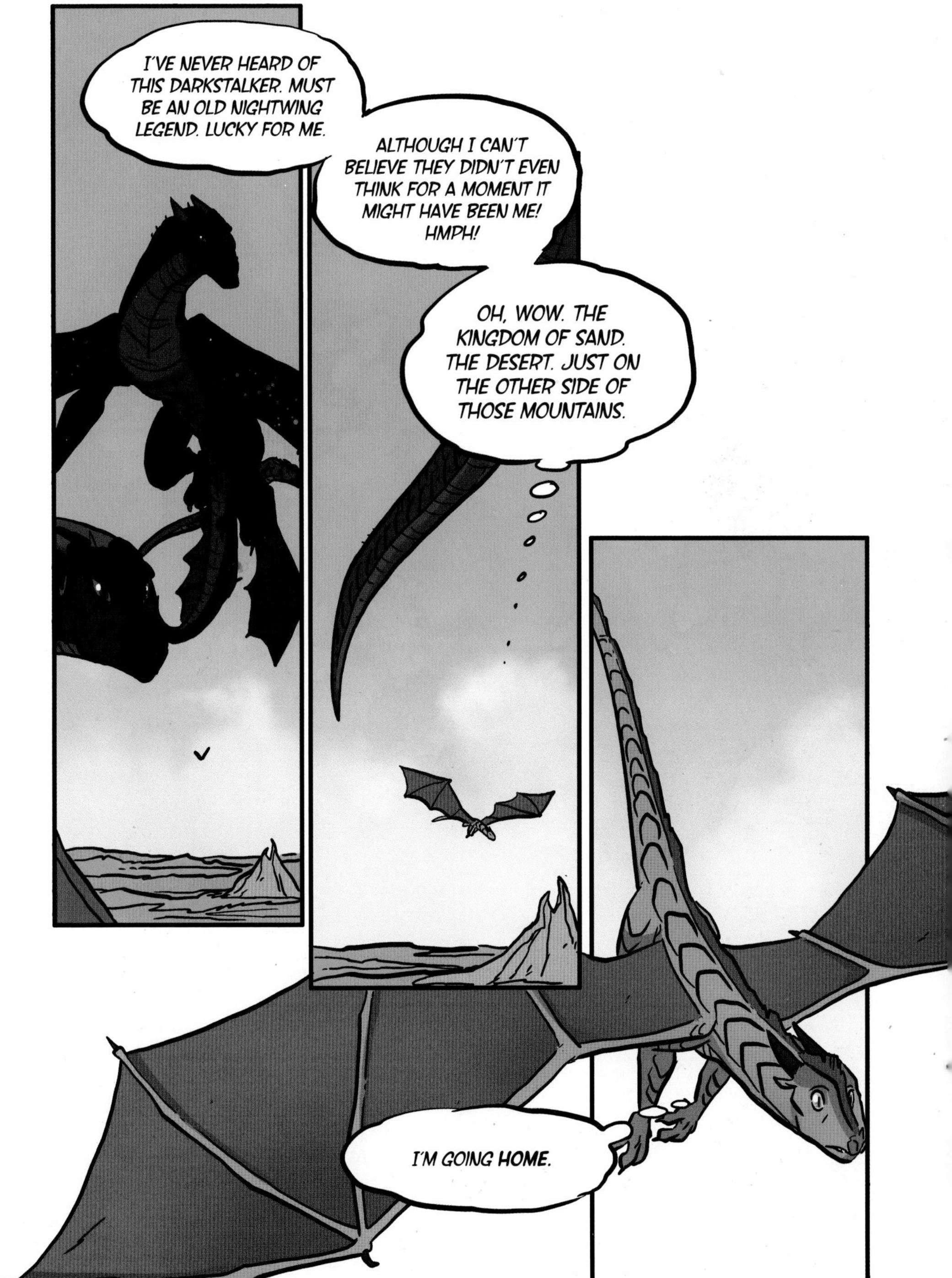
I'VE NEVER HEARD OF THIS DARKSTALKER. MUST BE AN OLD NIGHTWING LEGEND. LUCKY FOR ME.
ALTHOUGH I CAN'T BELIEVE THEY DIDN'T EVEN THINK FOR A MOMENT IT MIGHT HAVE BEEN ME! HMPH!
OH, WOW. THE KINGDOM OF SAND. THE DESERT. JUST ON THE OTHER SIDE OF THOSE MOUNTAINS.
I'M GOING **HOME**.

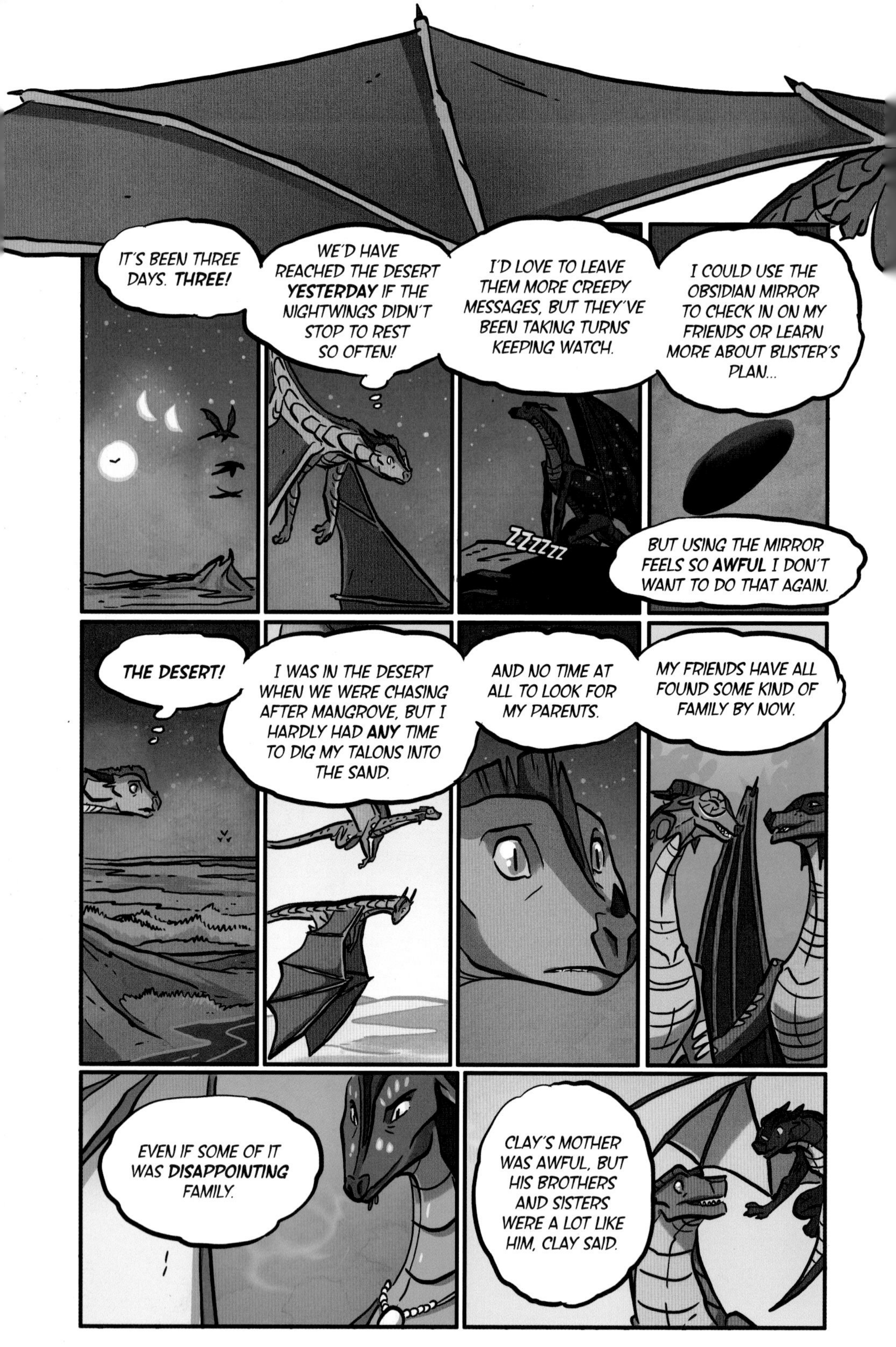
IT'S BEEN THREE DAYS. **THREE!**
WE'D HAVE REACHED THE DESERT **YESTERDAY** IF THE NIGHTWINGS DIDN'T STOP TO REST SO OFTEN!
I'D LOVE TO LEAVE THEM MORE CREEPY MESSAGES, BUT THEY'VE BEEN TAKING TURNS KEEPING WATCH.
ZZZZZZ
I COULD USE THE OBSIDIAN MIRROR TO CHECK IN ON MY FRIENDS OR LEARN MORE ABOUT BLISTER'S PLAN...
BUT USING THE MIRROR FEELS SO **AWFUL** I DON'T WANT TO DO THAT AGAIN.
THE DESERT!
I WAS IN THE DESERT WHEN WE WERE CHASING AFTER MANGROVE, BUT I HARDLY HAD **ANY** TIME TO DIG MY TALONS INTO THE SAND.
AND NO TIME AT ALL TO LOOK FOR MY PARENTS.
MY FRIENDS HAVE ALL FOUND SOME KIND OF FAMILY BY NOW.
EVEN IF SOME OF IT WAS **DISAPPOINTING** FAMILY.
CLAY'S MOTHER WAS AWFUL, BUT HIS BROTHERS AND SISTERS WERE A LOT LIKE HIM, CLAY SAID.

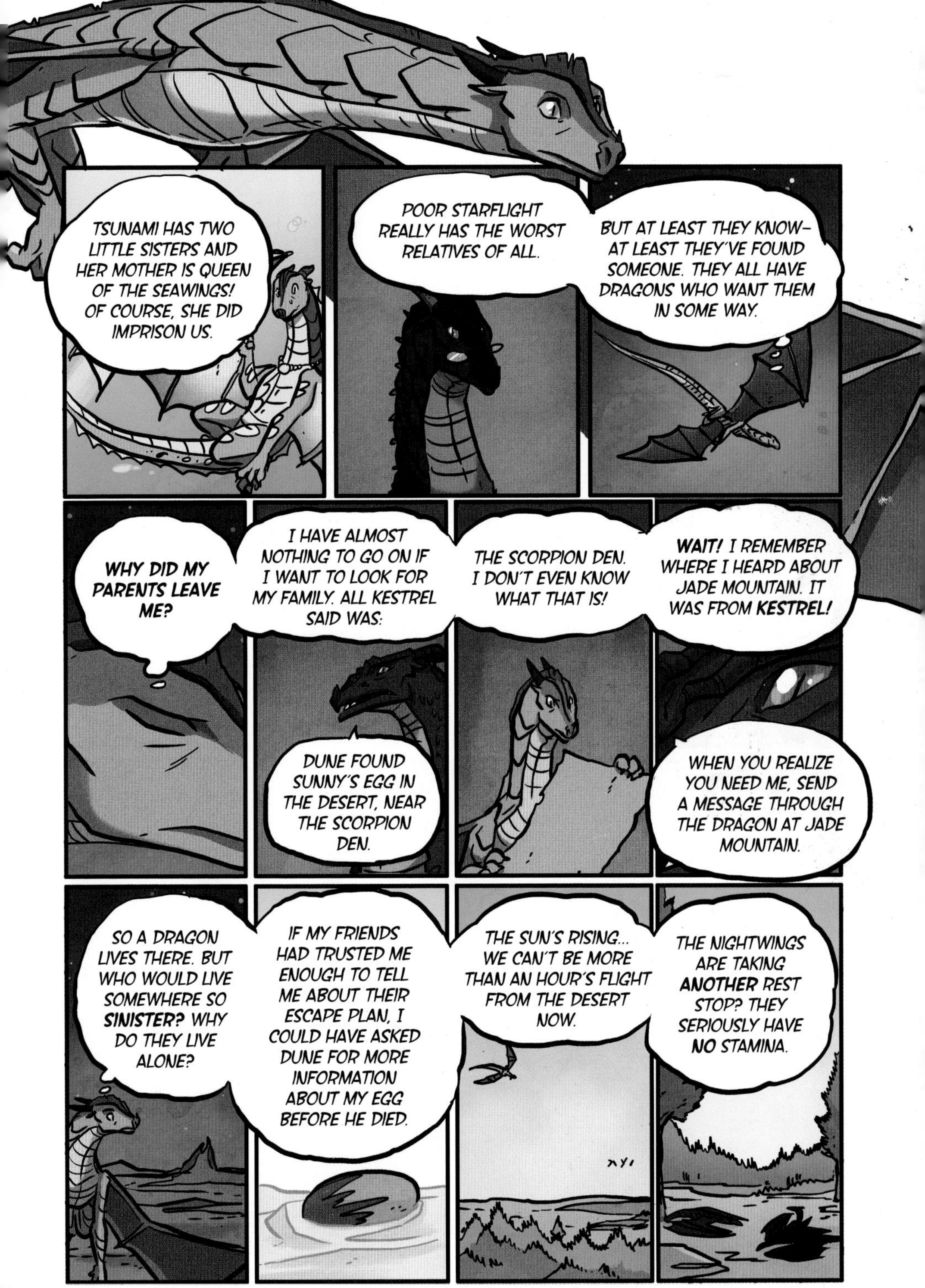
TSUNAMI HAS TWO LITTLE SISTERS AND HER MOTHER IS QUEEN OF THE SEAWINGS! OF COURSE, SHE DID IMPRISON US.
POOR STARFLIGHT REALLY HAS THE WORST RELATIVES OF ALL.
BUT AT LEAST THEY KNOW— AT LEAST THEY'VE FOUND SOMEONE. THEY ALL HAVE DRAGONS WHO WANT THEM IN SOME WAY.
WHY DID MY PARENTS LEAVE ME?
I HAVE ALMOST NOTHING TO GO ON IF I WANT TO LOOK FOR MY FAMILY. ALL KESTREL SAID WAS:
DUNE FOUND SUNNY'S EGG IN THE DESERT, NEAR THE SCORPION DEN.
THE SCORPION DEN. I DON'T EVEN KNOW WHAT THAT IS!
WAIT! I REMEMBER WHERE I HEARD ABOUT JADE MOUNTAIN. IT WAS FROM **KESTREL!**
WHEN YOU REALIZE YOU NEED ME, SEND A MESSAGE THROUGH THE DRAGON AT JADE MOUNTAIN.
SO A DRAGON LIVES THERE. BUT WHO WOULD LIVE SOMEWHERE SO **SINISTER?** WHY DO THEY LIVE ALONE?
IF MY FRIENDS HAD TRUSTED ME ENOUGH TO TELL ME ABOUT THEIR ESCAPE PLAN, I COULD HAVE ASKED DUNE FOR MORE INFORMATION ABOUT MY EGG BEFORE HE DIED.
THE SUN'S RISING... WE CAN'T BE MORE THAN AN HOUR'S FLIGHT FROM THE DESERT NOW.
THE NIGHTWINGS ARE TAKING **ANOTHER** REST STOP? THEY SERIOUSLY HAVE **NO** STAMINA.

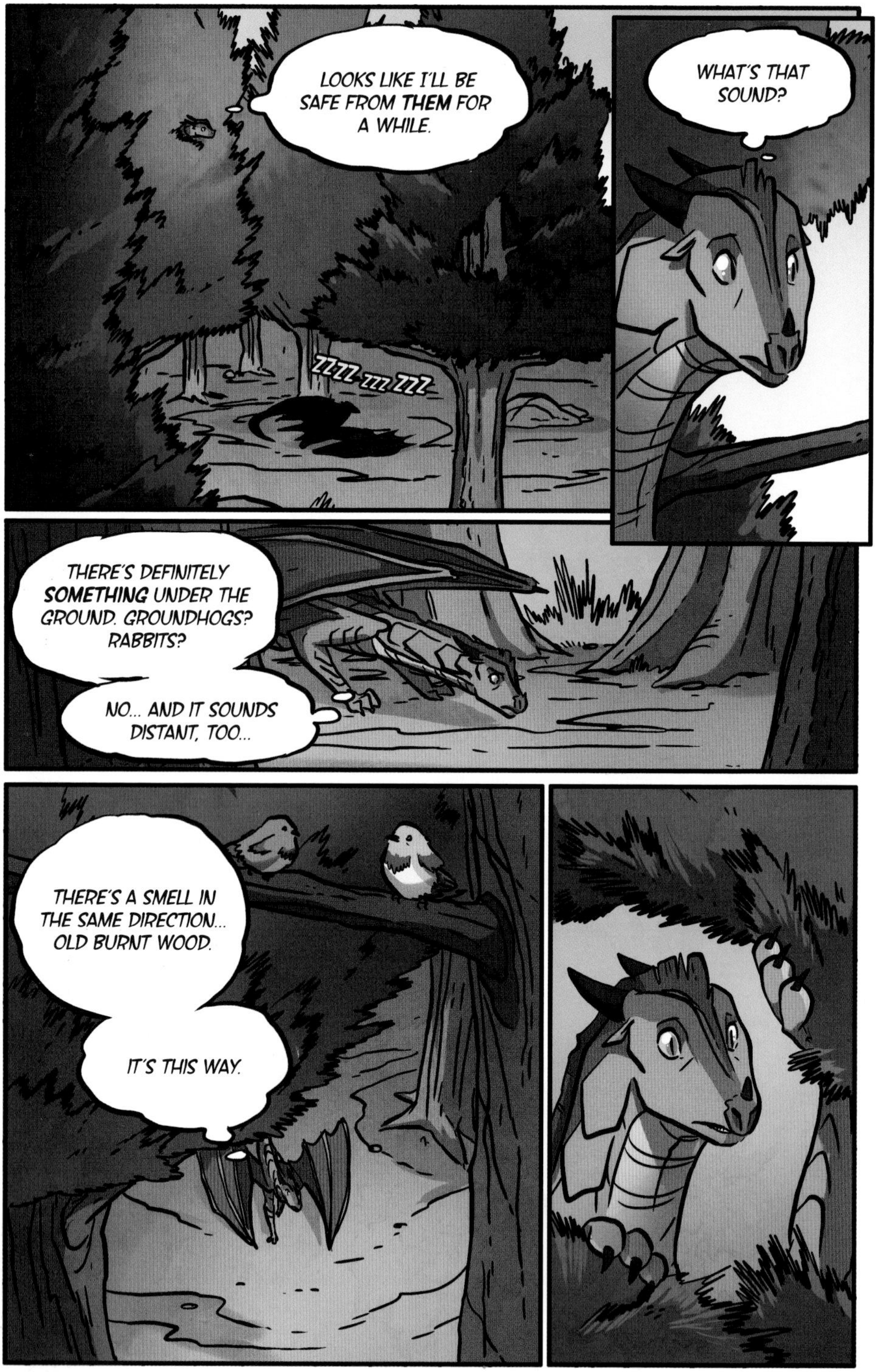
LOOKS LIKE I'LL BE SAFE FROM THEM FOR A WHILE.
ZZZZ zzz ZZZ
WHAT'S THAT SOUND?
THERE'S DEFINITELY SOMETHING UNDER THE GROUND. GROUNDHOGS? RABBITS?
NO... AND IT SOUNDS DISTANT, TOO...
THERE'S A SMELL IN THE SAME DIRECTION... OLD BURNT WOOD.
IT'S THIS WAY.

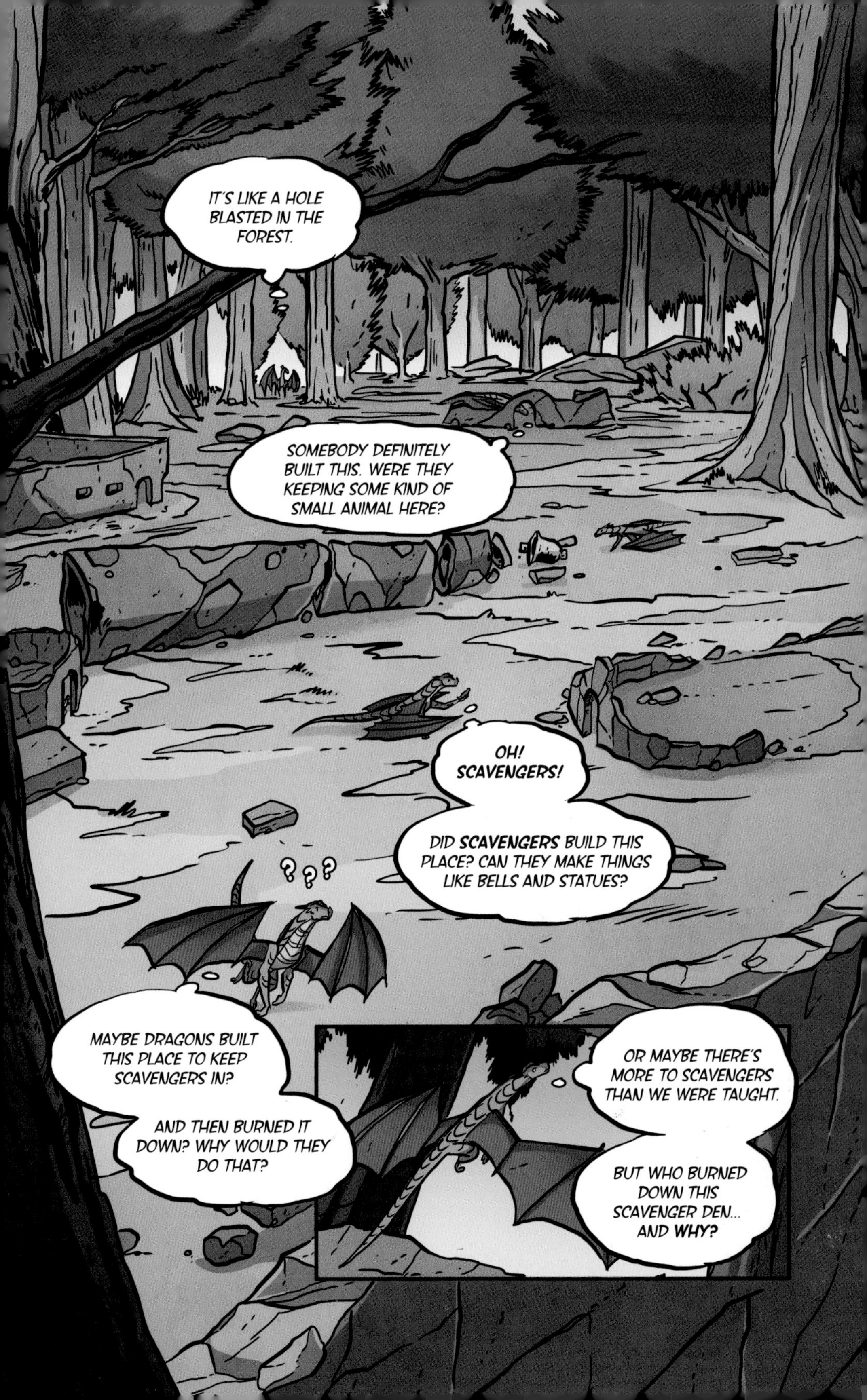
IT'S LIKE A HOLE BLASTED IN THE FOREST.
SOMEBODY DEFINITELY BUILT THIS. WERE THEY KEEPING SOME KIND OF SMALL ANIMAL HERE?
OH! SCAVENGERS!
DID **SCAVENGERS** BUILD THIS PLACE? CAN THEY MAKE THINGS LIKE BELLS AND STATUES?
???
MAYBE DRAGONS BUILT THIS PLACE TO KEEP SCAVENGERS IN?
AND THEN BURNED IT DOWN? WHY WOULD THEY DO THAT?
OR MAYBE THERE'S MORE TO SCAVENGERS THAN WE WERE TAUGHT.
BUT WHO BURNED DOWN THIS SCAVENGER DEN... AND **WHY?**

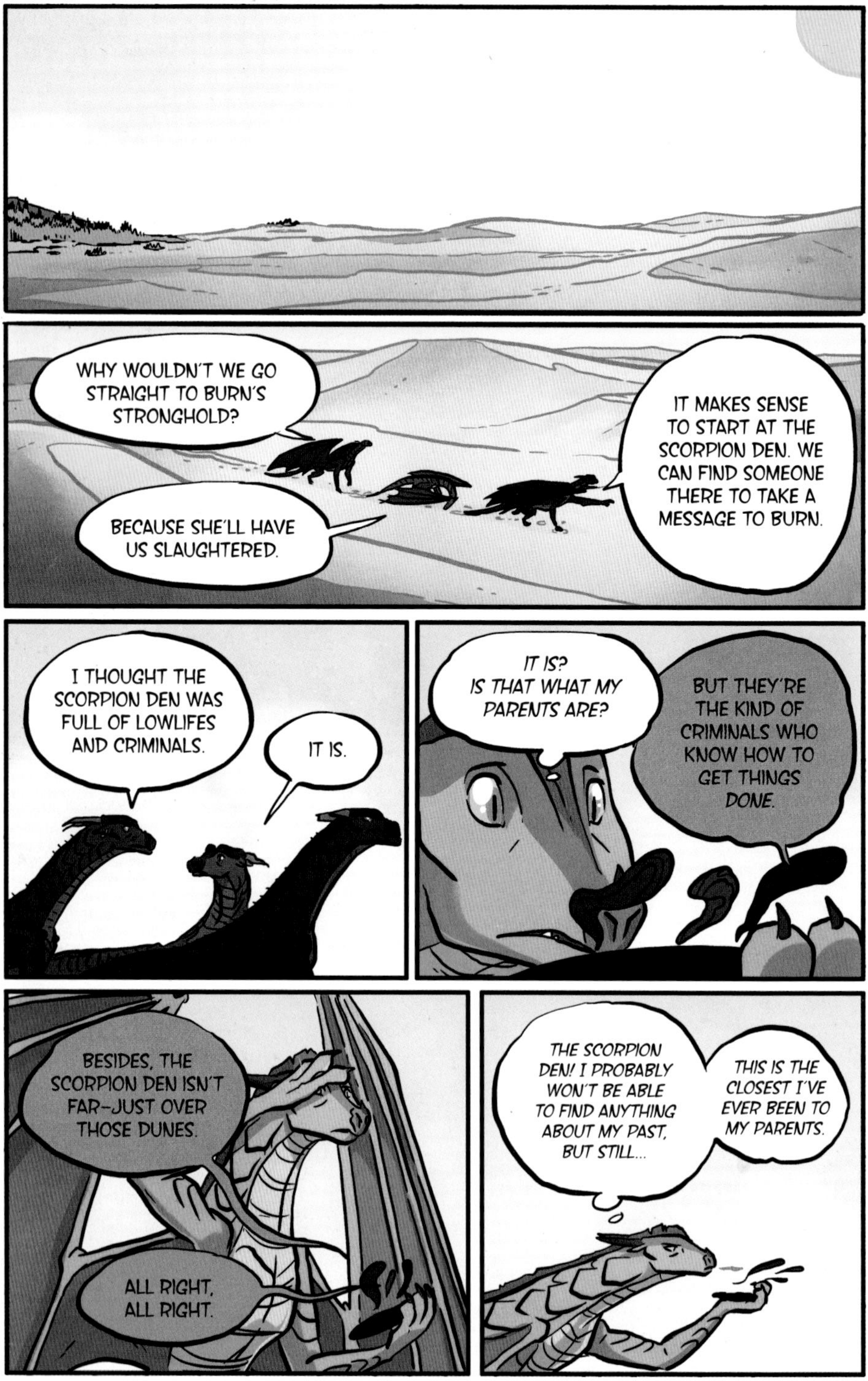
WHY WOULDN'T WE GO STRAIGHT TO BURN'S STRONGHOLD?
IT MAKES SENSE TO START AT THE SCORPION DEN. WE CAN FIND SOMEONE THERE TO TAKE A MESSAGE TO BURN.
BECAUSE SHE'LL HAVE US SLAUGHTERED.
I THOUGHT THE SCORPION DEN WAS FULL OF LOWLIFES AND CRIMINALS.
IT IS.
IT IS? IS THAT WHAT MY PARENTS ARE?
BUT THEY'RE THE KIND OF CRIMINALS WHO KNOW HOW TO GET THINGS DONE.
BESIDES, THE SCORPION DEN ISN'T FAR–JUST OVER THOSE DUNES.
ALL RIGHT, ALL RIGHT.
THE SCORPION DEN! I PROBABLY WON'T BE ABLE TO FIND ANYTHING ABOUT MY PAST, BUT STILL...
THIS IS THE CLOSEST I'VE EVER BEEN TO MY PARENTS.

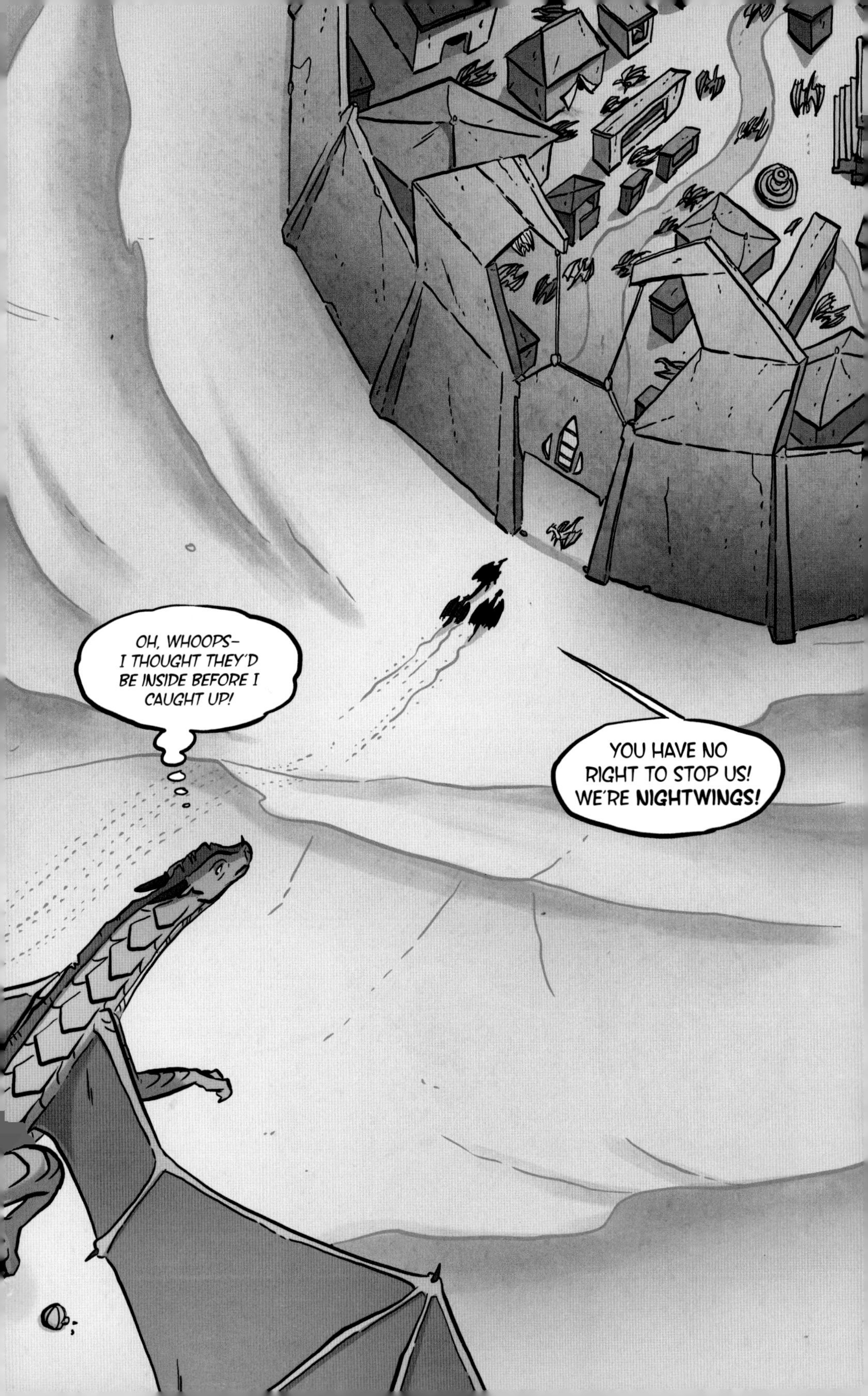
OH, WHOOPS– I THOUGHT THEY'D BE INSIDE BEFORE I CAUGHT UP!
YOU HAVE NO RIGHT TO STOP US! WE'RE **NIGHTWINGS!**

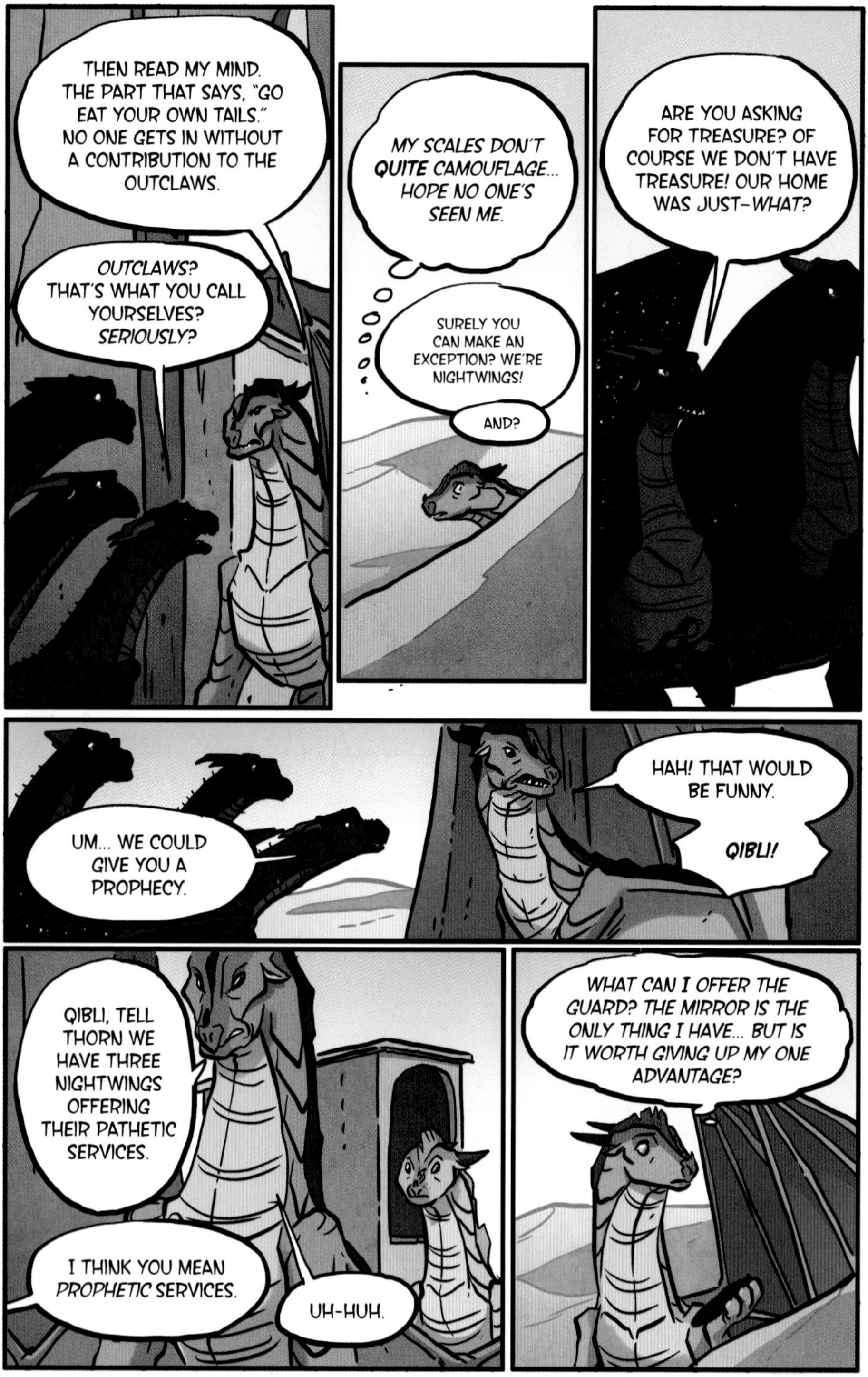
THEN READ MY MIND. THE PART THAT SAYS, "GO EAT YOUR OWN TAILS." NO ONE GETS IN WITHOUT A CONTRIBUTION TO THE OUTCLAWS.
OUTCLAWS? THAT'S WHAT YOU CALL YOURSELVES? *SERIOUSLY?*
*MY SCALES DON'T **QUITE** CAMOUFLAGE... HOPE NO ONE'S SEEN ME.*
SURELY YOU CAN MAKE AN EXCEPTION? WE'RE NIGHTWINGS!
AND?
ARE YOU ASKING FOR TREASURE? OF COURSE WE DON'T HAVE TREASURE! OUR HOME WAS JUST—*WHAT?*
UM... WE COULD GIVE YOU A PROPHECY.
HAH! THAT WOULD BE FUNNY.
QIBLI!
QIBLI, TELL THORN WE HAVE THREE NIGHTWINGS OFFERING THEIR PATHETIC SERVICES.
I THINK YOU MEAN *PROPHETIC* SERVICES.
UH-HUH.
*WHAT CAN **I** OFFER THE GUARD? THE MIRROR IS THE ONLY THING I HAVE... BUT IS IT WORTH GIVING UP MY ONE ADVANTAGE?*

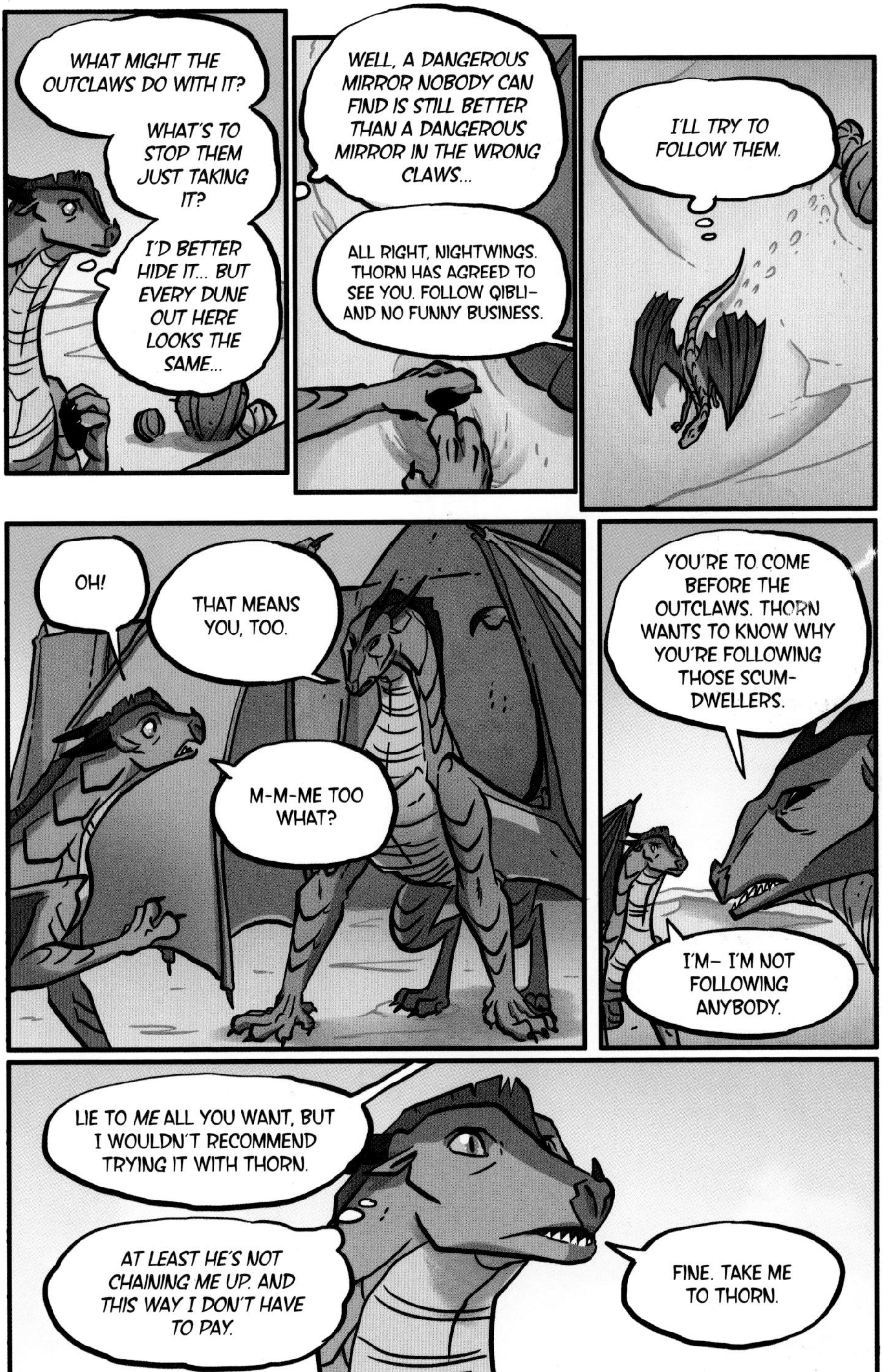
WHAT MIGHT THE OUTCLAWS DO WITH IT?
WHAT'S TO STOP THEM JUST TAKING IT?
I'D BETTER HIDE IT... BUT EVERY DUNE OUT HERE LOOKS THE SAME...
WELL, A DANGEROUS MIRROR NOBODY CAN FIND IS STILL BETTER THAN A DANGEROUS MIRROR IN THE WRONG CLAWS...
ALL RIGHT, NIGHTWINGS. THORN HAS AGREED TO SEE YOU. FOLLOW QIBLI— AND NO FUNNY BUSINESS.
I'LL TRY TO FOLLOW THEM.
OH!
THAT MEANS YOU, TOO.
M-M-ME TOO WHAT?
YOU'RE TO COME BEFORE THE OUTCLAWS. THORN WANTS TO KNOW WHY YOU'RE FOLLOWING THOSE SCUM-DWELLERS.
I'M— I'M NOT FOLLOWING ANYBODY.
LIE TO *ME* ALL YOU WANT, BUT I WOULDN'T RECOMMEND TRYING IT WITH THORN.
AT LEAST HE'S NOT CHAINING ME UP. AND THIS WAY I DON'T HAVE TO PAY.
FINE. TAKE ME TO THORN.

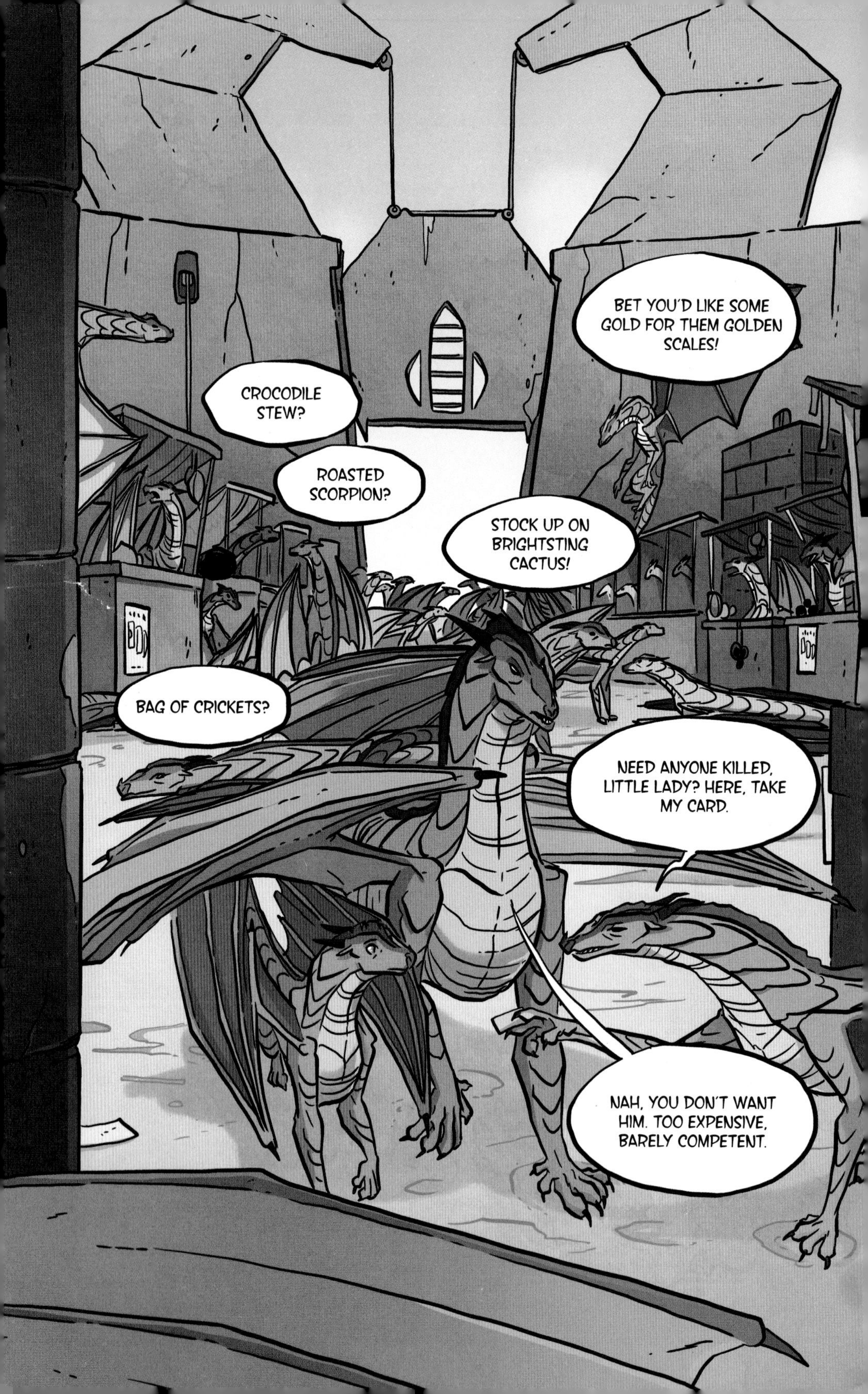
BET YOU'D LIKE SOME GOLD FOR THEM GOLDEN SCALES!
CROCODILE STEW?
ROASTED SCORPION?
STOCK UP ON BRIGHTSTING CACTUS!
BAG OF CRICKETS?
NEED ANYONE KILLED, LITTLE LADY? HERE, TAKE MY CARD.
NAH, YOU DON'T WANT HIM. TOO EXPENSIVE, BARELY COMPETENT.

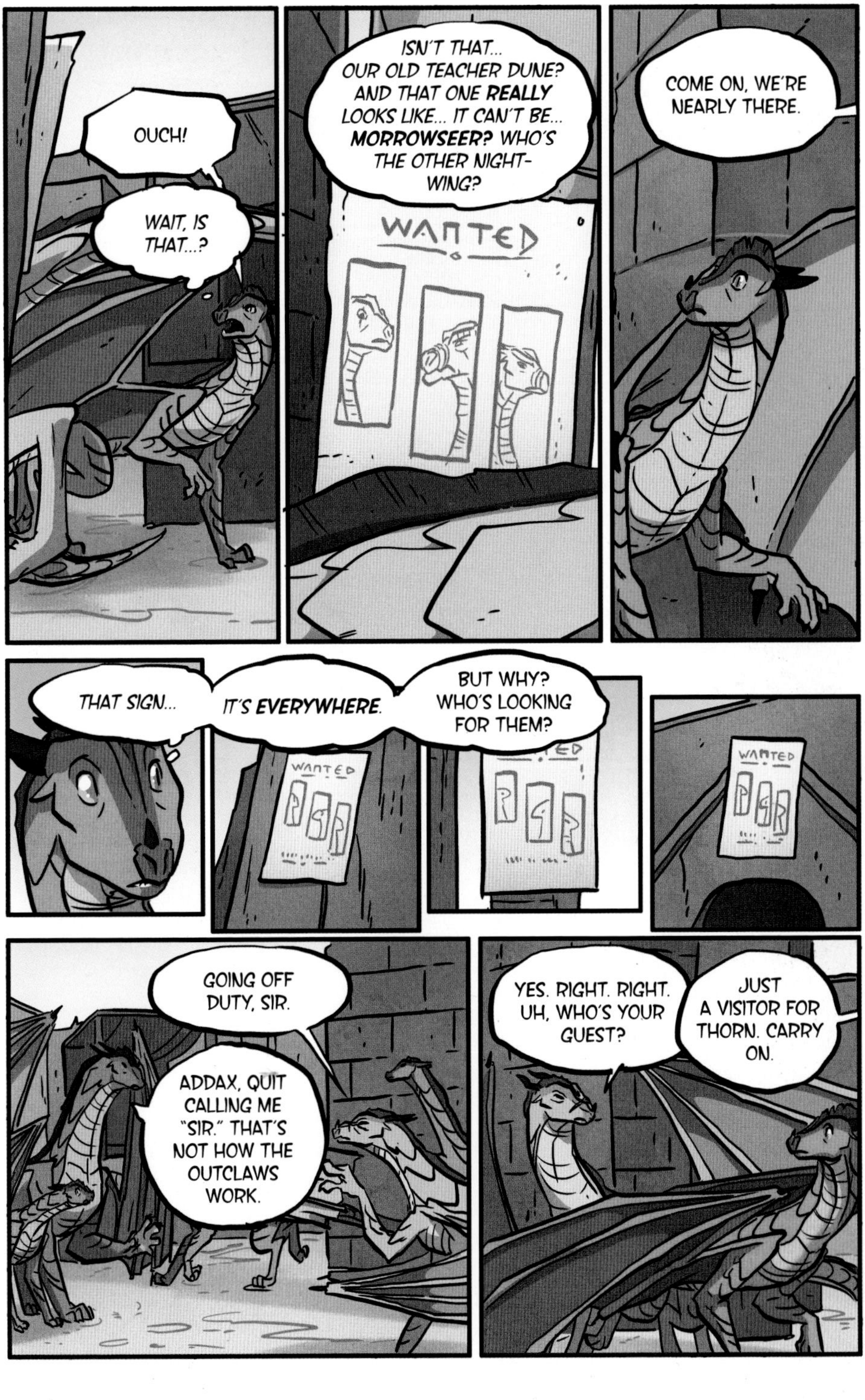
OUCH!
WAIT, IS THAT...?
ISN'T THAT... OUR OLD TEACHER DUNE? AND THAT ONE **REALLY** LOOKS LIKE... IT CAN'T BE... **MORROWSEER?** WHO'S THE OTHER NIGHT-WING?
WANTED
COME ON, WE'RE NEARLY THERE.
THAT SIGN...
IT'S **EVERYWHERE**.
BUT WHY? WHO'S LOOKING FOR THEM?
WANTED
WANTED
GOING OFF DUTY, SIR.
ADDAX, QUIT CALLING ME "SIR." THAT'S NOT HOW THE OUTCLAWS WORK.
YES. RIGHT. RIGHT. UH, WHO'S YOUR GUEST?
JUST A VISITOR FOR THORN. CARRY ON.

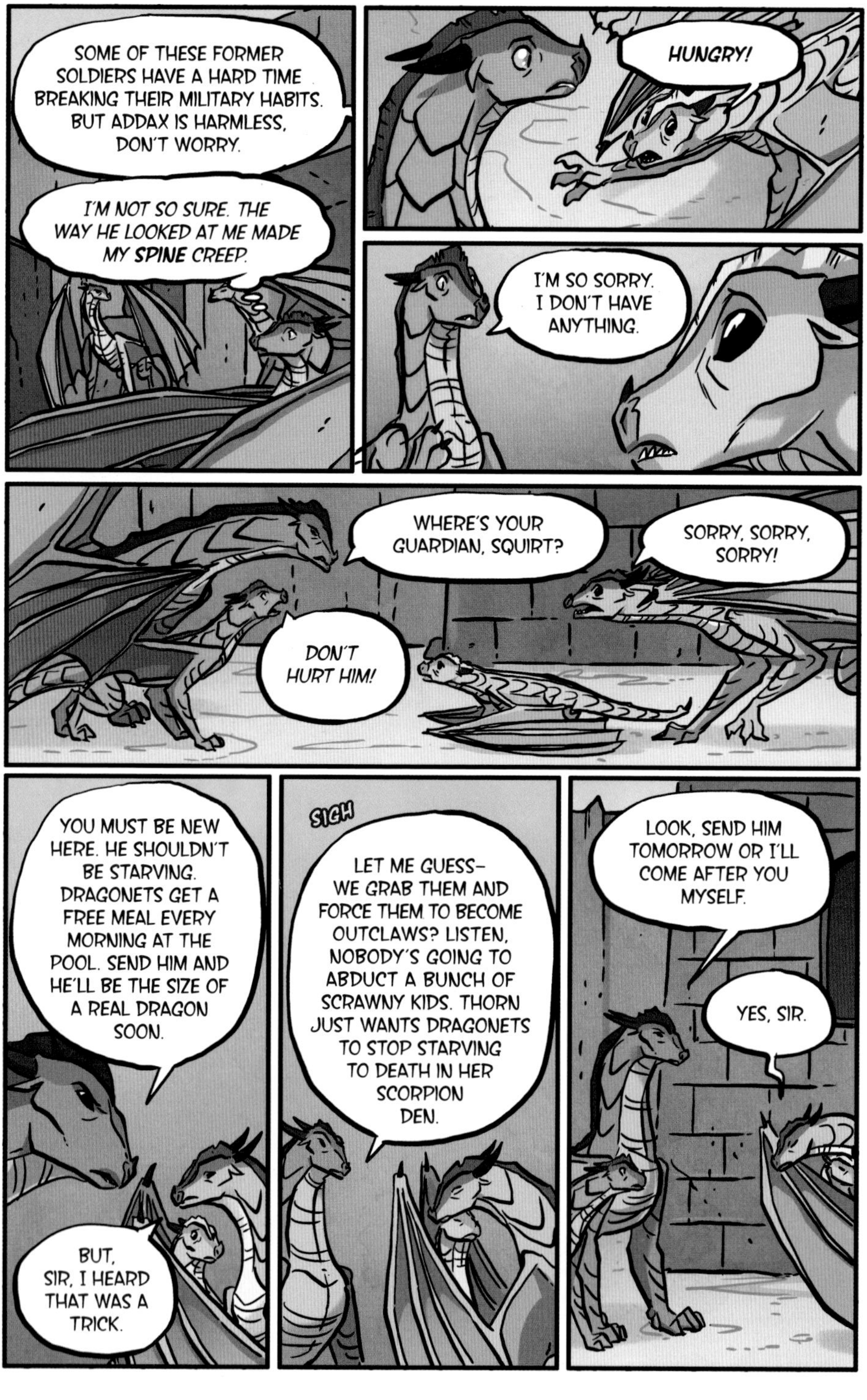

SOME OF THESE FORMER SOLDIERS HAVE A HARD TIME BREAKING THEIR MILITARY HABITS. BUT ADDAX IS HARMLESS, DON'T WORRY.
I'M NOT SO SURE. THE WAY HE LOOKED AT ME MADE MY SPINE CREEP.
HUNGRY!
I'M SO SORRY. I DON'T HAVE ANYTHING.
WHERE'S YOUR GUARDIAN, SQUIRT?
SORRY, SORRY, SORRY!
DON'T HURT HIM!
YOU MUST BE NEW HERE. HE SHOULDN'T BE STARVING. DRAGONETS GET A FREE MEAL EVERY MORNING AT THE POOL. SEND HIM AND HE'LL BE THE SIZE OF A REAL DRAGON SOON.
BUT, SIR, I HEARD THAT WAS A TRICK.
SIGH
LET ME GUESS– WE GRAB THEM AND FORCE THEM TO BECOME OUTCLAWS? LISTEN, NOBODY'S GOING TO ABDUCT A BUNCH OF SCRAWNY KIDS. THORN JUST WANTS DRAGONETS TO STOP STARVING TO DEATH IN HER SCORPION DEN.
LOOK, SEND HIM TOMORROW OR I'LL COME AFTER YOU MYSELF.
YES, SIR.

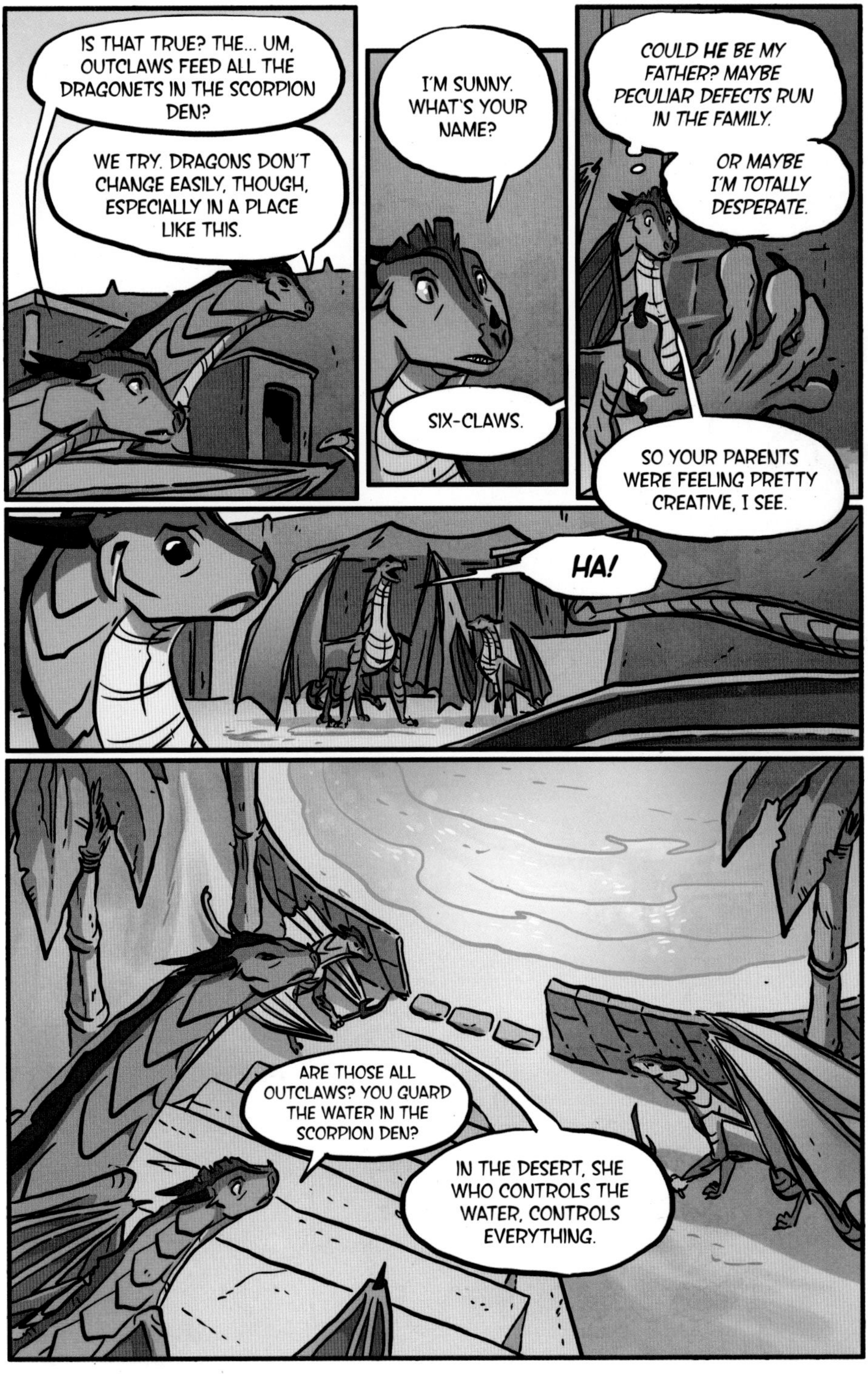
IS THAT TRUE? THE... UM, OUTCLAWS FEED ALL THE DRAGONETS IN THE SCORPION DEN?
WE TRY. DRAGONS DON'T CHANGE EASILY, THOUGH, ESPECIALLY IN A PLACE LIKE THIS.
I'M SUNNY. WHAT'S YOUR NAME?
SIX-CLAWS.
COULD **HE** BE MY FATHER? MAYBE PECULIAR DEFECTS RUN IN THE FAMILY.
OR MAYBE I'M TOTALLY DESPERATE.
SO YOUR PARENTS WERE FEELING PRETTY CREATIVE, I SEE.
HA!
ARE THOSE ALL OUTCLAWS? YOU GUARD THE WATER IN THE SCORPION DEN?
IN THE DESERT, SHE WHO CONTROLS THE WATER, CONTROLS EVERYTHING.

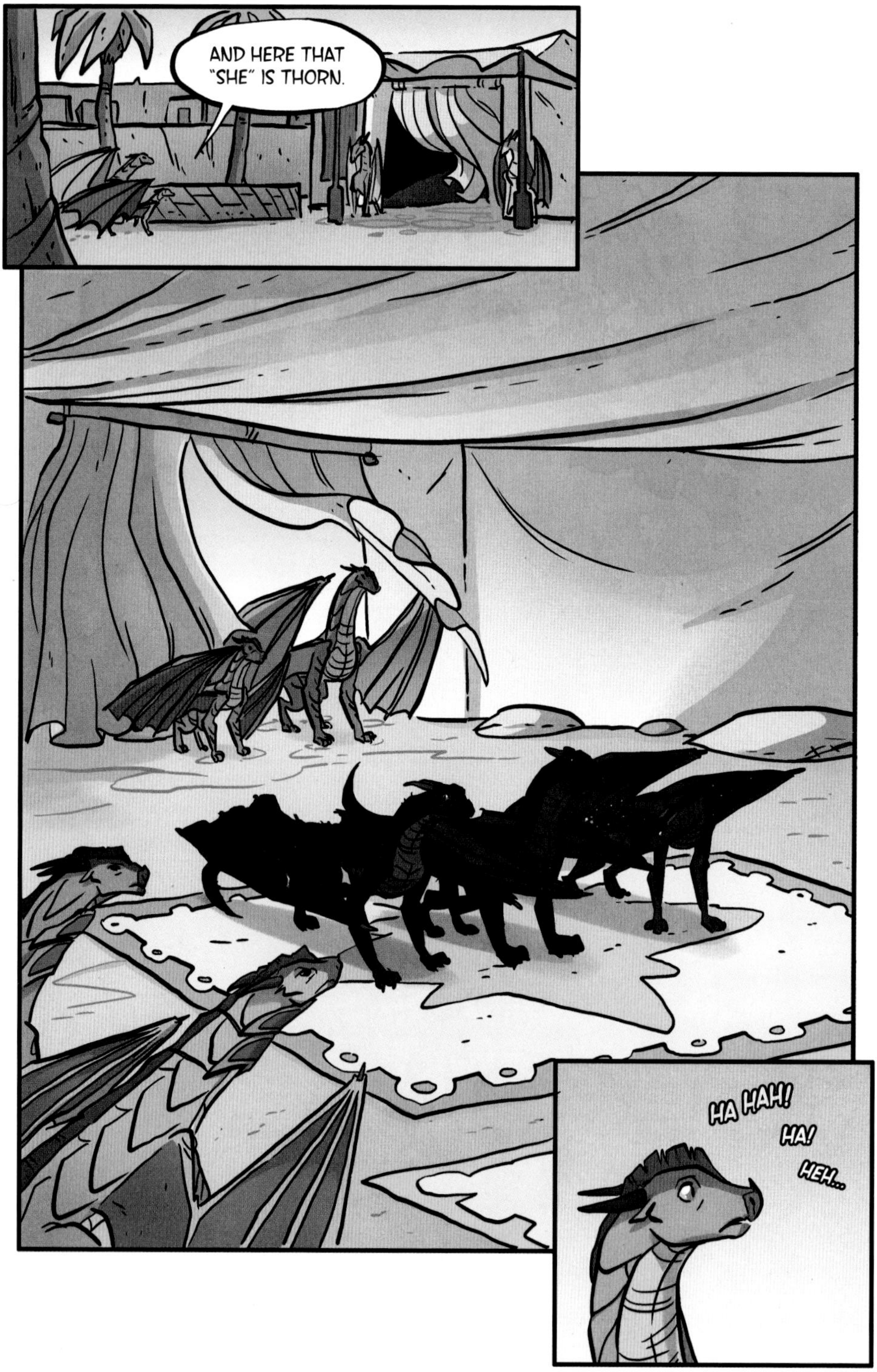
AND HERE THAT "SHE" IS THORN.
HA HAH!
HA!
HEH...

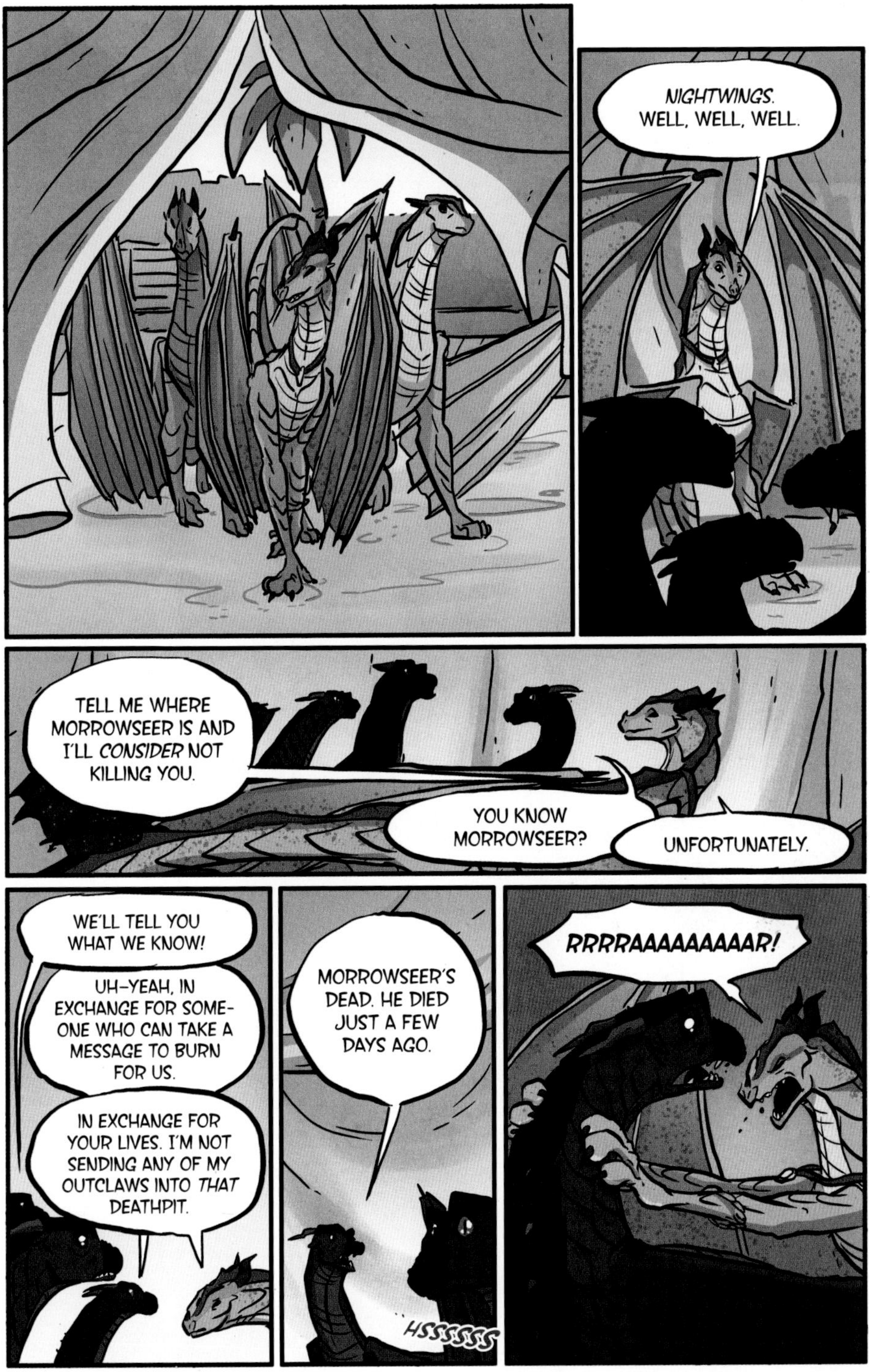
NIGHTWINGS. WELL, WELL, WELL.
TELL ME WHERE MORROWSEER IS AND I'LL *CONSIDER* NOT KILLING YOU.
YOU KNOW MORROWSEER?
UNFORTUNATELY.
WE'LL TELL YOU WHAT WE KNOW!
UH—YEAH, IN EXCHANGE FOR SOME-ONE WHO CAN TAKE A MESSAGE TO BURN FOR US.
IN EXCHANGE FOR YOUR LIVES. I'M NOT SENDING ANY OF MY OUTCLAWS INTO *THAT* DEATHPIT.
MORROWSEER'S DEAD. HE DIED JUST A FEW DAYS AGO.
HSSSSSS
RRRRAAAAAAAAAAR!

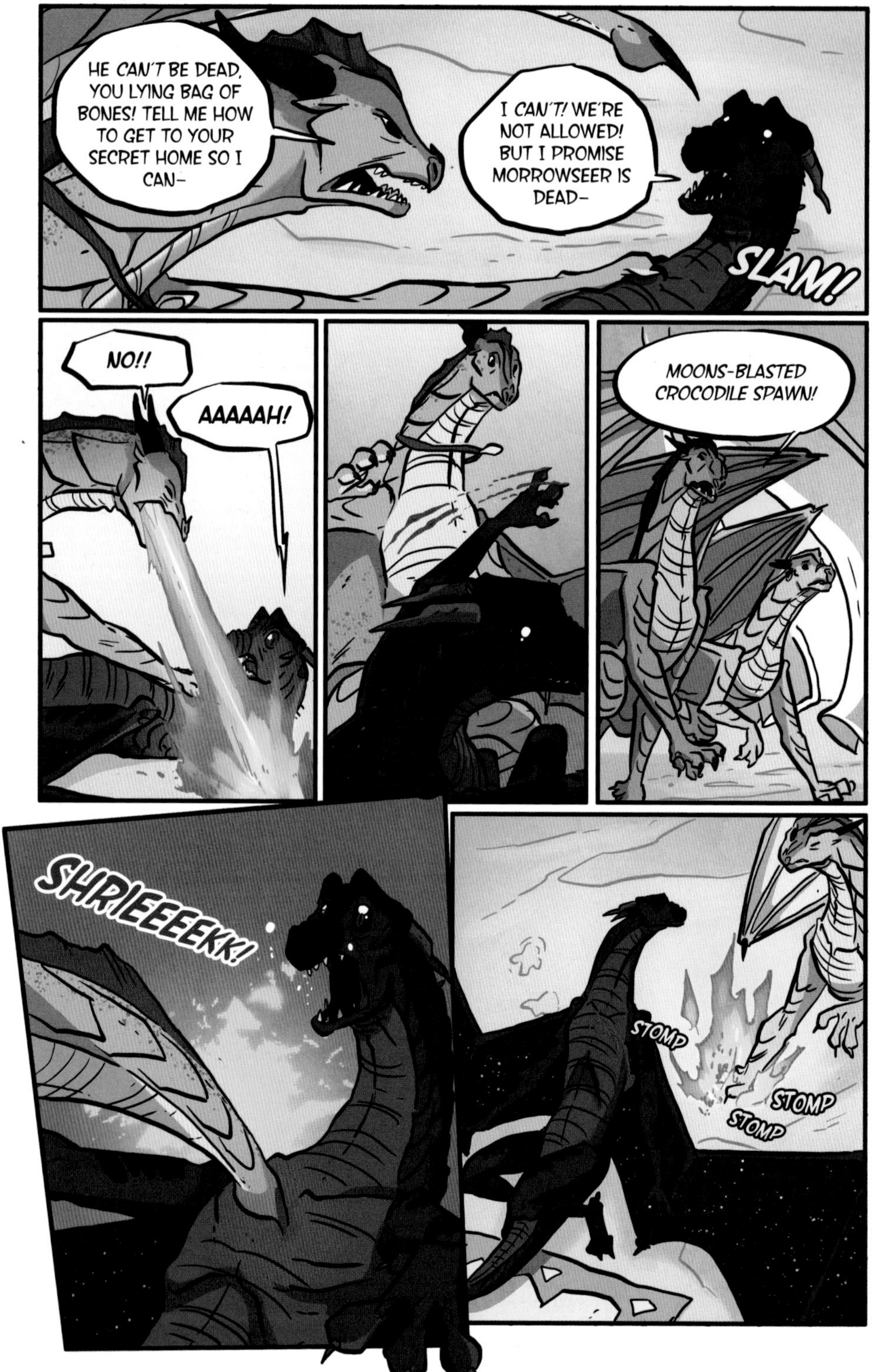
HE *CAN'T* BE DEAD, YOU LYING BAG OF BONES! TELL ME HOW TO GET TO YOUR SECRET HOME SO I CAN–
I *CAN'T!* WE'RE NOT ALLOWED! BUT I PROMISE MORROWSEER IS DEAD–
SLAM!
NO!!
AAAAAH!
MOONS-BLASTED CROCODILE SPAWN!
SHRIEEEEEKK!
STOMP
STOMP
STOMP

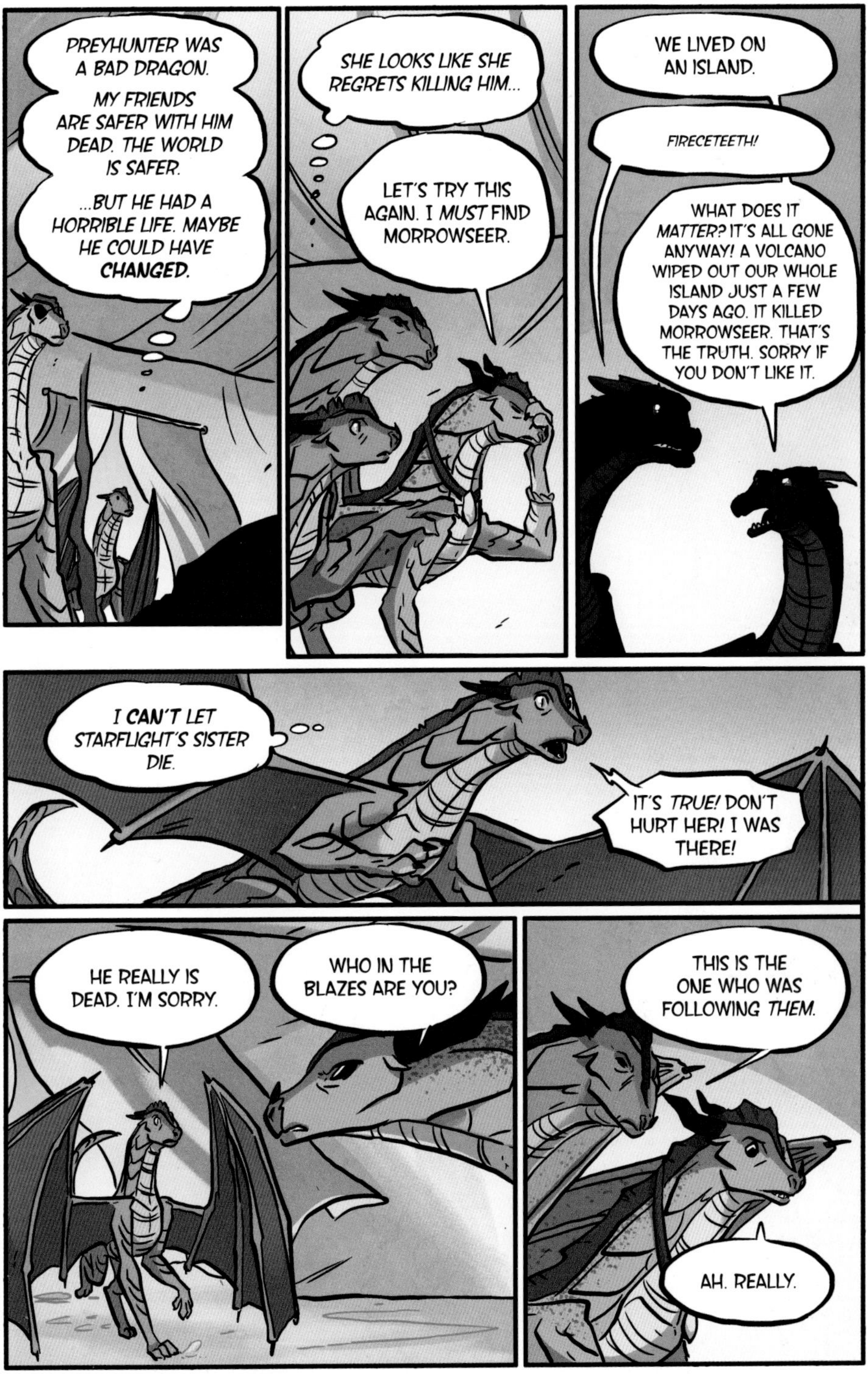
PREYHUNTER WAS A BAD DRAGON.
MY FRIENDS ARE SAFER WITH HIM DEAD. THE WORLD IS SAFER.
...BUT HE HAD A HORRIBLE LIFE. MAYBE HE COULD HAVE **CHANGED.**
SHE LOOKS LIKE SHE REGRETS KILLING HIM...
LET'S TRY THIS AGAIN. I *MUST* FIND MORROWSEER.
WE LIVED ON AN ISLAND.
FIRECETEETH!
WHAT DOES IT *MATTER?* IT'S ALL GONE ANYWAY! A VOLCANO WIPED OUT OUR WHOLE ISLAND JUST A FEW DAYS AGO. IT KILLED MORROWSEER. THAT'S THE TRUTH. SORRY IF YOU DON'T LIKE IT.
*I **CAN'T** LET STARFLIGHT'S SISTER DIE.*
IT'S *TRUE!* DON'T HURT HER! I WAS THERE!
HE REALLY IS DEAD. I'M SORRY.
WHO IN THE BLAZES ARE YOU?
THIS IS THE ONE WHO WAS FOLLOWING *THEM.*
AH. REALLY.

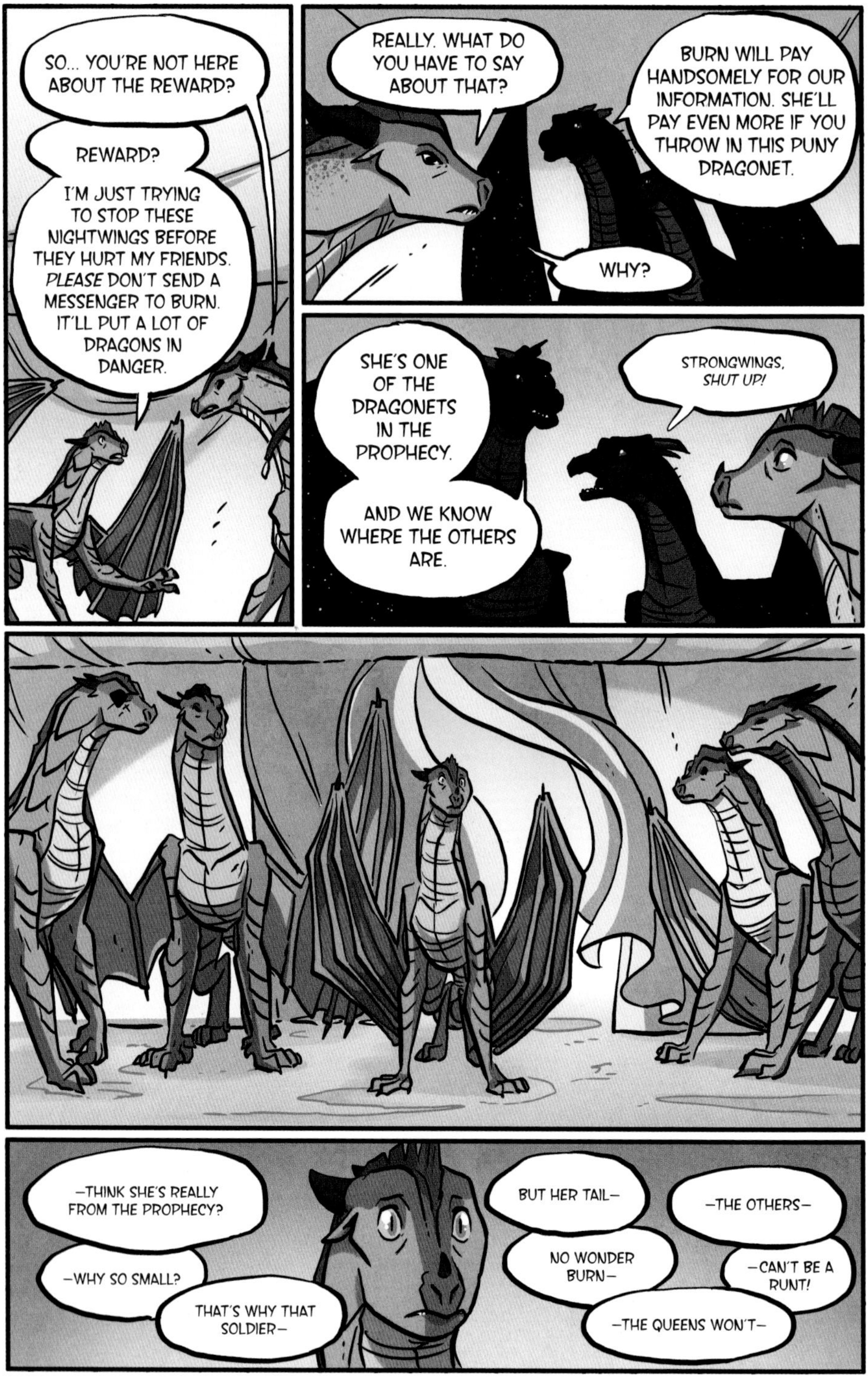
SO... YOU'RE NOT HERE ABOUT THE REWARD?
REWARD?
I'M JUST TRYING TO STOP THESE NIGHTWINGS BEFORE THEY HURT MY FRIENDS. *PLEASE* DON'T SEND A MESSENGER TO BURN. IT'LL PUT A LOT OF DRAGONS IN DANGER.
REALLY. WHAT DO YOU HAVE TO SAY ABOUT THAT?
BURN WILL PAY HANDSOMELY FOR OUR INFORMATION. SHE'LL PAY EVEN MORE IF YOU THROW IN THIS PUNY DRAGONET.
WHY?
SHE'S ONE OF THE DRAGONETS IN THE PROPHECY.
AND WE KNOW WHERE THE OTHERS ARE.
STRONGWINGS, *SHUT UP!*
—THINK SHE'S REALLY FROM THE PROPHECY?
—WHY SO SMALL?
THAT'S WHY THAT SOLDIER—
BUT HER TAIL—
NO WONDER BURN—
—THE OTHERS—
—CAN'T BE A RUNT!
—THE QUEENS WON'T—

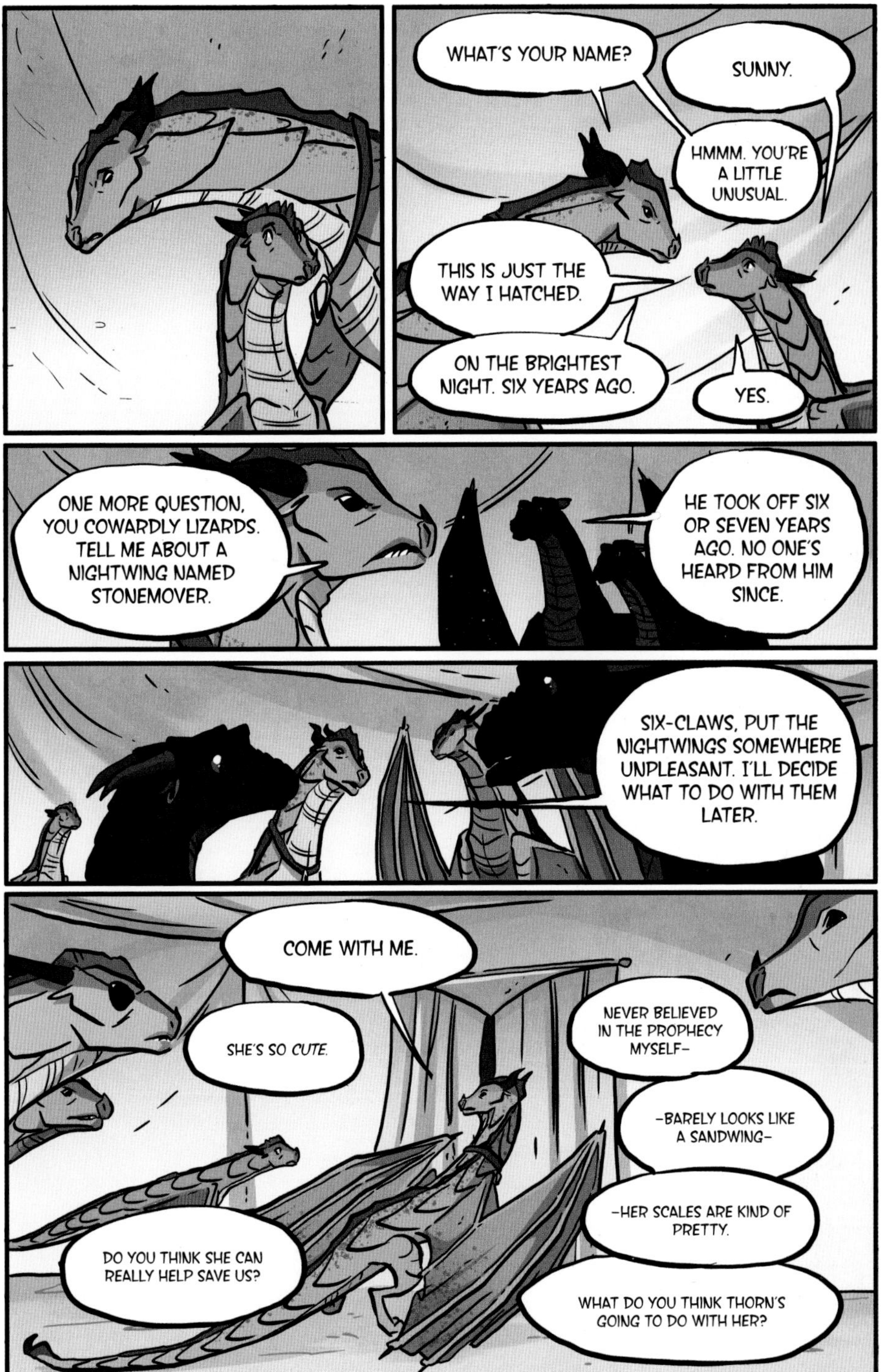
WHAT'S YOUR NAME?
SUNNY.
HMMM. YOU'RE A LITTLE UNUSUAL.
THIS IS JUST THE WAY I HATCHED.
ON THE BRIGHTEST NIGHT. SIX YEARS AGO.
YES.
ONE MORE QUESTION, YOU COWARDLY LIZARDS. TELL ME ABOUT A NIGHTWING NAMED STONEMOVER.
HE TOOK OFF SIX OR SEVEN YEARS AGO. NO ONE'S HEARD FROM HIM SINCE.
SIX-CLAWS, PUT THE NIGHTWINGS SOMEWHERE UNPLEASANT. I'LL DECIDE WHAT TO DO WITH THEM LATER.
COME WITH ME.
SHE'S SO *CUTE*.
NEVER BELIEVED IN THE PROPHECY MYSELF–
–BARELY LOOKS LIKE A SANDWING–
–HER SCALES ARE KIND OF PRETTY.
DO YOU THINK SHE CAN REALLY HELP SAVE US?
WHAT DO YOU THINK THORN'S GOING TO DO WITH HER?

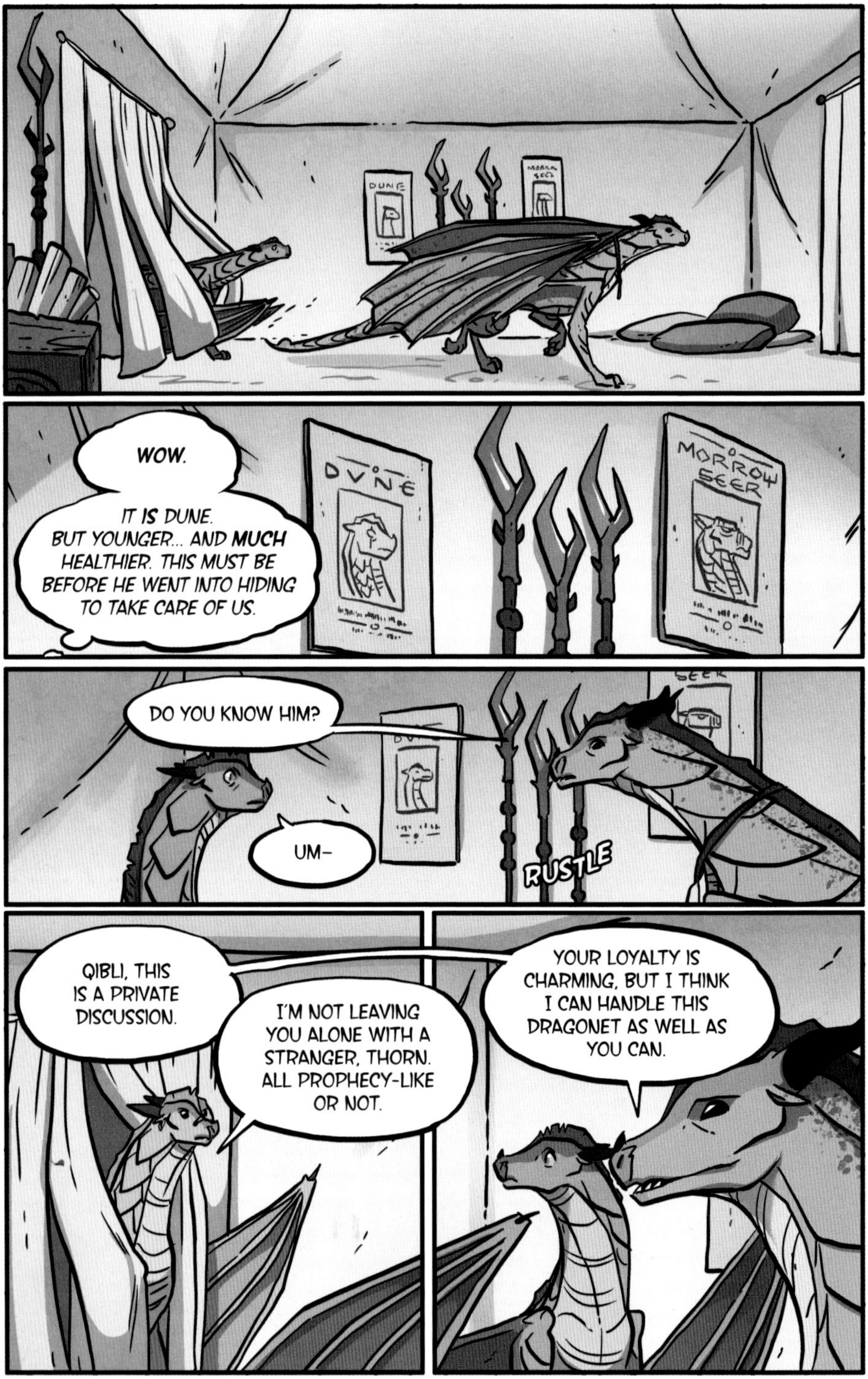
DUNE
MORROWSEER
WOW.
IT IS DUNE. BUT YOUNGER... AND MUCH HEALTHIER. THIS MUST BE BEFORE HE WENT INTO HIDING TO TAKE CARE OF US.
DO YOU KNOW HIM?
UM–
RUSTLE
QIBLI, THIS IS A PRIVATE DISCUSSION.
I'M NOT LEAVING YOU ALONE WITH A STRANGER, THORN. ALL PROPHECY-LIKE OR NOT.
YOUR LOYALTY IS CHARMING, BUT I THINK I CAN HANDLE THIS DRAGONET AS WELL AS YOU CAN.

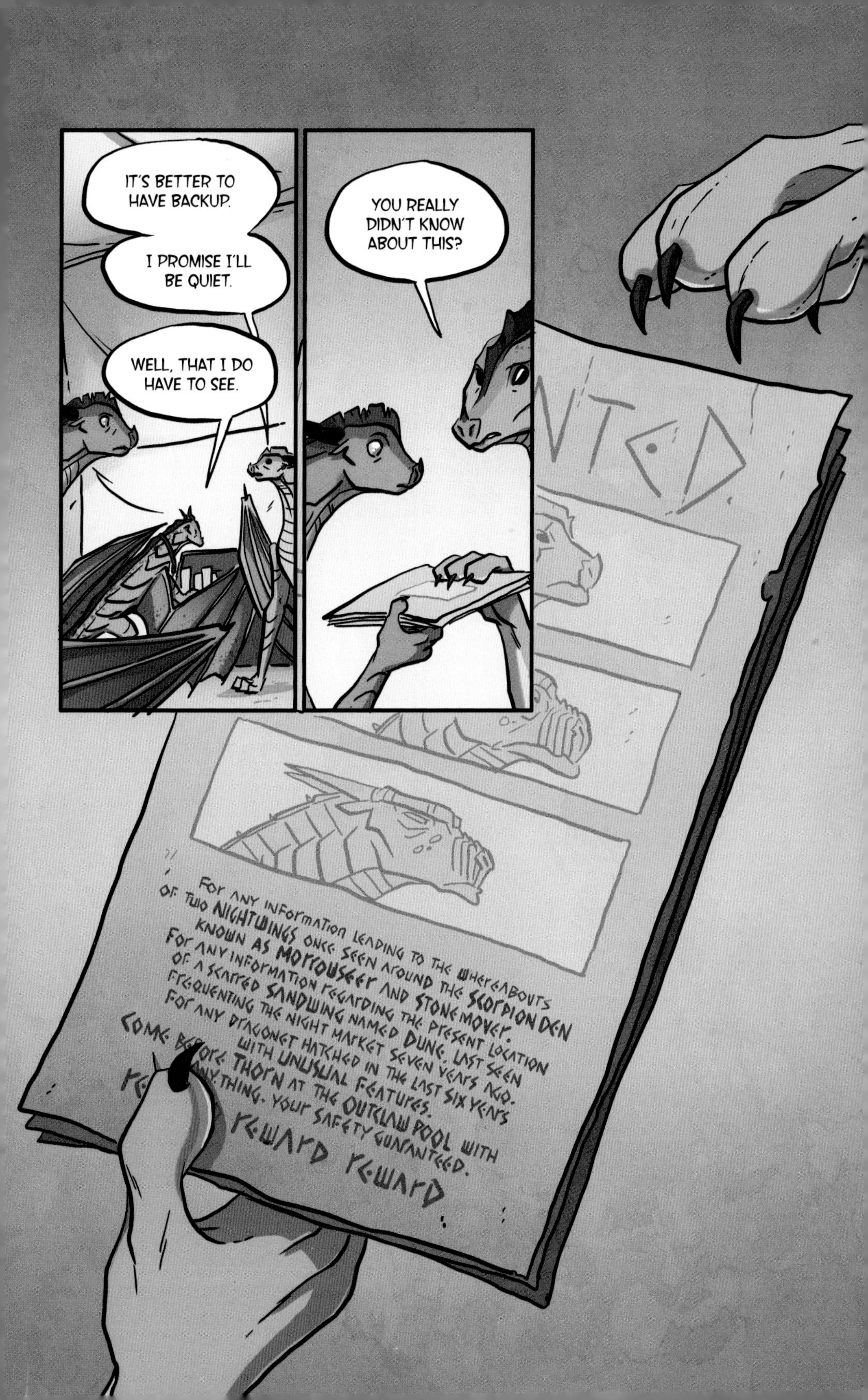
IT'S BETTER TO HAVE BACKUP.
I PROMISE I'LL BE QUIET.
WELL, THAT I DO HAVE TO SEE.
YOU REALLY DIDN'T KNOW ABOUT THIS?
FOR ANY INFORMATION LEADING TO THE WHEREABOUTS OF TWO NIGHTWINGS ONCE SEEN AROUND THE SCORPION DEN KNOWN AS MORROWSEER AND STONEMOVER.
FOR ANY INFORMATION REGARDING THE PRESENT LOCATION OF A SCARRED SANDWING NAMED DUNE, LAST SEEN FREQUENTING THE NIGHT MARKET SEVEN YEARS AGO.
FOR ANY DRAGONET HATCHED IN THE LAST SIX YEARS WITH UNUSUAL FEATURES.
COME B ORE THORN AT THE OUTCLAW POOL WITH
RE ANYTHING. YOUR SAFETY GUARANTEED.
REWARD REWARD

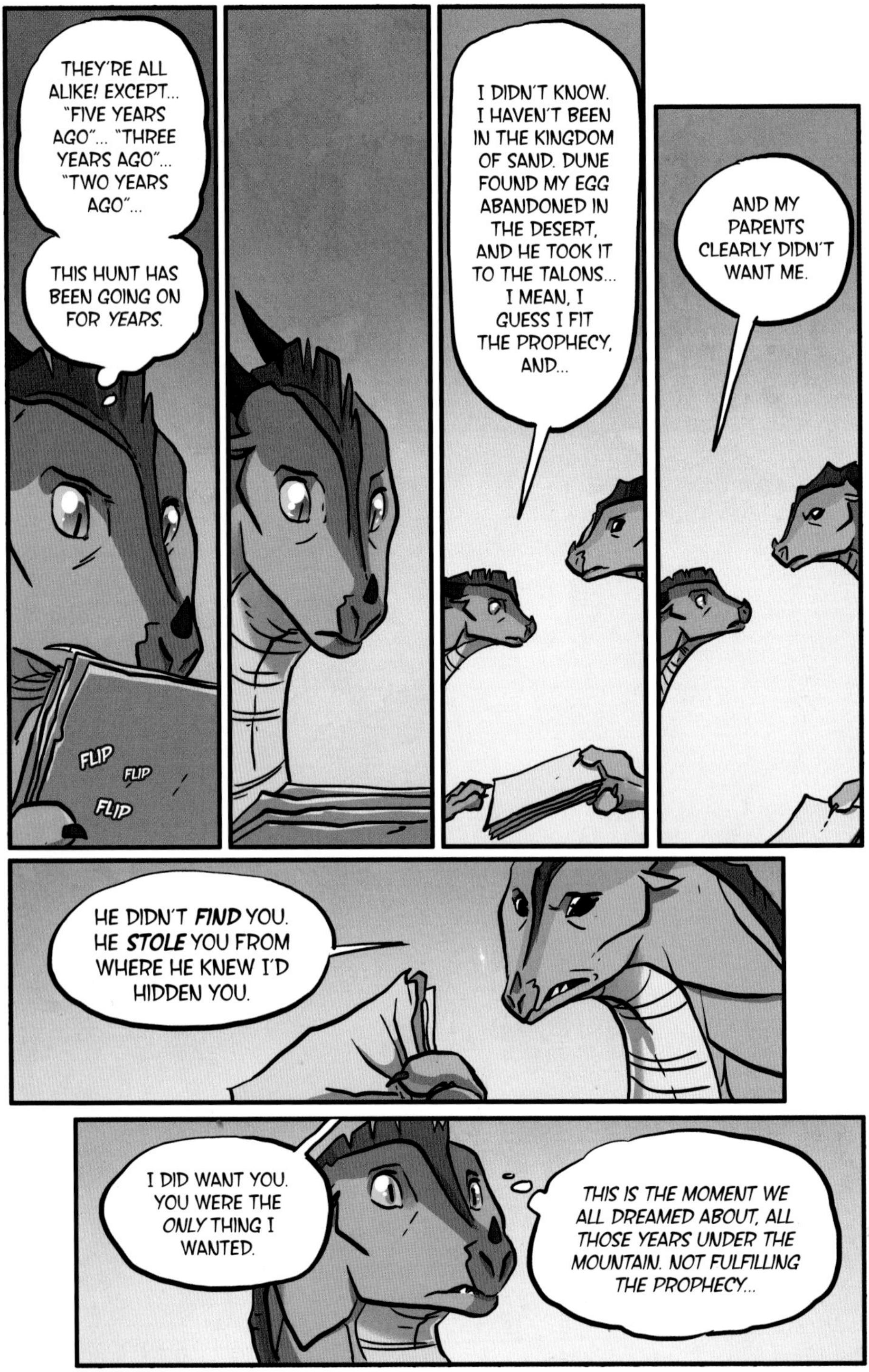
THEY'RE ALL ALIKE! EXCEPT... "FIVE YEARS AGO"... "THREE YEARS AGO"... "TWO YEARS AGO"...
THIS HUNT HAS BEEN GOING ON FOR *YEARS*.
FLIP
FLIP
FLIP
I DIDN'T KNOW. I HAVEN'T BEEN IN THE KINGDOM OF SAND. DUNE FOUND MY EGG ABANDONED IN THE DESERT, AND HE TOOK IT TO THE TALONS... I MEAN, I GUESS I FIT THE PROPHECY, AND...
AND MY PARENTS CLEARLY DIDN'T WANT ME.
HE DIDN'T ***FIND*** YOU. HE ***STOLE*** YOU FROM WHERE HE KNEW I'D HIDDEN YOU.
I DID WANT YOU. YOU WERE THE *ONLY* THING I WANTED.
THIS IS THE MOMENT WE ALL DREAMED ABOUT, ALL THOSE YEARS UNDER THE MOUNTAIN. NOT FULFILLING THE PROPHECY...

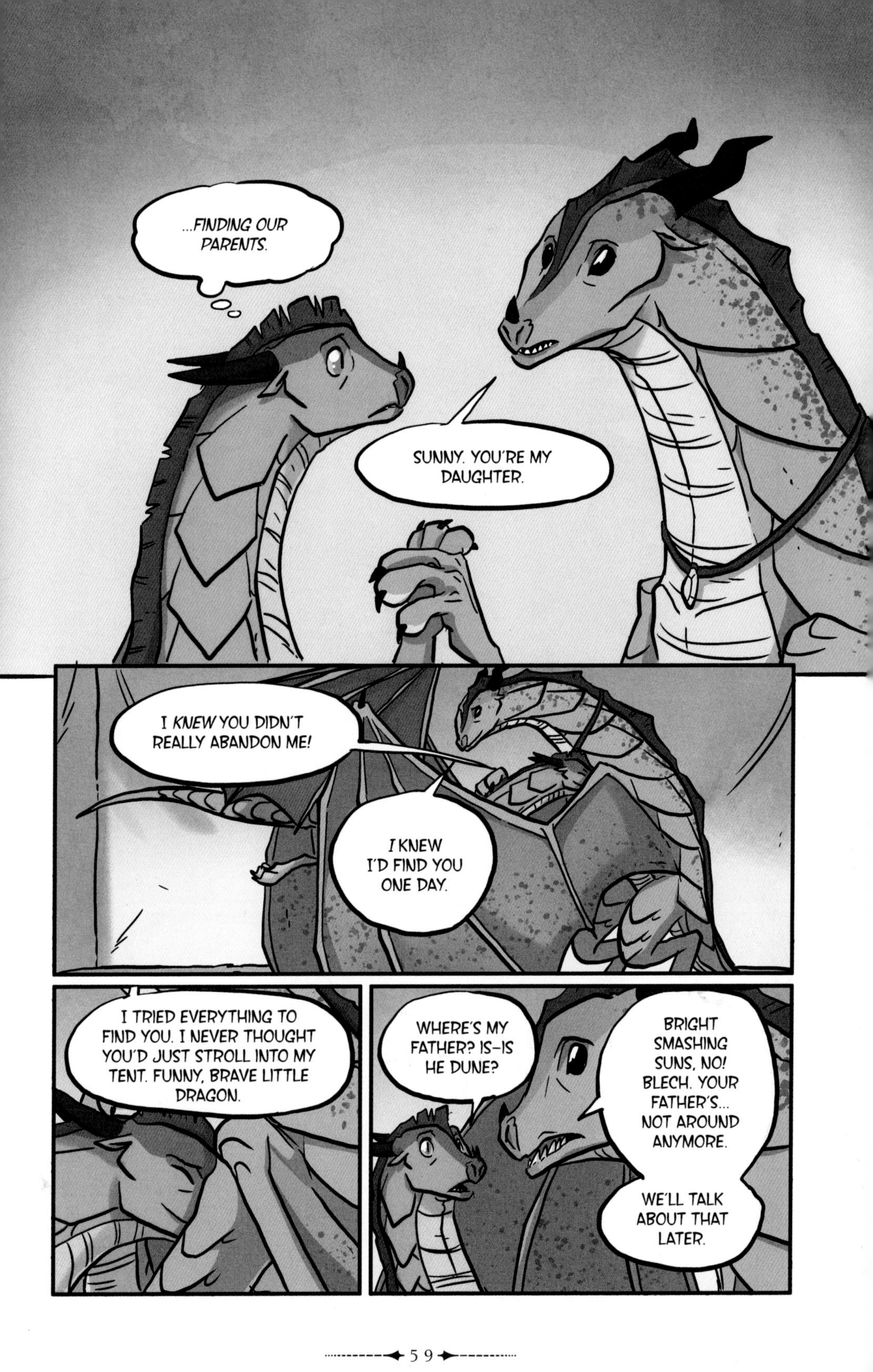
...FINDING OUR PARENTS.
SUNNY. YOU'RE MY DAUGHTER.
I KNEW YOU DIDN'T REALLY ABANDON ME!
I KNEW I'D FIND YOU ONE DAY.
I TRIED EVERYTHING TO FIND YOU. I NEVER THOUGHT YOU'D JUST STROLL INTO MY TENT. FUNNY, BRAVE LITTLE DRAGON.
WHERE'S MY FATHER? IS—IS HE DUNE?
BRIGHT SMASHING SUNS, NO! BLECH. YOUR FATHER'S... NOT AROUND ANYMORE.
WE'LL TALK ABOUT THAT LATER.

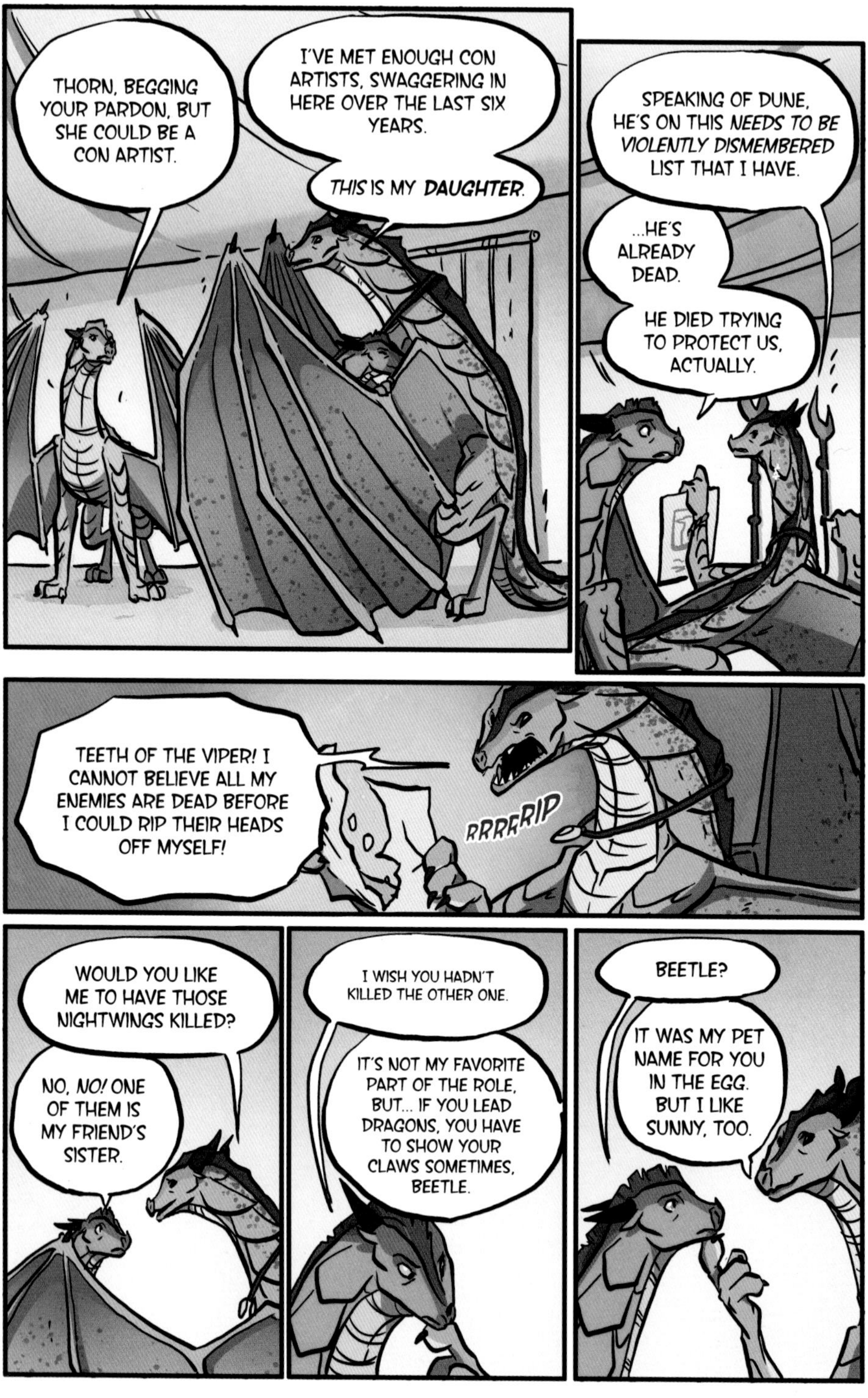
THORN, BEGGING YOUR PARDON, BUT SHE COULD BE A CON ARTIST.
I'VE MET ENOUGH CON ARTISTS, SWAGGERING IN HERE OVER THE LAST SIX YEARS.
THIS IS MY ***DAUGHTER***.
SPEAKING OF DUNE, HE'S ON THIS *NEEDS TO BE VIOLENTLY DISMEMBERED* LIST THAT I HAVE.
...HE'S ALREADY DEAD.
HE DIED TRYING TO PROTECT US, ACTUALLY.
TEETH OF THE VIPER! I CANNOT BELIEVE ALL MY ENEMIES ARE DEAD BEFORE I COULD RIP THEIR HEADS OFF MYSELF!
RRRRRIP
WOULD YOU LIKE ME TO HAVE THOSE NIGHTWINGS KILLED?
NO, *NO!* ONE OF THEM IS MY FRIEND'S SISTER.
I WISH YOU HADN'T KILLED THE OTHER ONE.
IT'S NOT MY FAVORITE PART OF THE ROLE, BUT... IF YOU LEAD DRAGONS, YOU HAVE TO SHOW YOUR CLAWS SOMETIMES, BEETLE.
BEETLE?
IT WAS MY PET NAME FOR YOU IN THE EGG. BUT I LIKE SUNNY, TOO.

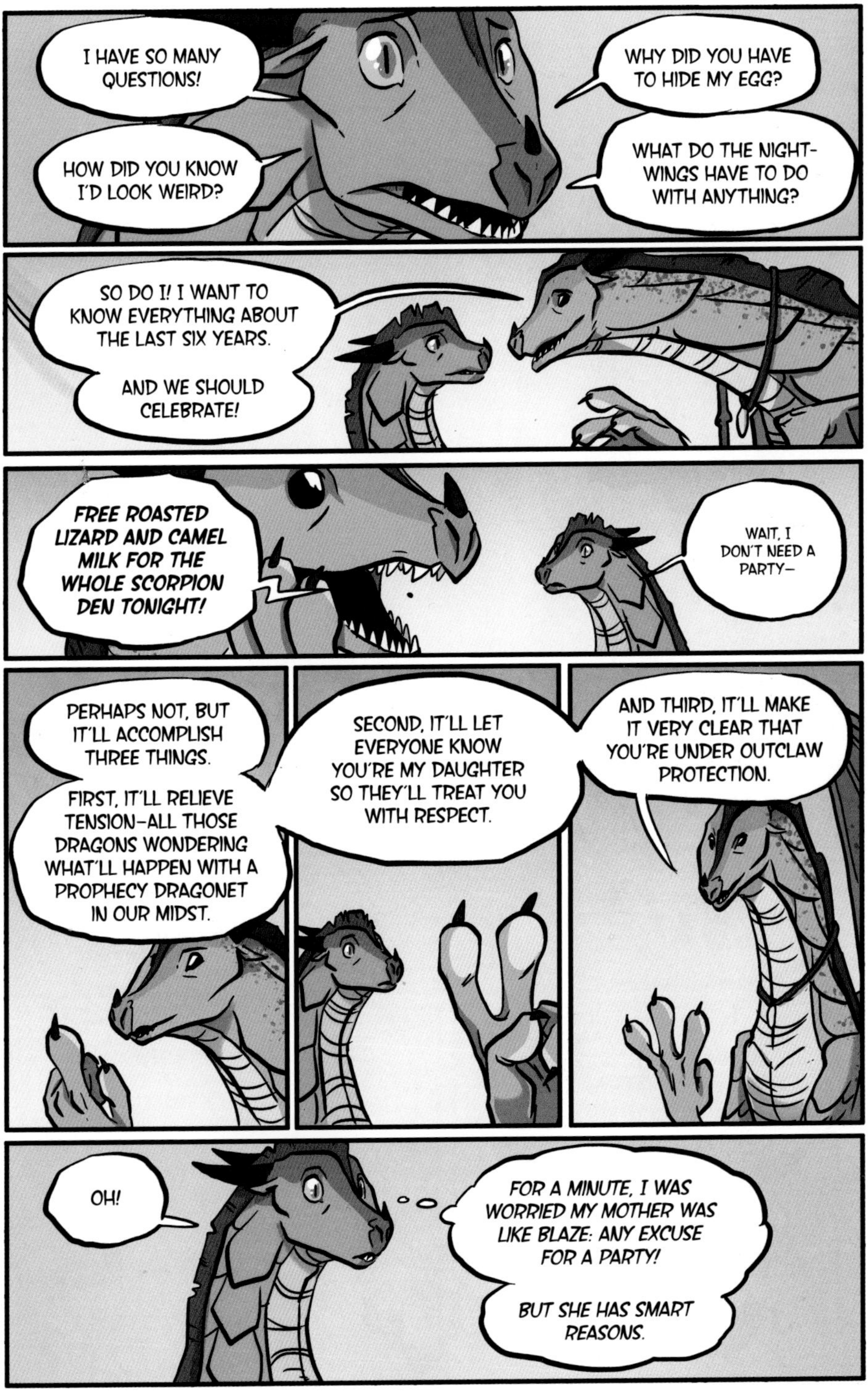
I HAVE SO MANY QUESTIONS!
HOW DID YOU KNOW I'D LOOK WEIRD?
WHY DID YOU HAVE TO HIDE MY EGG?
WHAT DO THE NIGHT-WINGS HAVE TO DO WITH ANYTHING?
SO DO I! I WANT TO KNOW EVERYTHING ABOUT THE LAST SIX YEARS.
AND WE SHOULD CELEBRATE!
FREE ROASTED LIZARD AND CAMEL MILK FOR THE WHOLE SCORPION DEN TONIGHT!
WAIT, I DON'T NEED A PARTY—
PERHAPS NOT, BUT IT'LL ACCOMPLISH THREE THINGS.
FIRST, IT'LL RELIEVE TENSION—ALL THOSE DRAGONS WONDERING WHAT'LL HAPPEN WITH A PROPHECY DRAGONET IN OUR MIDST.
SECOND, IT'LL LET EVERYONE KNOW YOU'RE MY DAUGHTER SO THEY'LL TREAT YOU WITH RESPECT.
AND THIRD, IT'LL MAKE IT VERY CLEAR THAT YOU'RE UNDER OUTCLAW PROTECTION.
OH!
FOR A MINUTE, I WAS WORRIED MY MOTHER WAS LIKE BLAZE: ANY EXCUSE FOR A PARTY!
BUT SHE HAS SMART REASONS.

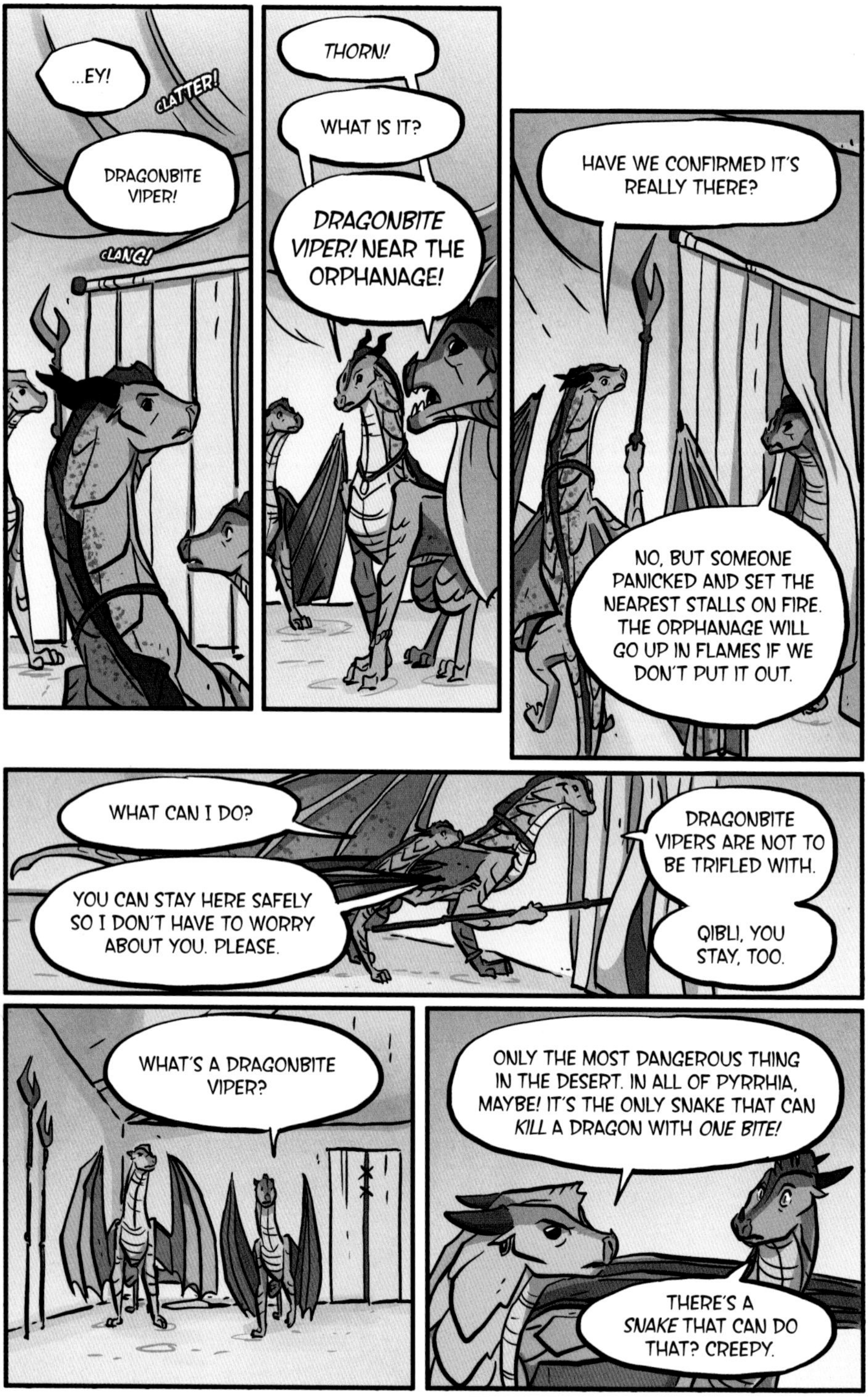
...EY!
CLATTER!
DRAGONBITE VIPER!
CLANG!
THORN!
WHAT IS IT?
DRAGONBITE VIPER! NEAR THE ORPHANAGE!
HAVE WE CONFIRMED IT'S REALLY THERE?
NO, BUT SOMEONE PANICKED AND SET THE NEAREST STALLS ON FIRE. THE ORPHANAGE WILL GO UP IN FLAMES IF WE DON'T PUT IT OUT.
WHAT CAN I DO?
YOU CAN STAY HERE SAFELY SO I DON'T HAVE TO WORRY ABOUT YOU. PLEASE.
DRAGONBITE VIPERS ARE NOT TO BE TRIFLED WITH.
QIBLI, YOU STAY, TOO.
WHAT'S A DRAGONBITE VIPER?
ONLY THE MOST DANGEROUS THING IN THE DESERT. IN ALL OF PYRRHIA, MAYBE! IT'S THE ONLY SNAKE THAT CAN KILL A DRAGON WITH ONE BITE!
THERE'S A SNAKE THAT CAN DO THAT? CREEPY.

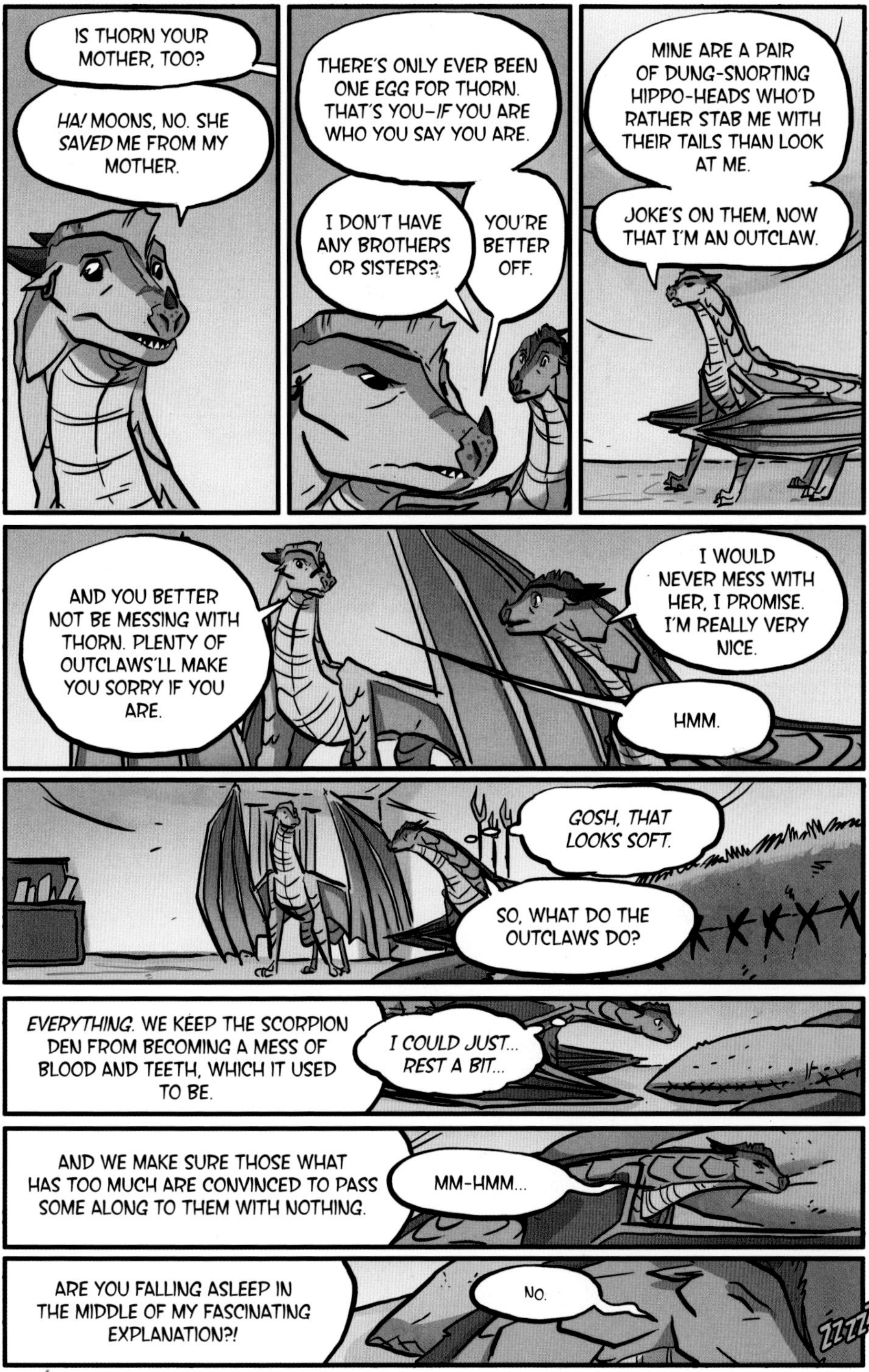

IS THORN YOUR MOTHER, TOO?
HA! MOONS, NO. SHE SAVED ME FROM MY MOTHER.
THERE'S ONLY EVER BEEN ONE EGG FOR THORN. THAT'S YOU–IF YOU ARE WHO YOU SAY YOU ARE.
I DON'T HAVE ANY BROTHERS OR SISTERS?
YOU'RE BETTER OFF.
MINE ARE A PAIR OF DUNG-SNORTING HIPPO-HEADS WHO'D RATHER STAB ME WITH THEIR TAILS THAN LOOK AT ME.
JOKE'S ON THEM, NOW THAT I'M AN OUTCLAW.
AND YOU BETTER NOT BE MESSING WITH THORN. PLENTY OF OUTCLAWS'LL MAKE YOU SORRY IF YOU ARE.
I WOULD NEVER MESS WITH HER, I PROMISE. I'M REALLY VERY NICE.
HMM.
GOSH, THAT LOOKS SOFT.
SO, WHAT DO THE OUTCLAWS DO?
EVERYTHING. WE KEEP THE SCORPION DEN FROM BECOMING A MESS OF BLOOD AND TEETH, WHICH IT USED TO BE.
I COULD JUST... REST A BIT...
AND WE MAKE SURE THOSE WHAT HAS TOO MUCH ARE CONVINCED TO PASS SOME ALONG TO THEM WITH NOTHING.
MM-HMM...
ARE YOU FALLING ASLEEP IN THE MIDDLE OF MY FASCINATING EXPLANATION?!
NO.
ZZZZ

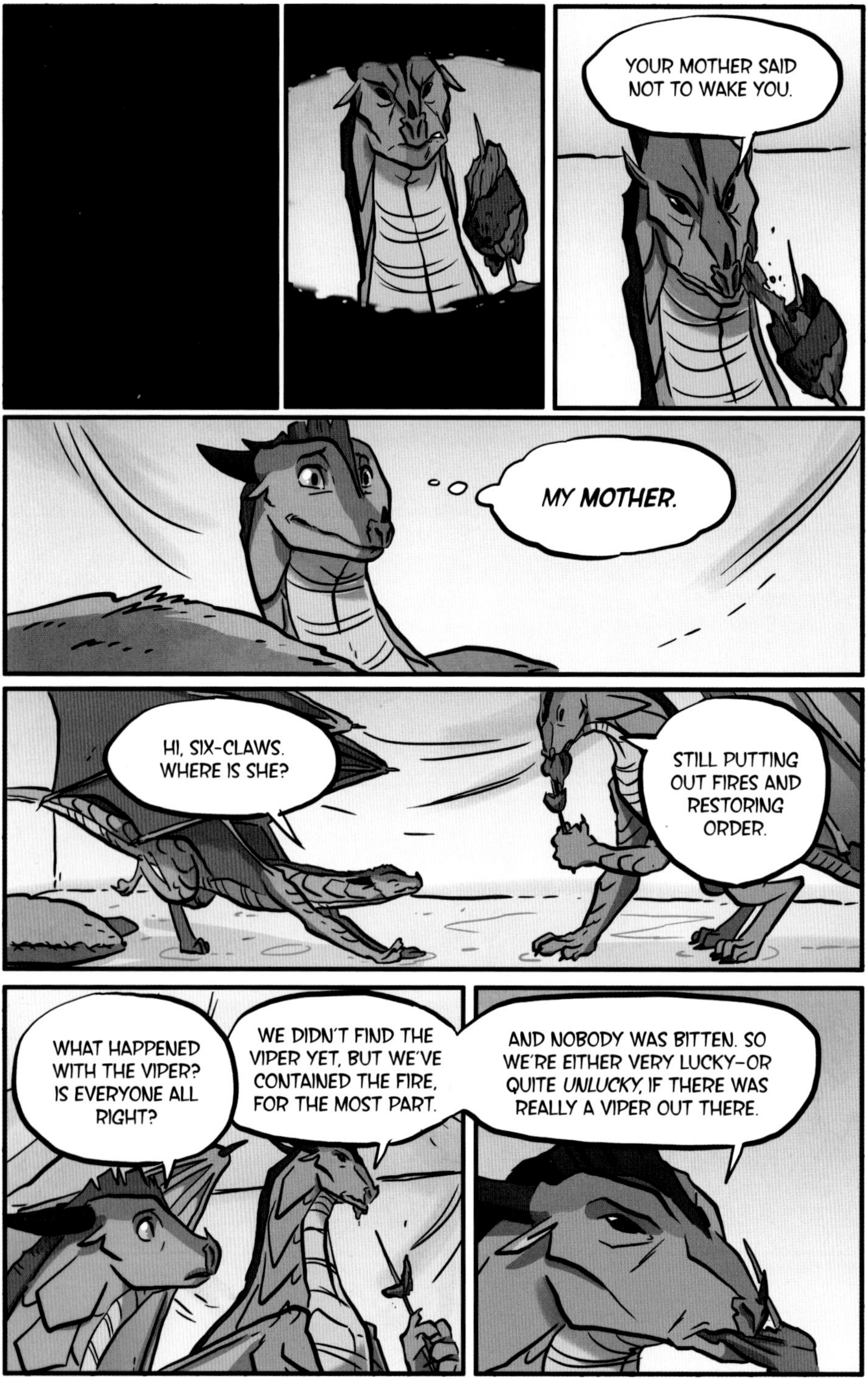
YOUR MOTHER SAID NOT TO WAKE YOU.
MY MOTHER.
HI, SIX-CLAWS. WHERE IS SHE?
STILL PUTTING OUT FIRES AND RESTORING ORDER.
WHAT HAPPENED WITH THE VIPER? IS EVERYONE ALL RIGHT?
WE DIDN'T FIND THE VIPER YET, BUT WE'VE CONTAINED THE FIRE, FOR THE MOST PART.
AND NOBODY WAS BITTEN. SO WE'RE EITHER VERY LUCKY—OR QUITE *UNLUCKY*, IF THERE WAS REALLY A VIPER OUT THERE.

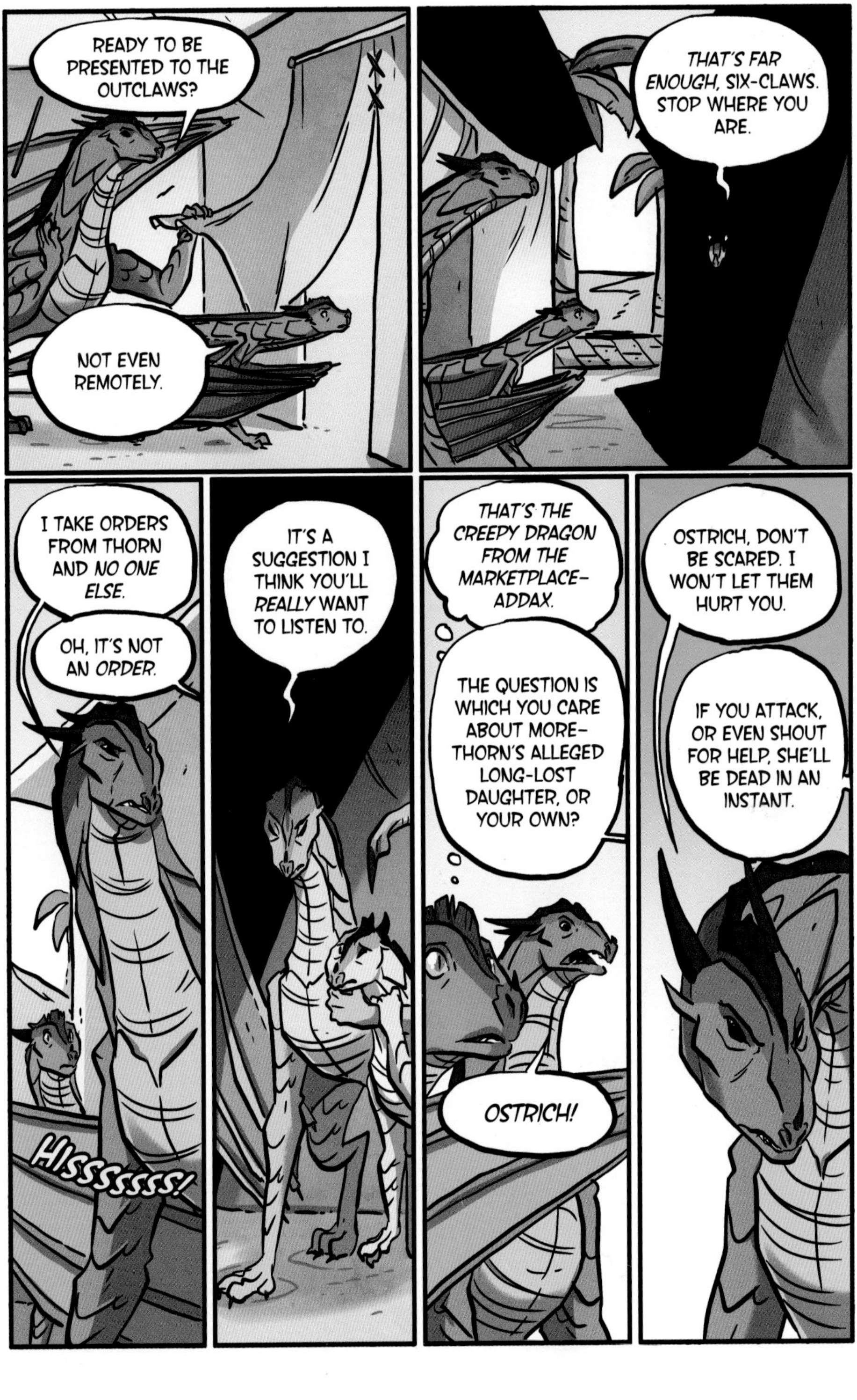
READY TO BE PRESENTED TO THE OUTCLAWS?
NOT EVEN REMOTELY.
THAT'S FAR ENOUGH, SIX-CLAWS. STOP WHERE YOU ARE.
I TAKE ORDERS FROM THORN AND NO ONE ELSE.
OH, IT'S NOT AN ORDER.
HISSSSSSS!
IT'S A SUGGESTION I THINK YOU'LL REALLY WANT TO LISTEN TO.
THAT'S THE CREEPY DRAGON FROM THE MARKETPLACE– ADDAX.
THE QUESTION IS WHICH YOU CARE ABOUT MORE– THORN'S ALLEGED LONG-LOST DAUGHTER, OR YOUR OWN?
OSTRICH!
OSTRICH, DON'T BE SCARED. I WON'T LET THEM HURT YOU.
IF YOU ATTACK, OR EVEN SHOUT FOR HELP, SHE'LL BE DEAD IN AN INSTANT.

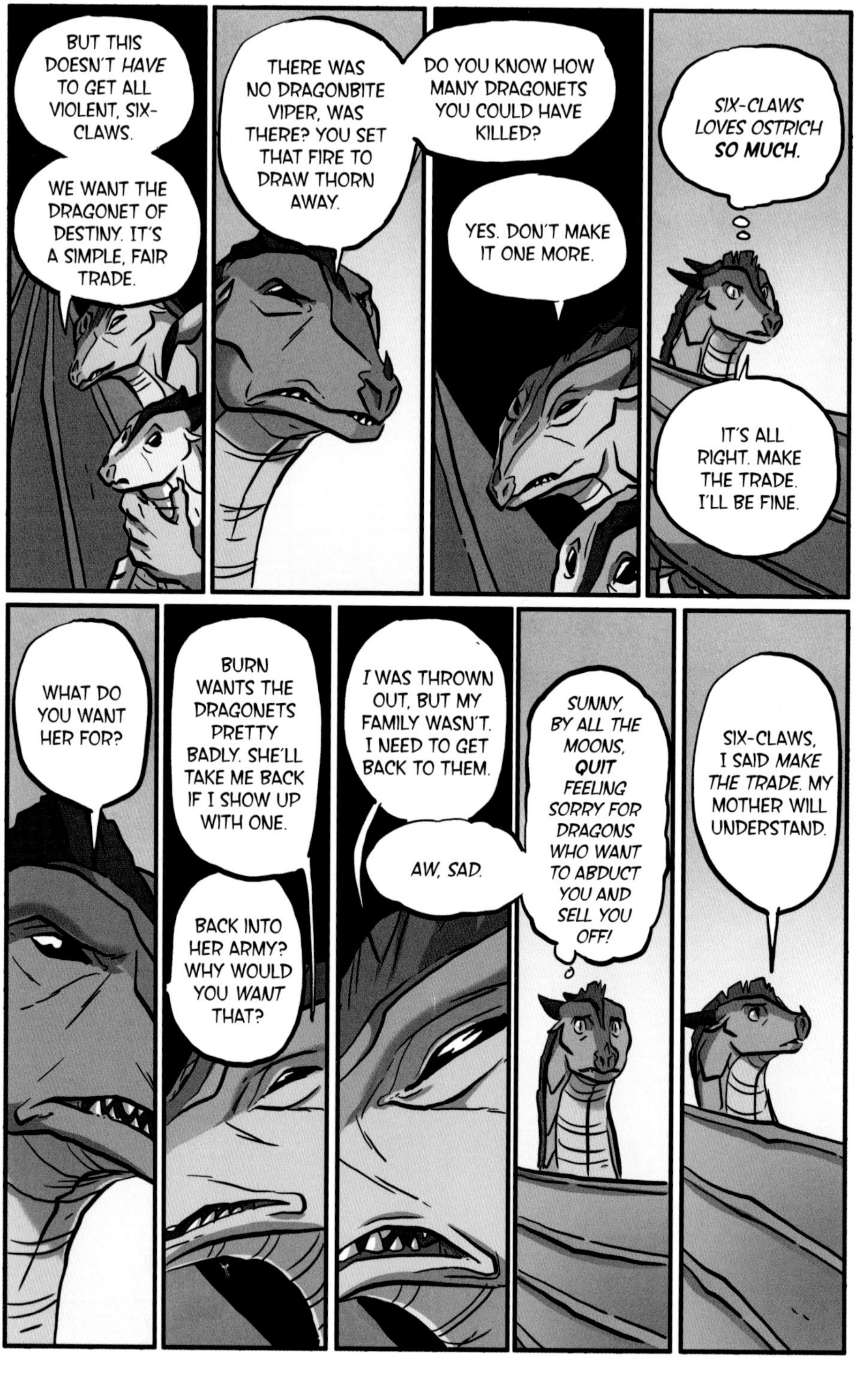
BUT THIS DOESN'T *HAVE* TO GET ALL VIOLENT, SIX-CLAWS.
WE WANT THE DRAGONET OF DESTINY. IT'S A SIMPLE, FAIR TRADE.
THERE WAS NO DRAGONBITE VIPER, WAS THERE? YOU SET THAT FIRE TO DRAW THORN AWAY.
DO YOU KNOW HOW MANY DRAGONETS YOU COULD HAVE KILLED?
YES. DON'T MAKE IT ONE MORE.
SIX-CLAWS LOVES OSTRICH ***SO MUCH.***
IT'S ALL RIGHT. MAKE THE TRADE. I'LL BE FINE.
WHAT DO YOU WANT HER FOR?
BURN WANTS THE DRAGONETS PRETTY BADLY. SHE'LL TAKE ME BACK IF I SHOW UP WITH ONE.
BACK INTO HER ARMY? WHY WOULD YOU *WANT* THAT?
I WAS THROWN OUT, BUT MY FAMILY WASN'T. I NEED TO GET BACK TO THEM.
AW, SAD.
SUNNY, BY ALL THE MOONS, ***QUIT*** *FEELING SORRY FOR DRAGONS WHO WANT TO ABDUCT YOU AND SELL YOU OFF!*
SIX-CLAWS, I SAID *MAKE THE TRADE.* MY MOTHER WILL UNDERSTAND.

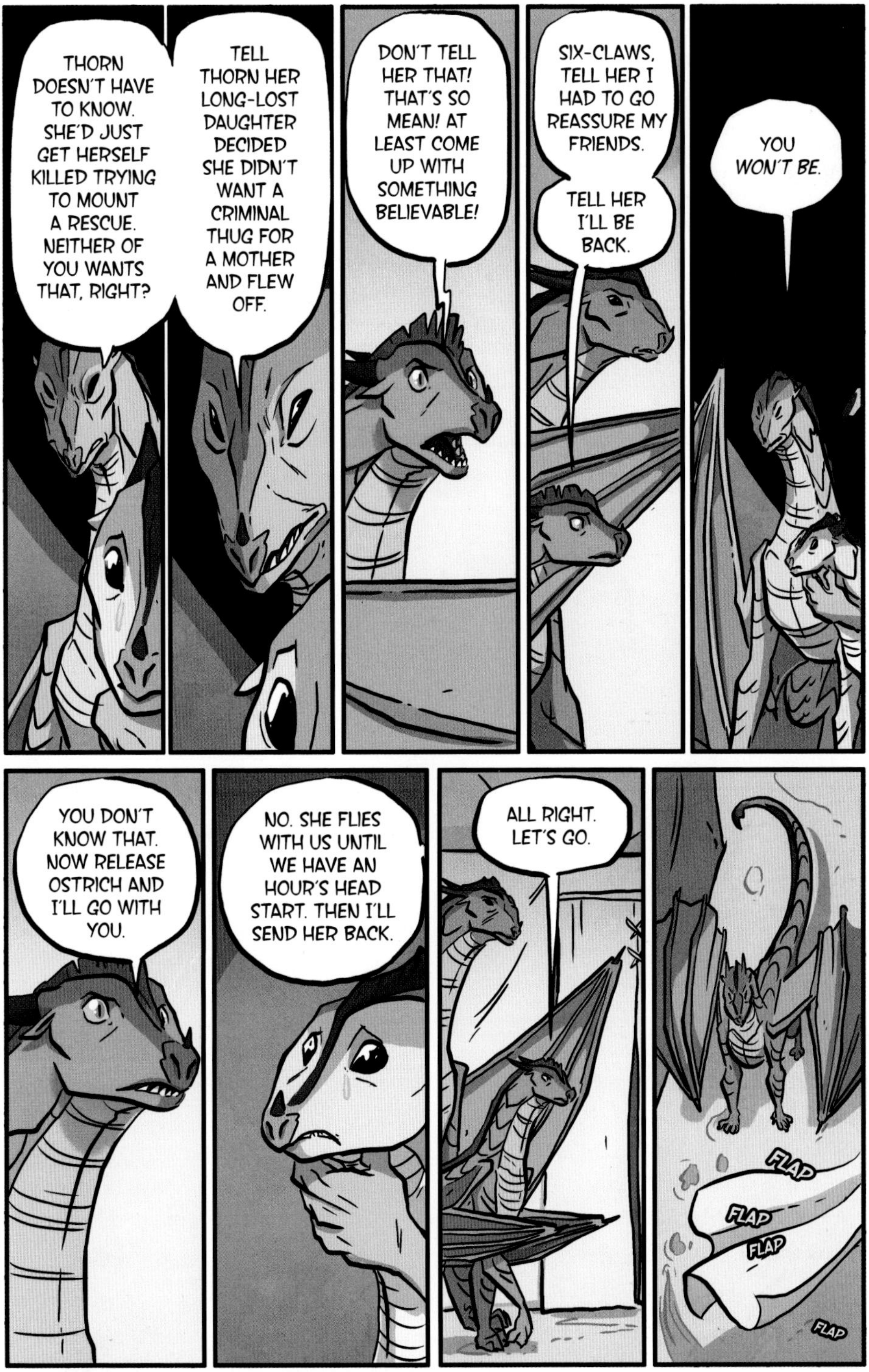
THORN DOESN'T HAVE TO KNOW. SHE'D JUST GET HERSELF KILLED TRYING TO MOUNT A RESCUE. NEITHER OF YOU WANTS THAT, RIGHT?
TELL THORN HER LONG-LOST DAUGHTER DECIDED SHE DIDN'T WANT A CRIMINAL THUG FOR A MOTHER AND FLEW OFF.
DON'T TELL HER THAT! THAT'S SO MEAN! AT LEAST COME UP WITH SOMETHING BELIEVABLE!
SIX-CLAWS, TELL HER I HAD TO GO REASSURE MY FRIENDS.
TELL HER I'LL BE BACK.
YOU *WON'T* BE.
YOU DON'T KNOW THAT. NOW RELEASE OSTRICH AND I'LL GO WITH YOU.
NO. SHE FLIES WITH US UNTIL WE HAVE AN HOUR'S HEAD START. THEN I'LL SEND HER BACK.
ALL RIGHT. LET'S GO.
FLAP
FLAP
FLAP
FLAP

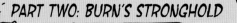

PART TWO: BURN'S STRONGHOLD

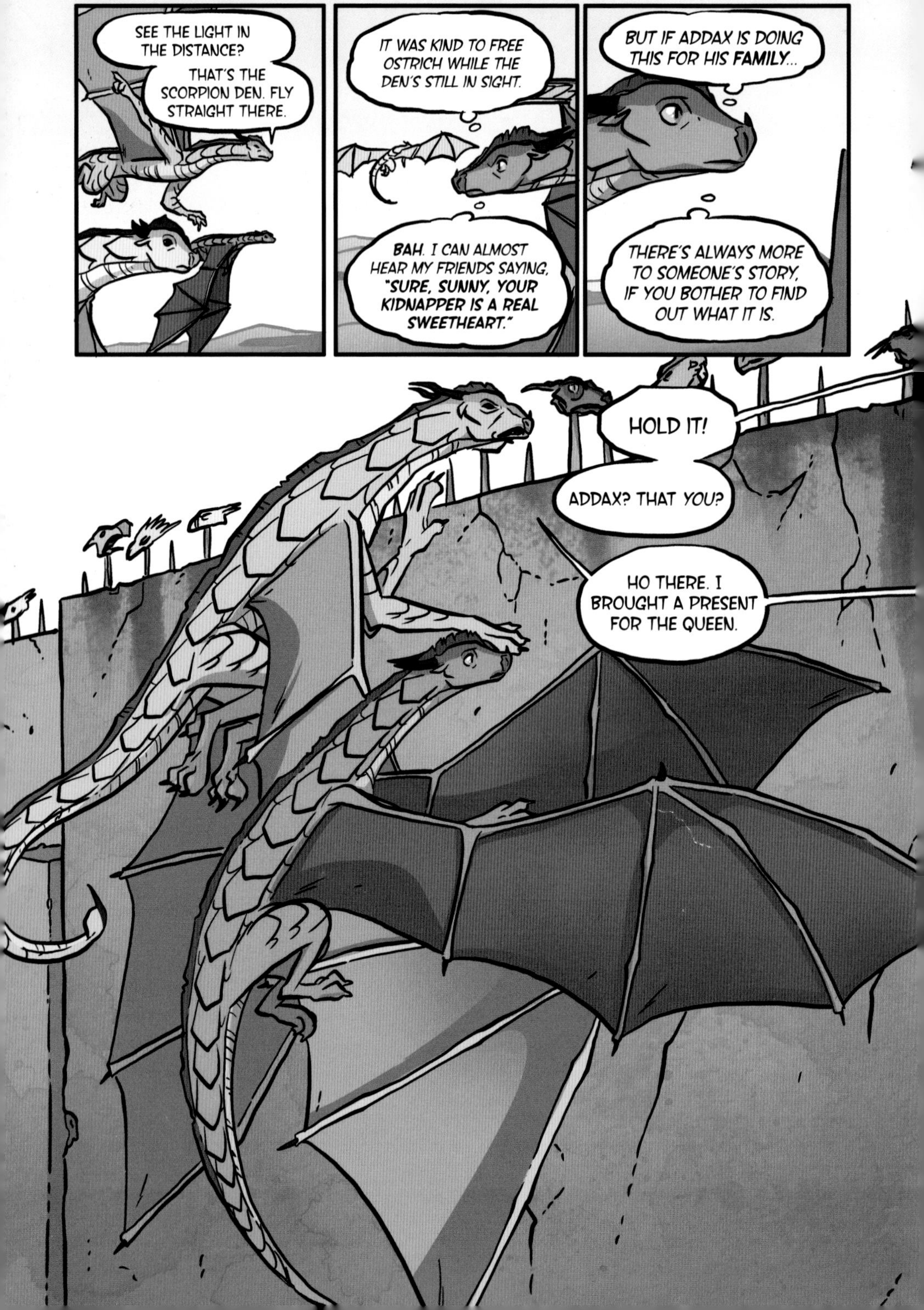
SEE THE LIGHT IN THE DISTANCE?
THAT'S THE SCORPION DEN. FLY STRAIGHT THERE.
IT WAS KIND TO FREE OSTRICH WHILE THE DEN'S STILL IN SIGHT.
BAH. I CAN ALMOST HEAR MY FRIENDS SAYING, "SURE, SUNNY, YOUR KIDNAPPER IS A REAL SWEETHEART."
BUT IF ADDAX IS DOING THIS FOR HIS FAMILY...
THERE'S ALWAYS MORE TO SOMEONE'S STORY, IF YOU BOTHER TO FIND OUT WHAT IT IS.
HOLD IT!
ADDAX? THAT YOU?
HO THERE. I BROUGHT A PRESENT FOR THE QUEEN.

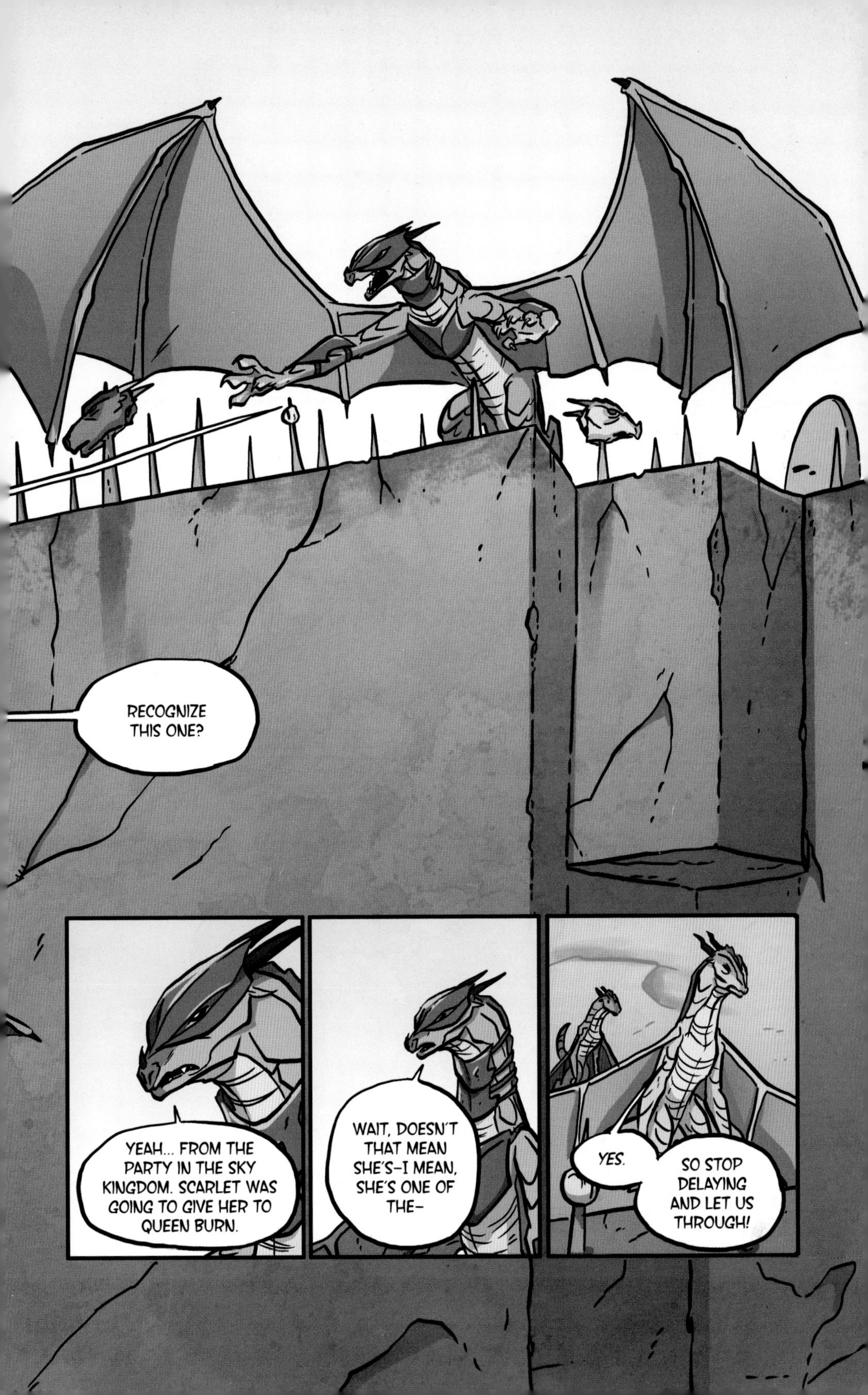
RECOGNIZE THIS ONE?
YEAH... FROM THE PARTY IN THE SKY KINGDOM. SCARLET WAS GOING TO GIVE HER TO QUEEN BURN.
WAIT, DOESN'T THAT MEAN SHE'S–I MEAN, SHE'S ONE OF THE–
YES.
SO STOP DELAYING AND LET US THROUGH!

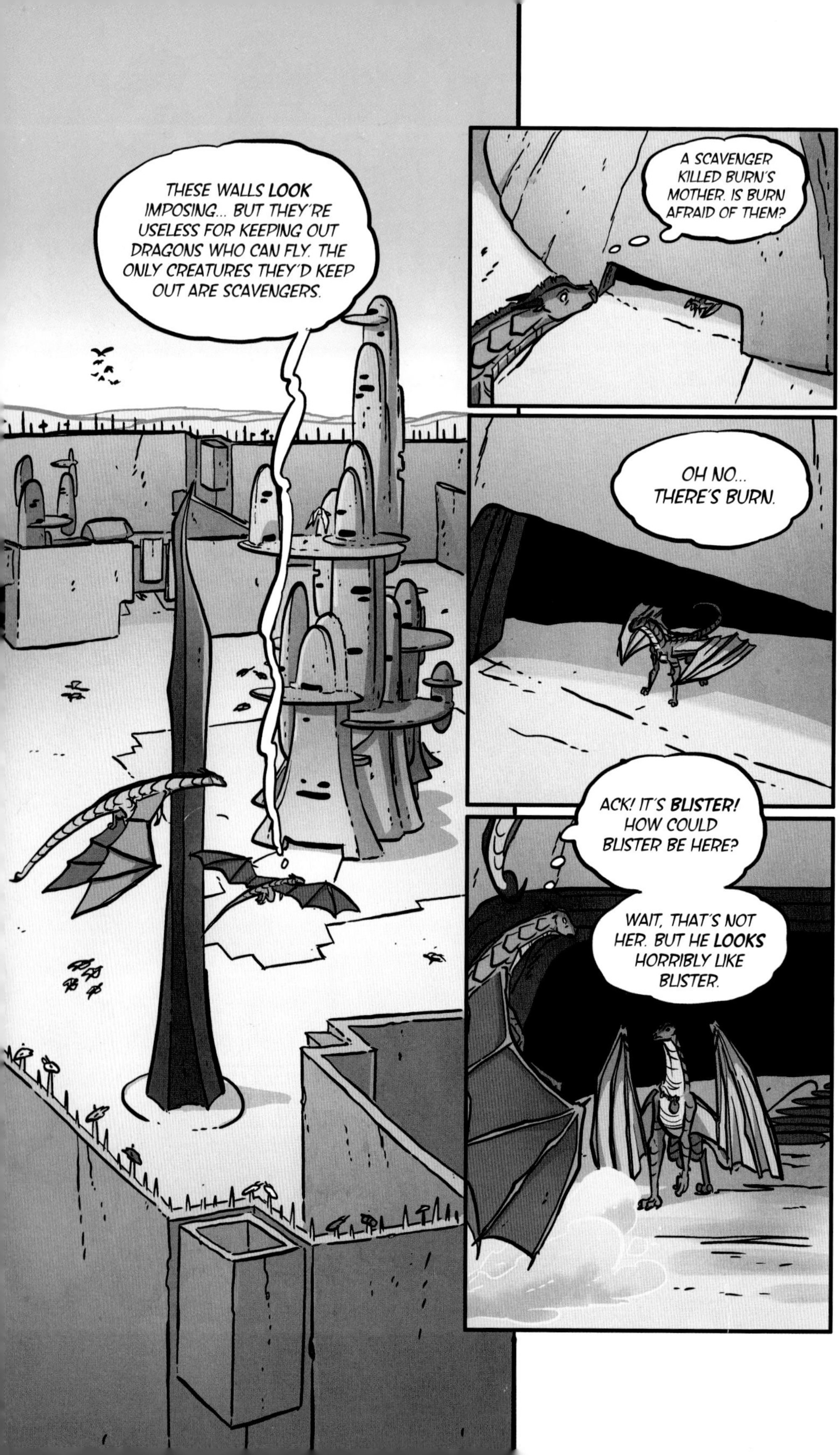
THESE WALLS LOOK IMPOSING... BUT THEY'RE USELESS FOR KEEPING OUT DRAGONS WHO CAN FLY. THE ONLY CREATURES THEY'D KEEP OUT ARE SCAVENGERS.
A SCAVENGER KILLED BURN'S MOTHER. IS BURN AFRAID OF THEM?
OH NO... THERE'S BURN.
ACK! IT'S BLISTER! HOW COULD BLISTER BE HERE?
WAIT, THAT'S NOT HER. BUT HE LOOKS HORRIBLY LIKE BLISTER.

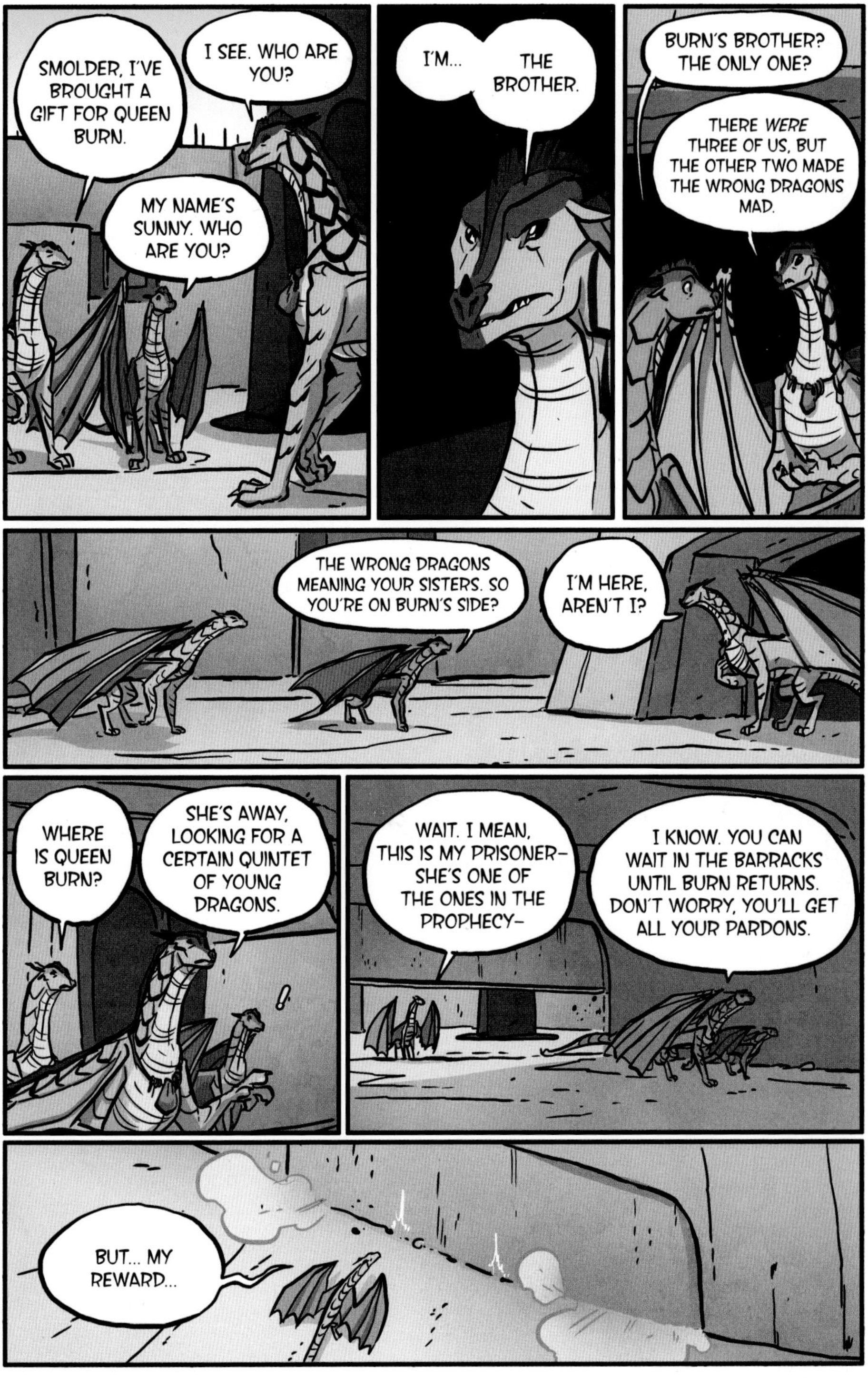
SMOLDER, I'VE BROUGHT A GIFT FOR QUEEN BURN.
I SEE. WHO ARE YOU?
MY NAME'S SUNNY. WHO ARE YOU?
I'M...
THE BROTHER.
BURN'S BROTHER? THE ONLY ONE?
THERE *WERE* THREE OF US, BUT THE OTHER TWO MADE THE WRONG DRAGONS MAD.
THE WRONG DRAGONS MEANING YOUR SISTERS. SO YOU'RE ON BURN'S SIDE?
I'M HERE, AREN'T I?
WHERE IS QUEEN BURN?
SHE'S AWAY, LOOKING FOR A CERTAIN QUINTET OF YOUNG DRAGONS.
!
WAIT. I MEAN, THIS IS MY PRISONER–SHE'S ONE OF THE ONES IN THE PROPHECY–
I KNOW. YOU CAN WAIT IN THE BARRACKS UNTIL BURN RETURNS. DON'T WORRY, YOU'LL GET ALL YOUR PARDONS.
BUT... MY REWARD...

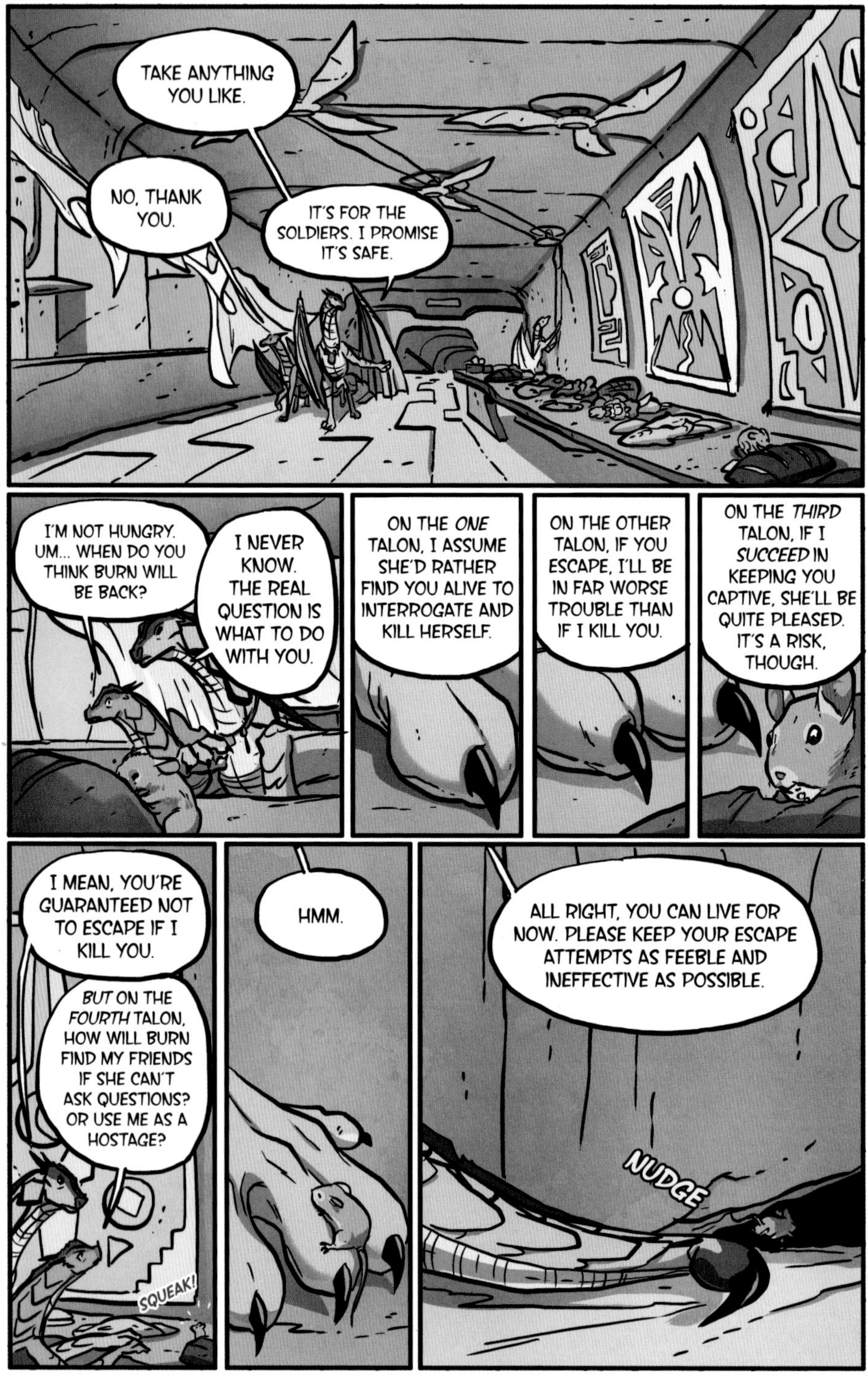
TAKE ANYTHING YOU LIKE.
NO, THANK YOU.
IT'S FOR THE SOLDIERS. I PROMISE IT'S SAFE.
I'M NOT HUNGRY. UM... WHEN DO YOU THINK BURN WILL BE BACK?
I NEVER KNOW. THE REAL QUESTION IS WHAT TO DO WITH YOU.
ON THE *ONE* TALON, I ASSUME SHE'D RATHER FIND YOU ALIVE TO INTERROGATE AND KILL HERSELF.
ON THE OTHER TALON, IF YOU ESCAPE, I'LL BE IN FAR WORSE TROUBLE THAN IF I KILL YOU.
ON THE *THIRD* TALON, IF I *SUCCEED* IN KEEPING YOU CAPTIVE, SHE'LL BE QUITE PLEASED. IT'S A RISK, THOUGH.
I MEAN, YOU'RE GUARANTEED NOT TO ESCAPE IF I KILL YOU.
BUT ON THE *FOURTH* TALON, HOW WILL BURN FIND MY FRIENDS IF SHE CAN'T ASK QUESTIONS? OR USE ME AS A HOSTAGE?
SQUEAK!
HMM.
ALL RIGHT, YOU CAN LIVE FOR NOW. PLEASE KEEP YOUR ESCAPE ATTEMPTS AS FEEBLE AND INEFFECTIVE AS POSSIBLE.
NUDGE

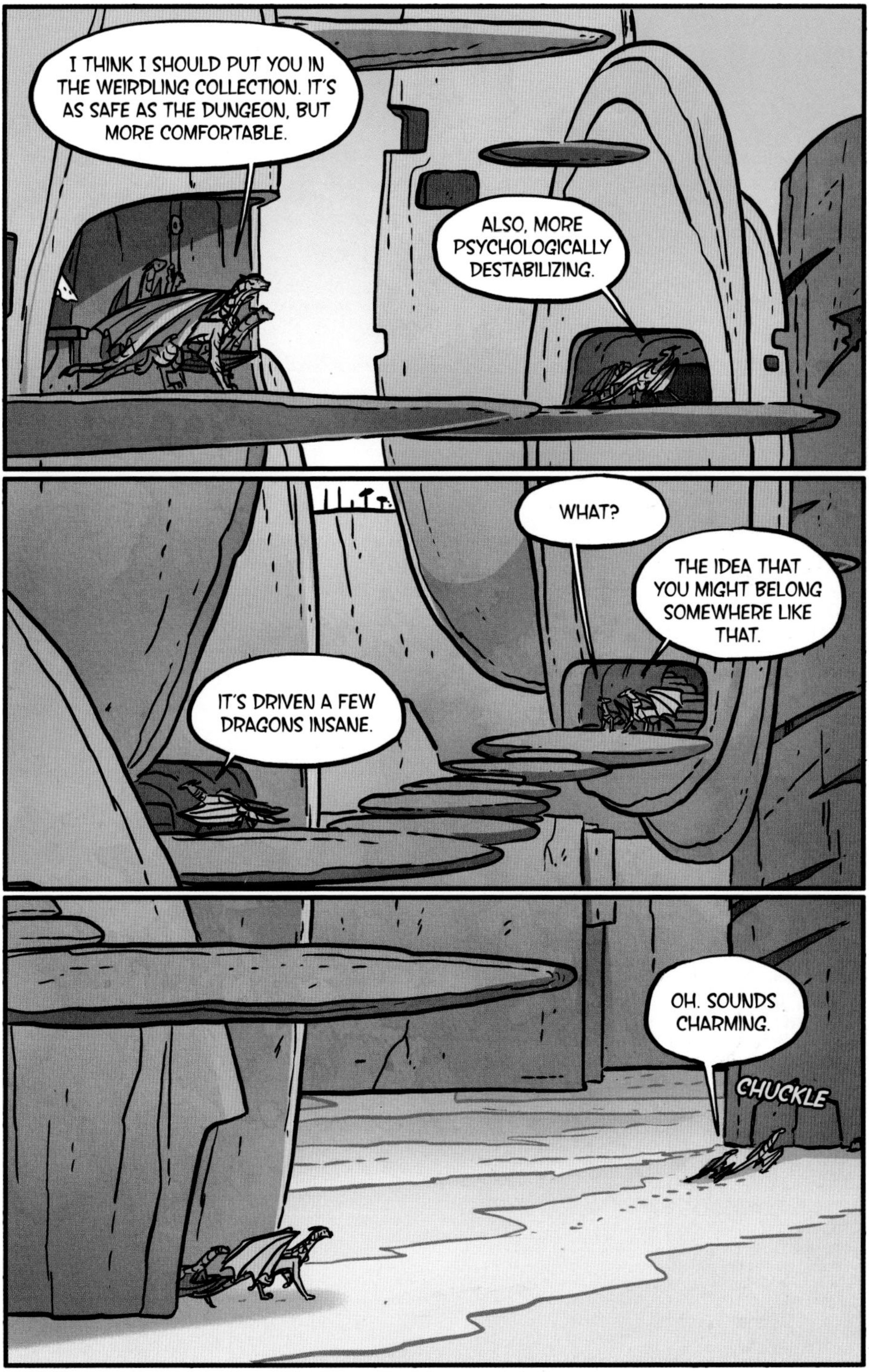
I THINK I SHOULD PUT YOU IN THE WEIRDLING COLLECTION. IT'S AS SAFE AS THE DUNGEON, BUT MORE COMFORTABLE.
ALSO, MORE PSYCHOLOGICALLY DESTABILIZING.
WHAT?
THE IDEA THAT YOU MIGHT BELONG SOMEWHERE LIKE THAT.
IT'S DRIVEN A FEW DRAGONS INSANE.
OH. SOUNDS CHARMING.
CHUCKLE

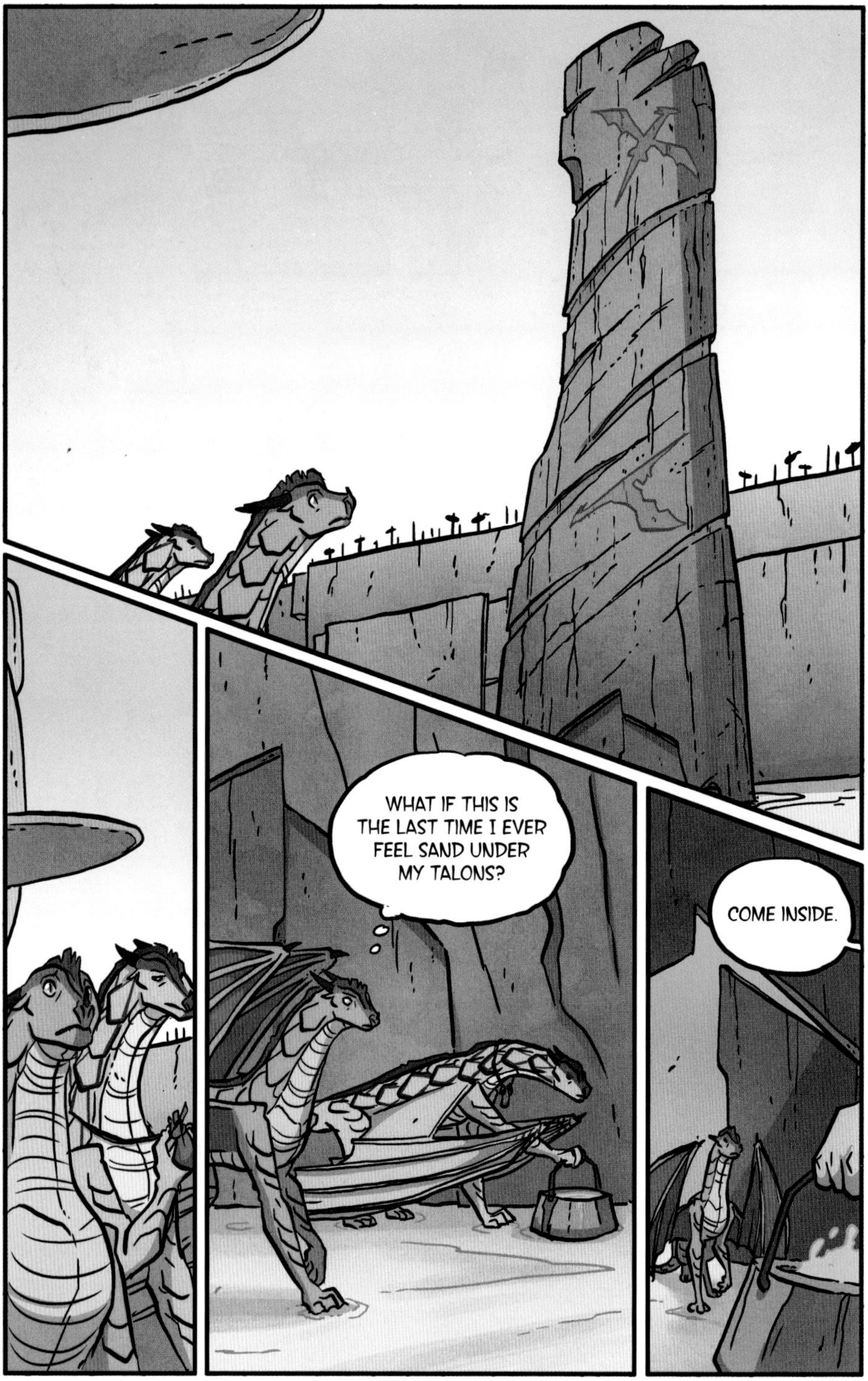
WHAT IF THIS IS THE LAST TIME I EVER FEEL SAND UNDER MY TALONS?
COME INSIDE.

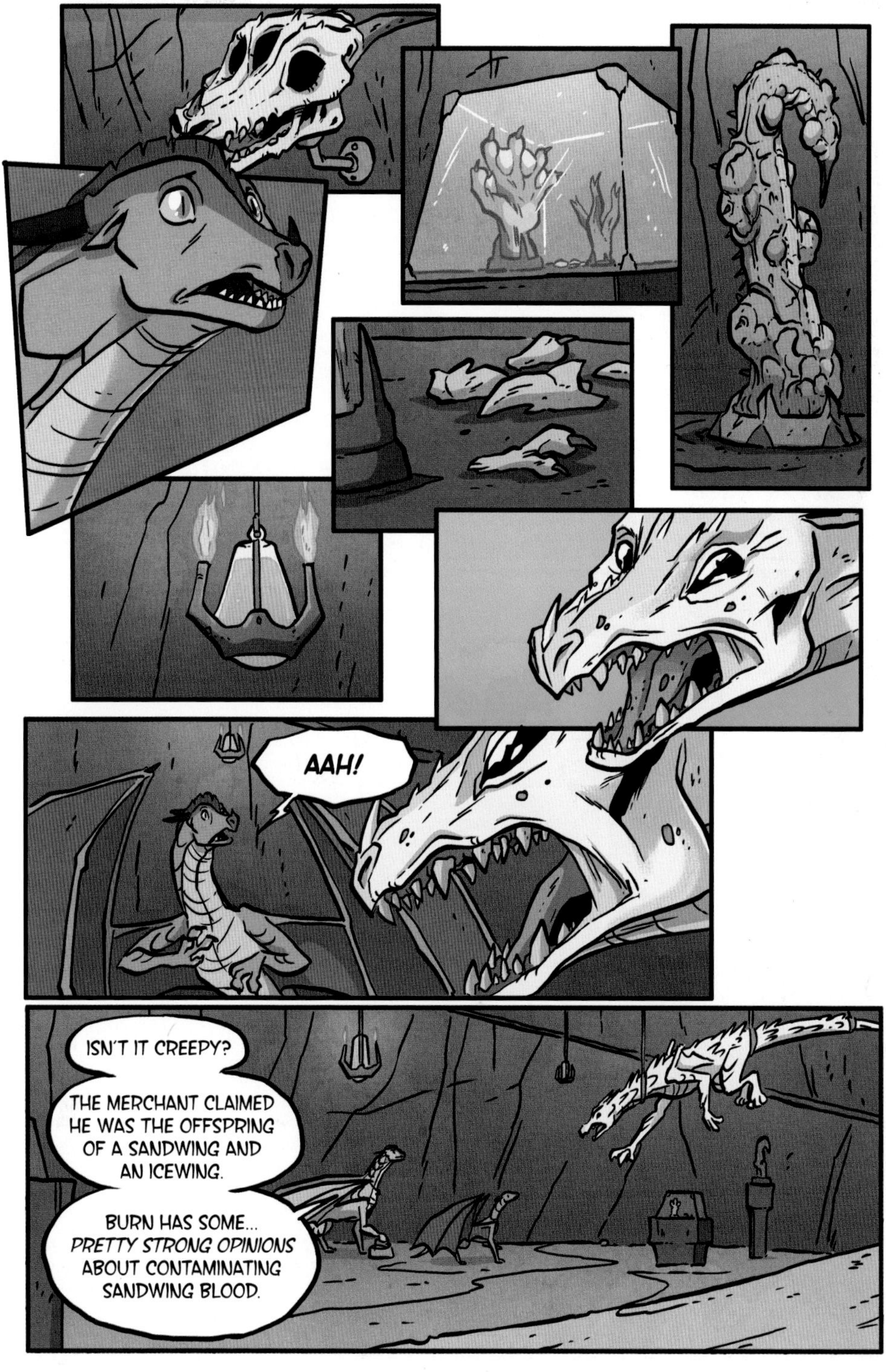
AAH!
ISN'T IT CREEPY?
THE MERCHANT CLAIMED HE WAS THE OFFSPRING OF A SANDWING AND AN ICEWING.
BURN HAS SOME... *PRETTY STRONG OPINIONS* ABOUT CONTAMINATING SANDWING BLOOD.

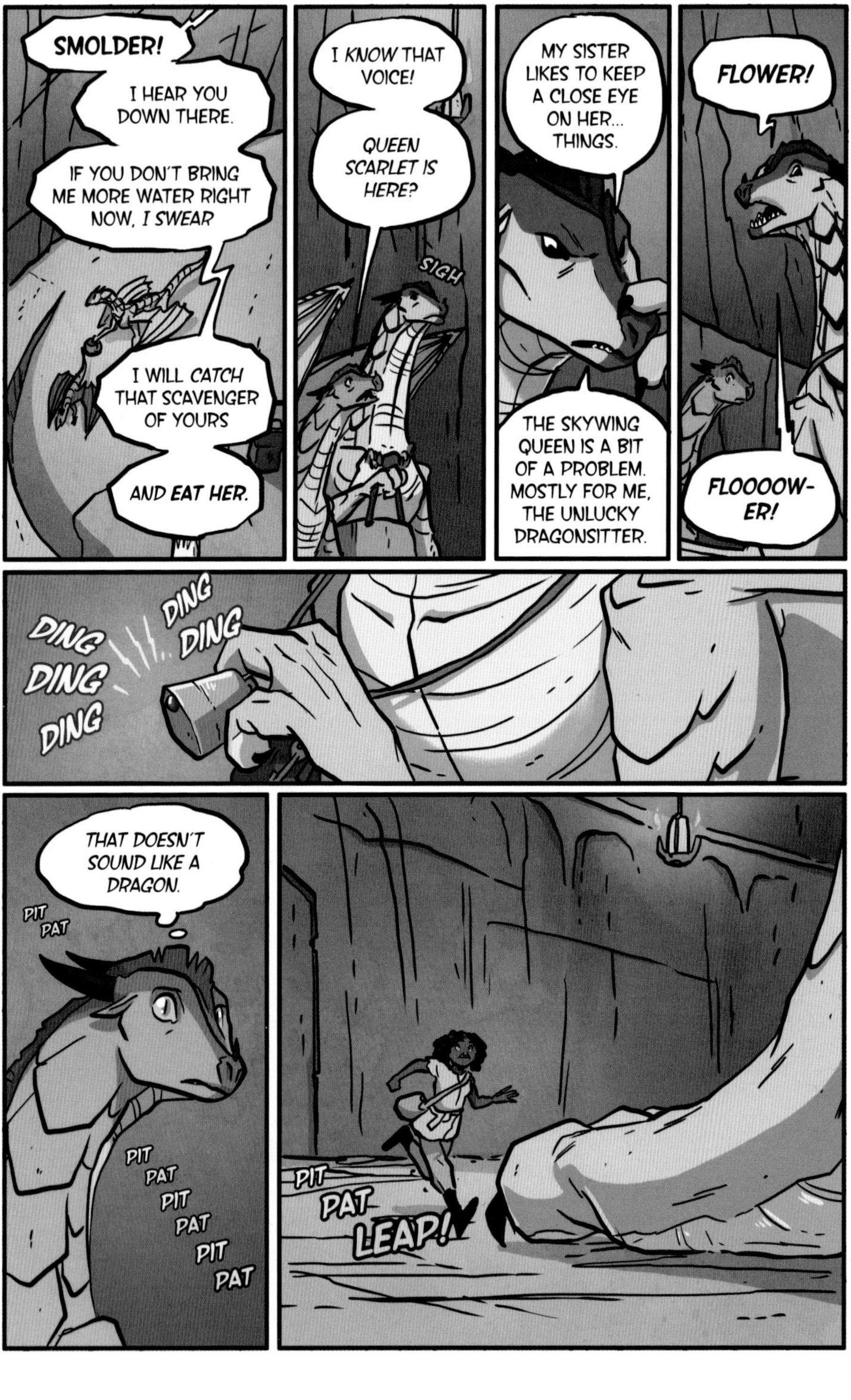
SMOLDER!
I HEAR YOU DOWN THERE.
IF YOU DON'T BRING ME MORE WATER RIGHT NOW, *I SWEAR*
I WILL *CATCH* THAT SCAVENGER OF YOURS
AND *EAT HER.*
I KNOW THAT VOICE!
QUEEN SCARLET IS HERE?
SIGH
MY SISTER LIKES TO KEEP A CLOSE EYE ON HER... THINGS.
THE SKYWING QUEEN IS A BIT OF A PROBLEM. MOSTLY FOR ME, THE UNLUCKY DRAGONSITTER.
FLOWER!
FLOOOOW-ER!
DING DING DING
DING DING
THAT DOESN'T SOUND LIKE A DRAGON.
PIT PAT
PIT PAT PIT PAT PIT PAT
PIT PAT LEAP!

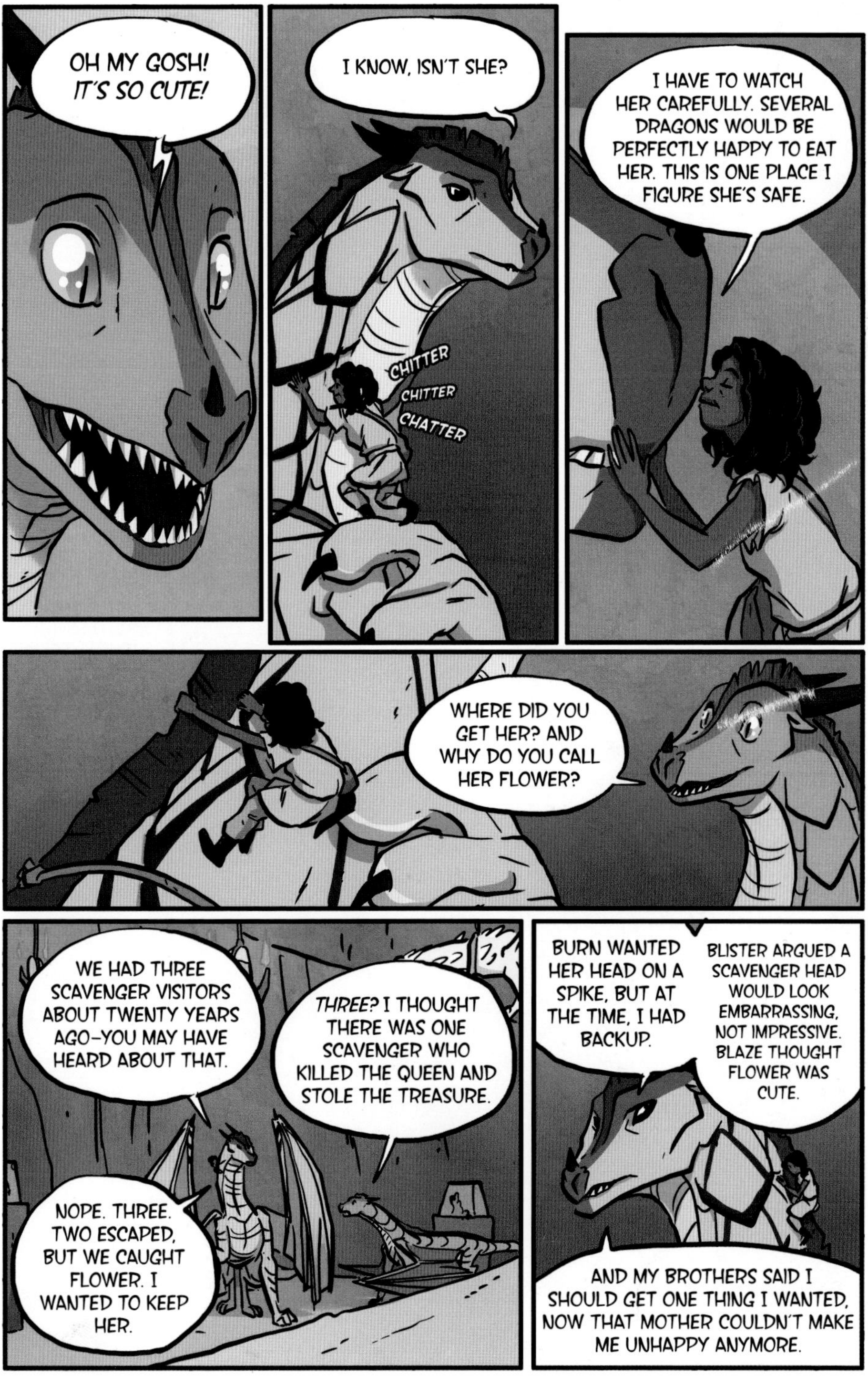
OH MY GOSH!
IT'S SO CUTE!
I KNOW, ISN'T SHE?
CHITTER
CHITTER
CHATTER
I HAVE TO WATCH HER CAREFULLY. SEVERAL DRAGONS WOULD BE PERFECTLY HAPPY TO EAT HER. THIS IS ONE PLACE I FIGURE SHE'S SAFE.
WHERE DID YOU GET HER? AND WHY DO YOU CALL HER FLOWER?
WE HAD THREE SCAVENGER VISITORS ABOUT TWENTY YEARS AGO—YOU MAY HAVE HEARD ABOUT THAT.
THREE? I THOUGHT THERE WAS ONE SCAVENGER WHO KILLED THE QUEEN AND STOLE THE TREASURE.
NOPE. THREE. TWO ESCAPED, BUT WE CAUGHT FLOWER. I WANTED TO KEEP HER.
BURN WANTED HER HEAD ON A SPIKE, BUT AT THE TIME, I HAD BACKUP.
BLISTER ARGUED A SCAVENGER HEAD WOULD LOOK EMBARRASSING, NOT IMPRESSIVE. BLAZE THOUGHT FLOWER WAS CUTE.
AND MY BROTHERS SAID I SHOULD GET ONE THING I WANTED, NOW THAT MOTHER COULDN'T MAKE ME UNHAPPY ANYMORE.

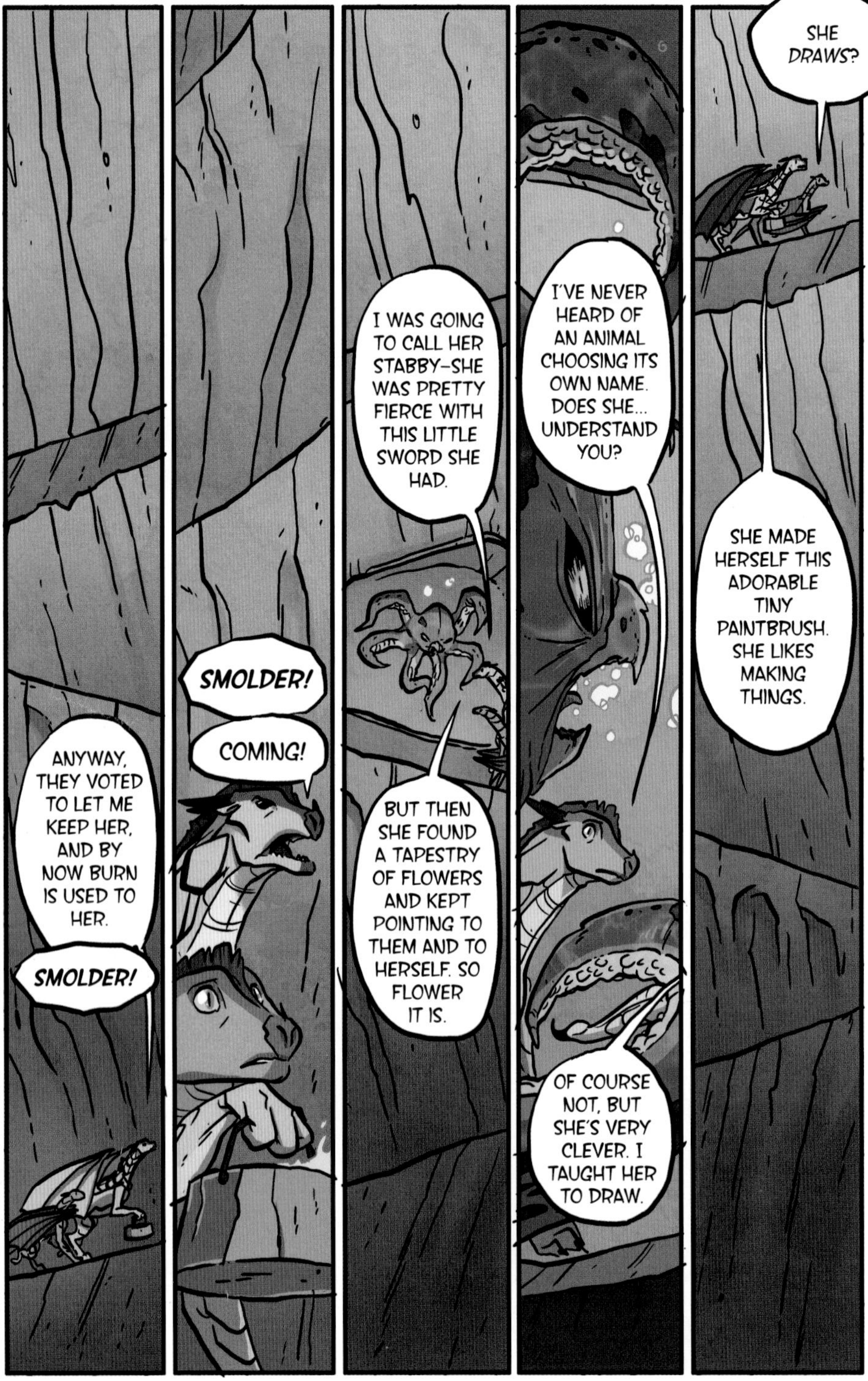
ANYWAY, THEY VOTED TO LET ME KEEP HER, AND BY NOW BURN IS USED TO HER.
SMOLDER!
SMOLDER!
COMING!
I WAS GOING TO CALL HER STABBY–SHE WAS PRETTY FIERCE WITH THIS LITTLE SWORD SHE HAD.
BUT THEN SHE FOUND A TAPESTRY OF FLOWERS AND KEPT POINTING TO THEM AND TO HERSELF. SO FLOWER IT IS.
I'VE NEVER HEARD OF AN ANIMAL CHOOSING ITS OWN NAME. DOES SHE... UNDERSTAND YOU?
OF COURSE NOT, BUT SHE'S VERY CLEVER. I TAUGHT HER TO DRAW.
SHE *DRAWS?*
SHE MADE HERSELF THIS ADORABLE TINY PAINTBRUSH. SHE LIKES MAKING THINGS.

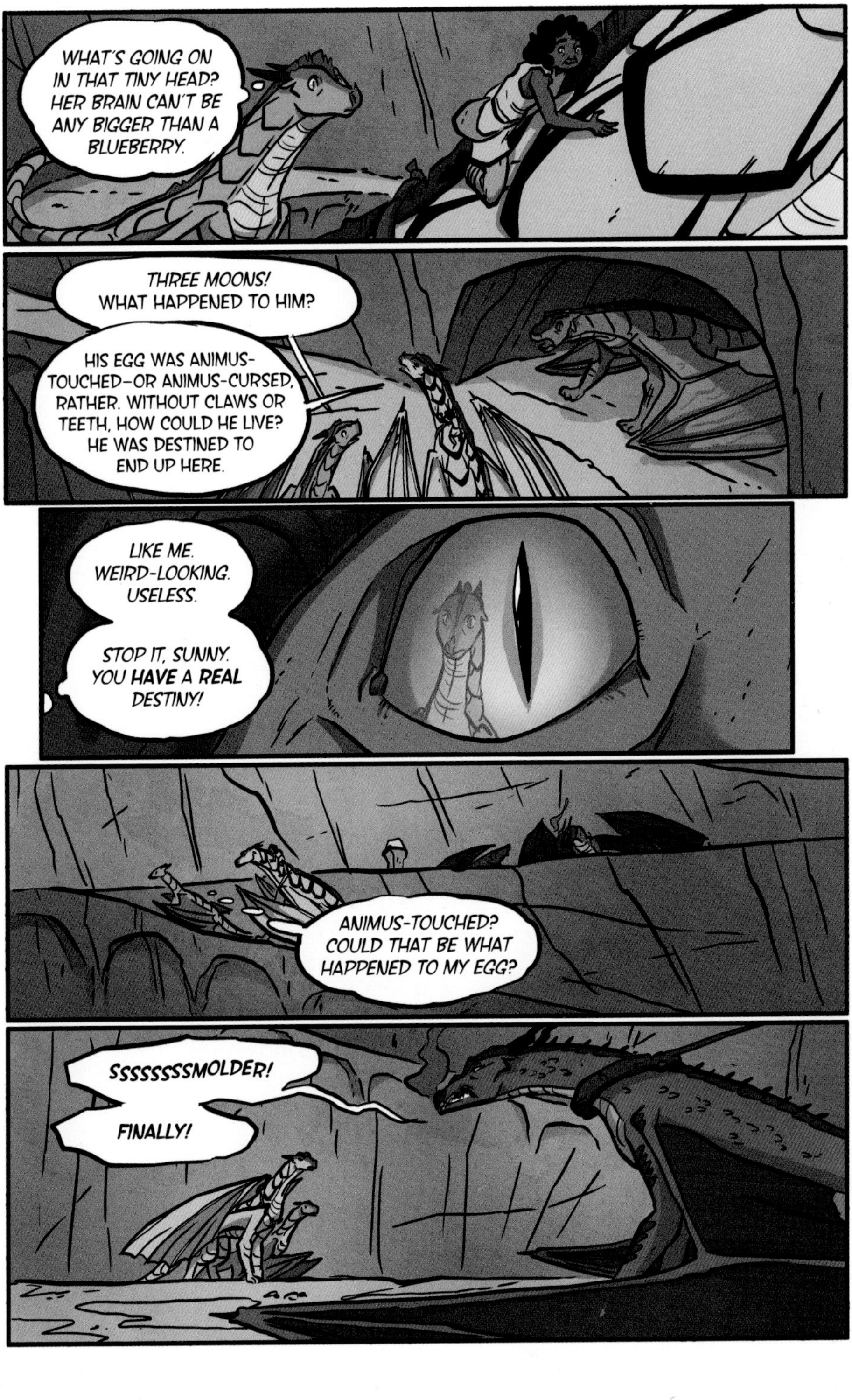
WHAT'S GOING ON IN THAT TINY HEAD? HER BRAIN CAN'T BE ANY BIGGER THAN A BLUEBERRY.
THREE MOONS! WHAT HAPPENED TO HIM?
HIS EGG WAS ANIMUS-TOUCHED—OR ANIMUS-CURSED, RATHER. WITHOUT CLAWS OR TEETH, HOW COULD HE LIVE? HE WAS DESTINED TO END UP HERE.
LIKE ME. WEIRD-LOOKING. USELESS.
STOP IT, SUNNY. YOU **HAVE** A **REAL** DESTINY!
ANIMUS-TOUCHED? COULD THAT BE WHAT HAPPENED TO MY EGG?
SSSSSSSSMOLDER!
FINALLY!

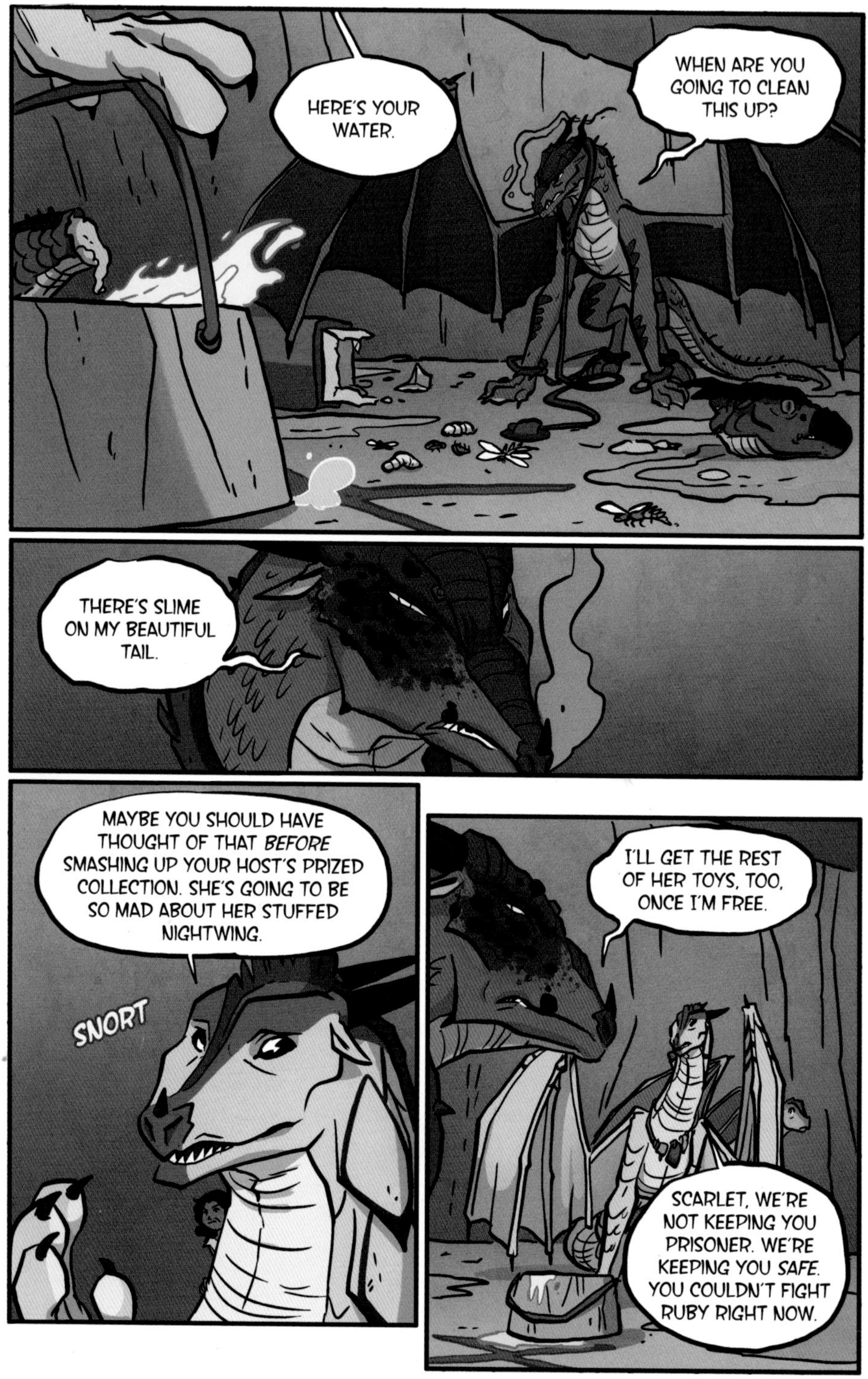
HERE'S YOUR WATER.
WHEN ARE YOU GOING TO CLEAN THIS UP?
THERE'S SLIME ON MY BEAUTIFUL TAIL.
MAYBE YOU SHOULD HAVE THOUGHT OF THAT *BEFORE* SMASHING UP YOUR HOST'S PRIZED COLLECTION. SHE'S GOING TO BE SO MAD ABOUT HER STUFFED NIGHTWING.
SNORT
I'LL GET THE REST OF HER TOYS, TOO, ONCE I'M FREE.
SCARLET, WE'RE NOT KEEPING YOU PRISONER. WE'RE KEEPING YOU *SAFE*. YOU COULDN'T FIGHT RUBY RIGHT NOW.

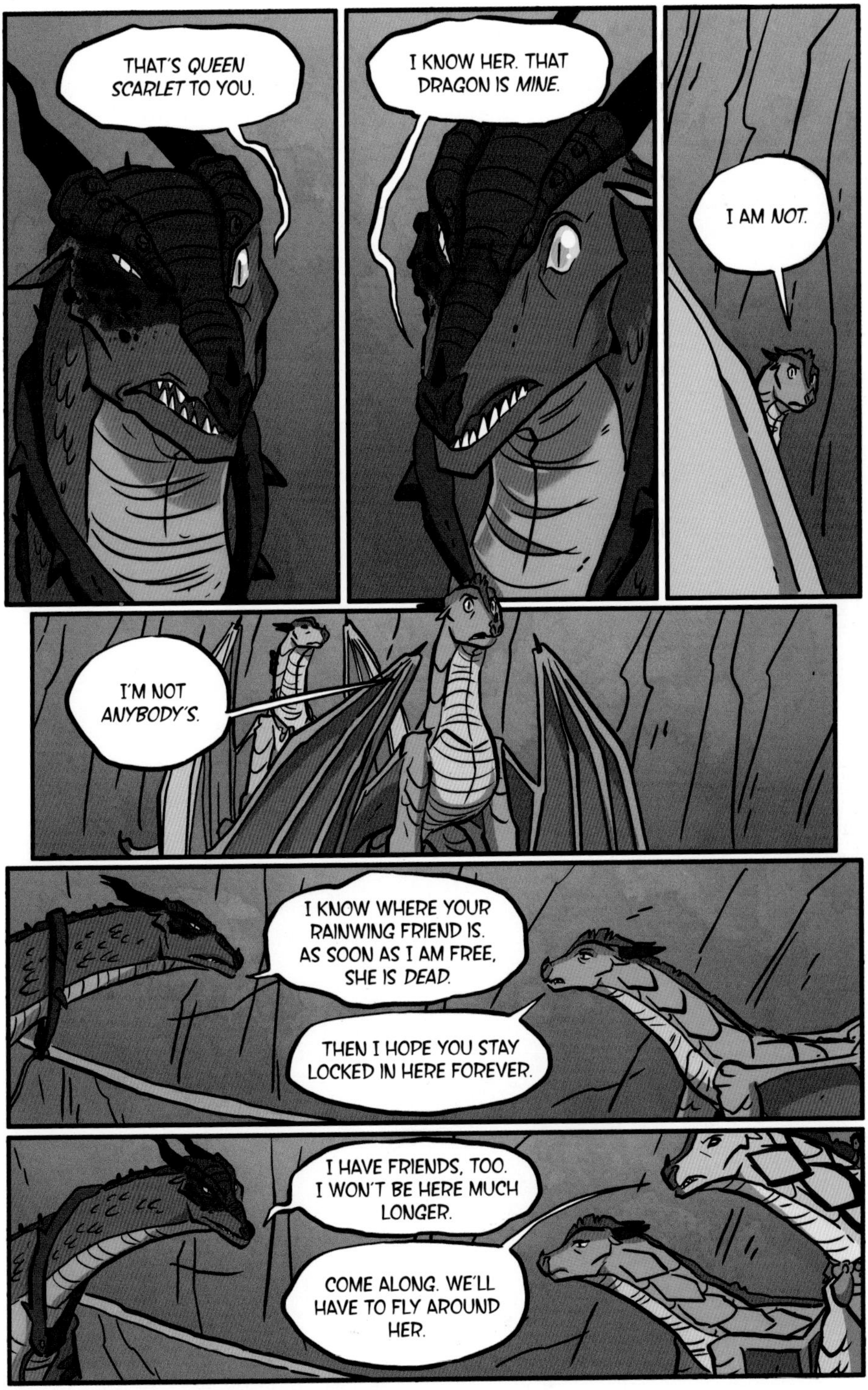
THAT'S QUEEN SCARLET TO YOU.
I KNOW HER. THAT DRAGON IS MINE.
I AM NOT.
I'M NOT ANYBODY'S.
I KNOW WHERE YOUR RAINWING FRIEND IS. AS SOON AS I AM FREE, SHE IS DEAD.
THEN I HOPE YOU STAY LOCKED IN HERE FOREVER.
I HAVE FRIENDS, TOO. I WON'T BE HERE MUCH LONGER.
COME ALONG. WE'LL HAVE TO FLY AROUND HER.

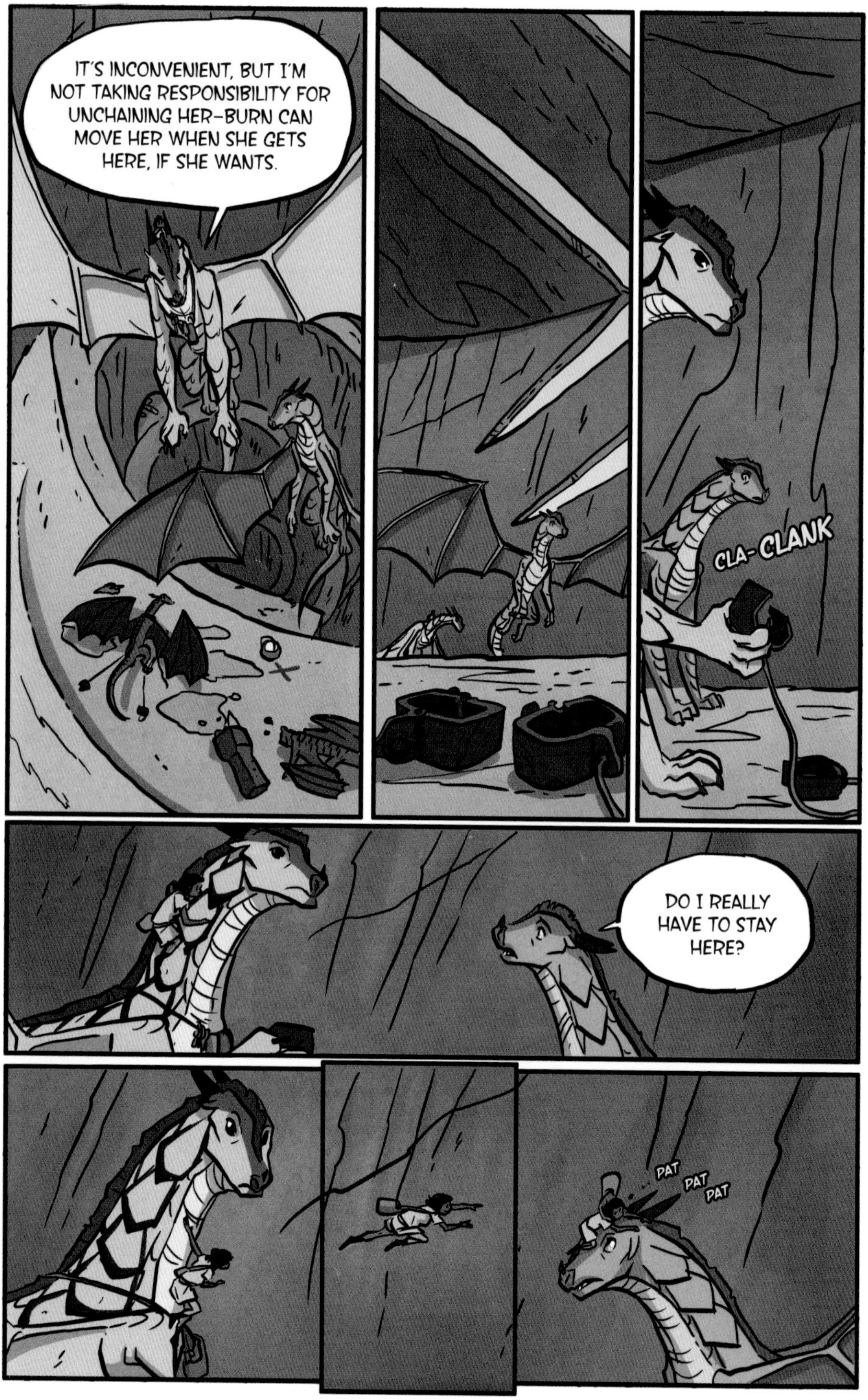
IT'S INCONVENIENT, BUT I'M NOT TAKING RESPONSIBILITY FOR UNCHAINING HER–BURN CAN MOVE HER WHEN SHE GETS HERE, IF SHE WANTS.
CLA-CLANK
DO I REALLY HAVE TO STAY HERE?
PAT
PAT
PAT

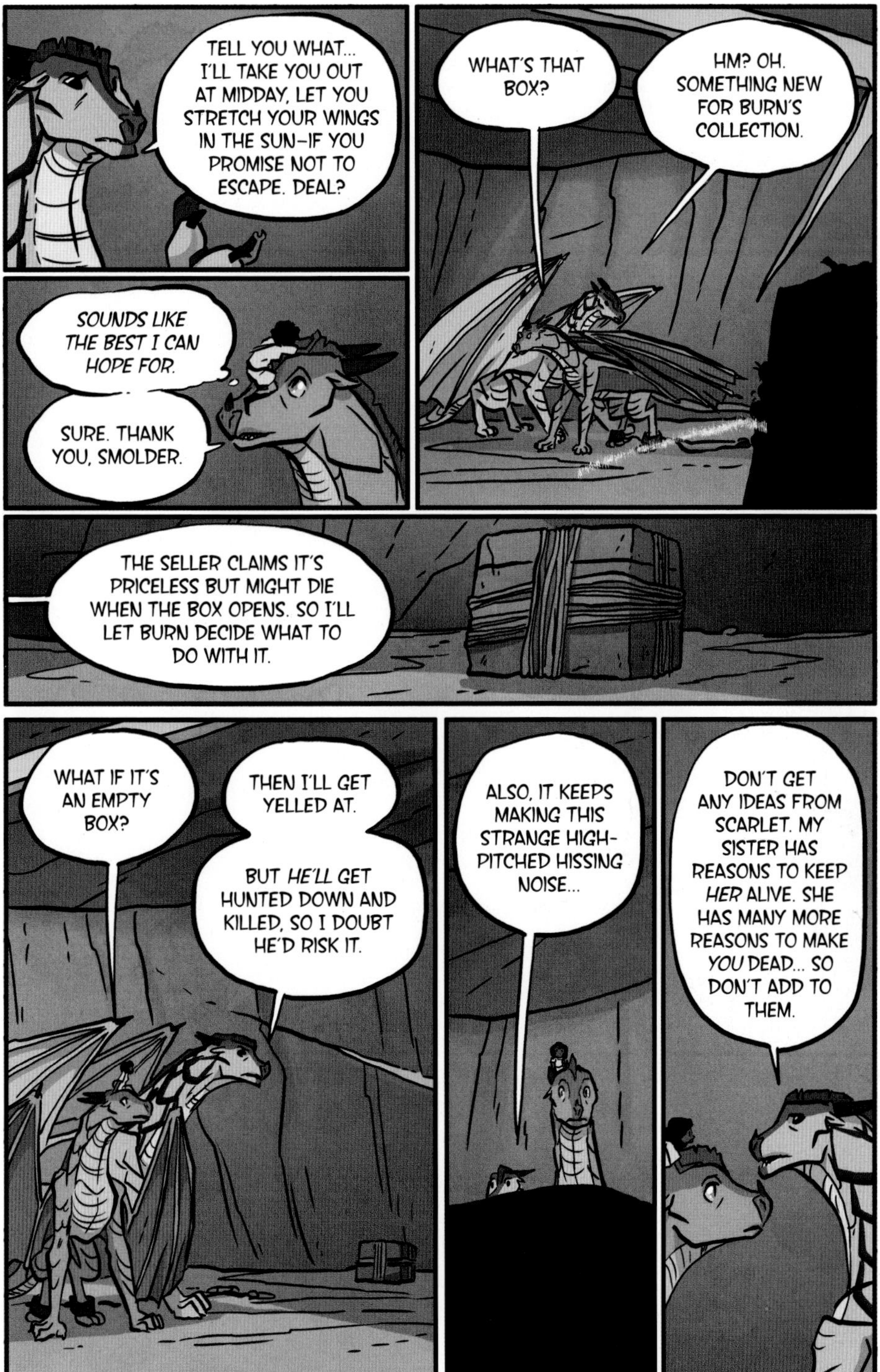
TELL YOU WHAT... I'LL TAKE YOU OUT AT MIDDAY, LET YOU STRETCH YOUR WINGS IN THE SUN–IF YOU PROMISE NOT TO ESCAPE. DEAL?
SOUNDS LIKE THE BEST I CAN HOPE FOR.
SURE. THANK YOU, SMOLDER.
WHAT'S THAT BOX?
HM? OH. SOMETHING NEW FOR BURN'S COLLECTION.
THE SELLER CLAIMS IT'S PRICELESS BUT MIGHT DIE WHEN THE BOX OPENS. SO I'LL LET BURN DECIDE WHAT TO DO WITH IT.
WHAT IF IT'S AN EMPTY BOX?
THEN I'LL GET YELLED AT.
BUT *HE'LL* GET HUNTED DOWN AND KILLED, SO I DOUBT HE'D RISK IT.
ALSO, IT KEEPS MAKING THIS STRANGE HIGH-PITCHED HISSING NOISE...
DON'T GET ANY IDEAS FROM SCARLET. MY SISTER HAS REASONS TO KEEP *HER* ALIVE. SHE HAS MANY MORE REASONS TO MAKE *YOU* DEAD... SO DON'T ADD TO THEM.

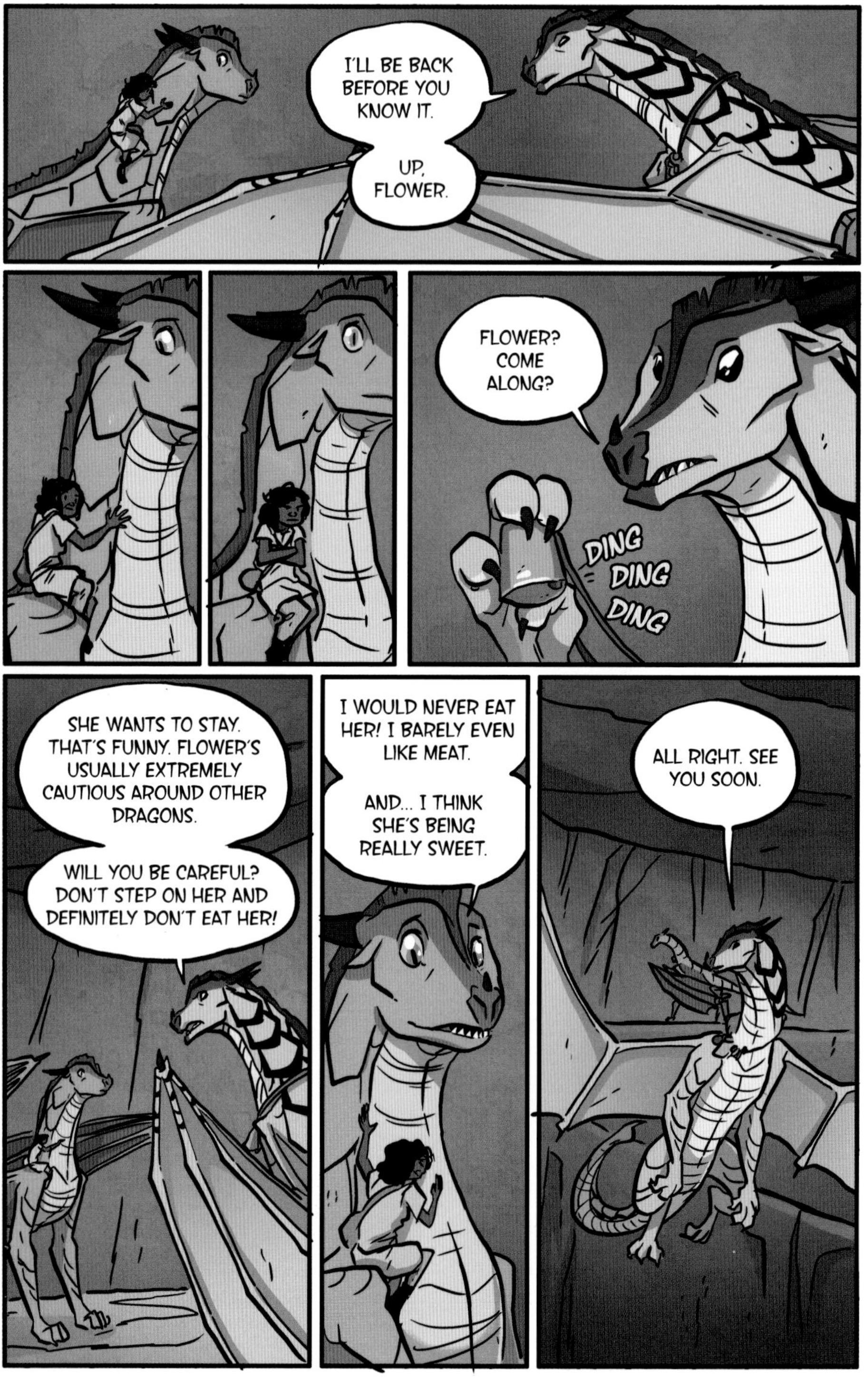
I'LL BE BACK BEFORE YOU KNOW IT.
UP, FLOWER.
FLOWER? COME ALONG?
DING DING DING
SHE WANTS TO STAY. THAT'S FUNNY. FLOWER'S USUALLY EXTREMELY CAUTIOUS AROUND OTHER DRAGONS.
WILL YOU BE CAREFUL? DON'T STEP ON HER AND DEFINITELY DON'T EAT HER!
I WOULD NEVER EAT HER! I BARELY EVEN LIKE MEAT.
AND... I THINK SHE'S BEING REALLY SWEET.
ALL RIGHT. SEE YOU SOON.

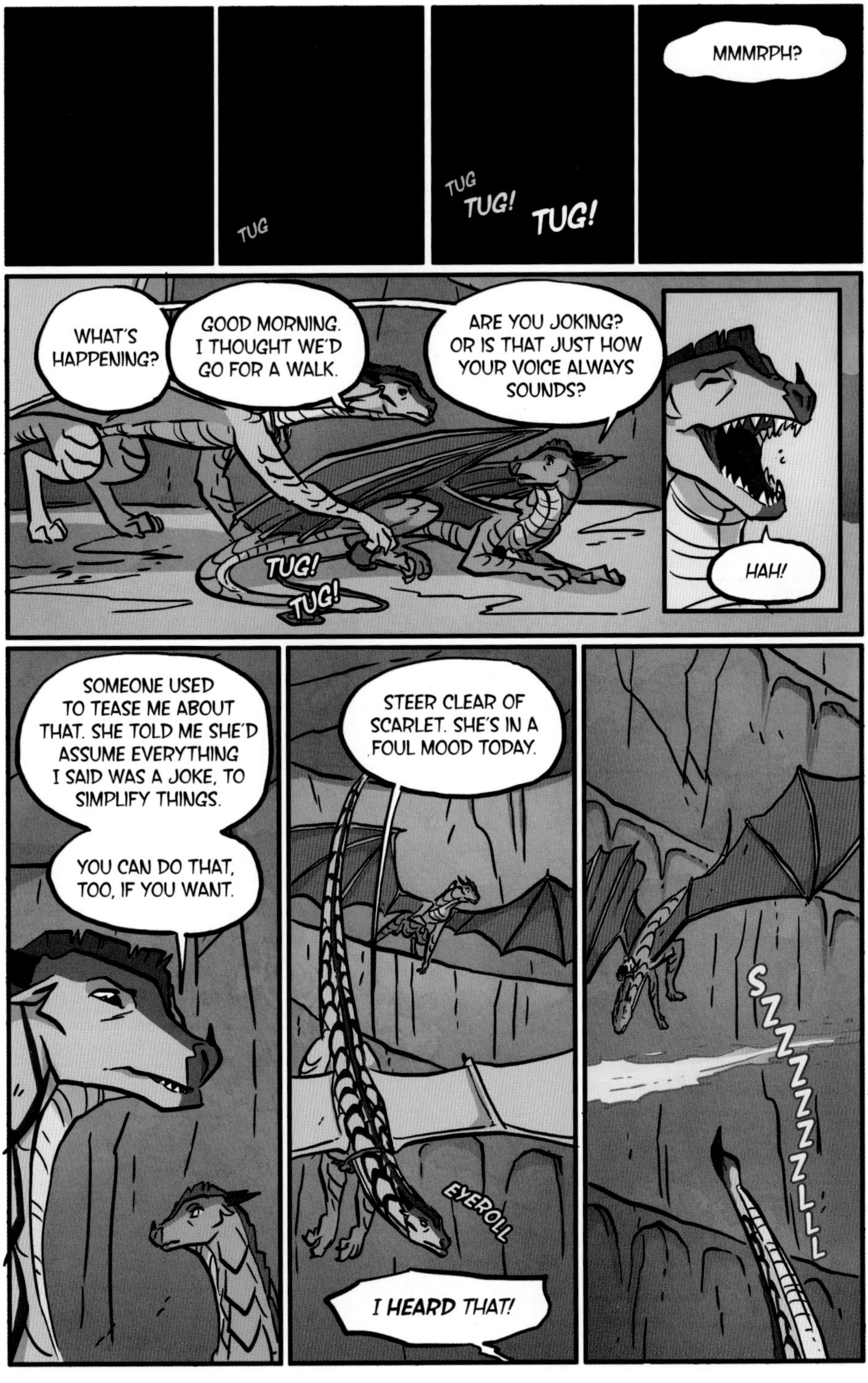
TUG
TUG
TUG!
TUG!
MMMRPH?
WHAT'S HAPPENING?
GOOD MORNING. I THOUGHT WE'D GO FOR A WALK.
TUG!
TUG!
ARE YOU JOKING? OR IS THAT JUST HOW YOUR VOICE ALWAYS SOUNDS?
HAH!
SOMEONE USED TO TEASE ME ABOUT THAT. SHE TOLD ME SHE'D ASSUME EVERYTHING I SAID WAS A JOKE, TO SIMPLIFY THINGS.
YOU CAN DO THAT, TOO, IF YOU WANT.
STEER CLEAR OF SCARLET. SHE'S IN A FOUL MOOD TODAY.
EYEROLL
I HEARD THAT!
SZZZZZZLLL

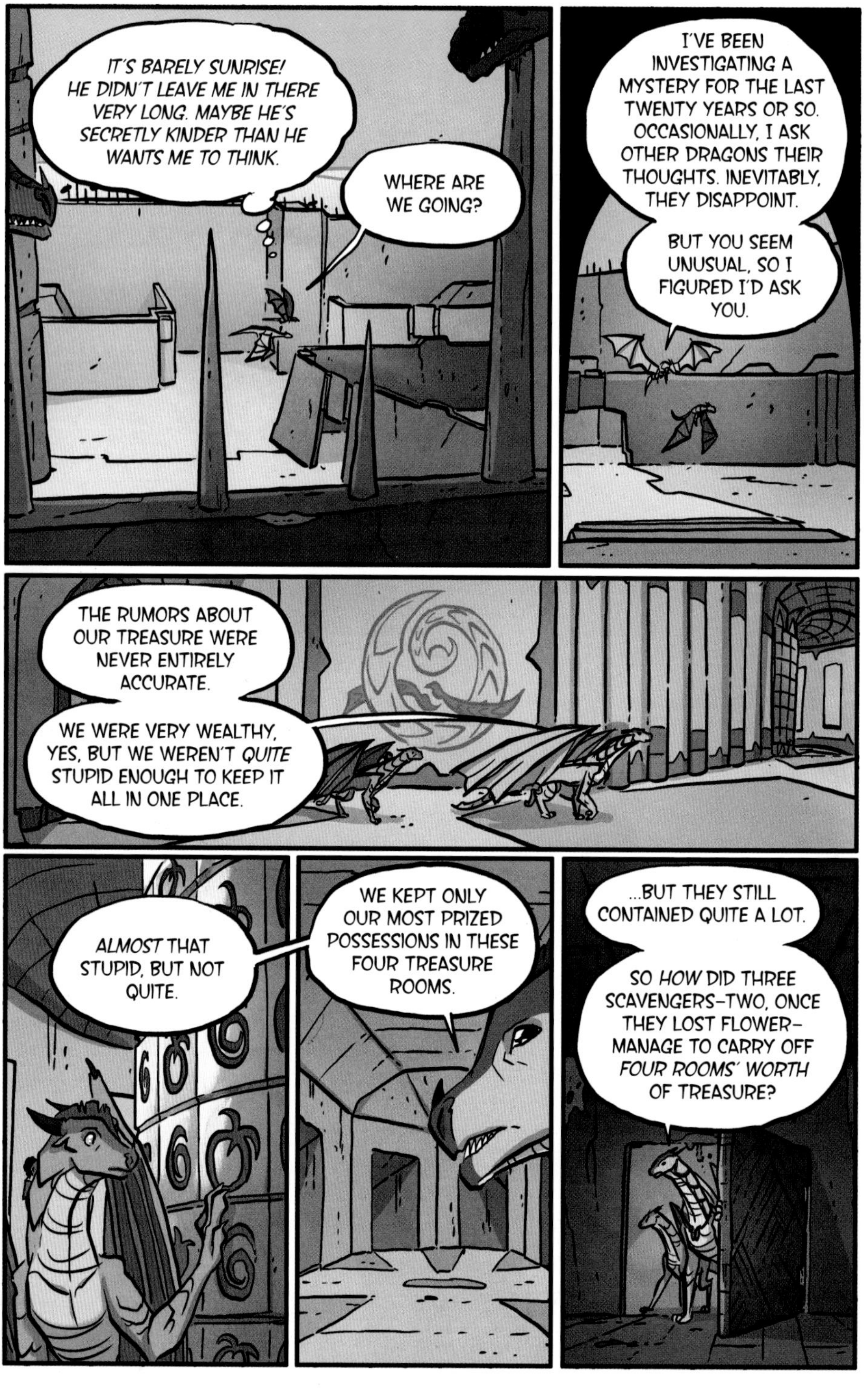
IT'S BARELY SUNRISE! HE DIDN'T LEAVE ME IN THERE VERY LONG. MAYBE HE'S SECRETLY KINDER THAN HE WANTS ME TO THINK.
WHERE ARE WE GOING?
I'VE BEEN INVESTIGATING A MYSTERY FOR THE LAST TWENTY YEARS OR SO. OCCASIONALLY, I ASK OTHER DRAGONS THEIR THOUGHTS. INEVITABLY, THEY DISAPPOINT.
BUT YOU SEEM UNUSUAL, SO I FIGURED I'D ASK YOU.
THE RUMORS ABOUT OUR TREASURE WERE NEVER ENTIRELY ACCURATE.
WE WERE VERY WEALTHY, YES, BUT WE WEREN'T *QUITE* STUPID ENOUGH TO KEEP IT ALL IN ONE PLACE.
ALMOST THAT STUPID, BUT NOT QUITE.
WE KEPT ONLY OUR MOST PRIZED POSSESSIONS IN THESE FOUR TREASURE ROOMS.
...BUT THEY STILL CONTAINED QUITE A LOT.
SO *HOW* DID THREE SCAVENGERS—TWO, ONCE THEY LOST FLOWER—MANAGE TO CARRY OFF *FOUR ROOMS' WORTH* OF TREASURE?

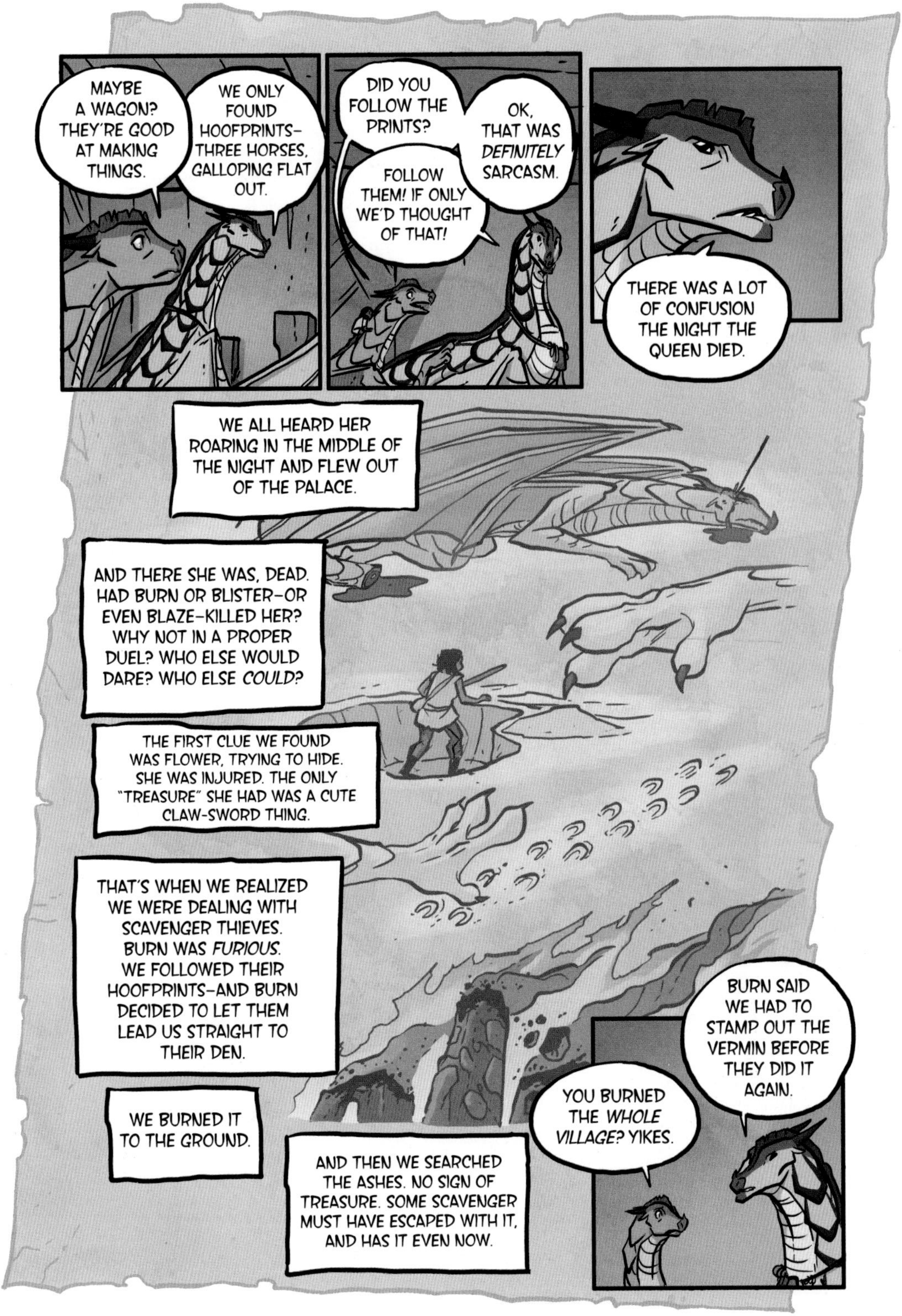
MAYBE A WAGON? THEY'RE GOOD AT MAKING THINGS.
WE ONLY FOUND HOOFPRINTS– THREE HORSES, GALLOPING FLAT OUT.
DID YOU FOLLOW THE PRINTS?
FOLLOW THEM! IF ONLY WE'D THOUGHT OF THAT!
OK, THAT WAS *DEFINITELY* SARCASM.
THERE WAS A LOT OF CONFUSION THE NIGHT THE QUEEN DIED.
WE ALL HEARD HER ROARING IN THE MIDDLE OF THE NIGHT AND FLEW OUT OF THE PALACE.
AND THERE SHE WAS, DEAD. HAD BURN OR BLISTER–OR EVEN BLAZE–KILLED HER? WHY NOT IN A PROPER DUEL? WHO ELSE WOULD DARE? WHO ELSE *COULD*?
THE FIRST CLUE WE FOUND WAS FLOWER, TRYING TO HIDE. SHE WAS INJURED. THE ONLY "TREASURE" SHE HAD WAS A CUTE CLAW-SWORD THING.
THAT'S WHEN WE REALIZED WE WERE DEALING WITH SCAVENGER THIEVES. BURN WAS *FURIOUS*. WE FOLLOWED THEIR HOOFPRINTS–AND BURN DECIDED TO LET THEM LEAD US STRAIGHT TO THEIR DEN.
WE BURNED IT TO THE GROUND.
AND THEN WE SEARCHED THE ASHES. NO SIGN OF TREASURE. SOME SCAVENGER MUST HAVE ESCAPED WITH IT, AND HAS IT EVEN NOW.
BURN SAID WE HAD TO STAMP OUT THE VERMIN BEFORE THEY DID IT AGAIN.
YOU BURNED THE *WHOLE VILLAGE*? YIKES.

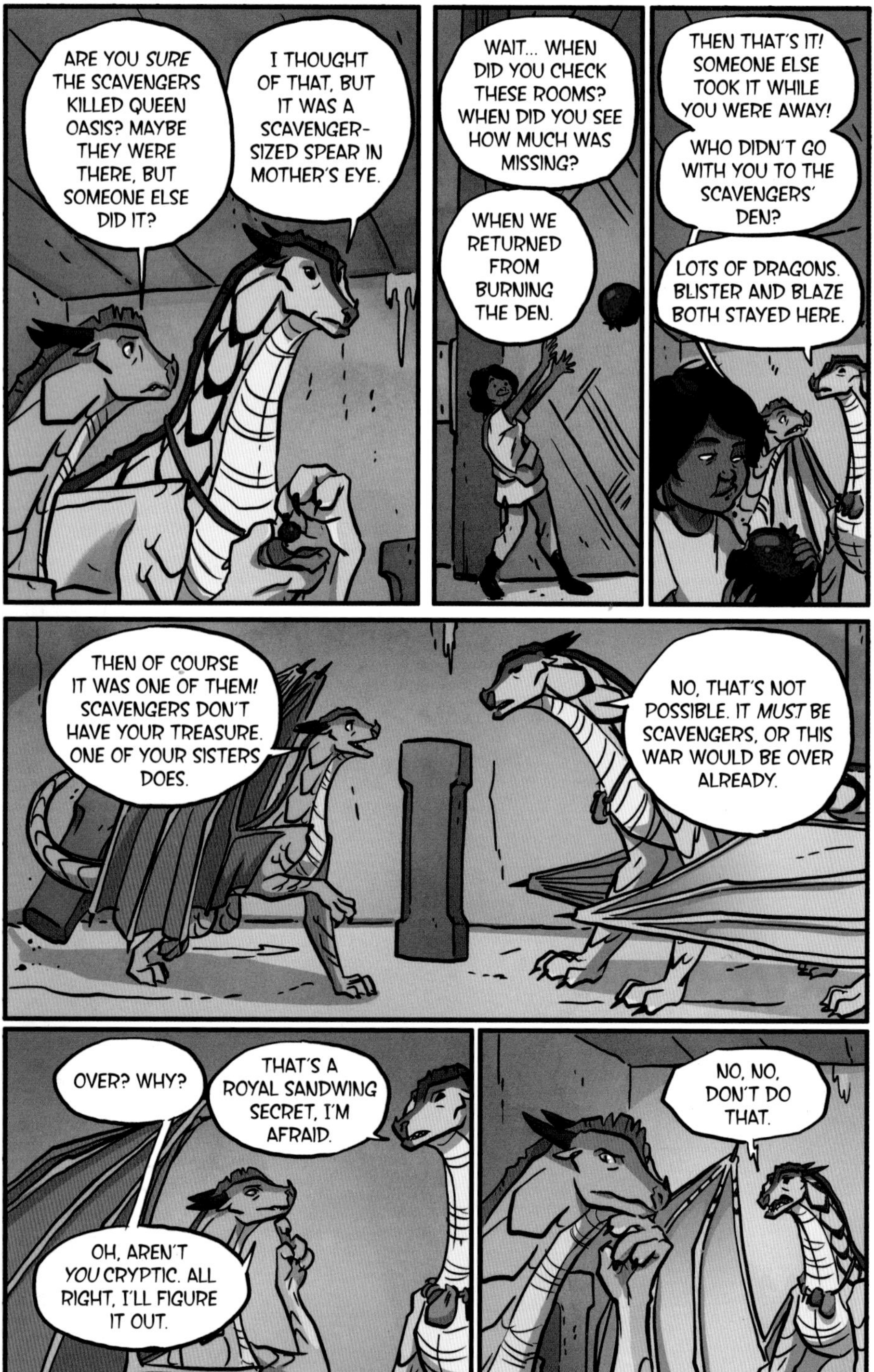
ARE YOU *SURE* THE SCAVENGERS KILLED QUEEN OASIS? MAYBE THEY WERE THERE, BUT SOMEONE ELSE DID IT?
I THOUGHT OF THAT, BUT IT WAS A SCAVENGER-SIZED SPEAR IN MOTHER'S EYE.
WAIT... WHEN DID YOU CHECK THESE ROOMS? WHEN DID YOU SEE HOW MUCH WAS MISSING?
WHEN WE RETURNED FROM BURNING THE DEN.
THEN THAT'S IT! SOMEONE ELSE TOOK IT WHILE YOU WERE AWAY!
WHO DIDN'T GO WITH YOU TO THE SCAVENGERS' DEN?
LOTS OF DRAGONS. BLISTER AND BLAZE BOTH STAYED HERE.
THEN OF COURSE IT WAS ONE OF THEM! SCAVENGERS DON'T HAVE YOUR TREASURE. ONE OF YOUR SISTERS DOES.
NO, THAT'S NOT POSSIBLE. IT *MUST* BE SCAVENGERS, OR THIS WAR WOULD BE OVER ALREADY.
OVER? WHY?
THAT'S A ROYAL SANDWING SECRET, I'M AFRAID.
OH, AREN'T *YOU* CRYPTIC. ALL RIGHT, I'LL FIGURE IT OUT.
NO, NO, DON'T DO THAT.

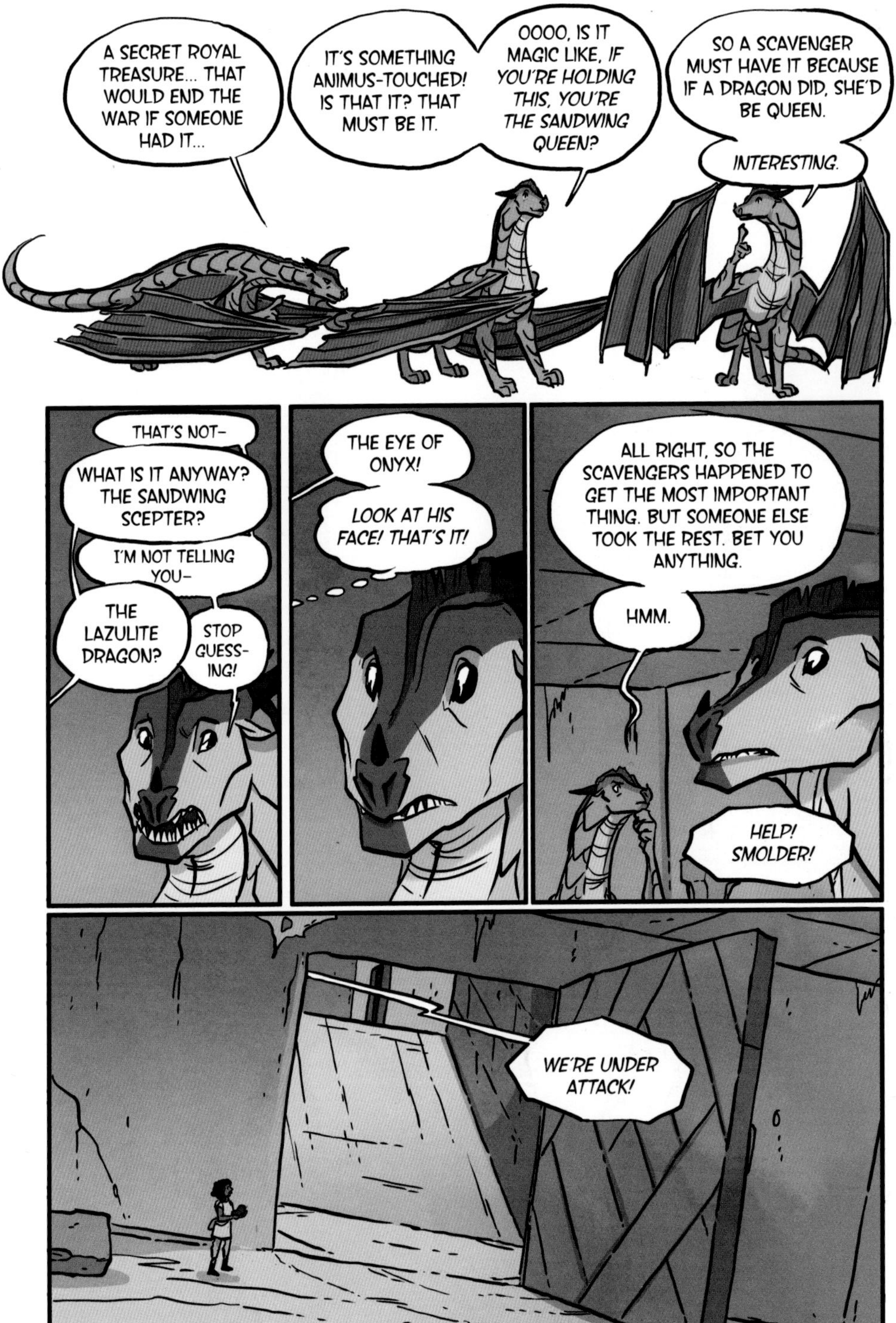
A SECRET ROYAL TREASURE... THAT WOULD END THE WAR IF SOMEONE HAD IT...
IT'S SOMETHING ANIMUS-TOUCHED! IS THAT IT? THAT MUST BE IT.
OOOO, IS IT MAGIC LIKE, IF YOU'RE HOLDING THIS, YOU'RE THE SANDWING QUEEN?
SO A SCAVENGER MUST HAVE IT BECAUSE IF A DRAGON DID, SHE'D BE QUEEN.
INTERESTING.
THAT'S NOT—
WHAT IS IT ANYWAY? THE SANDWING SCEPTER?
I'M NOT TELLING YOU—
THE LAZULITE DRAGON?
STOP GUESS-ING!
THE EYE OF ONYX!
LOOK AT HIS FACE! THAT'S IT!
ALL RIGHT, SO THE SCAVENGERS HAPPENED TO GET THE MOST IMPORTANT THING. BUT SOMEONE ELSE TOOK THE REST. BET YOU ANYTHING.
HMM.
HELP! SMOLDER!
WE'RE UNDER ATTACK!

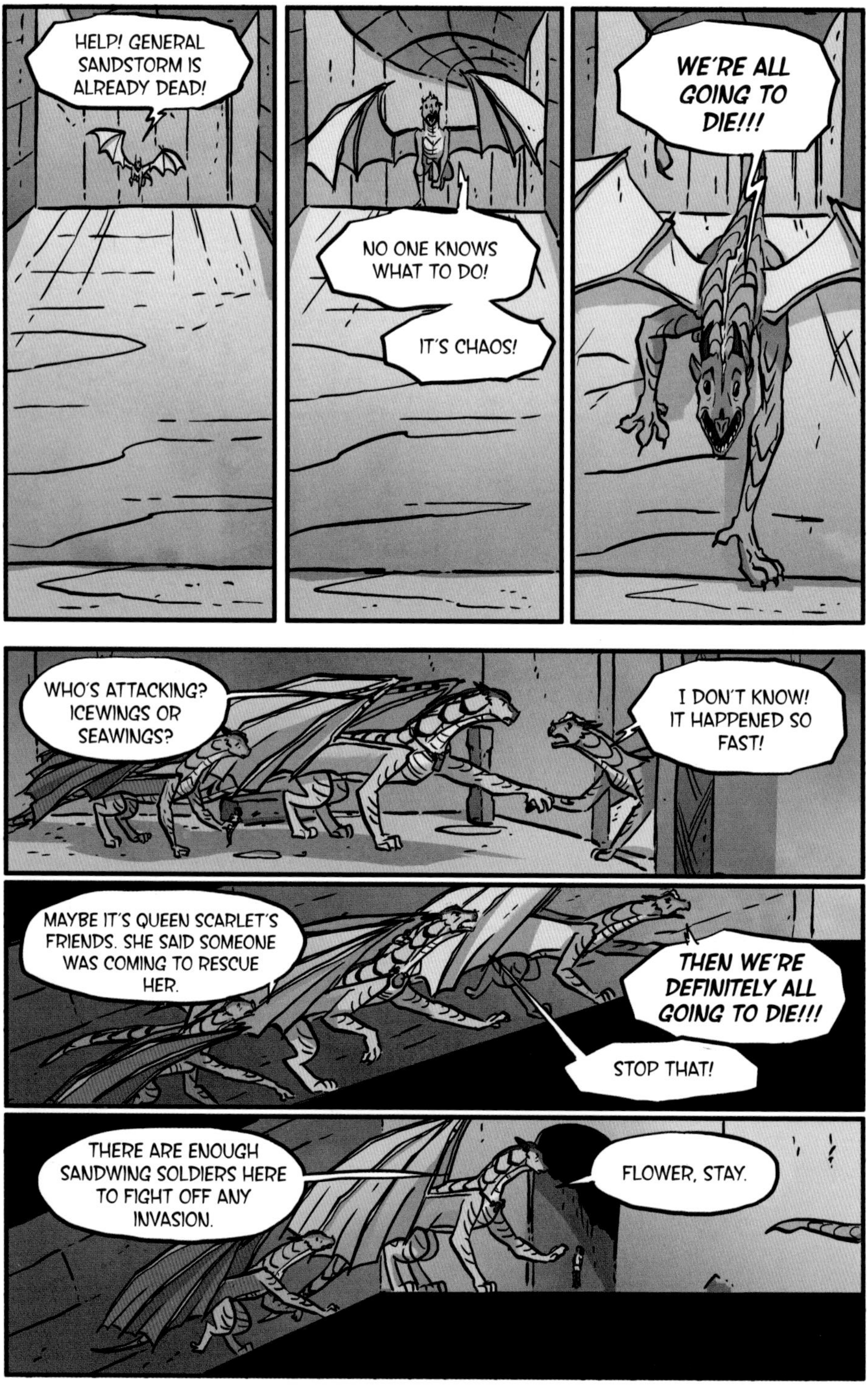
HELP! GENERAL SANDSTORM IS ALREADY DEAD!
NO ONE KNOWS WHAT TO DO!
IT'S CHAOS!
WE'RE ALL GOING TO DIE!!!
WHO'S ATTACKING? ICEWINGS OR SEAWINGS?
I DON'T KNOW! IT HAPPENED SO FAST!
MAYBE IT'S QUEEN SCARLET'S FRIENDS. SHE SAID SOMEONE WAS COMING TO RESCUE HER.
THEN WE'RE DEFINITELY ALL GOING TO DIE!!!
STOP THAT!
THERE ARE ENOUGH SANDWING SOLDIERS HERE TO FIGHT OFF ANY INVASION.
FLOWER, STAY.

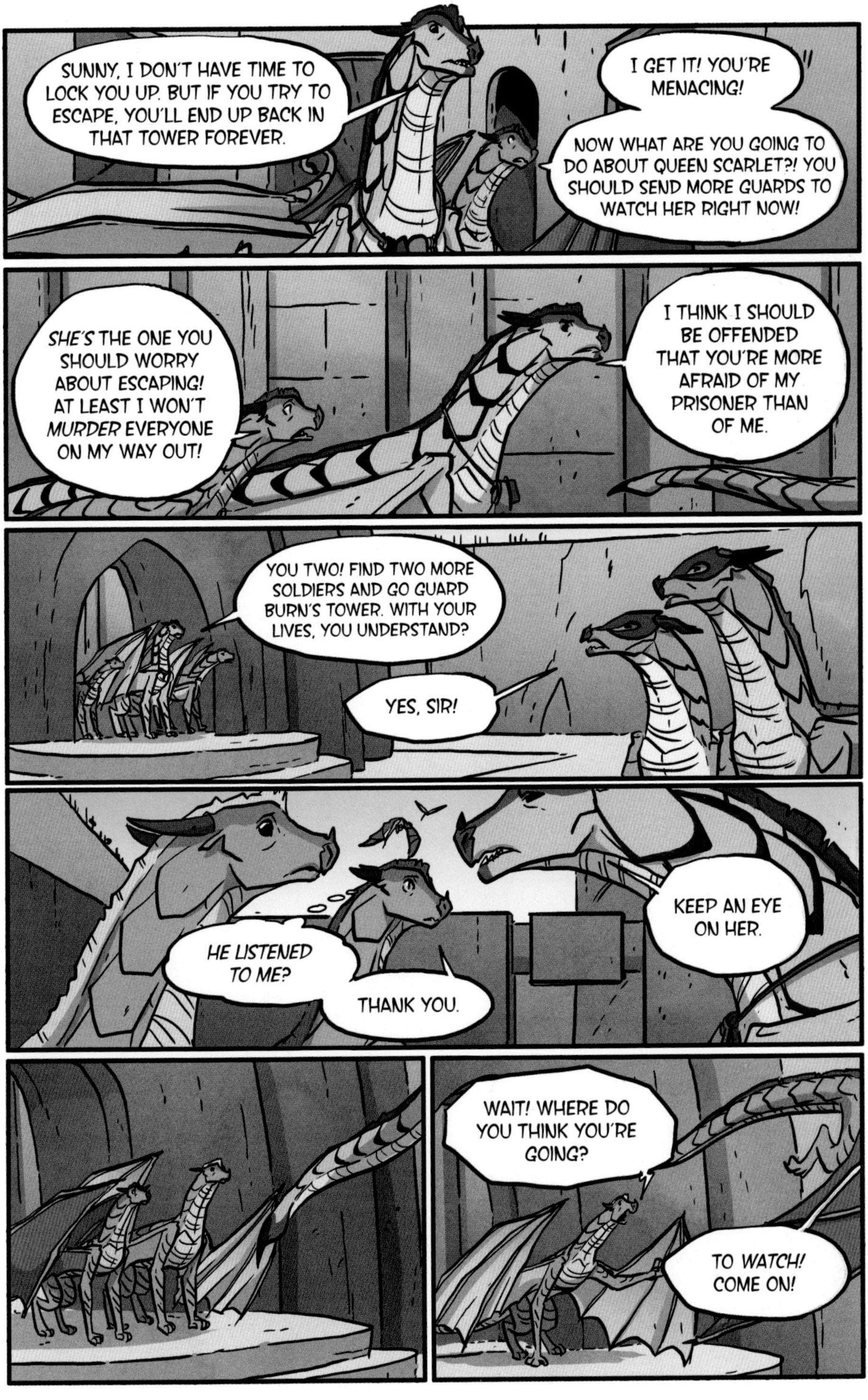
SUNNY, I DON'T HAVE TIME TO LOCK YOU UP. BUT IF YOU TRY TO ESCAPE, YOU'LL END UP BACK IN THAT TOWER FOREVER.
I GET IT! YOU'RE MENACING!
NOW WHAT ARE YOU GOING TO DO ABOUT QUEEN SCARLET?! YOU SHOULD SEND MORE GUARDS TO WATCH HER RIGHT NOW!
SHE'S THE ONE YOU SHOULD WORRY ABOUT ESCAPING! AT LEAST I WON'T *MURDER* EVERYONE ON MY WAY OUT!
I THINK I SHOULD BE OFFENDED THAT YOU'RE MORE AFRAID OF MY PRISONER THAN OF ME.
YOU TWO! FIND TWO MORE SOLDIERS AND GO GUARD BURN'S TOWER. WITH YOUR LIVES, YOU UNDERSTAND?
YES, SIR!
KEEP AN EYE ON HER.
HE LISTENED TO ME?
THANK YOU.
WAIT! WHERE DO YOU THINK YOU'RE GOING?
TO *WATCH!* COME ON!

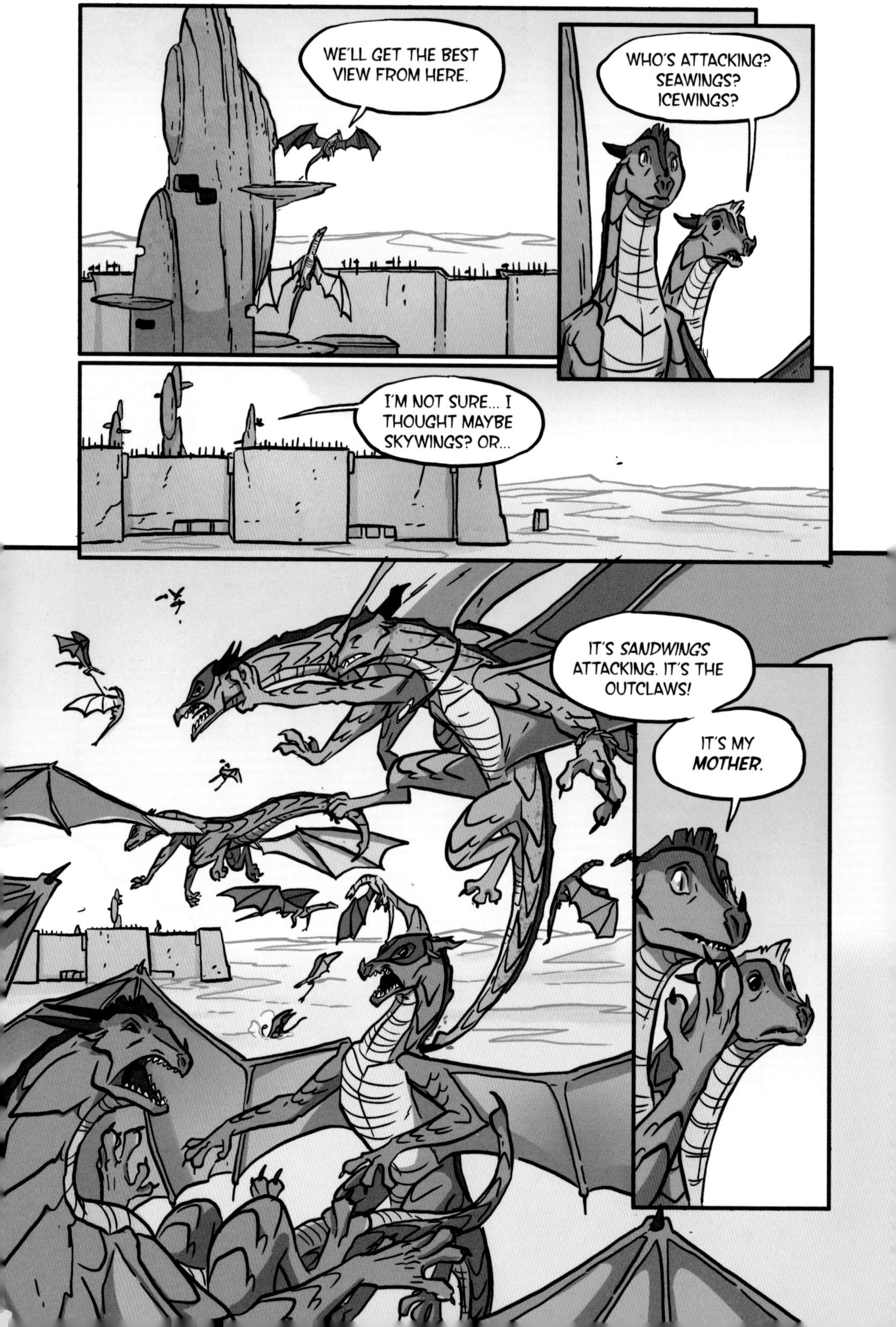
WE'LL GET THE BEST VIEW FROM HERE.
WHO'S ATTACKING? SEAWINGS? ICEWINGS?
I'M NOT SURE... I THOUGHT MAYBE SKYWINGS? OR...
IT'S *SANDWINGS* ATTACKING. IT'S THE OUTCLAWS!
IT'S MY ***MOTHER.***

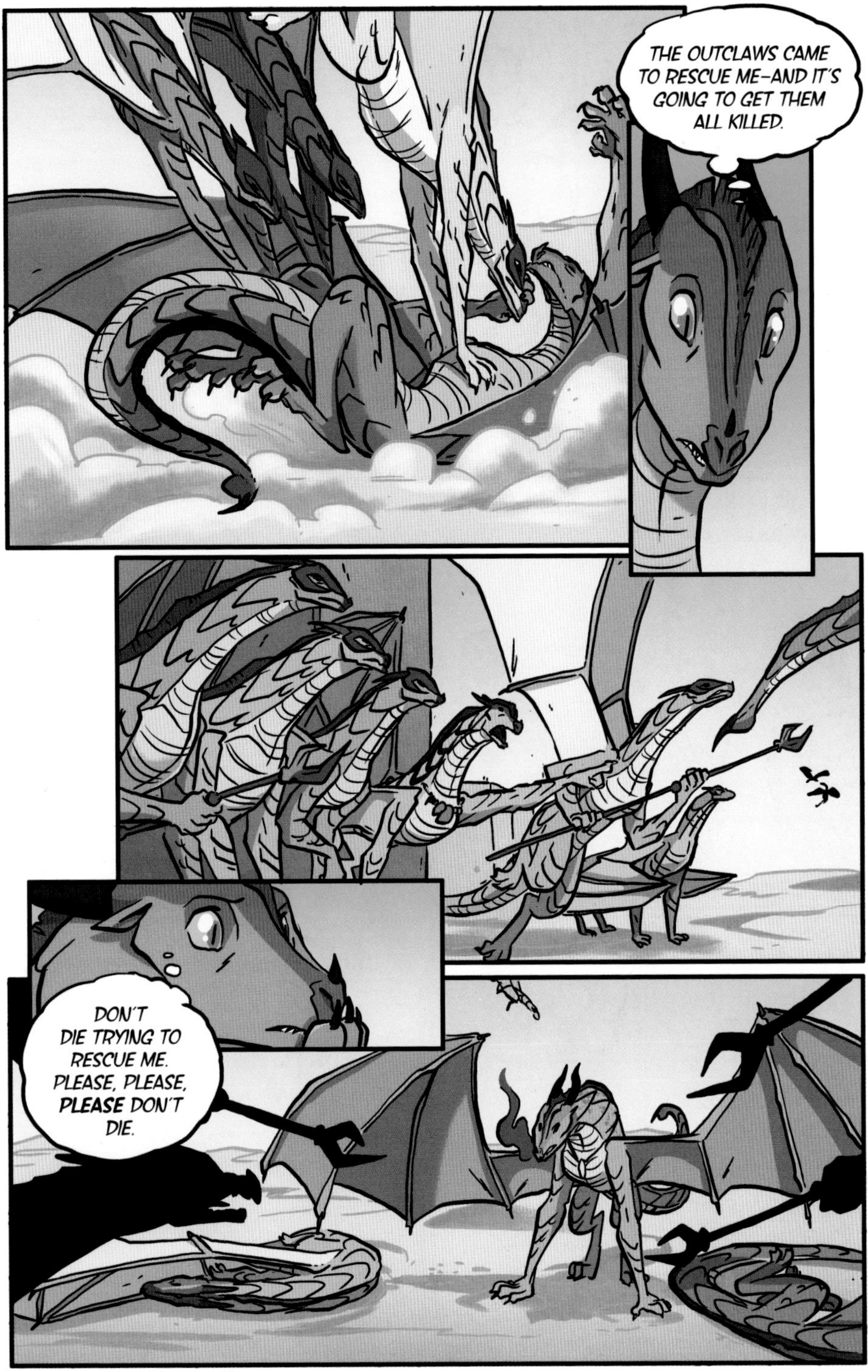
THE OUTCLAWS CAME TO RESCUE ME—AND IT'S GOING TO GET THEM ALL KILLED.
DON'T DIE TRYING TO RESCUE ME. PLEASE, PLEASE, **PLEASE** DON'T DIE.

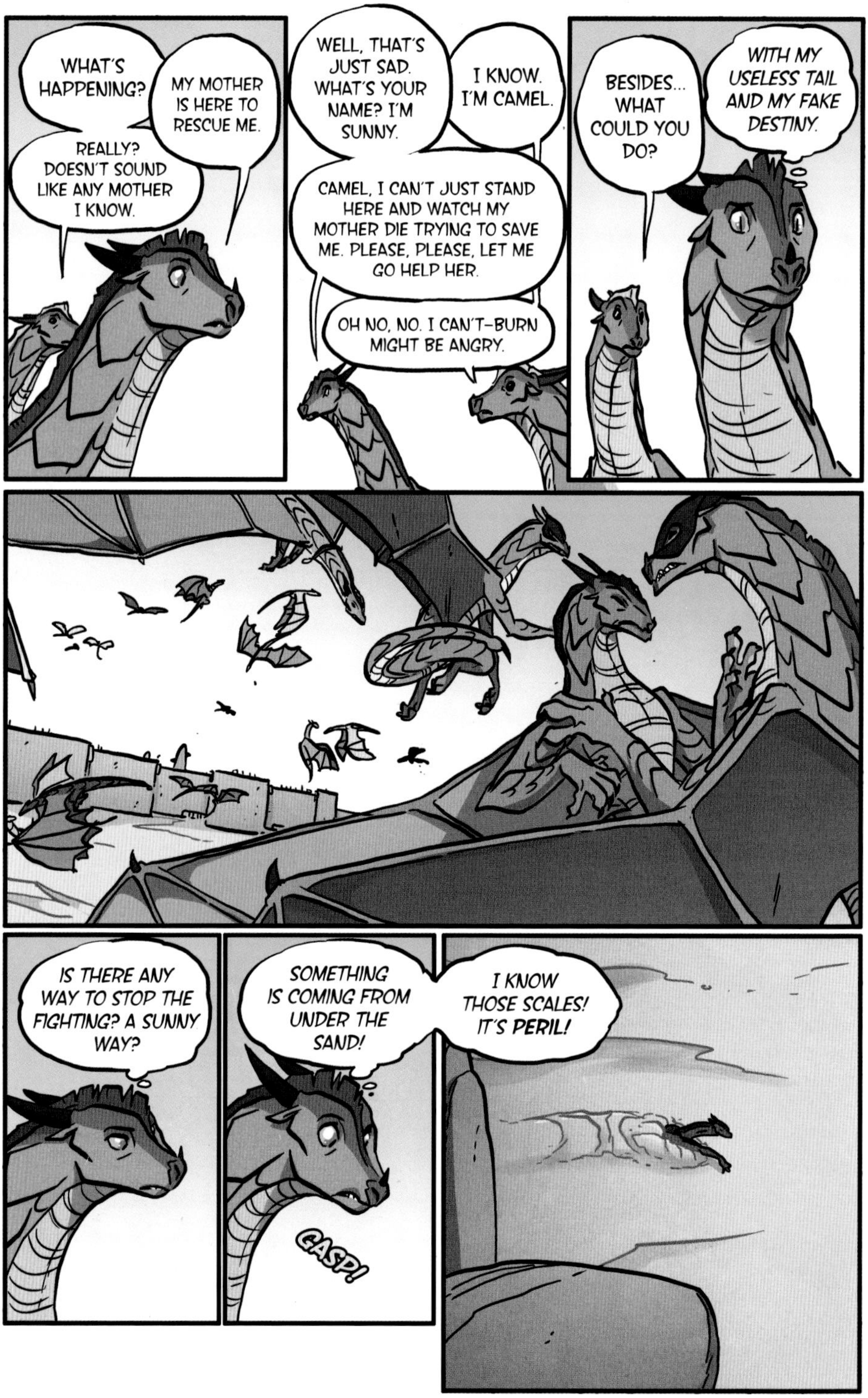
WHAT'S HAPPENING?
MY MOTHER IS HERE TO RESCUE ME.
REALLY? DOESN'T SOUND LIKE ANY MOTHER I KNOW.
WELL, THAT'S JUST SAD. WHAT'S YOUR NAME? I'M SUNNY.
I KNOW. I'M CAMEL.
CAMEL, I CAN'T JUST STAND HERE AND WATCH MY MOTHER DIE TRYING TO SAVE ME. PLEASE, PLEASE, LET ME GO HELP HER.
OH NO, NO. I CAN'T—BURN MIGHT BE ANGRY.
BESIDES... WHAT COULD YOU DO?
WITH MY USELESS TAIL AND MY FAKE DESTINY.
IS THERE ANY WAY TO STOP THE FIGHTING? A SUNNY WAY?
SOMETHING IS COMING FROM UNDER THE SAND!
GASP!
I KNOW THOSE SCALES! IT'S PERIL!

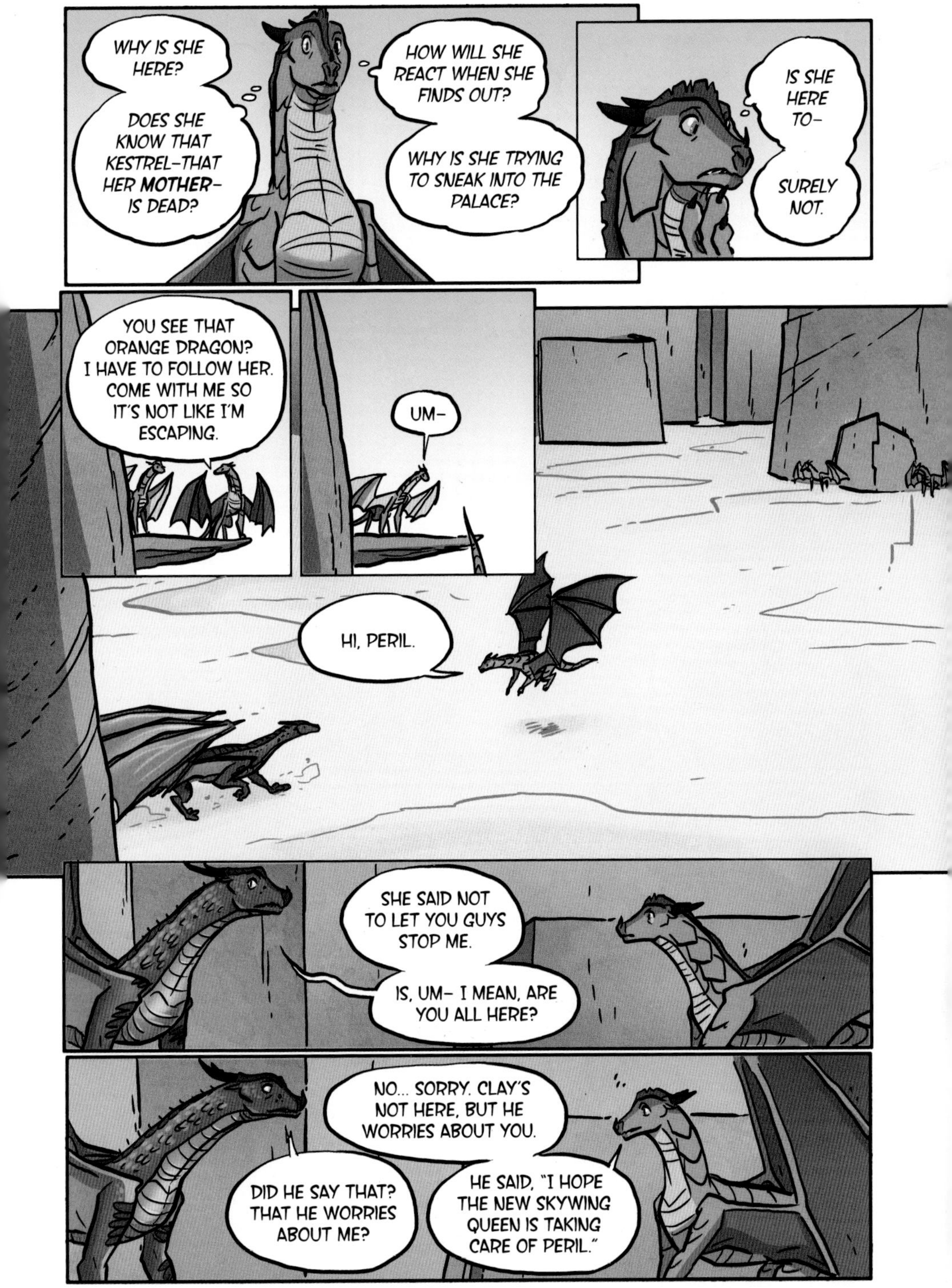
WHY IS SHE HERE?
DOES SHE KNOW THAT KESTREL—THAT HER **MOTHER**— IS DEAD?
HOW WILL SHE REACT WHEN SHE FINDS OUT?
WHY IS SHE TRYING TO SNEAK INTO THE PALACE?
IS SHE HERE TO—
SURELY NOT.
YOU SEE THAT ORANGE DRAGON? I HAVE TO FOLLOW HER. COME WITH ME SO IT'S NOT LIKE I'M ESCAPING.
UM—
HI, PERIL.
SHE SAID NOT TO LET YOU GUYS STOP ME.
IS, UM— I MEAN, ARE YOU ALL HERE?
NO... SORRY. CLAY'S NOT HERE, BUT HE WORRIES ABOUT YOU.
DID HE SAY THAT? THAT HE WORRIES ABOUT ME?
HE SAID, "I HOPE THE NEW SKYWING QUEEN IS TAKING CARE OF PERIL."

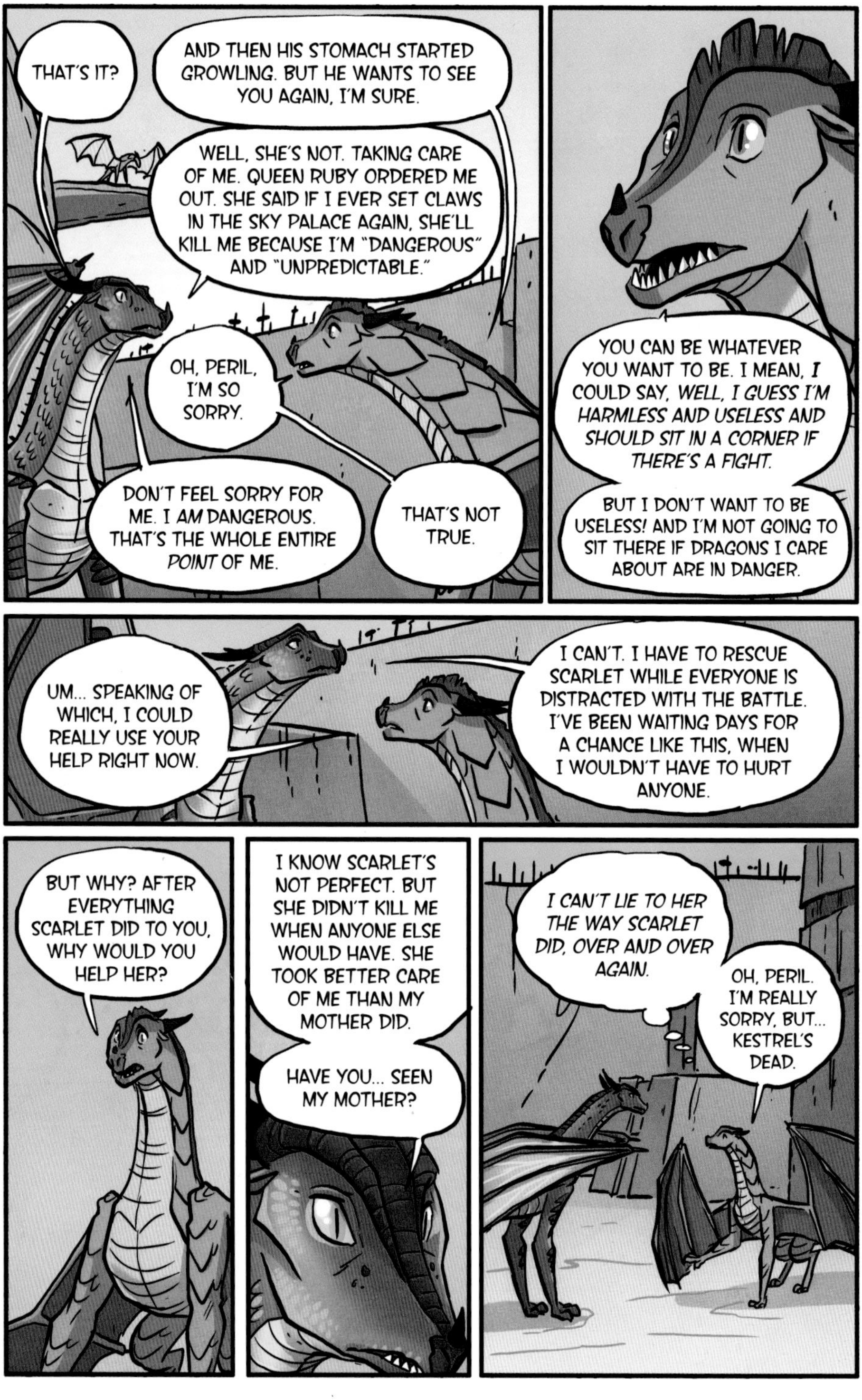
THAT'S IT?
AND THEN HIS STOMACH STARTED GROWLING. BUT HE WANTS TO SEE YOU AGAIN, I'M SURE.
WELL, SHE'S NOT. TAKING CARE OF ME. QUEEN RUBY ORDERED ME OUT. SHE SAID IF I EVER SET CLAWS IN THE SKY PALACE AGAIN, SHE'LL KILL ME BECAUSE I'M "DANGEROUS" AND "UNPREDICTABLE."
OH, PERIL, I'M SO SORRY.
DON'T FEEL SORRY FOR ME. I *AM* DANGEROUS. THAT'S THE WHOLE ENTIRE *POINT* OF ME.
THAT'S NOT TRUE.
YOU CAN BE WHATEVER YOU WANT TO BE. I MEAN, *I* COULD SAY, *WELL, I GUESS I'M HARMLESS AND USELESS AND SHOULD SIT IN A CORNER IF THERE'S A FIGHT.*
BUT I DON'T WANT TO BE USELESS! AND I'M NOT GOING TO SIT THERE IF DRAGONS I CARE ABOUT ARE IN DANGER.
UM... SPEAKING OF WHICH, I COULD REALLY USE YOUR HELP RIGHT NOW.
I CAN'T. I HAVE TO RESCUE SCARLET WHILE EVERYONE IS DISTRACTED WITH THE BATTLE. I'VE BEEN WAITING DAYS FOR A CHANCE LIKE THIS, WHEN I WOULDN'T HAVE TO HURT ANYONE.
BUT WHY? AFTER EVERYTHING SCARLET DID TO YOU, WHY WOULD YOU HELP HER?
I KNOW SCARLET'S NOT PERFECT. BUT SHE DIDN'T KILL ME WHEN ANYONE ELSE WOULD HAVE. SHE TOOK BETTER CARE OF ME THAN MY MOTHER DID.
HAVE YOU... SEEN MY MOTHER?
I CAN'T LIE TO HER THE WAY SCARLET DID, OVER AND OVER AGAIN.
OH, PERIL. I'M REALLY SORRY, BUT... KESTREL'S DEAD.

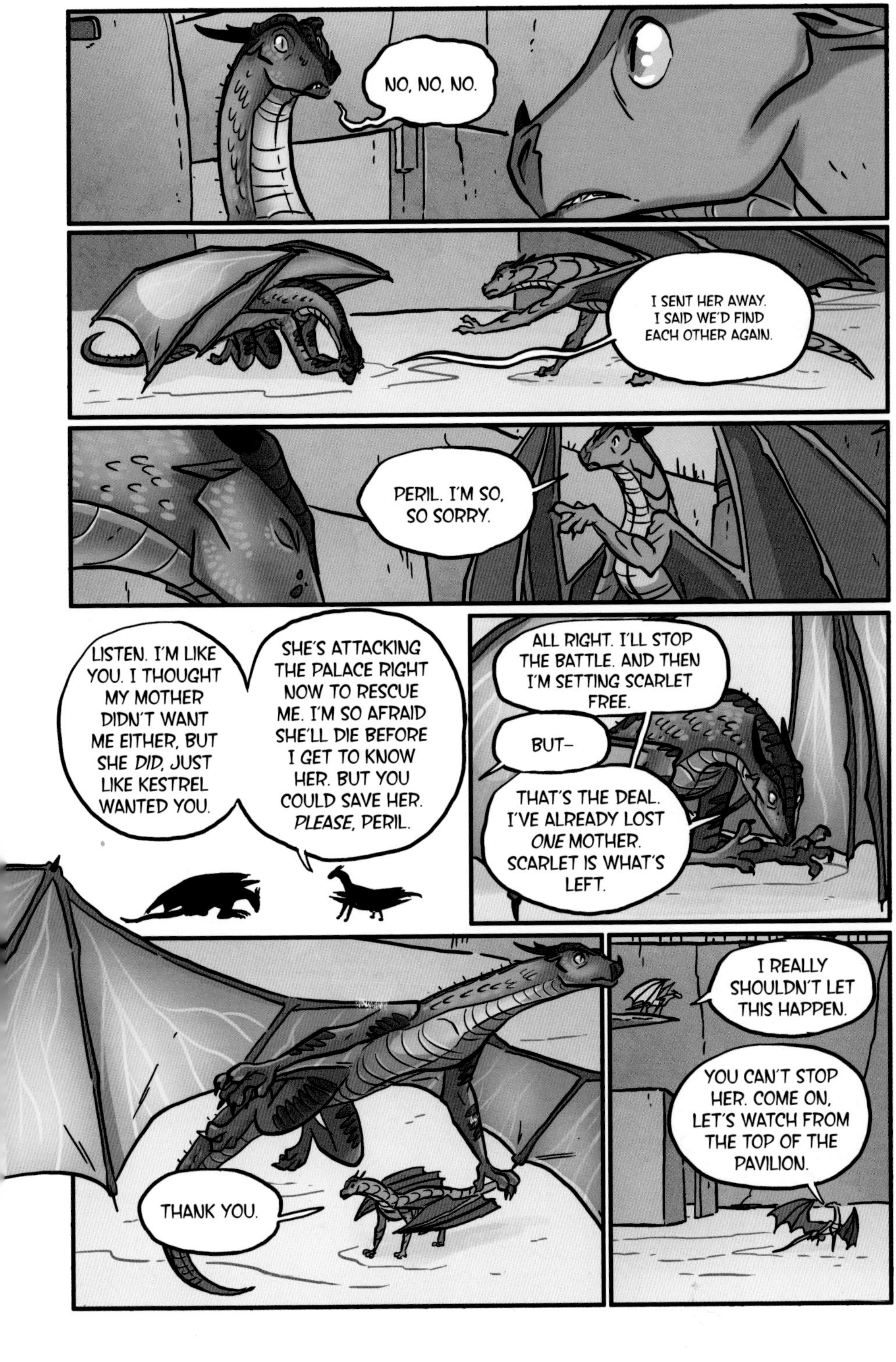
NO, NO, NO.
I SENT HER AWAY. I SAID WE'D FIND EACH OTHER AGAIN.
PERIL. I'M SO, SO SORRY.
LISTEN. I'M LIKE YOU. I THOUGHT MY MOTHER DIDN'T WANT ME EITHER, BUT SHE *DID*, JUST LIKE KESTREL WANTED YOU.
SHE'S ATTACKING THE PALACE RIGHT NOW TO RESCUE ME. I'M SO AFRAID SHE'LL DIE BEFORE I GET TO KNOW HER. BUT YOU COULD SAVE HER. *PLEASE*, PERIL.
ALL RIGHT. I'LL STOP THE BATTLE. AND THEN I'M SETTING SCARLET FREE.
BUT–
THAT'S THE DEAL. I'VE ALREADY LOST *ONE* MOTHER. SCARLET IS WHAT'S LEFT.
THANK YOU.
I REALLY SHOULDN'T LET THIS HAPPEN.
YOU CAN'T STOP HER. COME ON, LET'S WATCH FROM THE TOP OF THE PAVILION.

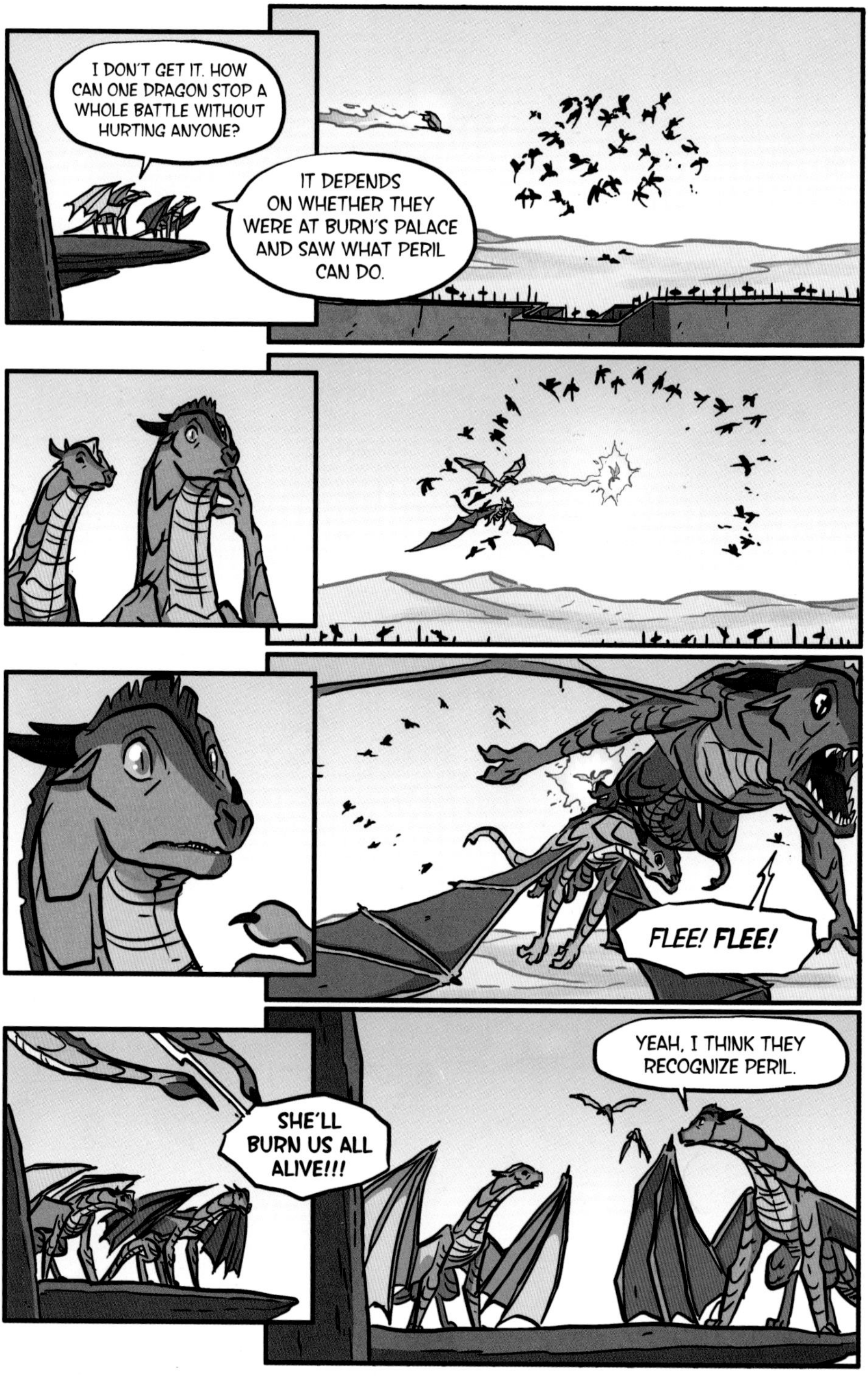
I DON'T GET IT. HOW CAN ONE DRAGON STOP A WHOLE BATTLE WITHOUT HURTING ANYONE?
IT DEPENDS ON WHETHER THEY WERE AT BURN'S PALACE AND SAW WHAT PERIL CAN DO.
FLEE! FLEE!
SHE'LL BURN US ALL ALIVE!!!
YEAH, I THINK THEY RECOGNIZE PERIL.

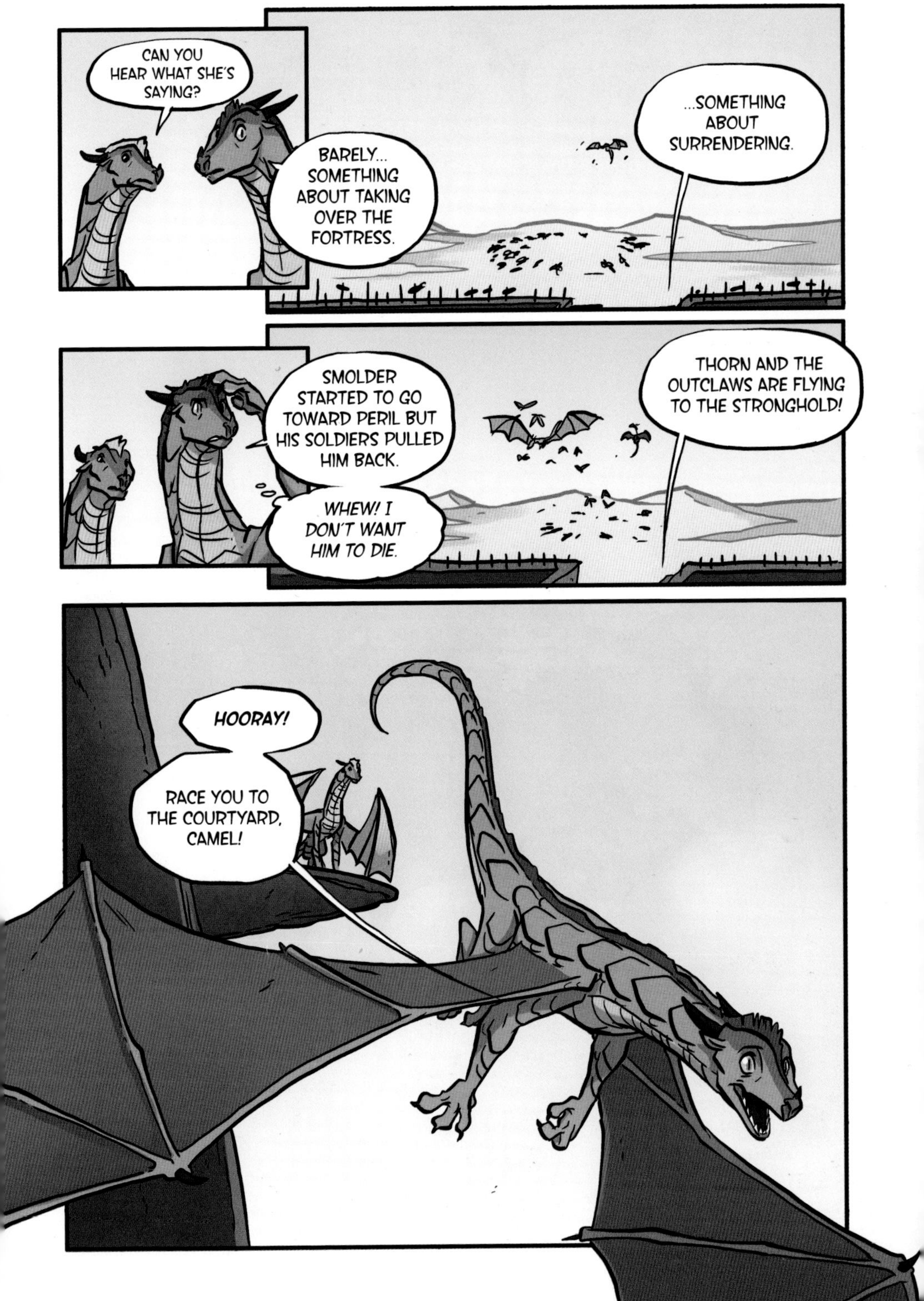
CAN YOU HEAR WHAT SHE'S SAYING?
BARELY... SOMETHING ABOUT TAKING OVER THE FORTRESS.
...SOMETHING ABOUT SURRENDERING.
SMOLDER STARTED TO GO TOWARD PERIL BUT HIS SOLDIERS PULLED HIM BACK.
WHEW! I DON'T WANT HIM TO DIE.
THORN AND THE OUTCLAWS ARE FLYING TO THE STRONGHOLD!
HOORAY!
RACE YOU TO THE COURTYARD, CAMEL!

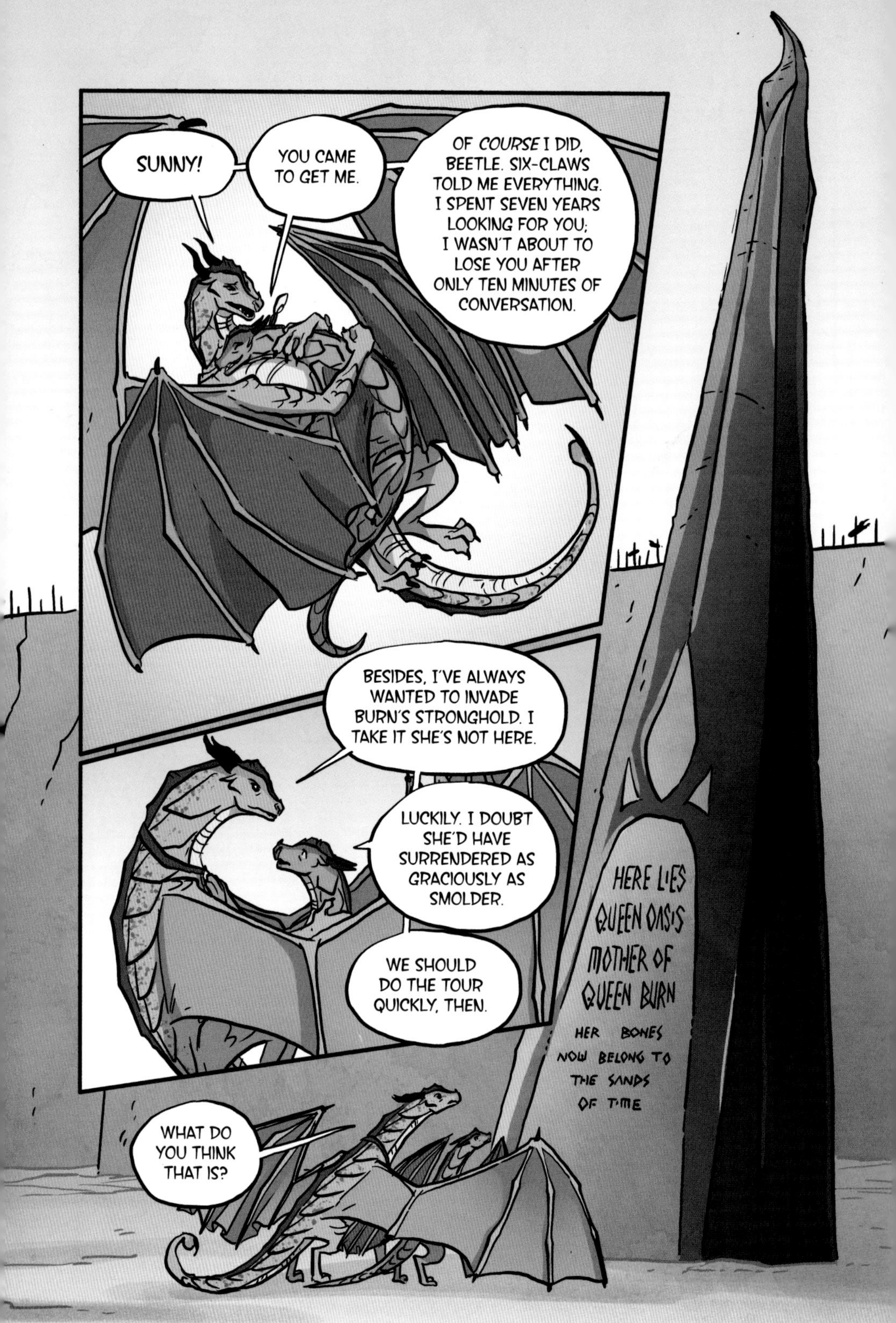
SUNNY!
YOU CAME TO GET ME.
OF *COURSE* I DID, BEETLE. SIX-CLAWS TOLD ME EVERYTHING. I SPENT SEVEN YEARS LOOKING FOR YOU; I WASN'T ABOUT TO LOSE YOU AFTER ONLY TEN MINUTES OF CONVERSATION.
BESIDES, I'VE ALWAYS WANTED TO INVADE BURN'S STRONGHOLD. I TAKE IT SHE'S NOT HERE.
LUCKILY. I DOUBT SHE'D HAVE SURRENDERED AS GRACIOUSLY AS SMOLDER.
WE SHOULD DO THE TOUR QUICKLY, THEN.
HERE LIES QUEEN OASIS MOTHER OF QUEEN BURN
HER BONES NOW BELONG TO THE SANDS OF TIME
WHAT DO YOU THINK THAT IS?

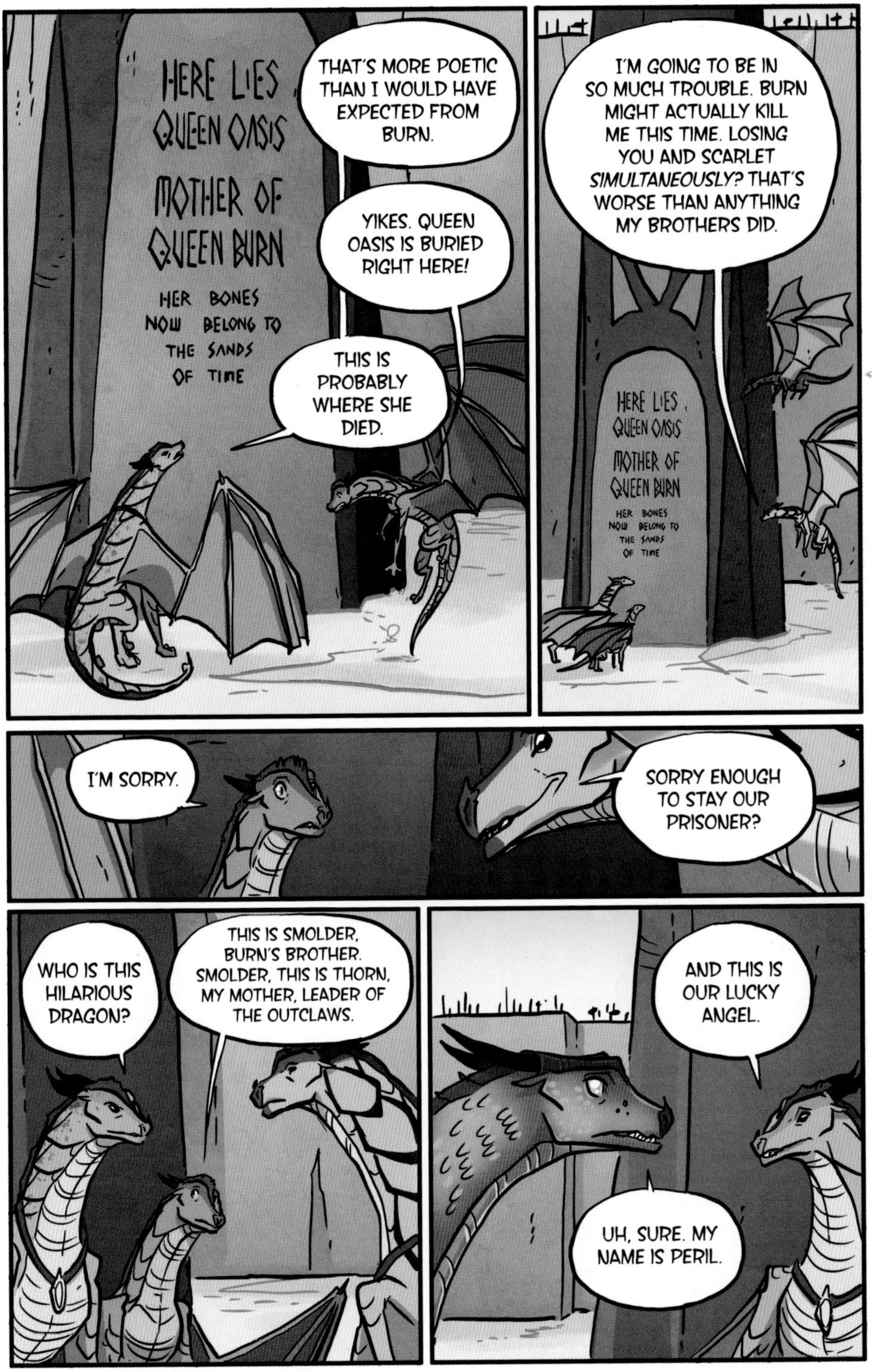
HERE LIES QUEEN OASIS
MOTHER OF QUEEN BURN
HER BONES NOW BELONG TO THE SANDS OF TIME
THAT'S MORE POETIC THAN I WOULD HAVE EXPECTED FROM BURN.
YIKES. QUEEN OASIS IS BURIED RIGHT HERE!
THIS IS PROBABLY WHERE SHE DIED.
I'M GOING TO BE IN SO MUCH TROUBLE. BURN MIGHT ACTUALLY KILL ME THIS TIME. LOSING YOU AND SCARLET *SIMULTANEOUSLY*? THAT'S WORSE THAN ANYTHING MY BROTHERS DID.
HERE LIES QUEEN OASIS
MOTHER OF QUEEN BURN
HER BONES NOW BELONG TO THE SANDS OF TIME
I'M SORRY.
SORRY ENOUGH TO STAY OUR PRISONER?
WHO IS THIS HILARIOUS DRAGON?
THIS IS SMOLDER, BURN'S BROTHER. SMOLDER, THIS IS THORN, MY MOTHER, LEADER OF THE OUTCLAWS.
AND THIS IS OUR LUCKY ANGEL.
UH, SURE. MY NAME IS PERIL.

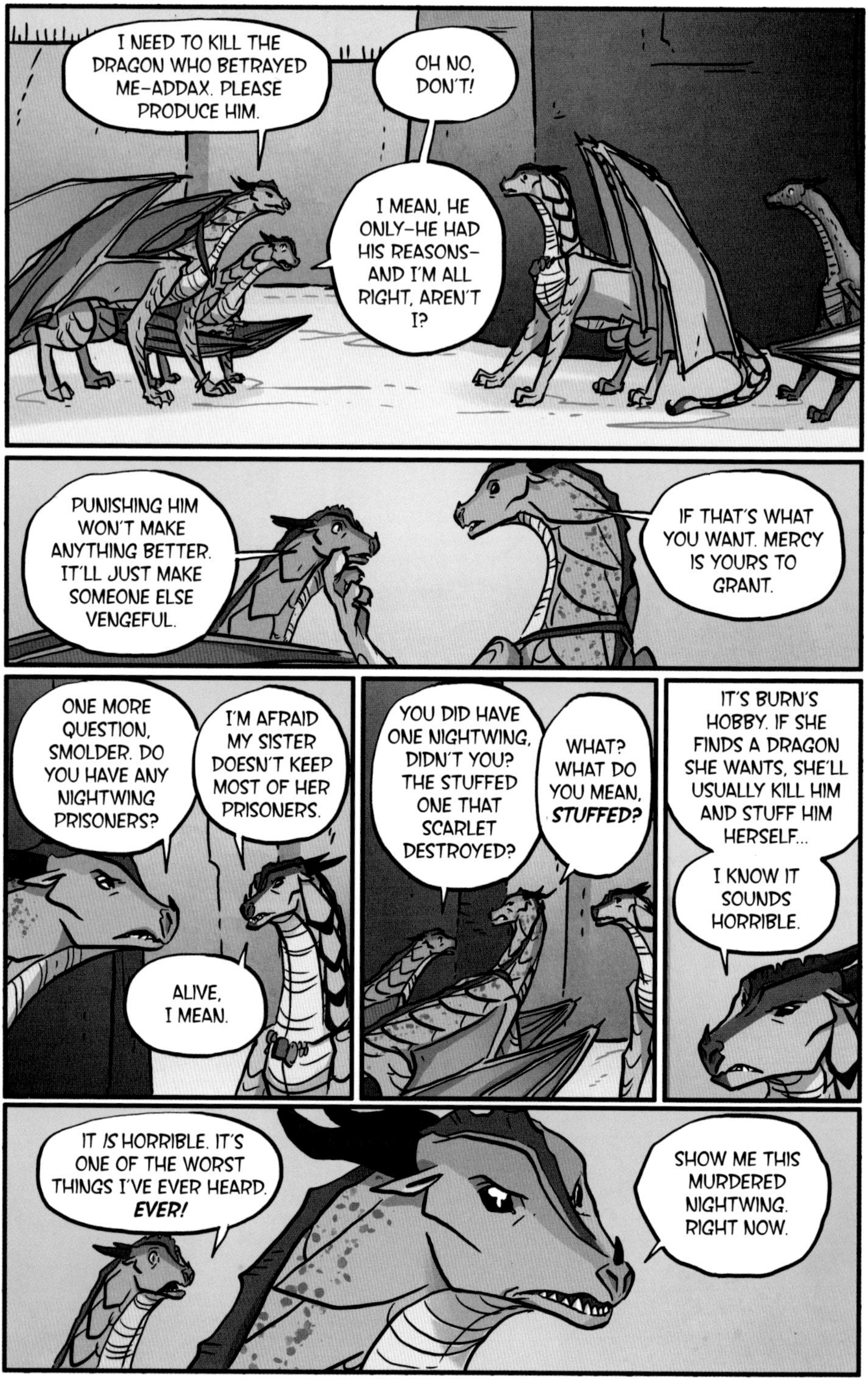
I NEED TO KILL THE DRAGON WHO BETRAYED ME—ADDAX. PLEASE PRODUCE HIM.
OH NO, DON'T!
I MEAN, HE ONLY—HE HAD HIS REASONS—AND I'M ALL RIGHT, AREN'T I?
PUNISHING HIM WON'T MAKE ANYTHING BETTER. IT'LL JUST MAKE SOMEONE ELSE VENGEFUL.
IF THAT'S WHAT YOU WANT. MERCY IS YOURS TO GRANT.
ONE MORE QUESTION, SMOLDER. DO YOU HAVE ANY NIGHTWING PRISONERS?
I'M AFRAID MY SISTER DOESN'T KEEP MOST OF HER PRISONERS.
ALIVE, I MEAN.
YOU DID HAVE ONE NIGHTWING, DIDN'T YOU? THE STUFFED ONE THAT SCARLET DESTROYED?
WHAT? WHAT DO YOU MEAN, ***STUFFED?***
IT'S BURN'S HOBBY. IF SHE FINDS A DRAGON SHE WANTS, SHE'LL USUALLY KILL HIM AND STUFF HIM HERSELF...
I KNOW IT SOUNDS HORRIBLE.
IT *IS* HORRIBLE. IT'S ONE OF THE WORST THINGS I'VE EVER HEARD. ***EVER!***
SHOW ME THIS MURDERED NIGHTWING. RIGHT NOW.

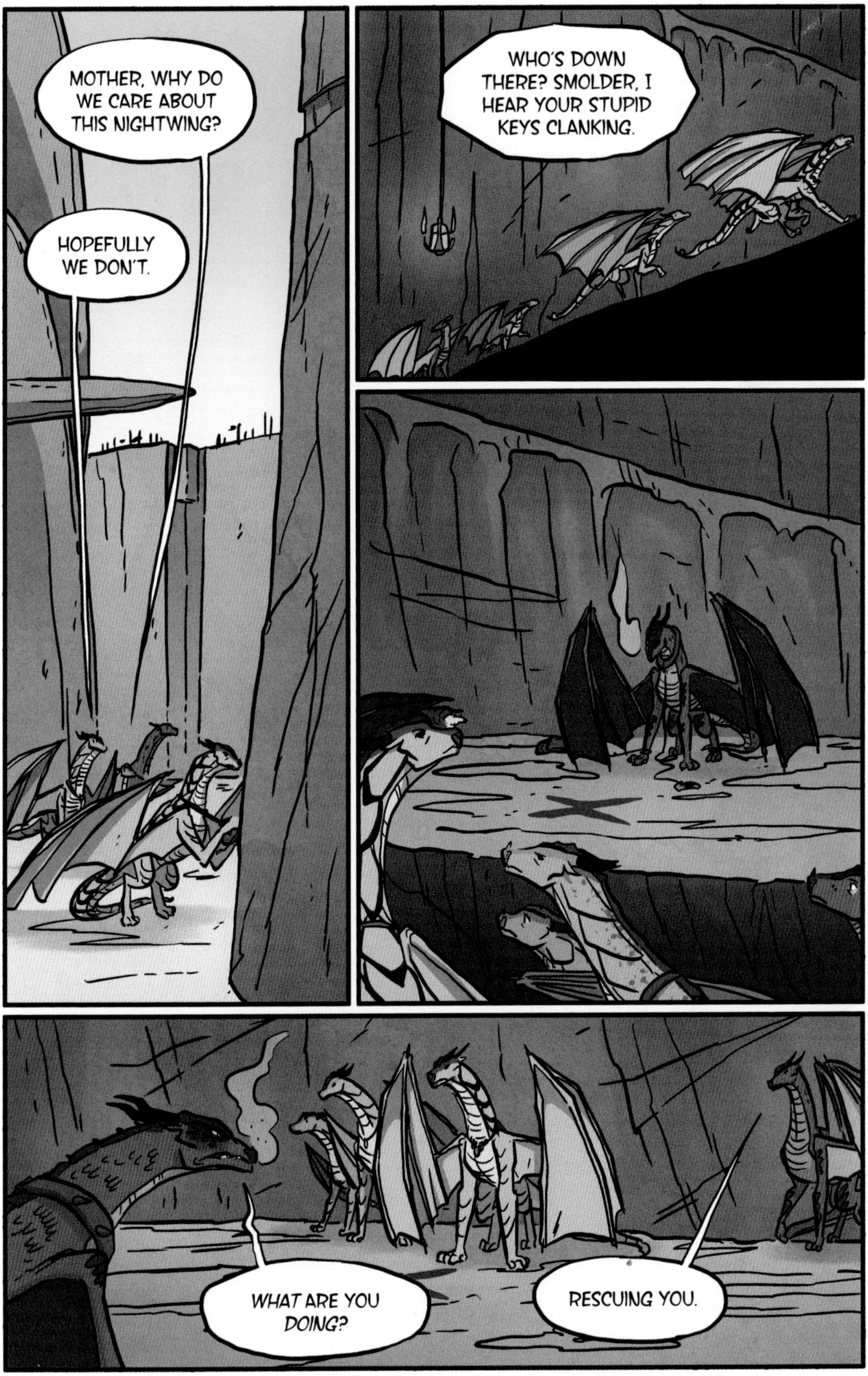
MOTHER, WHY DO WE CARE ABOUT THIS NIGHTWING?
HOPEFULLY WE DON'T.
WHO'S DOWN THERE? SMOLDER, I HEAR YOUR STUPID KEYS CLANKING.
WHAT ARE YOU DOING?
RESCUING YOU.

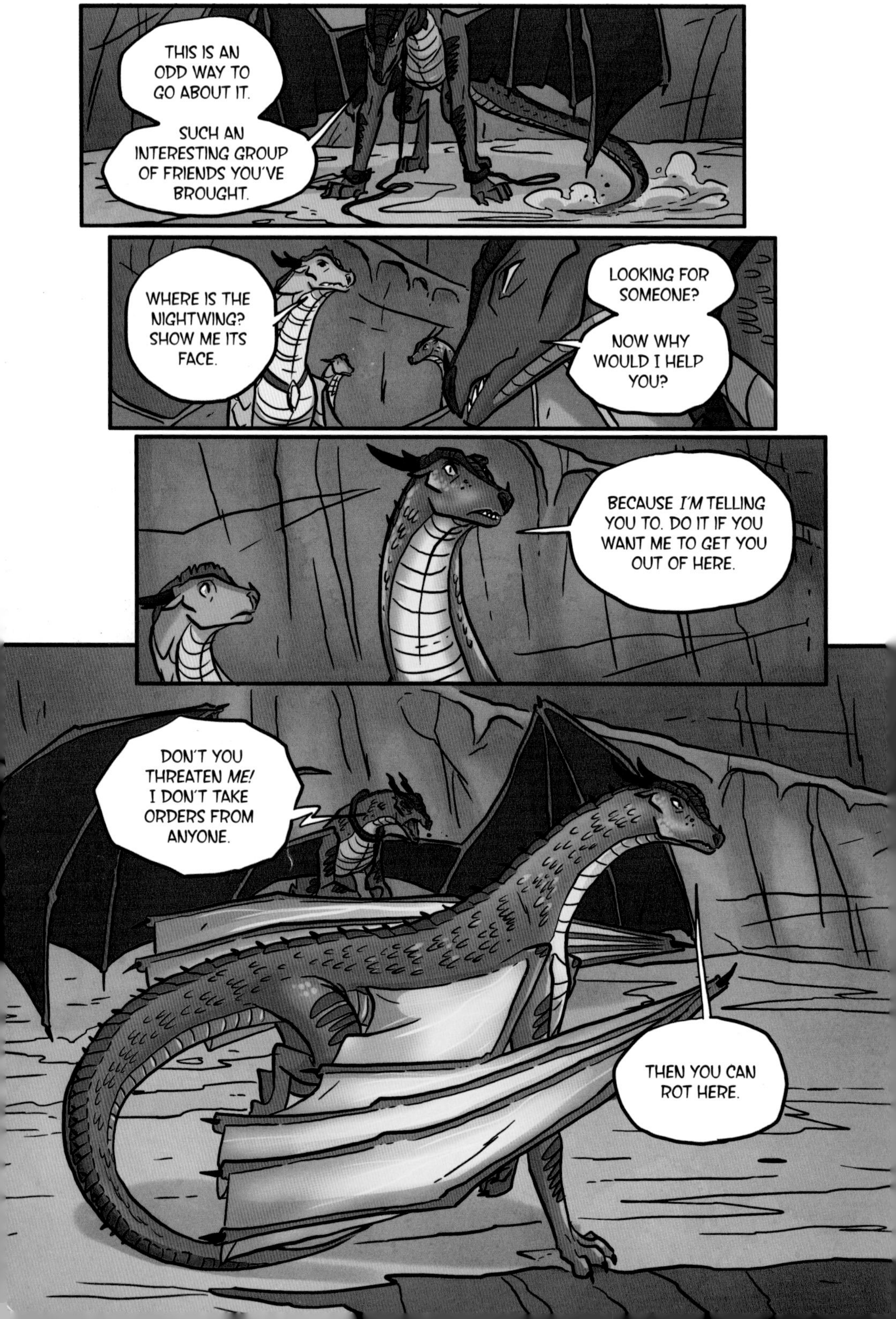
THIS IS AN ODD WAY TO GO ABOUT IT.
SUCH AN INTERESTING GROUP OF FRIENDS YOU'VE BROUGHT.
WHERE IS THE NIGHTWING? SHOW ME ITS FACE.
LOOKING FOR SOMEONE?
NOW WHY WOULD I HELP YOU?
BECAUSE *I'M* TELLING YOU TO. DO IT IF YOU WANT ME TO GET YOU OUT OF HERE.
DON'T YOU THREATEN *ME!* I DON'T TAKE ORDERS FROM ANYONE.
THEN YOU CAN ROT HERE.

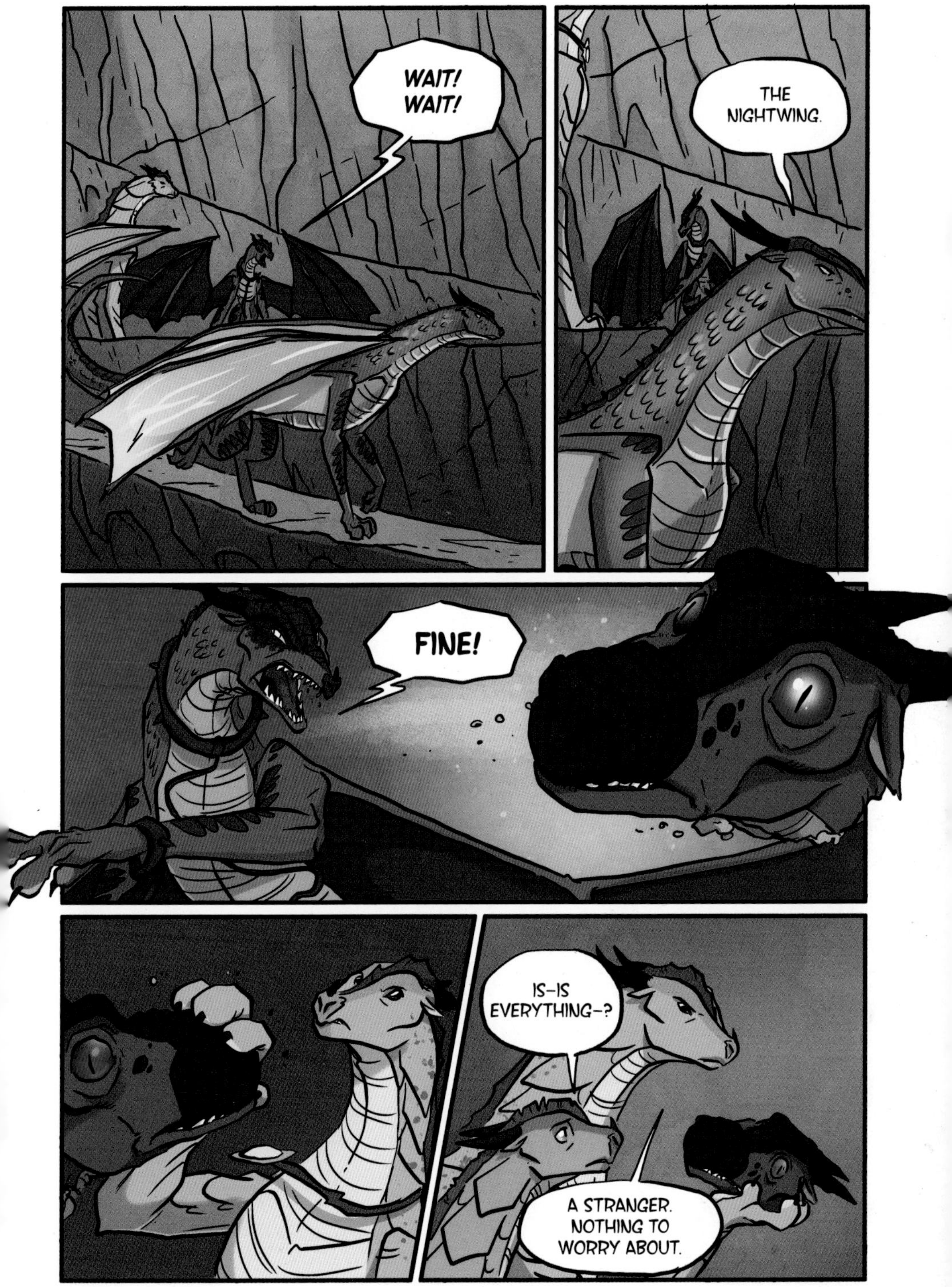
WAIT! WAIT!
THE NIGHTWING.
FINE!
IS—IS EVERYTHING—?
A STRANGER. NOTHING TO WORRY ABOUT.

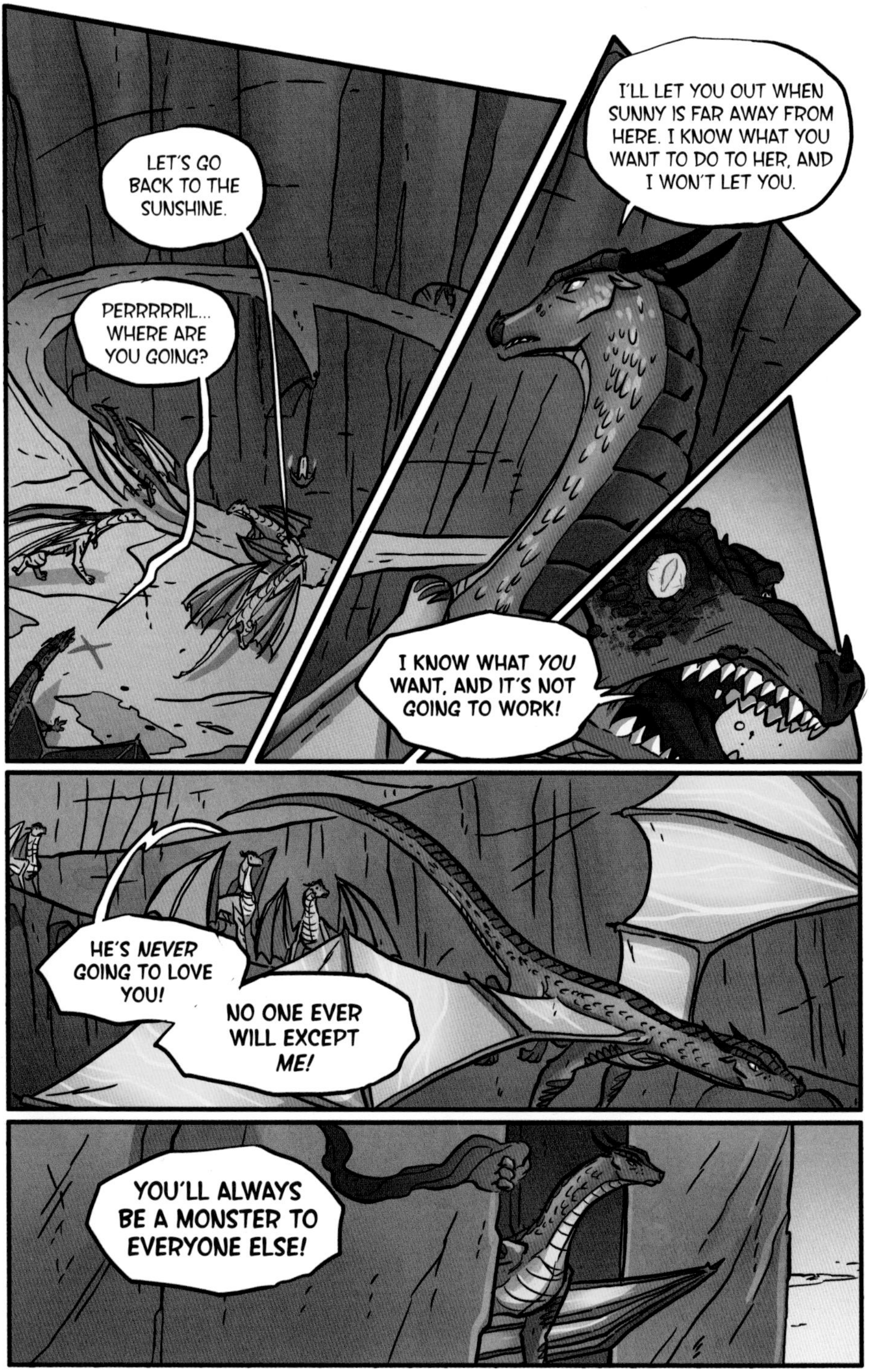
LET'S GO BACK TO THE SUNSHINE.
PERRRRRIL... WHERE ARE YOU GOING?
I'LL LET YOU OUT WHEN SUNNY IS FAR AWAY FROM HERE. I KNOW WHAT YOU WANT TO DO TO HER, AND I WON'T LET YOU.
I KNOW WHAT *YOU* WANT, AND IT'S NOT GOING TO WORK!
HE'S *NEVER* GOING TO LOVE YOU!
NO ONE EVER WILL EXCEPT *ME!*
YOU'LL ALWAYS BE A MONSTER TO EVERYONE ELSE!

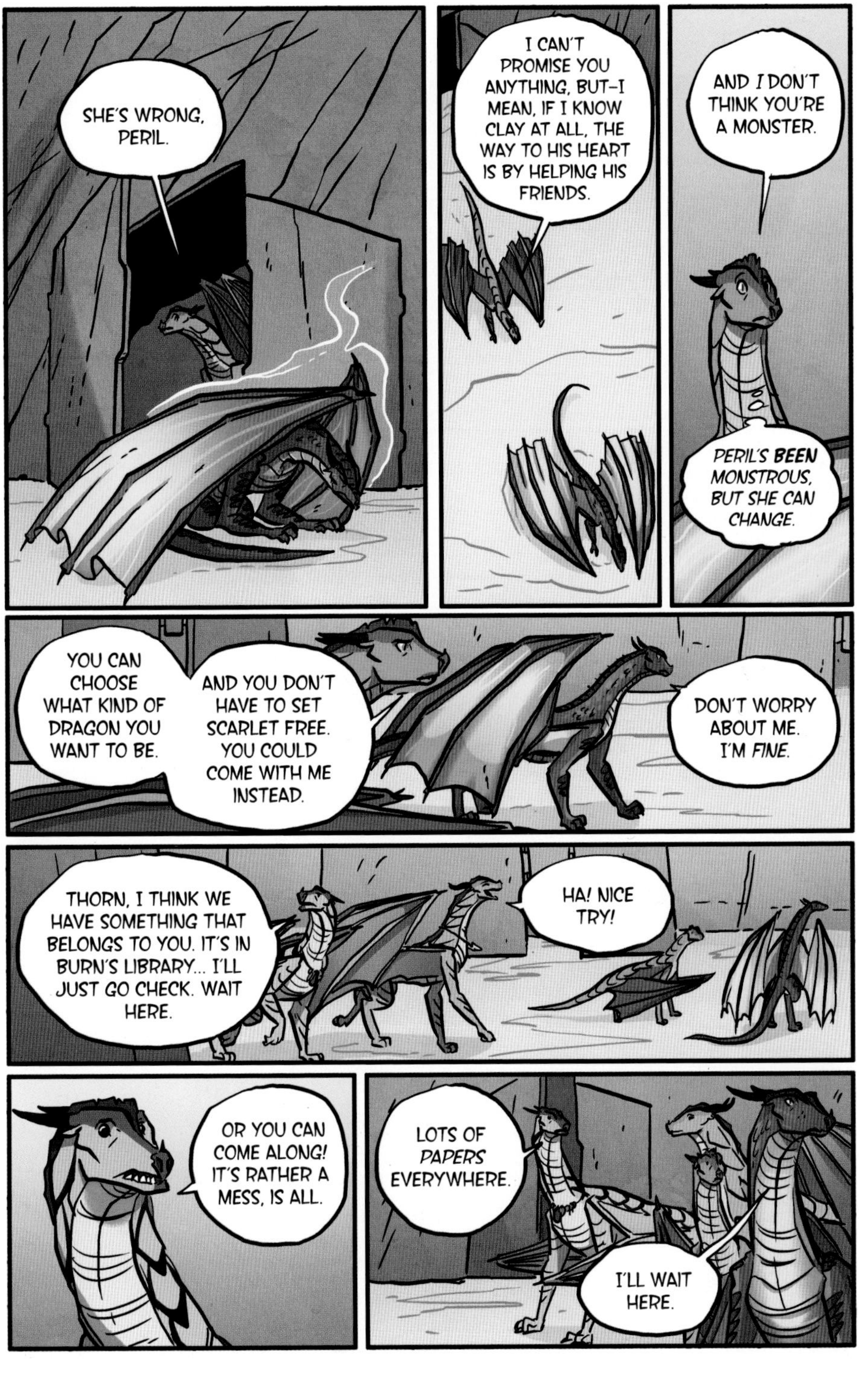
SHE'S WRONG, PERIL.
I CAN'T PROMISE YOU ANYTHING, BUT–I MEAN, IF I KNOW CLAY AT ALL, THE WAY TO HIS HEART IS BY HELPING HIS FRIENDS.
AND *I* DON'T THINK YOU'RE A MONSTER.
PERIL'S ***BEEN*** *MONSTROUS, BUT SHE CAN CHANGE.*
YOU CAN CHOOSE WHAT KIND OF DRAGON YOU WANT TO BE.
AND YOU DON'T HAVE TO SET SCARLET FREE. YOU COULD COME WITH ME INSTEAD.
DON'T WORRY ABOUT ME. I'M *FINE*.
THORN, I THINK WE HAVE SOMETHING THAT BELONGS TO YOU. IT'S IN BURN'S LIBRARY... I'LL JUST GO CHECK. WAIT HERE.
HA! NICE TRY!
OR YOU CAN COME ALONG! IT'S RATHER A MESS, IS ALL.
LOTS OF *PAPERS* EVERYWHERE.
I'LL WAIT HERE.

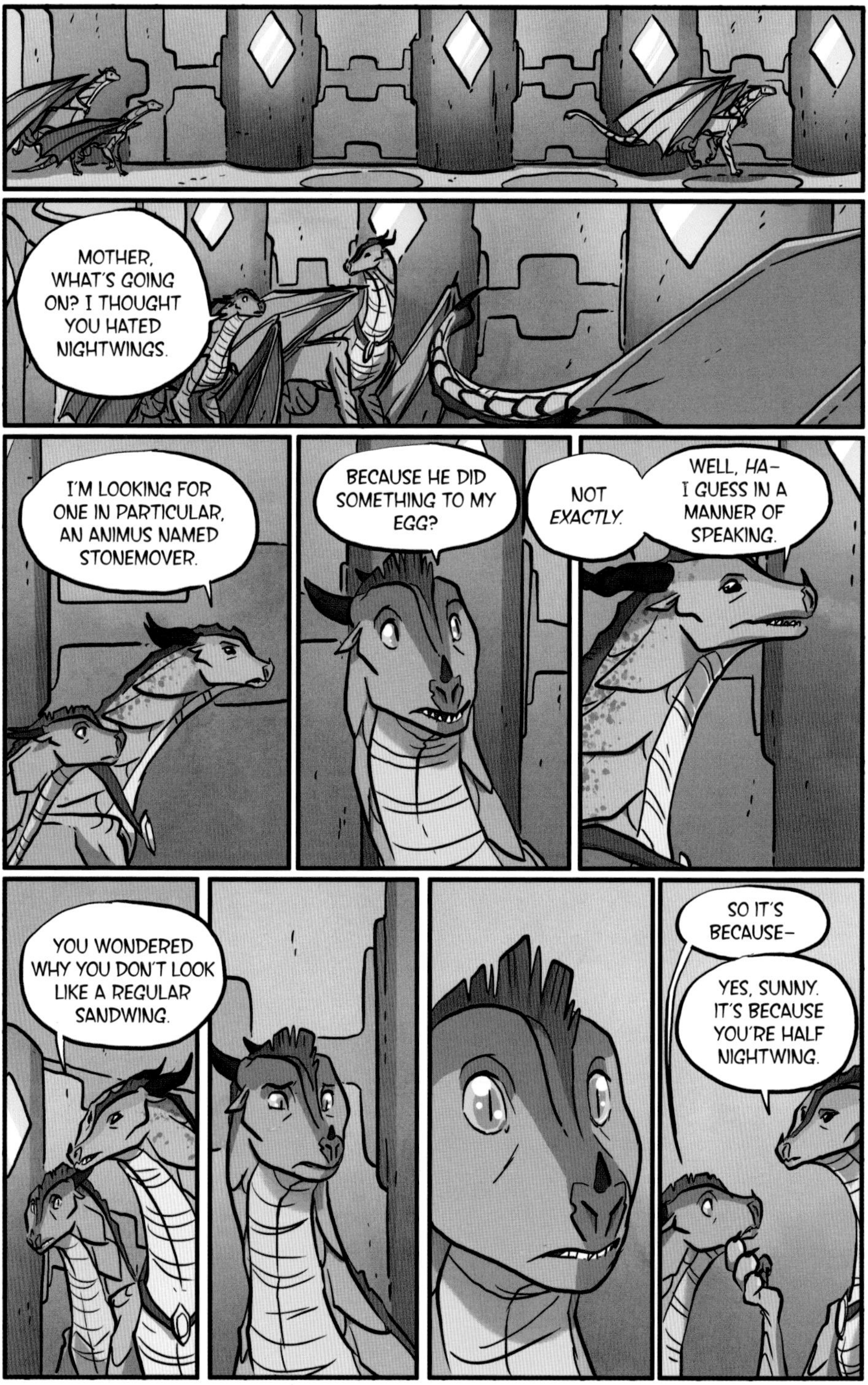
MOTHER, WHAT'S GOING ON? I THOUGHT YOU HATED NIGHTWINGS.
I'M LOOKING FOR ONE IN PARTICULAR, AN ANIMUS NAMED STONEMOVER.
BECAUSE HE DID SOMETHING TO MY EGG?
NOT *EXACTLY.*
WELL, *HA*- I GUESS IN A MANNER OF SPEAKING.
YOU WONDERED WHY YOU DON'T LOOK LIKE A REGULAR SANDWING.
SO IT'S BECAUSE-
YES, SUNNY. IT'S BECAUSE YOU'RE HALF NIGHTWING.

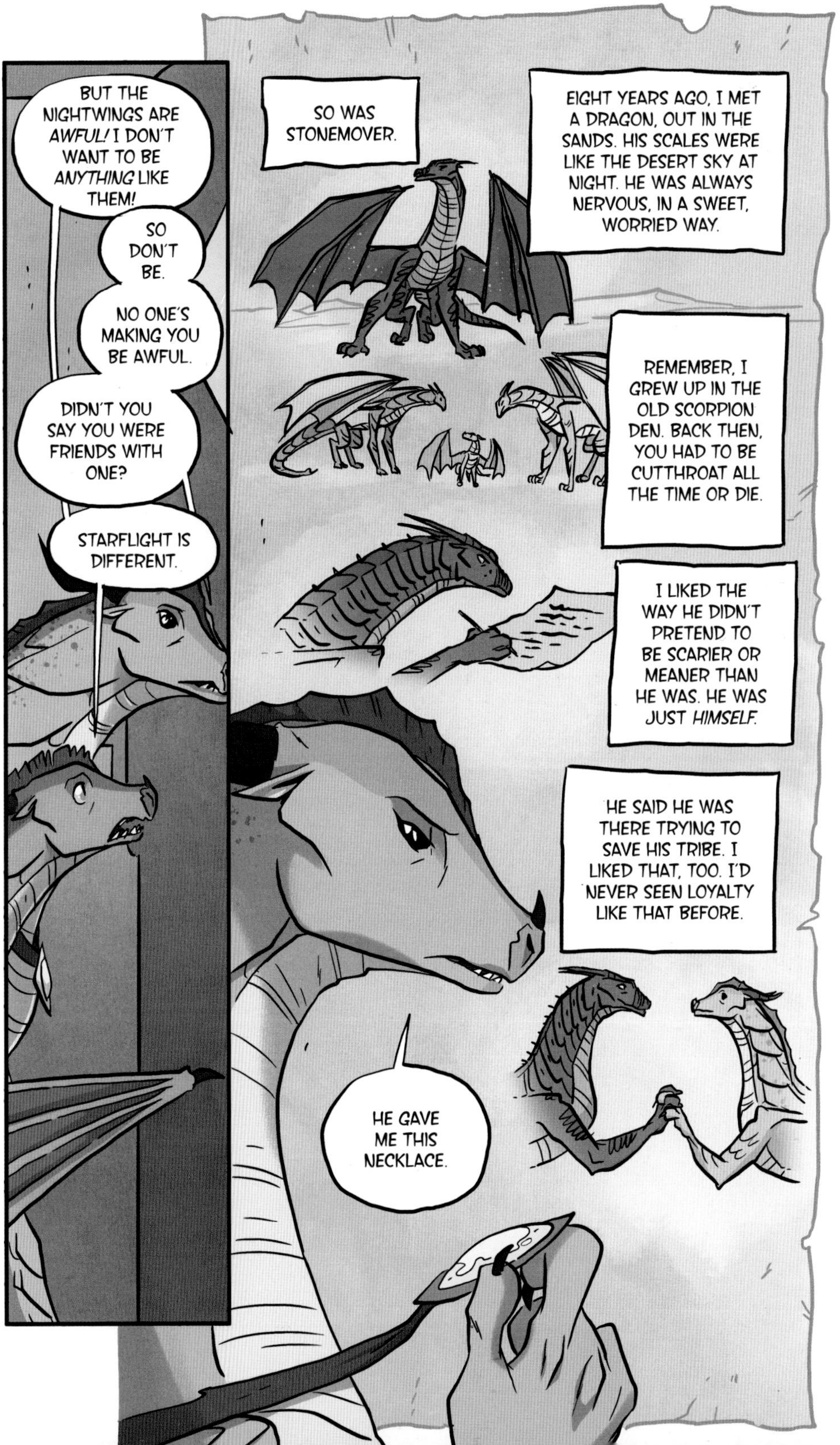

BUT THE NIGHTWINGS ARE *AWFUL!* I DON'T WANT TO BE *ANYTHING* LIKE THEM!
SO DON'T BE.
NO ONE'S MAKING YOU BE AWFUL.
DIDN'T YOU SAY YOU WERE FRIENDS WITH ONE?
STARFLIGHT IS DIFFERENT.
SO WAS STONEMOVER.
EIGHT YEARS AGO, I MET A DRAGON, OUT IN THE SANDS. HIS SCALES WERE LIKE THE DESERT SKY AT NIGHT. HE WAS ALWAYS NERVOUS, IN A SWEET, WORRIED WAY.
REMEMBER, I GREW UP IN THE OLD SCORPION DEN. BACK THEN, YOU HAD TO BE CUTTHROAT ALL THE TIME OR DIE.
I LIKED THE WAY HE DIDN'T PRETEND TO BE SCARIER OR MEANER THAN HE WAS. HE WAS JUST *HIMSELF.*
HE SAID HE WAS THERE TRYING TO SAVE HIS TRIBE. I LIKED THAT, TOO. I'D NEVER SEEN LOYALTY LIKE THAT BEFORE.
HE GAVE ME THIS NECKLACE.

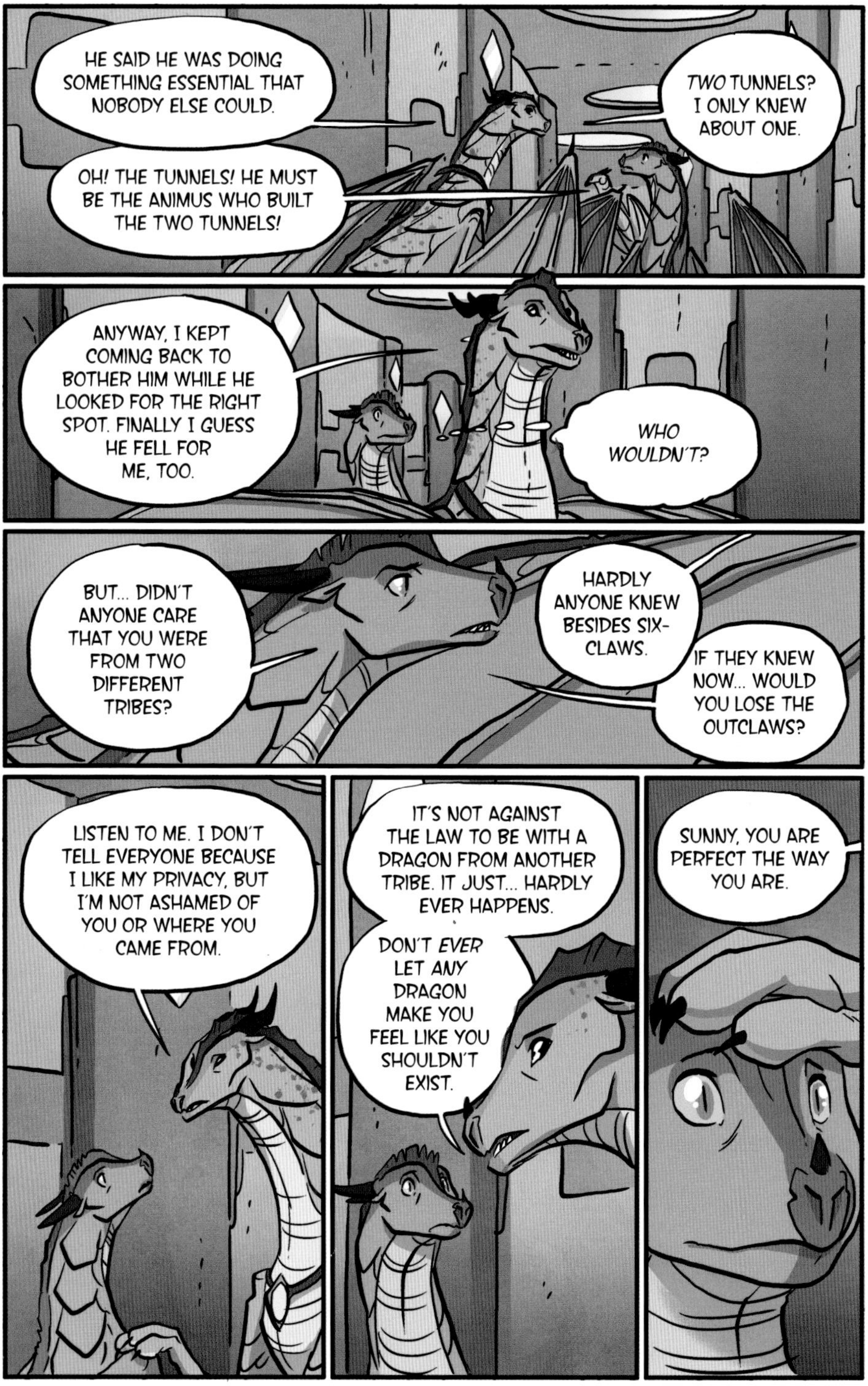
HE SAID HE WAS DOING SOMETHING ESSENTIAL THAT NOBODY ELSE COULD.
OH! THE TUNNELS! HE MUST BE THE ANIMUS WHO BUILT THE TWO TUNNELS!
TWO TUNNELS? I ONLY KNEW ABOUT ONE.
ANYWAY, I KEPT COMING BACK TO BOTHER HIM WHILE HE LOOKED FOR THE RIGHT SPOT. FINALLY I GUESS HE FELL FOR ME, TOO.
WHO WOULDN'T?
BUT... DIDN'T ANYONE CARE THAT YOU WERE FROM TWO DIFFERENT TRIBES?
HARDLY ANYONE KNEW BESIDES SIX-CLAWS.
IF THEY KNEW NOW... WOULD YOU LOSE THE OUTCLAWS?
LISTEN TO ME. I DON'T TELL EVERYONE BECAUSE I LIKE MY PRIVACY, BUT I'M NOT ASHAMED OF YOU OR WHERE YOU CAME FROM.
IT'S NOT AGAINST THE LAW TO BE WITH A DRAGON FROM ANOTHER TRIBE. IT JUST... HARDLY EVER HAPPENS.
DON'T EVER LET ANY DRAGON MAKE YOU FEEL LIKE YOU SHOULDN'T EXIST.
SUNNY, YOU ARE PERFECT THE WAY YOU ARE.

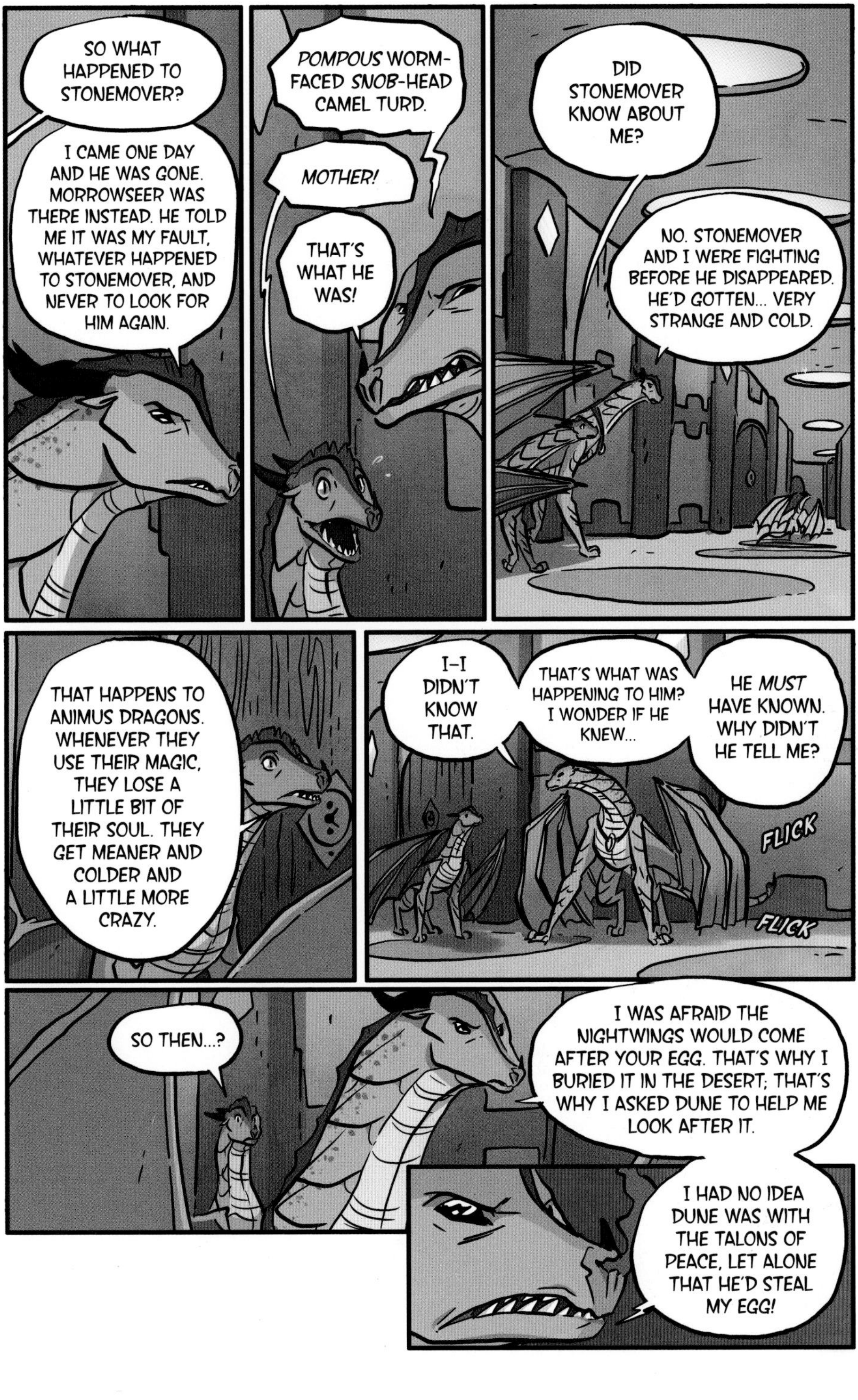
SO WHAT HAPPENED TO STONEMOVER?
I CAME ONE DAY AND HE WAS GONE. MORROWSEER WAS THERE INSTEAD. HE TOLD ME IT WAS MY FAULT, WHATEVER HAPPENED TO STONEMOVER, AND NEVER TO LOOK FOR HIM AGAIN.
POMPOUS WORM-FACED *SNOB*-HEAD CAMEL TURD.
MOTHER!
THAT'S WHAT HE WAS!
DID STONEMOVER KNOW ABOUT ME?
NO. STONEMOVER AND I WERE FIGHTING BEFORE HE DISAPPEARED. HE'D GOTTEN... VERY STRANGE AND COLD.
THAT HAPPENS TO ANIMUS DRAGONS. WHENEVER THEY USE THEIR MAGIC, THEY LOSE A LITTLE BIT OF THEIR SOUL. THEY GET MEANER AND COLDER AND A LITTLE MORE CRAZY.
I–I DIDN'T KNOW THAT.
THAT'S WHAT WAS HAPPENING TO HIM? I WONDER IF HE KNEW...
HE *MUST* HAVE KNOWN. WHY DIDN'T HE TELL ME?
FLICK
FLICK
SO THEN...?
I WAS AFRAID THE NIGHTWINGS WOULD COME AFTER YOUR EGG. THAT'S WHY I BURIED IT IN THE DESERT; THAT'S WHY I ASKED DUNE TO HELP ME LOOK AFTER IT.
I HAD NO IDEA DUNE WAS WITH THE TALONS OF PEACE, LET ALONE THAT HE'D STEAL MY EGG!

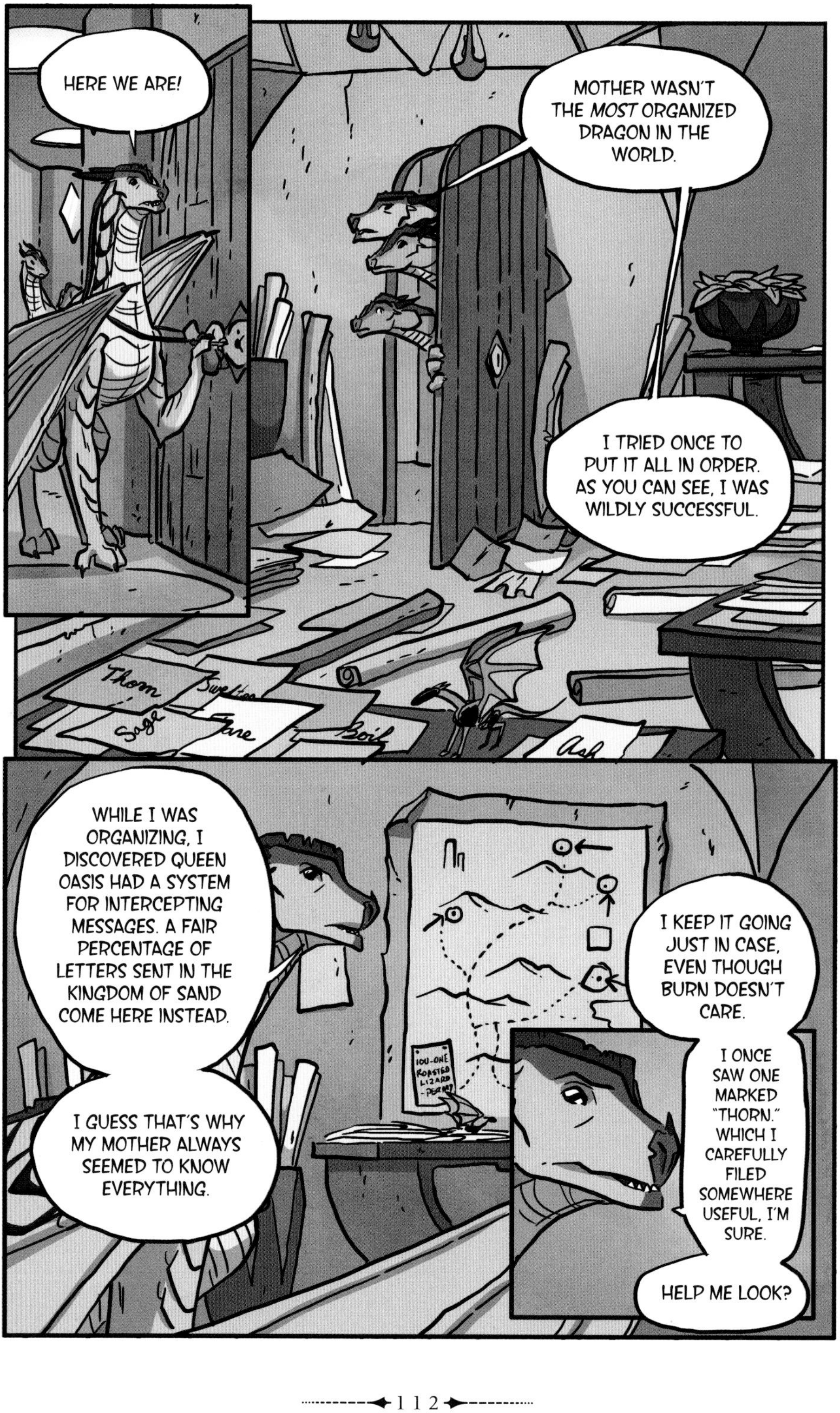
HERE WE ARE!
MOTHER WASN'T THE *MOST* ORGANIZED DRAGON IN THE WORLD.
I TRIED ONCE TO PUT IT ALL IN ORDER. AS YOU CAN SEE, I WAS WILDLY SUCCESSFUL.
Thorn
Sage
Boil
Ash
WHILE I WAS ORGANIZING, I DISCOVERED QUEEN OASIS HAD A SYSTEM FOR INTERCEPTING MESSAGES. A FAIR PERCENTAGE OF LETTERS SENT IN THE KINGDOM OF SAND COME HERE INSTEAD.
I GUESS THAT'S WHY MY MOTHER ALWAYS SEEMED TO KNOW EVERYTHING.
I KEEP IT GOING JUST IN CASE, EVEN THOUGH BURN DOESN'T CARE.
I ONCE SAW ONE MARKED "THORN." WHICH I CAREFULLY FILED SOMEWHERE USEFUL, I'M SURE.
HELP ME LOOK?

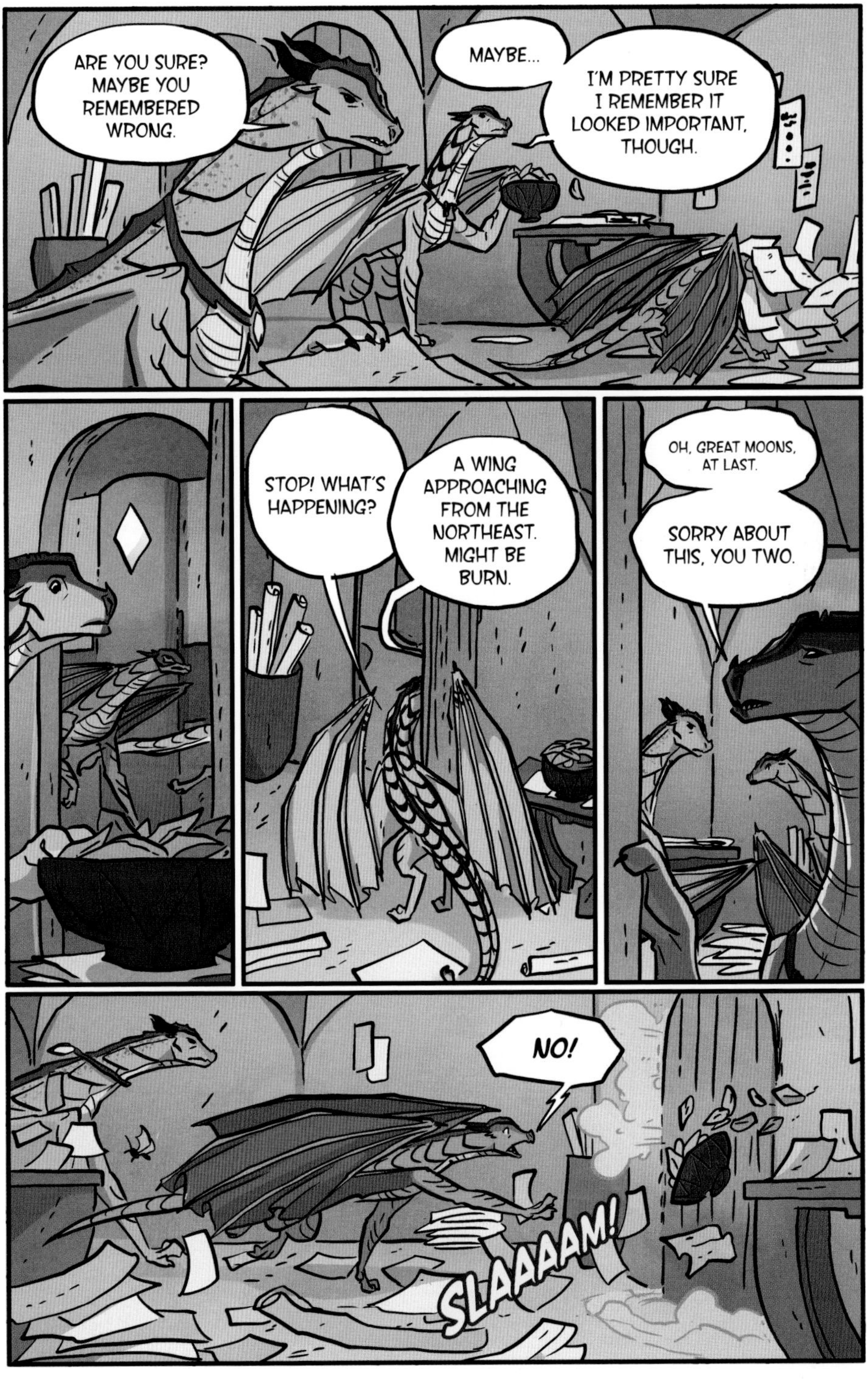
ARE YOU SURE? MAYBE YOU REMEMBERED WRONG.
MAYBE...
I'M PRETTY SURE I REMEMBER IT LOOKED IMPORTANT, THOUGH.
STOP! WHAT'S HAPPENING?
A WING APPROACHING FROM THE NORTHEAST. MIGHT BE BURN.
OH, GREAT MOONS, AT LAST.
SORRY ABOUT THIS, YOU TWO.
NO!
SLAAAAM!

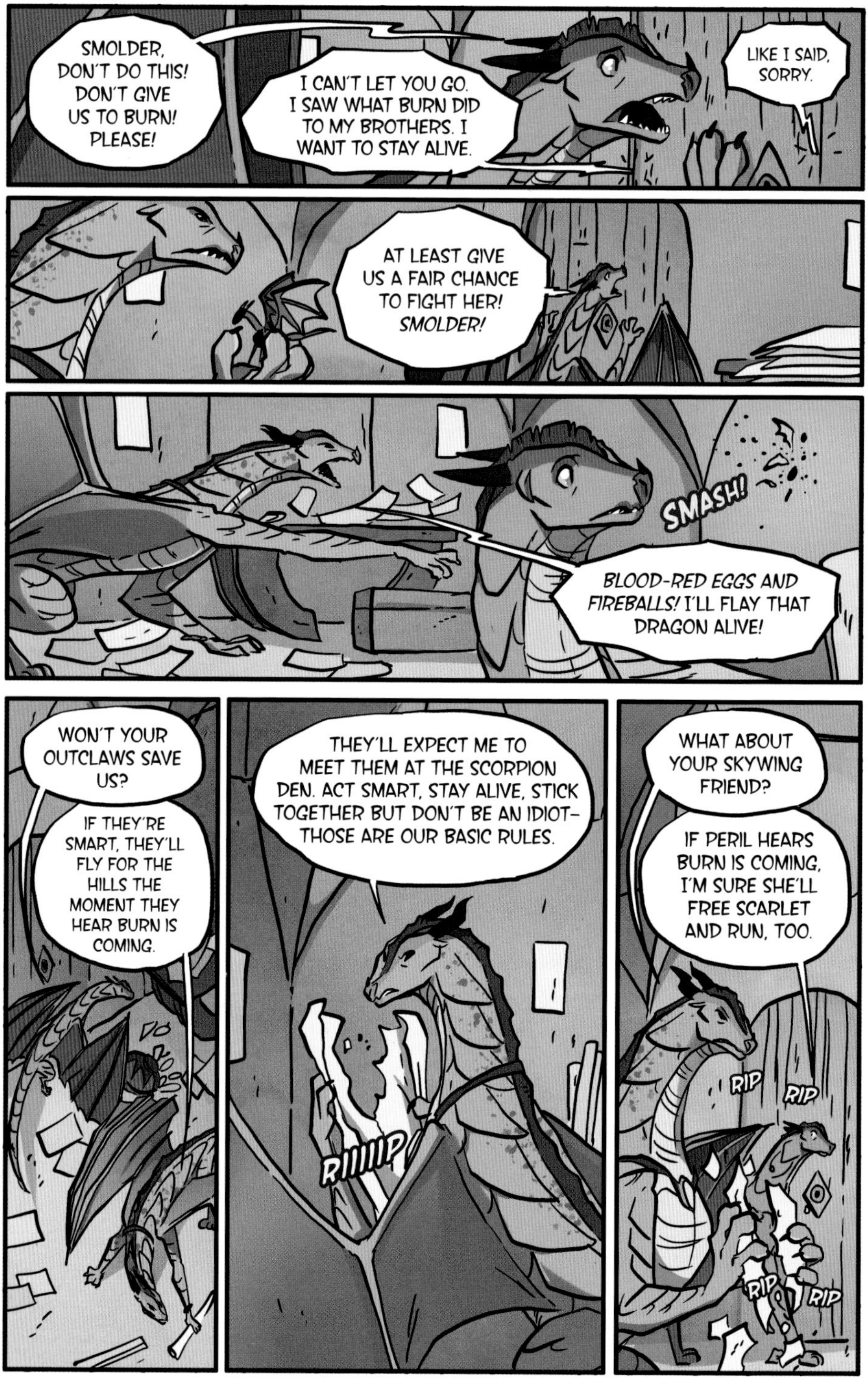
SMOLDER, DON'T DO THIS! DON'T GIVE US TO BURN! PLEASE!
I CAN'T LET YOU GO. I SAW WHAT BURN DID TO MY BROTHERS. I WANT TO STAY ALIVE.
LIKE I SAID, SORRY.
AT LEAST GIVE US A FAIR CHANCE TO FIGHT HER! SMOLDER!
SMASH!
BLOOD-RED EGGS AND FIREBALLS! I'LL FLAY THAT DRAGON ALIVE!
WON'T YOUR OUTCLAWS SAVE US?
IF THEY'RE SMART, THEY'LL FLY FOR THE HILLS THE MOMENT THEY HEAR BURN IS COMING.
THEY'LL EXPECT ME TO MEET THEM AT THE SCORPION DEN. ACT SMART, STAY ALIVE, STICK TOGETHER BUT DON'T BE AN IDIOT–THOSE ARE OUR BASIC RULES.
RIIIIIP
WHAT ABOUT YOUR SKYWING FRIEND?
IF PERIL HEARS BURN IS COMING, I'M SURE SHE'LL FREE SCARLET AND RUN, TOO.
RIP
RIP
RIP
RIP

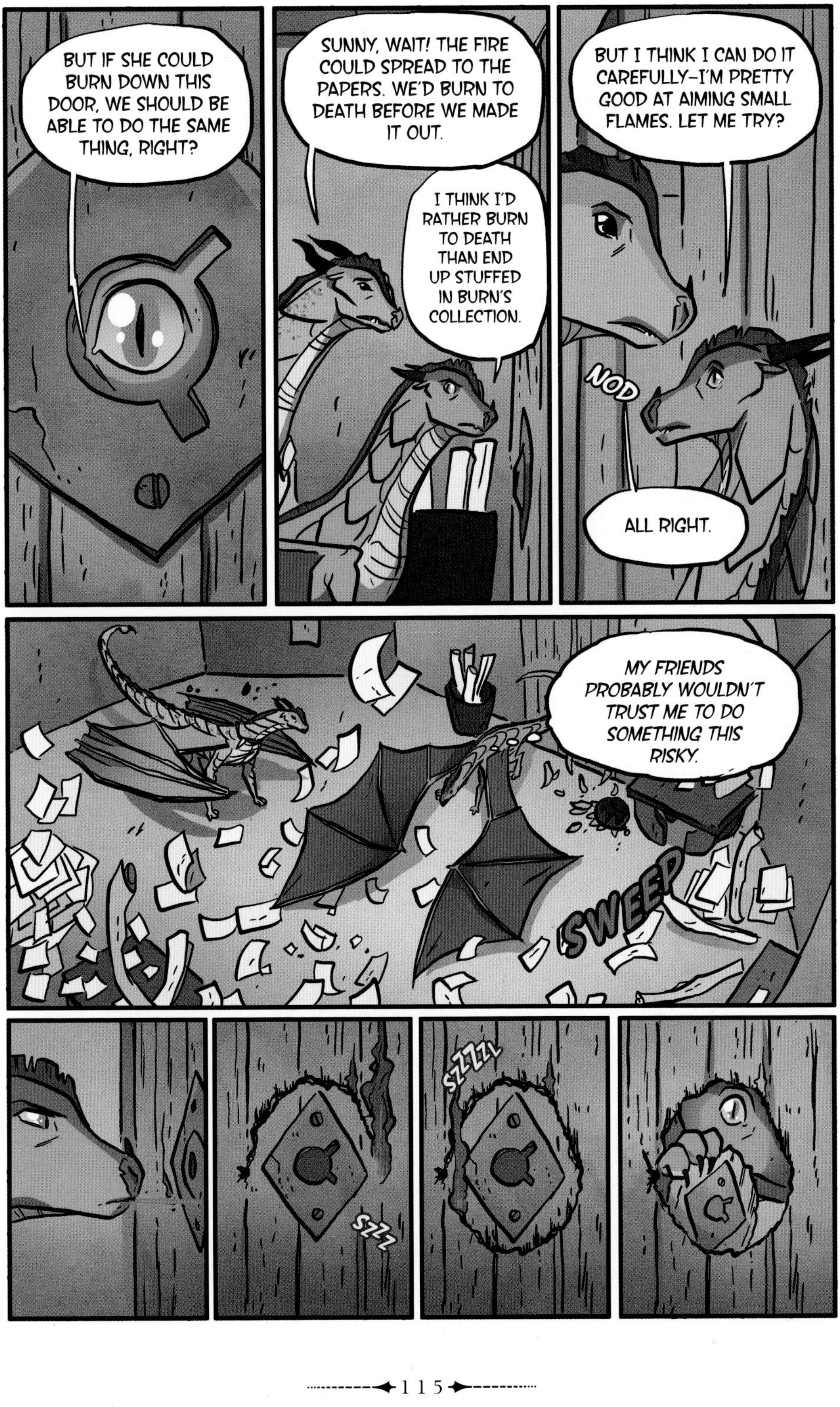
BUT IF SHE COULD BURN DOWN THIS DOOR, WE SHOULD BE ABLE TO DO THE SAME THING, RIGHT?
SUNNY, WAIT! THE FIRE COULD SPREAD TO THE PAPERS. WE'D BURN TO DEATH BEFORE WE MADE IT OUT.
I THINK I'D RATHER BURN TO DEATH THAN END UP STUFFED IN BURN'S COLLECTION.
BUT I THINK I CAN DO IT CAREFULLY–I'M PRETTY GOOD AT AIMING SMALL FLAMES. LET ME TRY?
NOD
ALL RIGHT.
MY FRIENDS PROBABLY WOULDN'T TRUST ME TO DO SOMETHING THIS RISKY.
SWEEP
SZZZ
SZZZZL

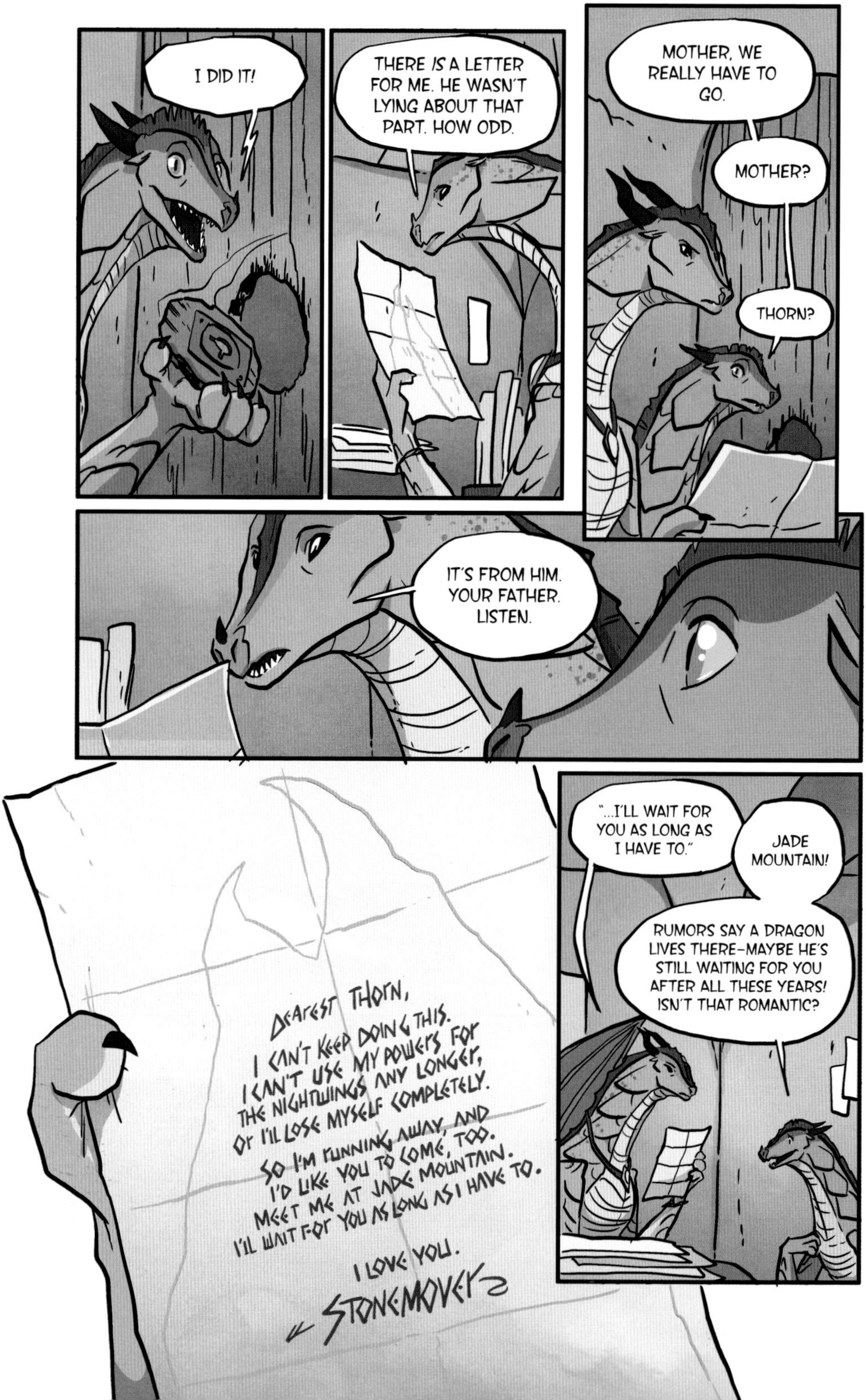
I DID IT!
THERE IS A LETTER FOR ME. HE WASN'T LYING ABOUT THAT PART. HOW ODD.
MOTHER, WE REALLY HAVE TO GO.
MOTHER?
THORN?
IT'S FROM HIM. YOUR FATHER. LISTEN.
Dearest Thorn,
I can't keep doing this. I can't use my powers for the NightWings any longer, or I'll lose myself completely.
So I'm running away, and I'd like you to come, too. Meet me at Jade Mountain. I'll wait for you as long as I have to.
I love you.
StoneMover
"...I'LL WAIT FOR YOU AS LONG AS I HAVE TO."
JADE MOUNTAIN!
RUMORS SAY A DRAGON LIVES THERE—MAYBE HE'S STILL WAITING FOR YOU AFTER ALL THESE YEARS! ISN'T THAT ROMANTIC?

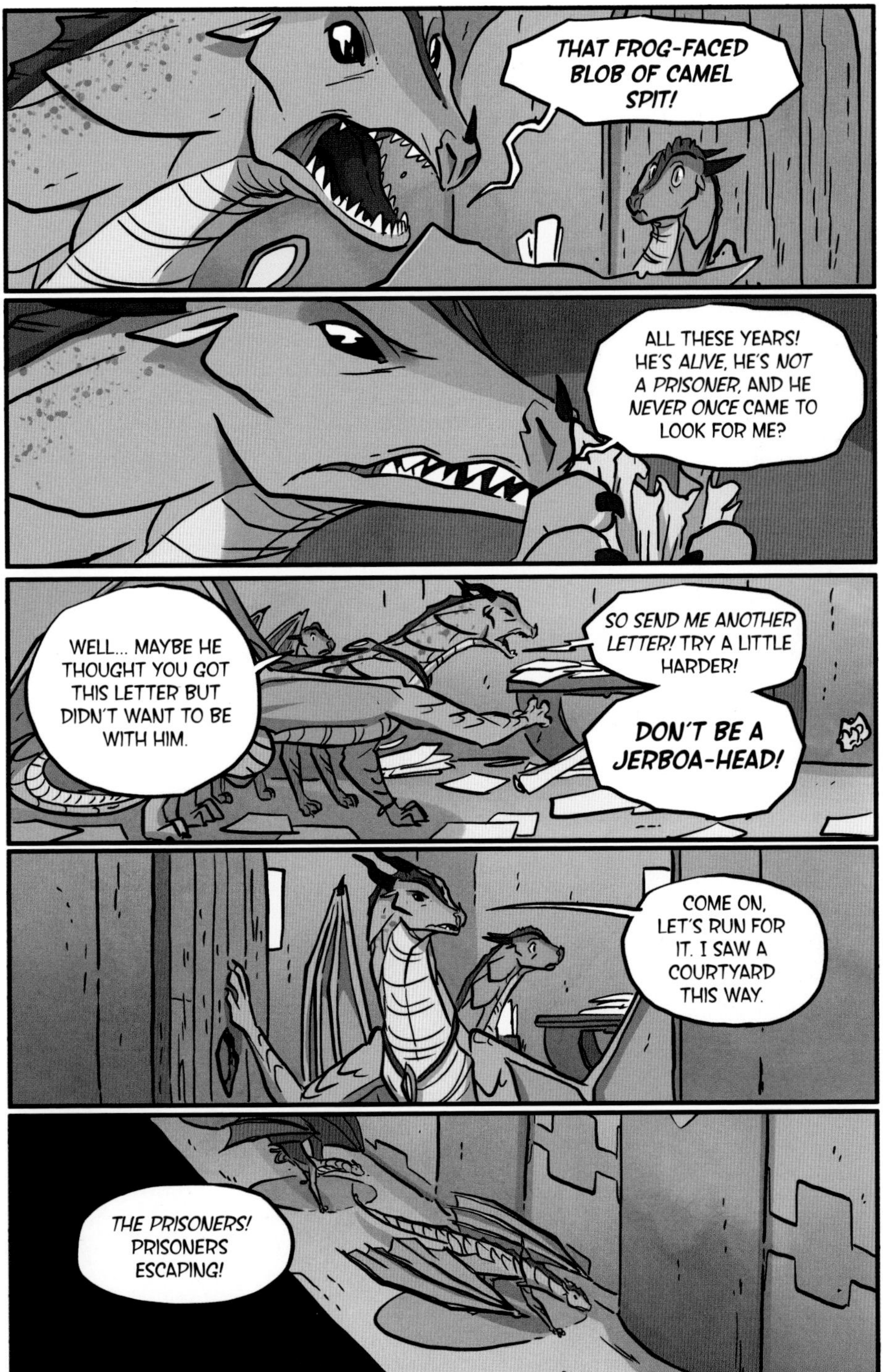
THAT FROG-FACED BLOB OF CAMEL SPIT!
ALL THESE YEARS! HE'S *ALIVE*, HE'S *NOT* A *PRISONER*, AND HE *NEVER ONCE* CAME TO LOOK FOR ME?
WELL... MAYBE HE THOUGHT YOU GOT THIS LETTER BUT DIDN'T WANT TO BE WITH HIM.
SO SEND ME ANOTHER LETTER! TRY A LITTLE HARDER!
DON'T BE A JERBOA-HEAD!
COME ON, LET'S RUN FOR IT. I SAW A COURTYARD THIS WAY.
THE PRISONERS! PRISONERS ESCAPING!

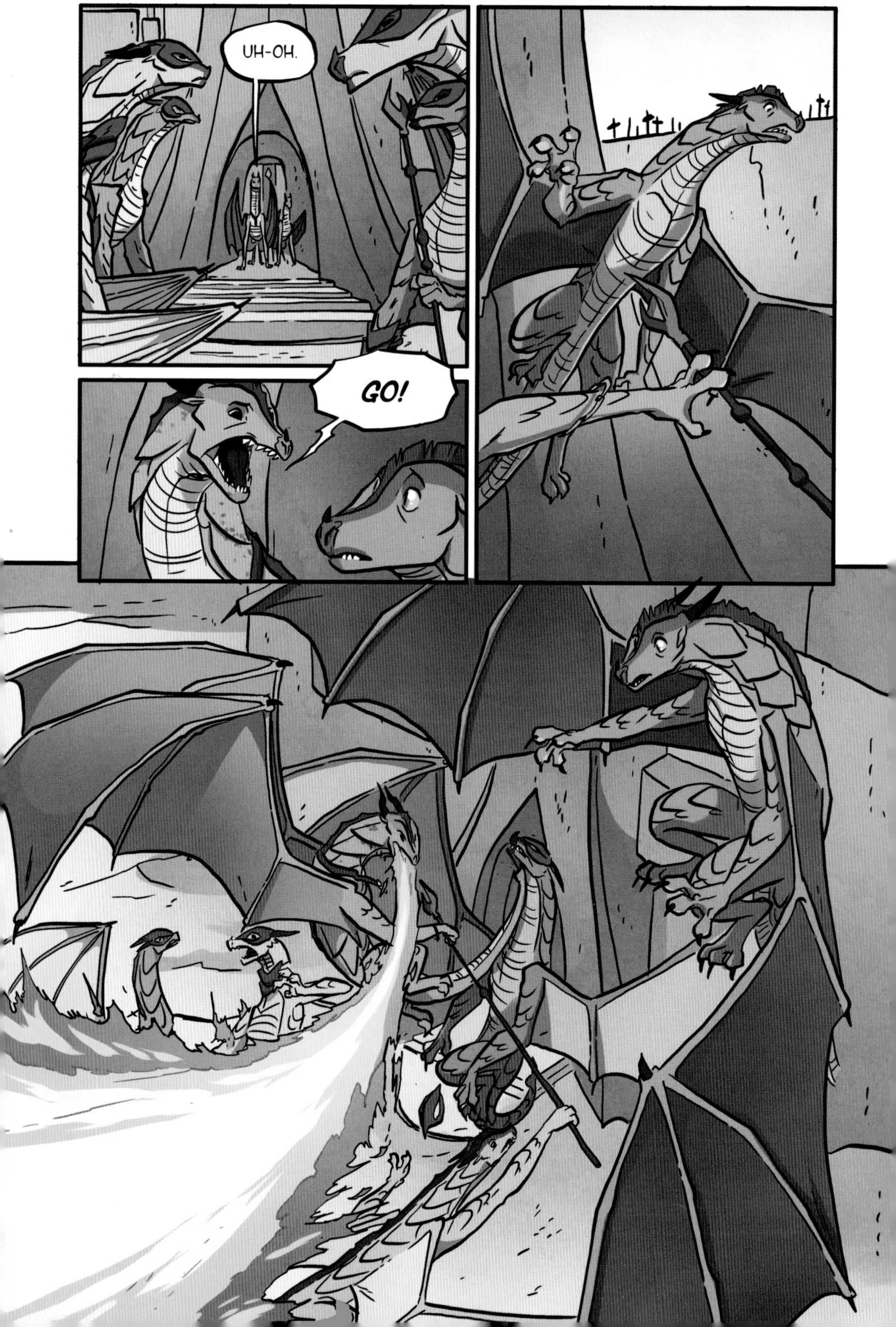
UH-OH.
GO!

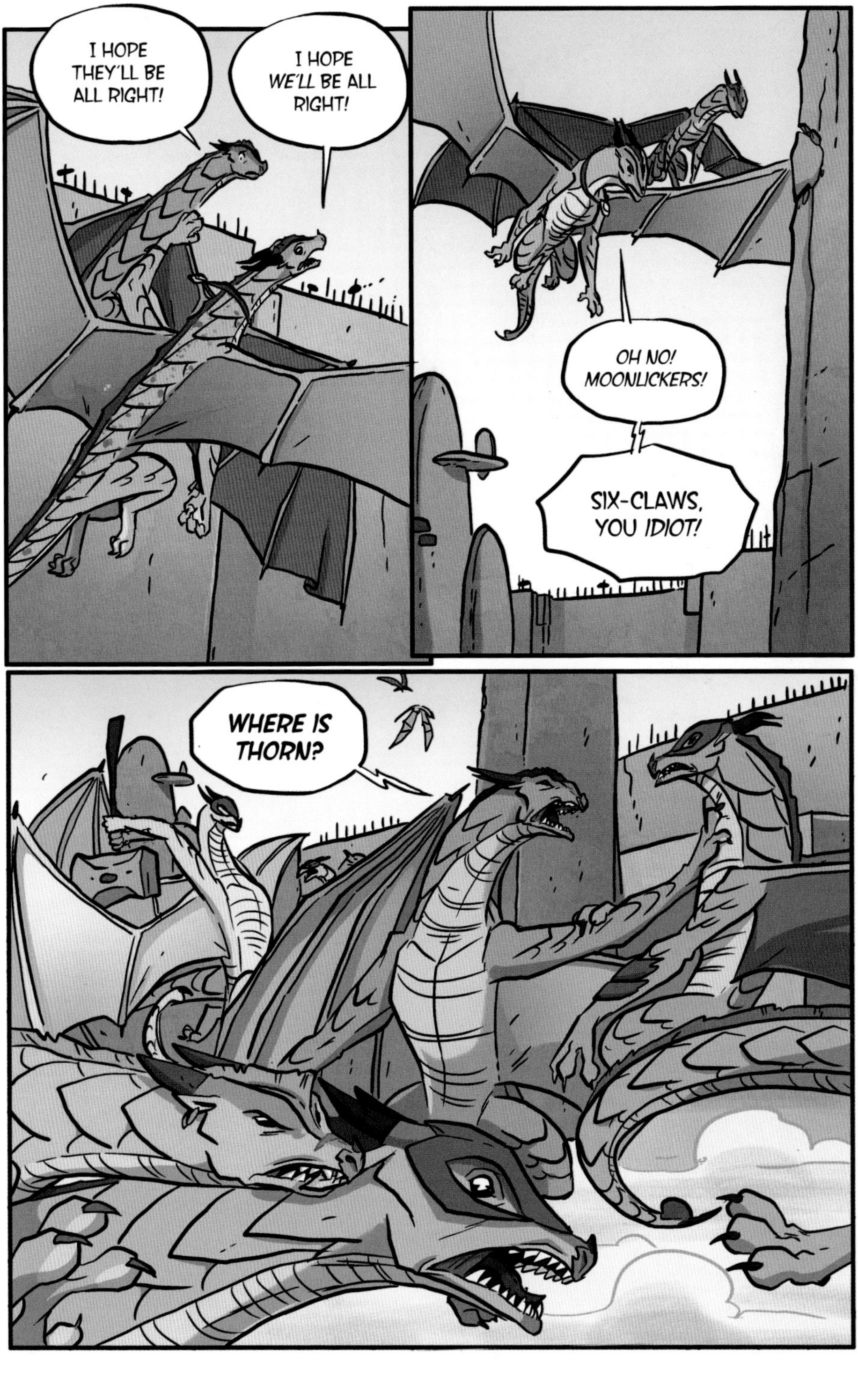
I HOPE THEY'LL BE ALL RIGHT!
I HOPE WE'LL BE ALL RIGHT!
OH NO! MOONLICKERS!
SIX-CLAWS, YOU IDIOT!
WHERE IS THORN?

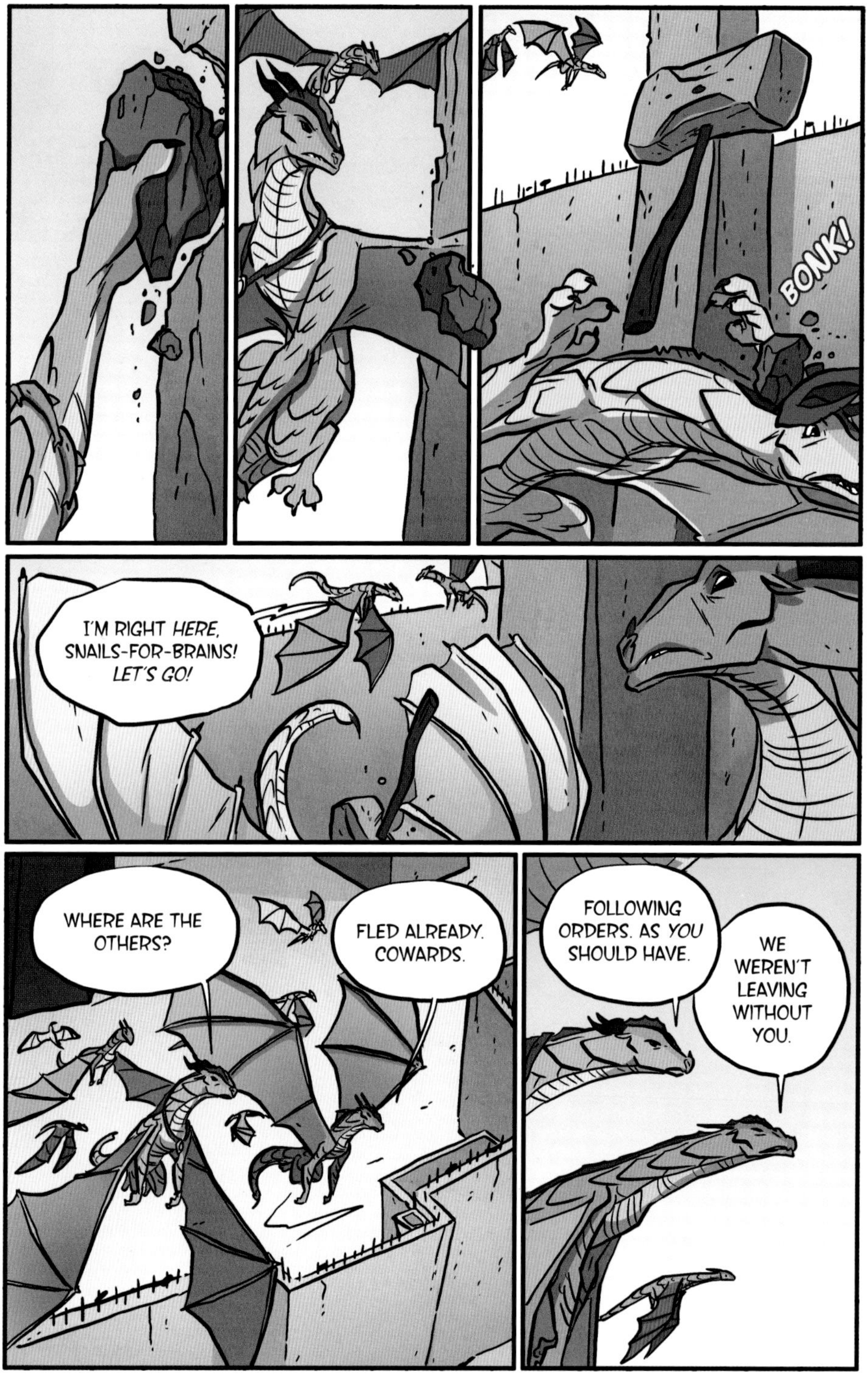
BONK!
I'M RIGHT *HERE*, SNAILS-FOR-BRAINS! *LET'S GO!*
WHERE ARE THE OTHERS?
FLED ALREADY. COWARDS.
FOLLOWING ORDERS. AS *YOU* SHOULD HAVE.
WE WEREN'T LEAVING WITHOUT YOU.

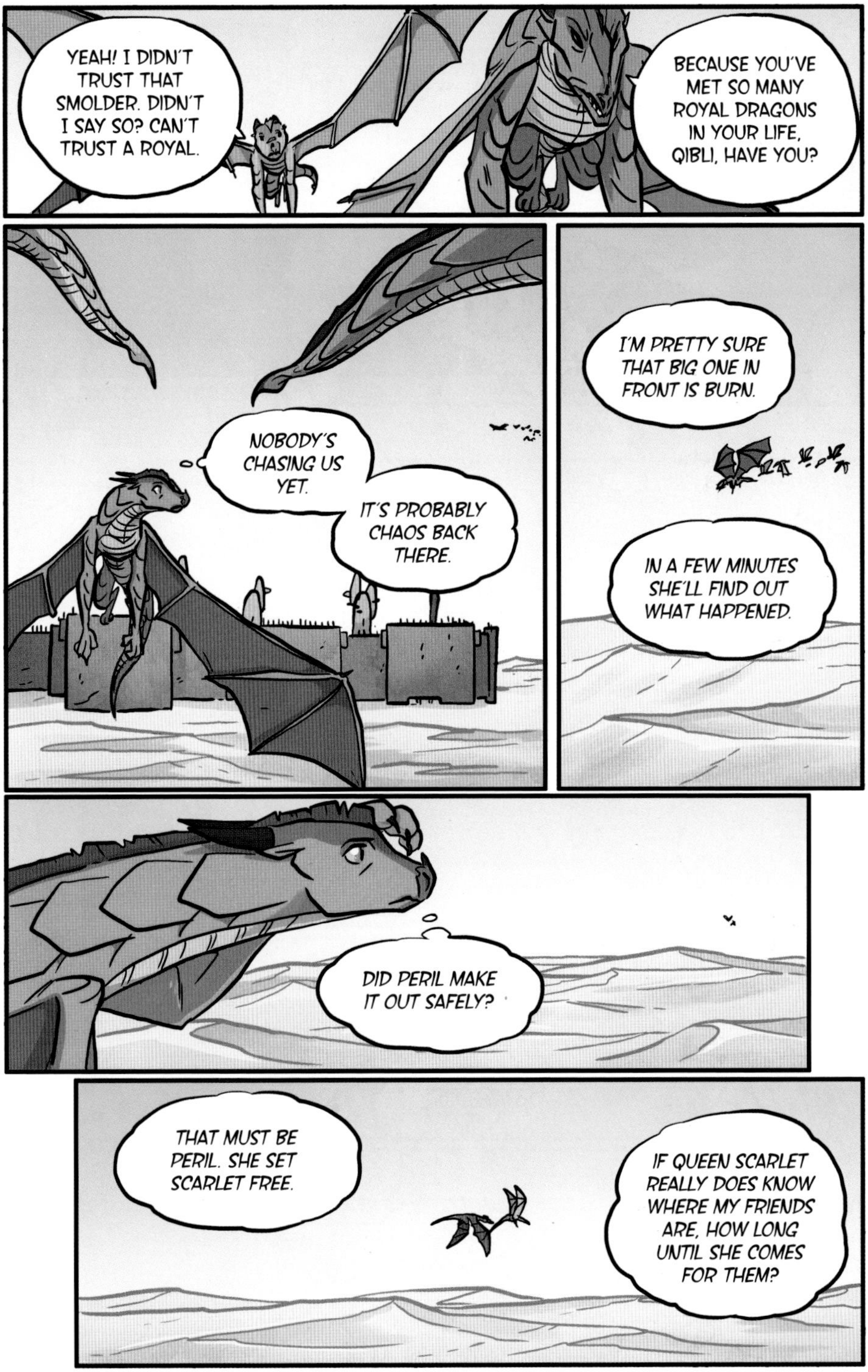
YEAH! I DIDN'T TRUST THAT SMOLDER. DIDN'T I SAY SO? CAN'T TRUST A ROYAL.
BECAUSE YOU'VE MET SO MANY ROYAL DRAGONS IN YOUR LIFE, QIBLI, HAVE YOU?
NOBODY'S CHASING US YET.
IT'S PROBABLY CHAOS BACK THERE.
I'M PRETTY SURE THAT BIG ONE IN FRONT IS BURN.
IN A FEW MINUTES SHE'LL FIND OUT WHAT HAPPENED.
DID PERIL MAKE IT OUT SAFELY?
THAT MUST BE PERIL. SHE SET SCARLET FREE.
IF QUEEN SCARLET REALLY DOES KNOW WHERE MY FRIENDS ARE, HOW LONG UNTIL SHE COMES FOR THEM?

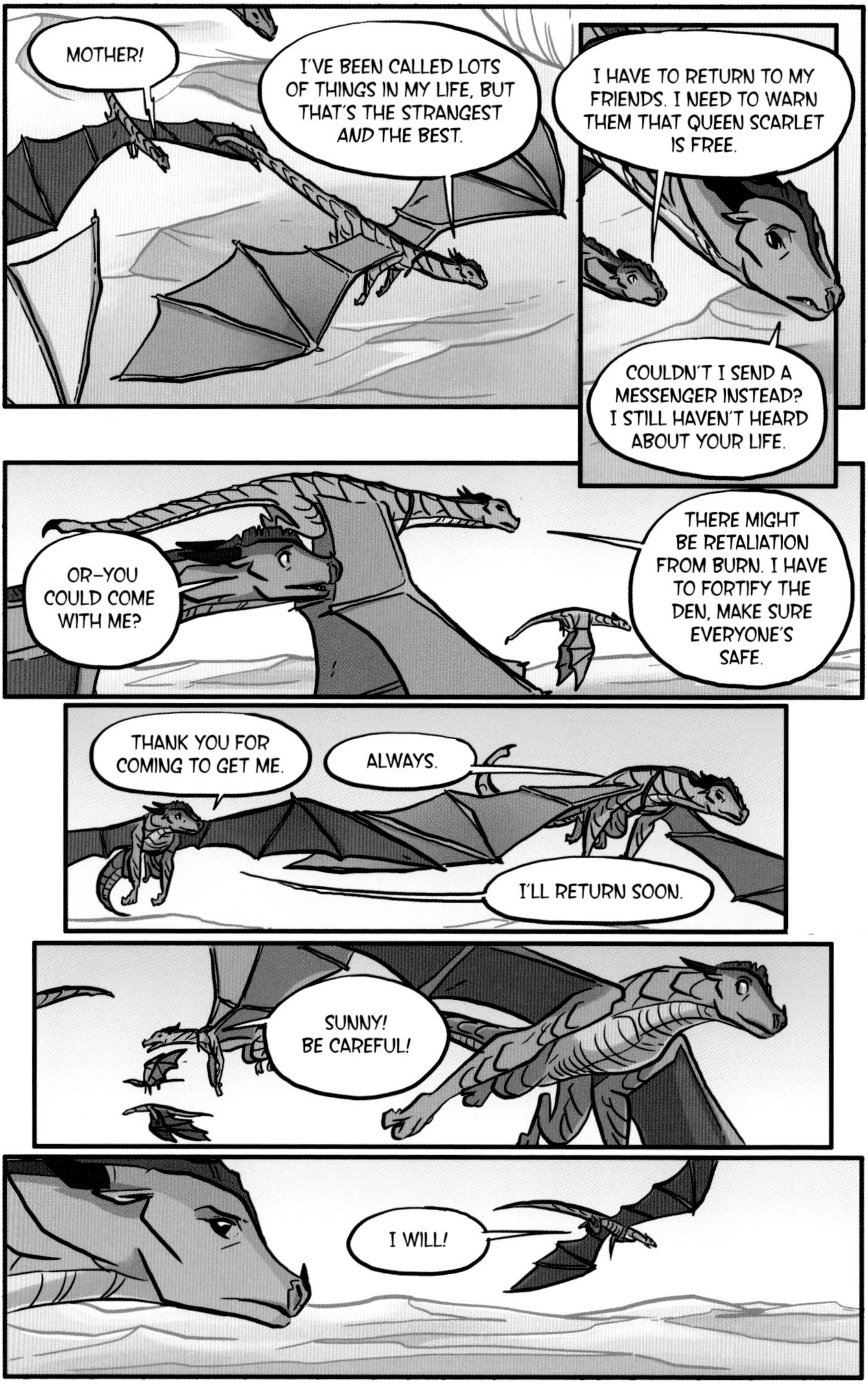
MOTHER!
I'VE BEEN CALLED LOTS OF THINGS IN MY LIFE, BUT THAT'S THE STRANGEST AND THE BEST.
I HAVE TO RETURN TO MY FRIENDS. I NEED TO WARN THEM THAT QUEEN SCARLET IS FREE.
COULDN'T I SEND A MESSENGER INSTEAD? I STILL HAVEN'T HEARD ABOUT YOUR LIFE.
OR–YOU COULD COME WITH ME?
THERE MIGHT BE RETALIATION FROM BURN. I HAVE TO FORTIFY THE DEN, MAKE SURE EVERYONE'S SAFE.
THANK YOU FOR COMING TO GET ME.
ALWAYS.
I'LL RETURN SOON.
SUNNY! BE CAREFUL!
I WILL!

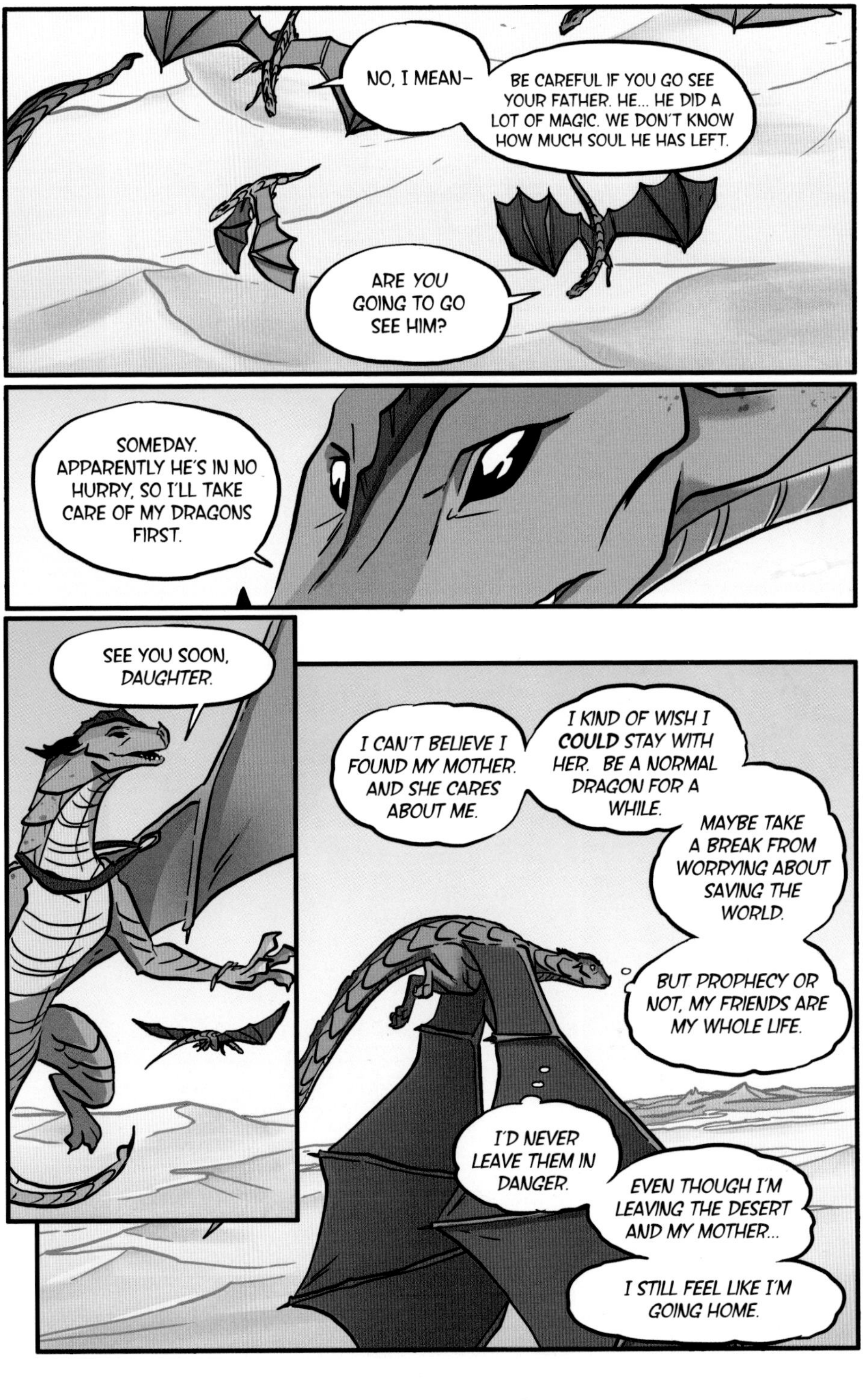
NO, I MEAN–
BE CAREFUL IF YOU GO SEE YOUR FATHER. HE... HE DID A LOT OF MAGIC. WE DON'T KNOW HOW MUCH SOUL HE HAS LEFT.
ARE YOU GOING TO GO SEE HIM?
SOMEDAY. APPARENTLY HE'S IN NO HURRY, SO I'LL TAKE CARE OF MY DRAGONS FIRST.
SEE YOU SOON, DAUGHTER.
I CAN'T BELIEVE I FOUND MY MOTHER. AND SHE CARES ABOUT ME.
I KIND OF WISH I **COULD** STAY WITH HER. BE A NORMAL DRAGON FOR A WHILE.
MAYBE TAKE A BREAK FROM WORRYING ABOUT SAVING THE WORLD.
BUT PROPHECY OR NOT, MY FRIENDS ARE MY WHOLE LIFE.
I'D NEVER LEAVE THEM IN DANGER.
EVEN THOUGH I'M LEAVING THE DESERT AND MY MOTHER...
I STILL FEEL LIKE I'M GOING HOME.

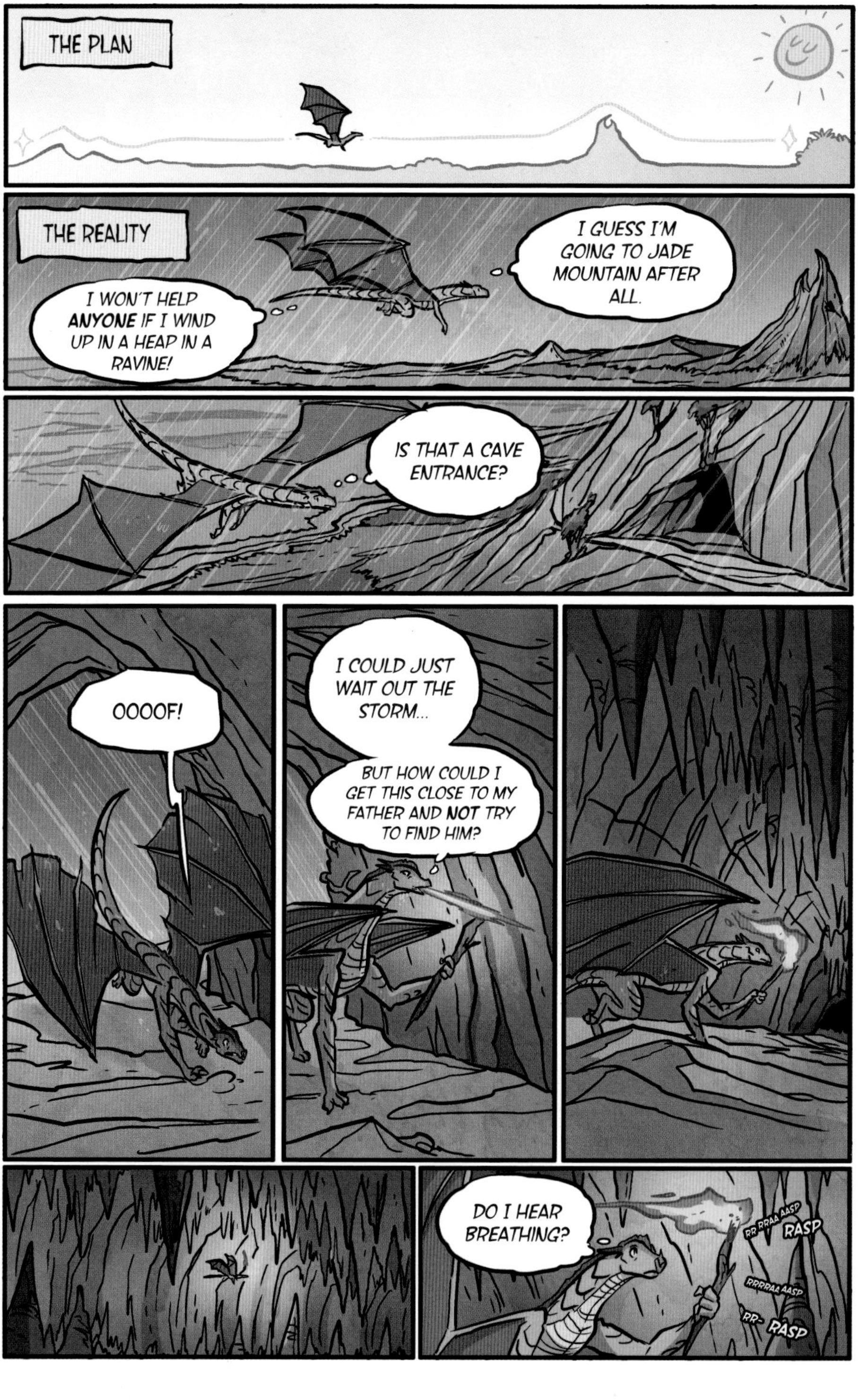
THE PLAN
THE REALITY
I WON'T HELP ANYONE IF I WIND UP IN A HEAP IN A RAVINE!
I GUESS I'M GOING TO JADE MOUNTAIN AFTER ALL.
IS THAT A CAVE ENTRANCE?
OOOOF!
I COULD JUST WAIT OUT THE STORM...
BUT HOW COULD I GET THIS CLOSE TO MY FATHER AND NOT TRY TO FIND HIM?
DO I HEAR BREATHING?
RR RRAA AASP RASP
RRRRAA AASP
RR- RASP

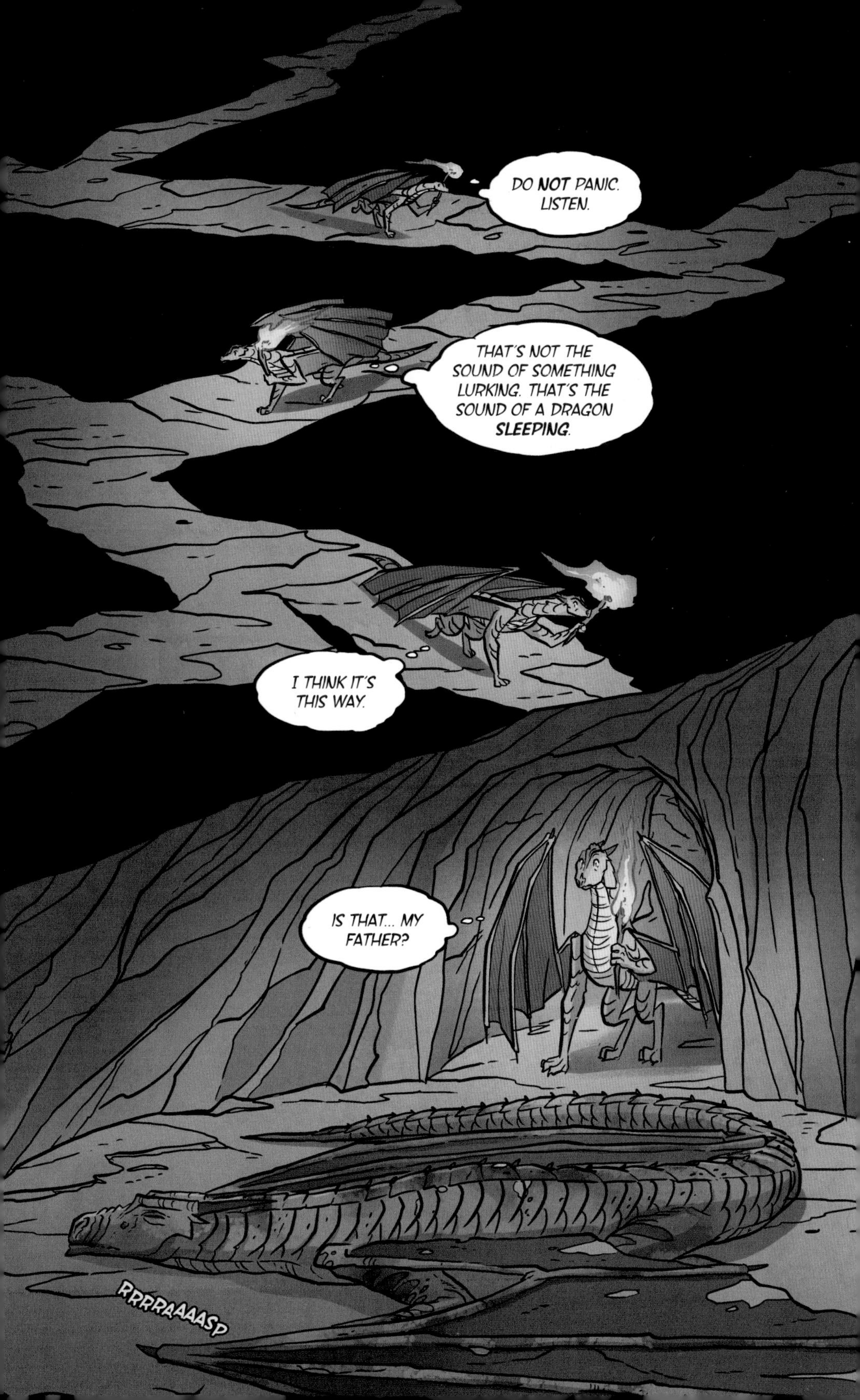
DO NOT PANIC. LISTEN.
THAT'S NOT THE SOUND OF SOMETHING LURKING. THAT'S THE SOUND OF A DRAGON SLEEPING.
I THINK IT'S THIS WAY.
IS THAT... MY FATHER?
RRRRAAAASP

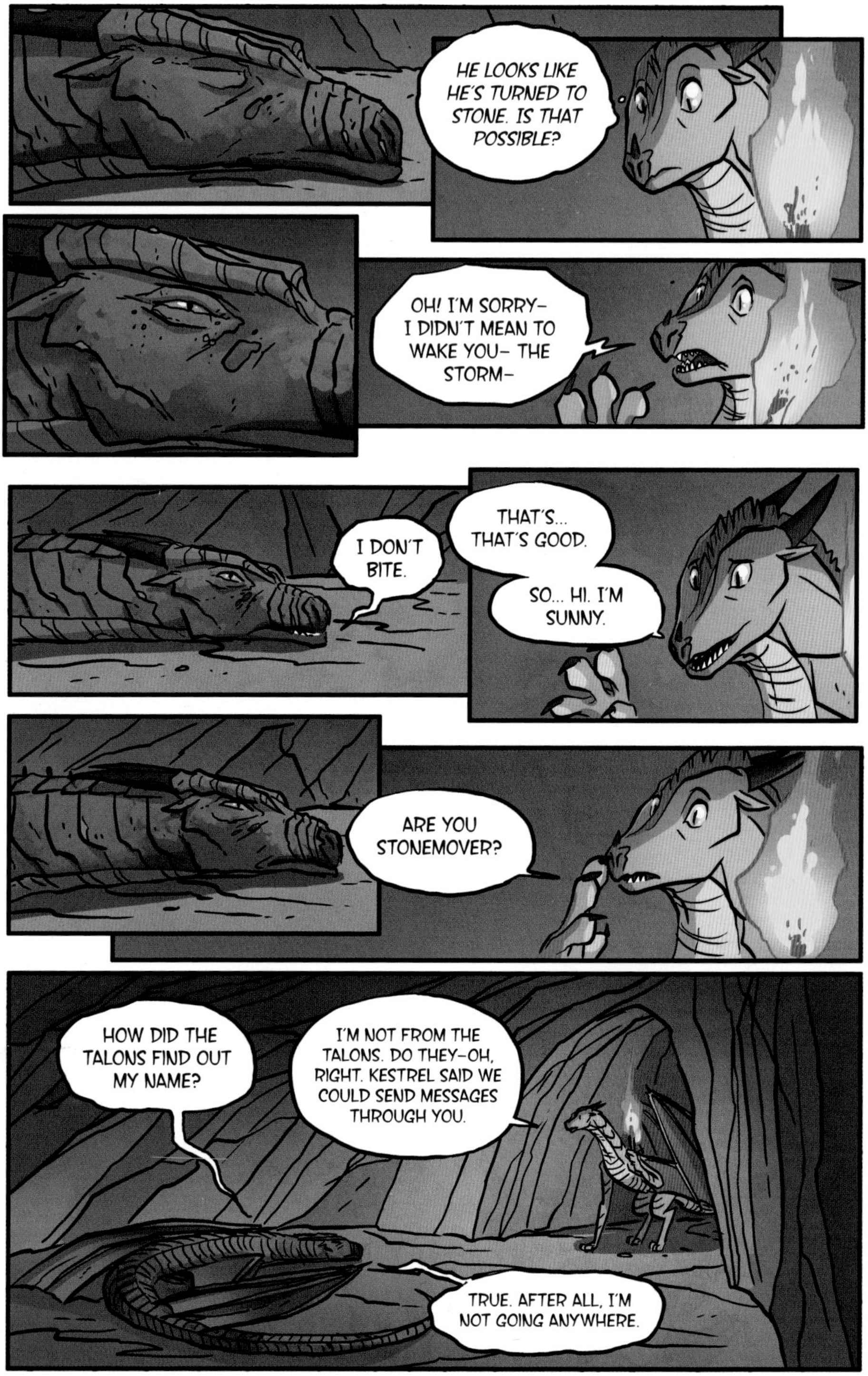
HE LOOKS LIKE HE'S TURNED TO STONE. IS THAT POSSIBLE?
OH! I'M SORRY– I DIDN'T MEAN TO WAKE YOU– THE STORM–
I DON'T BITE.
THAT'S... THAT'S GOOD.
SO... HI. I'M SUNNY.
ARE YOU STONEMOVER?
HOW DID THE TALONS FIND OUT MY NAME?
I'M NOT FROM THE TALONS. DO THEY–OH, RIGHT. KESTREL SAID WE COULD SEND MESSAGES THROUGH YOU.
TRUE. AFTER ALL, I'M NOT GOING ANYWHERE.

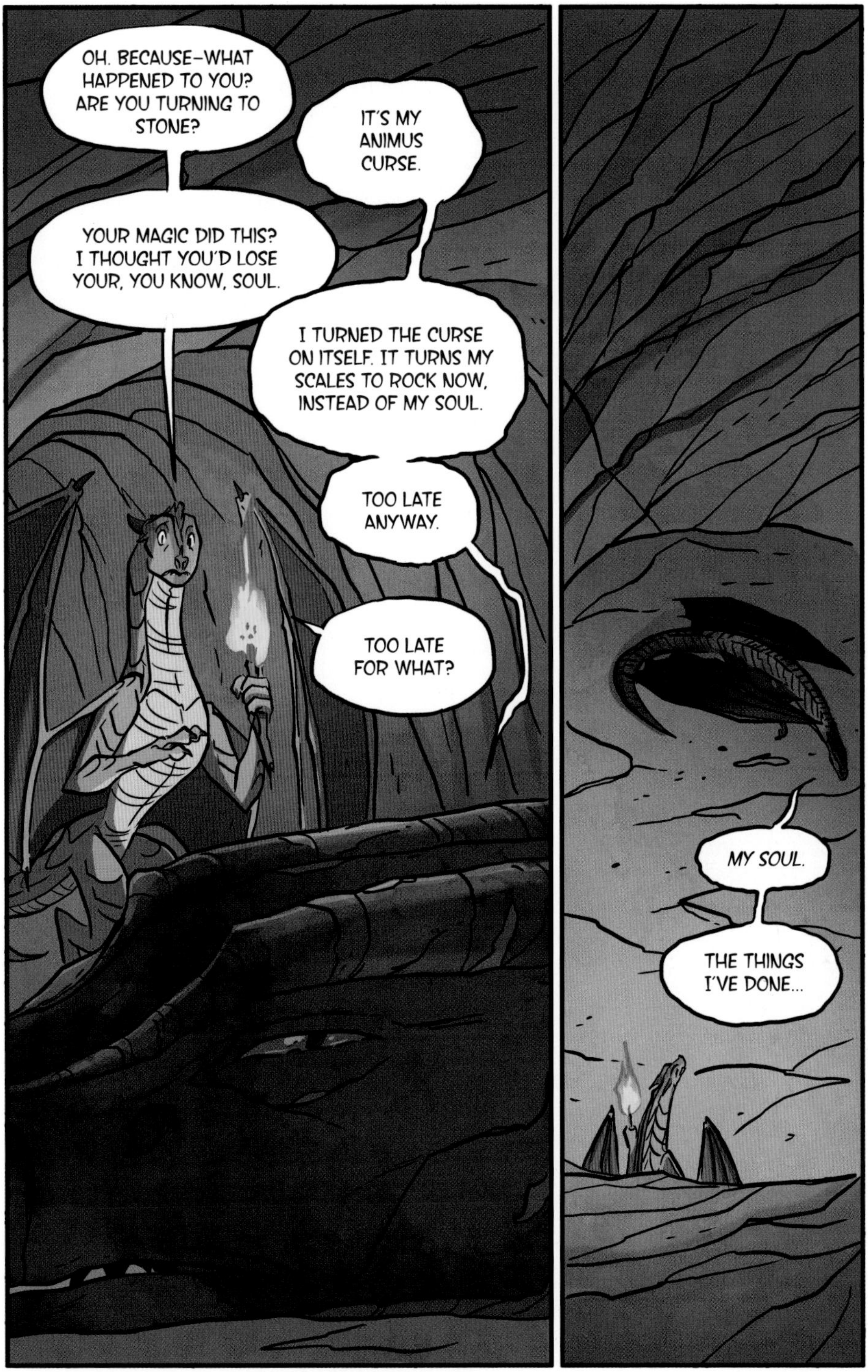
OH. BECAUSE—WHAT HAPPENED TO YOU? ARE YOU TURNING TO STONE?
IT'S MY ANIMUS CURSE.
YOUR MAGIC DID THIS? I THOUGHT YOU'D LOSE YOUR, YOU KNOW, SOUL.
I TURNED THE CURSE ON ITSELF. IT TURNS MY SCALES TO ROCK NOW, INSTEAD OF MY SOUL.
TOO LATE ANYWAY.
TOO LATE FOR WHAT?
MY SOUL.
THE THINGS I'VE DONE...

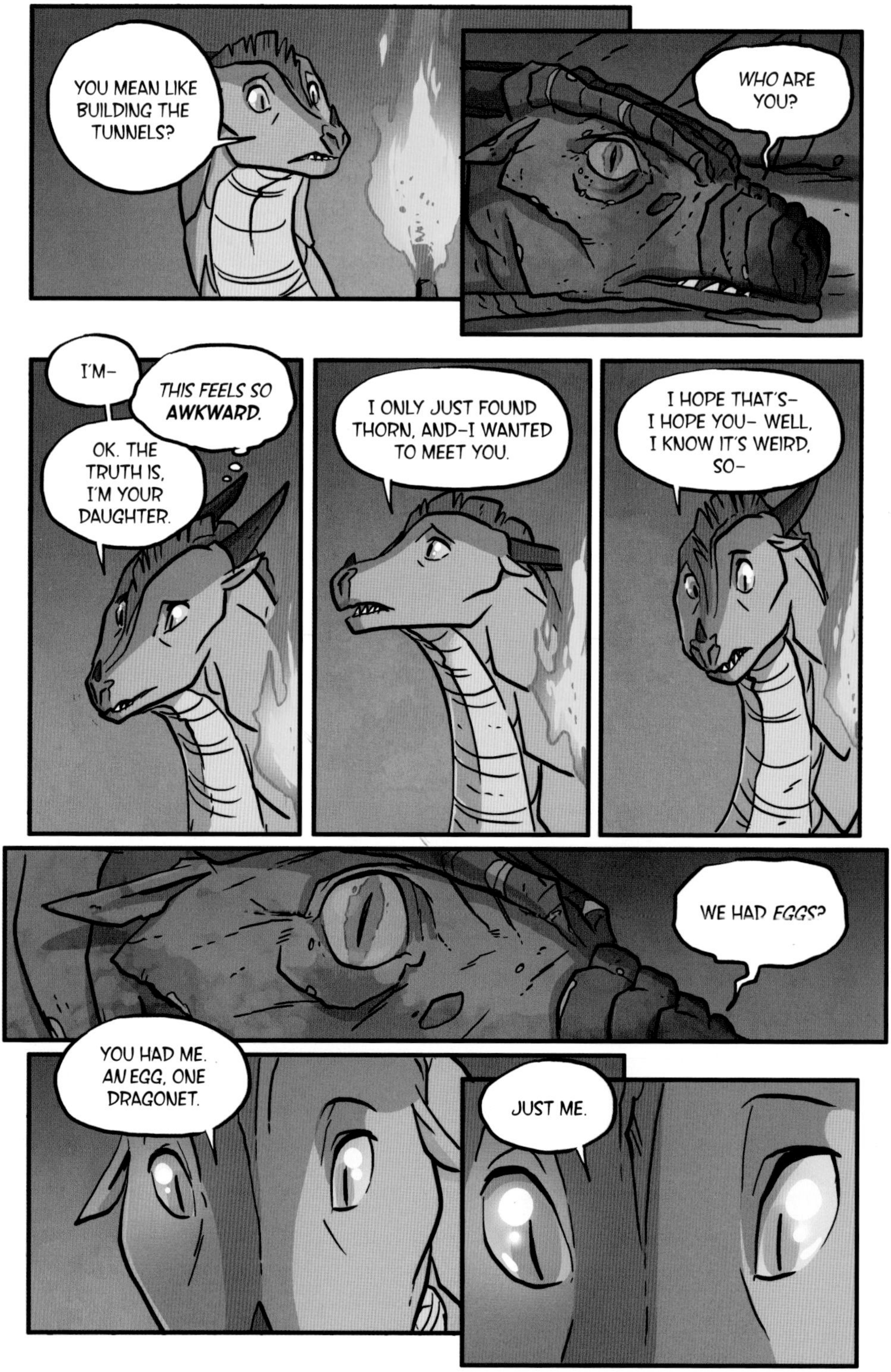
YOU MEAN LIKE BUILDING THE TUNNELS?
WHO ARE YOU?
I'M–
THIS FEELS SO AWKWARD.
OK. THE TRUTH IS, I'M YOUR DAUGHTER.
I ONLY JUST FOUND THORN, AND–I WANTED TO MEET YOU.
I HOPE THAT'S– I HOPE YOU– WELL, I KNOW IT'S WEIRD, SO–
WE HAD EGGS?
YOU HAD ME. AN EGG, ONE DRAGONET.
JUST ME.

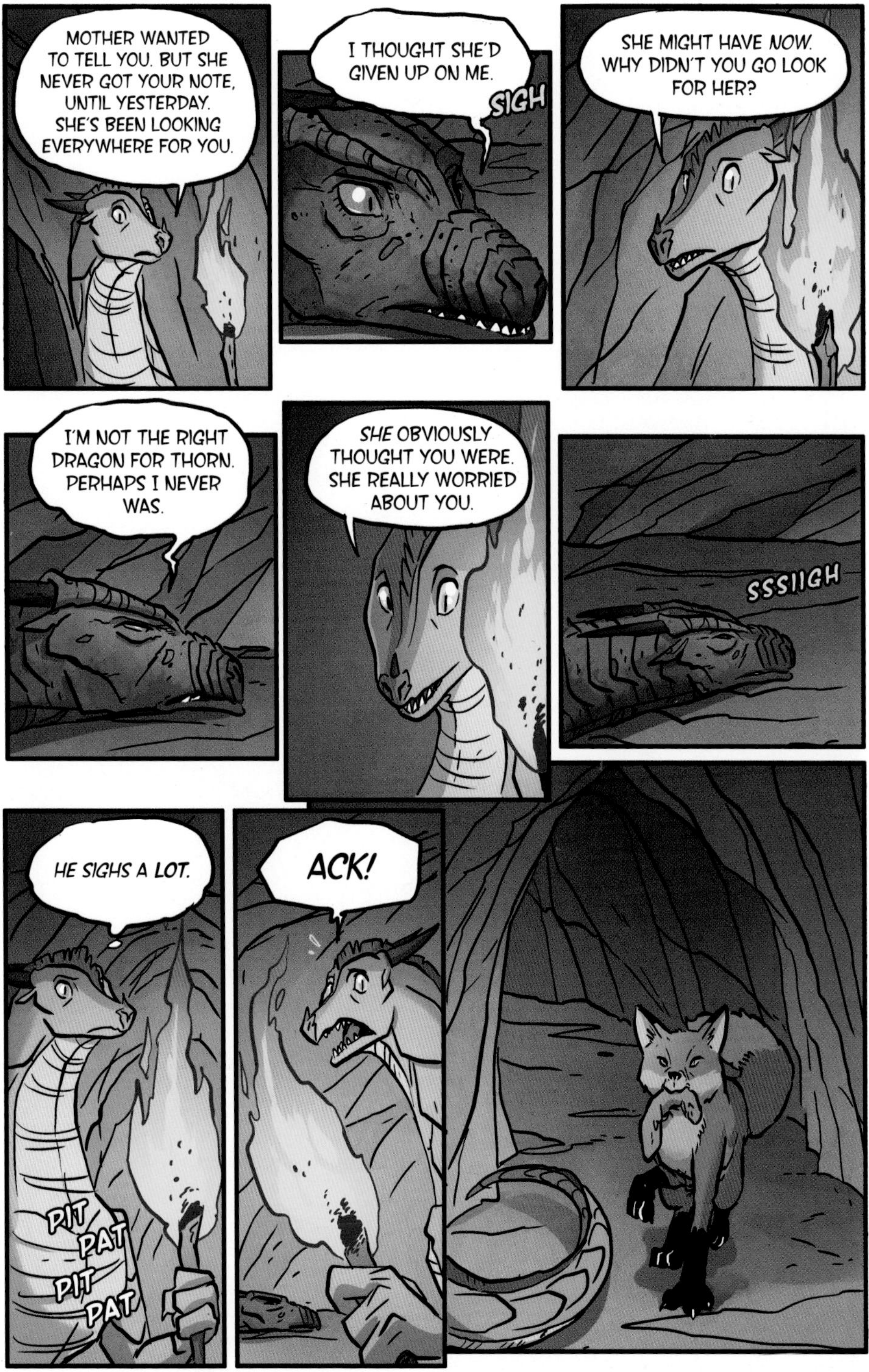
MOTHER WANTED TO TELL YOU. BUT SHE NEVER GOT YOUR NOTE, UNTIL YESTERDAY. SHE'S BEEN LOOKING EVERYWHERE FOR YOU.
I THOUGHT SHE'D GIVEN UP ON ME.
SIGH
SHE MIGHT HAVE NOW. WHY DIDN'T YOU GO LOOK FOR HER?
I'M NOT THE RIGHT DRAGON FOR THORN. PERHAPS I NEVER WAS.
SHE OBVIOUSLY THOUGHT YOU WERE. SHE REALLY WORRIED ABOUT YOU.
SSSIIGH
HE SIGHS A LOT.
PIT
PAT
PIT
PAT
ACK!

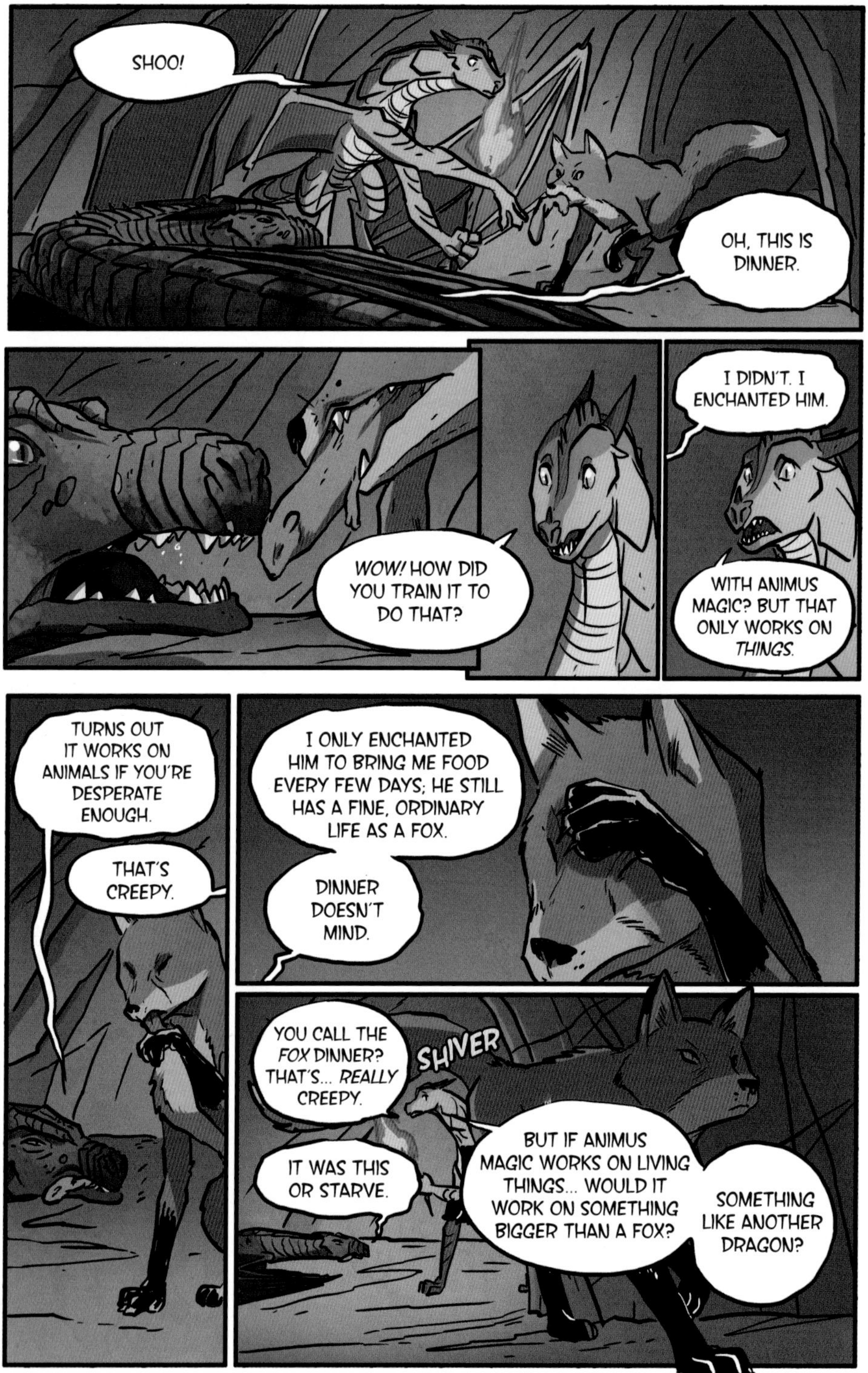
SHOO!
OH, THIS IS DINNER.
WOW! HOW DID YOU TRAIN IT TO DO THAT?
I DIDN'T. I ENCHANTED HIM.
WITH ANIMUS MAGIC? BUT THAT ONLY WORKS ON *THINGS*.
TURNS OUT IT WORKS ON ANIMALS IF YOU'RE DESPERATE ENOUGH.
THAT'S CREEPY.
I ONLY ENCHANTED HIM TO BRING ME FOOD EVERY FEW DAYS; HE STILL HAS A FINE, ORDINARY LIFE AS A FOX.
DINNER DOESN'T MIND.
YOU CALL THE *FOX* DINNER? THAT'S... *REALLY* CREEPY.
SHIVER
IT WAS THIS OR STARVE.
BUT IF ANIMUS MAGIC WORKS ON LIVING THINGS... WOULD IT WORK ON SOMETHING BIGGER THAN A FOX?
SOMETHING LIKE ANOTHER DRAGON?

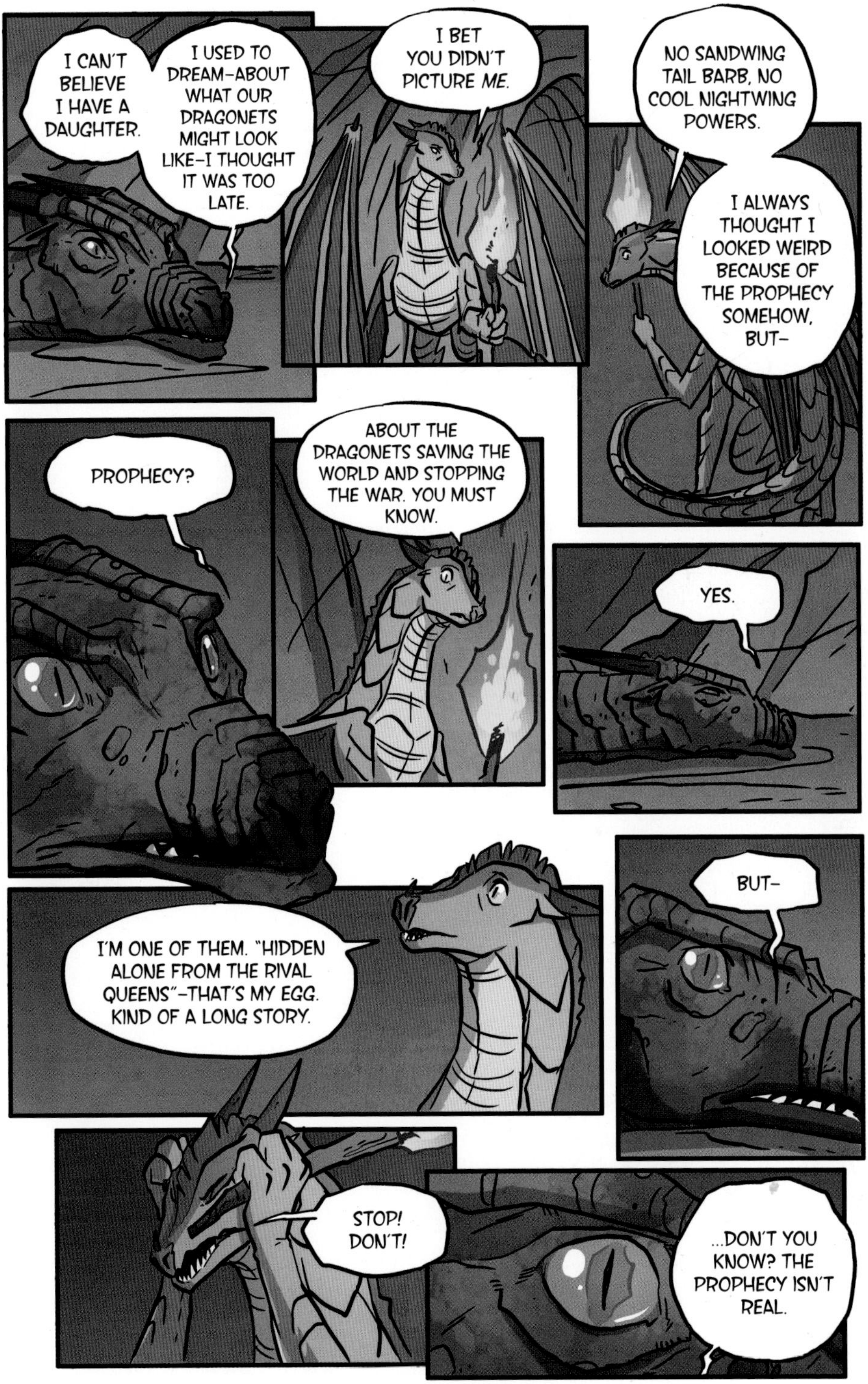
I CAN'T BELIEVE I HAVE A DAUGHTER.
I USED TO DREAM—ABOUT WHAT OUR DRAGONETS MIGHT LOOK LIKE—I THOUGHT IT WAS TOO LATE.
I BET YOU DIDN'T PICTURE *ME*.
NO SANDWING TAIL BARB, NO COOL NIGHTWING POWERS.
I ALWAYS THOUGHT I LOOKED WEIRD BECAUSE OF THE PROPHECY SOMEHOW, BUT—
PROPHECY?
ABOUT THE DRAGONETS SAVING THE WORLD AND STOPPING THE WAR. YOU MUST KNOW.
YES.
I'M ONE OF THEM. "HIDDEN ALONE FROM THE RIVAL QUEENS"—THAT'S MY EGG. KIND OF A LONG STORY.
BUT—
STOP! DON'T!
...DON'T YOU KNOW? THE PROPHECY ISN'T REAL.

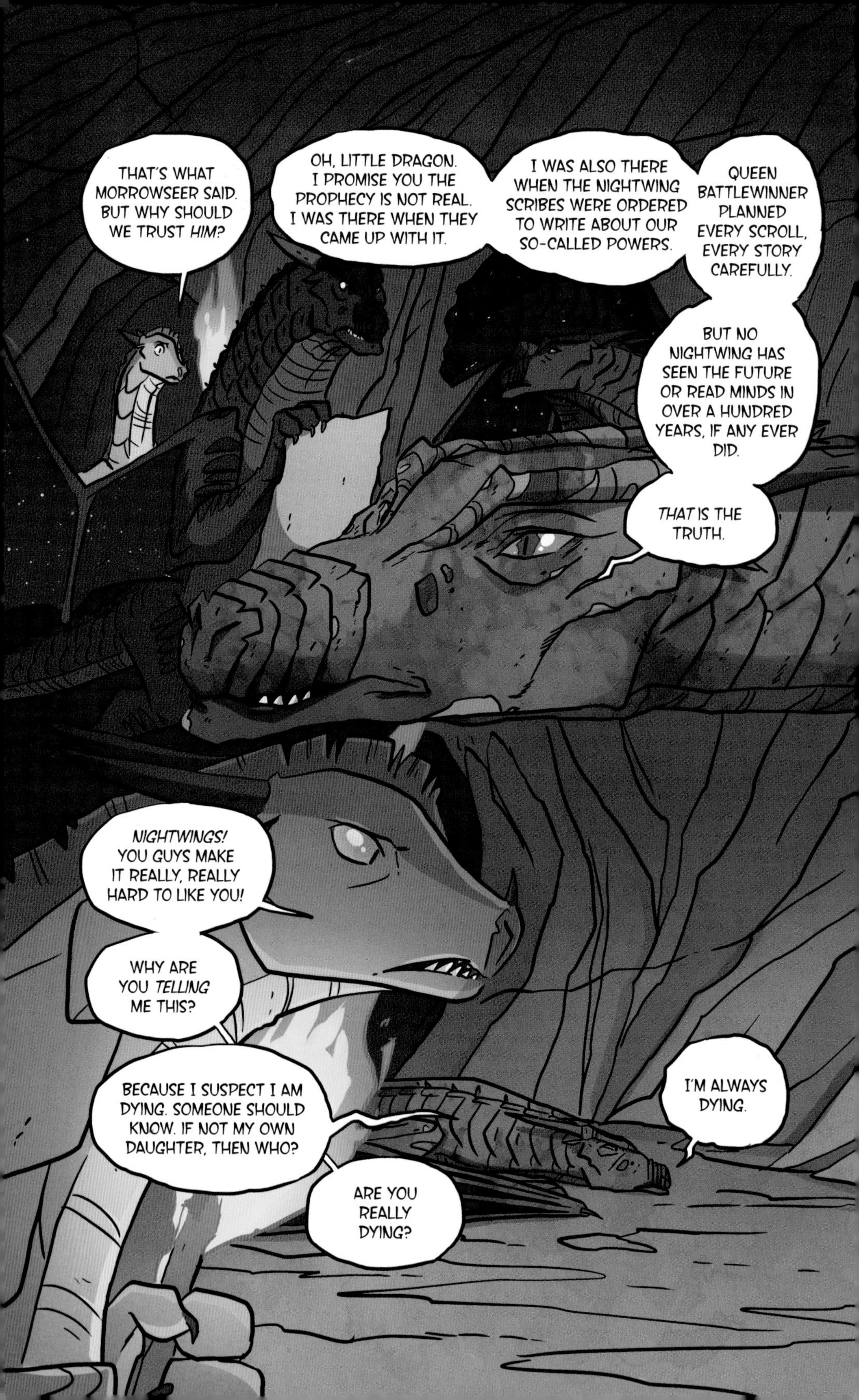
THAT'S WHAT MORROWSEER SAID. BUT WHY SHOULD WE TRUST *HIM*?
OH, LITTLE DRAGON. I PROMISE YOU THE PROPHECY IS NOT REAL. I WAS THERE WHEN THEY CAME UP WITH IT.
I WAS ALSO THERE WHEN THE NIGHTWING SCRIBES WERE ORDERED TO WRITE ABOUT OUR SO-CALLED POWERS.
QUEEN BATTLEWINNER PLANNED EVERY SCROLL, EVERY STORY CAREFULLY.
BUT NO NIGHTWING HAS SEEN THE FUTURE OR READ MINDS IN OVER A HUNDRED YEARS, IF ANY EVER DID.
THAT IS THE TRUTH.
NIGHTWINGS! YOU GUYS MAKE IT REALLY, REALLY HARD TO LIKE YOU!
WHY ARE YOU *TELLING* ME THIS?
BECAUSE I SUSPECT I AM DYING. SOMEONE SHOULD KNOW. IF NOT MY OWN DAUGHTER, THEN WHO?
I'M ALWAYS DYING.
ARE YOU REALLY DYING?

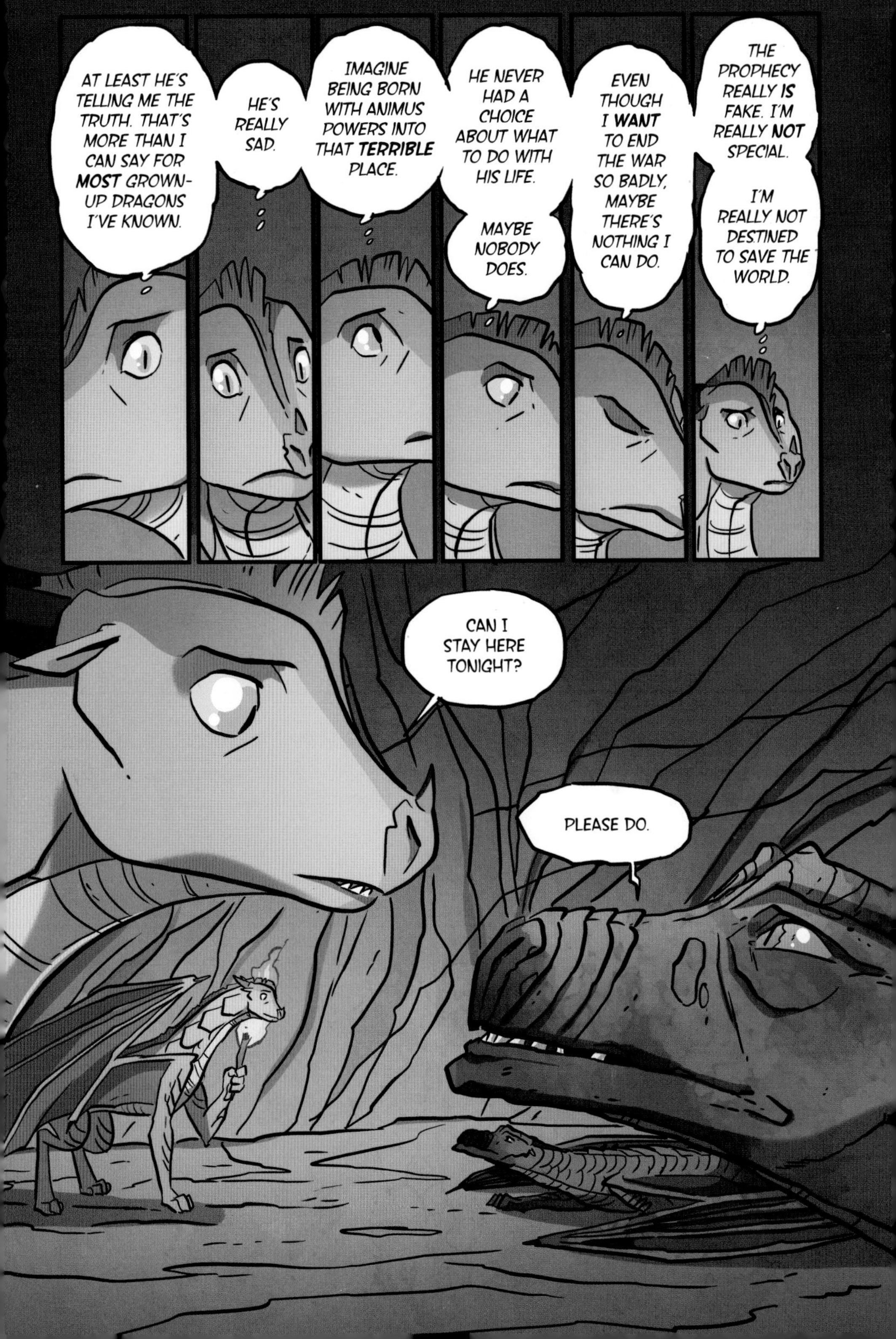
AT LEAST HE'S TELLING ME THE TRUTH. THAT'S MORE THAN I CAN SAY FOR **MOST** GROWN-UP DRAGONS I'VE KNOWN.
HE'S REALLY SAD.
IMAGINE BEING BORN WITH ANIMUS POWERS INTO THAT **TERRIBLE** PLACE.
HE NEVER HAD A CHOICE ABOUT WHAT TO DO WITH HIS LIFE.
MAYBE NOBODY DOES.
EVEN THOUGH I **WANT** TO END THE WAR SO BADLY, MAYBE THERE'S NOTHING I CAN DO.
THE PROPHECY REALLY **IS** FAKE. I'M REALLY **NOT** SPECIAL.
I'M REALLY NOT DESTINED TO SAVE THE WORLD.
CAN I STAY HERE TONIGHT?
PLEASE DO.

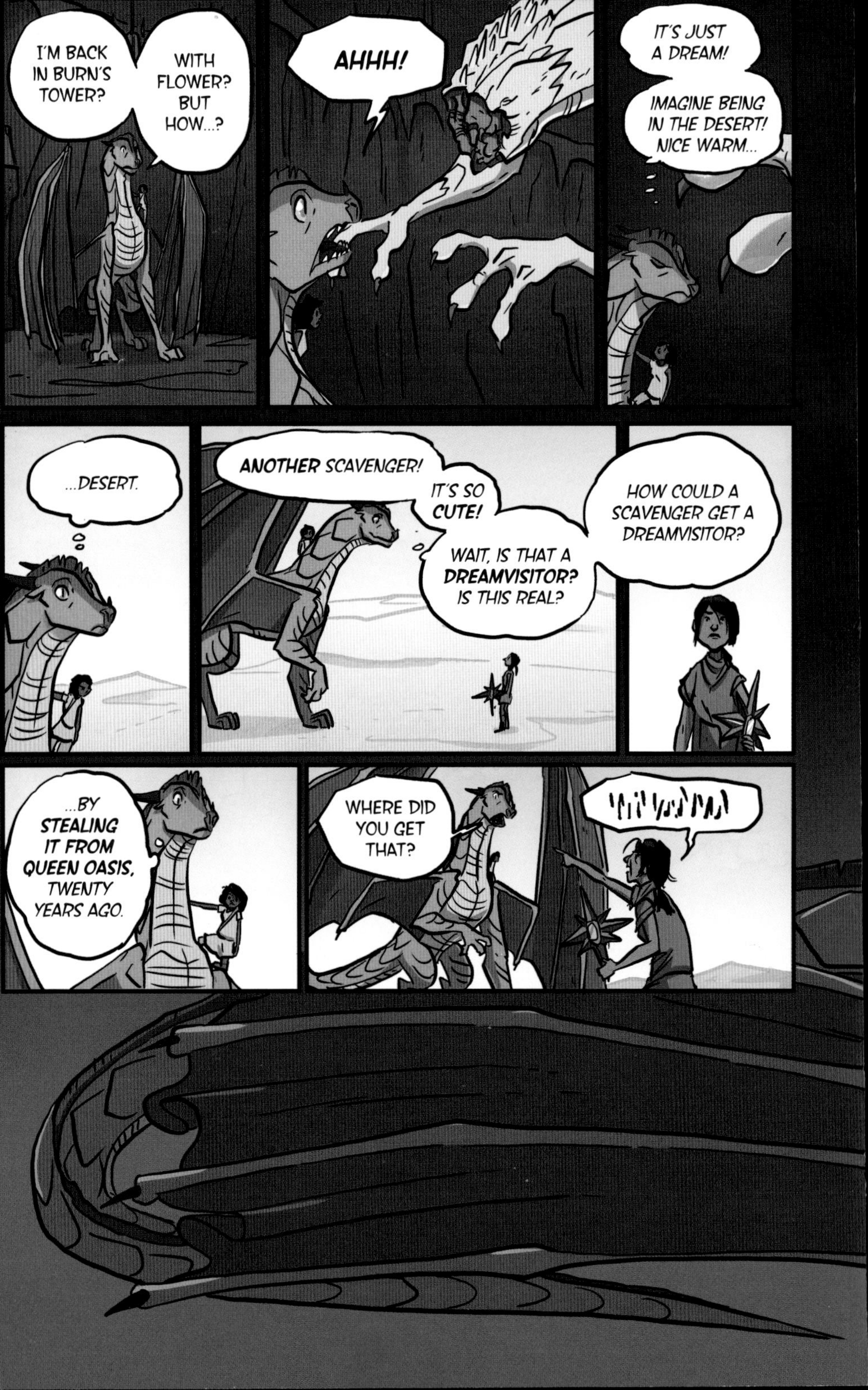
I'M BACK IN BURN'S TOWER?
WITH FLOWER? BUT HOW...?
AHHH!
IT'S JUST A DREAM!
IMAGINE BEING IN THE DESERT! NICE WARM...
...DESERT.
ANOTHER SCAVENGER!
IT'S SO CUTE!
WAIT, IS THAT A DREAMVISITOR? IS THIS REAL?
HOW COULD A SCAVENGER GET A DREAMVISITOR?
...BY STEALING IT FROM QUEEN OASIS, TWENTY YEARS AGO.
WHERE DID YOU GET THAT?

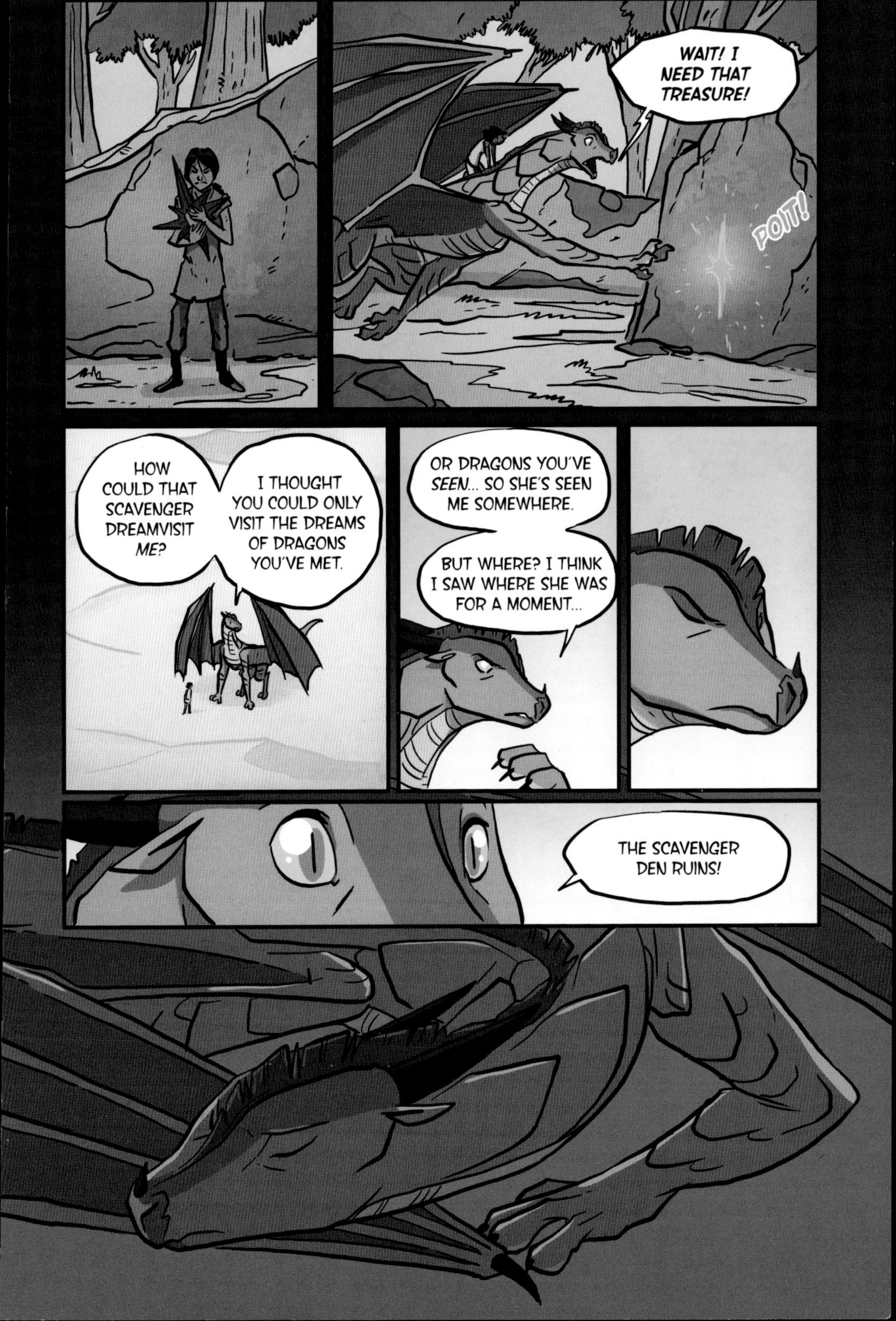
WAIT! I NEED THAT TREASURE!
POIT!
HOW COULD THAT SCAVENGER DREAMVISIT *ME*?
I THOUGHT YOU COULD ONLY VISIT THE DREAMS OF DRAGONS YOU'VE MET.
OR DRAGONS YOU'VE *SEEN*... SO SHE'S SEEN ME SOMEWHERE.
BUT WHERE? I THINK I SAW WHERE SHE WAS FOR A MOMENT...
THE SCAVENGER DEN RUINS!

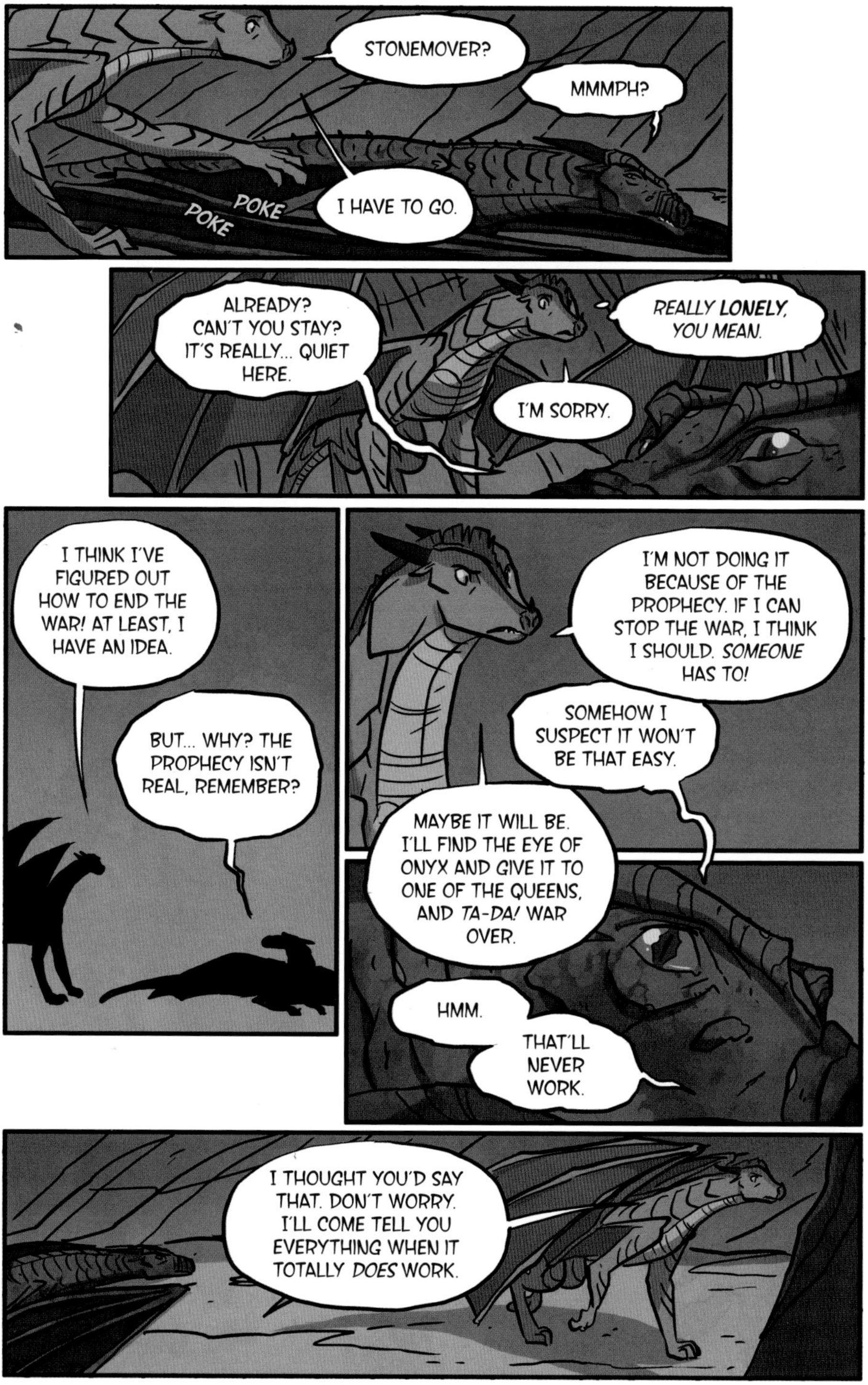
STONEMOVER?
MMMPH?
POKE
POKE
I HAVE TO GO.
ALREADY? CAN'T YOU STAY? IT'S REALLY... QUIET HERE.
*REALLY **LONELY,** YOU MEAN.*
I'M SORRY.
I THINK I'VE FIGURED OUT HOW TO END THE WAR! AT LEAST, I HAVE AN IDEA.
BUT... WHY? THE PROPHECY ISN'T REAL, REMEMBER?
I'M NOT DOING IT BECAUSE OF THE PROPHECY. IF I CAN STOP THE WAR, I THINK I SHOULD. *SOMEONE* HAS TO!
SOMEHOW I SUSPECT IT WON'T BE THAT EASY.
MAYBE IT WILL BE. I'LL FIND THE EYE OF ONYX AND GIVE IT TO ONE OF THE QUEENS, AND *TA-DA!* WAR OVER.
HMM.
THAT'LL NEVER WORK.
I THOUGHT YOU'D SAY THAT. DON'T WORRY. I'LL COME TELL YOU EVERYTHING WHEN IT TOTALLY *DOES* WORK.

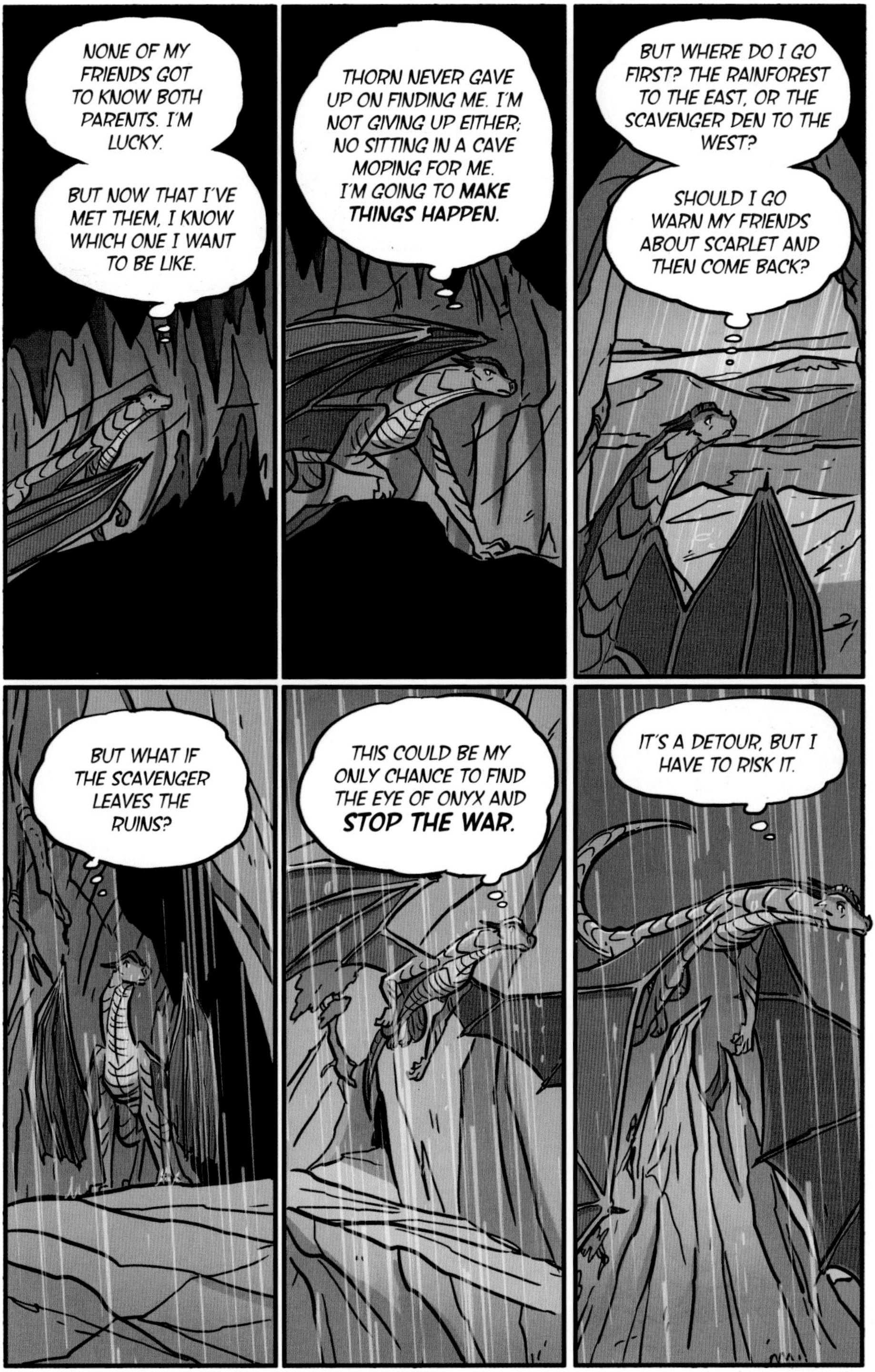
NONE OF MY FRIENDS GOT TO KNOW BOTH PARENTS. I'M LUCKY.
BUT NOW THAT I'VE MET THEM, I KNOW WHICH ONE I WANT TO BE LIKE.
THORN NEVER GAVE UP ON FINDING ME. I'M NOT GIVING UP EITHER; NO SITTING IN A CAVE MOPING FOR ME. I'M GOING TO **MAKE THINGS HAPPEN.**
BUT WHERE DO I GO FIRST? THE RAINFOREST TO THE EAST, OR THE SCAVENGER DEN TO THE WEST?
SHOULD I GO WARN MY FRIENDS ABOUT SCARLET AND THEN COME BACK?
BUT WHAT IF THE SCAVENGER LEAVES THE RUINS?
THIS COULD BE MY ONLY CHANCE TO FIND THE EYE OF ONYX AND **STOP THE WAR.**
IT'S A DETOUR, BUT I HAVE TO RISK IT.

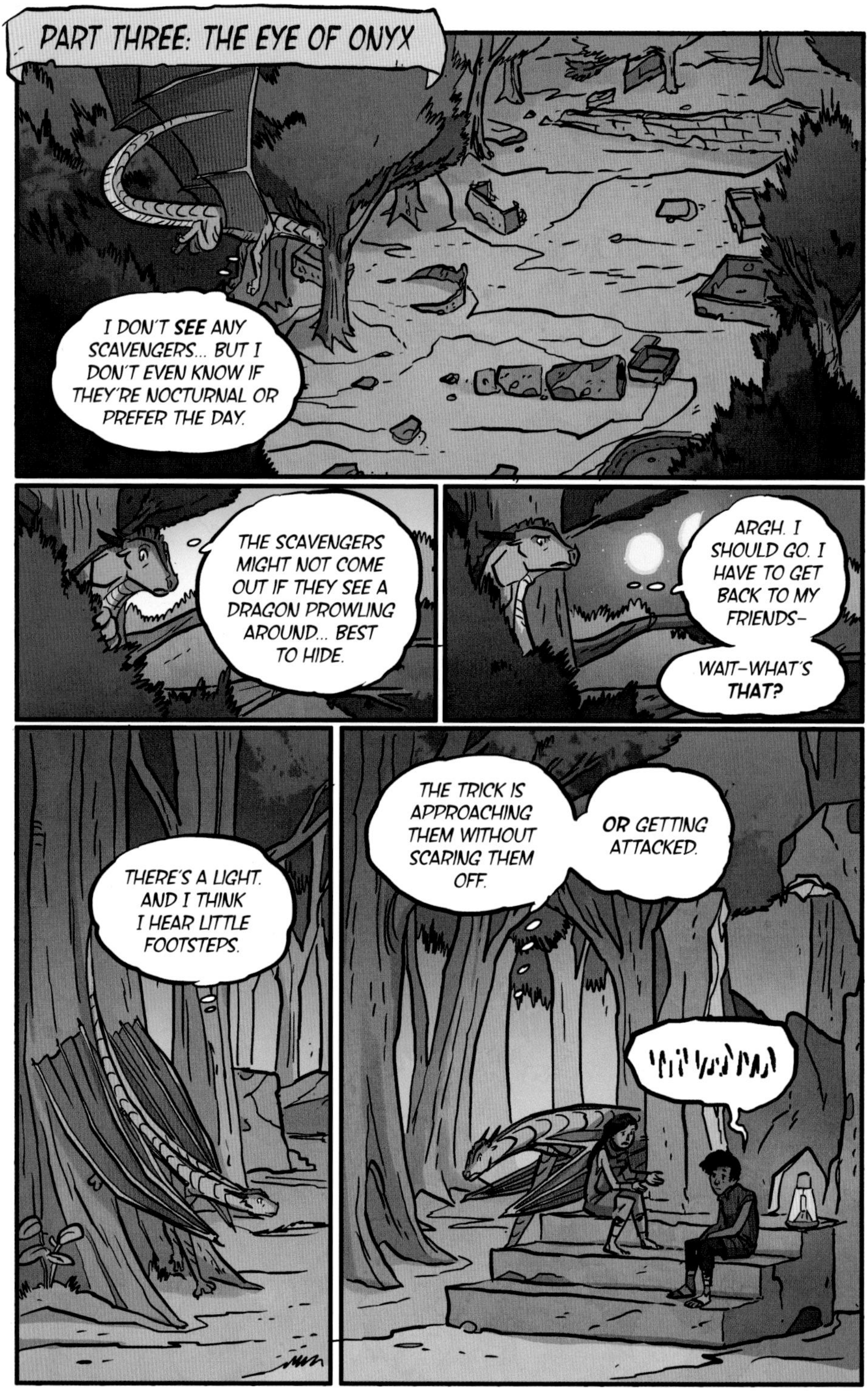
PART THREE: THE EYE OF ONYX
I DON'T **SEE** ANY SCAVENGERS... BUT I DON'T EVEN KNOW IF THEY'RE NOCTURNAL OR PREFER THE DAY.
THE SCAVENGERS MIGHT NOT COME OUT IF THEY SEE A DRAGON PROWLING AROUND... BEST TO HIDE.
ARGH. I SHOULD GO. I HAVE TO GET BACK TO MY FRIENDS–
WAIT–WHAT'S **THAT?**
THERE'S A LIGHT. AND I THINK I HEAR LITTLE FOOTSTEPS.
THE TRICK IS APPROACHING THEM WITHOUT SCARING THEM OFF.
OR GETTING ATTACKED.

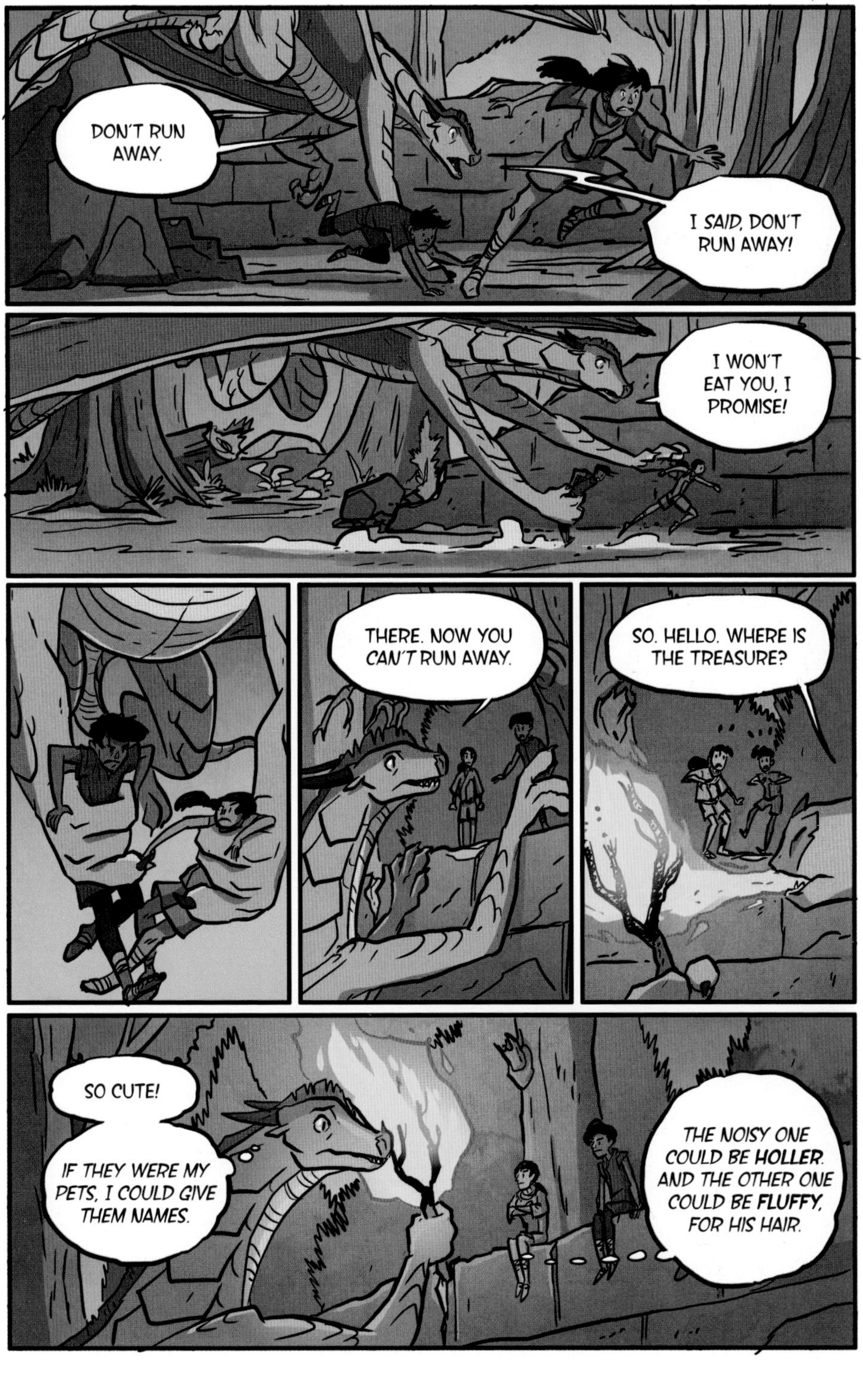
DON'T RUN AWAY.
I *SAID*, DON'T RUN AWAY!
I WON'T EAT YOU, I PROMISE!
THERE. NOW YOU *CAN'T* RUN AWAY.
SO. HELLO. WHERE IS THE TREASURE?
SO CUTE!
IF THEY WERE MY PETS, I COULD GIVE THEM NAMES.
*THE NOISY ONE COULD BE **HOLLER**. AND THE OTHER ONE COULD BE **FLUFFY**, FOR HIS HAIR.*

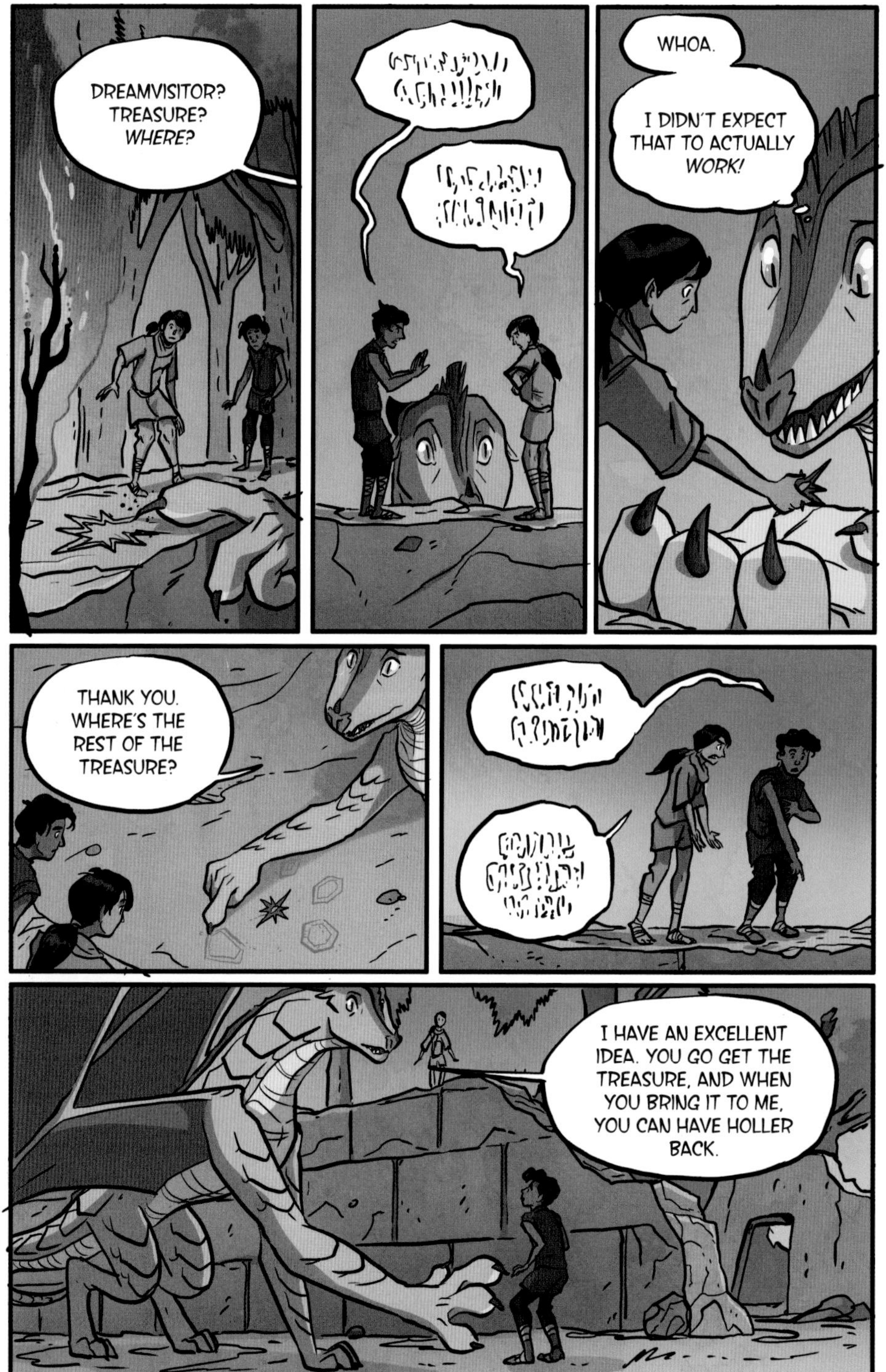
DREAMVISITOR? TREASURE? *WHERE?*
WHOA.
I DIDN'T EXPECT THAT TO ACTUALLY *WORK!*
THANK YOU. WHERE'S THE REST OF THE TREASURE?
I HAVE AN EXCELLENT IDEA. YOU GO GET THE TREASURE, AND WHEN YOU BRING IT TO ME, YOU CAN HAVE HOLLER BACK.

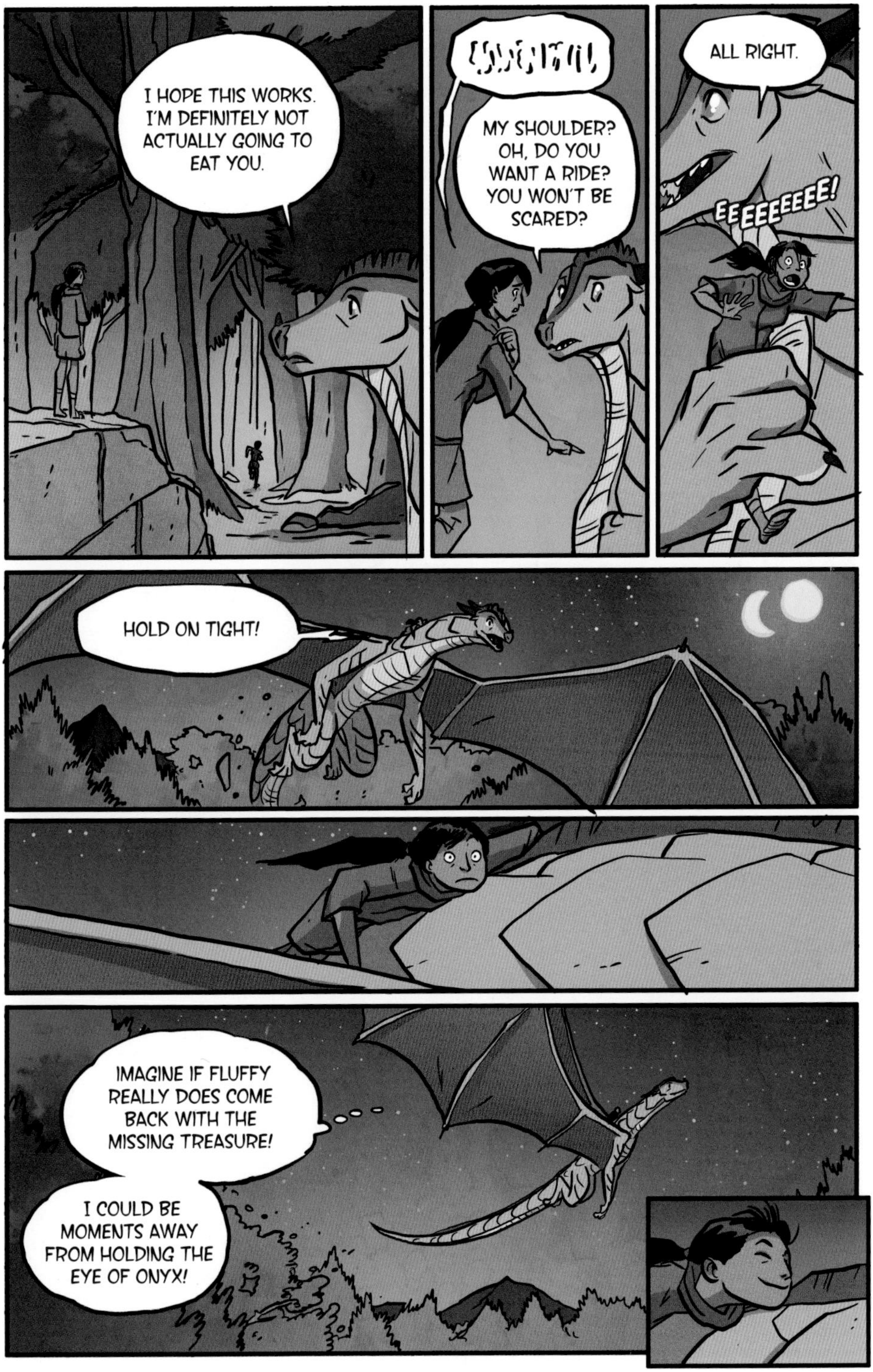
I HOPE THIS WORKS. I'M DEFINITELY NOT ACTUALLY GOING TO EAT YOU.
MY SHOULDER? OH, DO YOU WANT A RIDE? YOU WON'T BE SCARED?
ALL RIGHT.
EEEEEEEEE!
HOLD ON TIGHT!
IMAGINE IF FLUFFY REALLY DOES COME BACK WITH THE MISSING TREASURE!
I COULD BE MOMENTS AWAY FROM HOLDING THE EYE OF ONYX!

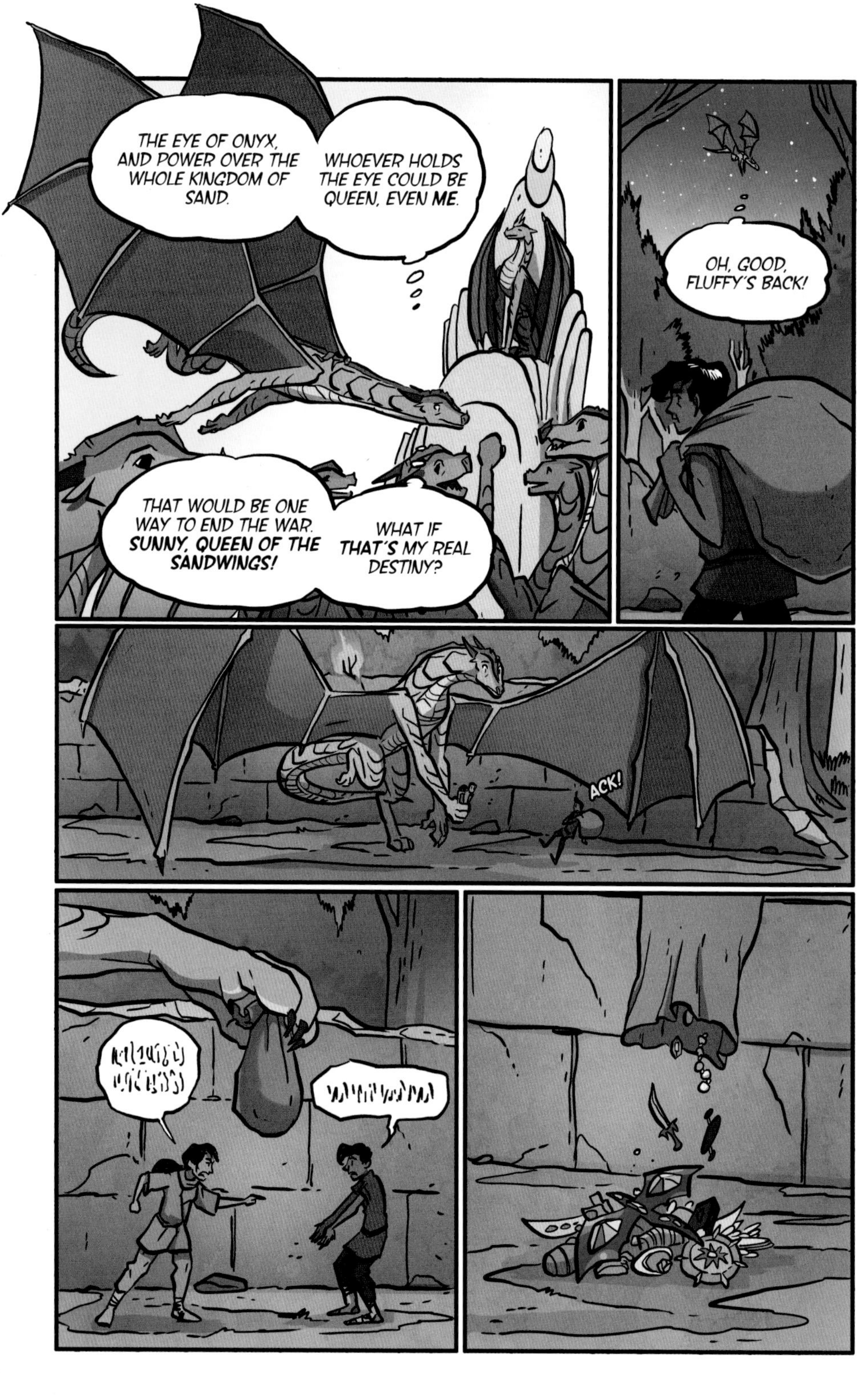
THE EYE OF ONYX, AND POWER OVER THE WHOLE KINGDOM OF SAND.
WHOEVER HOLDS THE EYE COULD BE QUEEN, EVEN ME.
THAT WOULD BE ONE WAY TO END THE WAR. SUNNY, QUEEN OF THE SANDWINGS!
WHAT IF THAT'S MY REAL DESTINY?
OH, GOOD, FLUFFY'S BACK!
ACK!

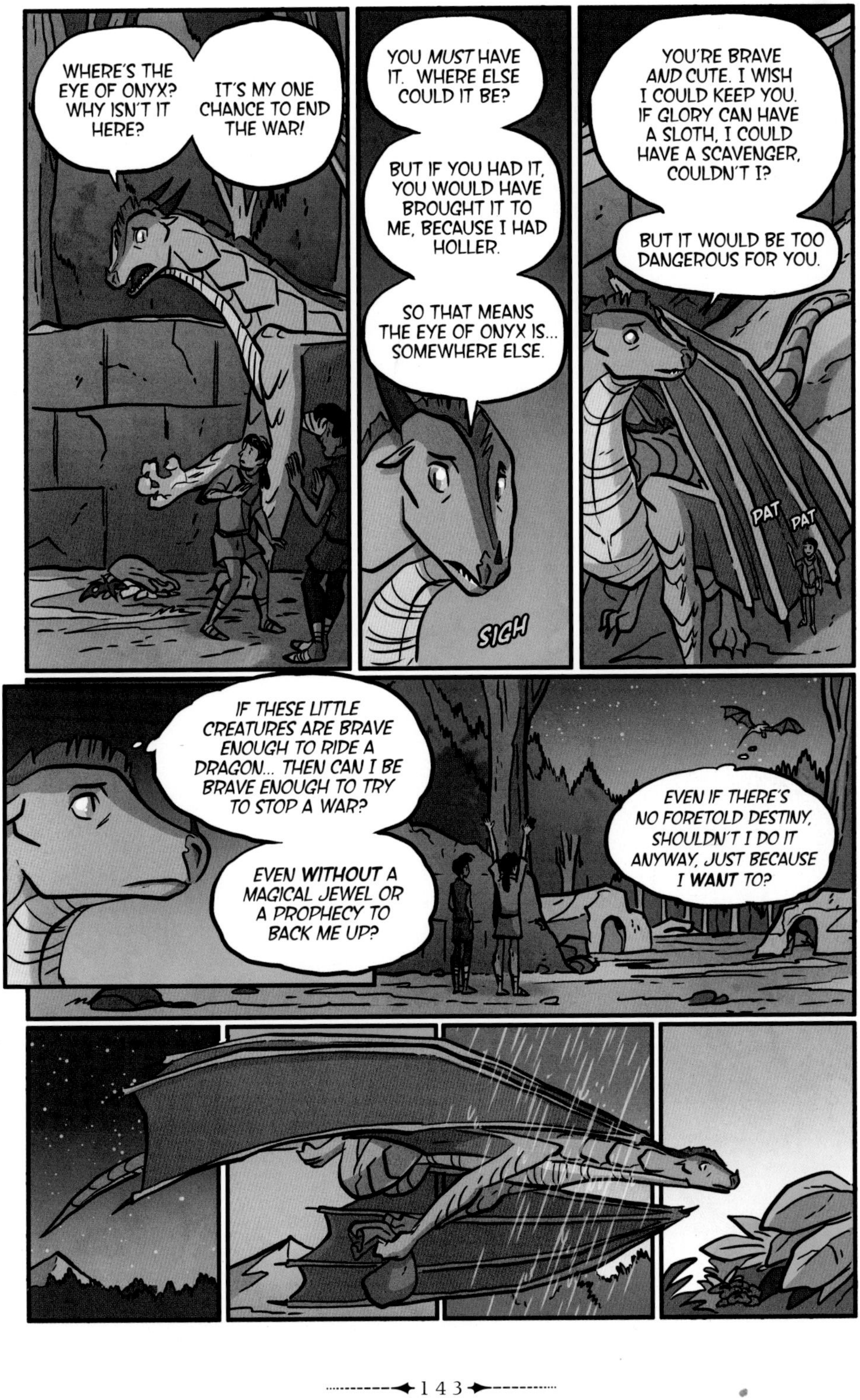
WHERE'S THE EYE OF ONYX? WHY ISN'T IT HERE?
IT'S MY ONE CHANCE TO END THE WAR!
YOU *MUST* HAVE IT. WHERE ELSE COULD IT BE?
BUT IF YOU HAD IT, YOU WOULD HAVE BROUGHT IT TO ME, BECAUSE I HAD HOLLER.
SO THAT MEANS THE EYE OF ONYX IS... SOMEWHERE ELSE.
SIGH
YOU'RE BRAVE AND CUTE. I WISH I COULD KEEP YOU. IF GLORY CAN HAVE A SLOTH, I COULD HAVE A SCAVENGER, COULDN'T I?
BUT IT WOULD BE TOO DANGEROUS FOR YOU.
PAT PAT
IF THESE LITTLE CREATURES ARE BRAVE ENOUGH TO RIDE A DRAGON... THEN CAN I BE BRAVE ENOUGH TO TRY TO STOP A WAR?
EVEN **WITHOUT** A MAGICAL JEWEL OR A PROPHECY TO BACK ME UP?
EVEN IF THERE'S NO FORETOLD DESTINY, SHOULDN'T I DO IT ANYWAY, JUST BECAUSE I **WANT** TO?

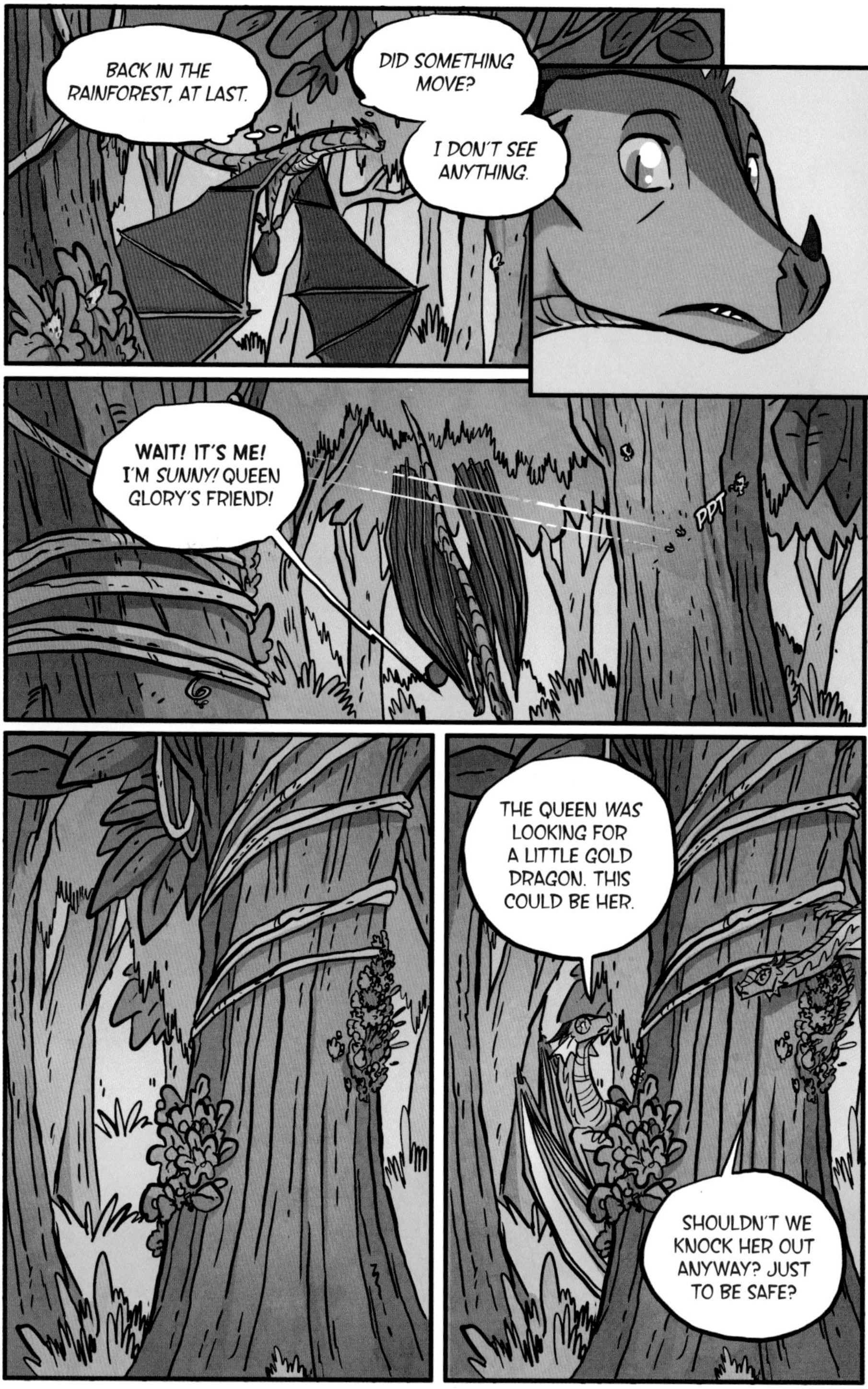
BACK IN THE RAINFOREST, AT LAST.
DID SOMETHING MOVE?
I DON'T SEE ANYTHING.
WAIT! IT'S ME! I'M *SUNNY!* QUEEN GLORY'S FRIEND!
PPT
THE QUEEN *WAS* LOOKING FOR A LITTLE GOLD DRAGON. THIS COULD BE HER.
SHOULDN'T WE KNOCK HER OUT ANYWAY? JUST TO BE SAFE?

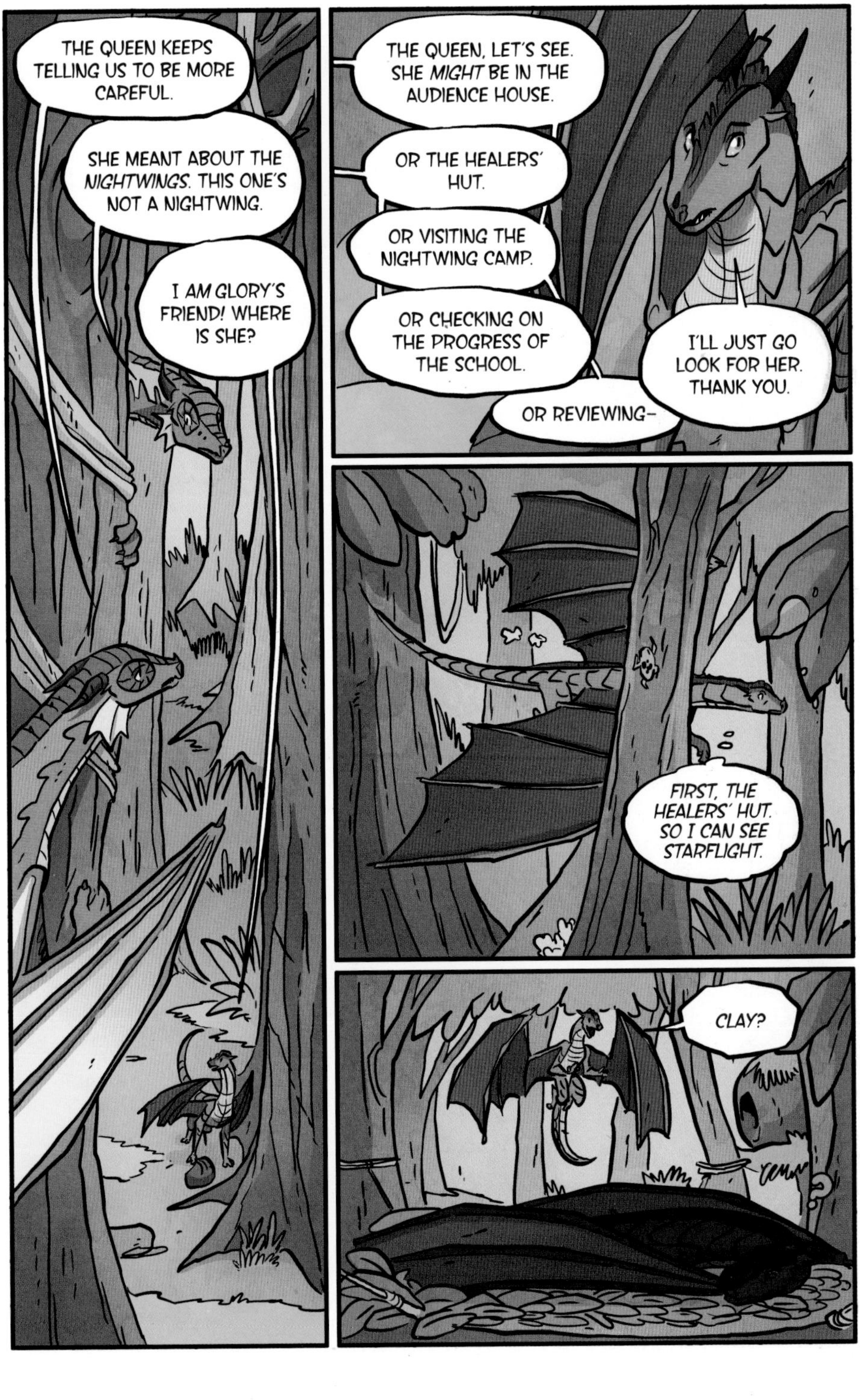
THE QUEEN KEEPS TELLING US TO BE MORE CAREFUL.
SHE MEANT ABOUT THE *NIGHTWINGS*. THIS ONE'S NOT A NIGHTWING.
I *AM* GLORY'S FRIEND! WHERE IS SHE?
THE QUEEN, LET'S SEE. SHE *MIGHT* BE IN THE AUDIENCE HOUSE.
OR THE HEALERS' HUT.
OR VISITING THE NIGHTWING CAMP.
OR CHECKING ON THE PROGRESS OF THE SCHOOL.
OR REVIEWING–
I'LL JUST GO LOOK FOR HER. THANK YOU.
FIRST, THE HEALERS' HUT. SO I CAN SEE STARFLIGHT.
CLAY?

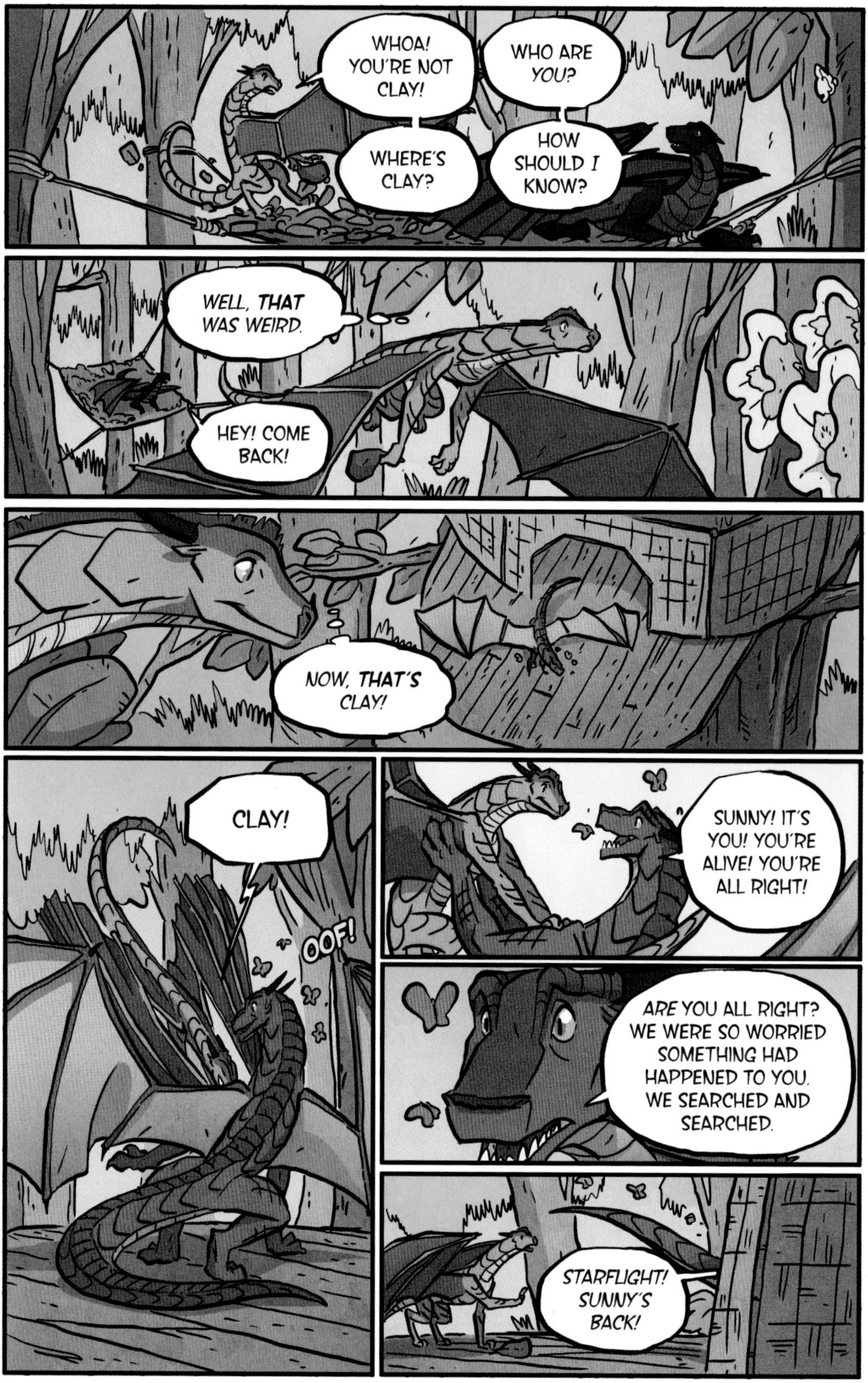
WHOA! YOU'RE NOT CLAY!
WHO ARE YOU?
WHERE'S CLAY?
HOW SHOULD I KNOW?
WELL, THAT WAS WEIRD.
HEY! COME BACK!
NOW, THAT'S CLAY!
CLAY!
OOF!
SUNNY! IT'S YOU! YOU'RE ALIVE! YOU'RE ALL RIGHT!
ARE YOU ALL RIGHT? WE WERE SO WORRIED SOMETHING HAD HAPPENED TO YOU. WE SEARCHED AND SEARCHED.
STARFLIGHT! SUNNY'S BACK!

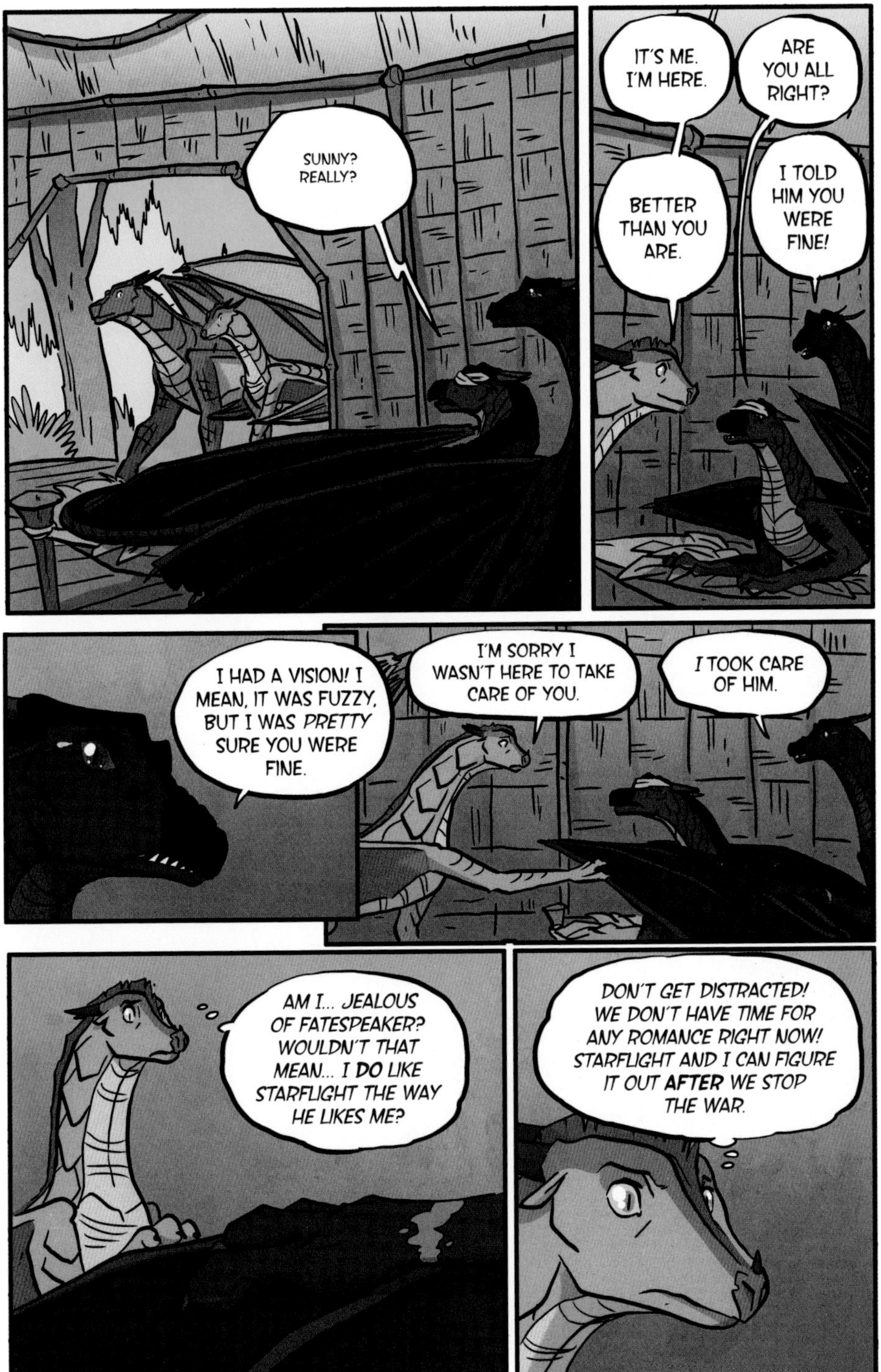
SUNNY? REALLY?
IT'S ME. I'M HERE.
ARE YOU ALL RIGHT?
BETTER THAN YOU ARE.
I TOLD HIM YOU WERE FINE!
I HAD A VISION! I MEAN, IT WAS FUZZY, BUT I WAS *PRETTY* SURE YOU WERE FINE.
I'M SORRY I WASN'T HERE TO TAKE CARE OF YOU.
I TOOK CARE OF HIM.
AM I... JEALOUS OF FATESPEAKER? WOULDN'T THAT MEAN... I **DO** LIKE STARFLIGHT THE WAY HE LIKES ME?
DON'T GET DISTRACTED! WE DON'T HAVE TIME FOR ANY ROMANCE RIGHT NOW! STARFLIGHT AND I CAN FIGURE IT OUT **AFTER** WE STOP THE WAR.

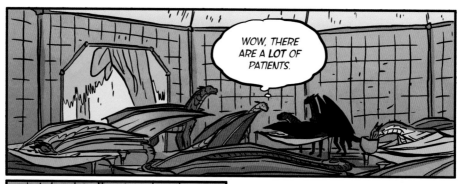

WOW, THERE ARE A **LOT** OF PATIENTS.

WEBS LOOKS LIKE HE'S DOING WELL.

THAT'S FLAME, ISN'T IT? THE SKYWING FROM THE ALTERNATE DRAGONETS. HIS POOR FACE. HE LOOKS SO ANGRY.

THOSE RAINWINGS MUST HAVE BEEN PRISONERS OF THE NIGHTWINGS.

LOOK AT WHAT THE NIGHTWINGS **DID** TO THEM.

HOW WILL THE RAINWINGS EVER FORGIVE THEM?

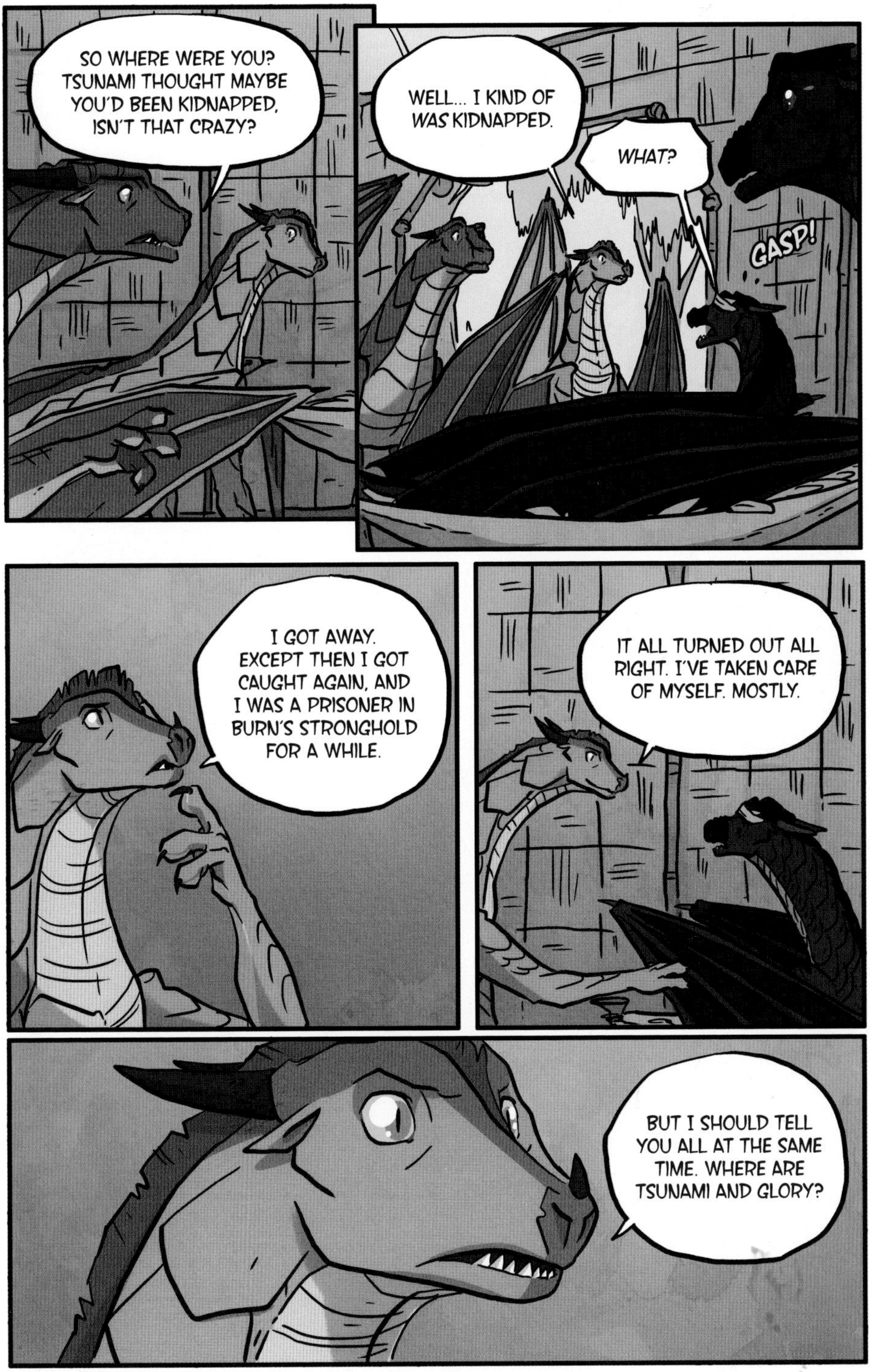
SO WHERE WERE YOU? TSUNAMI THOUGHT MAYBE YOU'D BEEN KIDNAPPED, ISN'T THAT CRAZY?
WELL... I KIND OF WAS KIDNAPPED.
WHAT?
GASP!
I GOT AWAY. EXCEPT THEN I GOT CAUGHT AGAIN, AND I WAS A PRISONER IN BURN'S STRONGHOLD FOR A WHILE.
IT ALL TURNED OUT ALL RIGHT. I'VE TAKEN CARE OF MYSELF. MOSTLY.
BUT I SHOULD TELL YOU ALL AT THE SAME TIME. WHERE ARE TSUNAMI AND GLORY?

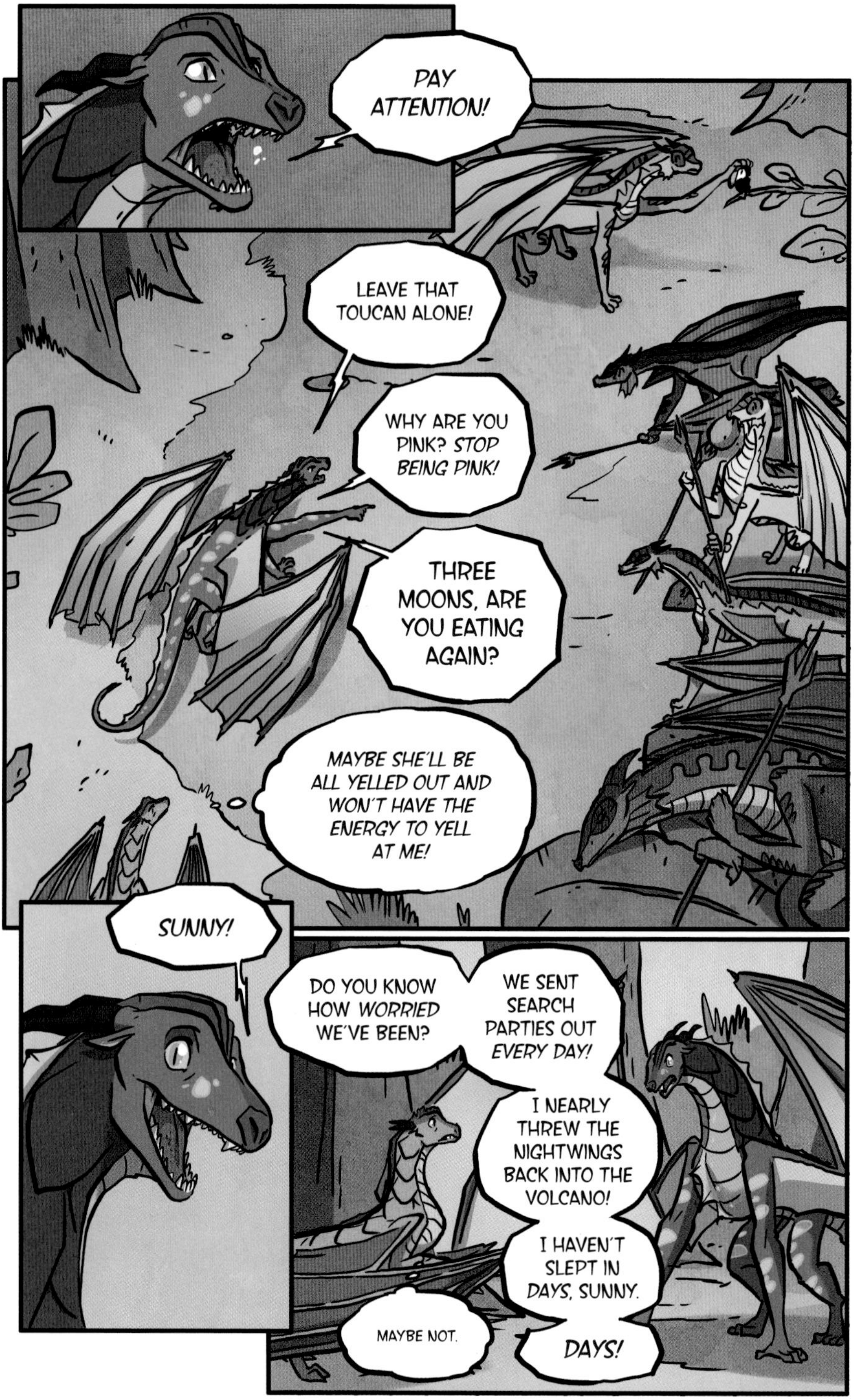
PAY ATTENTION!
LEAVE THAT TOUCAN ALONE!
WHY ARE YOU PINK? STOP BEING PINK!
THREE MOONS, ARE YOU EATING AGAIN?
MAYBE SHE'LL BE ALL YELLED OUT AND WON'T HAVE THE ENERGY TO YELL AT ME!
SUNNY!
DO YOU KNOW HOW WORRIED WE'VE BEEN?
WE SENT SEARCH PARTIES OUT EVERY DAY!
I NEARLY THREW THE NIGHTWINGS BACK INTO THE VOLCANO!
I HAVEN'T SLEPT IN DAYS, SUNNY.
DAYS!
MAYBE NOT.

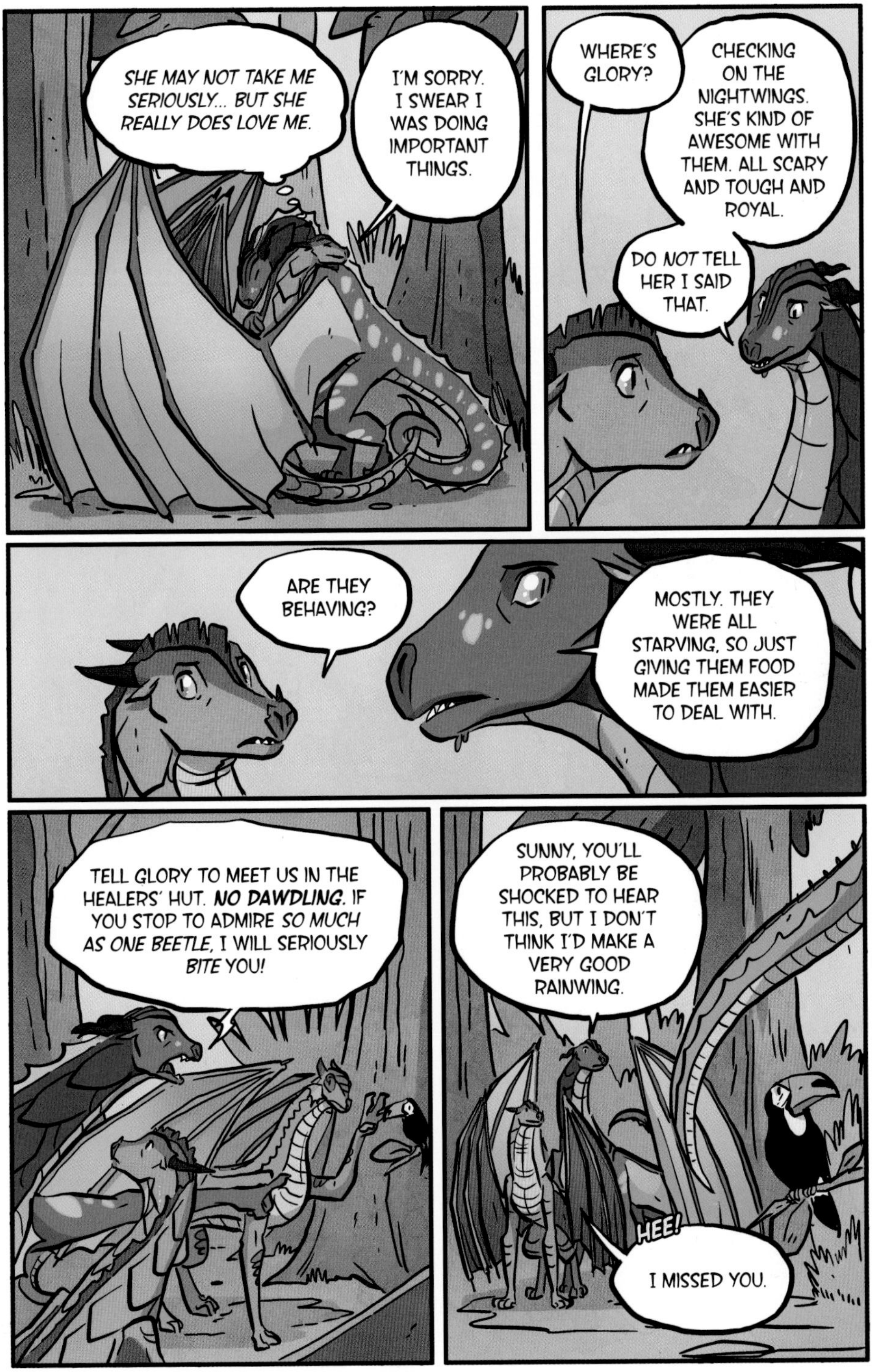
SHE MAY NOT TAKE ME SERIOUSLY... BUT SHE REALLY DOES LOVE ME.
I'M SORRY. I SWEAR I WAS DOING IMPORTANT THINGS.
WHERE'S GLORY?
CHECKING ON THE NIGHTWINGS. SHE'S KIND OF AWESOME WITH THEM. ALL SCARY AND TOUGH AND ROYAL.
DO NOT TELL HER I SAID THAT.
ARE THEY BEHAVING?
MOSTLY. THEY WERE ALL STARVING, SO JUST GIVING THEM FOOD MADE THEM EASIER TO DEAL WITH.
TELL GLORY TO MEET US IN THE HEALERS' HUT. NO DAWDLING. IF YOU STOP TO ADMIRE SO MUCH AS ONE BEETLE, I WILL SERIOUSLY BITE YOU!
SUNNY, YOU'LL PROBABLY BE SHOCKED TO HEAR THIS, BUT I DON'T THINK I'D MAKE A VERY GOOD RAINWING.
HEE!
I MISSED YOU.

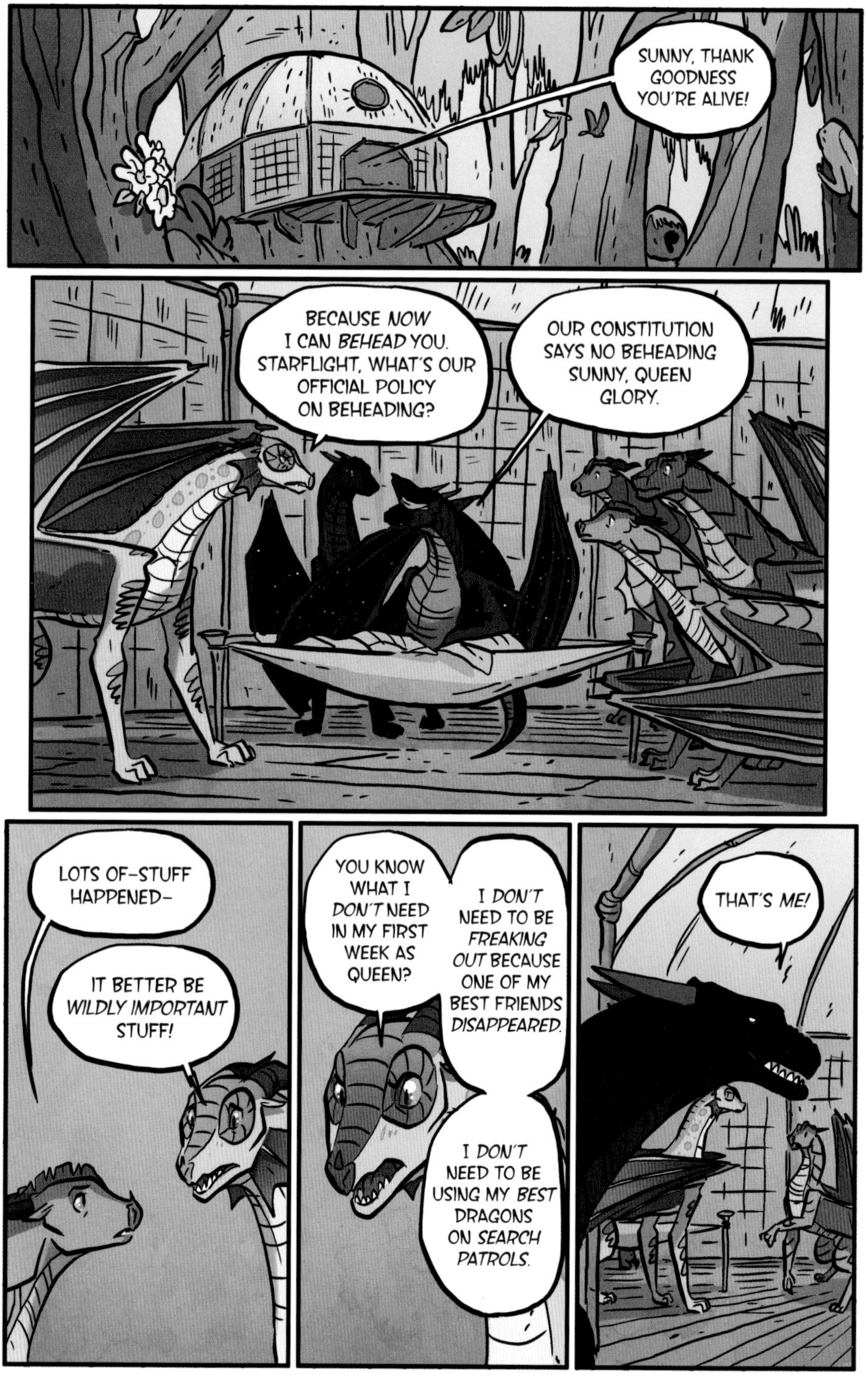
SUNNY, THANK GOODNESS YOU'RE ALIVE!
BECAUSE *NOW* I CAN *BEHEAD* YOU. STARFLIGHT, WHAT'S OUR OFFICIAL POLICY ON BEHEADING?
OUR CONSTITUTION SAYS NO BEHEADING SUNNY, QUEEN GLORY.
LOTS OF—STUFF HAPPENED—
IT BETTER BE *WILDLY IMPORTANT* STUFF!
YOU KNOW WHAT I *DON'T* NEED IN MY FIRST WEEK AS QUEEN?
I *DON'T* NEED TO BE *FREAKING OUT* BECAUSE ONE OF MY BEST FRIENDS *DISAPPEARED.*
I *DON'T* NEED TO BE USING MY *BEST* DRAGONS ON *SEARCH PATROLS.*
THAT'S *ME!*

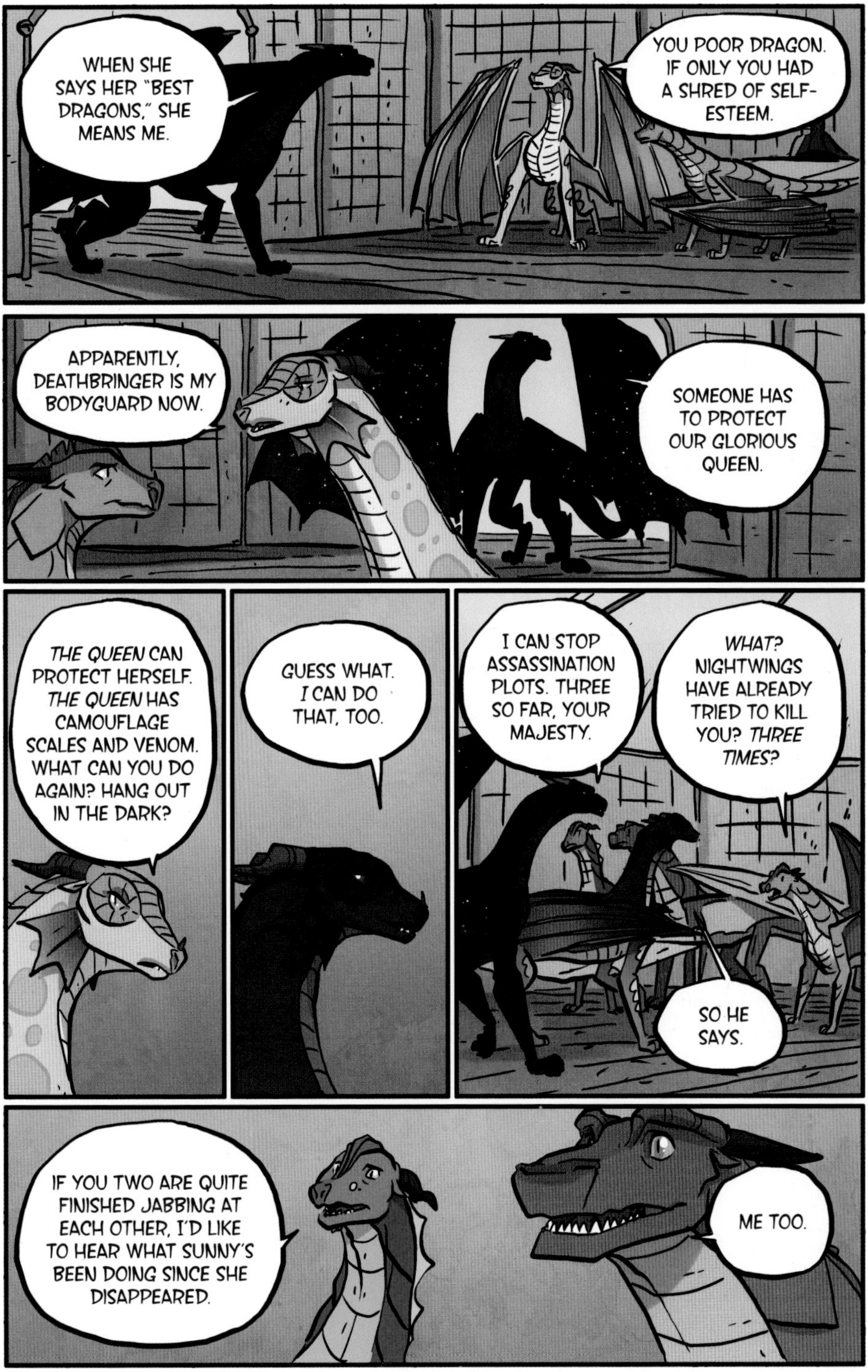
WHEN SHE SAYS HER "BEST DRAGONS," SHE MEANS ME.
YOU POOR DRAGON. IF ONLY YOU HAD A SHRED OF SELF-ESTEEM.
APPARENTLY, DEATHBRINGER IS MY BODYGUARD NOW.
SOMEONE HAS TO PROTECT OUR GLORIOUS QUEEN.
THE QUEEN CAN PROTECT HERSELF. *THE QUEEN* HAS CAMOUFLAGE SCALES AND VENOM. WHAT CAN YOU DO AGAIN? HANG OUT IN THE DARK?
GUESS WHAT. *I* CAN DO THAT, TOO.
I CAN STOP ASSASSINATION PLOTS. THREE SO FAR, YOUR MAJESTY.
WHAT? NIGHTWINGS HAVE ALREADY TRIED TO KILL YOU? *THREE TIMES?*
SO HE SAYS.
IF YOU TWO ARE QUITE FINISHED JABBING AT EACH OTHER, I'D LIKE TO HEAR WHAT SUNNY'S BEEN DOING SINCE SHE DISAPPEARED.
ME TOO.

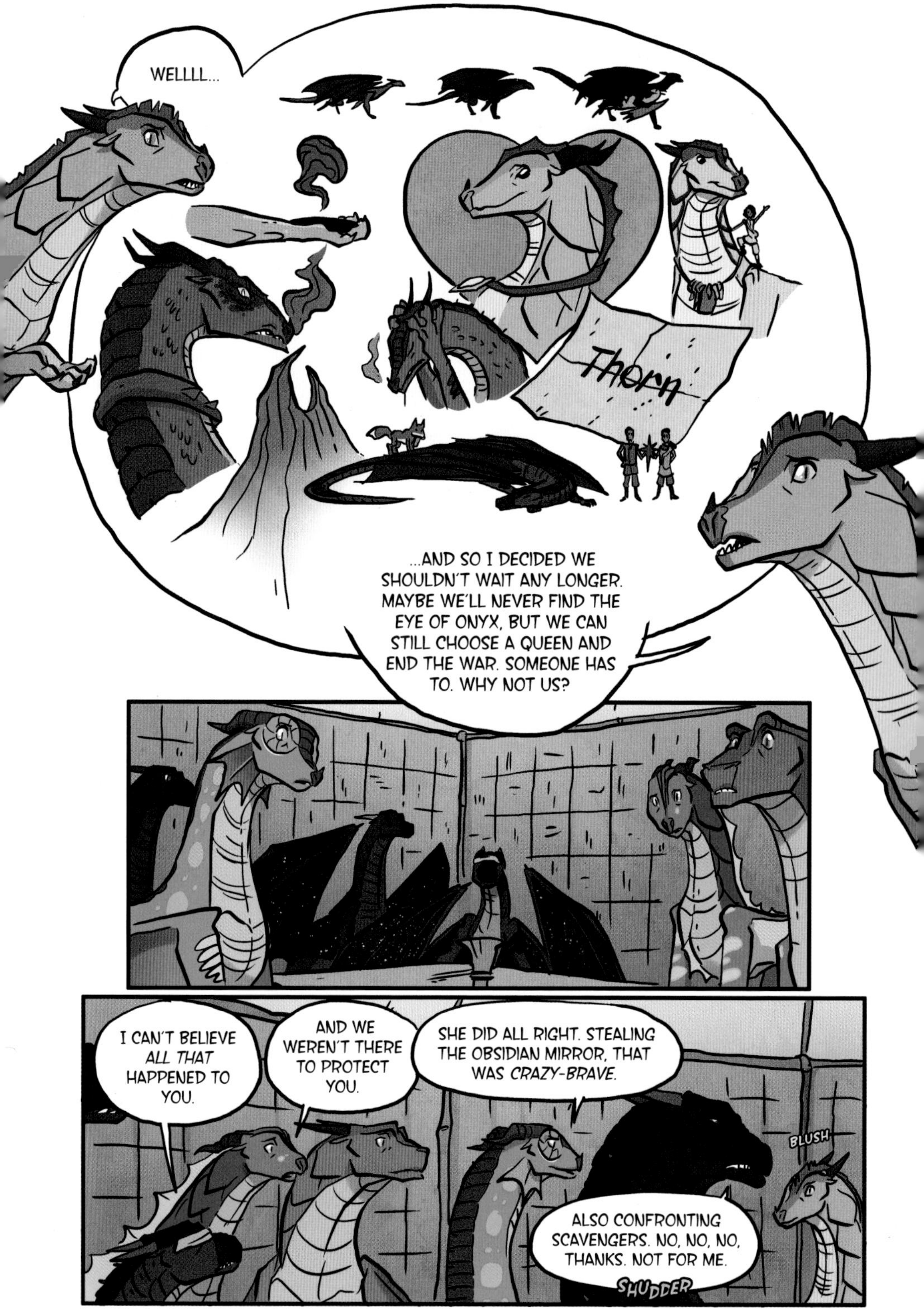
WELLLL...
Thorn
...AND SO I DECIDED WE SHOULDN'T WAIT ANY LONGER. MAYBE WE'LL NEVER FIND THE EYE OF ONYX, BUT WE CAN STILL CHOOSE A QUEEN AND END THE WAR. SOMEONE HAS TO. WHY NOT US?
I CAN'T BELIEVE *ALL THAT* HAPPENED TO YOU.
AND WE WEREN'T THERE TO PROTECT YOU.
SHE DID ALL RIGHT. STEALING THE OBSIDIAN MIRROR, THAT WAS *CRAZY-BRAVE*.
BLUSH
ALSO CONFRONTING SCAVENGERS. NO, NO, NO, THANKS. NOT FOR ME.
SHUDDER

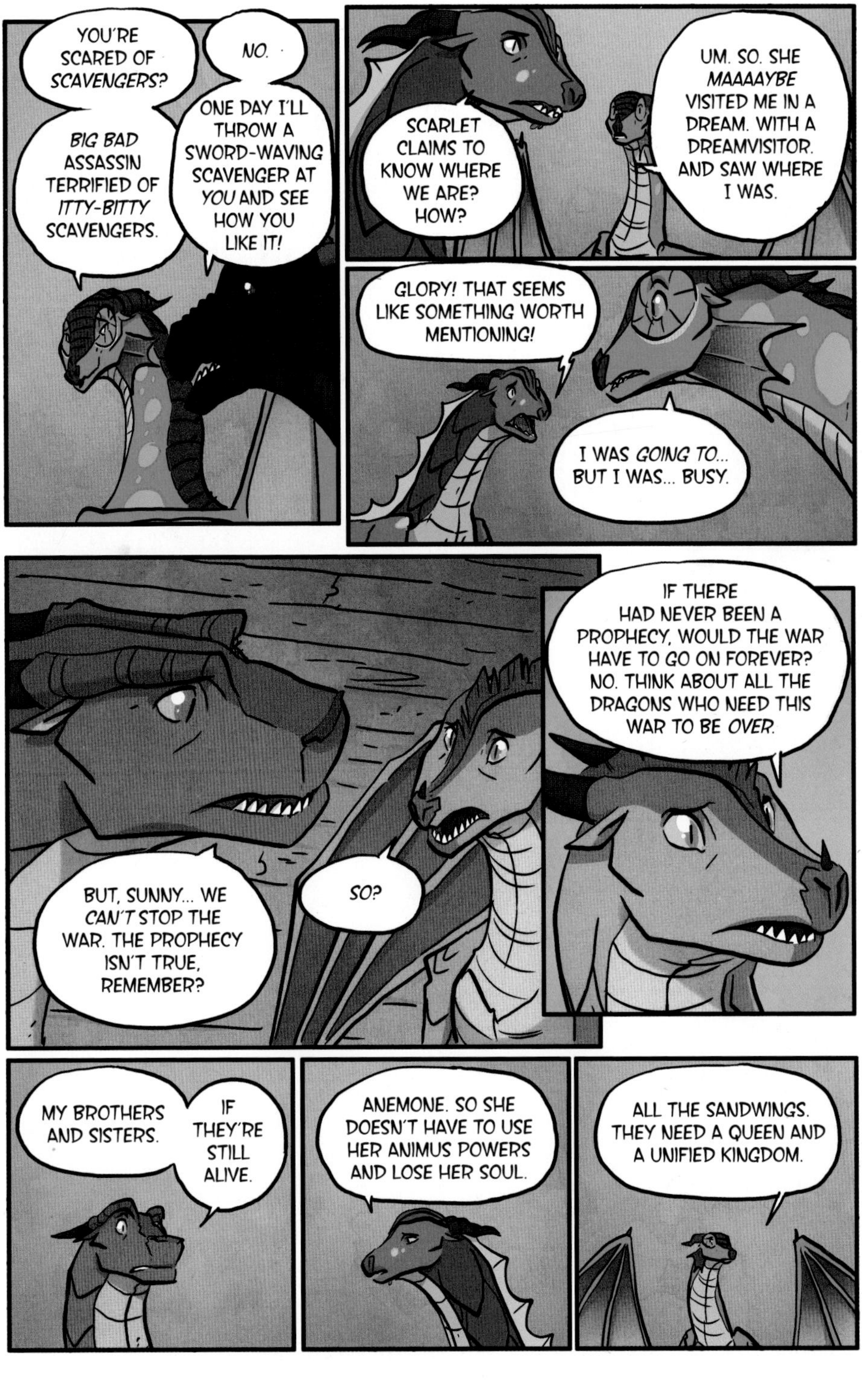
YOU'RE SCARED OF SCAVENGERS?
BIG BAD ASSASSIN TERRIFIED OF *ITTY-BITTY* SCAVENGERS.
NO.
ONE DAY I'LL THROW A SWORD-WAVING SCAVENGER AT *YOU* AND SEE HOW YOU LIKE IT!
SCARLET CLAIMS TO KNOW WHERE WE ARE? HOW?
UM. SO. SHE *MAAAAYBE* VISITED ME IN A DREAM. WITH A DREAMVISITOR. AND SAW WHERE I WAS.
GLORY! THAT SEEMS LIKE SOMETHING WORTH MENTIONING!
I WAS *GOING TO...* BUT I WAS... BUSY.
BUT, SUNNY... WE *CAN'T* STOP THE WAR. THE PROPHECY ISN'T TRUE, REMEMBER?
SO?
IF THERE HAD NEVER BEEN A PROPHECY, WOULD THE WAR HAVE TO GO ON FOREVER? NO. THINK ABOUT ALL THE DRAGONS WHO NEED THIS WAR TO BE *OVER*.
MY BROTHERS AND SISTERS.
IF THEY'RE STILL ALIVE.
ANEMONE. SO SHE DOESN'T HAVE TO USE HER ANIMUS POWERS AND LOSE HER SOUL.
ALL THE SANDWINGS. THEY NEED A QUEEN AND A UNIFIED KINGDOM.

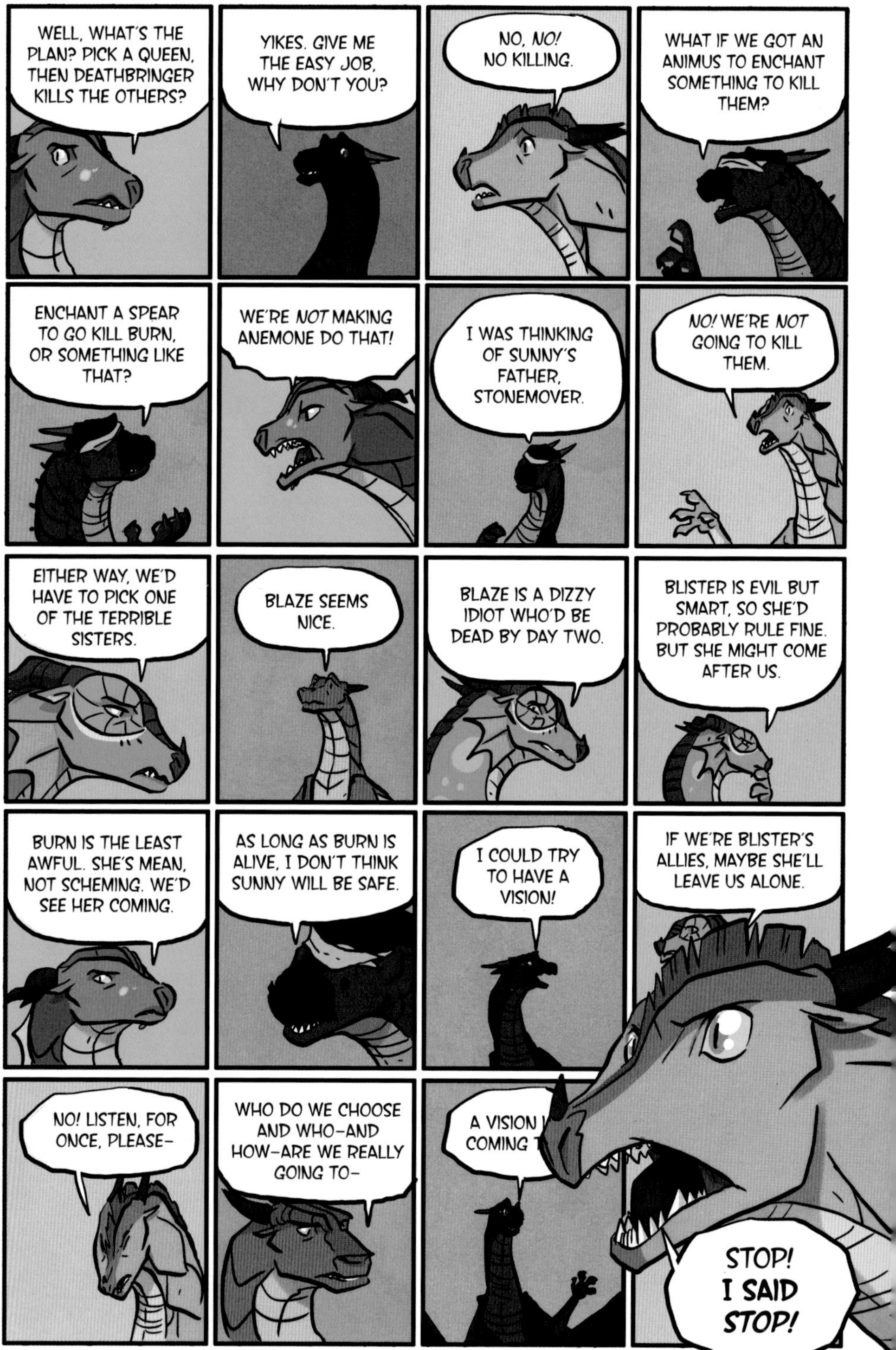
WELL, WHAT'S THE PLAN? PICK A QUEEN, THEN DEATHBRINGER KILLS THE OTHERS?
YIKES. GIVE ME THE EASY JOB, WHY DON'T YOU?
NO, *NO!* NO KILLING.
WHAT IF WE GOT AN ANIMUS TO ENCHANT SOMETHING TO KILL THEM?
ENCHANT A SPEAR TO GO KILL BURN, OR SOMETHING LIKE THAT?
WE'RE *NOT* MAKING ANEMONE DO THAT!
I WAS THINKING OF SUNNY'S FATHER, STONEMOVER.
NO! WE'RE *NOT* GOING TO KILL THEM.
EITHER WAY, WE'D HAVE TO PICK ONE OF THE TERRIBLE SISTERS.
BLAZE SEEMS NICE.
BLAZE IS A DIZZY IDIOT WHO'D BE DEAD BY DAY TWO.
BLISTER IS EVIL BUT SMART, SO SHE'D PROBABLY RULE FINE. BUT SHE MIGHT COME AFTER US.
BURN IS THE LEAST AWFUL. SHE'S MEAN, NOT SCHEMING. WE'D SEE HER COMING.
AS LONG AS BURN IS ALIVE, I DON'T THINK SUNNY WILL BE SAFE.
I COULD TRY TO HAVE A VISION!
IF WE'RE BLISTER'S ALLIES, MAYBE SHE'LL LEAVE US ALONE.
NO! LISTEN, FOR ONCE, PLEASE–
WHO DO WE CHOOSE AND WHO–AND HOW–ARE WE REALLY GOING TO–
STOP! **I SAID STOP!**

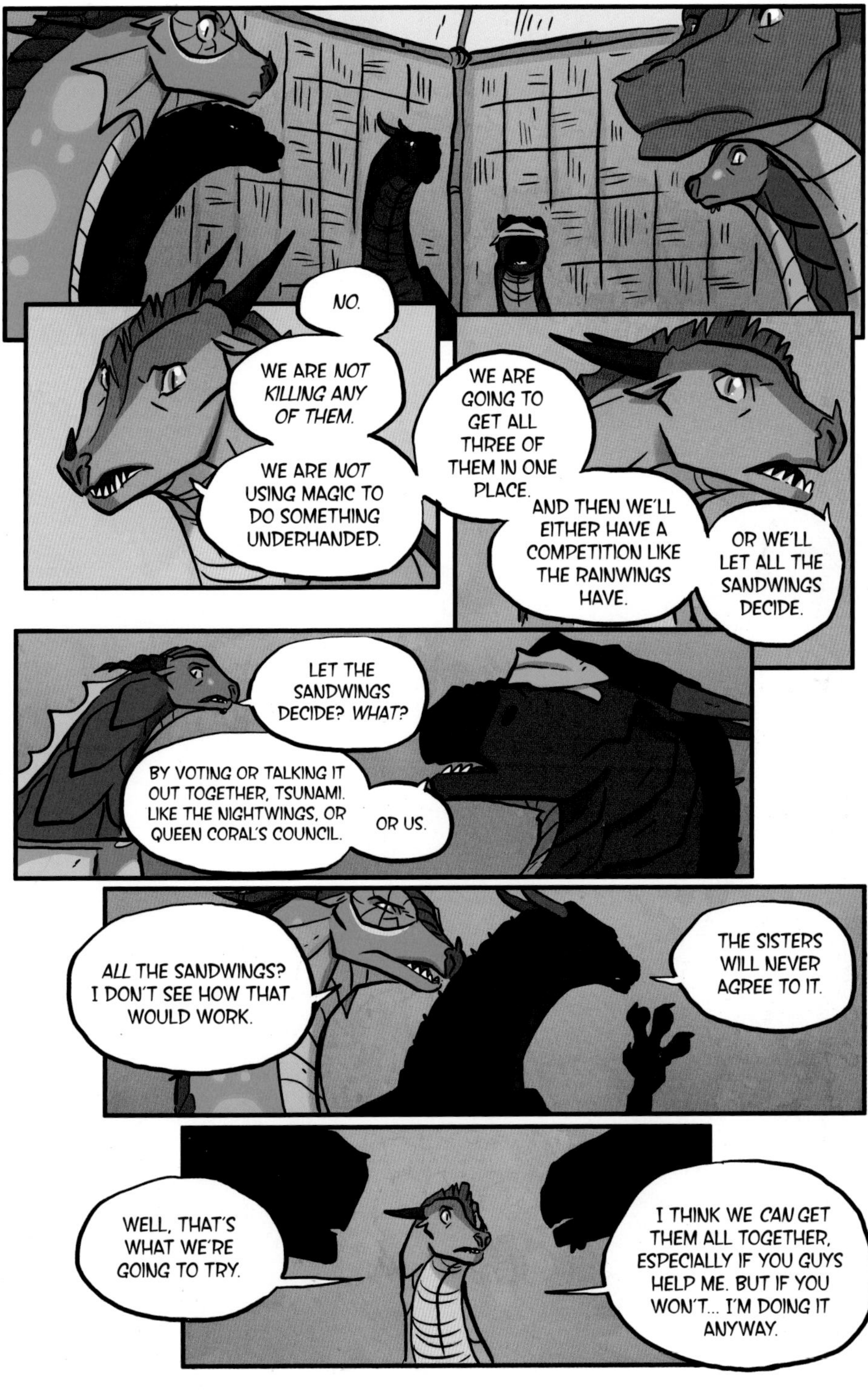
NO.
WE ARE NOT KILLING ANY OF THEM.
WE ARE NOT USING MAGIC TO DO SOMETHING UNDERHANDED.
WE ARE GOING TO GET ALL THREE OF THEM IN ONE PLACE.
AND THEN WE'LL EITHER HAVE A COMPETITION LIKE THE RAINWINGS HAVE.
OR WE'LL LET ALL THE SANDWINGS DECIDE.
LET THE SANDWINGS DECIDE? WHAT?
BY VOTING OR TALKING IT OUT TOGETHER, TSUNAMI. LIKE THE NIGHTWINGS, OR QUEEN CORAL'S COUNCIL.
OR US.
ALL THE SANDWINGS? I DON'T SEE HOW THAT WOULD WORK.
THE SISTERS WILL NEVER AGREE TO IT.
WELL, THAT'S WHAT WE'RE GOING TO TRY.
I THINK WE CAN GET THEM ALL TOGETHER, ESPECIALLY IF YOU GUYS HELP ME. BUT IF YOU WON'T... I'M DOING IT ANYWAY.

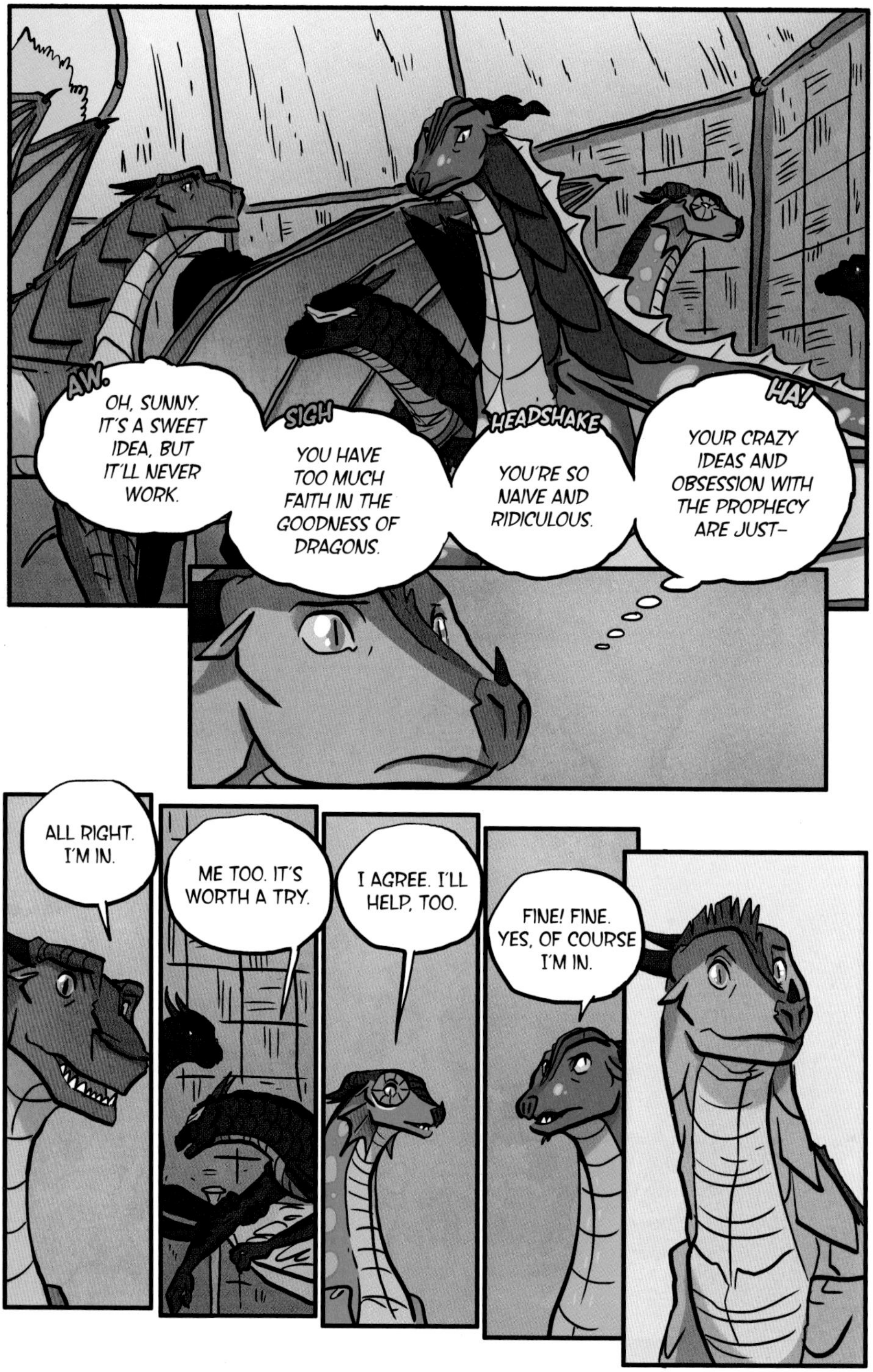
AW.
OH, SUNNY. IT'S A SWEET IDEA, BUT IT'LL NEVER WORK.
SIGH
YOU HAVE TOO MUCH FAITH IN THE GOODNESS OF DRAGONS.
HEADSHAKE
YOU'RE SO NAIVE AND RIDICULOUS.
HA!
YOUR CRAZY IDEAS AND OBSESSION WITH THE PROPHECY ARE JUST–
ALL RIGHT. I'M IN.
ME TOO. IT'S WORTH A TRY.
I AGREE. I'LL HELP, TOO.
FINE! FINE. YES, OF COURSE I'M IN.

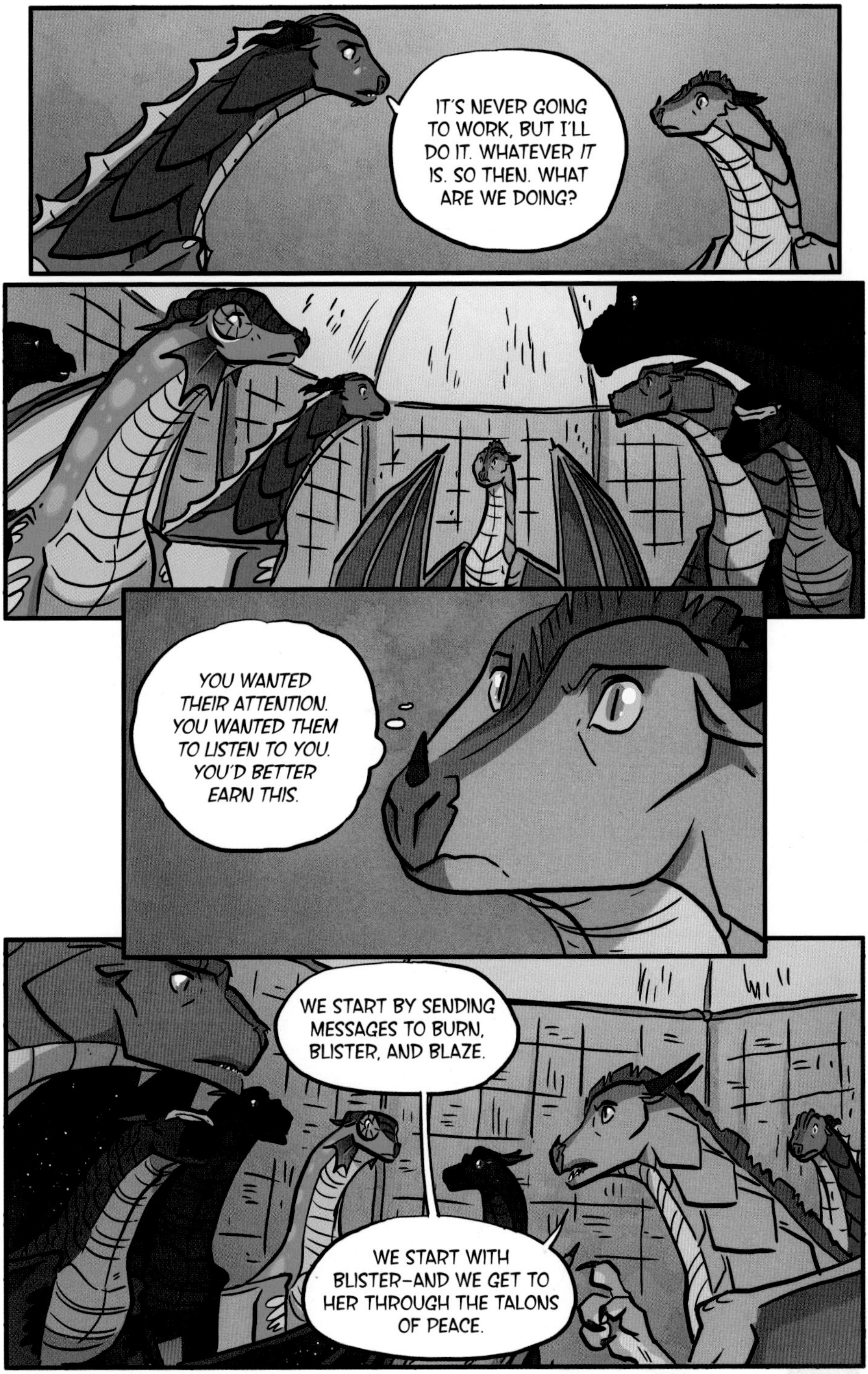
IT'S NEVER GOING TO WORK, BUT I'LL DO IT. WHATEVER *IT* IS. SO THEN. WHAT ARE WE DOING?
YOU WANTED THEIR ATTENTION. YOU WANTED THEM TO LISTEN TO YOU. YOU'D BETTER EARN THIS.
WE START BY SENDING MESSAGES TO BURN, BLISTER, AND BLAZE.
WE START WITH BLISTER—AND WE GET TO HER THROUGH THE TALONS OF PEACE.

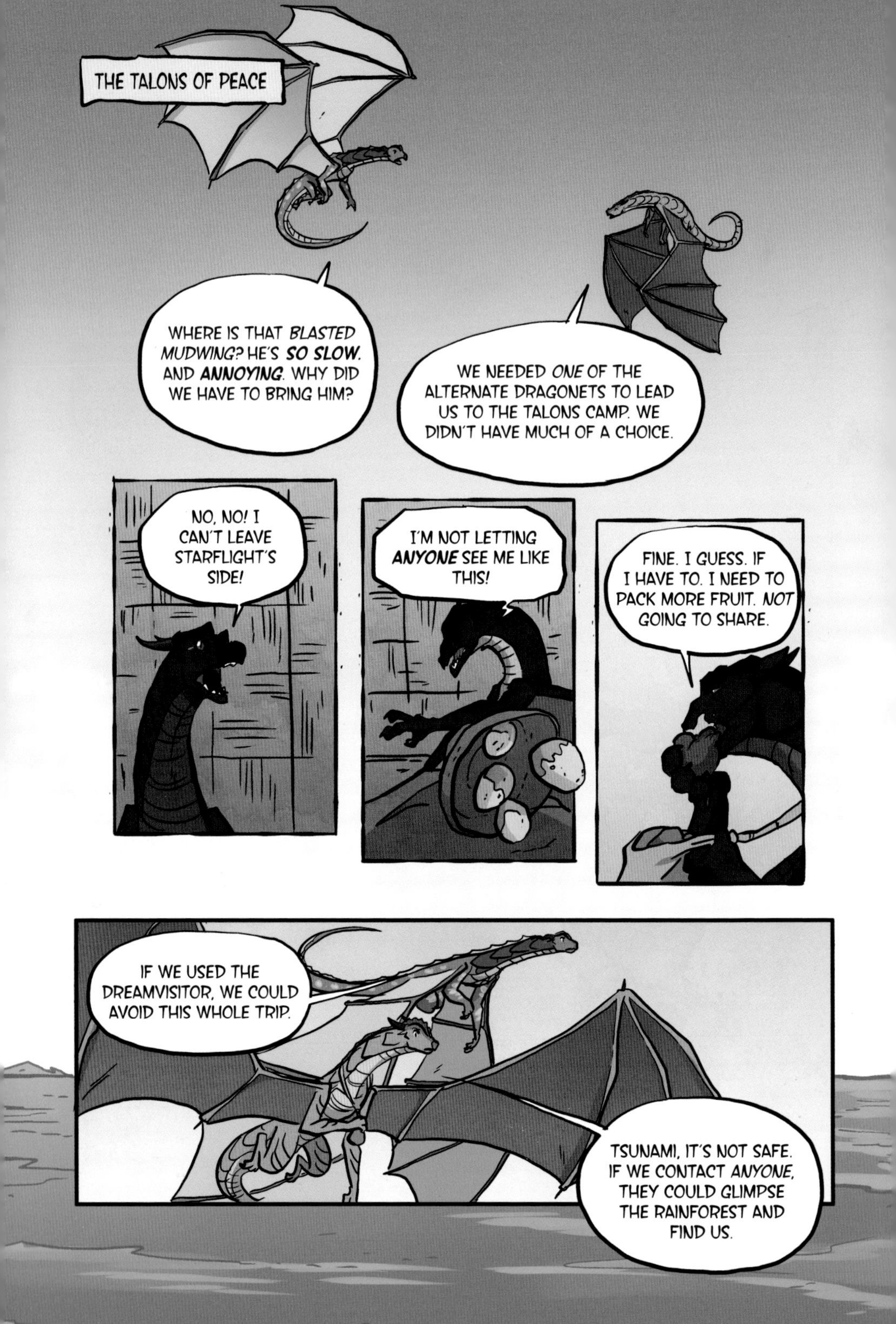
THE TALONS OF PEACE
WHERE IS THAT *BLASTED MUDWING*? HE'S ***SO SLOW.*** AND ***ANNOYING***. WHY DID WE HAVE TO BRING HIM?
WE NEEDED *ONE* OF THE ALTERNATE DRAGONETS TO LEAD US TO THE TALONS CAMP. WE DIDN'T HAVE MUCH OF A CHOICE.
NO, NO*!* I CAN'T LEAVE STARFLIGHT'S SIDE!
I'M NOT LETTING ***ANYONE*** SEE ME LIKE THIS!
FINE. I GUESS. IF I HAVE TO. I NEED TO PACK MORE FRUIT. *NOT* GOING TO SHARE.
IF WE USED THE DREAMVISITOR, WE COULD AVOID THIS WHOLE TRIP.
TSUNAMI, IT'S NOT SAFE. IF WE CONTACT *ANYONE*, THEY COULD GLIMPSE THE RAINFOREST AND FIND US.

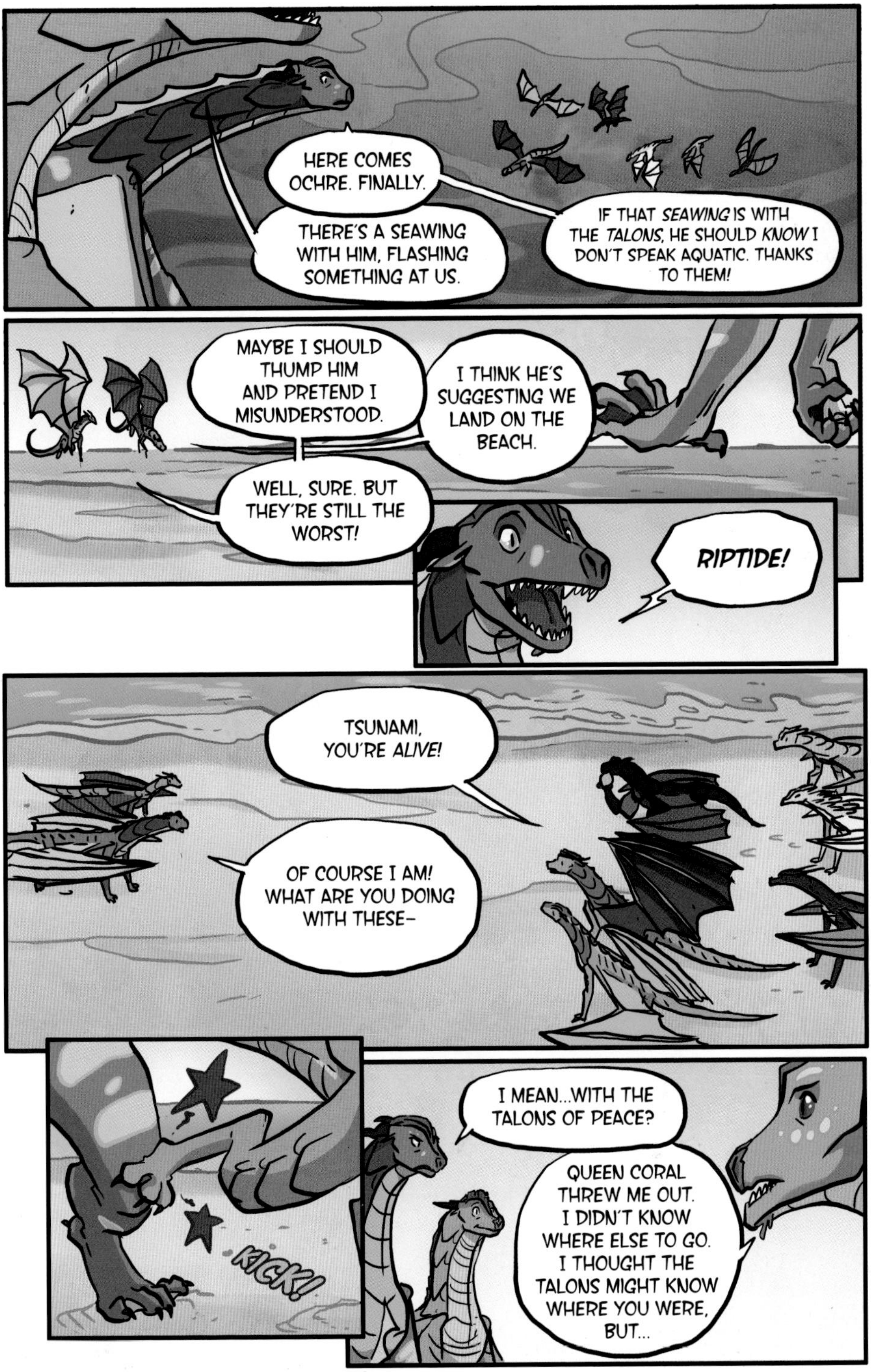
HERE COMES OCHRE. FINALLY.
THERE'S A SEAWING WITH HIM, FLASHING SOMETHING AT US.
IF THAT *SEAWING* IS WITH THE *TALONS*, HE SHOULD *KNOW* I DON'T SPEAK AQUATIC. THANKS TO THEM!
MAYBE I SHOULD THUMP HIM AND PRETEND I MISUNDERSTOOD.
I THINK HE'S SUGGESTING WE LAND ON THE BEACH.
WELL, SURE. BUT THEY'RE STILL THE WORST!
RIPTIDE!
TSUNAMI, YOU'RE *ALIVE!*
OF COURSE I AM! WHAT ARE YOU DOING WITH THESE–
KICK!
I MEAN...WITH THE TALONS OF PEACE?
QUEEN CORAL THREW ME OUT. I DIDN'T KNOW WHERE ELSE TO GO. I THOUGHT THE TALONS MIGHT KNOW WHERE YOU WERE, BUT...

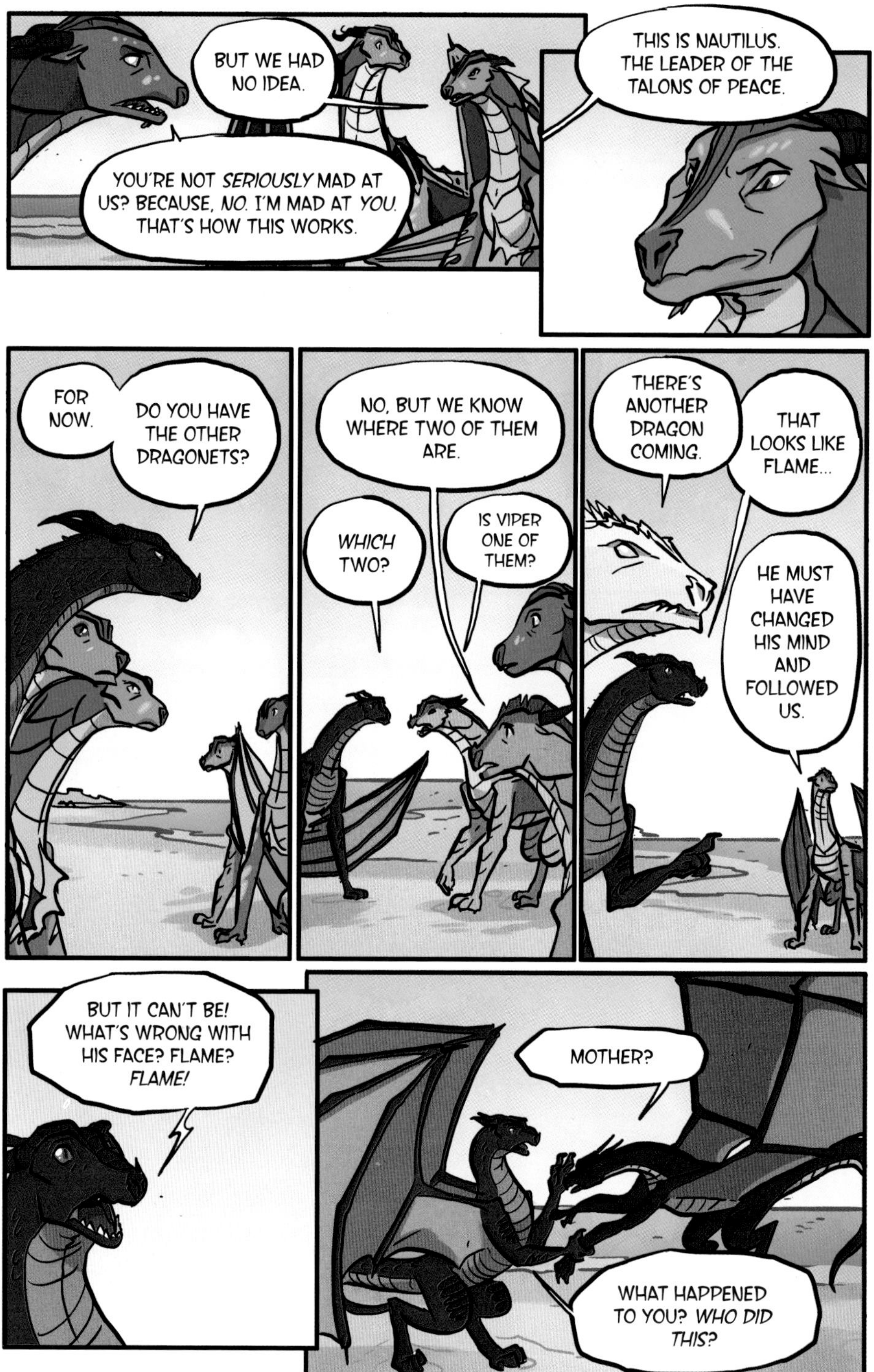
BUT WE HAD NO IDEA.
YOU'RE NOT *SERIOUSLY* MAD AT US? BECAUSE, *NO.* I'M MAD AT *YOU.* THAT'S HOW THIS WORKS.
THIS IS NAUTILUS. THE LEADER OF THE TALONS OF PEACE.
FOR NOW.
DO YOU HAVE THE OTHER DRAGONETS?
NO, BUT WE KNOW WHERE TWO OF THEM ARE.
WHICH TWO?
IS VIPER ONE OF THEM?
THERE'S ANOTHER DRAGON COMING.
THAT LOOKS LIKE FLAME...
HE MUST HAVE CHANGED HIS MIND AND FOLLOWED US.
BUT IT CAN'T BE! WHAT'S WRONG WITH HIS FACE? FLAME? *FLAME!*
MOTHER?
WHAT HAPPENED TO YOU? *WHO DID THIS?*

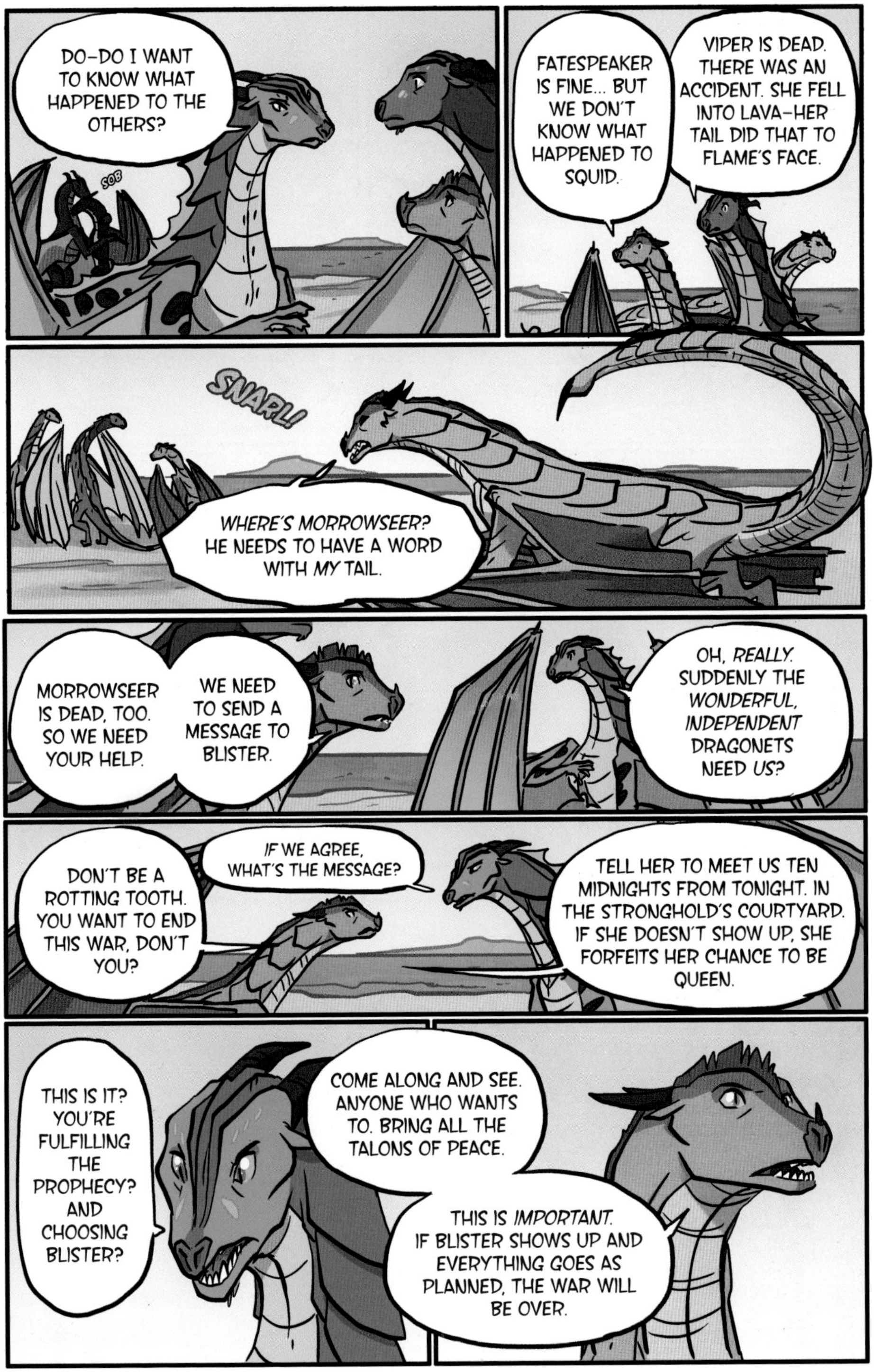

DO–DO I WANT TO KNOW WHAT HAPPENED TO THE OTHERS?
SOB
FATESPEAKER IS FINE... BUT WE DON'T KNOW WHAT HAPPENED TO SQUID.
VIPER IS DEAD. THERE WAS AN ACCIDENT. SHE FELL INTO LAVA–HER TAIL DID THAT TO FLAME'S FACE.
SNARL!
WHERE'S MORROWSEER? HE NEEDS TO HAVE A WORD WITH *MY* TAIL.
MORROWSEER IS DEAD, TOO. SO WE NEED YOUR HELP.
WE NEED TO SEND A MESSAGE TO BLISTER.
OH, *REALLY.* SUDDENLY THE *WONDERFUL, INDEPENDENT* DRAGONETS NEED US?
DON'T BE A ROTTING TOOTH. YOU WANT TO END THIS WAR, DON'T YOU?
IF WE AGREE, WHAT'S THE MESSAGE?
TELL HER TO MEET US TEN MIDNIGHTS FROM TONIGHT. IN THE STRONGHOLD'S COURTYARD. IF SHE DOESN'T SHOW UP, SHE FORFEITS HER CHANCE TO BE QUEEN.
THIS IS IT? YOU'RE FULFILLING THE PROPHECY? AND CHOOSING BLISTER?
COME ALONG AND SEE. ANYONE WHO WANTS TO. BRING ALL THE TALONS OF PEACE.
THIS IS *IMPORTANT.* IF BLISTER SHOWS UP AND EVERYTHING GOES AS PLANNED, THE WAR WILL BE OVER.

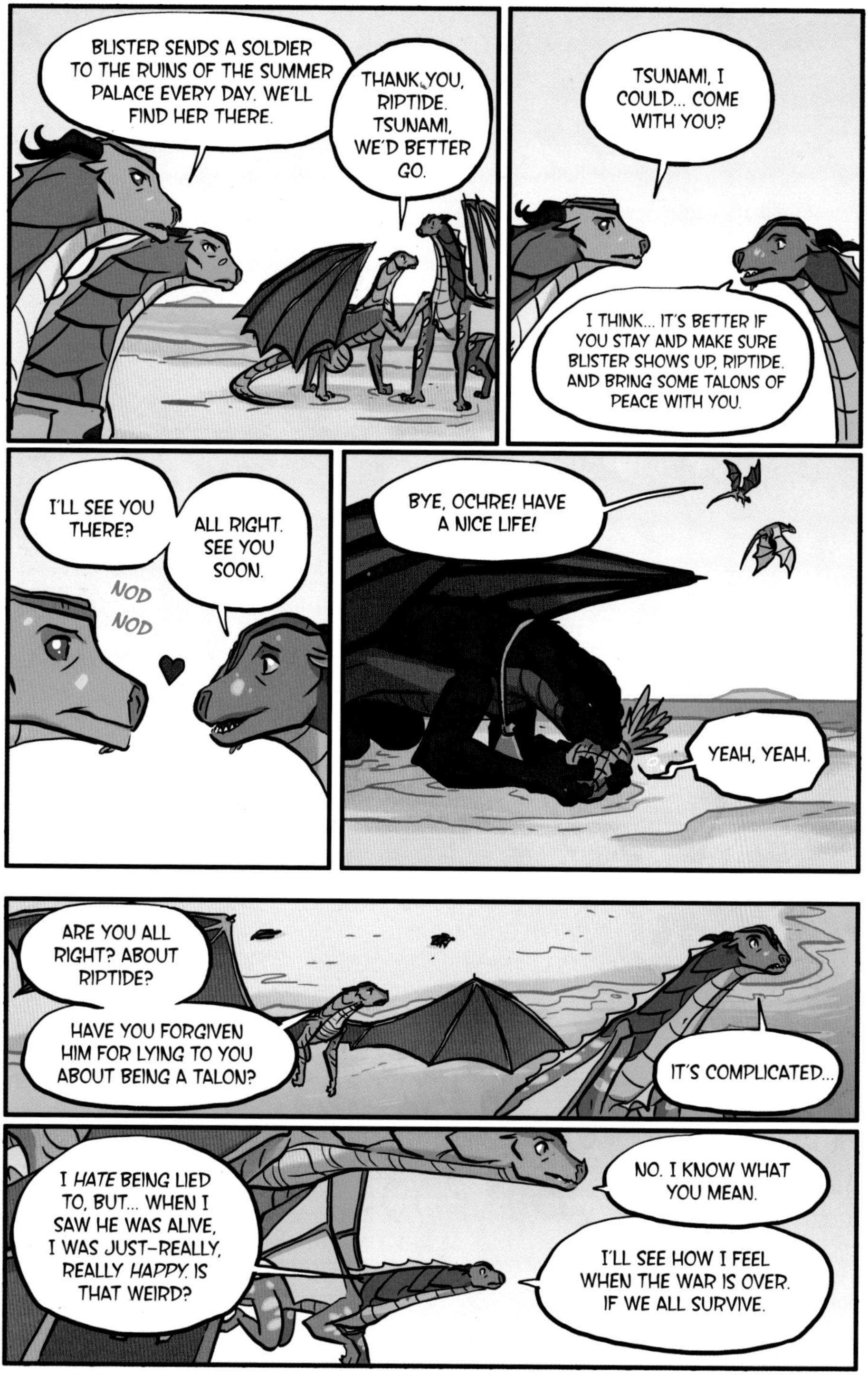
BLISTER SENDS A SOLDIER TO THE RUINS OF THE SUMMER PALACE EVERY DAY. WE'LL FIND HER THERE.
THANK YOU, RIPTIDE. TSUNAMI, WE'D BETTER GO.
TSUNAMI, I COULD... COME WITH YOU?
I THINK... IT'S BETTER IF YOU STAY AND MAKE SURE BLISTER SHOWS UP, RIPTIDE. AND BRING SOME TALONS OF PEACE WITH YOU.
I'LL SEE YOU THERE?
ALL RIGHT. SEE YOU SOON.
NOD
NOD
BYE, OCHRE! HAVE A NICE LIFE!
YEAH, YEAH.
ARE YOU ALL RIGHT? ABOUT RIPTIDE?
HAVE YOU FORGIVEN HIM FOR LYING TO YOU ABOUT BEING A TALON?
IT'S COMPLICATED...
I *HATE* BEING LIED TO, BUT... WHEN I SAW HE WAS ALIVE, I WAS JUST—REALLY, REALLY *HAPPY*. IS THAT WEIRD?
NO. I KNOW WHAT YOU MEAN.
I'LL SEE HOW I FEEL WHEN THE WAR IS OVER. IF WE ALL SURVIVE.

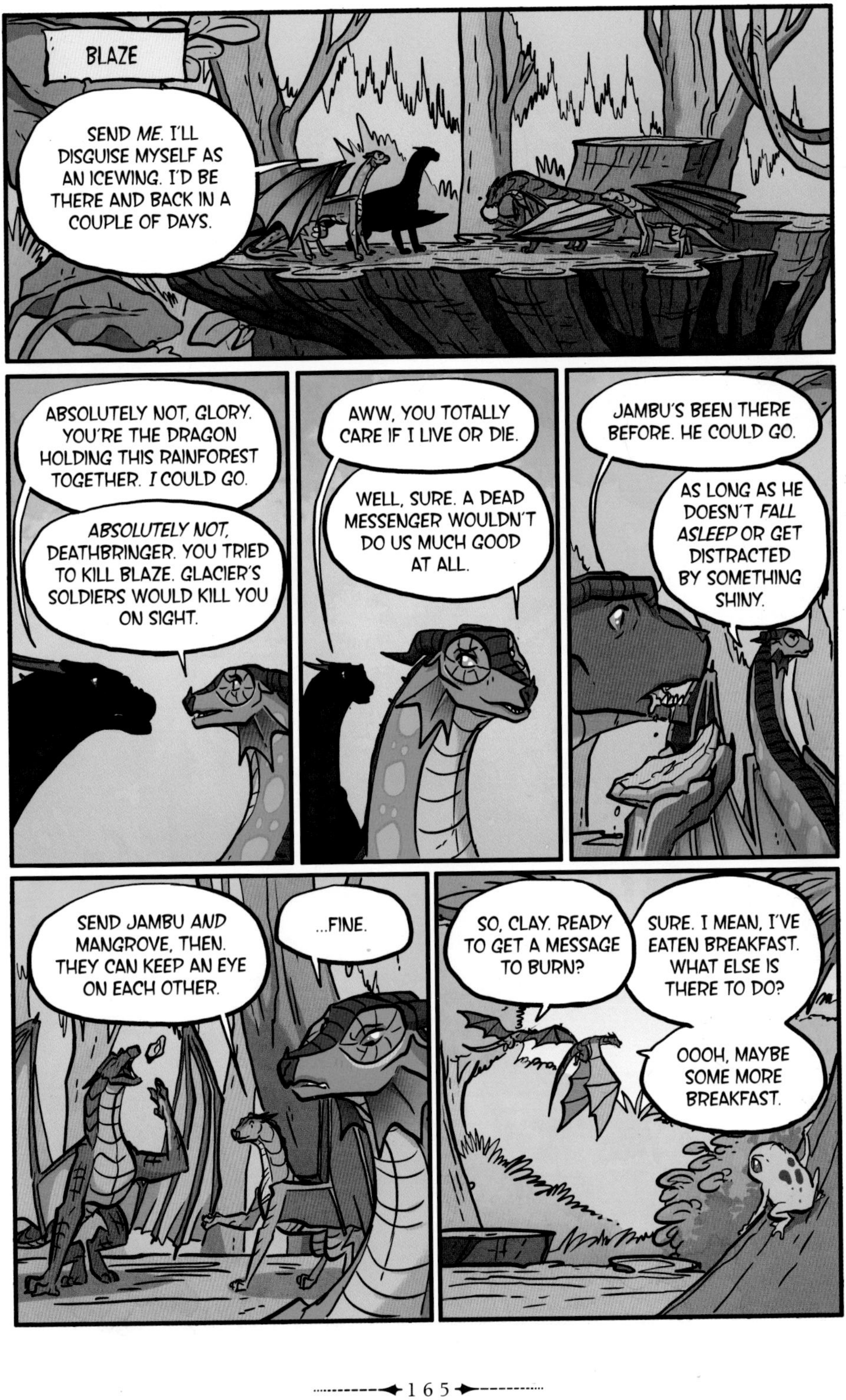
BLAZE
SEND *ME*. I'LL DISGUISE MYSELF AS AN ICEWING. I'D BE THERE AND BACK IN A COUPLE OF DAYS.
ABSOLUTELY NOT, GLORY. YOU'RE THE DRAGON HOLDING THIS RAINFOREST TOGETHER. *I* COULD GO.
ABSOLUTELY NOT, DEATHBRINGER. YOU TRIED TO KILL BLAZE. GLACIER'S SOLDIERS WOULD KILL YOU ON SIGHT.
AWW, YOU TOTALLY CARE IF I LIVE OR DIE.
WELL, SURE. A DEAD MESSENGER WOULDN'T DO US MUCH GOOD AT ALL.
JAMBU'S BEEN THERE BEFORE. HE COULD GO.
AS LONG AS HE DOESN'T *FALL ASLEEP* OR GET DISTRACTED BY SOMETHING SHINY.
SEND JAMBU *AND* MANGROVE, THEN. THEY CAN KEEP AN EYE ON EACH OTHER.
...FINE.
SO, CLAY. READY TO GET A MESSAGE TO BURN?
SURE. I MEAN, I'VE EATEN BREAKFAST. WHAT ELSE IS THERE TO DO?
OOOH, MAYBE SOME MORE BREAKFAST.

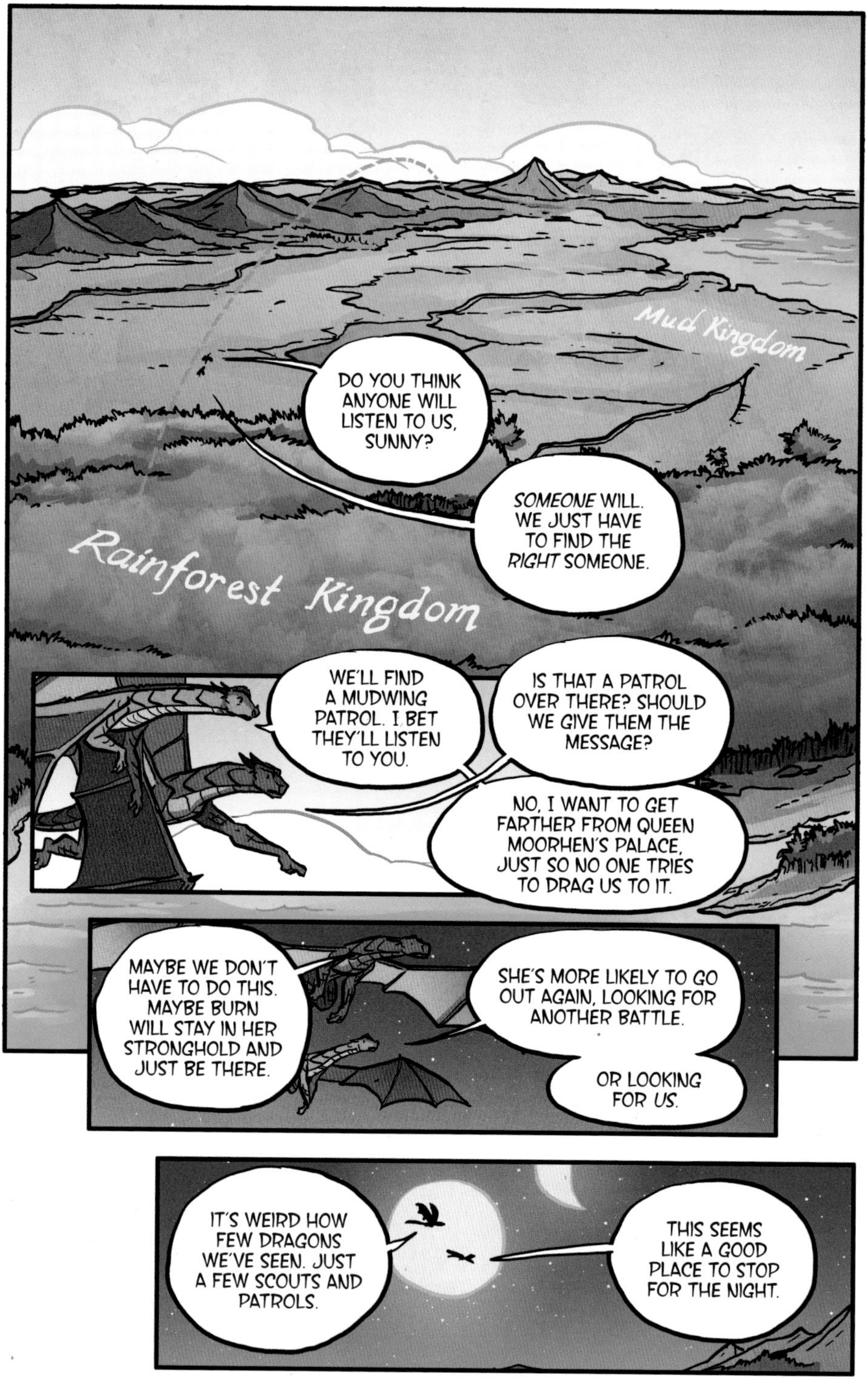
Mud Kingdom
Rainforest Kingdom
DO YOU THINK ANYONE WILL LISTEN TO US, SUNNY?
SOMEONE WILL. WE JUST HAVE TO FIND THE *RIGHT* SOMEONE.
WE'LL FIND A MUDWING PATROL. I BET THEY'LL LISTEN TO YOU.
IS THAT A PATROL OVER THERE? SHOULD WE GIVE THEM THE MESSAGE?
NO, I WANT TO GET FARTHER FROM QUEEN MOORHEN'S PALACE, JUST SO NO ONE TRIES TO DRAG US TO IT.
MAYBE WE DON'T HAVE TO DO THIS. MAYBE BURN WILL STAY IN HER STRONGHOLD AND JUST BE THERE.
SHE'S MORE LIKELY TO GO OUT AGAIN, LOOKING FOR ANOTHER BATTLE.
OR LOOKING FOR *US*.
IT'S WEIRD HOW FEW DRAGONS WE'VE SEEN. JUST A FEW SCOUTS AND PATROLS.
THIS SEEMS LIKE A GOOD PLACE TO STOP FOR THE NIGHT.

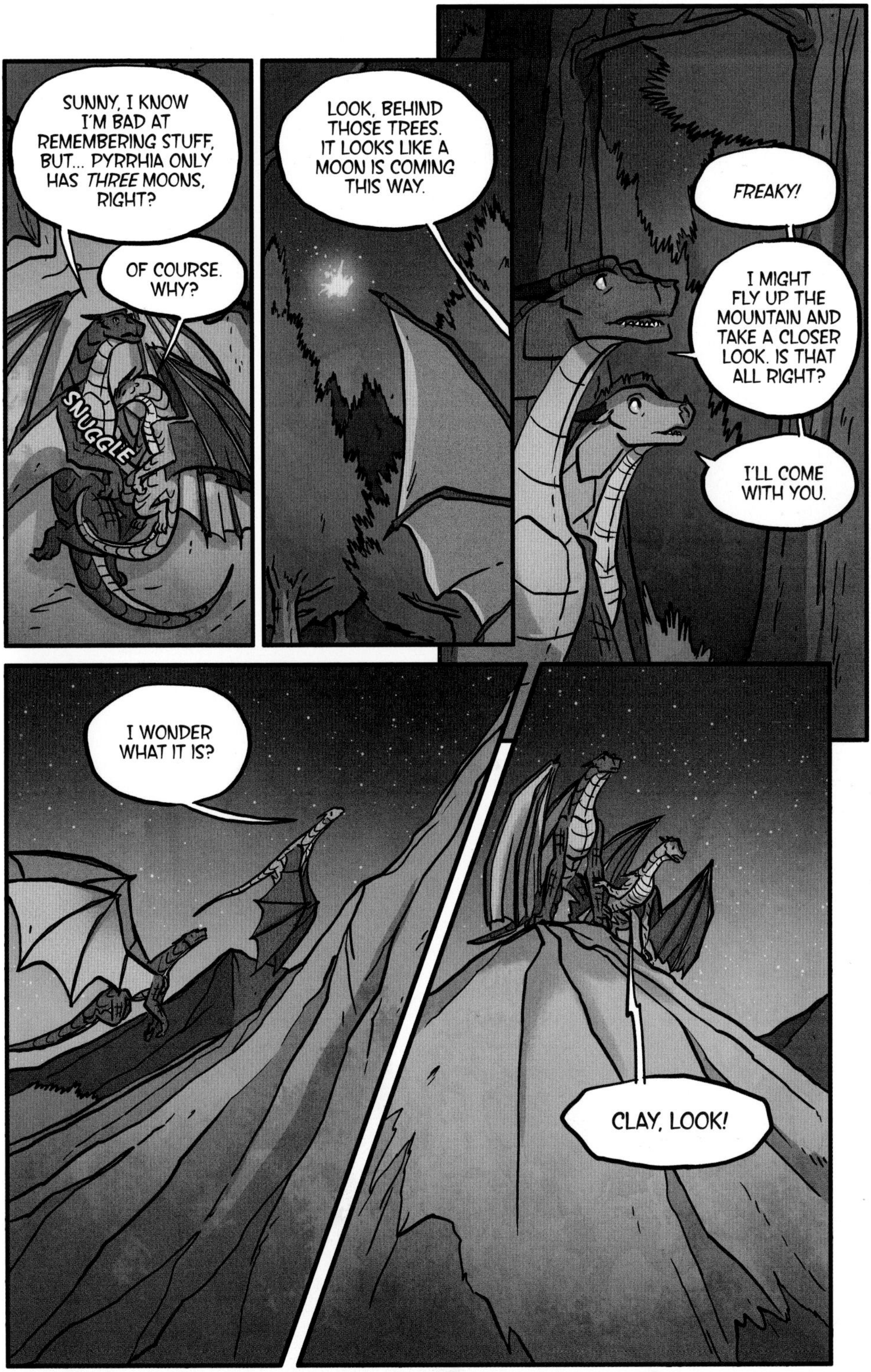
SUNNY, I KNOW I'M BAD AT REMEMBERING STUFF, BUT... PYRRHIA ONLY HAS *THREE* MOONS, RIGHT?
OF COURSE. WHY?
SNUGGLE
LOOK, BEHIND THOSE TREES. IT LOOKS LIKE A MOON IS COMING THIS WAY.
FREAKY!
I MIGHT FLY UP THE MOUNTAIN AND TAKE A CLOSER LOOK. IS THAT ALL RIGHT?
I'LL COME WITH YOU.
I WONDER WHAT IT IS?
CLAY, LOOK!

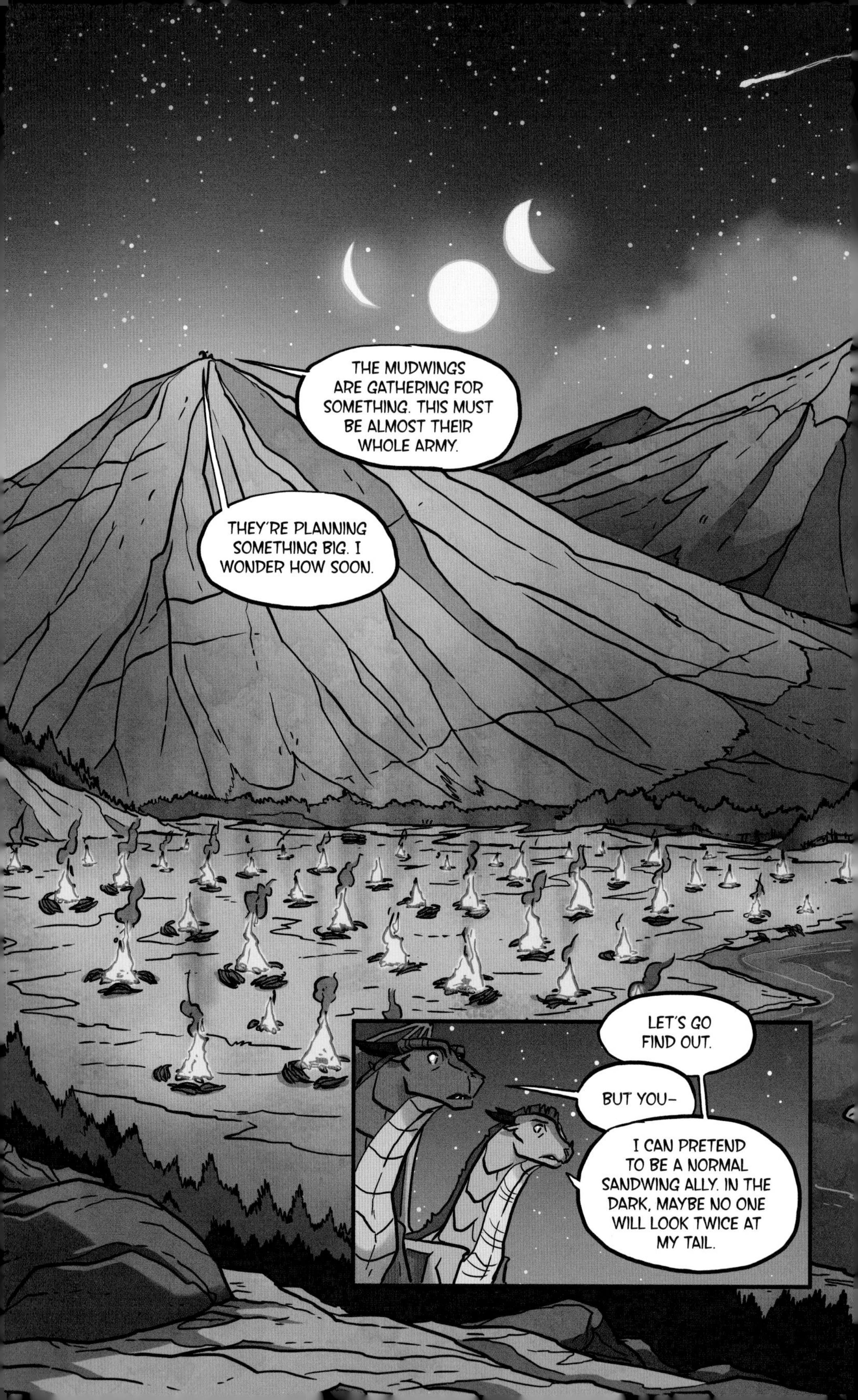
THE MUDWINGS ARE GATHERING FOR SOMETHING. THIS MUST BE ALMOST THEIR WHOLE ARMY.
THEY'RE PLANNING SOMETHING BIG. I WONDER HOW SOON.
LET'S GO FIND OUT.
BUT YOU–
I CAN PRETEND TO BE A NORMAL SANDWING ALLY. IN THE DARK, MAYBE NO ONE WILL LOOK TWICE AT MY TAIL.

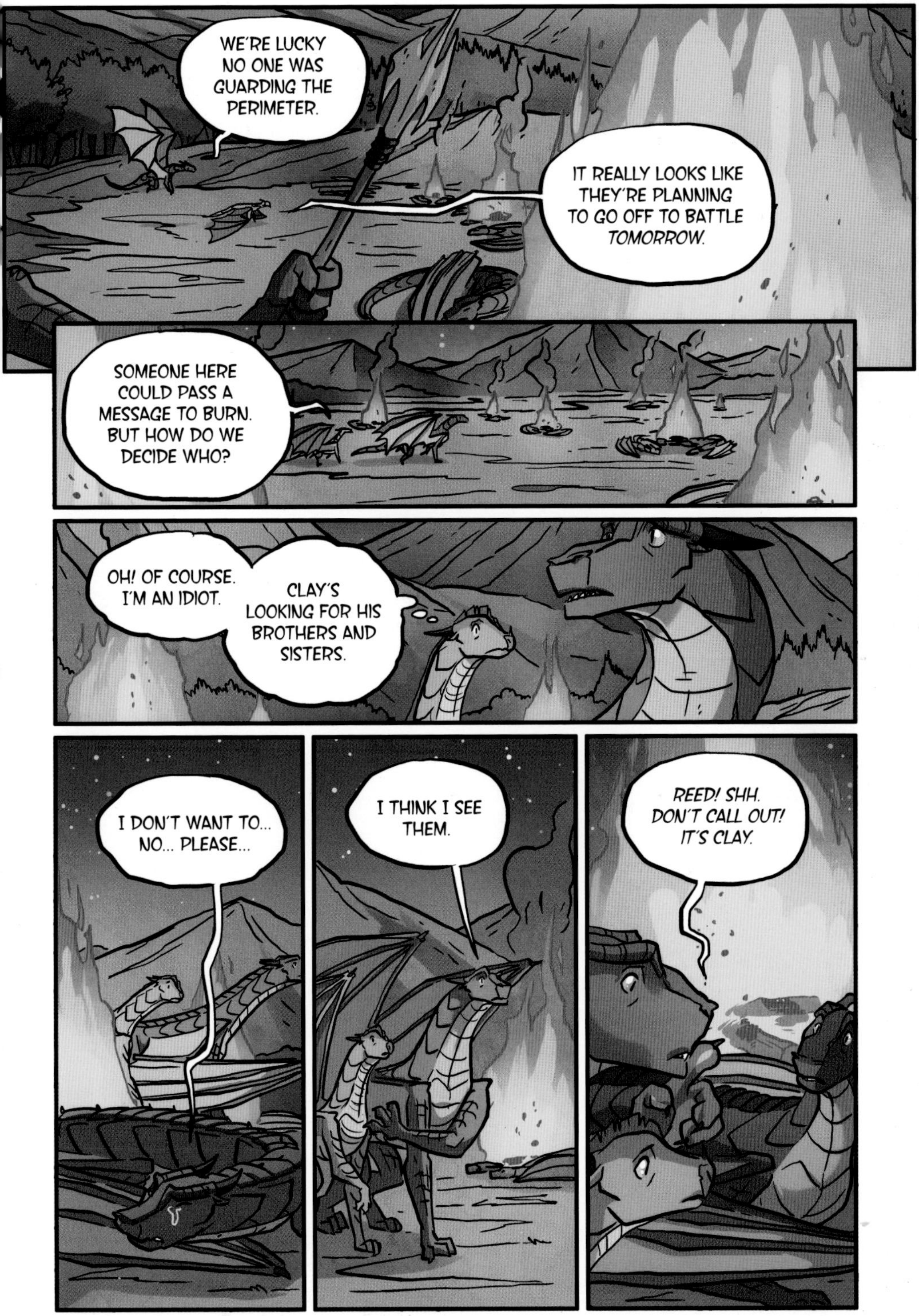
WE'RE LUCKY NO ONE WAS GUARDING THE PERIMETER.
IT REALLY LOOKS LIKE THEY'RE PLANNING TO GO OFF TO BATTLE *TOMORROW*.
SOMEONE HERE COULD PASS A MESSAGE TO BURN. BUT HOW DO WE DECIDE WHO?
OH! OF COURSE. I'M AN IDIOT.
CLAY'S LOOKING FOR HIS BROTHERS AND SISTERS.
I DON'T WANT TO... NO... PLEASE...
I THINK I SEE THEM.
REED! SHH. DON'T CALL OUT! IT'S CLAY.

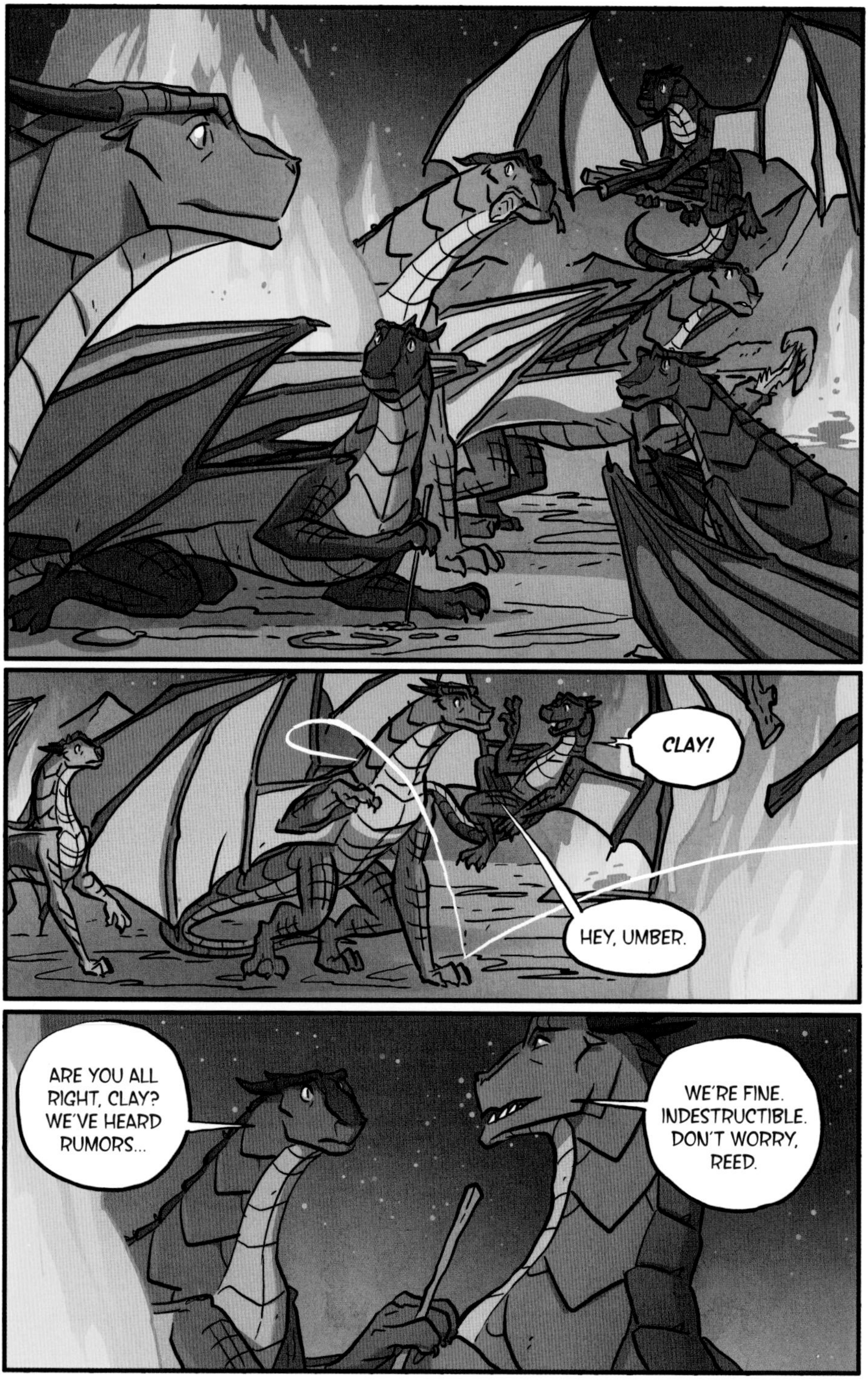
CLAY!
HEY, UMBER.
ARE YOU ALL RIGHT, CLAY? WE'VE HEARD RUMORS...
WE'RE FINE. INDESTRUCTIBLE. DON'T WORRY, REED.

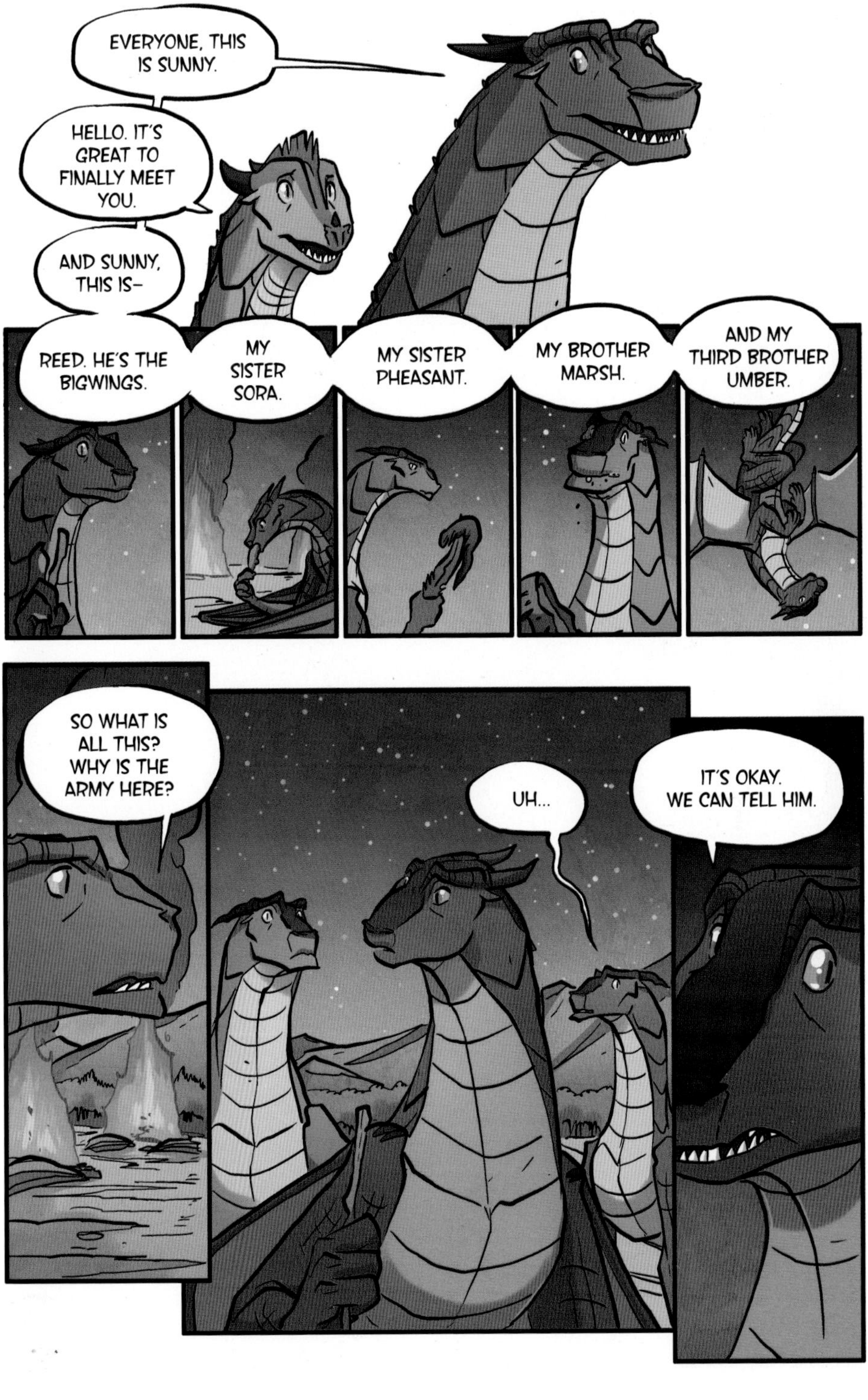
EVERYONE, THIS IS SUNNY.
HELLO. IT'S GREAT TO FINALLY MEET YOU.
AND SUNNY, THIS IS–
REED. HE'S THE BIGWINGS.
MY SISTER SORA.
MY SISTER PHEASANT.
MY BROTHER MARSH.
AND MY THIRD BROTHER UMBER.
SO WHAT IS ALL THIS? WHY IS THE ARMY HERE?
UH...
IT'S OKAY. WE CAN TELL HIM.

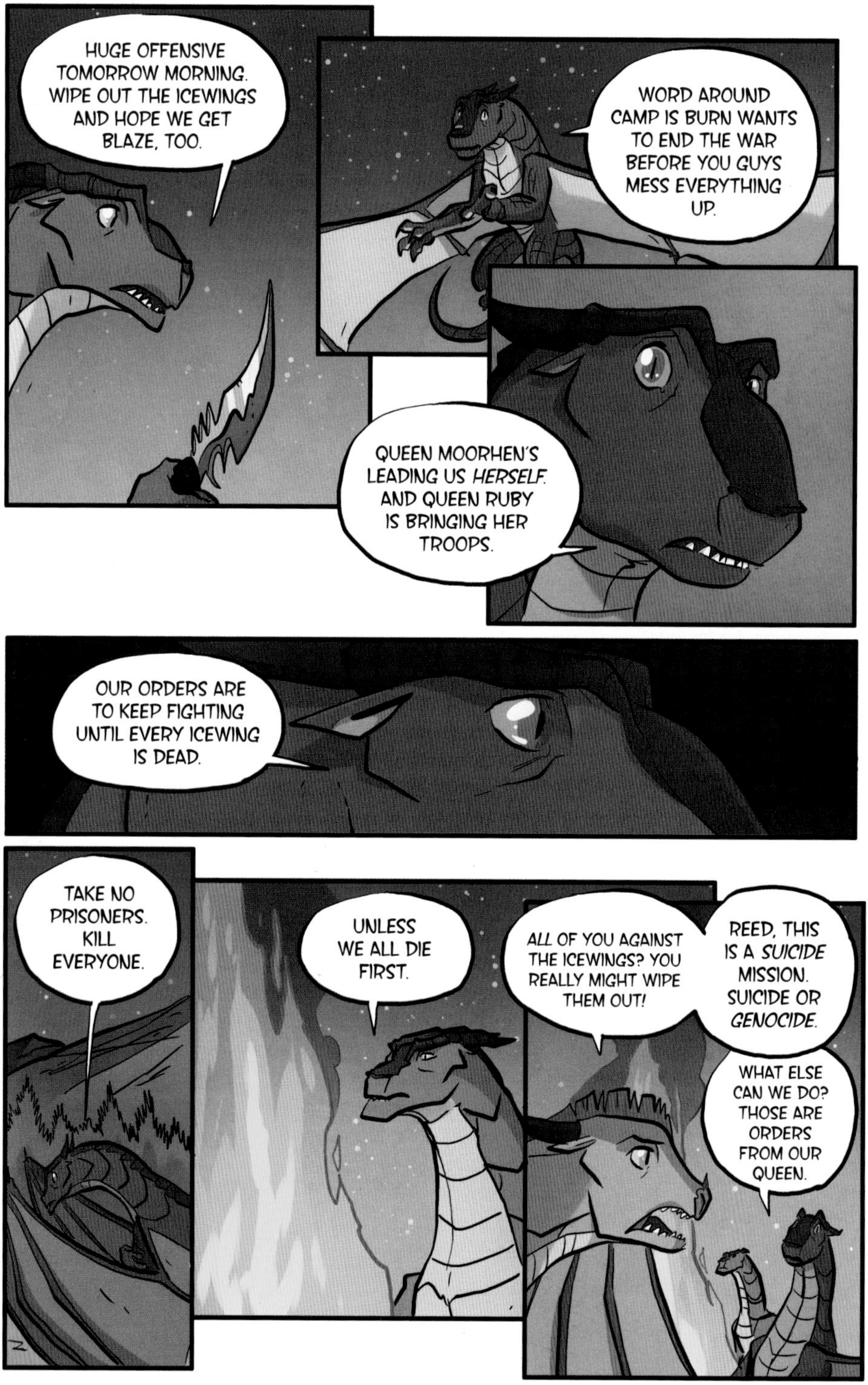
HUGE OFFENSIVE TOMORROW MORNING. WIPE OUT THE ICEWINGS AND HOPE WE GET BLAZE, TOO.
WORD AROUND CAMP IS BURN WANTS TO END THE WAR BEFORE YOU GUYS MESS EVERYTHING UP.
QUEEN MOORHEN'S LEADING US *HERSELF*. AND QUEEN RUBY IS BRINGING HER TROOPS.
OUR ORDERS ARE TO KEEP FIGHTING UNTIL EVERY ICEWING IS DEAD.
TAKE NO PRISONERS. KILL EVERYONE.
UNLESS WE ALL DIE FIRST.
ALL OF YOU AGAINST THE ICEWINGS? YOU REALLY MIGHT WIPE THEM OUT!
REED, THIS IS A *SUICIDE* MISSION. SUICIDE OR *GENOCIDE*.
WHAT ELSE CAN WE DO? THOSE ARE ORDERS FROM OUR QUEEN.

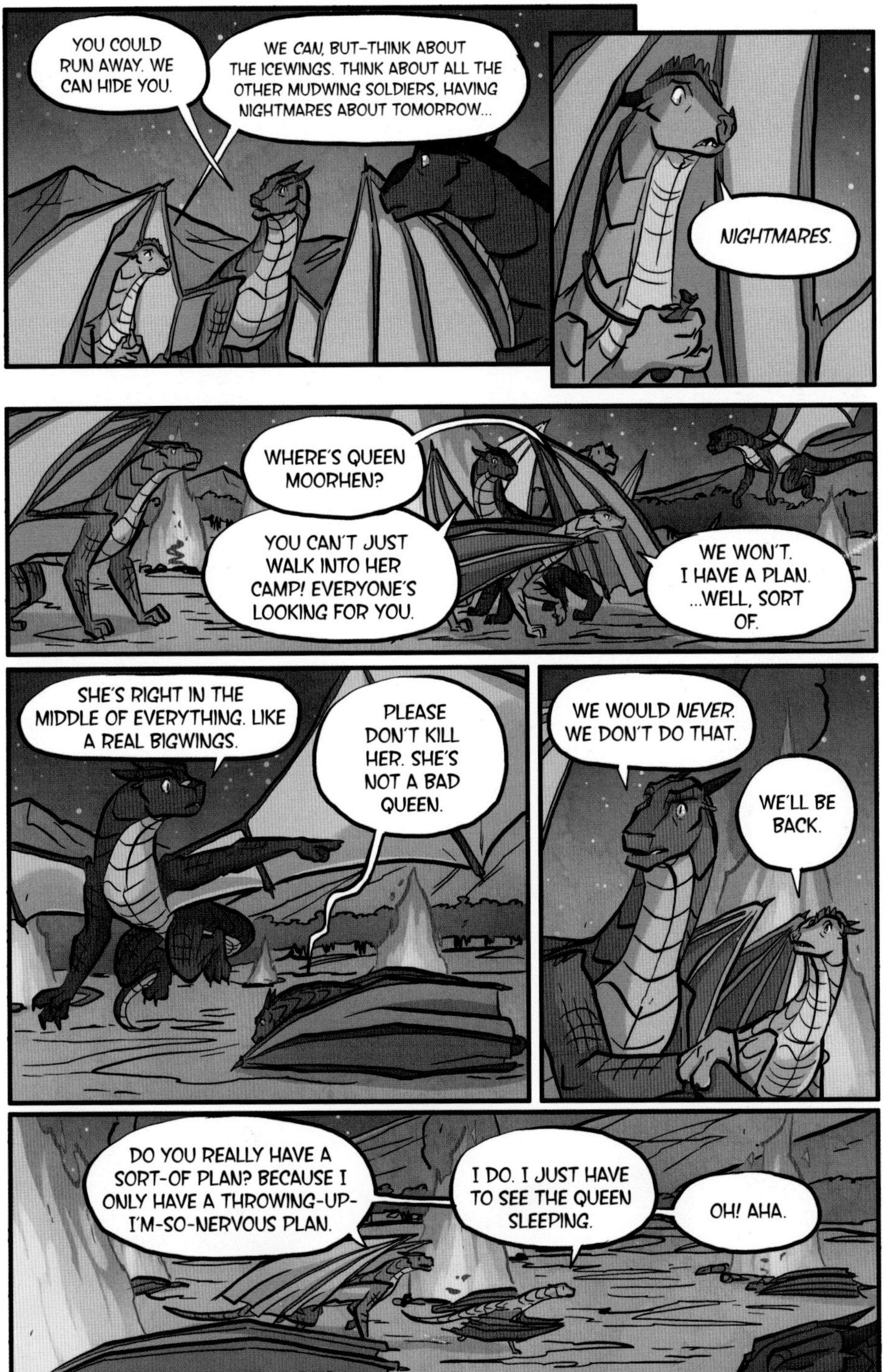
YOU COULD RUN AWAY. WE CAN HIDE YOU.
WE *CAN,* BUT–THINK ABOUT THE ICEWINGS. THINK ABOUT ALL THE OTHER MUDWING SOLDIERS, HAVING NIGHTMARES ABOUT TOMORROW...
NIGHTMARES.
WHERE'S QUEEN MOORHEN?
YOU CAN'T JUST WALK INTO HER CAMP! EVERYONE'S LOOKING FOR YOU.
WE WON'T. I HAVE A PLAN. ...WELL, SORT OF.
SHE'S RIGHT IN THE MIDDLE OF EVERYTHING. LIKE A REAL BIGWINGS.
PLEASE DON'T KILL HER. SHE'S NOT A BAD QUEEN.
WE WOULD *NEVER.* WE DON'T DO THAT.
WE'LL BE BACK.
DO YOU REALLY HAVE A SORT-OF PLAN? BECAUSE I ONLY HAVE A THROWING-UP-I'M-SO-NERVOUS PLAN.
I DO. I JUST HAVE TO SEE THE QUEEN SLEEPING.
OH! AHA.

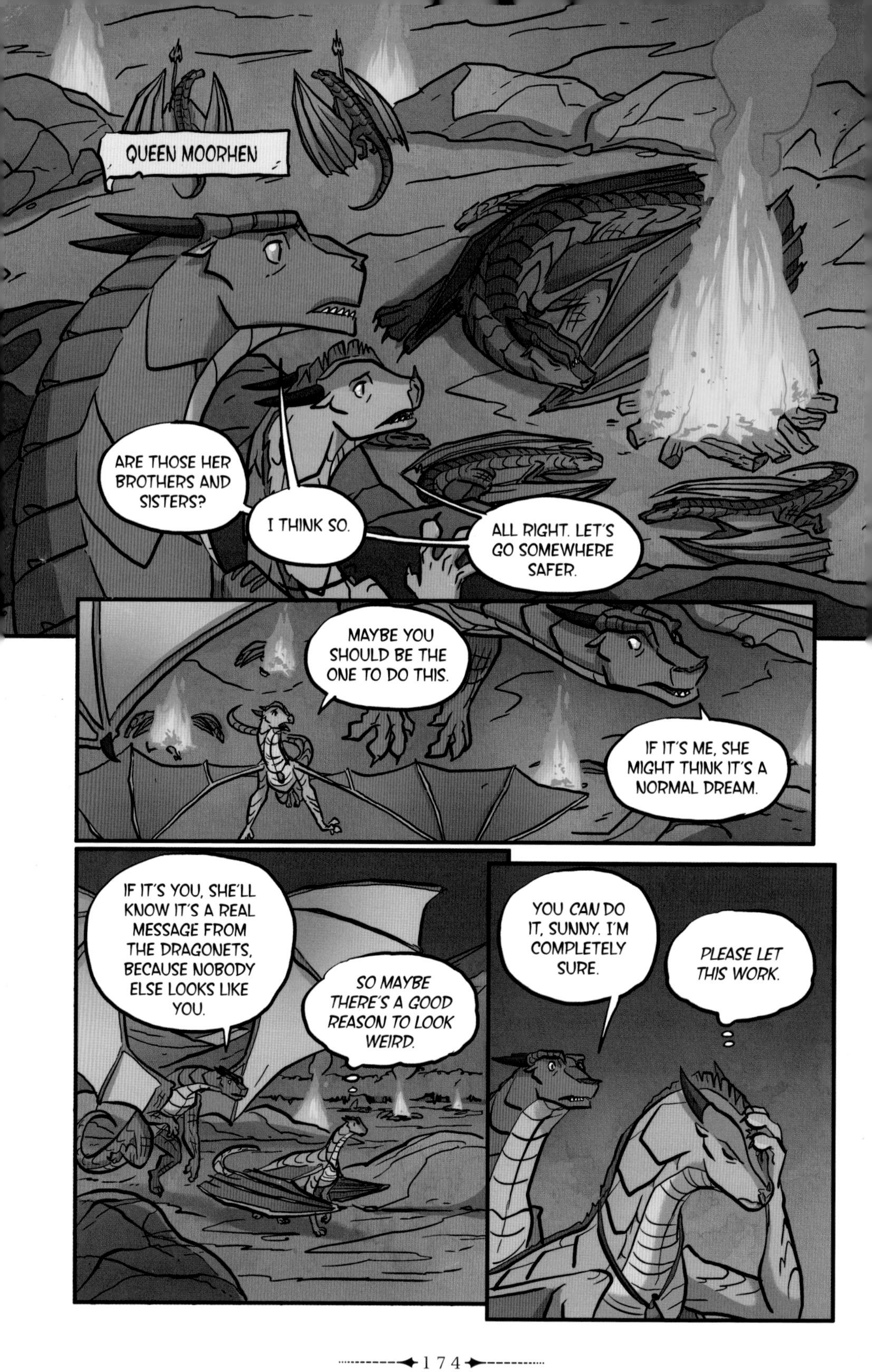
QUEEN MOORHEN
ARE THOSE HER BROTHERS AND SISTERS?
I THINK SO.
ALL RIGHT. LET'S GO SOMEWHERE SAFER.
MAYBE YOU SHOULD BE THE ONE TO DO THIS.
IF IT'S ME, SHE MIGHT THINK IT'S A NORMAL DREAM.
IF IT'S YOU, SHE'LL KNOW IT'S A REAL MESSAGE FROM THE DRAGONETS, BECAUSE NOBODY ELSE LOOKS LIKE YOU.
SO MAYBE THERE'S A GOOD REASON TO LOOK WEIRD.
YOU CAN DO IT, SUNNY. I'M COMPLETELY SURE.
PLEASE LET THIS WORK.

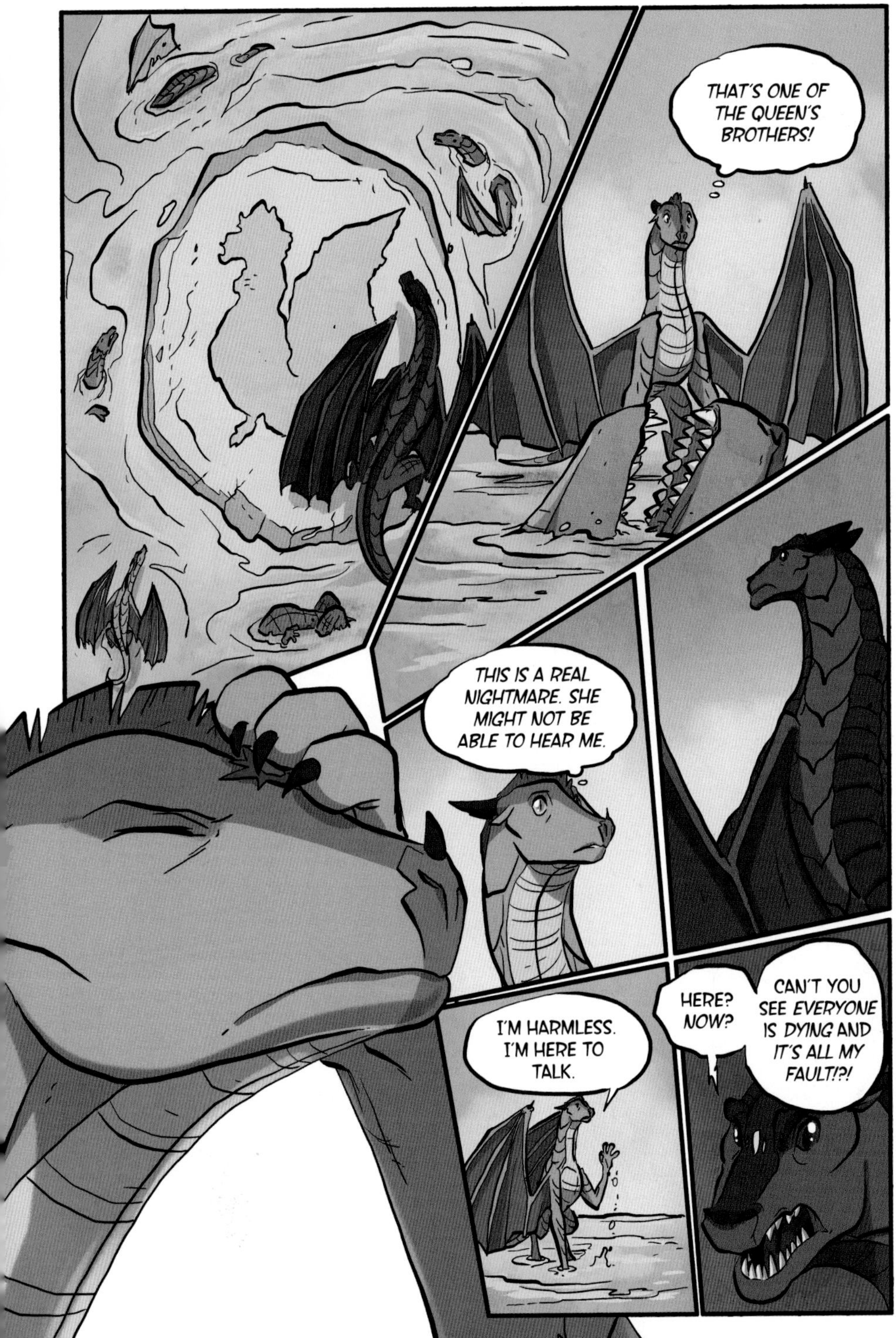
THAT'S ONE OF THE QUEEN'S BROTHERS!
THIS IS A REAL NIGHTMARE. SHE MIGHT NOT BE ABLE TO HEAR ME.
I'M HARMLESS. I'M HERE TO TALK.
HERE? NOW?
CAN'T YOU SEE *EVERYONE* IS *DYING* AND IT'S ALL MY FAULT!?!

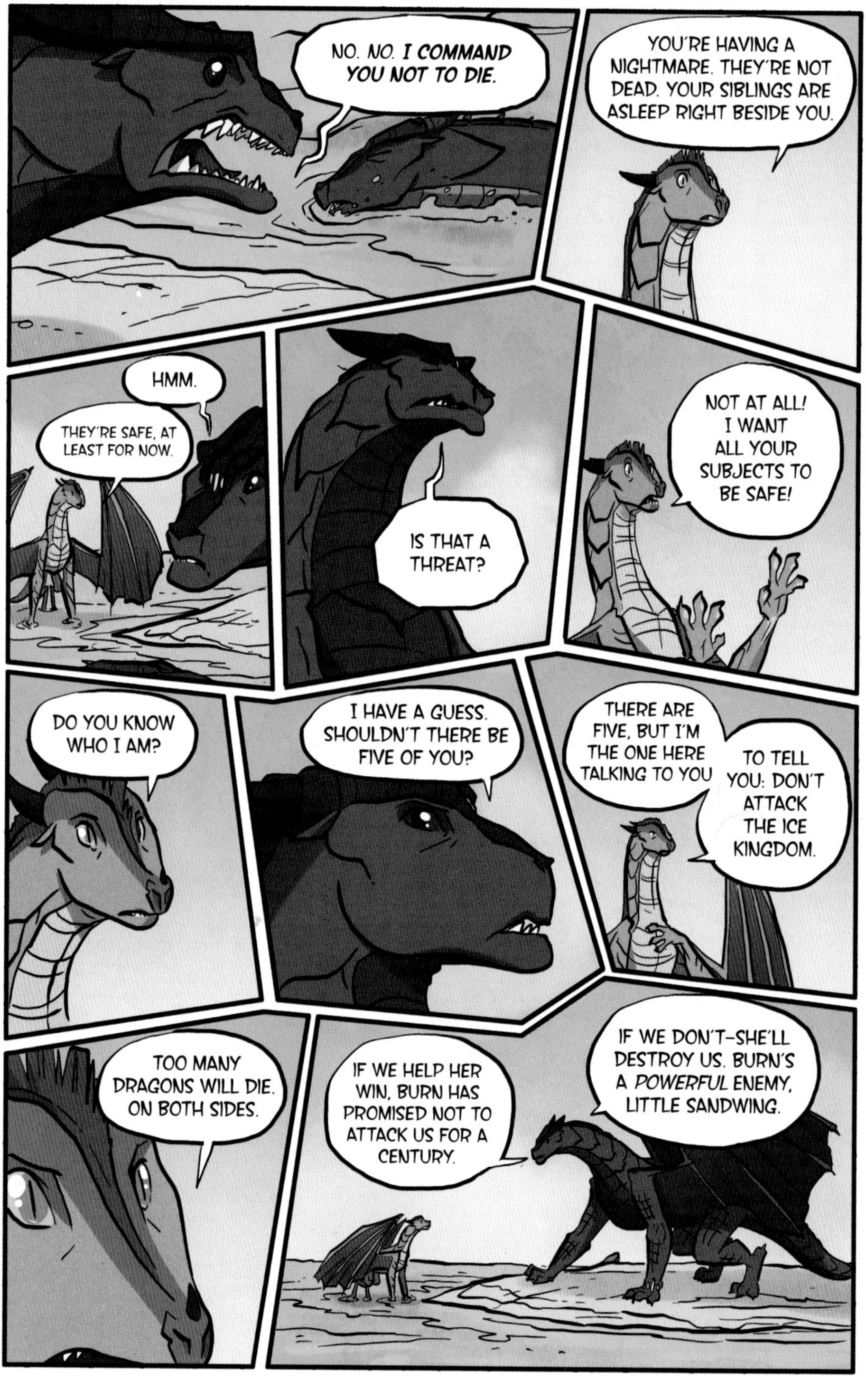
NO. NO. **I COMMAND YOU NOT TO DIE.**
YOU'RE HAVING A NIGHTMARE. THEY'RE NOT DEAD. YOUR SIBLINGS ARE ASLEEP RIGHT BESIDE YOU.
HMM.
THEY'RE SAFE, AT LEAST FOR NOW.
IS THAT A THREAT?
NOT AT ALL! I WANT ALL YOUR SUBJECTS TO BE SAFE!
DO YOU KNOW WHO I AM?
I HAVE A GUESS. SHOULDN'T THERE BE FIVE OF YOU?
THERE ARE FIVE, BUT I'M THE ONE HERE TALKING TO YOU
TO TELL YOU: DON'T ATTACK THE ICE KINGDOM.
TOO MANY DRAGONS WILL DIE. ON BOTH SIDES.
IF WE HELP HER WIN, BURN HAS PROMISED NOT TO ATTACK US FOR A CENTURY.
IF WE DON'T—SHE'LL DESTROY US. BURN'S A *POWERFUL* ENEMY, LITTLE SANDWING.

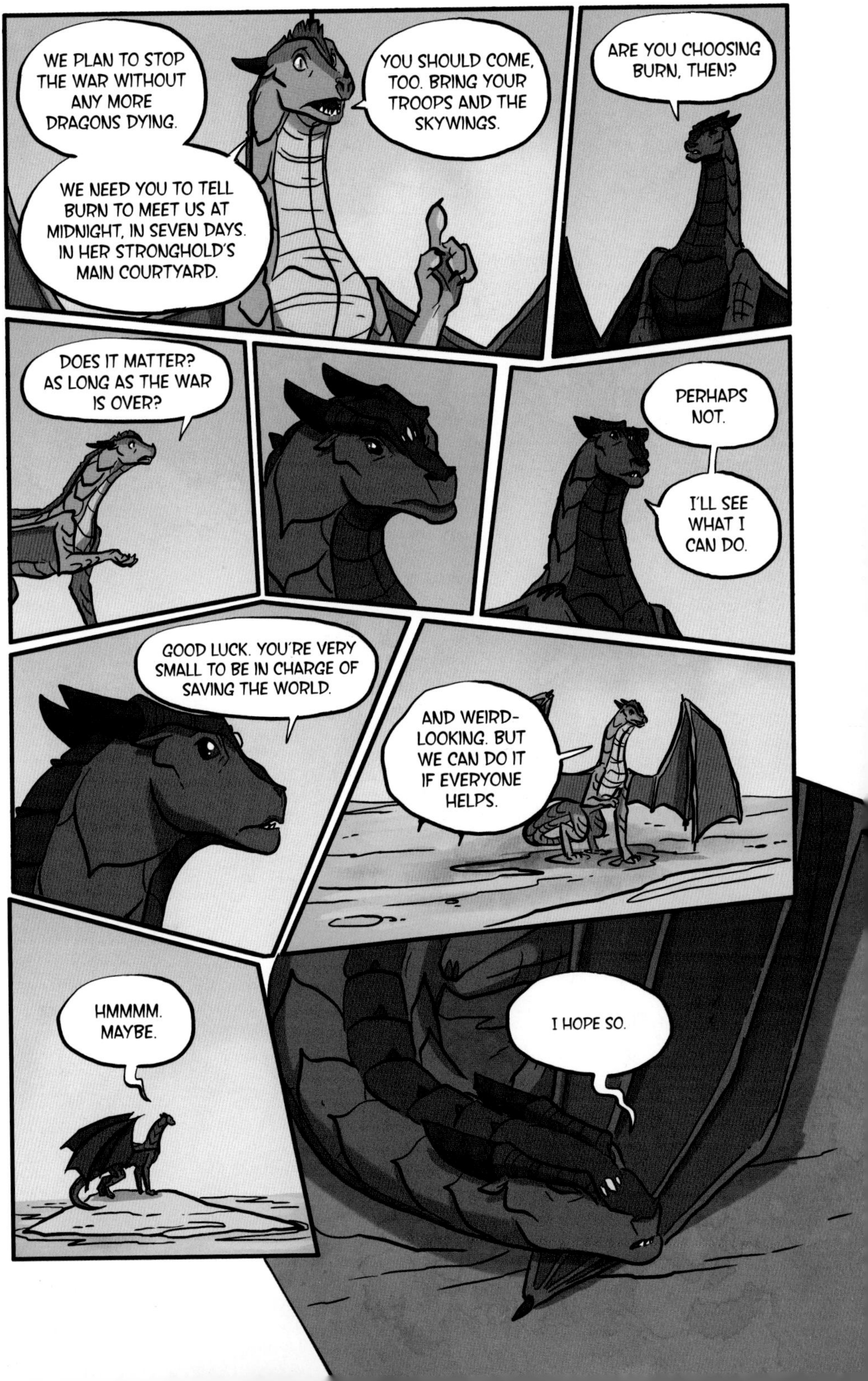
WE PLAN TO STOP THE WAR WITHOUT ANY MORE DRAGONS DYING.
WE NEED YOU TO TELL BURN TO MEET US AT MIDNIGHT, IN SEVEN DAYS. IN HER STRONGHOLD'S MAIN COURTYARD.
YOU SHOULD COME, TOO. BRING YOUR TROOPS AND THE SKYWINGS.
ARE YOU CHOOSING BURN, THEN?
DOES IT MATTER? AS LONG AS THE WAR IS OVER?
PERHAPS NOT.
I'LL SEE WHAT I CAN DO.
GOOD LUCK. YOU'RE VERY SMALL TO BE IN CHARGE OF SAVING THE WORLD.
AND WEIRD-LOOKING. BUT WE CAN DO IT IF EVERYONE HELPS.
HMMMM. MAYBE.
I HOPE SO.

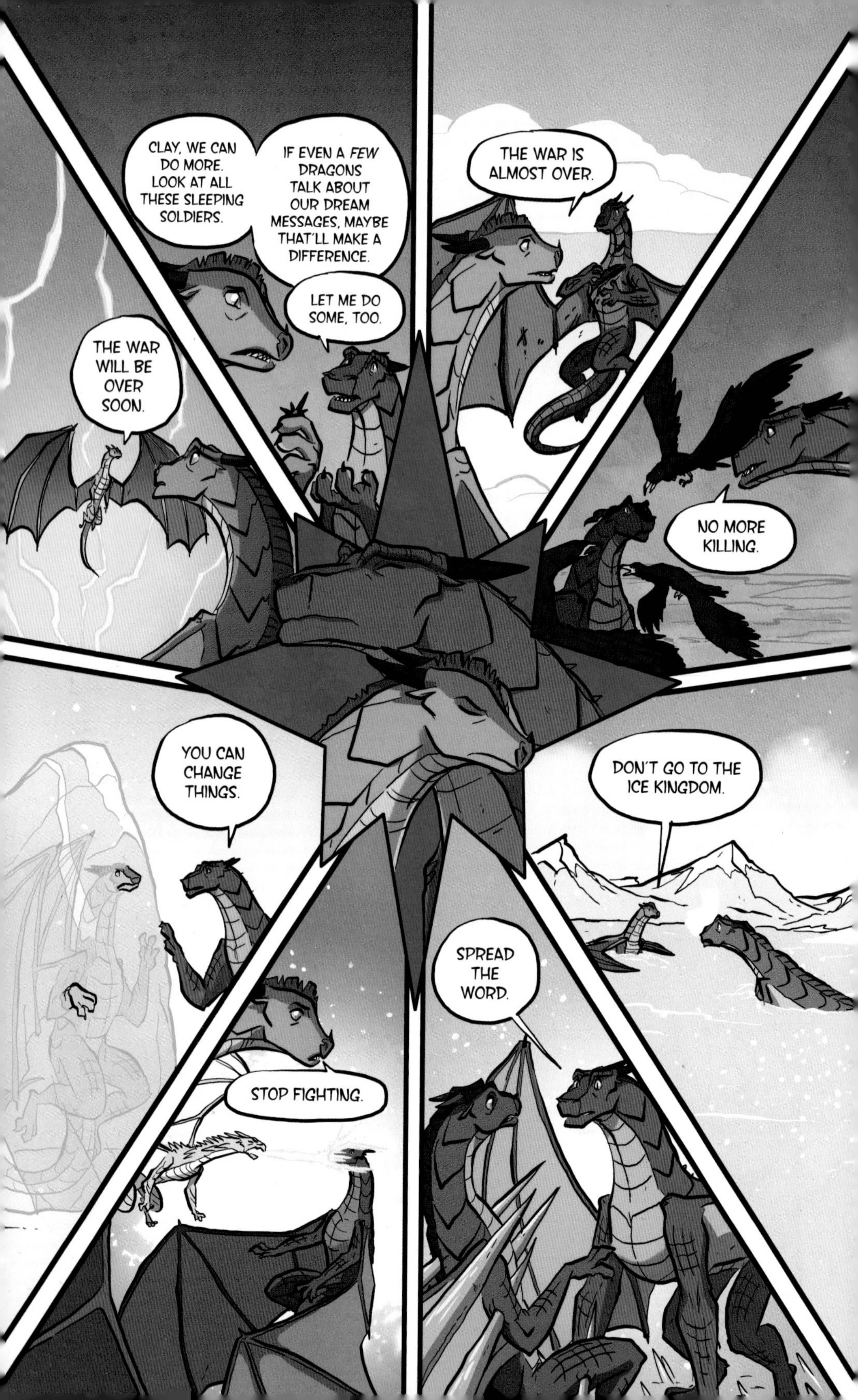
CLAY, WE CAN DO MORE. LOOK AT ALL THESE SLEEPING SOLDIERS.
IF EVEN A *FEW* DRAGONS TALK ABOUT OUR DREAM MESSAGES, MAYBE THAT'LL MAKE A DIFFERENCE.
LET ME DO SOME, TOO.
THE WAR WILL BE OVER SOON.
THE WAR IS ALMOST OVER.
NO MORE KILLING.
YOU CAN CHANGE THINGS.
DON'T GO TO THE ICE KINGDOM.
SPREAD THE WORD.
STOP FIGHTING.

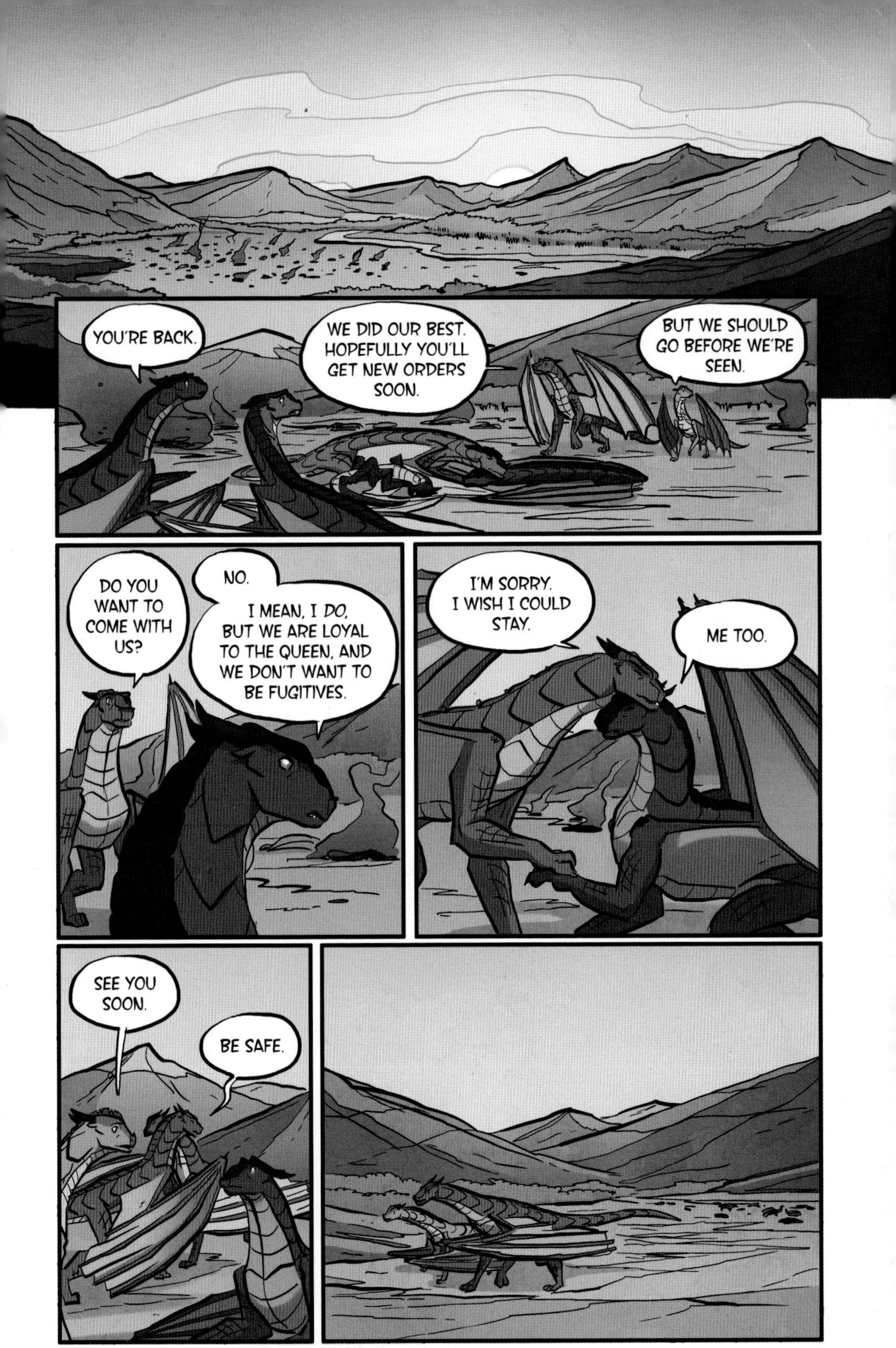
YOU'RE BACK.
WE DID OUR BEST. HOPEFULLY YOU'LL GET NEW ORDERS SOON.
BUT WE SHOULD GO BEFORE WE'RE SEEN.
DO YOU WANT TO COME WITH US?
NO.
I MEAN, I *DO*, BUT WE ARE LOYAL TO THE QUEEN, AND WE DON'T WANT TO BE FUGITIVES.
I'M SORRY. I WISH I COULD STAY.
ME TOO.
SEE YOU SOON.
BE SAFE.

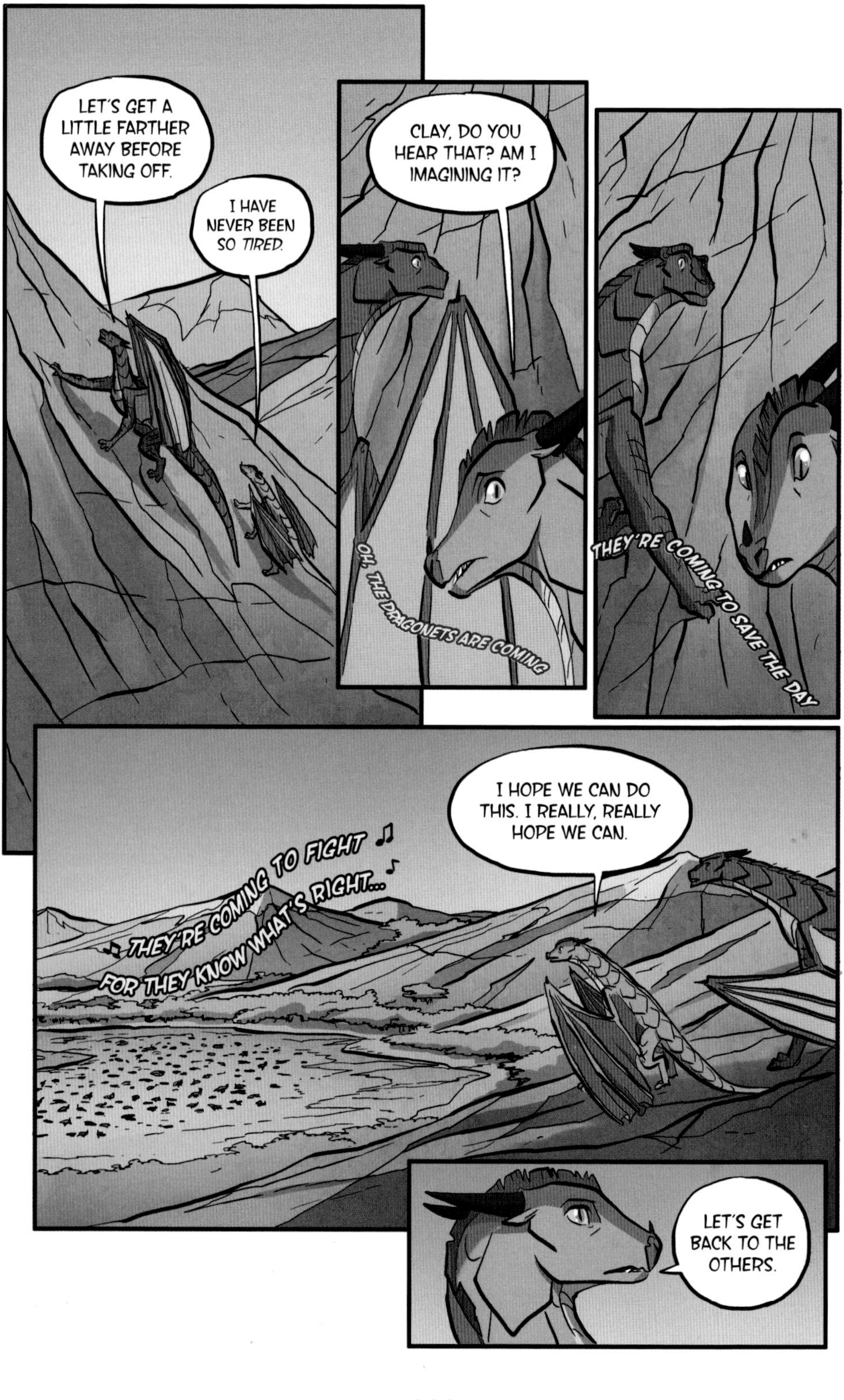
LET'S GET A LITTLE FARTHER AWAY BEFORE TAKING OFF.
I HAVE NEVER BEEN SO TIRED.
CLAY, DO YOU HEAR THAT? AM I IMAGINING IT?
OH, THE DRAGONETS ARE COMING
THEY'RE COMING TO SAVE THE DAY
THEY'RE COMING TO FIGHT
FOR THEY KNOW WHAT'S RIGHT...
I HOPE WE CAN DO THIS. I REALLY, REALLY HOPE WE CAN.
LET'S GET BACK TO THE OTHERS.

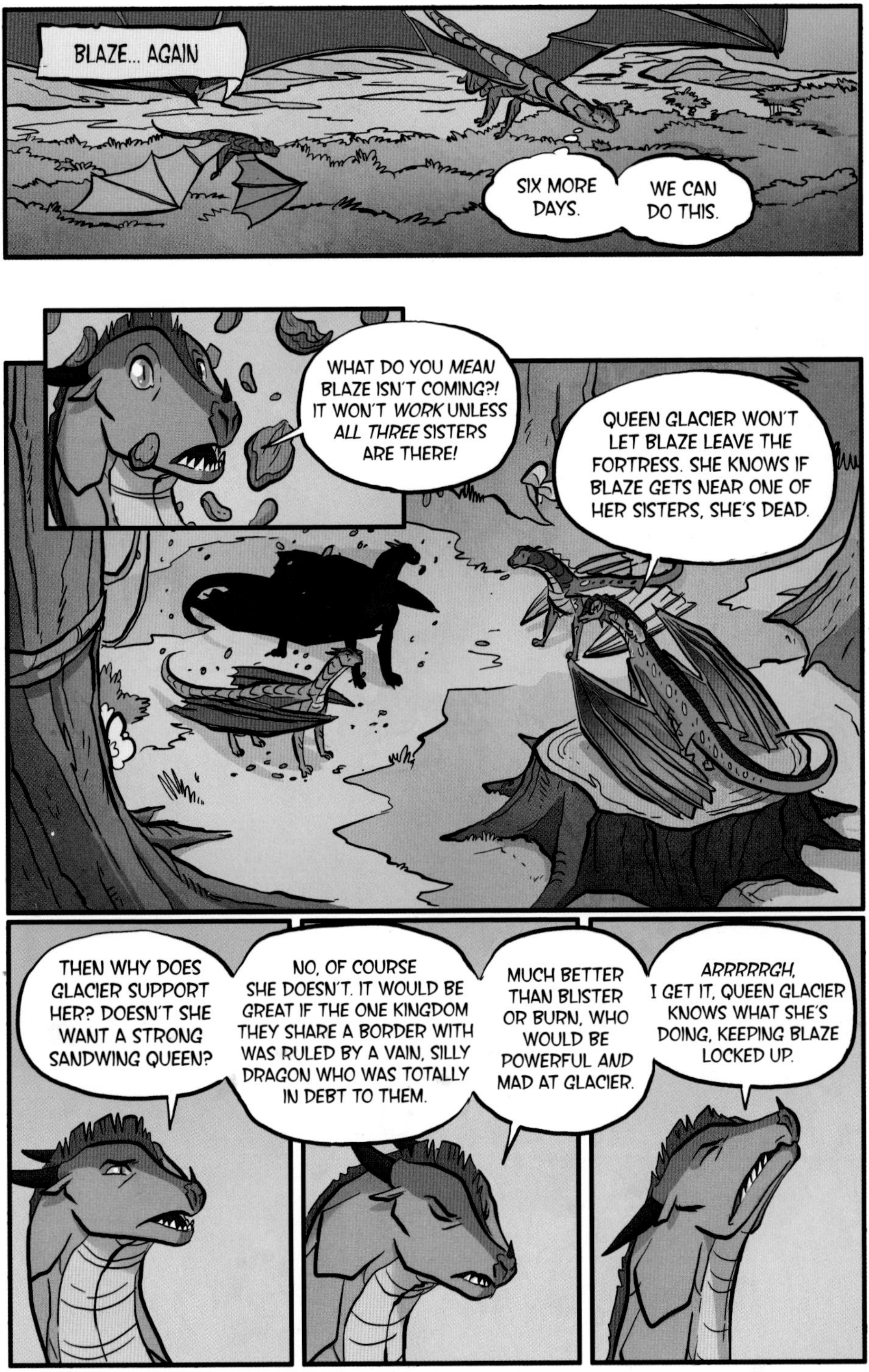
BLAZE... AGAIN
SIX MORE DAYS.
WE CAN DO THIS.
WHAT DO YOU *MEAN* BLAZE ISN'T COMING?! IT WON'T *WORK* UNLESS *ALL THREE* SISTERS ARE THERE!
QUEEN GLACIER WON'T LET BLAZE LEAVE THE FORTRESS. SHE KNOWS IF BLAZE GETS NEAR ONE OF HER SISTERS, SHE'S DEAD.
THEN WHY DOES GLACIER SUPPORT HER? DOESN'T SHE WANT A STRONG SANDWING QUEEN?
NO, OF COURSE SHE DOESN'T. IT WOULD BE GREAT IF THE ONE KINGDOM THEY SHARE A BORDER WITH WAS RULED BY A VAIN, SILLY DRAGON WHO WAS TOTALLY IN DEBT TO THEM.
MUCH BETTER THAN BLISTER OR BURN, WHO WOULD BE POWERFUL *AND* MAD AT GLACIER.
ARRRRRGH, I GET IT, QUEEN GLACIER KNOWS WHAT SHE'S DOING, KEEPING BLAZE LOCKED UP.

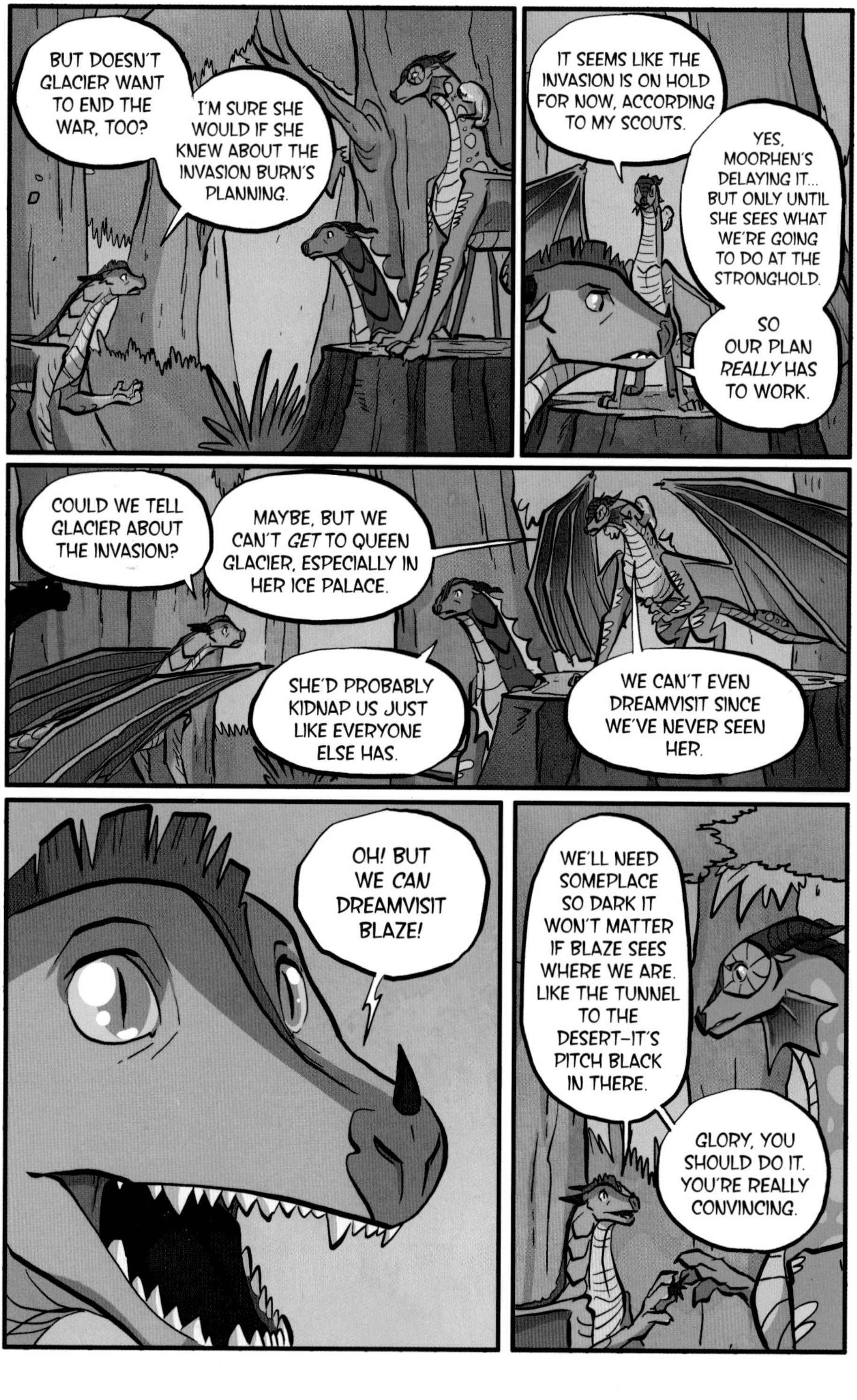
BUT DOESN'T GLACIER WANT TO END THE WAR, TOO?
I'M SURE SHE WOULD IF SHE KNEW ABOUT THE INVASION BURN'S PLANNING.
IT SEEMS LIKE THE INVASION IS ON HOLD FOR NOW, ACCORDING TO MY SCOUTS.
YES, MOORHEN'S DELAYING IT... BUT ONLY UNTIL SHE SEES WHAT WE'RE GOING TO DO AT THE STRONGHOLD.
SO OUR PLAN *REALLY* HAS TO WORK.
COULD WE TELL GLACIER ABOUT THE INVASION?
MAYBE, BUT WE CAN'T *GET* TO QUEEN GLACIER, ESPECIALLY IN HER ICE PALACE.
SHE'D PROBABLY KIDNAP US JUST LIKE EVERYONE ELSE HAS.
WE CAN'T EVEN DREAMVISIT SINCE WE'VE NEVER SEEN HER.
OH! BUT WE *CAN* DREAMVISIT BLAZE!
WE'LL NEED SOMEPLACE SO DARK IT WON'T MATTER IF BLAZE SEES WHERE WE ARE. LIKE THE TUNNEL TO THE DESERT—IT'S PITCH BLACK IN THERE.
GLORY, YOU SHOULD DO IT. YOU'RE REALLY CONVINCING.

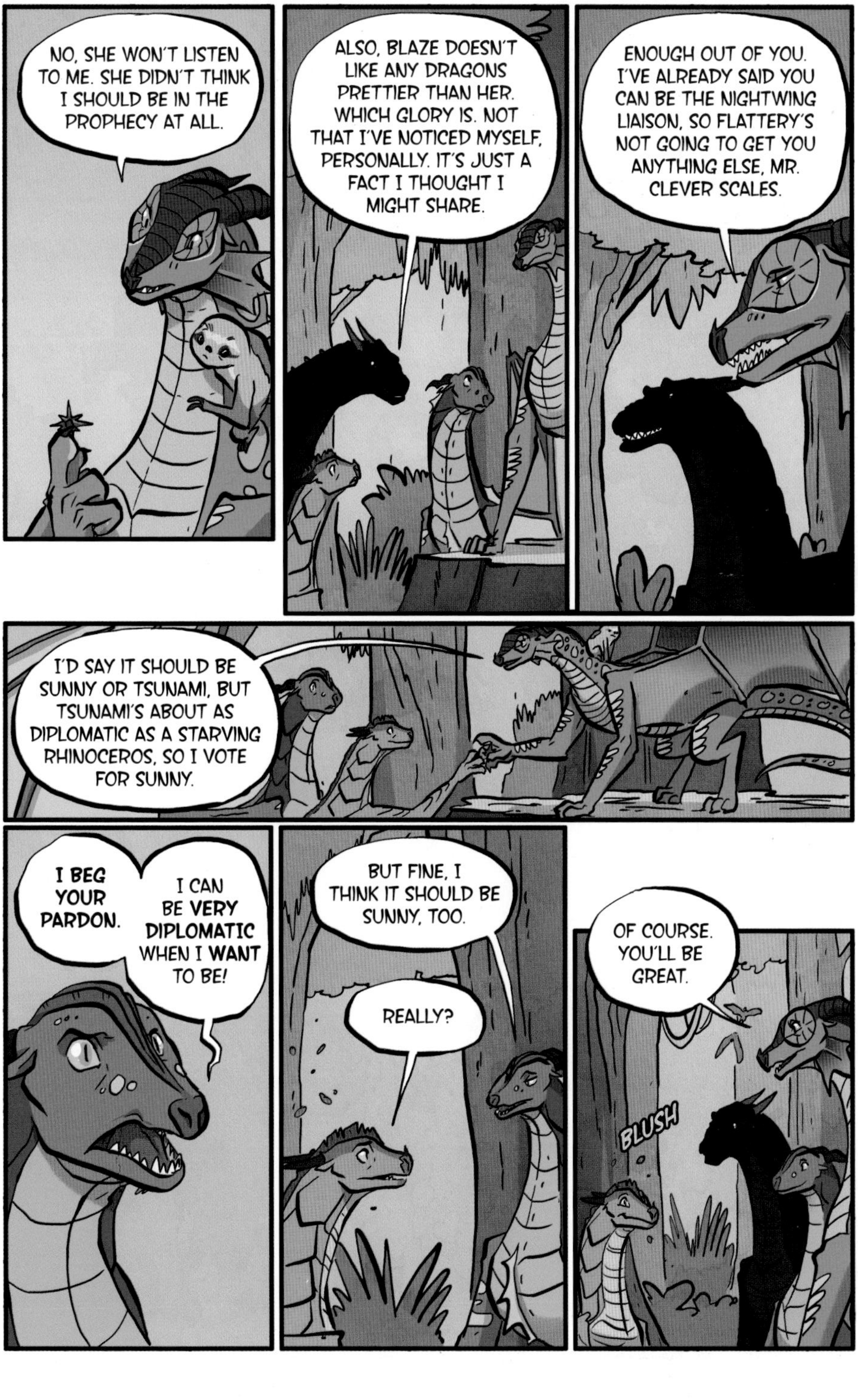
NO, SHE WON'T LISTEN TO ME. SHE DIDN'T THINK I SHOULD BE IN THE PROPHECY AT ALL.
ALSO, BLAZE DOESN'T LIKE ANY DRAGONS PRETTIER THAN HER. WHICH GLORY IS. NOT THAT I'VE NOTICED MYSELF, PERSONALLY. IT'S JUST A FACT I THOUGHT I MIGHT SHARE.
ENOUGH OUT OF YOU. I'VE ALREADY SAID YOU CAN BE THE NIGHTWING LIAISON, SO FLATTERY'S NOT GOING TO GET YOU ANYTHING ELSE, MR. CLEVER SCALES.
I'D SAY IT SHOULD BE SUNNY OR TSUNAMI, BUT TSUNAMI'S ABOUT AS DIPLOMATIC AS A STARVING RHINOCEROS, SO I VOTE FOR SUNNY.
I BEG YOUR PARDON.
I CAN BE VERY DIPLOMATIC WHEN I WANT TO BE!
BUT FINE, I THINK IT SHOULD BE SUNNY, TOO.
REALLY?
OF COURSE. YOU'LL BE GREAT.
BLUSH

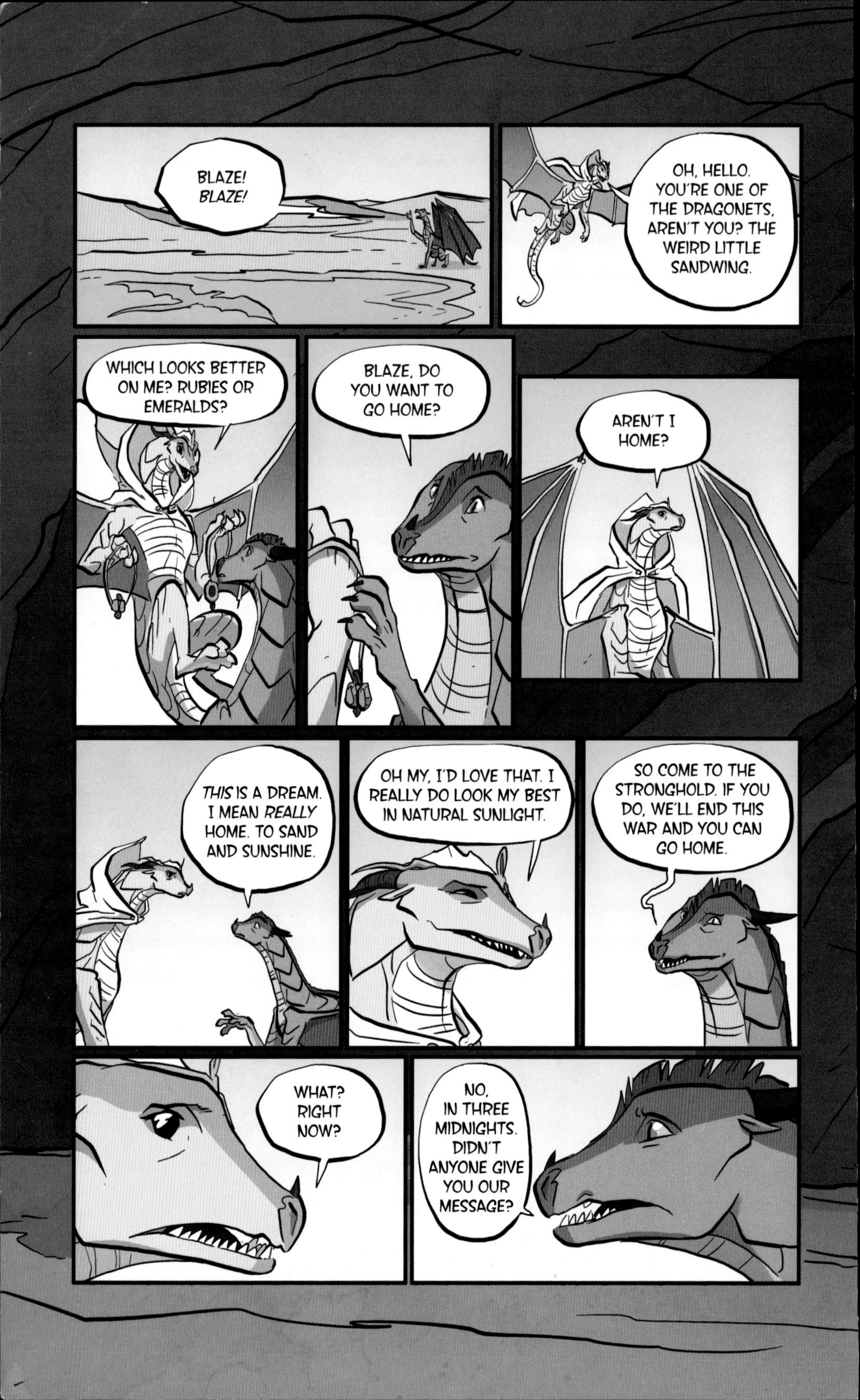
BLAZE!
BLAZE!
OH, HELLO. YOU'RE ONE OF THE DRAGONETS, AREN'T YOU? THE WEIRD LITTLE SANDWING.
WHICH LOOKS BETTER ON ME? RUBIES OR EMERALDS?
BLAZE, DO YOU WANT TO GO HOME?
AREN'T I HOME?
THIS IS A DREAM. I MEAN *REALLY* HOME. TO SAND AND SUNSHINE.
OH MY, I'D LOVE THAT. I REALLY DO LOOK MY BEST IN NATURAL SUNLIGHT.
SO COME TO THE STRONGHOLD. IF YOU DO, WE'LL END THIS WAR AND YOU CAN GO HOME.
WHAT? RIGHT NOW?
NO, IN THREE MIDNIGHTS. DIDN'T ANYONE GIVE YOU OUR MESSAGE?

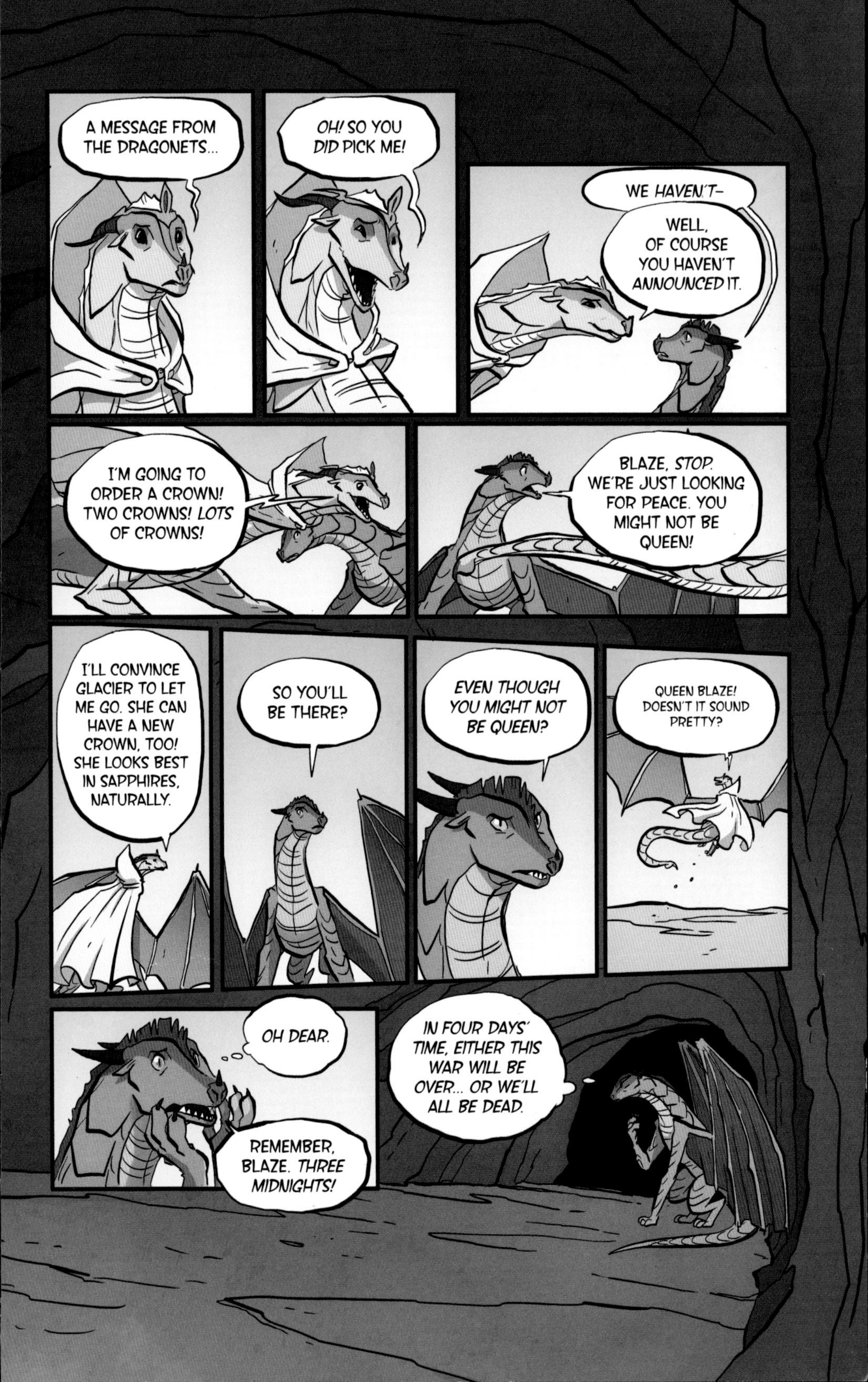
A MESSAGE FROM THE DRAGONETS...
OH! SO YOU *DID* PICK ME!
WE *HAVEN'T*–
WELL, OF COURSE YOU HAVEN'T *ANNOUNCED* IT.
I'M GOING TO ORDER A CROWN! TWO CROWNS! *LOTS* OF CROWNS!
BLAZE, *STOP.* WE'RE JUST LOOKING FOR PEACE. YOU MIGHT NOT BE QUEEN!
I'LL CONVINCE GLACIER TO LET ME GO. SHE CAN HAVE A NEW CROWN, TOO! SHE LOOKS BEST IN SAPPHIRES, NATURALLY.
SO YOU'LL BE THERE?
EVEN THOUGH YOU MIGHT NOT BE QUEEN?
QUEEN BLAZE! DOESN'T IT SOUND PRETTY?
OH DEAR.
REMEMBER, BLAZE. *THREE MIDNIGHTS!*
IN FOUR DAYS' TIME, EITHER THIS WAR WILL BE OVER... OR WE'LL ALL BE DEAD.

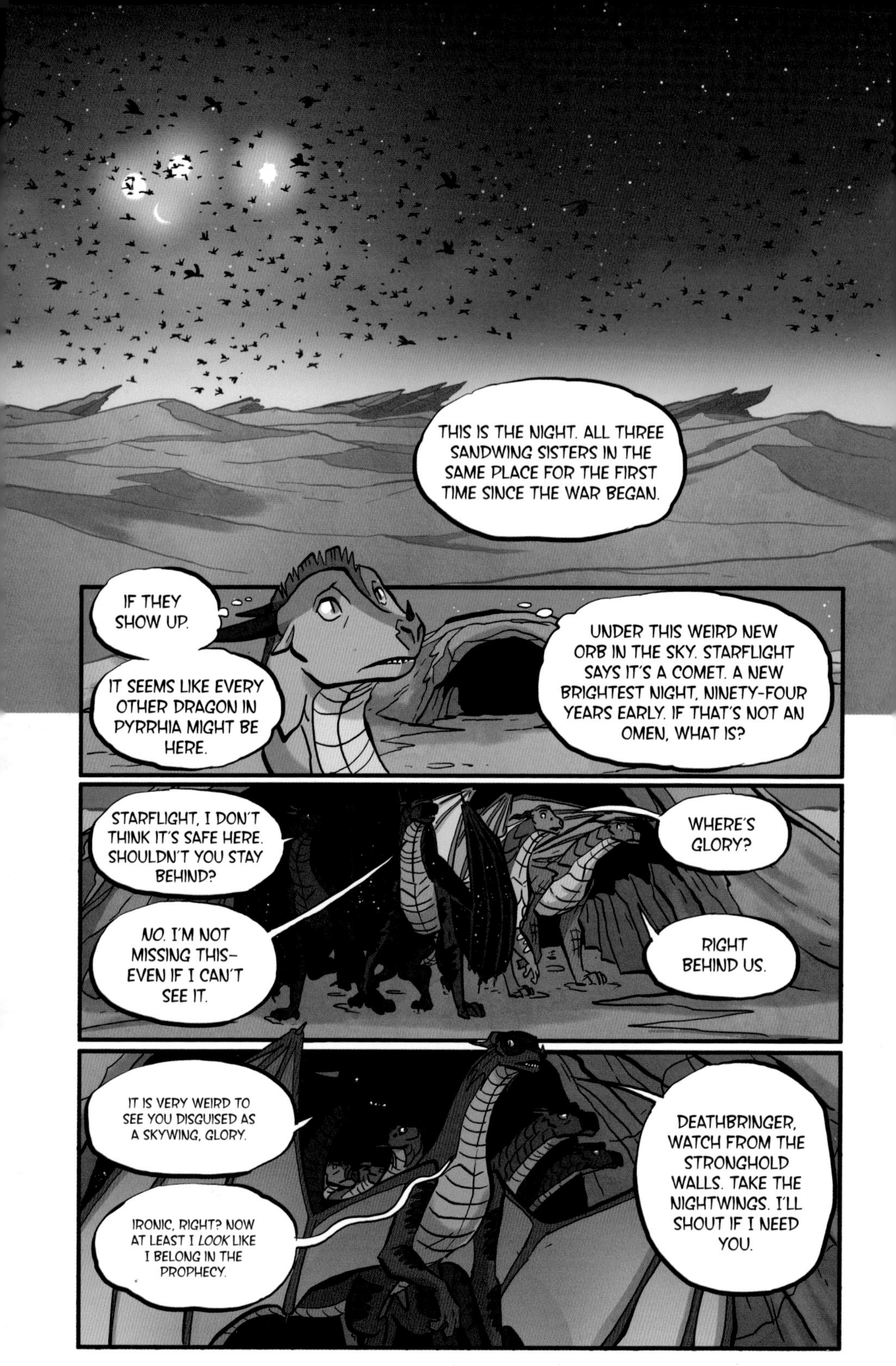
THIS IS THE NIGHT. ALL THREE SANDWING SISTERS IN THE SAME PLACE FOR THE FIRST TIME SINCE THE WAR BEGAN.
IF THEY SHOW UP.
IT SEEMS LIKE EVERY OTHER DRAGON IN PYRRHIA MIGHT BE HERE.
UNDER THIS WEIRD NEW ORB IN THE SKY. STARFLIGHT SAYS IT'S A COMET. A NEW BRIGHTEST NIGHT, NINETY-FOUR YEARS EARLY. IF THAT'S NOT AN OMEN, WHAT IS?
STARFLIGHT, I DON'T THINK IT'S SAFE HERE. SHOULDN'T YOU STAY BEHIND?
NO. I'M NOT MISSING THIS— EVEN IF I CAN'T SEE IT.
WHERE'S GLORY?
RIGHT BEHIND US.
IT IS VERY WEIRD TO SEE YOU DISGUISED AS A SKYWING, GLORY.
IRONIC, RIGHT? NOW AT LEAST I *LOOK* LIKE I BELONG IN THE PROPHECY.
DEATHBRINGER, WATCH FROM THE STRONGHOLD WALLS. TAKE THE NIGHTWINGS. I'LL SHOUT IF I NEED YOU.

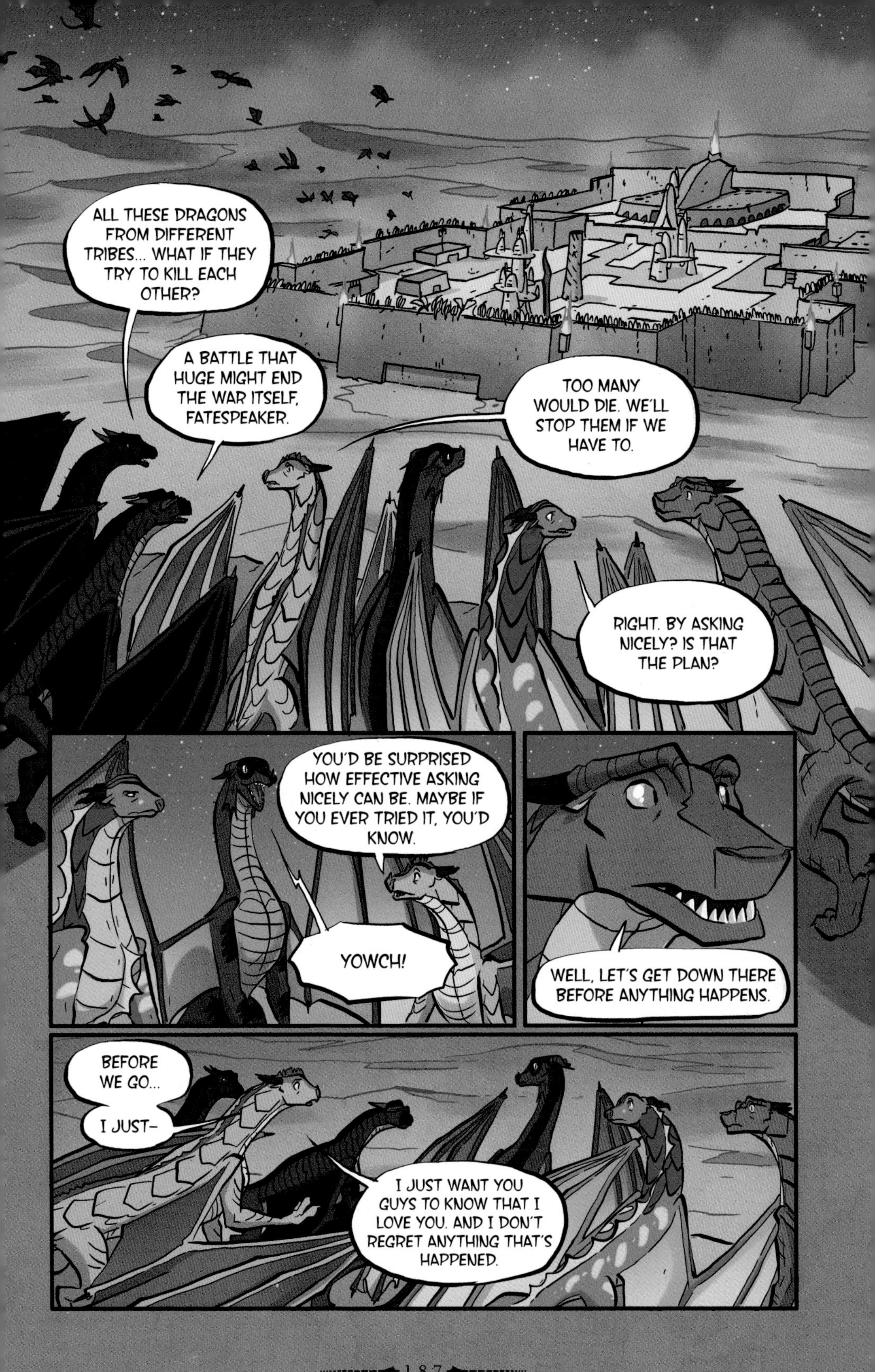
ALL THESE DRAGONS FROM DIFFERENT TRIBES... WHAT IF THEY TRY TO KILL EACH OTHER?
A BATTLE THAT HUGE MIGHT END THE WAR ITSELF, FATESPEAKER.
TOO MANY WOULD DIE. WE'LL STOP THEM IF WE HAVE TO.
RIGHT. BY ASKING NICELY? IS THAT THE PLAN?
YOU'D BE SURPRISED HOW EFFECTIVE ASKING NICELY CAN BE. MAYBE IF YOU EVER TRIED IT, YOU'D KNOW.
YOWCH!
WELL, LET'S GET DOWN THERE BEFORE ANYTHING HAPPENS.
BEFORE WE GO...
I JUST–
I JUST WANT YOU GUYS TO KNOW THAT I LOVE YOU. AND I DON'T REGRET ANYTHING THAT'S HAPPENED.

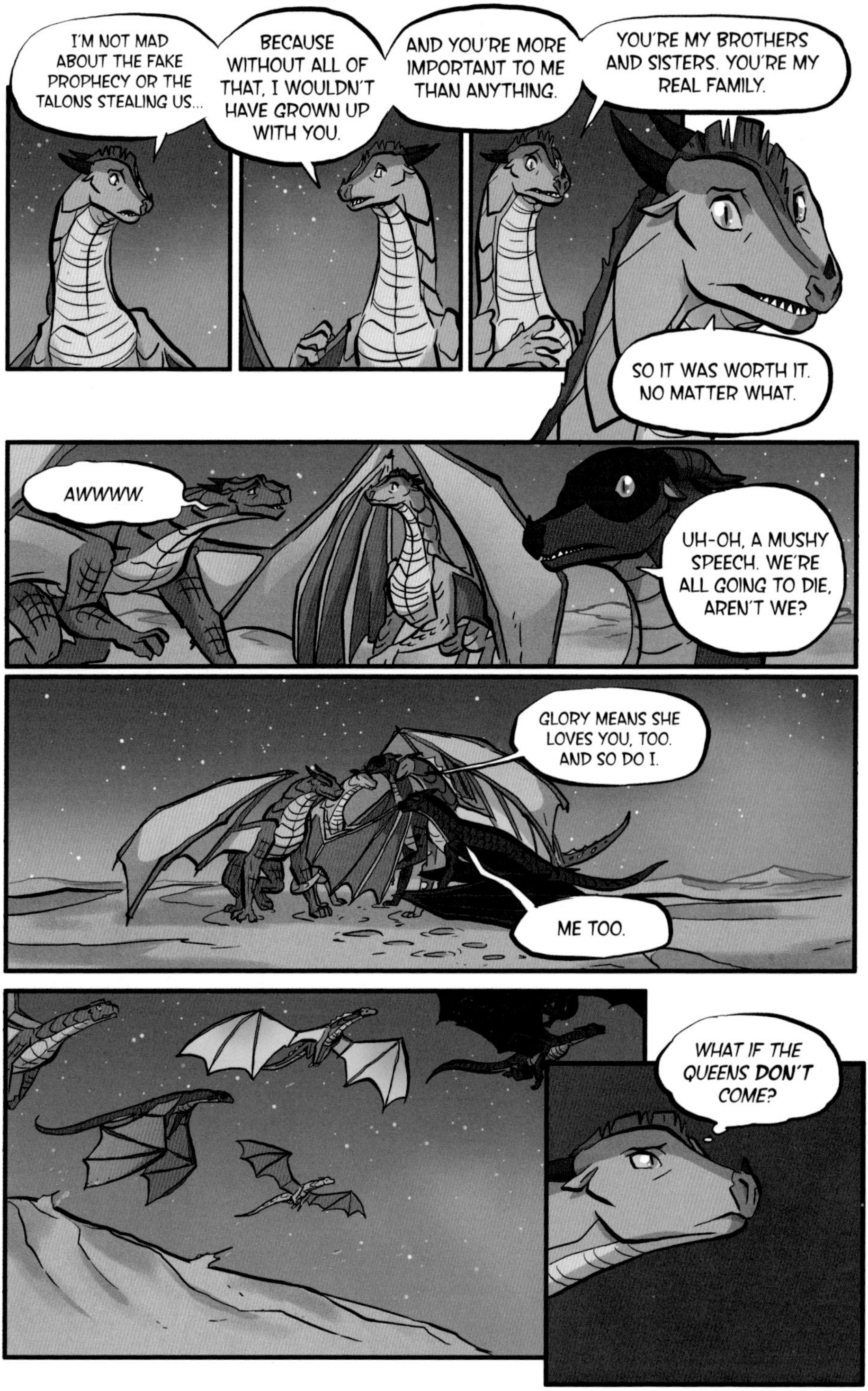
I'M NOT MAD ABOUT THE FAKE PROPHECY OR THE TALONS STEALING US...
BECAUSE WITHOUT ALL OF THAT, I WOULDN'T HAVE GROWN UP WITH YOU.
AND YOU'RE MORE IMPORTANT TO ME THAN ANYTHING.
YOU'RE MY BROTHERS AND SISTERS. YOU'RE MY REAL FAMILY.
SO IT WAS WORTH IT. NO MATTER WHAT.
AWWWW.
UH-OH, A MUSHY SPEECH. WE'RE ALL GOING TO DIE, AREN'T WE?
GLORY MEANS SHE LOVES YOU, TOO. AND SO DO I.
ME TOO.
WHAT IF THE QUEENS ***DON'T*** *COME?*

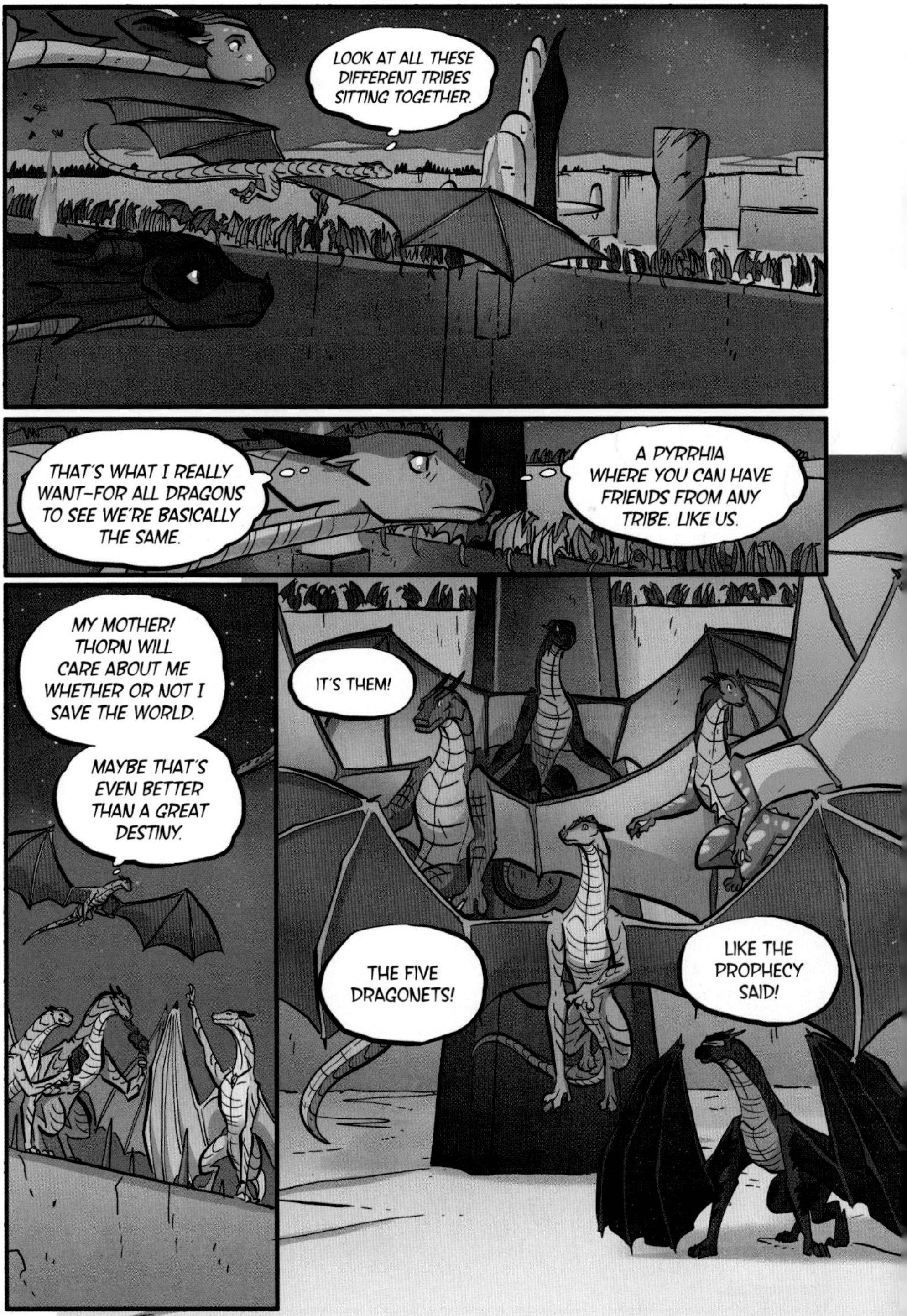
LOOK AT ALL THESE DIFFERENT TRIBES SITTING TOGETHER.
THAT'S WHAT I REALLY WANT—FOR ALL DRAGONS TO SEE WE'RE BASICALLY THE SAME.
A PYRRHIA WHERE YOU CAN HAVE FRIENDS FROM ANY TRIBE. LIKE US.
MY MOTHER! THORN WILL CARE ABOUT ME WHETHER OR NOT I SAVE THE WORLD.
MAYBE THAT'S EVEN BETTER THAN A GREAT DESTINY.
IT'S THEM!
THE FIVE DRAGONETS!
LIKE THE PROPHECY SAID!

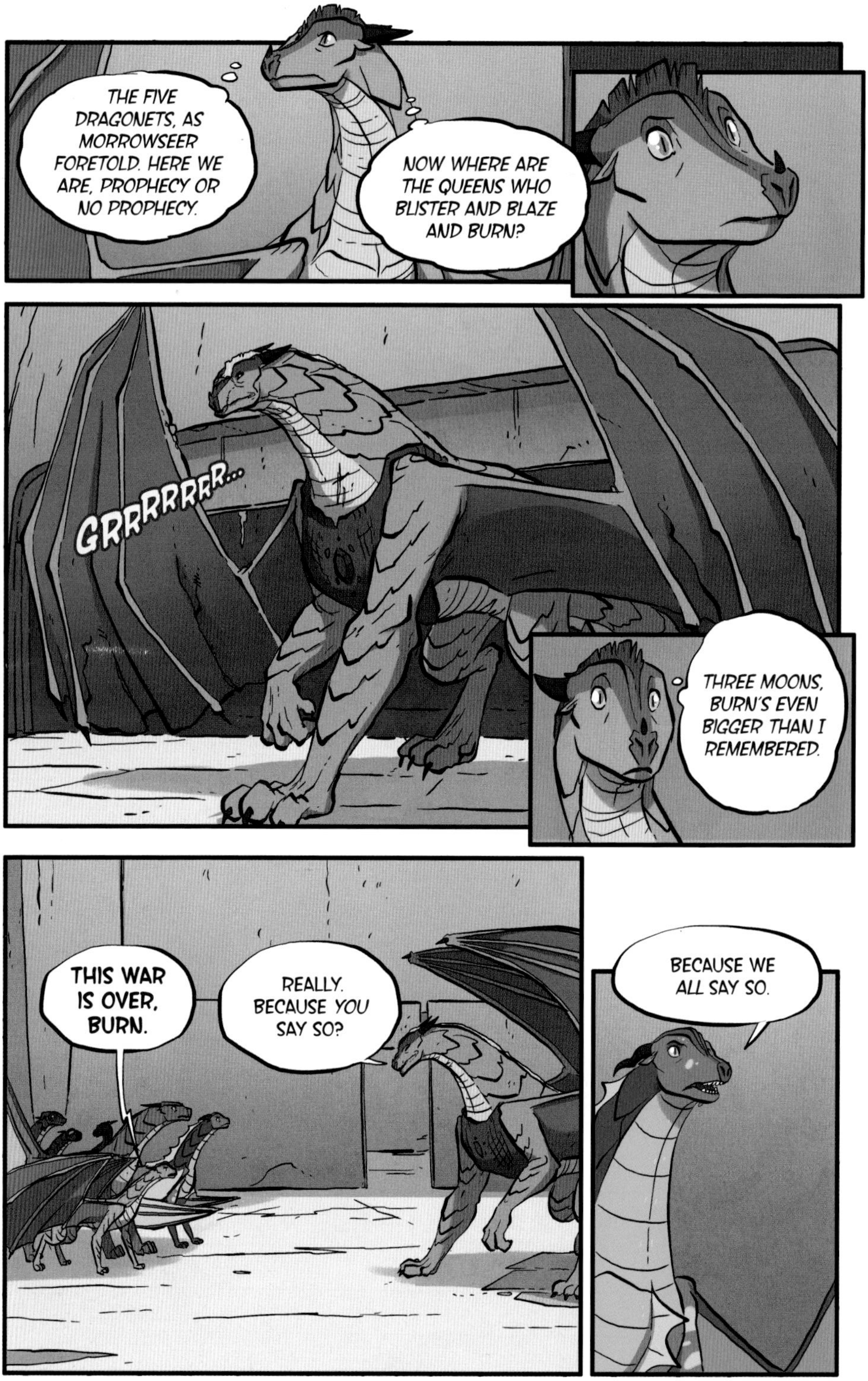
THE FIVE DRAGONETS, AS MORROWSEER FORETOLD. HERE WE ARE, PROPHECY OR NO PROPHECY.
NOW WHERE ARE THE QUEENS WHO BLISTER AND BLAZE AND BURN?
GRRRRRRR...
THREE MOONS, BURN'S EVEN BIGGER THAN I REMEMBERED.
THIS WAR IS OVER, BURN.
REALLY. BECAUSE YOU SAY SO?
BECAUSE WE ALL SAY SO.

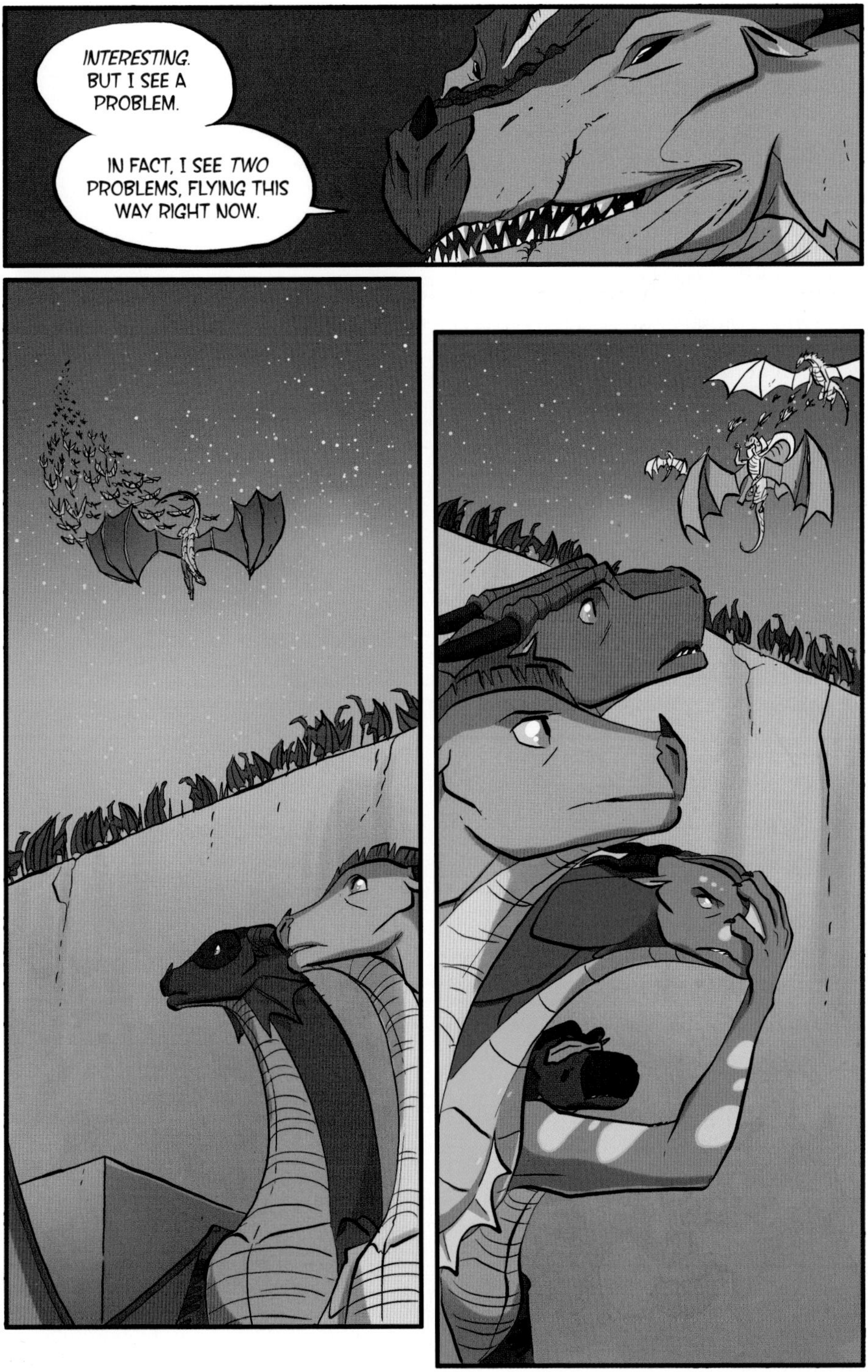
INTERESTING. BUT I SEE A PROBLEM.
IN FACT, I SEE TWO PROBLEMS, FLYING THIS WAY RIGHT NOW.

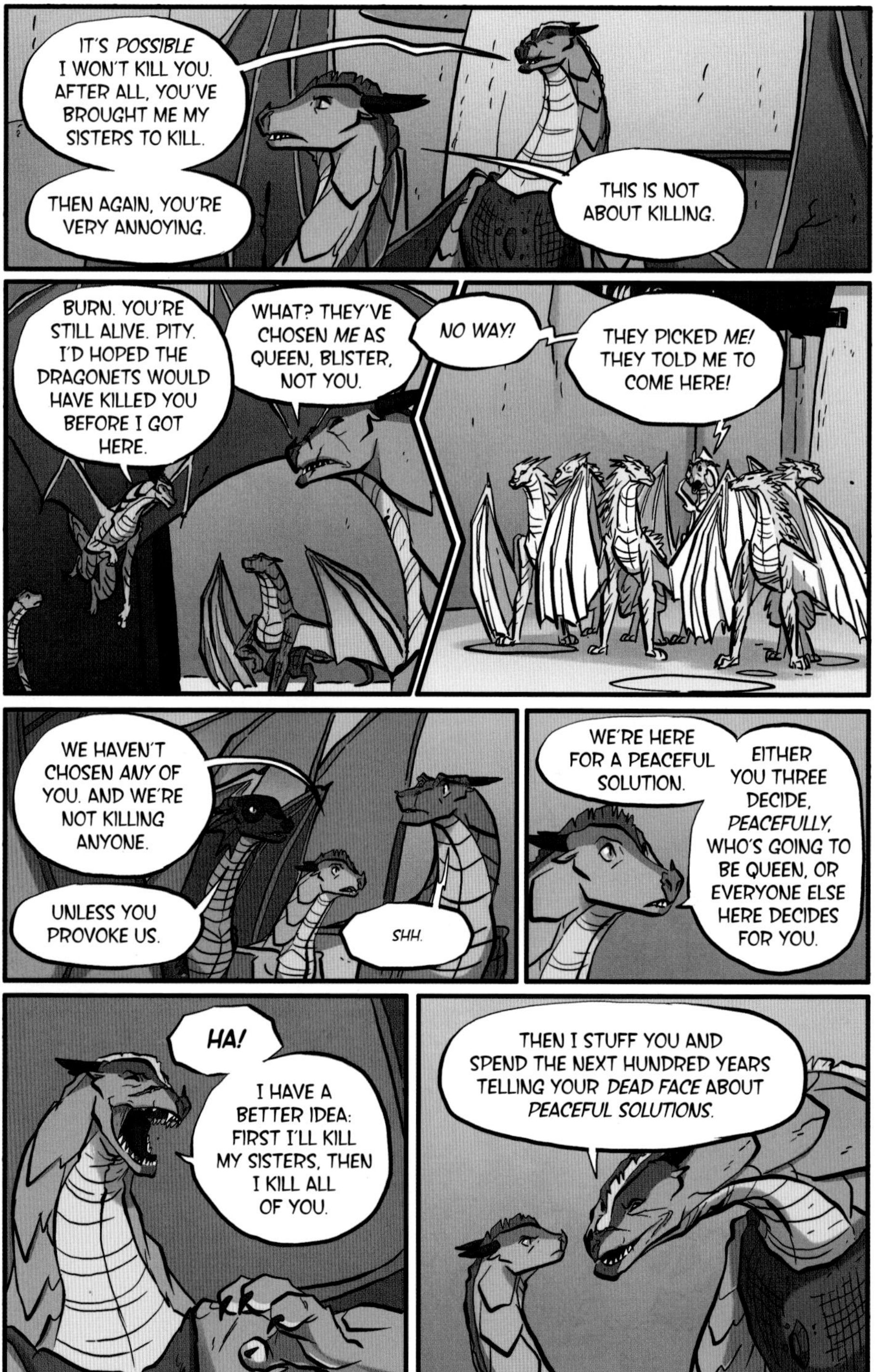
IT'S POSSIBLE I WON'T KILL YOU. AFTER ALL, YOU'VE BROUGHT ME MY SISTERS TO KILL.
THEN AGAIN, YOU'RE VERY ANNOYING.
THIS IS NOT ABOUT KILLING.
BURN. YOU'RE STILL ALIVE. PITY. I'D HOPED THE DRAGONETS WOULD HAVE KILLED YOU BEFORE I GOT HERE.
WHAT? THEY'VE CHOSEN ME AS QUEEN, BLISTER, NOT YOU.
NO WAY!
THEY PICKED ME! THEY TOLD ME TO COME HERE!
WE HAVEN'T CHOSEN ANY OF YOU. AND WE'RE NOT KILLING ANYONE.
UNLESS YOU PROVOKE US.
SHH.
WE'RE HERE FOR A PEACEFUL SOLUTION.
EITHER YOU THREE DECIDE, PEACEFULLY, WHO'S GOING TO BE QUEEN, OR EVERYONE ELSE HERE DECIDES FOR YOU.
HA!
I HAVE A BETTER IDEA: FIRST I'LL KILL MY SISTERS, THEN I KILL ALL OF YOU.
THEN I STUFF YOU AND SPEND THE NEXT HUNDRED YEARS TELLING YOUR DEAD FACE ABOUT PEACEFUL SOLUTIONS.

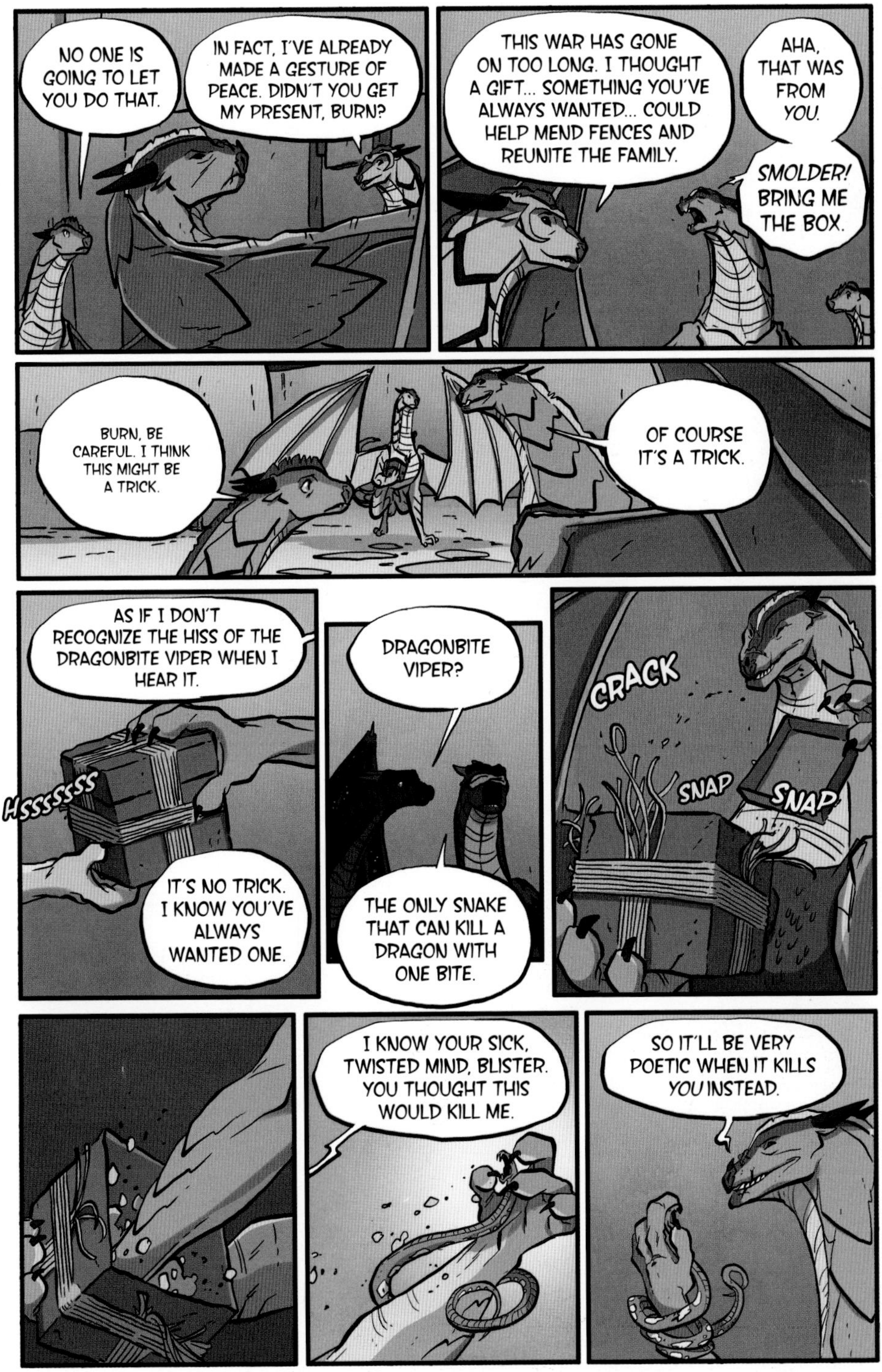
NO ONE IS GOING TO LET YOU DO THAT.
IN FACT, I'VE ALREADY MADE A GESTURE OF PEACE. DIDN'T YOU GET MY PRESENT, BURN?
THIS WAR HAS GONE ON TOO LONG. I THOUGHT A GIFT... SOMETHING YOU'VE ALWAYS WANTED... COULD HELP MEND FENCES AND REUNITE THE FAMILY.
AHA, THAT WAS FROM *YOU.*
SMOLDER! BRING ME THE BOX.
BURN, BE CAREFUL. I THINK THIS MIGHT BE A TRICK.
OF COURSE IT'S A TRICK.
AS IF I DON'T RECOGNIZE THE HISS OF THE DRAGONBITE VIPER WHEN I HEAR IT.
HSSSSSSS
IT'S NO TRICK. I KNOW YOU'VE ALWAYS WANTED ONE.
DRAGONBITE VIPER?
THE ONLY SNAKE THAT CAN KILL A DRAGON WITH ONE BITE.
CRACK
SNAP
SNAP
I KNOW YOUR SICK, TWISTED MIND, BLISTER. YOU THOUGHT THIS WOULD KILL ME.
SO IT'LL BE VERY POETIC WHEN IT KILLS *YOU* INSTEAD.

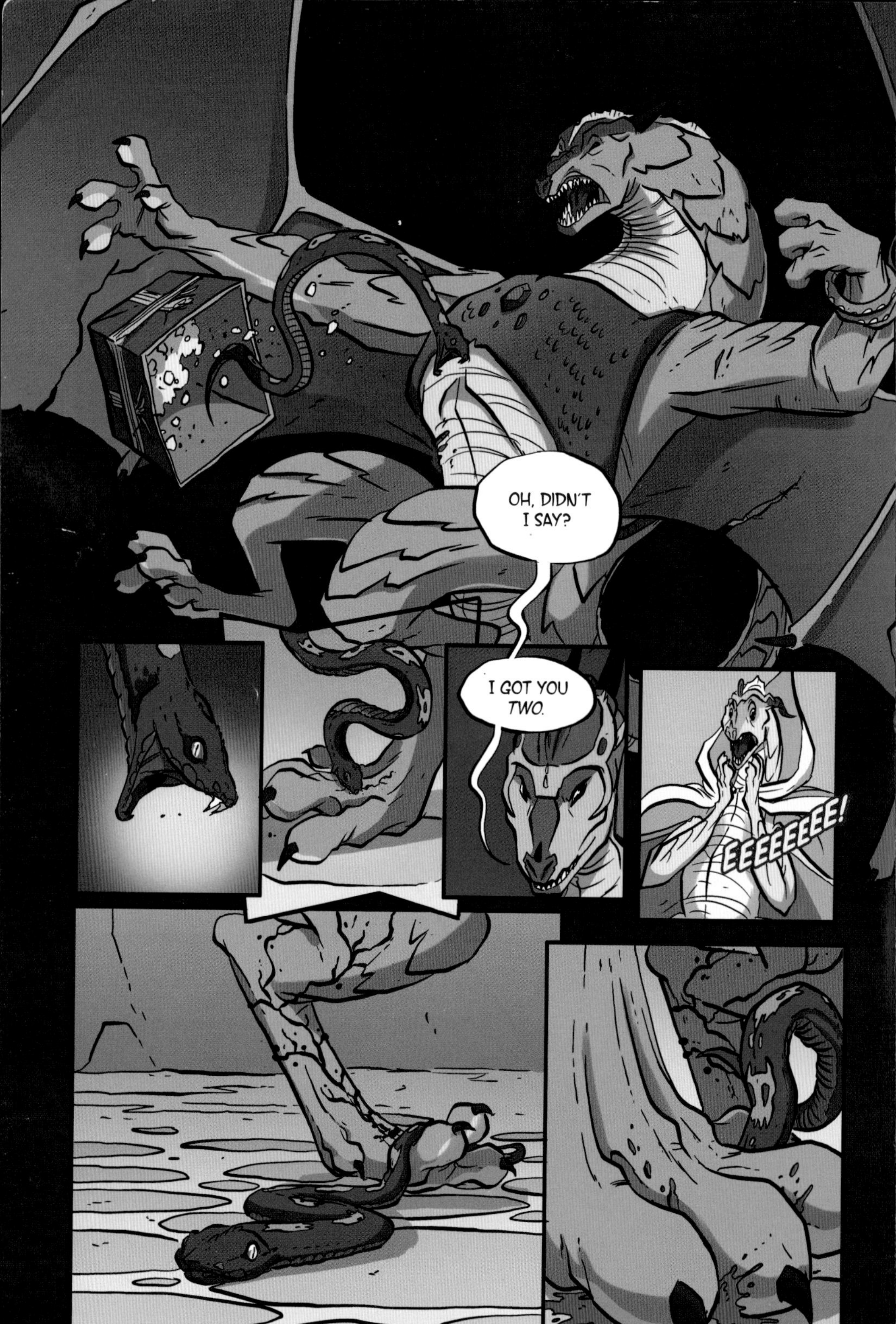
OH, DIDN'T I SAY?
I GOT YOU TWO.
EEEEEEEE!

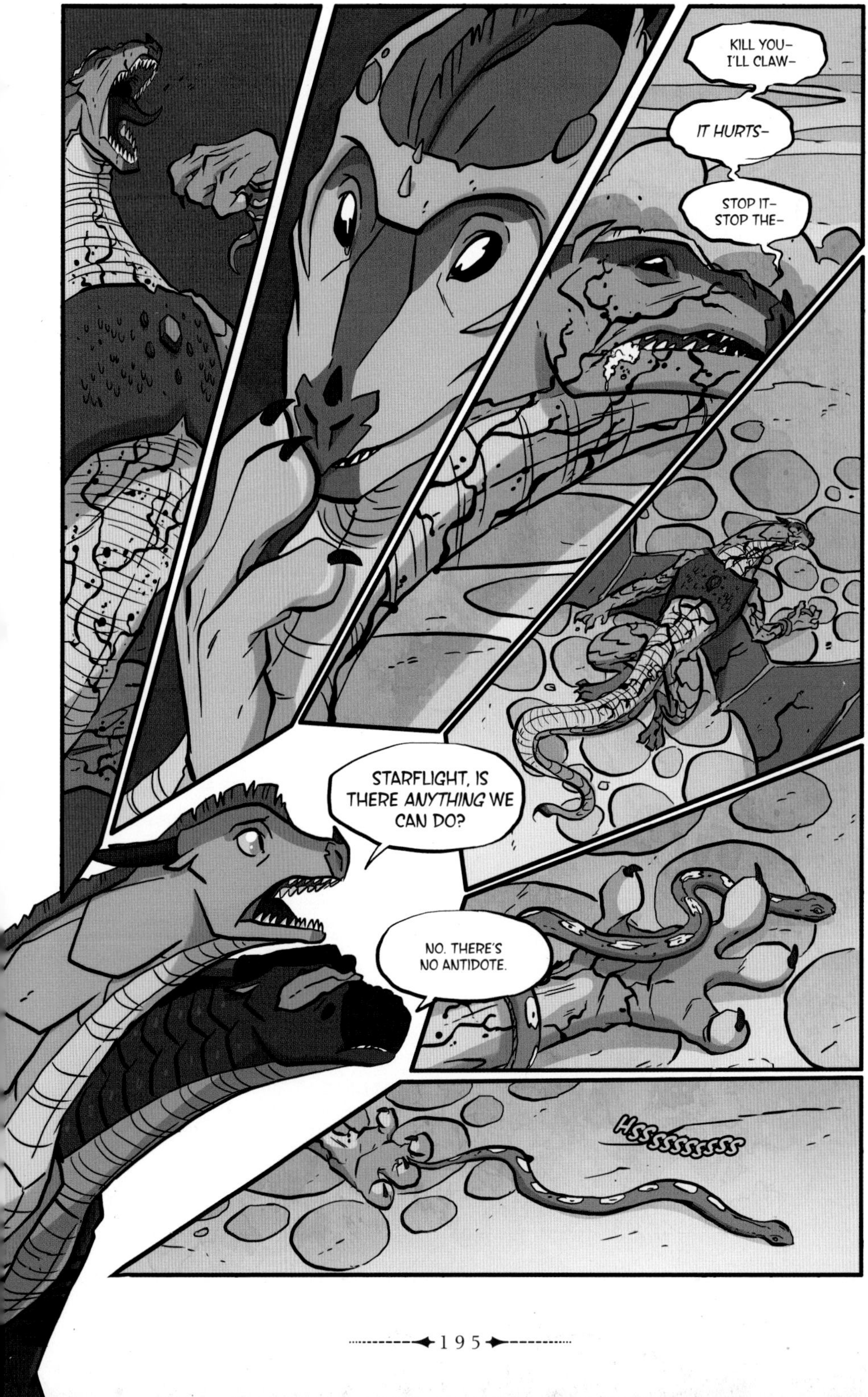
KILL YOU–
I'LL CLAW–
IT HURTS–
STOP IT–
STOP THE–
STARFLIGHT, IS THERE *ANYTHING* WE CAN DO?
NO. THERE'S NO ANTIDOTE.
HSSSSSSSSS

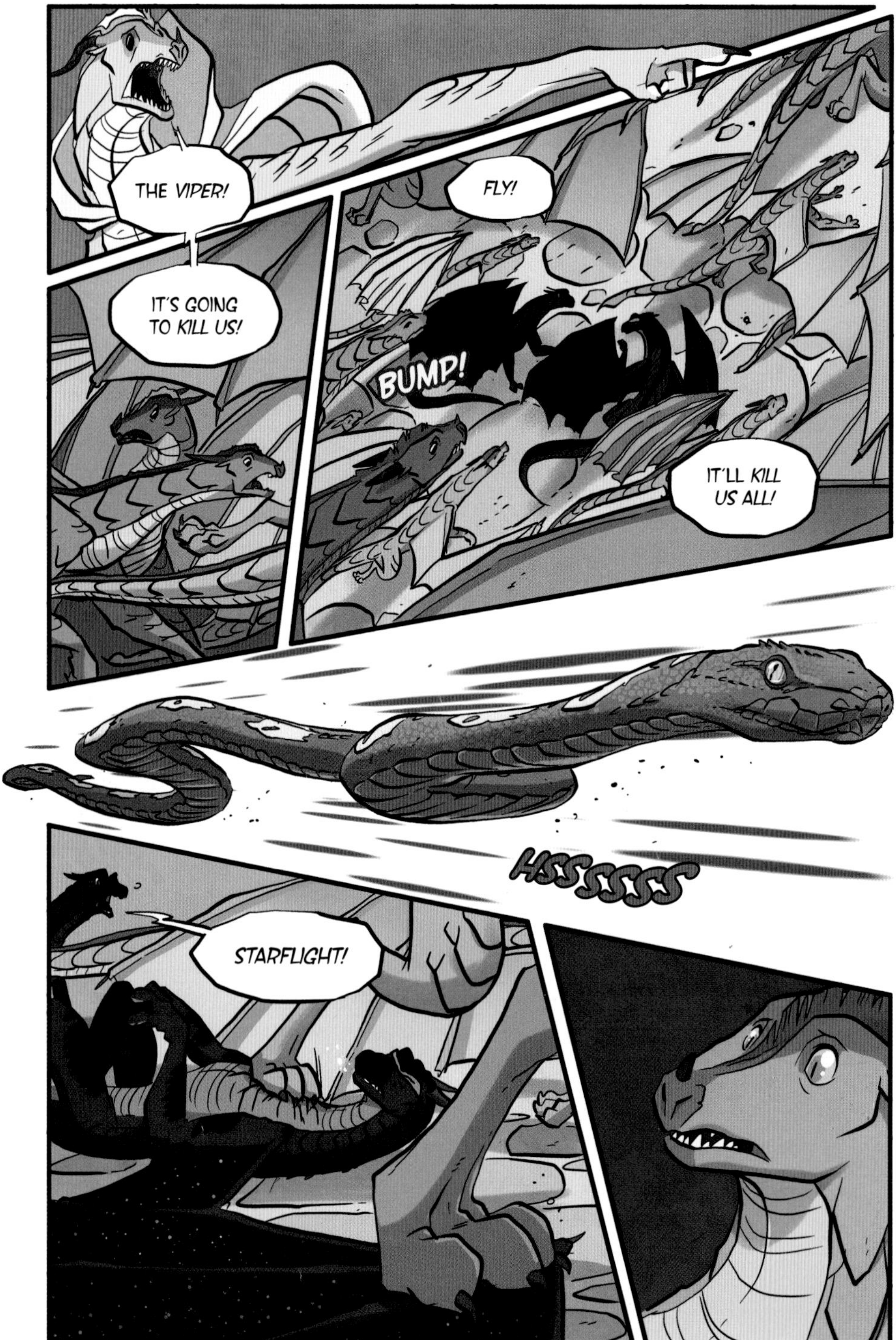
THE VIPER!
IT'S GOING TO KILL US!
FLY!
BUMP!
IT'LL KILL US ALL!
HSSSSSS
STARFLIGHT!

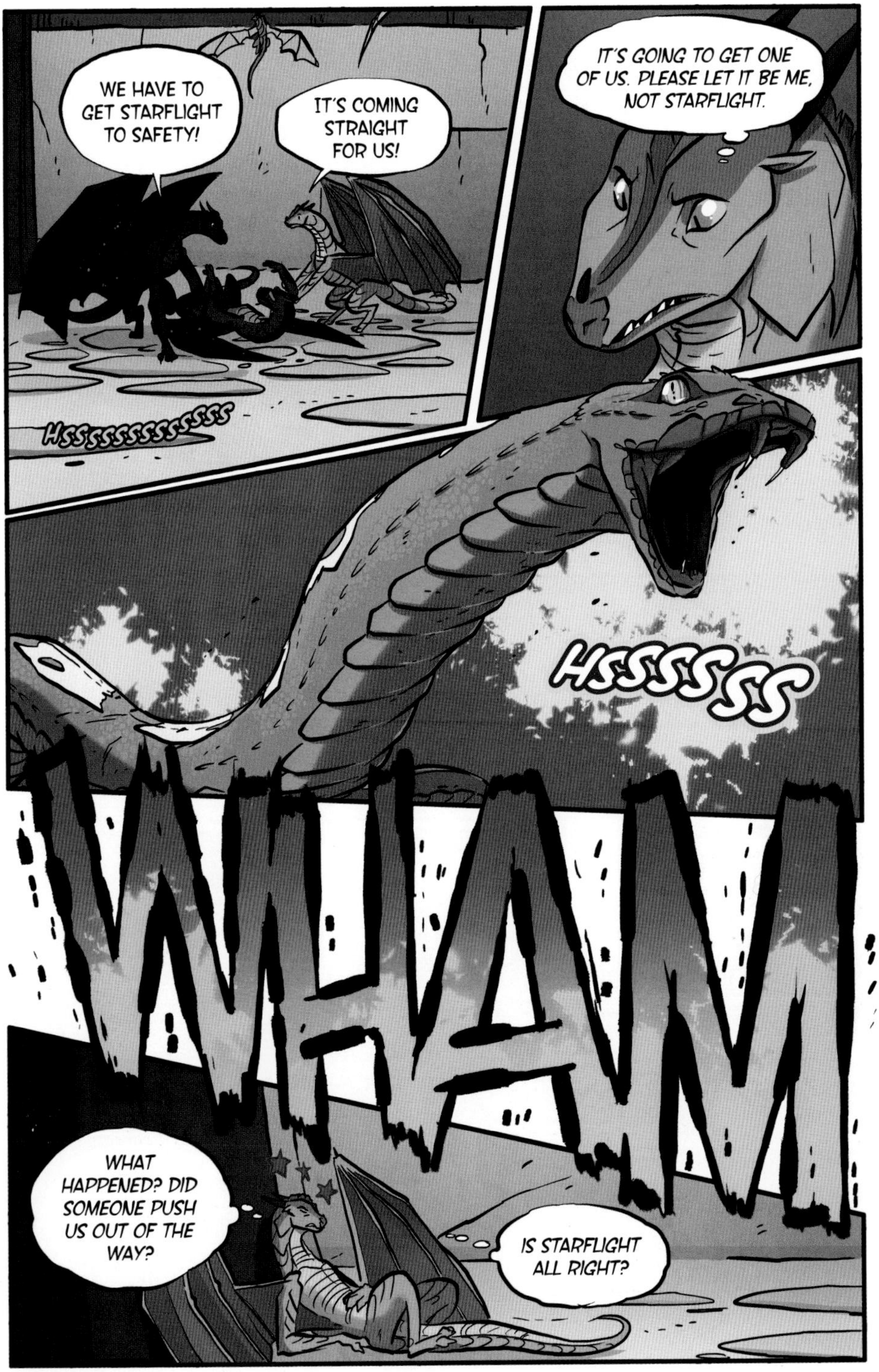
WE HAVE TO GET STARFLIGHT TO SAFETY!
IT'S COMING STRAIGHT FOR US!
HSSSSSSSSSSSSS
IT'S GOING TO GET ONE OF US. PLEASE LET IT BE ME, NOT STARFLIGHT.
HSSSSS
WHAM
WHAT HAPPENED? DID SOMEONE PUSH US OUT OF THE WAY?
IS STARFLIGHT ALL RIGHT?

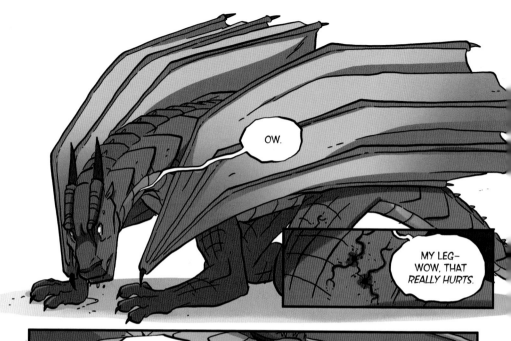

OW.

MY LEG– WOW, THAT REALLY HURTS.

CLAY!

SUNNY! STAY BACK! THE VIPER'S STILL ALIVE!

CLAY, PLEASE DON'T DIE.

I'M– I'M, UH– OPEN TO SUGGESTIONS.

WHERE'S THE SNAKE?

IT'S NOT... SUCH A BAD DESTINY, SUNNY. I'D DIE TO SAVE YOU AND STARFLIGHT OVER AND OVER.

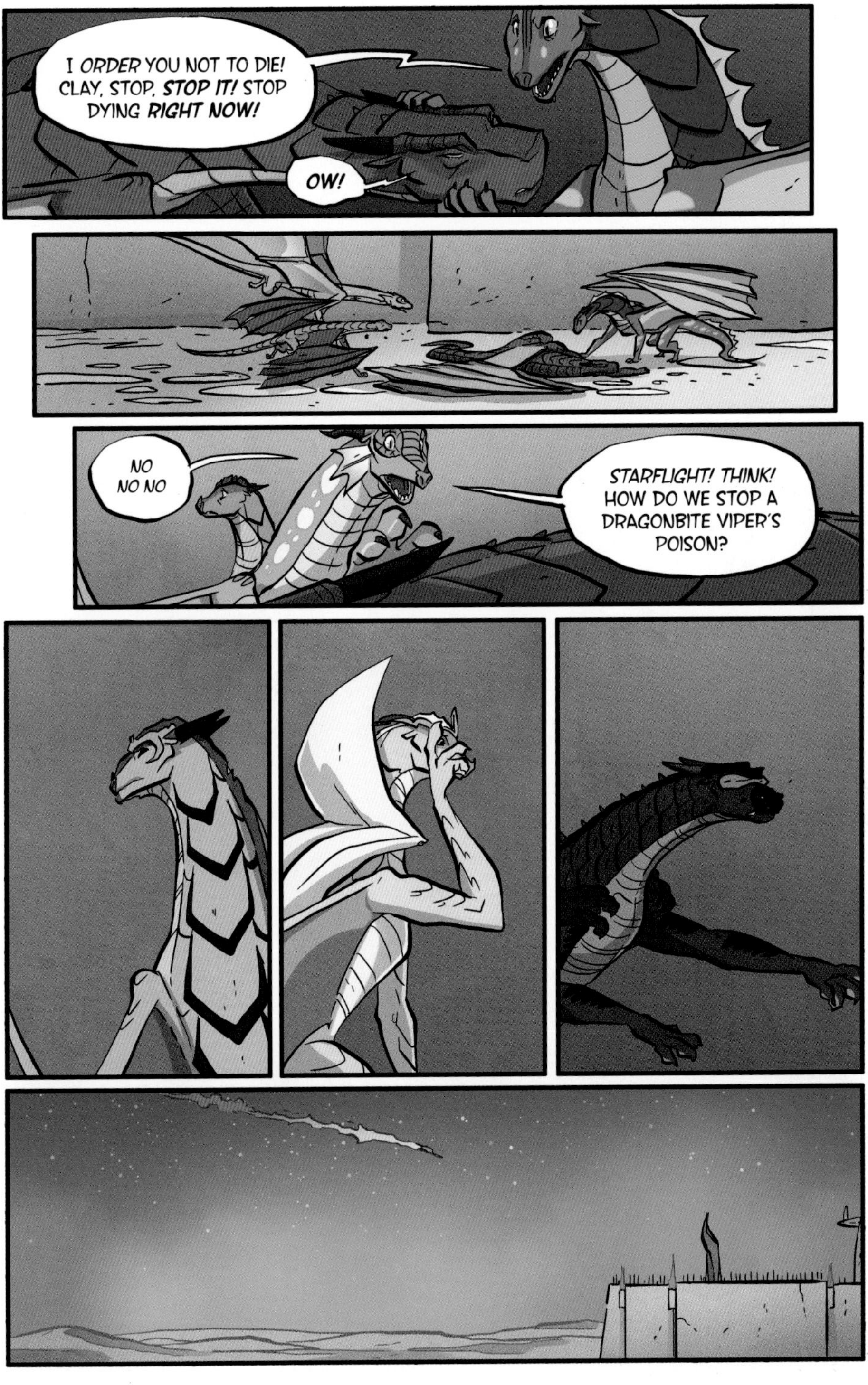
I ORDER YOU NOT TO DIE! CLAY, STOP, STOP IT! STOP DYING RIGHT NOW!
OW!
NO NO NO
STARFLIGHT! THINK! HOW DO WE STOP A DRAGONBITE VIPER'S POISON?

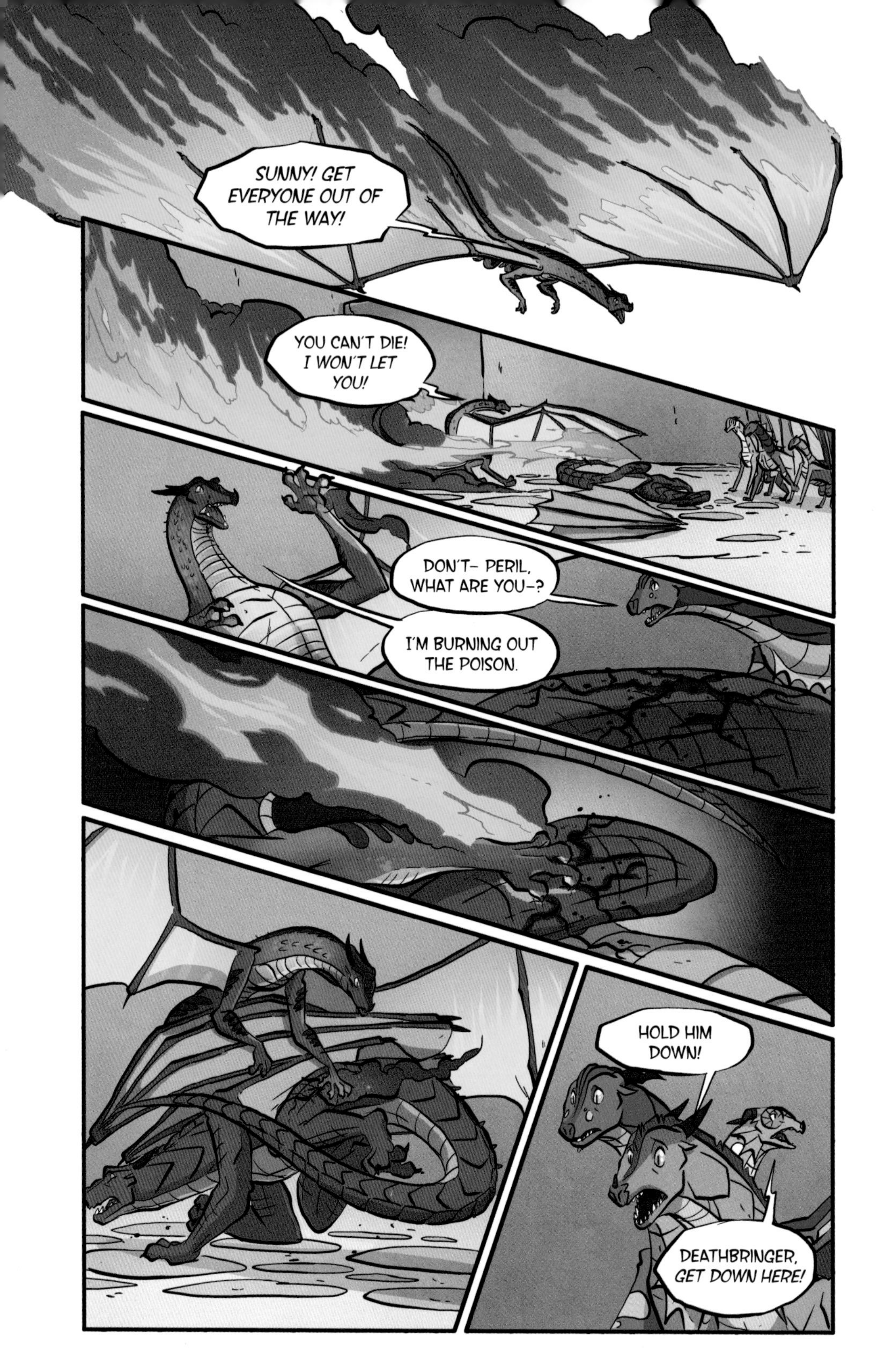
SUNNY! GET EVERYONE OUT OF THE WAY!
YOU CAN'T DIE! I WON'T LET YOU!
DON'T– PERIL, WHAT ARE YOU–?
I'M BURNING OUT THE POISON.
HOLD HIM DOWN!
DEATHBRINGER, GET DOWN HERE!

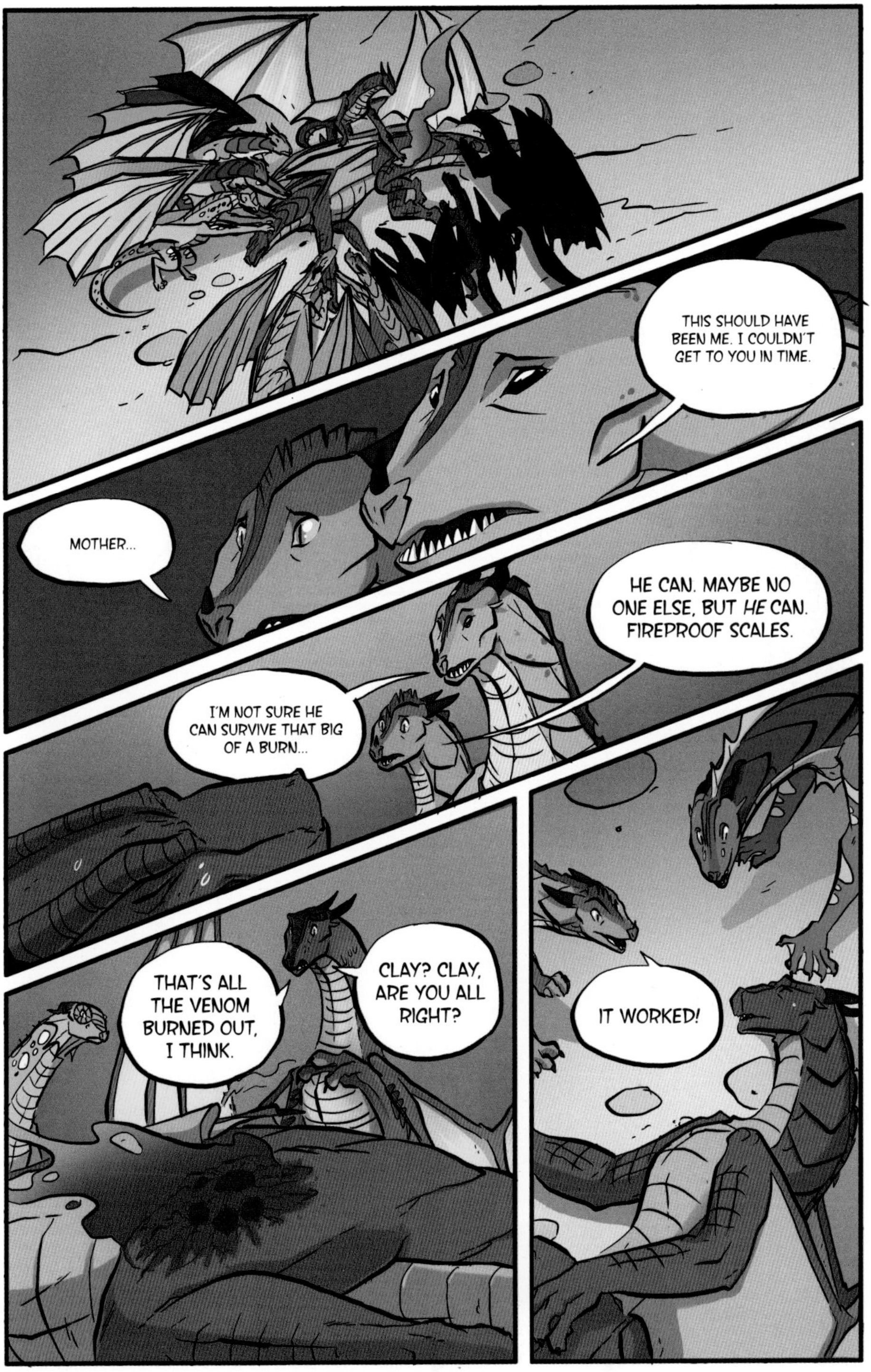
THIS SHOULD HAVE BEEN ME. I COULDN'T GET TO YOU IN TIME.
MOTHER...
HE CAN. MAYBE NO ONE ELSE, BUT *HE* CAN. FIREPROOF SCALES.
I'M NOT SURE HE CAN SURVIVE THAT BIG OF A BURN...
THAT'S ALL THE VENOM BURNED OUT, I THINK.
CLAY? CLAY, ARE YOU ALL RIGHT?
IT WORKED!

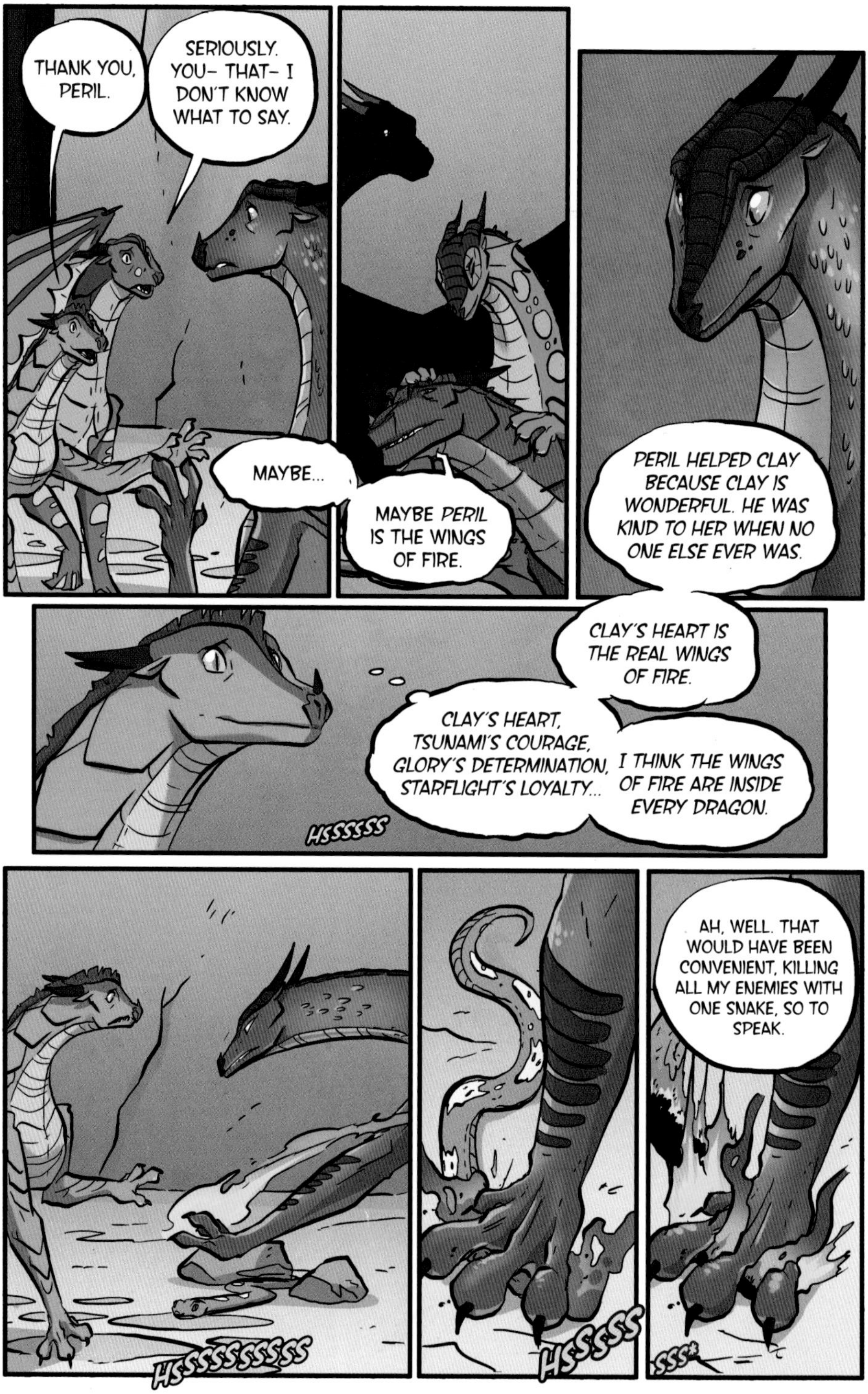
THANK YOU, PERIL.
SERIOUSLY. YOU– THAT– I DON'T KNOW WHAT TO SAY.
MAYBE...
MAYBE *PERIL* IS THE WINGS OF FIRE.
PERIL HELPED CLAY BECAUSE CLAY IS WONDERFUL. HE WAS KIND TO HER WHEN NO ONE ELSE EVER WAS.
CLAY'S HEART IS THE REAL WINGS OF FIRE.
CLAY'S HEART, TSUNAMI'S COURAGE, GLORY'S DETERMINATION, STARFLIGHT'S LOYALTY...
I THINK THE WINGS OF FIRE ARE INSIDE EVERY DRAGON.
HSSSSSS
HSSSSSSSSSS
HSSSSS
AH, WELL. THAT WOULD HAVE BEEN CONVENIENT, KILLING ALL MY ENEMIES WITH ONE SNAKE, SO TO SPEAK.
SSS*

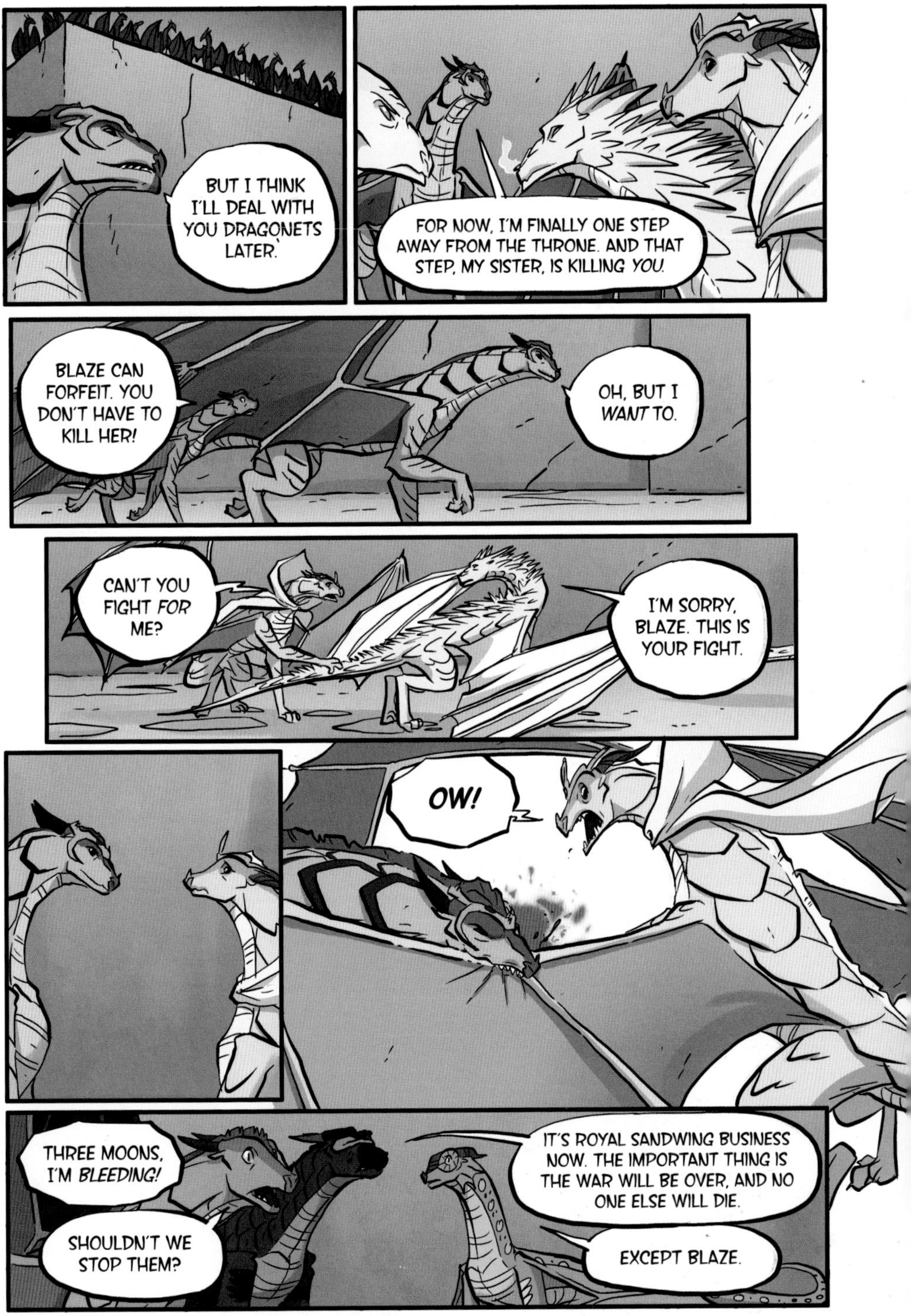
BUT I THINK I'LL DEAL WITH YOU DRAGONETS LATER.
FOR NOW, I'M FINALLY ONE STEP AWAY FROM THE THRONE. AND THAT STEP, MY SISTER, IS KILLING *YOU*.
BLAZE CAN FORFEIT. YOU DON'T HAVE TO KILL HER!
OH, BUT I *WANT* TO.
CAN'T YOU FIGHT *FOR* ME?
I'M SORRY, BLAZE. THIS IS YOUR FIGHT.
OW!
THREE MOONS, I'M *BLEEDING!*
SHOULDN'T WE STOP THEM?
IT'S ROYAL SANDWING BUSINESS NOW. THE IMPORTANT THING IS THE WAR WILL BE OVER, AND NO ONE ELSE WILL DIE.
EXCEPT BLAZE.

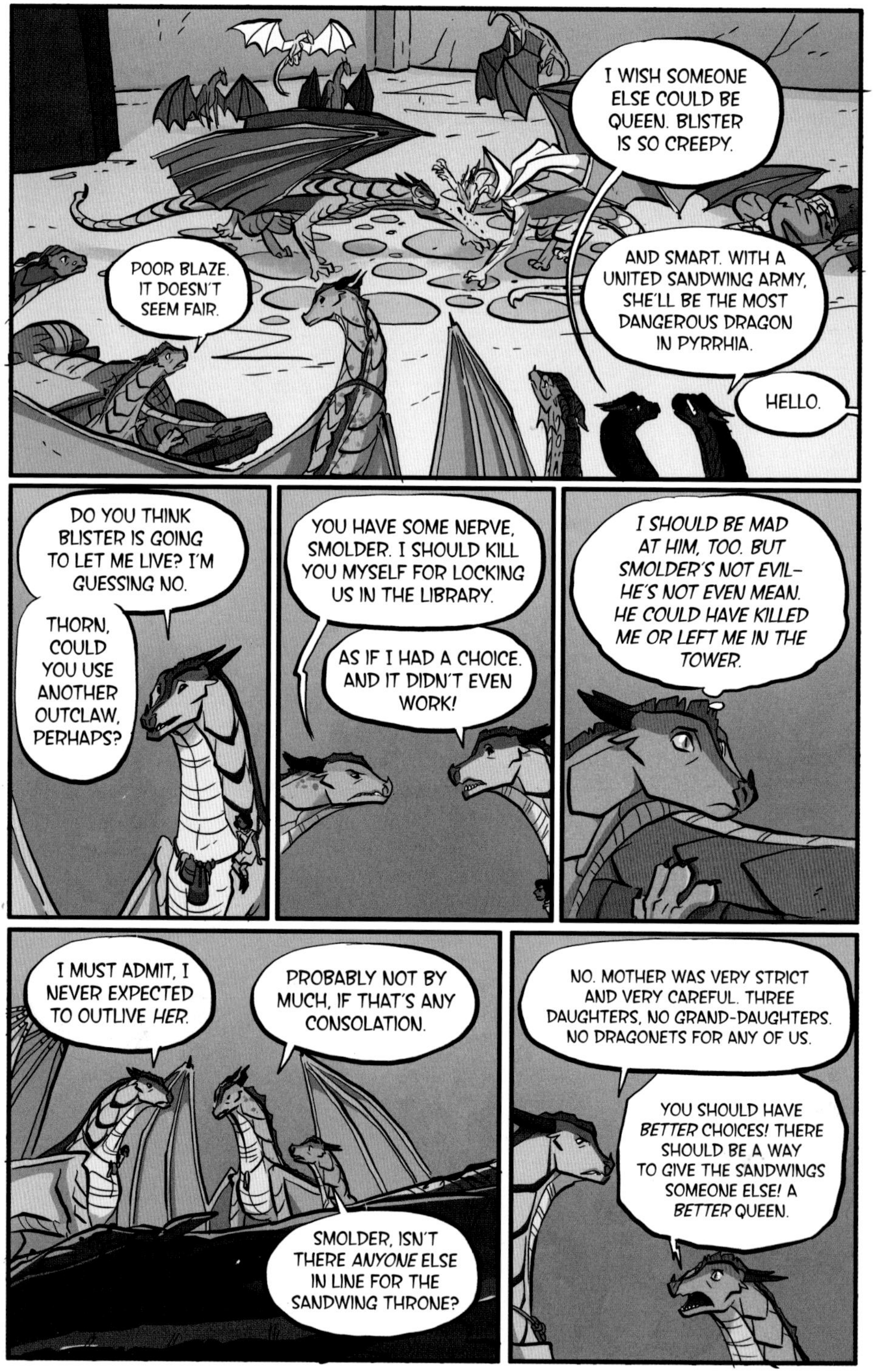
I WISH SOMEONE ELSE COULD BE QUEEN. BLISTER IS SO CREEPY.
POOR BLAZE. IT DOESN'T SEEM FAIR.
AND SMART. WITH A UNITED SANDWING ARMY, SHE'LL BE THE MOST DANGEROUS DRAGON IN PYRRHIA.
HELLO.
DO YOU THINK BLISTER IS GOING TO LET ME LIVE? I'M GUESSING NO.
THORN, COULD YOU USE ANOTHER OUTCLAW, PERHAPS?
YOU HAVE SOME NERVE, SMOLDER. I SHOULD KILL YOU MYSELF FOR LOCKING US IN THE LIBRARY.
AS IF I HAD A CHOICE. AND IT DIDN'T EVEN WORK!
I SHOULD BE MAD AT HIM, TOO. BUT SMOLDER'S NOT EVIL—HE'S NOT EVEN MEAN. HE COULD HAVE KILLED ME OR LEFT ME IN THE TOWER.
I MUST ADMIT, I NEVER EXPECTED TO OUTLIVE *HER*.
PROBABLY NOT BY MUCH, IF THAT'S ANY CONSOLATION.
SMOLDER, ISN'T THERE *ANYONE* ELSE IN LINE FOR THE SANDWING THRONE?
NO. MOTHER WAS VERY STRICT AND VERY CAREFUL. THREE DAUGHTERS, NO GRAND-DAUGHTERS. NO DRAGONETS FOR ANY OF US.
YOU SHOULD HAVE *BETTER* CHOICES! THERE SHOULD BE A WAY TO GIVE THE SANDWINGS SOMEONE ELSE! A *BETTER* QUEEN.

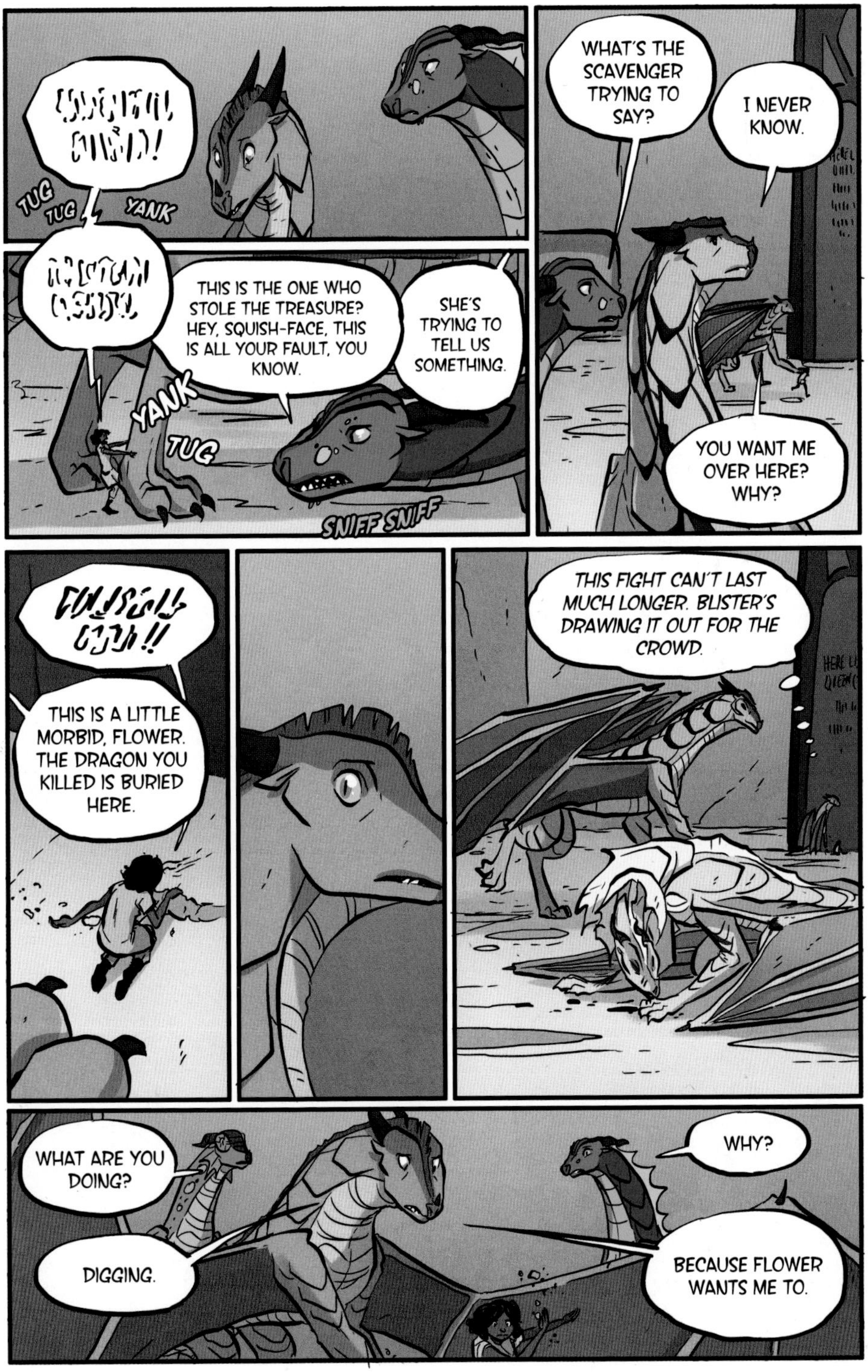
TUG
TUG
YANK
THIS IS THE ONE WHO STOLE THE TREASURE? HEY, SQUISH-FACE, THIS IS ALL YOUR FAULT, YOU KNOW.
SHE'S TRYING TO TELL US SOMETHING.
YANK
TUG
SNIFF SNIFF
WHAT'S THE SCAVENGER TRYING TO SAY?
I NEVER KNOW.
YOU WANT ME OVER HERE? WHY?
THIS IS A LITTLE MORBID, FLOWER. THE DRAGON YOU KILLED IS BURIED HERE.
THIS FIGHT CAN'T LAST MUCH LONGER. BLISTER'S DRAWING IT OUT FOR THE CROWD.
WHAT ARE YOU DOING?
DIGGING.
WHY?
BECAUSE FLOWER WANTS ME TO.

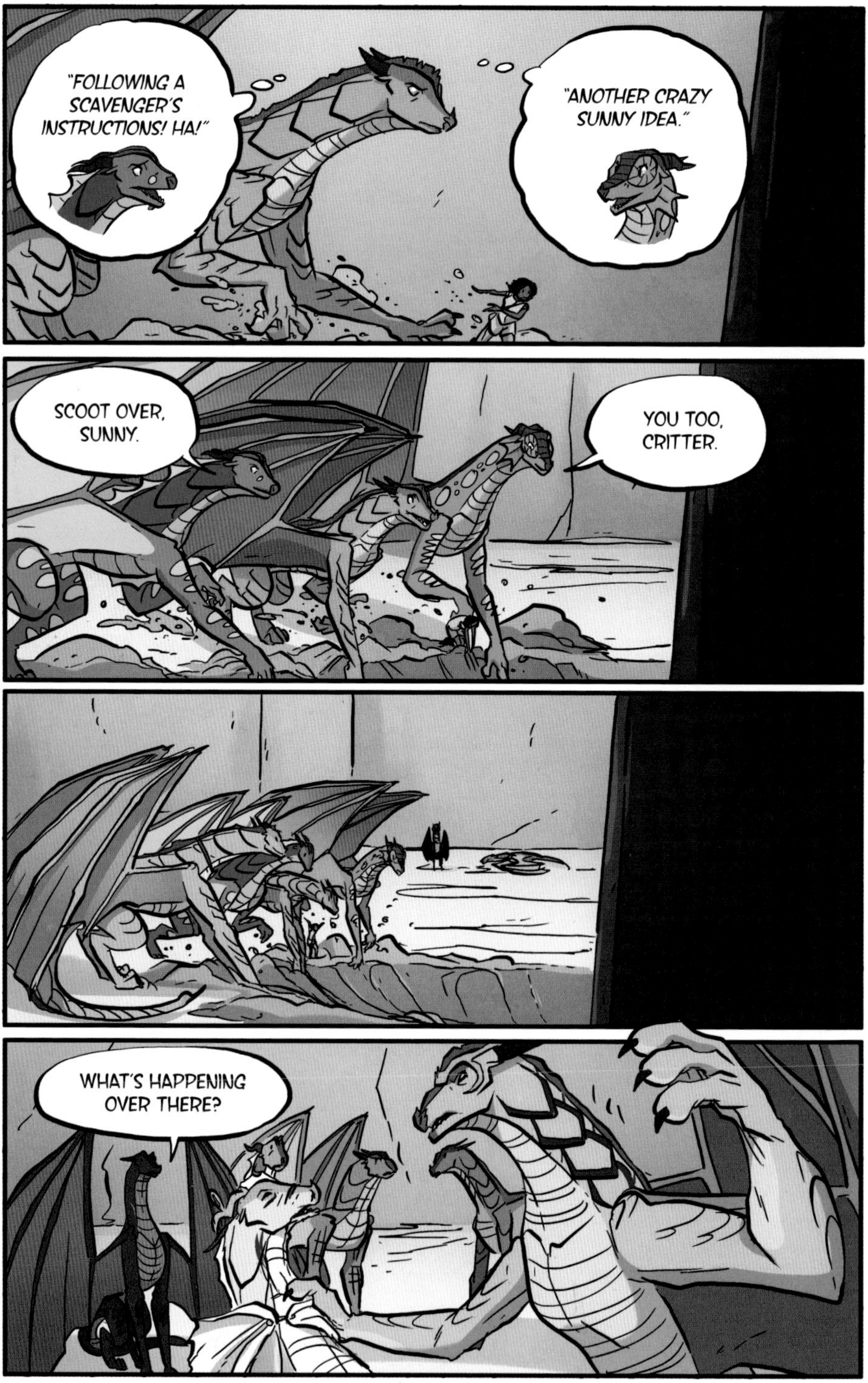
"FOLLOWING A SCAVENGER'S INSTRUCTIONS! HA!"
"ANOTHER CRAZY SUNNY IDEA."
SCOOT OVER, SUNNY.
YOU TOO, CRITTER.
WHAT'S HAPPENING OVER THERE?

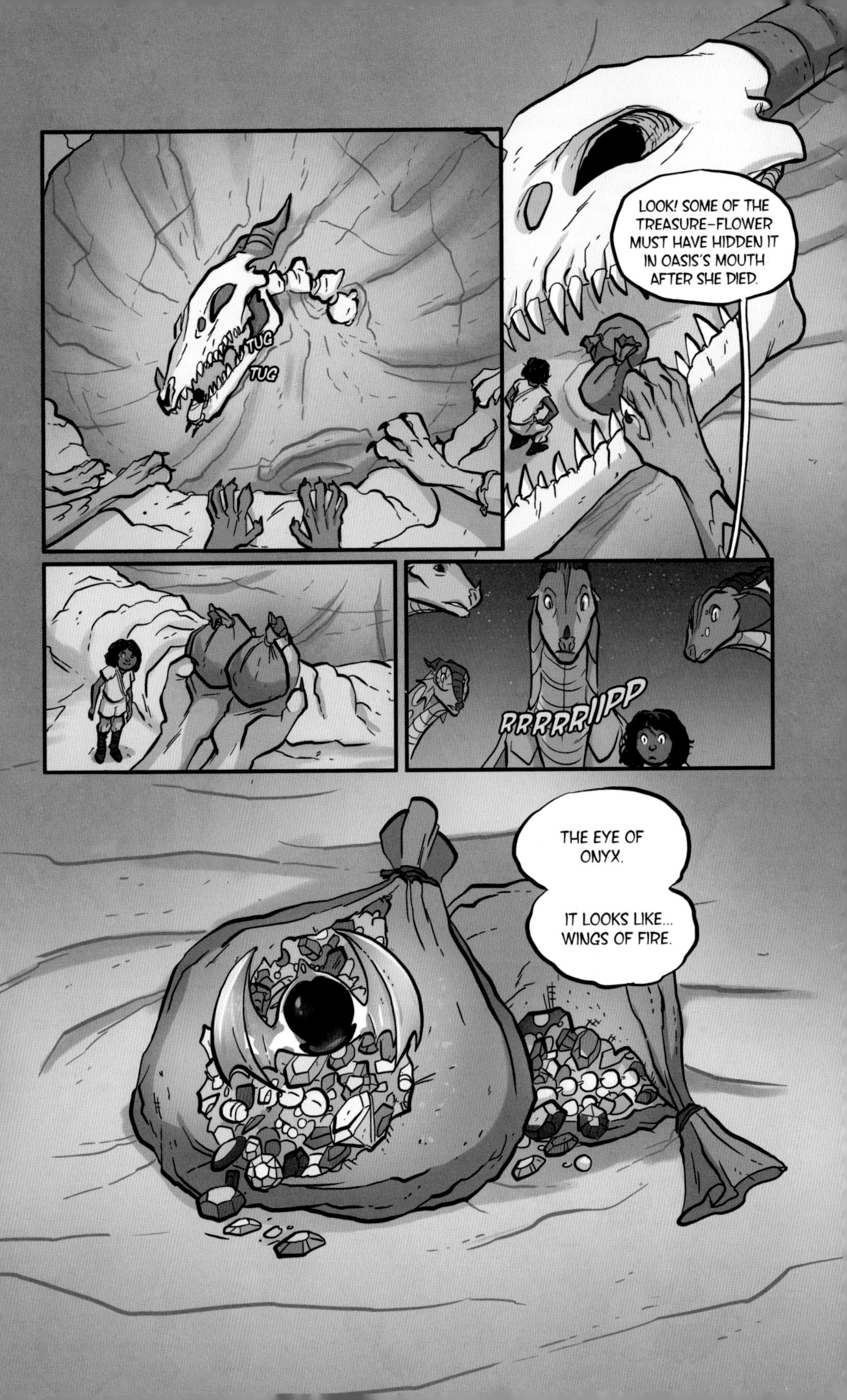
TUG
TUG
LOOK! SOME OF THE TREASURE-FLOWER MUST HAVE HIDDEN IT IN OASIS'S MOUTH AFTER SHE DIED.
RRRRRIIPP
THE EYE OF ONYX.
IT LOOKS LIKE... WINGS OF FIRE.

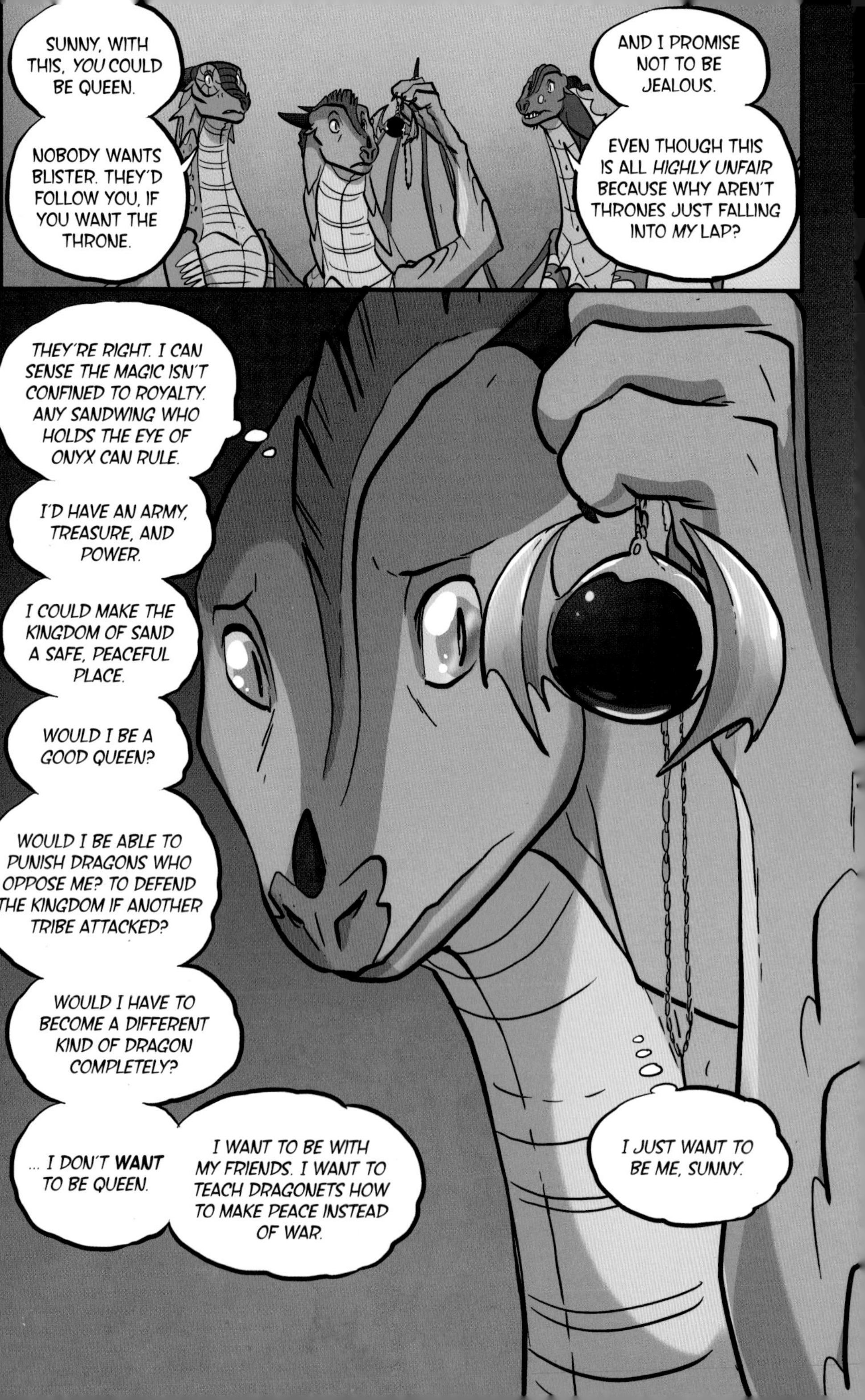
SUNNY, WITH THIS, *YOU* COULD BE QUEEN.
NOBODY WANTS BLISTER. THEY'D FOLLOW YOU, IF YOU WANT THE THRONE.
AND I PROMISE NOT TO BE JEALOUS.
EVEN THOUGH THIS IS ALL *HIGHLY UNFAIR* BECAUSE WHY AREN'T THRONES JUST FALLING INTO *MY* LAP?
THEY'RE RIGHT. I CAN SENSE THE MAGIC ISN'T CONFINED TO ROYALTY. ANY SANDWING WHO HOLDS THE EYE OF ONYX CAN RULE.
I'D HAVE AN ARMY, TREASURE, AND POWER.
I COULD MAKE THE KINGDOM OF SAND A SAFE, PEACEFUL PLACE.
WOULD I BE A GOOD QUEEN?
WOULD I BE ABLE TO PUNISH DRAGONS WHO OPPOSE ME? TO DEFEND THE KINGDOM IF ANOTHER TRIBE ATTACKED?
WOULD I HAVE TO BECOME A DIFFERENT KIND OF DRAGON COMPLETELY?
... I DON'T **WANT** TO BE QUEEN.
I WANT TO BE WITH MY FRIENDS. I WANT TO TEACH DRAGONETS HOW TO MAKE PEACE INSTEAD OF WAR.
I JUST WANT TO BE ME, SUNNY.

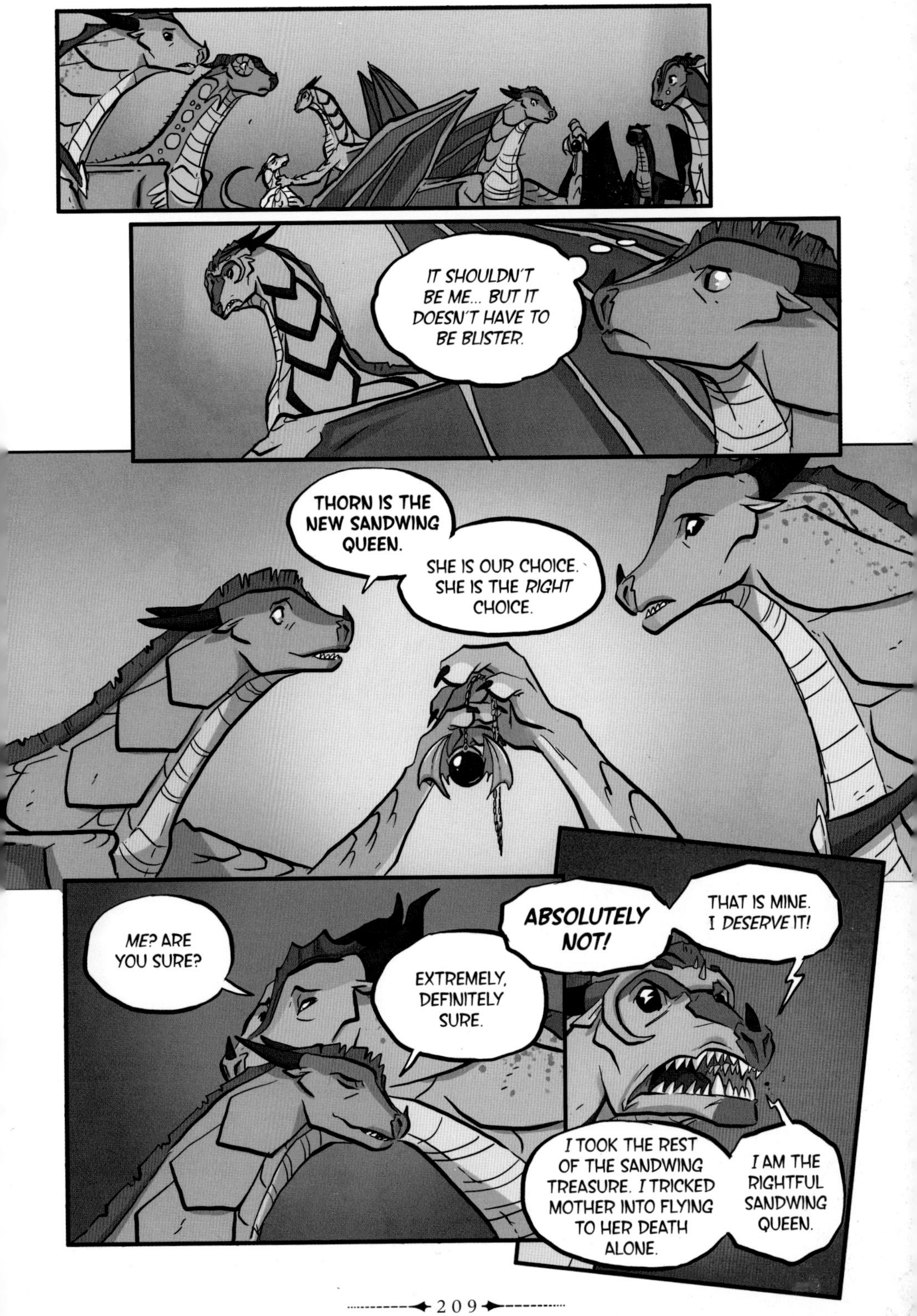
IT SHOULDN'T BE ME... BUT IT DOESN'T HAVE TO BE BLISTER.
THORN IS THE NEW SANDWING QUEEN.
SHE IS OUR CHOICE. SHE IS THE *RIGHT* CHOICE.
ME? ARE YOU SURE?
EXTREMELY, DEFINITELY SURE.
ABSOLUTELY NOT!
THAT IS MINE. I *DESERVE* IT!
I TOOK THE REST OF THE SANDWING TREASURE. *I* TRICKED MOTHER INTO FLYING TO HER DEATH ALONE.
I AM THE RIGHTFUL SANDWING QUEEN.

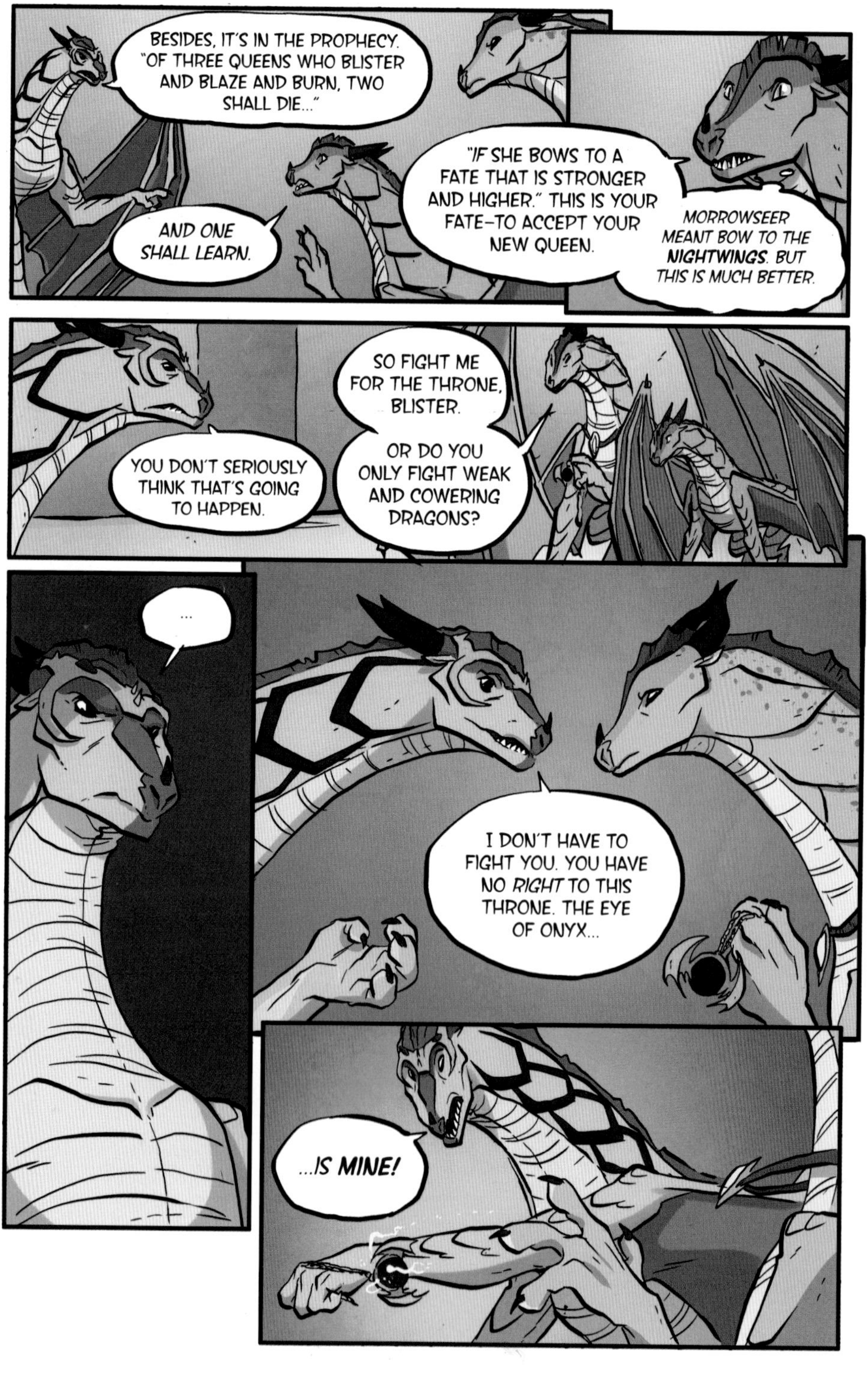
BESIDES, IT'S IN THE PROPHECY. "OF THREE QUEENS WHO BLISTER AND BLAZE AND BURN, TWO SHALL DIE..."
AND ONE SHALL LEARN.
"*IF* SHE BOWS TO A FATE THAT IS STRONGER AND HIGHER." THIS IS YOUR FATE—TO ACCEPT YOUR NEW QUEEN.
MORROWSEER MEANT BOW TO THE **NIGHTWINGS**. BUT THIS IS MUCH BETTER.
YOU DON'T SERIOUSLY THINK THAT'S GOING TO HAPPEN.
SO FIGHT ME FOR THE THRONE, BLISTER.
OR DO YOU ONLY FIGHT WEAK AND COWERING DRAGONS?
...
I DON'T HAVE TO FIGHT YOU. YOU HAVE NO *RIGHT* TO THIS THRONE. THE EYE OF ONYX...
...IS **MINE!**

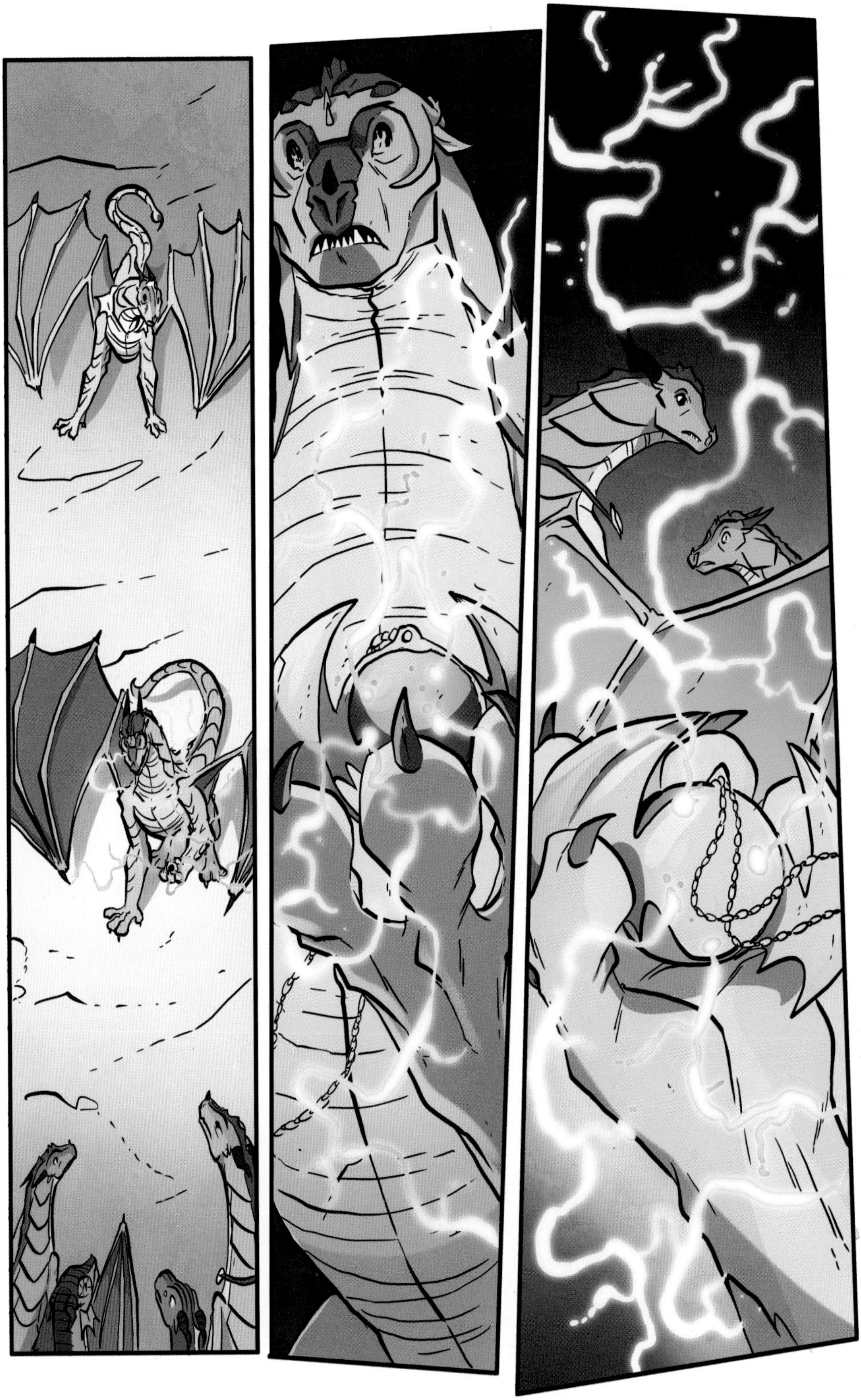

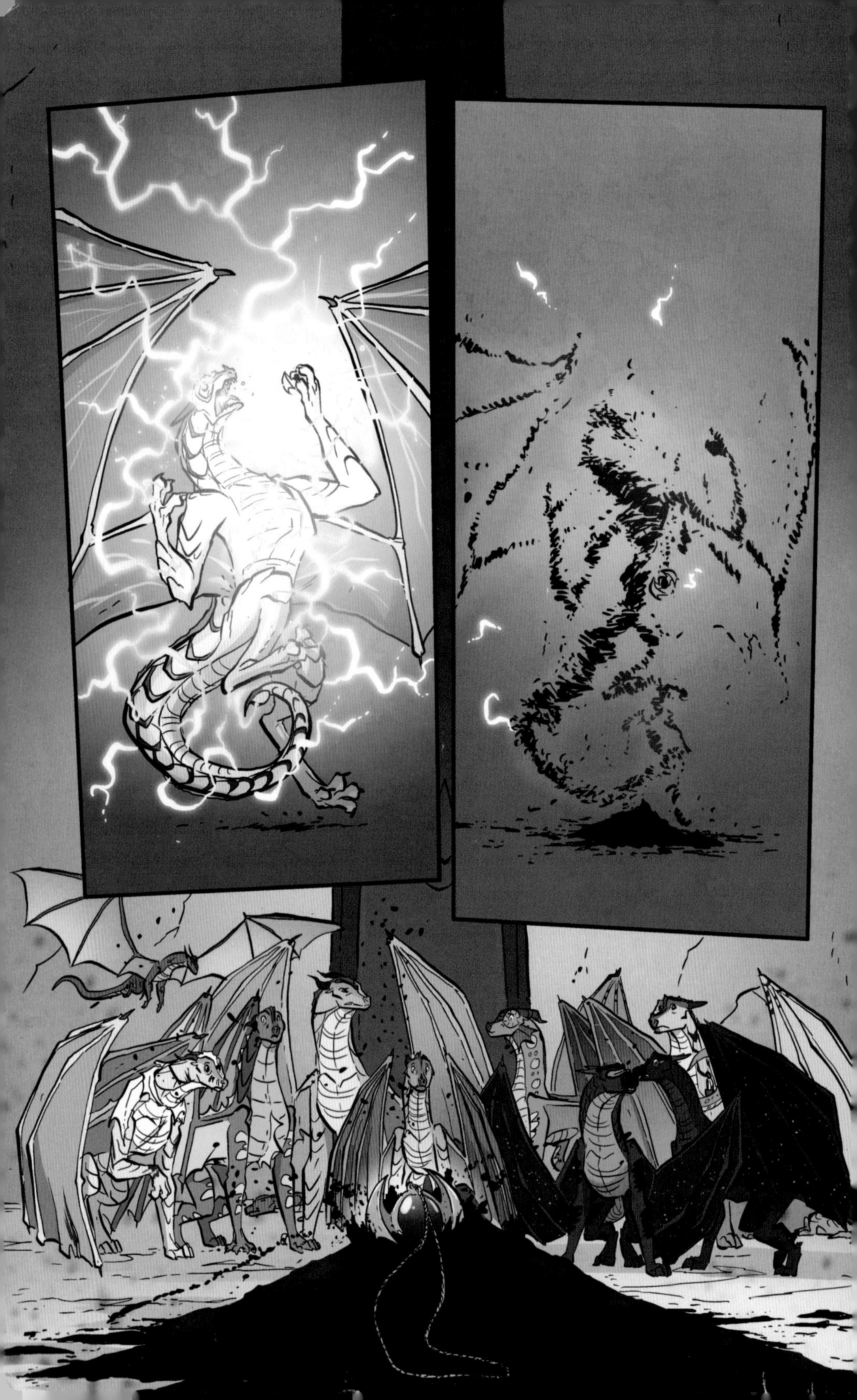

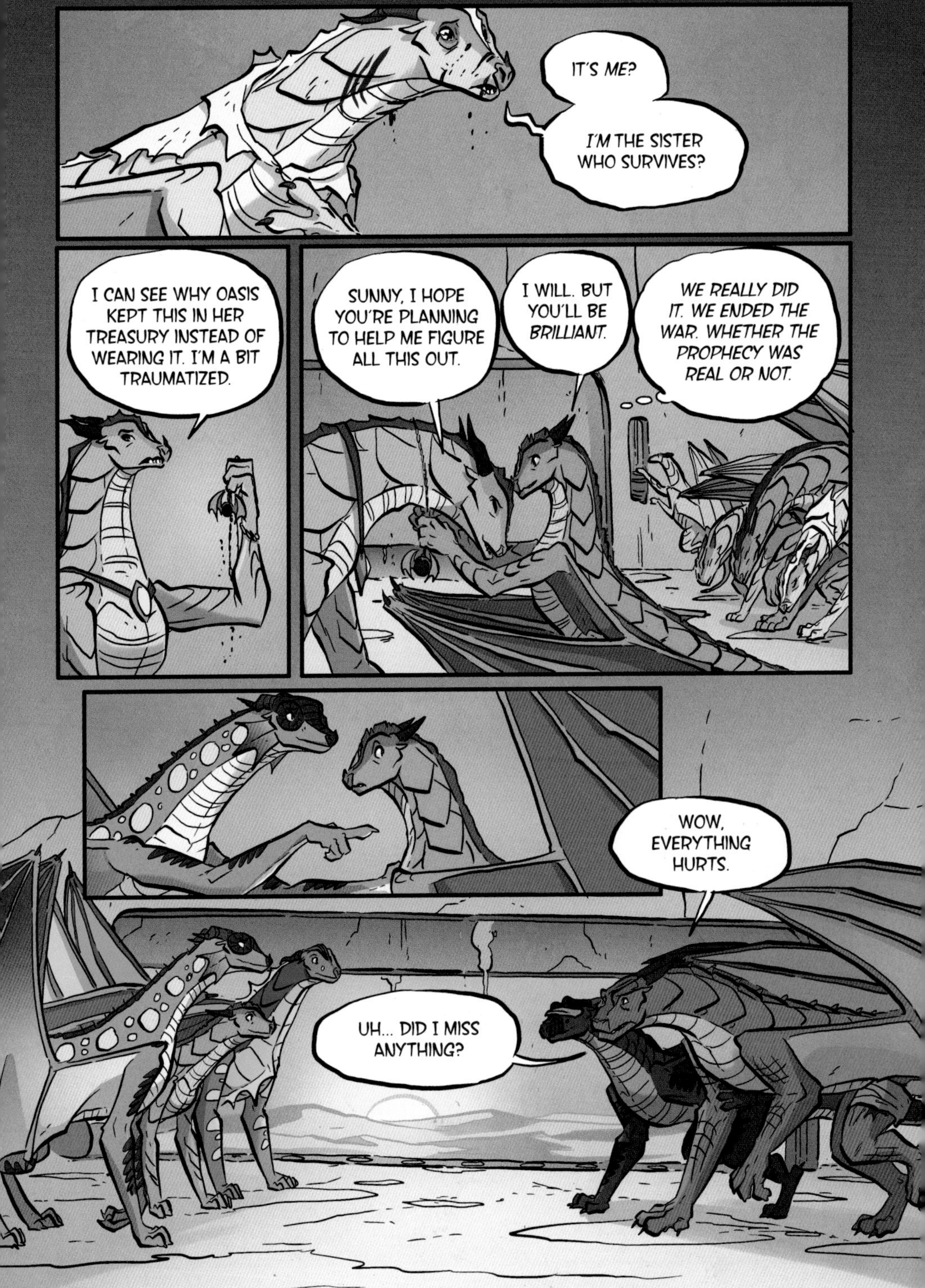

IT'S ME?
I'M THE SISTER WHO SURVIVES?
I CAN SEE WHY OASIS KEPT THIS IN HER TREASURY INSTEAD OF WEARING IT. I'M A BIT TRAUMATIZED.
SUNNY, I HOPE YOU'RE PLANNING TO HELP ME FIGURE ALL THIS OUT.
I WILL. BUT YOU'LL BE BRILLIANT.
WE REALLY DID IT. WE ENDED THE WAR. WHETHER THE PROPHECY WAS REAL OR NOT.
WOW, EVERYTHING HURTS.
UH... DID I MISS ANYTHING?

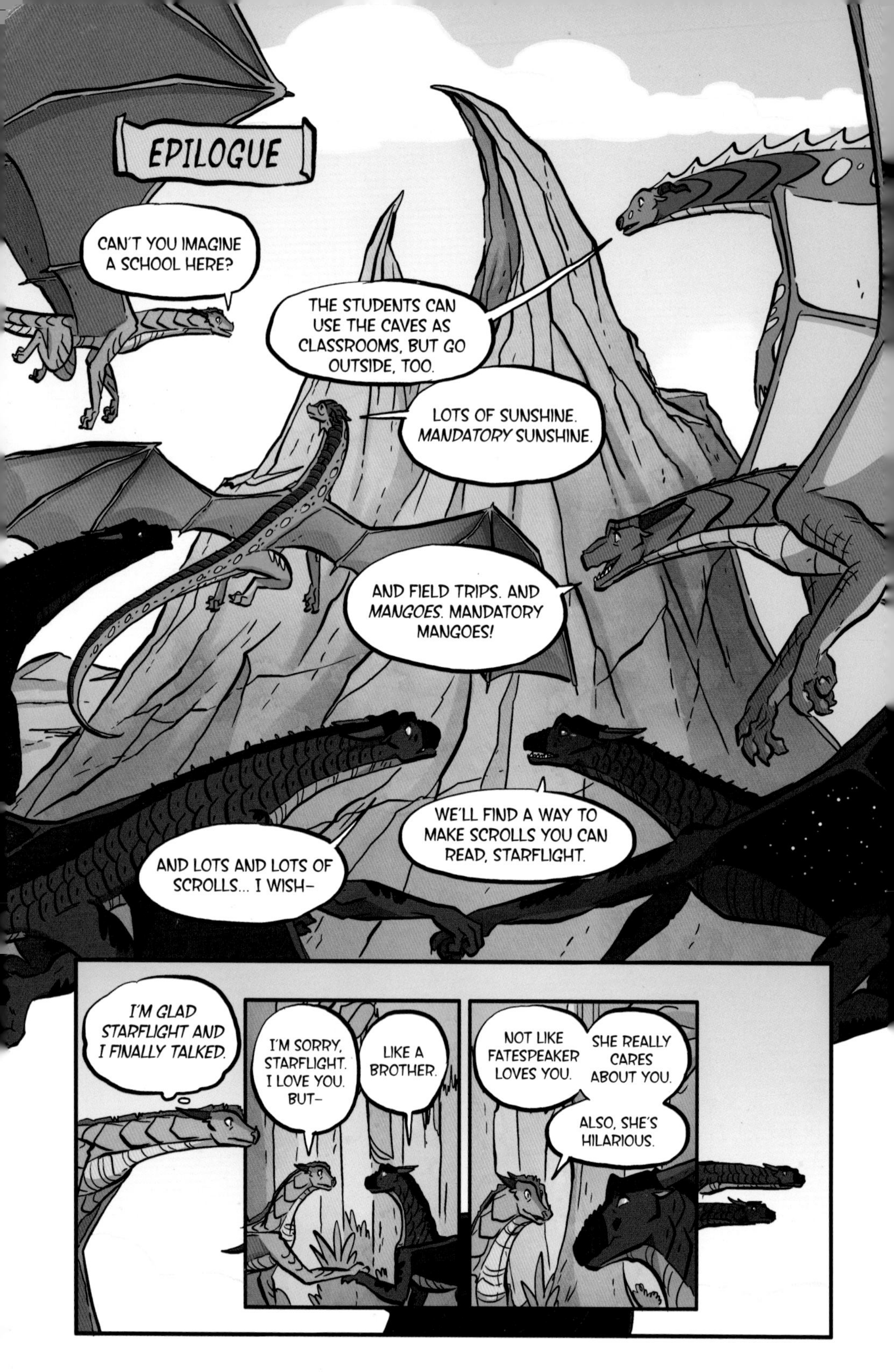
EPILOGUE
CAN'T YOU IMAGINE A SCHOOL HERE?
THE STUDENTS CAN USE THE CAVES AS CLASSROOMS, BUT GO OUTSIDE, TOO.
LOTS OF SUNSHINE. *MANDATORY* SUNSHINE.
AND FIELD TRIPS. AND *MANGOES*. MANDATORY MANGOES!
AND LOTS AND LOTS OF SCROLLS... I WISH–
WE'LL FIND A WAY TO MAKE SCROLLS YOU CAN READ, STARFLIGHT.
I'M GLAD STARFLIGHT AND I FINALLY TALKED.
I'M SORRY, STARFLIGHT. I LOVE YOU. BUT–
LIKE A BROTHER.
NOT LIKE FATESPEAKER LOVES YOU.
SHE REALLY CARES ABOUT YOU.
ALSO, SHE'S HILARIOUS.

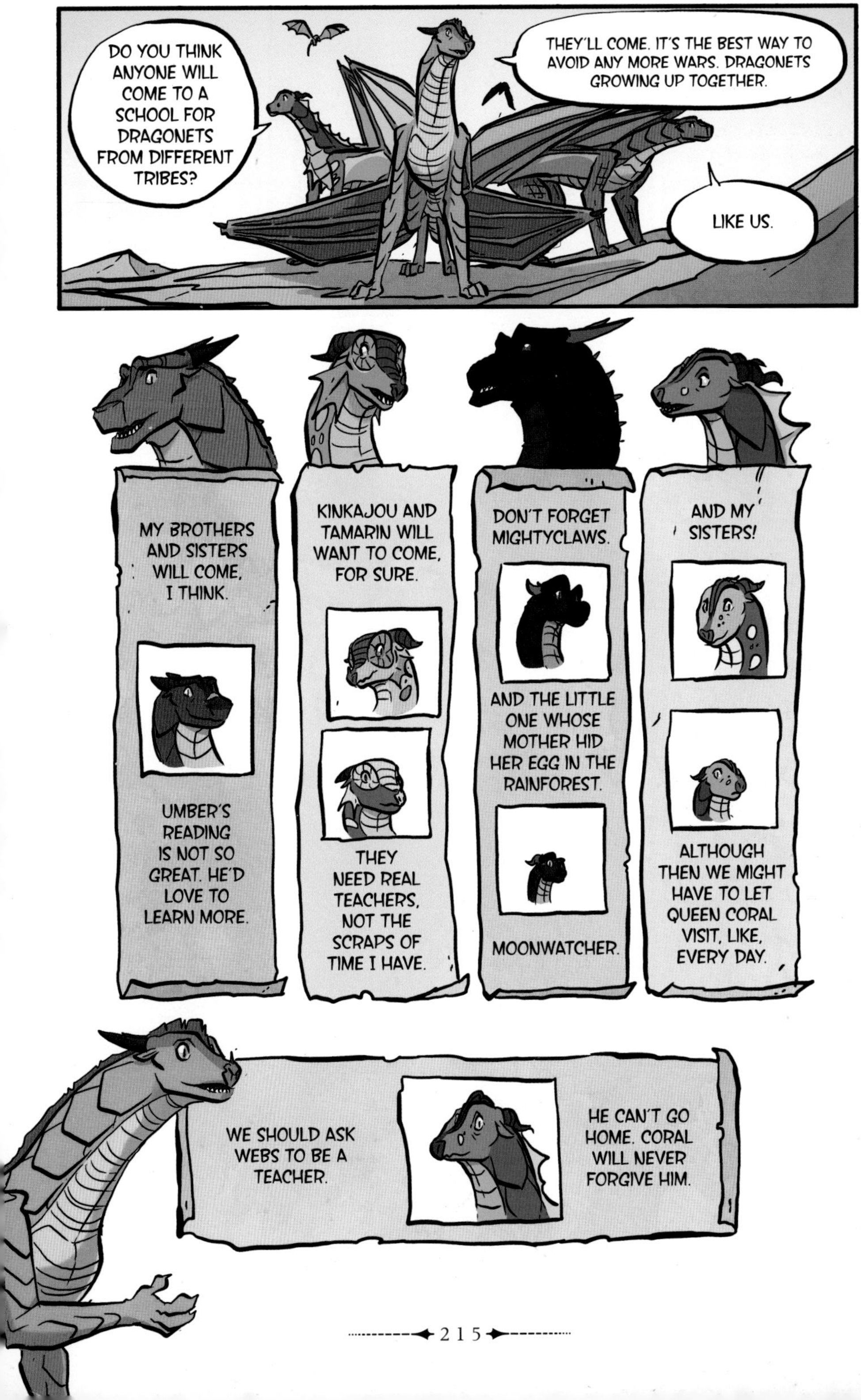

DO YOU THINK ANYONE WILL COME TO A SCHOOL FOR DRAGONETS FROM DIFFERENT TRIBES?
THEY'LL COME. IT'S THE BEST WAY TO AVOID ANY MORE WARS. DRAGONETS GROWING UP TOGETHER.
LIKE US.
MY BROTHERS AND SISTERS WILL COME, I THINK.
UMBER'S READING IS NOT SO GREAT. HE'D LOVE TO LEARN MORE.
KINKAJOU AND TAMARIN WILL WANT TO COME, FOR SURE.
THEY NEED REAL TEACHERS, NOT THE SCRAPS OF TIME I HAVE.
DON'T FORGET MIGHTYCLAWS.
AND THE LITTLE ONE WHOSE MOTHER HID HER EGG IN THE RAINFOREST.
MOONWATCHER.
AND MY SISTERS!
ALTHOUGH THEN WE MIGHT HAVE TO LET QUEEN CORAL VISIT, LIKE, EVERY DAY.
WE SHOULD ASK WEBS TO BE A TEACHER.
HE CAN'T GO HOME. CORAL WILL NEVER FORGIVE HIM.

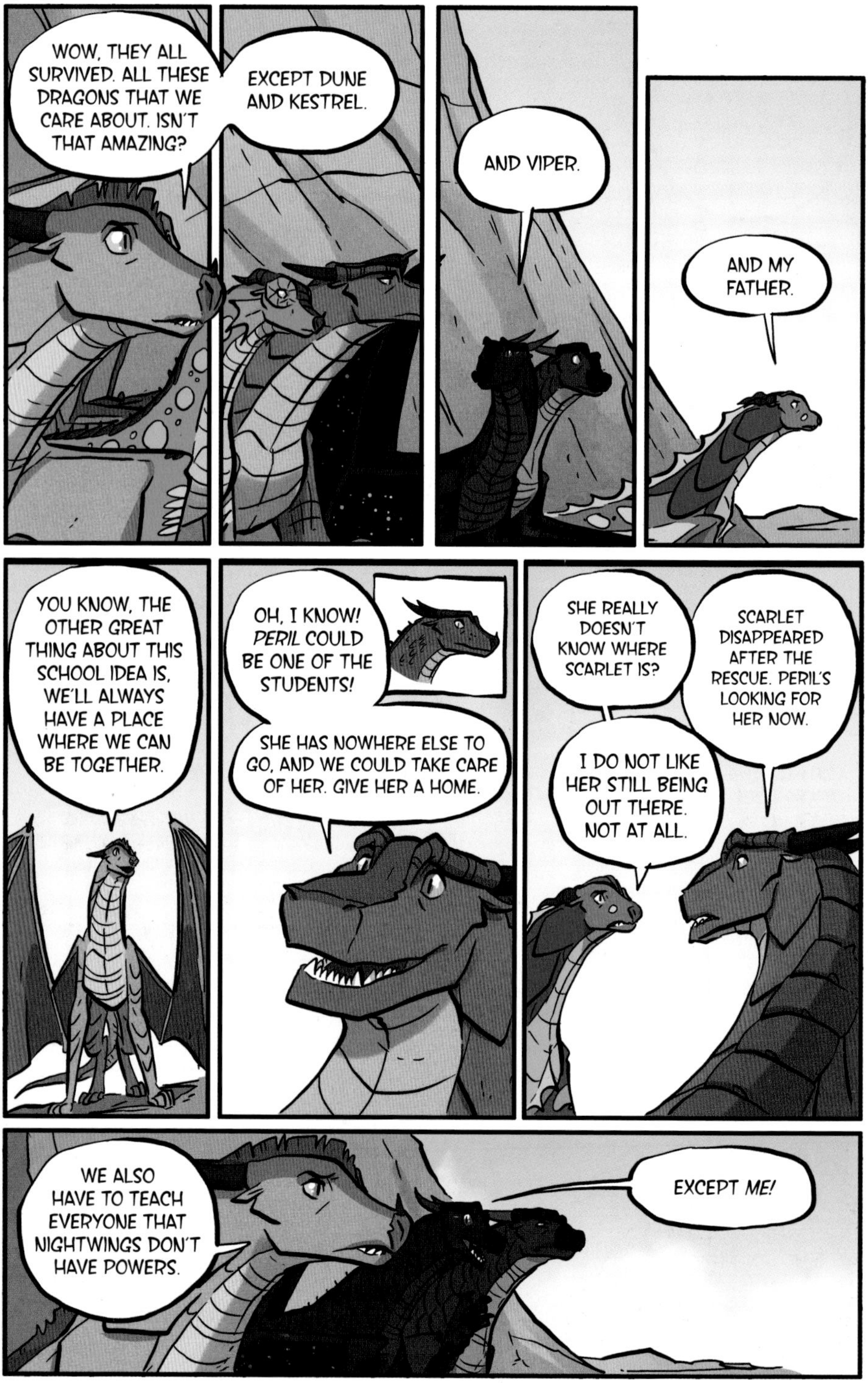
WOW, THEY ALL SURVIVED. ALL THESE DRAGONS THAT WE CARE ABOUT. ISN'T THAT AMAZING?
EXCEPT DUNE AND KESTREL.
AND VIPER.
AND MY FATHER.
YOU KNOW, THE OTHER GREAT THING ABOUT THIS SCHOOL IDEA IS, WE'LL ALWAYS HAVE A PLACE WHERE WE CAN BE TOGETHER.
OH, I KNOW! *PERIL* COULD BE ONE OF THE STUDENTS!
SHE HAS NOWHERE ELSE TO GO, AND WE COULD TAKE CARE OF HER. GIVE HER A HOME.
SHE REALLY DOESN'T KNOW WHERE SCARLET IS?
SCARLET DISAPPEARED AFTER THE RESCUE. PERIL'S LOOKING FOR HER NOW.
I DO NOT LIKE HER STILL BEING OUT THERE. NOT AT ALL.
WE ALSO HAVE TO TEACH EVERYONE THAT NIGHTWINGS DON'T HAVE POWERS.
EXCEPT *ME!*

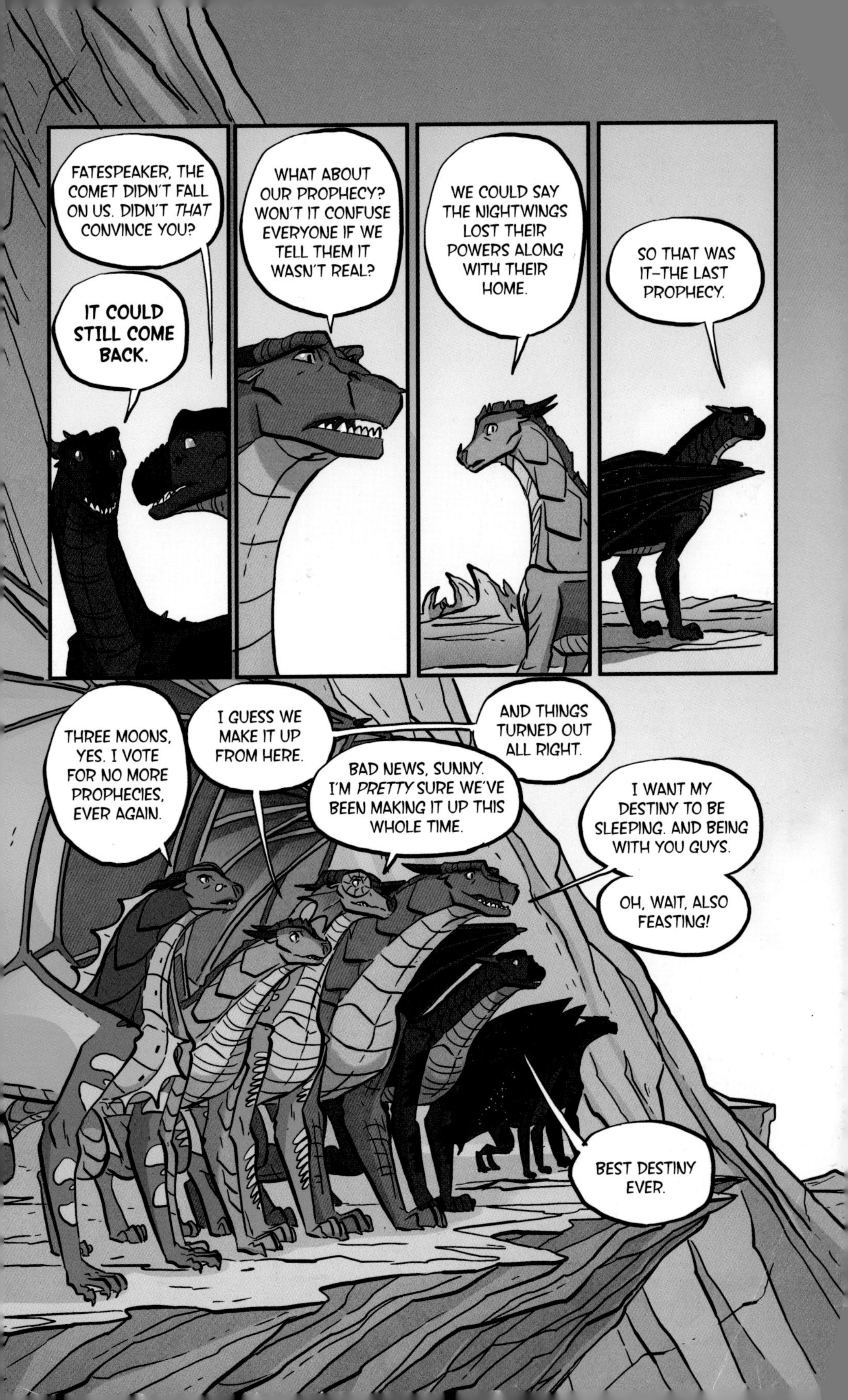
FATESPEAKER, THE COMET DIDN'T FALL ON US. DIDN'T *THAT* CONVINCE YOU?
IT COULD STILL COME BACK.
WHAT ABOUT OUR PROPHECY? WON'T IT CONFUSE EVERYONE IF WE TELL THEM IT WASN'T REAL?
WE COULD SAY THE NIGHTWINGS LOST THEIR POWERS ALONG WITH THEIR HOME.
SO THAT WAS IT—THE LAST PROPHECY.
THREE MOONS, YES. I VOTE FOR NO MORE PROPHECIES, EVER AGAIN.
I GUESS WE MAKE IT UP FROM HERE.
AND THINGS TURNED OUT ALL RIGHT.
BAD NEWS, SUNNY. I'M *PRETTY* SURE WE'VE BEEN MAKING IT UP THIS WHOLE TIME.
I WANT MY DESTINY TO BE SLEEPING. AND BEING WITH YOU GUYS.
OH, WAIT, ALSO FEASTING!
BEST DESTINY EVER.

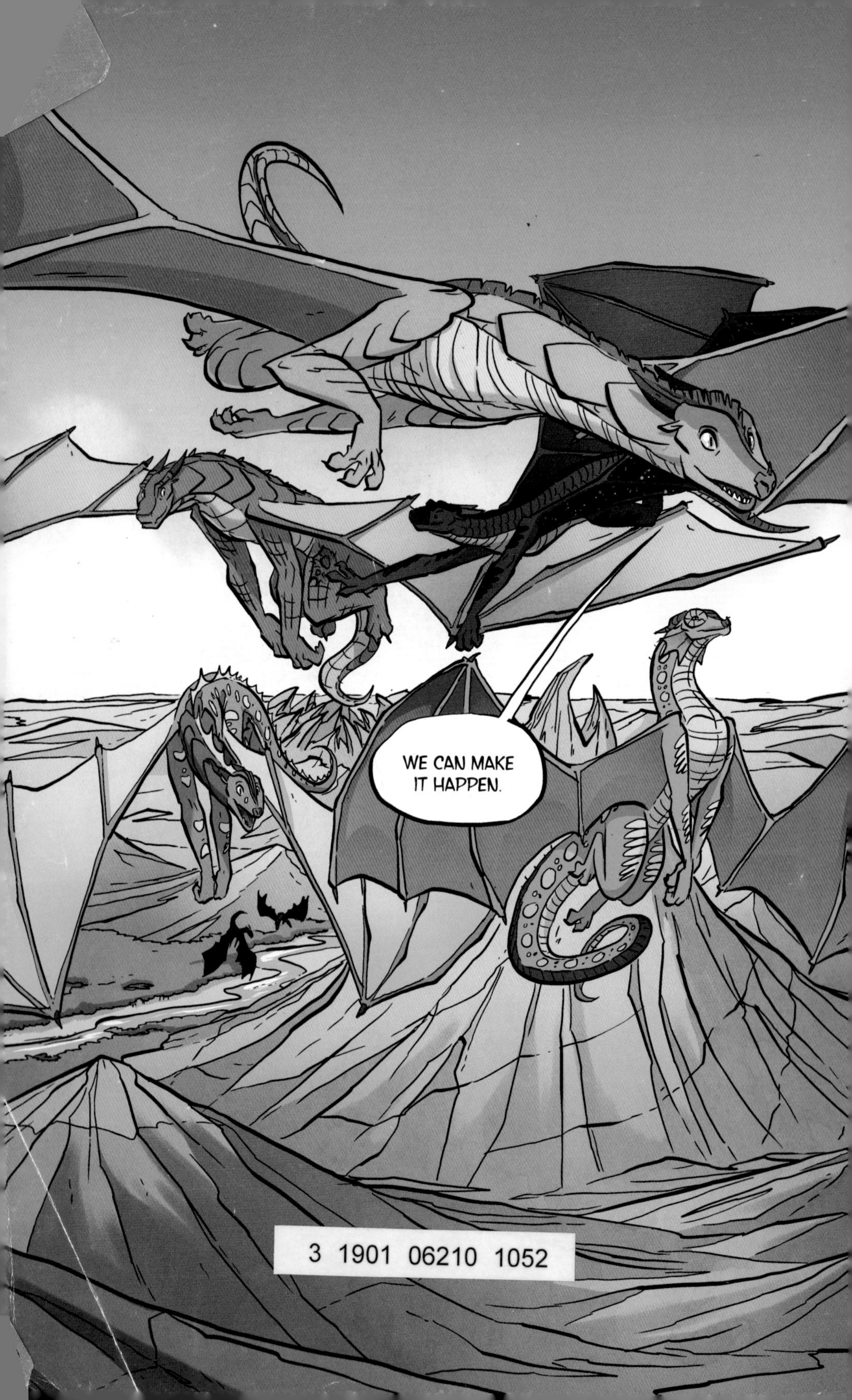
WE CAN MAKE IT HAPPEN.